Ben, David ... men prepa ... lives for wl ... Men much too attractive to resist!

They are

DANGEROUS TO LOVE

Three wonderful novels of
romantic suspense from
award-winning novelists
Marie Ferrarella, Beverly Barton
and Lindsay McKenna.

MARIE FERRARELLA

sold her first contemporary romance to Silhouette Books seventeen years ago and has now written more than one hundred books for the company. Her stories are beloved by fans worldwide and have been translated into many different languages. She has a master's degree in Shakespearean comedy, and her writing is distinguished by humour and realistic dialogue; she loves nothing more than to entertain her readers. Marie describes herself as the proud mother of two and the lucky wife of a man who still knows how to make the room fade away for her.

BEVERLY BARTON

has been in love with romance ever since her grandfather gave her an illustrated book of *Beauty and the Beast*. After marriage to her own 'hero', and the births of her daughter and son, Beverly chose to be a full-time homemaker, aka wife, mother, friend and volunteer. This author of over thirty books has won numerous awards and made several bestseller lists.

LINDSAY McKENNA

is a practising homeopath on the Navajo Reservation in Arizona. She is also a certified EMT in the state of Arizona. She comes from an Eastern Cherokee medicine family and is a member of the Wolf Clan. The idea for her latest series grew out of her experiences as a meteorologist for the US Navy. To her the military is like an extended family. Lindsay divides her energy between alternative medicine and writing. She feels that books about love are the greatest positive healing force in the world.

DANGEROUS
TO LOVE

MARIE
FERRARELLA

BEVERLY
BARTON

LINDSAY
McKENNA

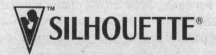

*Silhouette and Colophon are registered trademarks of
Harlequin Books S.A., used under licence.*

*First published in Great Britain 2002
Silhouette Books, Eton House, 18-24 Paradise Road,
Richmond, Surrey TW9 1SR*

DANGEROUS TO LOVE © Harlequin Books S.A. 2002

The publisher acknowledges the copyright holders of the
individual works as follows:

An Uncommon Hero © Marie Rydzynski-Ferrarella 2001
(Original title ChildFinders, Inc.: An Uncommon Hero)

Sweet Caroline's Keeper © Beverly Beaver 2001
(Original title The Protectors: Sweet Caroline's Keeper)

Heart of Stone © Lindsay McKenna 2001
(Original title Morgan's Mercenaries: Heart of Stone)

ISBN 0 373 04774 6

81-0702

*Printed and bound in Spain
by Litografia Rosés S.A., Barcelona*

An Uncommon Hero

MARIE FERRARELLA

Dear Reader,

Welcome to my latest instalment of ChildFinders, Inc. Since I'm an overprotective mother, it's always been my recurring nightmare that I've 'misplaced' my children who, when they were younger, enjoyed hiding in department store clothes racks and the like just long enough to give me a heart attack. Losing your kids is a very real fear that most mothers live with. The newspapers, sadly, are full of kidnapping stories that are not resolved happily. I thought it might be nice to create a safe haven where one could go and have potentially heinous situations brought to a happy ending. The people at ChildFinders, Inc. never met a case they couldn't solve.

Each time I finish writing a ChildFinders, Inc. book I think to myself, 'That's it. I've exhausted all the possibilities for this kind of a case.' And then, after a while, I get this itch to do one more, to find just another twist so that the story is interesting enough to demand its own space, its own book. And so it was with Ben's story. Ben Underwood appeared in the first ChildFinders, Inc. story as a policeman on the force, newly divorced and feeling his way around. He sparked my interest, and I threaded him through the second and third stories. By the time I was into my fourth story, dealing with Chad Andreini, Ben was part of the agency and comfortable with his single life. But he was a family man at heart, and I just had to find him a family worthy of the kind of caring man Ben actually was. I think I succeeded when I put him on this newest case. I hope you agree. Once again, I thank you for revisiting me, and from the bottom of my heart I wish you love.

Love,

Marie Ferrarella

Marie Ferrarella

CHILDFINDERS, INC.

A HERO FOR ALL SEASONS
A FOREVER KIND OF HERO
HERO IN THE NICK OF TIME

HERO FOR HIRE

AN UNCOMMON HERO
(in *Dangerous to Love*)

Coming Soon:
A HERO IN HER EYES - *August 2002*
Silhouette Sensation

HEART OF A HERO - *September 2002*
Silhouette Sensation

To
S. Cloud Hsueh, PhD
For guidance and warmth
over and above
the call of duty

Prologue

She wasn't going to cry, she wasn't.

There was no time to waste on tears. No time for anything. Only the hasty gathering of the very most important things. The things she couldn't leave behind along with everything else.

With the rest of her life.

She should have seen this coming, Gloria upbraided herself, tossing essentials into the suitcase that lay open on her bed. It wasn't as if this had suddenly materialized out of the blue. There had been signs. Signs she'd refused to acknowledge because things like this only happened in the movies. Or to people she read about in the newspaper. They didn't happen to people she knew. They didn't happen to her.

Except that now they were.

She glanced over at the small boy lying in the center of her bed, curled up right next to the suitcase. Poor baby, he'd dozed off and on the entire time she'd dressed him, waking just enough to ask her if he was having a dream. She'd told him yes.

It was better this way. She wouldn't have to field the tearful questions until later.

Maybe later, she could come up with answers that he could accept. Right now, she couldn't even come up with any that she could accept.

Regardless, she knew she had to hurry. If Stephen came looking for her here before she could get away, it would be too late.

She flipped the suitcase lid closed, pushing down on the locks. She prayed she knew what she was doing.

It was time to go.

Chapter 1

"You can name your own price, just find my son."

Ben Underwood studied the well-dressed man sitting in front of his desk. There was a time when the words *name your own price* would have been extremely tempting to him. A time, a little more than a decade ago, when he had stood at the crossroads of his life, wondering whether or not to take the easy road, the road his cousin and best friend, Vinnie, was taking. Or to take the road that, for the most part, followed a straight-and-narrow path.

It had been more of a mental wrestling match than he would have liked to admit now, but finally, Ben, in deference to his conscience and his mother and three sisters, had chosen the latter road. Only to "un-choose" it when he and the Bedford Police Department had come to a parting of the ways because of his untamable, independent methods. He'd gone from the department straight to ChildFinders, Inc. without so much as a breather and without looking back. He'd never regretted it.

It had been a very long time since money had had any sort of allure for him beyond providing for the basic creature comforts. Principles counted for so much more and were, in the end, longer-lasting.

Besides, Ben thought, he had a tendency to let money pass through his hands if he had it. He'd always been an easy touch.

He figured he'd better set this newest client, a man who seemed to fill up the room with his presence and who Megan Andreini, one of the agency's partners, would have undoubtedly referred to as a silver fox, straight.

"The fee depends on the length of time and expense it takes to locate your son, Mr. McNair." Ben smiled, comfortingly, he hoped. It wasn't that he didn't feel for these people who came into his office, quite the contrary. He just had never managed to master expressing his feelings satisfactorily. It was easier just tucking them away. "It's not determined by your net worth."

The last part wasn't strictly true, but not in any way that Stephen McNair could appreciate, Ben thought. On occasion, the agency took on cases pro bono. Cade Townsend, the original founder of the agency, didn't believe that lack of funds was any reason not to try to reunite a family with their missing child. Cade had been on the raw end of that situation, and knew the anguish of looking for a child who'd been kidnapped.

But there was no point in mentioning any of that to their newest client. McNair wasn't here to discuss the agency's policies, or its history. He had come here for the same reason everyone came to ChildFinders, Inc.—

to find his missing child. In McNair's case, it was a six-year-old blond-haired boy named Andrew.

Stephen McNair looked somewhat displeased at being lumped in with the general populace. Ben had a hunch the man had gotten accustomed to being able to buy anything he wanted, people and time included. If it were that easy, Ben mused, his son would have been back to him in minutes.

McNair's eyes narrowed a fraction. Ben felt himself being sized up. He couldn't say he liked it any. Given the circumstances, Ben decided McNair was entitled to some slack.

"Surely I'm permitted to throw a bonus into the agreement?"

"So we'll work a little faster?" Ben guessed, trying hard not to take offense.

McNair smiled triumphantly. "Exactly."

Ben shifted his lanky frame in his chair. He wasn't here to pass judgment. It was a given that the people who came into these offices were usually at their worst. It wasn't his place to like or dislike any of them. For the most part, he had to admit he felt for them and liked them. He didn't care for McNair. But that didn't matter one way or another. It was finding the boy that counted.

He couldn't help wondering if the boy would grow up to be like his father.

The man sitting before him in the six-hundred-dollar suit was about ten years older than Ben and gave new meaning to the word *polished.* The card McNair had made a point of presenting to him even before they had shaken hands identified him as Stephen W. McNair, president and CEO of IndieCorp, a fast-rising company that was, if he remembered correctly, on the cusp of a colossal merger with Mercury Electronics. The talk was that between the two giants, the semiconductor market was just about covered.

Ben rocked back in his chair, studying McNair in silence for a moment, questions occurring to him. A man like McNair could easily have a hundred agencies at his beck and call, including the FBI. Considering that kidnapping was every parent's nightmare and had become a reality for McNair, Ben couldn't help wondering what the man was doing here. Granted, ChildFinders had a heretofore unbelievable track record for solving kidnapping cases. For every closed case, there had been a happy ending. Not many places could boast a record like that. But the FBI had more manpower.

Ben leaned forward. "If you don't mind my asking, why haven't you gone to the police?"

There was a flash of annoyance in Stephen McNair's piercing blue eyes, but it was gone so quickly, Ben thought he might have imagined it. McNair looked the soul of cooperation as he answered, "Perhaps you're aware of the merger Indie is about to make with Mercury?"

Ben had found he learned a great deal when he pretended to be ignorant of things. "I don't keep up with the financial section of the newspaper, Mr. McNair. In my line of work, there's not much time for things that aren't directly relevant to the cases I'm working on."

A slight frown twitched McNair's lips before he proceeded to enlighten Ben. "Yes, well, my company is at a crucial stage of its development right now. We're to merge with Mercury Electronics. Any hint of scandal and the entire negotiations could be placed in jeopardy."

"I don't know the kind of people you're dealing

with, Mr. McNair, but I don't think they'd consider the kidnapping of a child as scandalous.''

In response, Stephen McNair merely shook his head. ''It's not the kidnapping they'd consider scandalous, it's the circumstances surrounding it.''

Now they were getting somewhere, Ben thought. He took out the tape recorder that was part of each office's furnishings and placed it on the desk beside him.

''Tell me about the circumstances.'' He pressed the red button down on the recorder and the tape began to whir softly.

McNair froze. He glared at the small rectangle on the desk as if it were an offending lower life-form. ''Turn that off.'' The three terse words were not a request. They were an order.

Despite his affable demeanor, Ben didn't respond well to being ordered around. That had been one of the reasons he and the Bedford Police Department hadn't remained on intimate terms. He made no move to comply with McNair's order. ''Sorry, company policy.''

''I said turn it off.'' Rather than wait, McNair leaned over and switched off the recorder himself. He met Ben's barely veiled annoyed look with a passionate verbal volley. ''I won't be recorded. I—'' He lowered his voice as he searched for the right words. ''This is very delicate, Mr. Underwood. Haven't you ever been in a delicate situation you didn't want broadcast?''

''This doesn't get broadcast, Mr. McNair.'' He indicated the tape recorder. ''The only reason the initial interview is taped is to help us go over the case. Sometimes things are said that are forgotten later. Other times, playing the tape back might inadvertently remind you of a detail or event you forgot to mention.''

McNair remained unmovable. ''I have a photographic

memory, Mr. Underwood. I assure you I do not forget anything.'' He paused, then added a bit more softly, ''Except, perhaps, discretion.'' His eyes met Ben's. ''But I am paying dearly for my error now.''

Ben made a judgment call. He left the tape recorder off. Curiosity had gotten the better of him. His mother had always warned him it would be his undoing.

''All right, we'll leave it off for the time being. Now, do you have any idea who might have kidnapped your son?''

''Any idea who kidnapped my son?'' McNair parroted the question incredulously. ''Of course I have an idea who kidnapped my son. I know exactly who's responsible. Gloria Prescott kidnapped my son.''

''Gloria Prescott,'' Ben repeated, and McNair nodded adamantly. It was a toss-up whether to ask first who the woman was or why she would abduct his son. Ben went with the more important of the two. ''And do you have any idea why she would kidnap your son?''

McNair passed his hand slowly over his face, a man struggling with his secrets, buying himself a tiny fragment of time in which to compose himself and frame his answer.

''She kidnapped Andrew to get back at me. She is— was,'' McNair said, correcting himself, ''Andrew's nanny.'' Just for an instant, his eyes grew soft, as if he were visualizing her. ''She's quite a stunning young woman.'' The laugh that followed was self-mocking. ''Too young for me, really.''

Mentally, Ben filled in the blanks. He had heard it often enough before. Older man, younger woman. The combination rarely yielded satisfactory results. According to his mother, that was why his own father had left. In pursuit of youth. In this case, youth had a name.

Claudia Gershon. Ben had a half brother named Jason who was half his age. For his father, things had worked out. Obviously, for McNair it hadn't.

"Go on," he encouraged when McNair continued to remain silent.

The older man shrugged. "You've heard it before, I'm sure. Older man trying to hang on to his youth, beautiful young woman bringing it to him in a gift-wrapped box." There was a faraway look in his eyes as he spoke.

The man had gotten it bad, Ben thought. He thought of his own mother. "And how did Mrs. McNair feel about you hanging on to your youth? Or Gloria's," he amended wryly.

McNair's eyes went flat as he regarded him. "She didn't feel anything."

"And why is that?" Ben was playing devil's advocate, but there was something a little too pat about the man sitting before him. He seemed a little too held together. Ben was used to people coming unraveled under the pressure of the crisis they were enduring. This man looked annoyed, nothing more. Fathers didn't look annoyed or inconvenienced when their sons were taken— they looked angry. Distraught, capable of mayhem themselves. On occasion, they looked lost. But not annoyed.

He wanted to get to the bottom of Stephen McNair.

"Because there is no Mrs. McNair." The annoyance deepened as McNair moved to the edge of his seat. "Look, I'm going to be perfectly frank with you. I'm rather new at this father business. Andrew is the result of a liaison I had with a young woman seven years ago. One of those flash-and-fire things. The whole thing lasted perhaps three weeks, perhaps less. I hadn't heard from her since. She died nine months ago, leaving me a letter and the boy. Both came to me via her lawyer. I had some lab tests done, DNA, that sort of thing, and the results were conclusive. Andrew was mine. Naturally, I saw him as my responsibility.''

''Naturally.''

McNair stopped, narrowing his eyes. ''Are you mocking me?''

Ben straightened, all business. His remark had been a slip. ''I'm not here to mock, Mr. McNair, or to sit in judgment. My only function is to help. I'm sorry if I gave you any other impression.'' He was going to have to work on his poker face, Ben thought.

''Look, I'm sorry if I don't live up to your expectations of the grieving father. It's not easy for me to show my emotions. But make no mistake about it, I am worried about my son and I want him back.''

Ben nodded. ''You were saying about Gloria…''

Scrubbing a well-manicured hand over his face, McNair sighed and continued. ''I was completely besotted with her for several months.''

Besotted. Now, there was a word he didn't run into every day, Ben thought. But somehow, coming from McNair, it seemed to fit the narrative. ''What happened after several months?''

''I came to my senses. Realized that a man in my position—responsible for the livelihood of so many people—couldn't continue behaving like some smitten adolescent. I tried to let her down as gently as possible, make her see reason.'' McNair looked at Ben to see if he understood the awkward position he'd been in. ''Unfortunately, Gloria didn't choose to be reasonable about it. I don't think she really cared about me as much as

she did about the money. I think she thought I was
going to marry her.''

''And you weren't.'' Ben waited for him to continue.

He shook his head. ''She wasn't wife material.'' His
expression became superior. ''Gloria became very possessive, flying into jealous rages when she thought that
I was seeing someone else.''

Ben was undecided whether the man thought himself
to be a much-abused saint, or was only trying to present
himself as one. ''And were you?''

''No.'' The response was indignant. ''And whether I
was seeing someone or not is not the point.''

''No, but everything is a piece of this puzzle. In the
interest of brevity, why don't you shorten the story for
the time being. Why did Gloria suddenly kidnap your
son? Why now, rather than last month or next week?''

''Because I officially broke off our relationship in no
uncertain terms last Thursday.''

''Thursday,'' Ben echoed.

''I see why you might need a recorder,'' McNair
commented impatiently. ''Yes, Thursday. I told her I
couldn't have a woman stalking my every move no matter how beautiful she was.''

Ben toyed with the carved paperweight one of his
sisters had made for him when she was twelve as he
played with logistics in his head. ''What did she do with
Andrew while she was stalking you?''

The question took McNair aback for a moment before
he responded. ''She had him with her.'' He continued
with his narrative, impatient to be done with it. ''Of
course, I took total responsibility for the affair even
though she was the one who seduced me, and I offered
her quite a sizable severance package to tide her over

until she found another position. After all, I wasn't heartless.''

Ben wondered if Stephen McNair actually saw himself as benevolent and blame-free. ''But that didn't fly with her.''

''No, it didn't 'fly.''' McNair wrapped his tongue around the word disdainfully. ''When I came home two nights ago from a business trip to Washington, D.C., I found that Gloria was gone and she'd taken Andrew with her.''

''Did she leave a note?''

The question caught McNair off guard. ''No.''

''Then you just assumed she'd kidnapped Andrew.''

''She was gone, he was gone, her clothes were gone. I came to the logical conclusion.'' He paused as if debating something, or hunting through the photographic memory he'd boasted of. ''And she'd threatened me earlier.''

''Threatened?'' Ben said, instantly alert. ''What kind of a threat?''

''She said she'd take Andrew away where I could never find him if I didn't marry her. That she was going to make me pay for what I 'did' to her.''

He supposed if the woman was being completely irrational, she might forget to write a note, although in his experience, writing a note would have added to the drama. Perhaps twisted the knife in a little harder. A woman making a dramatic statement wasn't apt to overlook writing a note.

But this woman hadn't. The minor point bothered Ben.

Something else was bothering him, too. Ben looked at the other man. ''And you waited almost five days before reporting this to anyone?''

It was an outright challenge and Ben half expected McNair to explode. Instead, the man looked contrite. "I was hoping that she was just angry. That she'd return him. I wanted to spare her being arrested if it was at all possible. I still do. You might have trouble understanding this because you're still young and not in my position, but I find I still have some residual feelings regarding Gloria."

For the first time, Stephen McNair seemed human to Ben. "Have you gotten in contact with her friends?"

The gesture was short, indicating a degree of helplessness that McNair looked unaccustomed to acknowledging.

"She's not from around here. As far as I know, she has no friends in the area. None that she ever went out with or even mentioned. For the most part, she stayed on the estate. She was very devoted to me and to Andrew."

Ben noted the order McNair had used. *To me and to Andrew.* But then, as the man said, he was new at being a father and hadn't had the luxury of experience to fall back on.

Sometimes all the experience and time in the world didn't help change the overall picture, Ben thought. His father had walked out on not only his mother, but on him, when he was thirteen. Being a father of four children hadn't made Jake Underwood any less the center of his own universe.

Still, whatever the order used, the word *devoted* had certain connotations. Ben was counting on them. "So you're pretty certain that she wouldn't hurt Andrew?"

There wasn't even a moment's hesitation. "Yes, I'm reasonably certain that she wouldn't do anything crazy like that. As I said, she's just doing this to get back at me.''

''Are you sure there wasn't some sort of note?'' Ben prodded. ''Conditions she wanted met before she returned your son?''

Maybe, for his own reasons, McNair was lying about there not being a note. It did seem highly unlikely that, given the circumstances, Gloria Prescott would allow this opportunity to slip by. Kidnappings happened for a variety of reasons, the least of which was revenge. But if this was for revenge, it was running atypical to form.

''No.'' Exasperation peppered McNair's voice. ''I suspect she was too angry to write anything. Besides, I already know her conditions. She'd want to take up where we'd left off. She wanted me to marry her.''

In his experience, grasping people tended to want money, Ben thought. Or at least power. Silence was not the order of the day. He wondered again if there was something McNair was holding back. ''And she hasn't attempted to get in contact with you?'' Ben asked.

''No,'' McNair snapped. He took a deep breath, composing himself. With shaky fingers he dug into his pocket and took out a half-empty pack of cigarettes. ''My one vice,'' he explained, holding the pack up. ''Other than falling for beautiful women. Do you mind?''

Ben was surprised that the man even bothered to ask. McNair struck him as someone who did as he pleased. Ben inclined his head, taking out a small ceramic ashtray from his side drawer and placing it on the desk. He didn't smoke, but he understood the need.

''Thanks.'' McNair lit up and inhaled. His eyes closed for a moment, as if he were having a spiritual experience. When he opened them again, he looked calmer, more capable of continuing. "If Gloria had left a note, I would have been taking care of this myself." He glanced toward the closed door. "Is Townsend around? Maybe he…?"

It obviously rankled McNair to deal with anyone who wasn't the top man. "Cade's out of town on a case. The caseload is pretty heavy. Right now, I appear to be all you have at your disposal."

McNair wouldn't have been where he was if he wasn't good at damage control. A smile nothing short of charming creased his lips. "Sorry, didn't mean to fly off the handle that way earlier. I can usually keep my temper under wraps, it's just that this is all completely new to me. Being a father, being a kidnap victim…"

"Strictly speaking, Andrew's the kidnap victim, but don't feel bad, this kind of thing usually is new to everyone. Now, if you'll make yourself comfortable, I still have a few more questions to ask you." Ben saw the slight frown on McNair's face reemerge. "I'll try to make this as painless for you as possible."

McNair looked at his watch before answering. Ben saw the flash of a Rolex. Nothing but the best, he thought.

"All right," Stephen agreed. "But I have to be back at a meeting in an hour."

He'd never run into a kidnap victim's father who'd set a time limit before. Took all kinds, Ben supposed. "You'll be back sooner than that."

As Ben got out his pad, he wondered just when Stephen McNair had found the time to even father a child.

She frowned slightly as she settled in. She wasn't used to lying and this was certainly lying. Big time. It was going to take a great deal of practice and care on her part. One misstep and people were going to begin suspecting that something wasn't right.

And once suspicions were aroused…

She didn't want to go there. There was far too much at stake for her to dwell on the consequences. There was no point in thinking about losing everything, it would only paralyze her.

For a moment, she paused in the doorway, looking into the small room the little boy had taken as his own. It was remarkable how resilient he was. She could stand to learn a thing or two from him about rolling with the punches and bouncing back.

He'd thrown off the covers again. Quietly, she crept into the room, careful not to make any noise that might wake him.

Very softly, she draped the comforter around his small body. Pressing a kiss to her fingertips, she passed it ever so lightly against his cheek. He meant everything to her.

"Sweet dreams, sweet prince," she whispered before withdrawing.

She kept the door slightly ajar so she could hear him calling if he needed her. He was having those nightmares again.

She slipped into bed. It was early, but she was tired. Lately, she'd been so drained. But then, she had reason enough to be. Before she fell asleep, as she did every night now, she thanked God for a new chance. A new chance to finally, perhaps, find peace and make her life work.

Work for her and for the little boy she loved.

About to leave, Ben saw a pencil-thin ray of light slipping out from beneath the door of Eliza's office.

Savannah had mentioned that the woman had just wrapped up the case she'd been working on.

Rapping once on her door, Ben opened it and peeked in. Eliza was looking through one of the files that were spread out all over her desk and glanced in his direction. Her smile was warmth itself.

"I didn't think there'd be anyone still in the office. Don't you have a home to go to?" Ben asked.

"I could say the same to you," she replied.

He leaned against the doorjamb. "Caught a new case this afternoon." He peered at the agency's newest partner. "You feeling all right?"

"Not enough sleep lately," she confessed with a shrug. "I've been having dreams lately."

"Dreams, or *dreams?*" he asked.

They both knew what he meant by the emphasis. One of her "seeing" dreams. The ones that crept up out of the dark and wouldn't give her peace until she solved the puzzle they came from. The ones she'd been blessed, or plagued with, depending on the point of view, since she'd turned twelve. "The latter."

He looked at her with eyes that silently communicated his sympathy. "Know what it's about yet?"

She shook her head. All she knew was that there was a child somewhere who needed her. But where and who and why, she hadn't a clue and it was tormenting her.

"No, but I will. Eventually." Eliza changed the topic. "So, you didn't answer me. What are you still doing here?"

He noticed that she hadn't given him an answer, either, but he let it pass. "Gathering some background information. I'm going to be out of town for a couple of days. Let the others know when they come in tomorrow, will you?"

"Sure thing." She swung her chair around to face him. "Going somewhere good?"

He laughed. "Depends on what you think of Saratoga."

Interest highlighted her delicate face. She assumed he was talking about the tiny town up north from Bedford, California. "Why Saratoga?"

"Our main kidnapping suspect has a relative there. Only living one I can come up with at the moment. A widowed great-aunt named—" he grinned "—Sugarland Malone. Not sure if she knows where the suspect is, but it's worth a shot." Even if the great-aunt did know, she might not be willing to disclose the information, Ben thought. Blood was thicker than water and he was an outsider.

Eliza smiled. It didn't take a clairvoyant to guess what was on his mind. "If anyone can get the lady to loosen her tongue, you can."

He wondered how much of that was flattery and how much was intuition. Eliza was a genuine psychic, one whom the police had brought in on more than a few of their unsolvable cases. He'd been as skeptical of her as anyone when he'd first met Eliza, but she'd eventually made a believer out of him. "You give me too much credit."

Her smile deepened, the shy edge fading. "No, I don't."

Amused, he cocked his head. "Your psychic intuition, I take it?"

She shook her head. "More like female intuition. Some things are just self-evident." Like a man who could charm the feathers off a bird, she thought with a smile. She doubted if he knew just how persuasive those dark blue eyes of his really were. "I'll tell the others—and good hunting."

"Thanks."

That was the word for it, all right, he thought as he closed the door behind him. Hunting.

Chapter 2

The jarring noise pushed its way into his consciousness.

It was the phone, Ben realized as his brain surfaced out of a dreamless sleep. The phone was ringing. Groping for the receiver, he tried to locate and focus in on his clock.

Four-thirty.

In the morning?

He scrubbed his hand over his face, trying to pull himself together. "Hello, you'd better be an obscene phone call to make this worth my while."

"I've already offered to make it worth your while, Underwood."

The voice—cool and official—jarred loose a memory. "Mr. McNair?" Ben looked at the clock again. A hint of annoyance entered his voice. He'd come home and done further background work for his intended trip today. He'd slept for less than three hours and he liked his rest. "Do you have any idea what time it is?"

The voice on the other end of the phone grew cooler. "I always know what time it is. I'm on my way to a meeting in Seattle and will be back by this evening. What I don't know is if you've made any progress yet." Ben sat up, annoyed now. Who the hell made phone calls at four-thirty in the morning? If he'd had any doubts about the man being a control freak, this cinched it.

"Some," Ben replied in answer to McNair's question.

"You've found her?" Excitement echoed in the receiver against Ben's ear.

Ben sighed, pulling up the comforter. Outside, the January rain was beating against his window. Telling him to go back to sleep. "No, but I might have located a relative."

"Where?"

The question echoed like a command for disclosure. Maybe it was because he was half asleep, but the tone rubbed him the wrong way. Instincts surfaced, making him just the slightest bit wary. McNair, polished CEO though he might be, was in this case a loose cannon. Loose cannons had a way of going off at precisely the worst time. Ben wasn't about to take the chance of having things blown apart by an overzealous parent.

"Let me check it out and I'll let you know."

The answer irritated McNair. "I'm not paying you to play games, Underwood."

Ben cut him yet a little more slack, though it galled him to do so. Stress did strange things to people, he reminded himself. Maybe, under ordinary circumstances, Stephen McNair was a completely likable person, although Ben sincerely doubted it.

In any event, rules had to be set and boundaries defined. "No, Mr. McNair, you're paying me to find your son and I intend to do that. But it'll have to be my way. Again, that's what you're paying me for."

He heard the man bite off a retort he couldn't make out, then say in a guarded voice, "You'll call as soon as you have anything?"

"I'll call," Ben promised, just as he had yesterday as McNair left the office. The man had tried to bully him into making reports at regular intervals. That might have been standard procedure at McNair's company, but that wasn't the way he operated and Ben had made his position perfectly clear. Or so he thought.

"Speaking of calling, how did you get my home number?" It was unlisted, and although he'd given out his number on occasion to more than one distraught parent, something had prevented Ben from offering it to McNair. Self-preservation, most likely.

"I have ways." There was a smug note in the other man's voice. And then he reiterated his earlier point. "I would appreciate you checking in with me regularly."

Maybe the agency should refine its screening process, Ben thought, growing closer to the end of his patience. At the moment, the agency took on all comers. Maybe it was time for Cade to rethink that when he got back from the case he was working on.

"There's nothing regular about my line of work. I'll call when there's something to call about. Goodbye, Mr. McNair."

Ben let the receiver fall back into the cradle, then slid back down on the bed. Less than five minutes of tossing and turning made him acknowledge that he was too irritated to go back to sleep.

Muttering under his breath, Ben got up to take a shower. The last time he'd been up on the wrong side of four-thirty, it'd been to get ready for his paper route before going to school. The nuns at St. Mary's, aware of his mother's financial situation, had said paying part of his own tuition at the parochial school would make a man out of him.

He didn't feel very manly right now. Just tired.

With a sigh, he turned on the hot water and stepped into the shower. There was no sense wasting time.

The drive up Interstate 5 from Bedford to Saratoga would have been scenic had it not been for the early morning fog that hung about the winding road. He was a careful driver by nature. It wasn't often, though, that he worried about the road and the hazards caused by careless drivers.

But a fog this thick made him aware of every inch of road. And the possibility of his own quickly snuffed-out mortality.

Ben slowed his vehicle down to a crawl.

He supposed he could have gone later, but the word itself held a foreboding threat within it. *Later* was too close to *never* when it came to kidnappings. It was always best to follow every lead as soon as it occurred. Later might be too late.

He didn't ever intend to be too late. So far, he'd been lucky. He'd never had to face a parent and say those gut-wrenching, eternally tormenting words that would forever cut them off from hope. He'd found every child he'd set out to locate. Which was what made his job at

ChildFinders so much more rewarding than the time he'd spent in the homicide division on the police force.

The coffee nestled in his cup holder had grown cold and stagnant by the time the fog had lifted, and he felt confident enough to risk taking one hand off the wheel to take a drink. By then, he was fifteen miles out of Saratoga.

The small town created an immediate impression the moment he entered it. Saratoga looked as if it should have been the subject of a fairy tale. Or, at the very least, a Frank Capra movie. There was a picturesque, storybook quality about it. The climate was cooler up here, and what had been rain in Bedford had transformed into light flurries in Saratoga.

The light layer of fresh snow on the trees and ground made Ben think of a Currier and Ives painting.

The woman he was looking for lived ten miles on the other side of Saratoga.

"I do so like getting visitors," the small, cherubic woman said, smiling at Ben. "Have another cookie." She pushed the near-full plate toward him. "I just wind up eating them myself half the time." Her eyes twinkled and she gave the illusion of lucidity as she smiled at her girth. "But I suspect you've already guessed that."

The wan afternoon sun had finally withdrawn from the parlor they were in, after losing a hopeless battle for space within a room crammed full of knickknacks and memorabilia. It was a room where an old woman sat, surrounded by things that reminded her that she had once been young, with the world at her feet. Too heavy-set to be called elfin, she still had that way about her. She was charming, and maybe, at some other time, Ben wouldn't have minded spending an afternoon talking to her about nothing.

But he didn't have time. Because of McNair's admitted reticence, too much had already elapsed. The longer it took him to find Andrew McNair, the harder it would become.

"No." The lie came easily to him. It harmed nothing to pretend that she was not heavy. The woman's smile became wider. "No, I hadn't guessed." Picking up another one of the cookies she was pushing on him, he took a bite. The cookies, laced liberally with macadamia nuts, were quite possibly the best he'd ever had. Andrea would have killed for these, he thought, chocolate chip cookies being a particular weakness for his middle sister. "And much as I'd like to load up on these, Mrs. Malone—"

"Oh, please, everyone calls me Sugar. I forget exactly why. Sugarland isn't my given name, you know."

"I rather suspected that," he said, smiling. "But as to the reason I'm here—"

"Oh, yes, your reason." Her smile faded a little. "And once you tell me, you'll be gone, won't you?"

He'd met her less than twenty minutes ago. Knocking on her door, he'd been surprised when she'd ushered him in like a long-lost friend. Asking for his name had been an after-thought. It had left him wondering if there was anyone who looked in on the old woman from time to time to make sure she hadn't given up the deed to the old Victorian house, or its surrounding fields. He hoped that the foreman who managed her field hands was a decent sort.

"I'm afraid—"

Sugar waved away the excuse magnanimously. "That's all right, Gloria was the same way, flitting in and out before I could so much as blink twice. I expect it's the same with all young people.''

"Gloria.'' He hadn't expected it to be this easy. Ben maintained a poker face as he asked, "Then she's been here?''

"Why, yes. Here and gone.'' Sugar brushed away the crumbs that had collected on her ample bosom. "But you were going to tell me something.''

Was she really as vague as she let on, or was it all an elaborate act? She seemed genuine enough, but Ben kept his eyes on the woman's face, watching for a tell-tale shift in expression as he said, "As a matter of fact, I'm looking for your grand-niece.''

"Why?'' It wasn't a challenge. Curiosity filtered into her eyes.

He began to give Sugar the story he'd rehearsed on his way up here. "I represent Jacob Marley's estate—''

"Jacob Marley....'' She closed her eyes, rolling the name over in her mind. Then, opening them again, she shook her head. "I don't believe I know the man.''

"No, ma'am, probably not.'' Especially since he'd borrowed the name from Dickens' *A Christmas Carol*, Ben thought. "But he's left Gloria a sizable amount of money—''

Sugar clapped her hands together in simple, childish delight. "How wonderful. The poor dear could so use the money. I couldn't give her very much when she came. She promised to pay me back, but I told her I wouldn't hear of it. I'm the only family she has, you know.''

"Yes, I do.'' Ben tried to press on before the woman became distracted again. "We have no forwarding ad-dress for her—''

Fluffy, cloudlike white hair bobbed up and down as Sugar nodded in agreement.

"That's because she's not where she used to be." She leaned forward, her voice dropping for a moment. "Can't be, you know. Too bad, it made her sad to leave."

This had to be what Alice felt like, trying to carry on a conversation with the creatures inhabiting Wonderland, Ben thought. Still, he was making some progress. "Do you know where she is now?"

"Not really." Sugar paused to nibble thoughtfully on one of her cookies. "But she said something about San Francisco. That's where she went to school, you know. Bright, bright girl." She sighed as that memory, too, slipped away from her. "Worked in a bookstore during those years. Practically ran the place. Don't know when she ever slept. The manager liked her, I could tell. Never acted on it, though." Suddenly realizing that her visitor was no longer chewing, she pushed the plate a little closer still. "Another cookie?" This time, the plate practically landed in his lap.

"Would you happen to know the name of the bookstore?" Gloria had to work, he thought. Maybe she'd touched base with the owner of the store, asking for a job. It was a long shot to say the least, but long shots had a way of paying off if you were persistent enough. Besides, it was a starting point. San Francisco was a big city to wander around in aimlessly.

"Why, as a matter of fact I do." Proudly, she recited the name of a popular chain that was currently sweeping the country, replacing older, independent stores. "It's located at Taylor and Turk. Or is it Turk and Taylor? I never know which way to say that." She looked pleased with herself for remembering the location. "I went there a few times myself. The bookstore,'' she clarified, almost more for her benefit than for his.

It was time to go, Ben thought. He could see she was about to push another cookie on him. ''One last question. Did Gloria have a little boy with her?''

Sugar blinked, staring at him as if he had just asked her if the sky was blue on a sunny day. ''Well, of course she did. Why wouldn't she? She was moving, you know.''

''Yes, so I gathered.'' On his feet, he extended his hand to her. ''Well, you've been a great help.''

Sugar took the compliment as her due. ''That's what Gloria said. But I couldn't help enough. Not her. Here.'' She slipped three large cookies into his pocket. ''For later. You might get hungry.''

He left feeling somewhat guilty about deceiving a woman who seemed bent on helping everyone who crossed her path.

The sun grazed off the window as she passed, catching her attention. Raising her eyes, surprise drenched her when she saw the reflection.

Idiot.

It still startled her, at unguarded moments, to see the different face looking back at her. To realize that the woman with the short, dark hair and blue eyes was not someone else, but her. In her mind's eye, she was still a blonde, still green-eyed. Yet now she was a woman with a life that held promise instead of one who had come full circle, returning to what she'd once felt was the beginning of the road.

Not the end, just a breather. She had to remember that.

With effort, she shook herself free of the morose

mood. It wasn't like her. No matter what, she'd always looked on the positive side. Stopping, she tucked a book back into place on the shelf.

There was more reason than ever to focus on the positive side. There wasn't just herself to think of. Her son needed her.

Her son.

She looked at her watch. The last customer she'd helped had taken more time than she'd judged. If she was going to be at the school in time to pick Andrew— no, Jesse, she upbraided herself. If she was going to be in time to pick Jesse up, she was going to have to get going. Now.

"I'm taking my break now, Jon," she called out to the burly man nursing a cup of espresso at the information counter.

The bald-headed man gave a half nod in acknowledgment to her announcement and went back to perusing a copy of one of the books UPS had dropped off this morning.

She smiled to herself. Some things never changed. Jon Peterson was lost to the world when he had his nose stuck in a good mystery. He'd been that way during the four years she'd worked here while she'd attended college. Heaven help anyone if they approached him with a question. Like as not, Jon was apt to send them into the self-help section even if they asked for a cookbook.

She blessed Jon for the umpteenth time since she'd arrived more than three weeks ago. If not for him and his calming influence, she could very well have come unglued that first night in San Francisco. If he had been away on one of his many minivacations that he'd always loved to take...well, she didn't want to think about it.

Trying to get to the front doors, she found her path blocked by a well-built man in his early twenties wearing a pricey sheepskin jacket and a cheap smile. He made no effort to move out of her way.

"Since you're free, why don't I buy you a cup of coffee to go along with that break?"

She'd been uncomfortably aware that the man had been sizing her up for at least the last fifteen minutes, meandering closely behind her as she stocked new books on the shelves. She'd caught him looking at her at least three times, attempting to make eye contact. She'd looked away each time. He gave her the shivers. Not the good kind.

Maybe it was her situation that made her so edgy, so suspect of every man who looked her way. Maybe she was being unduly sensitive and the man was just trying to strike up a conversation, nothing more.

But whatever he was attempting to do, she had no time for it. As it was, if she didn't hurry, she was going to be late.

Since he was a potential customer, she strove to remain polite. "No, thank you, I have an errand to run." Sidestepping him, she tried to get by.

One quick movement and he was in front of her again, blocking her path. He was not a man who was about to take no for an answer. "You work here, don't you?"

She glanced toward Jon, but his nose was buried in the book. None of the other people who worked in the store were within eye-contact range. She raised her head defiantly as she looked back at the man.

"Yes."

His eyes washing over her, he was obviously taken

with what he saw. "Well then, whatever happened to that old saying, the customer is always right?"

"That depends on what the customer wants."

A smile split his handsome face, failing to reach his eyes. "Guess."

If she called out to Jon, she'd cause a scene. The last thing she wanted was a scene. Just peaceful anonymity. "I'm afraid I don't have the time right now." She tried to move past him again, but the man swayed, blocking her every move. "I need to be somewhere else," she said.

He put up his hand against a shelf, cutting her off from making an exit. "Yes, with me."

Suddenly, he found himself being spun around and looking up at a stranger who was several inches taller than he was.

"The lady said no. What part of 'no' didn't you understand?" Ben asked.

Cold fury contorted the man's handsome features. It was evident he wasn't accustomed to being turned down, or opposed. "This doesn't concern you."

Ben's hand tightened around his arm. He gave the man no reason to doubt he meant business. "Lack of manners always concerns me. Now, apologize to the lady and let her pass."

She'd always loved westerns as a child. The rugged hero in the white hat coming to the aid of the wronged, put-upon but feisty heroine. Time and again, she'd eat up the stories even though they were always the same. Only the faces and names changed.

And now she had her very own cowboy riding to her rescue.

Annoyed but smart enough to know when he was

outmatched, the man glared sullenly at her. "I didn't mean anything by it."

Ben slowly nodded his head, as if evaluating the words. "A little lacking in poetry, but it'll do." Releasing his hold on the man's arm, Ben held his hand up. "You can go. Now."

Embarrassed, the man stalked out.

Ben shook his head, watching to make sure he left before turning back to the sultry-looking woman. He had no doubt she had more than her share of run-ins like that. Women with faces and figures as beautiful as hers generally did. "I apologize for my species. Just because we all walk upright doesn't make us all civilized."

The laugh that bubbled up in her throat was just a little nervous. "Thank you."

"My pleasure—" he glanced down at the small, square name tag "—Gina Wassel." He raised his eyes to hers. "And now, would you mind pointing me in the direction of the manager?"

She would have liked to stay and ask him if she could help, but the jerk who had tried to put the moves on her had eaten up her margin of time. She should have already been on her way.

"He's right over there." She pointed toward Jon. "Now, if you'll excuse me."

Ben nodded, stepping aside. "You have an errand to run."

"Emphasis on *run*," she said, tossing the words over her shoulder as she hurried out.

He allowed himself exactly half a second to take in the view. The woman looked just as good going as she did coming.

But he wasn't there to pass judgment on form. He was tracking a kidnapper.

With that in mind, Ben made his way over to the man the woman named Gina had pointed out to him.

Chapter 3

Jon Peterson slowly stroked his small goatee as he stared at the reprinted photograph of a woman with a little boy that Ben had handed him.

Longer than was necessary, in Ben's estimation. Gloria Prescott had either come in and applied for a job in the last few days, or she hadn't. Granted, the photograph wasn't a very good one, but it was the only one McNair had had of either Gloria, or his son. Ben could see not having photographs of the nanny, but it was difficult for him to understand why McNair had no available photographs of his son. He supposed that the man's excuse, that he wasn't the kind to take pictures, held some water. But he bet that McNair had plenty of photographs of himself around.

Blurred photograph or not, Peterson knew what Gloria looked like. According to her great-aunt, she'd worked here for four years. The man was either stalling for dramatic effect, or was debating something. Not knowing him made it next to impossible for Ben to tell.

When the bookstore manager finally raised his eyes to his, Ben had the impression that he was being scrutinized far more closely than the photograph had been.

''Nope, sorry, can't help you.'' Placing the photograph on the counter, Jon pushed it back toward him. He paused as if thinking. ''Haven't seen Gloria in, what? I guess about four, five years now.'' The small, dark eyes gave no indication of what was going on in his mind as they looked at Ben. ''Maybe even longer.''

''Then she didn't come here looking for a job,'' Ben reiterated.

The meeting apparently over, Peterson drew his book back to him and lowered his head, effectively blocking out any noise and any unwanted inquiries.

''That would have meant I'd seen her, wouldn't it? Sorry, she's not here. Wish she was. Best damn employee I ever had here. She actually wanted to work, not like some of the others.'' He turned a page in his book. Because Ben wasn't leaving, Peterson raised his eyes to look at him again. This time, his displeasure was not that difficult to discern. ''Anything else I can do for you?''

Ben had come across more sociable pit bulls. He slipped the photograph back into his pocket. ''Would you happen to know where Gloria might have gone if she'd returned to San Francisco?''

''Nope. Never meddle.'' Peterson returned to his mystery, making it painfully obvious that he considered Ben an annoying obstacle to his reading pleasure. ''Keeping your nose out of other people's lives is the secret to a long, healthy one of your own.'' Bent over his book, Peterson spared him one more pointed glance. "Know what I mean?"

"Yeah." He knew exactly what the older man meant. Get lost. Ben took one last look around the store. He'd already walked up and down the aisles methodically, not once but twice. That was how he'd happened to notice the college preppie putting the moves on the salesclerk. Not that he could actually blame him. The woman had been a looker in a classy sort of way. "Thanks for your help."

Engrossed in the book he was reading, the store manager grunted his acknowledgment.

There was nothing for Ben to do but retreat to his car.

Rather than drive off immediately, Ben put in a quick call to Savannah and came up empty there as well.

"If Gloria Prescott's in San Francisco, Ben, she's not using her charge cards," she told him.

"No paper trail of any kind?"

"Not unless she's leaving bread crumbs behind her on her way to the forest," Savannah quipped. "The canvassing down here's coming up dry, too. Rusty's been showing the photograph around in the area and he said to tell you that nobody's seen Gloria or the boy. I'm sorry, Ben."

"Not your fault," he murmured before hanging up.

Putting his cell phone back in his pocket, Ben stared at the bookstore across the street, not really seeing it. He doubted that driving back to Saratoga to ask Sugar any more questions would yield any further insight into finding Gloria.

That only left one other person to talk to.

The expression on Stephen McNair's face was far from welcoming when his secretary admitted Ben into his office. The man's countenance made Ben think of Zeus, presiding over Mount Olympus and bringing Mercury to task for failing to deliver the message he'd been anticipating. Ben had a hunch that even the man's furniture had been chosen with an eye toward intimidating anyone entering the office. Massive, opulent and expensive. The man certainly didn't assume his present position in life graciously.

Sitting as straight as a spear in his gray, imported leather office chair, McNair gripped the armrests as he scowled at him.

"Shut the door."

The tone rankled Ben, but he closed the door behind him. This was supposed to be private, anyway. The instant the door met the jamb, McNair was on his feet.

"Why are you coming to see me here?"

Definitely not a Mr. Congeniality candidate, Ben thought. In his book it would have had to have taken one hell of a greedy woman to have slept with this man for monetary gain. But then, it took all kinds, and he had yet to figure out just what "kind" his quarry was. Aside from cookies, her aunt had filled him in with stories of Gloria as well, all told with an abundance of affection and filial pride. Given the woman's state, though, he figured he had to take a great deal with a grain of salt.

"Because I didn't want to waste time making an appointment."

About to say something, McNair changed his tone. "Did you find her?"

Again, "her," not "him." "If you don't mind my saying so, Mr. McNair, you seem to be a great deal more interested in my finding Gloria Prescott than you are in my finding your son."

"Of course I'm interested in you finding Gloria. She has what belongs to me and no one, *no one* gets away with that. Now, did you find her or didn't you?"

"Not yet." Ben wanted to add that he wasn't a magician, but let the remark slide. It would only lead to an escalation of tempers.

"Then I repeat, what are you doing here in my office?"

Ben was beginning to feel really sorry for the little boy he was looking for. He had a feeling that McNair was probably just as cold and abrasive with the son he never actually wanted as he was with someone who was "displeasing" him. "I need more information."

Exasperation creased the remarkably unlined brow. "I already told you everything I could think of."

There had to be something, some tiny piece that would lead Ben to clues that would help him find the boy. He'd seen it happen often enough. The trick was finding that one scrap that eventually opened up everything. Maybe the answers he was looking for were in Gloria's recent past. "Where did Gloria work before she came to you?"

The annoyance on McNair's face deepened. "I don't remember."

He was being evasive, Ben thought, and wondered why. In any event, there was an easy-enough solution. "Check your references."

With an angry huff, McNair turned away. There was tension in the back Ben found himself looking at. "I don't know where they are."

He would have thought that McNair knew how to lay his hands on almost anything that remotely concerned him. "What about the agency that sent her? Can you remember its name?"

McNair swung around. "What does where she worked before have to do with finding her now?"

It was on the tip of Ben's tongue to say that he didn't appreciate having his methods questioned, but he thought better of it. He hadn't come here to argue, but to search for a lead. The sooner McNair gave him what he wanted, the sooner he could get going.

"There might be some sort of connection we've overlooked." McNair looked unconvinced. "No one we've questioned in the area has seen her, and her only relative sent me in the wrong direction."

"Relative?" He said the word as if he hadn't thought that Gloria had any, Ben noted. "Well, go back to him or her and get the truth."

"It's a her," Ben told him. "And I think the sky's a different color in her world than it is in the world the rest of us reside in."

"You mean she's crazy?" Surprise imprinted the distinguished features.

"No, just somewhat off. Eccentric." Ben had no idea why he suddenly felt protective of a woman he hardly knew. Maybe it was McNair's manner. He pressed on. "What I need right now is someone else who knew her, someone who might have a decent idea where Gloria might have gone with your son."

McNair blew out a breath as he scrubbed his hand over his face. Searching his memory. Or debating over something that he'd felt better about keeping obscure. Ben couldn't tell.

Finally, McNair said, "I think she used to work in a social security office."

Something to go on, Ben thought. "Locally?"

"I think so." The scowl returned. "Look, I'm doing all the work here."

Ben was already at the door, more than eager to leave. "We'll arrange for a discount." He didn't bother sublimating the sarcasm.

It wasn't wasted on McNair. His expression bordered on malevolence. "Damn straight you will. And don't forget, I want to be kept posted," he called after Ben.

"As soon as I find out anything, you'll be the first to know."

No one was more eager than he was to wrap this all up, Ben thought.

There was only one social security building in the county. Even if Gloria hadn't worked in this particular one, Ben figured that with a little coaxing applied to the right people, he could find out which office she had worked in.

He didn't need to coax.

The section supervisor, Anna Philbert, a robustly built woman in her forties who had once been an Olympic shot-put alternate if he was to believe the certificate that hung on the cubicle wall directly behind her, instantly recognized the photograph he showed her.

"Oh, sure, Gloria worked here." She looked at the photograph again before handing it back to him. "Is anything wrong?"

He didn't think the story he'd given Gloria's great-aunt sounded sufficiently credible in the government building, so he had created another one on his way over.

"She's missing and her fiancé's very worried about her."

"Missing? You mean kidnapped?" Anna asked, genuinely horrified. A beringed hand fluttered to her ample bosom. "Gloria? You're kidding." She shook her head in pure disbelief even as she clearly reveled in the drama of the situation. "The poor thing. She was the sweetest person in the world."

Apparently Gloria's fan club was growing. Why would someone regarded as "the sweetest person in the world" kidnap a child no matter how upset and angry she was? It didn't make sense to him.

"It might not be a kidnapping," he said quickly. "It just might be a case of cold feet." He deliberately exchanged a conspiratorial look with the woman, drawing her further into his camp. "Tell me, if Gloria did want to get away, would you have any idea where she might go?"

As much as she looked as if she wanted to help him, Anna was forced to shake her head. "No, but I really wasn't very close to her." She thought a moment. "You might have better luck talking to Carla Wassel."

"Wassel?" An image of the woman at the bookstore came to him. If he closed his eyes, he could see the name tag she'd worn against her shapely breast. It wasn't all that common a name. He wondered if the women were somehow related. Maybe he'd finally stumbled onto a connection. "Is she in?"

Rising from behind her desk, Anna peered over the tops of the maze of cubicles.

"She's right over there." Anna pointed to the far end of the corridor, to a desk on the extreme right. "She and Gloria were pretty tight while Gloria was here."

"Thank you." He started to leave. "Oh, by the way, when did Gloria leave her job?"

"About nine months ago." Anna smiled affectionately. "She always called this her day job, though you wouldn't have known by the way she worked. I wished I had ten of her."

Day job. That meant she was trying to make a go of

something else. But what? It obviously wasn't being a nanny. Could she have plotted to kidnap Andrew all along in order to get a stake of some sort? It sounded like a shot in the dark, but he'd come across wilder theories that had turned out to be true.

He probed a little further into the woman's testimonial. "What do you mean? She put in a lot of overtime?"

"Oh, no, she never worked overtime. Couldn't. She kept regular hours, but she gave a hundred twenty-five percent when she was here. I tried to talk her into staying, but she was adamant. Now or never, she said."

Now or never. What was that supposed to mean? The nine-month time frame coincided with when she came to work for McNair. Had she seen the CEO as her ticket to better things?

He was holding two different puzzle pieces in his hand. So far, he'd gotten two unofficial testimonials. Both of which painted the image of a woman who believed in giving her employer everything she felt was due him or her. Giving, not taking. People like that didn't just wake up one morning and steal their employer's child.

Or did they?

Thanking Anna for her help, he made his way through the maze to Carla Wassel's cubicle. He could feel Anna's eyes following him.

Because there was no door, he rapped once on the side of the cubicle to get the woman's attention. "Ms. Wassel?"

A dark-haired woman with striking bright blue eyes turned from her computer screen to look up at him. The smile tinged in curiosity came a beat afterward.

Ben could see the resemblance instantly. Not so much

the hair, although both the woman he'd met in the bookstore and Carla Wassel were brunettes who wore their hair short, but in the eyes. A man didn't readily forget eyes like that. They had the exact same shade of blue. Like bits of cobalt.

"Yes?"

"I'm Ben Underwood." He indicated the chair within her cubicle. "Mind if I sit down?" Still curious, she gestured for him to take a seat. "I'm trying to locate a friend of yours. Gloria Prescott."

"Gloria?" Her eyes widened. "Why? Has something happened to her?"

Ben stopped before reaching for Gloria's photograph. He saw no reason for her to get as upset as she did. "What makes you ask that?"

Carla flushed, embarrassed. "I'm sorry, ever since my sister died, I'm afraid I overreact to things. The first thing I think of is..." Her voice trailed off as she let the end of her thought go. "Never mind." She waved away the rest of her sentence. "Why are you trying to find Gloria?"

For simplicity, and because there was a chance he might have to return for more information, Ben gave Carla the same story he'd given her supervisor.

"Her fiancé's trying to find her. They were supposed to go away together to Hawaii last week and Gloria never showed up. Personally," he said, leaning in a little closer, "I think it might be cold feet, but we have to investigate these things."

Caution entered her voice. "Are you a policeman?"

For a second he debated going that route. But the closer he remained to the truth, the easier it was to remember details. "A private one."

Carla took the information in stride. "I don't think I

can help you. I haven't been in touch with Gloria since shortly after she left the office.'' She raised her shoulder in a semihelpless movement. ''I meant to, but you know how that goes. I suppose I wasn't much fun to be around at the time. But I'm better now.''

''Nice to hear.'' He tried to sound sympathetic. Another dead end, he thought. But there was still the coincidence of the names. No stone unturned. ''How do you spell your last name?''

Carla's dark eyebrows drew together over a Roman nose. ''W-a-s-s-e-l, why?''

He jotted it down in the small notepad he carried. Tucking it back into his pocket, his fingers came in contact with the cookies Aunt Sugar had slipped in. He had to remember to take them out.

''Just for the record,'' he assured her. ''Do you have any relatives in San Francisco?''

The answer required no extensive deliberation. ''No, I don't think so. Why?''

It was probably a meaningless coincidence, but he'd learned never to ignore or omit anything that seemed the slightest bit unusual. He'd gone to the bookstore where Gloria had once worked only to run into a woman with her best friend's last name. There could be a connection. At the very least, the woman in San Francisco might know Gloria.

''I ran into someone with the exact same last name as yours just yesterday. You have to admit, it's not exactly in the same realm as Smith or Jones.''

Curious, Carla asked gamely, ''Maybe we are related. What was his name?''

''Her,'' he corrected the woman. ''Gina Wassel.''

Carla turned pale and grabbed the edge of her desk. Ben saw her eyes roll toward the back of her head, and for a second he thought he was going to have to catch her to keep her from sliding off her chair, onto the floor.

He grabbed her arms. "Take a deep breath," he ordered. "Again." He waited until she exhaled slowly. "Are you all right?"

When she looked at him, there was an accusation in her eyes. "Is this some kind of a cruel joke?"

He had no idea what she was talking about, but he'd obviously stumbled onto something. "Not that I'm aware of," he said slowly.

"Gina's my sister. Was my sister," she corrected herself. The pain was obvious. "She's been gone for ten months. Wait." Agitated, blinking back tears that were threatening to overwhelm her, Carla dug into the purse she kept under her desk. "Here, here's her picture." She shoved her wallet at him and showed him a photograph of herself and her sister standing in front of an old house. A beat later he realized that it was the Victorian-looking house he'd gone to yesterday. "That's Gina." She indicated the slender young woman on the right.

"Who took this picture?"

"Gloria. We went to visit her aunt on her seventieth birthday."

The resemblance between the woman in the photograph and the one he'd met yesterday was unmistakable. They could have been the same person. Folding the wallet closed, he handed it back to Carla.

"Ms. Wassel," he began as gently as he could, "I have to ask—"

Carla cut him off. She couldn't bear to hear the words. "I was driving the car when the camper sideswiped us. Gina was killed instantly." Her breathing was ragged as she spoke. "It was Gloria who helped me through that, who let me sleep on her sofa and kept me sane.'' Without looking, she dropped the wallet back into her purse. ''If she hadn't been around, I probably would have killed myself.'' Her eyes held his for a moment. ''If Gloria's in some sort of danger, you've got to find her.''

Ben had a feeling he already had.

There were huge, gaping holes in the puzzle he found himself working. ''You have access to all sorts of information here, don't you?''

Carla's expression told him she wasn't sure where he was going with this, or what she should answer. ''Depending on your level of clearance, yes.''

''Such as social security numbers.''

She laughed nervously, still uncertain. ''Well, of course. We're a social security office.''

''Does that mean social security numbers that are no longer in use?'' This would have been the perfect place for Gloria to forge a new identity.

''Yes.'' The single word emerged slowly.

He had a feeling he was on the right track. ''Ms. Wassel, I know this might sound rather strange to you, but would you be able to give me your sister's social security number?''

''Yes, but I already told you, Gina's dead.'' Carla began to access a program for him, then stopped and looked at him. ''You think Gloria's using Gina's social security number.''

''Yes.''

It didn't make any sense. ''But why?''

To hide from Stephen McNair until he agreed to her terms. But he couldn't tell the woman that. She wouldn't give him the social security number he needed, and right now, he didn't know if Savannah had access to inactive files.

"I won't be able to answer any questions until I have all the facts," he told her.

Confusion furrowed her brow as she looked at the keys, undecided. "If Gloria's in some sort of trouble, maybe I shouldn't be helping you."

His voice was quiet and authoritative. "If Gloria's in some sort of trouble, I might be the only one who *can* help her."

Carla sat looking at him for a long moment, then began typing.

The electronic doors opened and closed.

The chill that ran up her back was immediate, drenching her with an icy wave. Though she was in one of the aisles, her eyes darted toward the front.

How long before that reaction would leave her? Before she could hear the doors opening and not be compelled to look, holding her breath and praying. It wasn't natural to feel this way, as if she were doomed to cross and recross a tightrope stretched over a bottomless pit with slippery shoes.

He wouldn't track her here, she insisted silently. He didn't know enough about her to know about this place. And even if he did and was still looking for her, she wasn't really here. Not the way he knew her.

She was safe.

The breath she'd been holding escaped as recognition came. Gina's mouth curved. The man who had gotten between her and that pushy jerk the day before yesterday had returned.

What was he was doing back? When she'd left, he'd asked her to point Jon out, or rather, the store manager.

That meant Jon and the stranger didn't know each other, so it wasn't personal. Jon hadn't mentioned anything to her, but then, he'd been in a real rush to leave after taking that call from his brother.

He told her he had to take some time off and left her in charge, just like that.

Funny how you could work with someone for so long and not know anything about him. She'd spent all four college years working in the store, and in all that time, Jon had never mentioned even having a family. He'd been closemouthed as far as things like that went.

Pot calling the kettle black. She certainly wasn't in a position to throw rocks right now, she mused. Jon didn't know all that much about her, either. Nor had he asked anything, not even when she'd suddenly appeared out of the blue three weeks ago, asking for her old job back. All he'd said was sure, then added an addendum: If she needed him, he was around. To prove it, he'd gotten her in contact with a friend of his who was trying to sublet his condo. She had a job and a home within one day, thanks to Jon. He was one in a million.

He hadn't even made any comment about her changed appearance when she came in the first day. Just asked her what name she wanted to go under. Nothing more.

Gina suspected that World War Three could probably break out right in front of the bookstore and as long as it didn't intrude within the doors, Jon would remain oblivious to it.

Lucky for her.

Pushing the book she was holding back into its space, she walked up to the man who had just entered and smiled at him. "I see you're back. Come to see if I needed rescuing again?"

He'd taken measure of her as he'd walked in and still wondered if there was some sort of mistake. But it was too much of a coincidence for him to shrug off. What he needed was to find a way to find out her social security number. That might be more difficult than he'd anticipated if the store manager had agreed to pay her off the books.

"Oh, you strike me as someone who can take care of herself. If I hadn't intervened yesterday, you probably would have decked him."

He had a dimple, she realized. And a sense of humor. She found that an extremely sexy trait. "My boxing gloves are in the shop," she said wryly. "Jon's not here if you came to see him."

"Jon?"

"The store manager." Obviously the name meant nothing to him. "I'm sorry, I'm just taking a stab at why you're here."

He wondered what she would say if he answered her truthfully. If he told her that he was looking for Gloria Prescott and the little boy she'd abducted. Probably nothing. At close quarters, the woman looked cool enough to be able to pull it off. If she was Gloria.

"To do some research, actually."

Savannah had managed to access Gloria Prescott's transcript at the University of San Francisco for him. He'd discovered that while her degree was in the field of studio arts, specifically sculpting, she'd minored in American history. He'd guessed that the preponderance of courses on Native Americans meant her interest lay there. The drive up from Bedford had given him ample time to come up with a scenario.

He looked around. "Do you have a Native American

section? I'm working on a project and I'm kind of stuck. I need all the input I can get.''

Ben saw interest enter her eyes. ''Native American? What kind of a project is it?''

He pretended to hesitate. ''You'd probably laugh.''

That made her smile. ''No, I wouldn't, try me.''

He'd chosen his story carefully. ''It's a screenplay—you probably hear that all the time. Everybody and his brother is writing one, or knows someone who's writing one.''

Her smile was nothing short of encouraging. If this was Gloria, he could easily see why McNair had lost his head. Whether she was blonde or brunette, there was something about the woman's smile that got to a man, made him want to puff up his chest and do something extraordinary to make her take notice.

''I don't,'' she told him.

He caught her off guard by putting out his hand. ''Ben Underwood. Now you know me, so you know someone who's writing one.''

The smile turned into a soft laugh that wafted around him like the first breeze of spring, full of promise at what was to be.

''All right, Ben Underwood, what's your screenplay about?''

''The Battle of Wounded Knee.'' Other than Custer's last stand at Little Big Horn, it was the only Indian battle that he was vaguely aware of.

She caught her lower lip between her teeth, holding back a laugh.

''You're not going to believe this, but I minored in Native American studies at UCSF.''

''You're kidding.'' He looked properly impressed.

"Damn, but this is my lucky day. Maybe you can help fill in the gaps for me."

"Maybe," she echoed, her mouth curving.

He did his best not to notice how inviting that looked.

Chapter 4

So far, so good, Ben thought, returning her smile. He'd managed to establish a beachhead, however small. But he was a long way from winning the battle yet.

What he needed was to gain her trust so he could get to the bottom of what was going on. As of right now, he still wasn't a hundred percent certain that he had the right woman. All he had to go on was the slightly out-of-focus photograph McNair had given him and a likeness of Gloria Prescott that Savannah had lifted from the DMV records she'd accessed. The only similarity between that and the woman he was looking at was they looked to be approximately the same age.

Ben summoned what latent acting talents he had and infused his voice with what he hoped was the right amount of enthusiasm. One of his best friends was a would-be screenwriter. Ben did his best to imitate the way he'd heard Nick talk when he was going on about his project of the moment.

"You know, this is almost like fate, meeting you."

He touched her shoulder lightly as he spoke, initiating contact, but making certain that it couldn't be misconstrued as anything remotely sexual. If the other day was any indication, she probably had more than her share of that, but he'd noted that the slightest bit of physical contact between people instantly brought them to a more familiar plane. He did his best to walk the fine line.

"Listen, I've got an idea." Ben dropped his hand, as if suddenly aware of what he was doing. He saw a hint of a smile on Gina's face and congratulated himself on his instincts. "I know you're working right now, but maybe we could grab a bite to eat later when you knock off and—"

Having displayed what he thought was just the right amount of eagerness, he stopped, as if realizing how his words had to sound to her.

"I know you're probably thinking that this is a come-on, but it's really not. I really do need your help. I want to be accurate about this and I'm willing to pay you for your time." He shoved his hands into his pockets. "Not much, I'm afraid—unless you're willing to take percentage points in my script."

Though she was trying to maintain her distance, Gina had to admit that this eager screenwriter did sound cute, stumbling over his words. She hoped he was better on paper. But she did appreciate that he realized she might be getting the wrong impression about his offer. Not many men would have picked up on that.

From the look of him, Ben Underwood seemed like the last word in manliness. Someone Aunt Sugar would have referred to as "a man's man—and a lady's heartthrob." Yet he was unapologetically sensitive to her feelings. After what she'd been through, he seemed more like a figment of her imagination than a real person.

Still, she had to turn him down.

"I can't tonight, I've got to close up." She was surprised at the regret she felt. Gina chalked it up to loneliness. "But I think I can manage tomorrow night after work, if that's all right." She could see he looked disappointed. "Unless you're in a hurry."

Ben noticed one of the other clerks looking their way and turned just slightly so that his body blocked her view of the other man. He didn't want her getting distracted while he made his pitch.

"I am—I'm getting close to my deadline." He paused, thinking that it was a lucky thing he'd decided to get a motel room close by. "But tomorrow night will be great," he added genially.

Intrigued, she cocked her head. "Deadline?"

The shrug was self-deprecating, with just enough boyishness thrown in to captivate her. Mischievous as a boy, he'd spent his childhood pleading his case to a tough audience. Looking sincere had become an art form. Dominican nuns ordinarily brooked no nonsense.

"I gave myself a deadline. If I didn't make it as a screenwriter within five years, I was going to stop fooling myself and go into the family business. I've got six months left."

She surprised him by whistling softly. His eyes lingered on her puckered lips.

"That's cutting it pretty close." She moved to the right, out of the way of a customer who was browsing through the section where they were standing. Perforce, she moved closer to Ben. "What's the family business?"

He silently apologized to Nick, whose life he was plagiarizing. ''Furniture-making.''

Gina studied him. She could definitely see this handsome stranger doing that. Wearing a leather apron over worn jeans and a checkered work shirt that was rolled up at the sleeves. Goggles perched atop his thick, black hair, the smell of freshly sawed wood about him. *You're getting carried away,* she warned herself. ''Are you any good at it?''

Humor glinted in his eyes as he laughed, thinking of Nick. Every time Nick attempted to make something, it was inevitably reduced to a pile of splinters and wood chips. He had no idea why Nick's father was so adamant about his joining the business.

''I would be if the family had a sideline making and selling toothpicks. My creativity lies in other directions, but if I can't make a go of it, my father insists I come into the business. Maybe as a sales rep.''

He made it sound like a life sentence with no possibility of parole. She found herself warming to him. ''We'll see what we can do. I'm not free tonight,'' she repeated, ''but I can point you toward an excellent book to get you started.''

''Sounds great.''

She led him to the American history section. One of the shelves was labeled Native American Studies. Eight years ago, it had been her personal baby, the one section she'd convinced Jon to set up. Now that she was back, she intended to keep on top of it religiously, making sure any new, relevant books were ordered while old standards were kept in stock.

She noticed two books were out of alphabetical order. Switching them to the right place, Gina selected one title and handed it to him. "This should be very help-ful."

"Thanks." He nodded toward the small table that was off to the side. There were several throughout the store, besides the ones at the coffee shop in the center of the store. "Mind if I...?"

Reading sections of a book before you bought it had become an accepted custom. "Help yourself. That's why the tables and chairs are here."

Ben made himself comfortable and opened the book to the first page. This was going to be slower going than he would have liked, he thought, but he felt he had no option. He needed something more to go on than just a glaring coincidence before he brought McNair in or the police down on the bookstore clerk. What if, by some strange twist of fate, he was wrong? Truth had been known to be stranger than fiction.

And if he was right, if this woman was Gloria Prescott and she was impersonating a dead woman, he needed to find out where she was keeping Andrew. His proceeding cautiously could mean the difference between life or death.

Mixed into all this was the question that was beginning to hound him. How could someone whom everyone he'd spoken with so far thought was a saint, have done something so heinous as to kidnap a child, no matter what her motive? If this woman with the winning smile and the killer figure was Gloria Prescott, she was either a consummate actress who had managed to fool her co-workers, her friend and her aunt, or something just wasn't right.

Any way he looked at it, he had a puzzle whose pieces weren't fitting together.

With a sigh, Ben lowered his eyes to his book and returned to playing his role.

Darkness pressed its face against the bookstore's large bay windows, peering in forlornly. It was a few minutes shy of nine o'clock, and except for Gina, he was the last one in the store. He'd spent the last few hours watching her interact with people, trying to form an opinion. Trying, also, to be objective and not swayed by the fact that she moved with the grace of a spring breeze, or that when she smiled or laughed, everyone around her seemed to light up. Him included.

He'd also wound up reading the book she had recommended. Even though his mind wasn't really on it, he had to admit that parts of it had managed to catch his attention and seep in. Maybe he'd mention the subject matter to Nick when he got home. Most success stories began as accidents. Who knew, this might be Nick's long-awaited accident.

Glancing at his watch, he verified the time. Nine. That meant she'd be closing up and going home soon. Maybe he could change her mind about tonight. The sooner he gained her confidence, the sooner he could get to the bottom of this.

He rose to his feet, feeling stiff. He'd stayed in one position too long. The wound he had gotten when he was shot in the line of duty, protecting his partner, whispered its presence along his body. He rotated his shoulders, trying to work out the discomfort.

Gina was at the register. Ben made his way over to her and placed the book on the counter between them, then took out his wallet.

"You're right, it's an excellent book." Handing her a twenty, he watched her ring the sale up. The last of the day. "Maybe we could go get that dinner now and discuss it."

She was tempted, she realized in surprise. What's more, it felt good to be tempted. She'd thought that perhaps, all things considered, she would never entertain that sensation again. But tempted or not, there was no way she could say yes, not tonight. Betty, her teenage baby-sitter, could only stay until nine-thirty. Jesse was asleep and she wasn't about to wake him. Besides, she doubted that this would-be screenwriter, sensitive or not, would welcome a six-year-old's company at dinner.

Handing him his change, she slipped the book into a bag with the store's logo on it. "I'm afraid I can't. There're…complications."

He played it as if she wasn't the suspect he'd been sent to track. "Husband?"

"No." She held up her left hand to substantiate her answer.

"Boyfriend?"

This time, Gina smiled as she shook her head, thinking him sweet and wondering if she was a fool for thinking it. "No."

Ben raised his brows in a supposed last-ditch, far-out guess. "Strict parents?"

She laughed. "No. Just…complications."

Gina wondered how her son would take to being referred to as a complication. In reality, he was the most uncomplicated, most wonderful part of her life. But arranging her schedule around him, picking him up at school and making sure he was safe at all times, did lead to a great many complications.

"If you come by the store tomorrow," she told him, hoping that he would, "I'll let you know about dinner."

"Why don't you just give me your home phone number and I'll call you?" He made the suggestion as casually as he could.

He seemed like a nice person, but she'd made a costly error in judgment before. It was better to be safe than sorry. "Coming by the shop would be easier."

"Here, let me give you my cell phone number just in case you need to get in touch with me." He wrote it down on a slip of paper and handed it to her. Folding it, she slipped it into her pocket. "You've aroused my curiosity, you know." Ben realized his mistake the instant the teasing remark left his lips. A wary look had entered her eyes. He immediately went into damage control. "Will I have to guess anyone's name, climb up a ladder made of golden hair or slay a dragon before I earn the pleasure of your company and get access to your knowledge?"

Ben silently breathed a sigh of relief as he saw her smile again. "No, nothing like that, I promise." Taking out the day's cash, she put it into a metal strongbox, then slipped a cover over the cash register.

The cop in him had him glancing toward the front door. This wasn't known to be the most savory location in San Francisco. "Should you be here by yourself doing that?"

The note of concern caught her off guard. So did the warmth stirring in response. "I've done this before. The front door locks automatically at nine. I'm going to have to use a key to let you out."

"Why don't I wait until you're finished and walk you to your car?" He wasn't certain if it was the man he was pretending to be or the man he was who made the offer.

There was a part of her that yearned for just that. To

have someone walk her to her car, to offer her his protection by mutual agreement. But there was a part, a much larger part, that had become very leery of protectiveness because it could so easily turn into possessiveness. And that led to dark places.

So, very politely but firmly, she turned him down. "Thank you, but there's no need for that." Gina cut him off before he could offer a protest. "And Jon would be upset if I let someone remain in the store when I put the money into the safe." Slipping the strongbox beneath the counter, she came out from behind it and deliberately led the way to the front doors. Unlocking them, she pushed one open and held it for him. "I'll see you tomorrow, Ben."

"Count on it."

Walking to his car, he thought of following Gina when she left the bookstore. But it was harder tailing someone at night than in the light of day, and if for some reason she spotted him, it would definitely spook her. He didn't want to undo the groundwork he'd just spent the last few hours laying down. He was going to have to wait. Tomorrow night, he'd find a way to get himself invited back to her place. Once he knew where she lived, he could return and nose around while she was at work.

Chapter 5

Despite the fact that it had been busy ever since they'd opened their doors this morning, Gina's eyes darted toward the electronic doors when she head the tiny buzzer sound, announcing the entrance of a new customer. It was a woman in her late forties. The rise in adrenaline leveled off.

This was stupid.

She had a great many more important things on her mind than a good-looking man supposedly writing a screenplay about the massacre at Wounded Knee. A very good-looking man, her mind amended automatically and entirely against her will.

"Next, please," she called to the orderly line of people who stood behind the deep purple plush ropes strung up solely to keep them in their place.

A heavyset man with an armload of books walked up, depositing them on the counter. Tilted, the books scattered every which way, mostly sprawling out on her side of the counter, some falling beneath. Offering a vague, sympathetic smile at the flustered man, Gina gathered the books up.

For all she knew, Gina thought as she began ringing up the sale for the hapless customer, Ben's story about needing to do research for his screenplay could have all been just an elaborate pickup line. When she'd turned him down for dinner, not once but twice, that might have been the end of it.

Gina scanned two more books quickly, punching in the total, telling herself it was just as well that he hadn't returned.

No, it hadn't been just about a pickup, she thought, still carrying on the internal debate. He'd sounded sincere. She knew it. Besides, he'd come to her rescue the first time she'd met him and he hadn't tried to come on to her then. Sure he was sexy, but he didn't seem to be deceitful. Maybe he was exactly what he seemed, an earnest dreamer pursuing his dream. An earnest, sweet, good-looking dreamer.

Ben Underwood might be a dreamer, but she couldn't be, Gina reminded herself, slipping all the books she'd just rung up into a shopping bag and then handing it to the man with a vague smile.

"Have a nice day," she told him. She was in no position to daydream like normal people. She wasn't normal people. Not right now, at any rate. She was a woman on the run and she had to remember that.

Maybe not, a small voice whispered within her. Maybe the running was finally over. Maybe the man who'd robbed her of so many nights' sleep had decided she was too much trouble to pursue any further and had given up looking for her. Maybe she was finally safe.

Safe.

God, but she'd never realized how overwhelmingly seductive the four-letter word could be. Safe. Safe to go about her life doing everyday things, safe not to be constantly looking over her shoulder, wondering, worrying. Safe not to see shapes hidden in the shadows, afraid that she was being followed.

The front door buzzer sounded. She lost her place in counting out the next customer's change.

"Sorry," she murmured, beginning again.

The man buying the massive cookbook looked at her as if she were incapable of counting beyond five. "Maybe I should have given you a charge card."

The slightly condescending tone and tolerant expression on his patrician face made her want to whip out her college diploma to show him that she was quite capable of conducting monetary transactions of any amount.

A lot of good that would do, she realized ruefully. The name on the diploma didn't match the one on her name tag.

"Please come again," she murmured as cheerfully as she could muster.

The man mumbled something in response that was lost on her as she found herself looking up into eyes that were almost Wedgwood blue. Ben had come up on her blind side and was now leaning against the counter, blocking the next customer.

"Hi, are we still on?"

Was it possible for him to look better today than he had yesterday? Or was that just the self-imposed drought in her life that was making her suddenly thirsty? Thirsty for the companionship of a personable man who wanted nothing more from her than just her mind.

"On?" she echoed.

The customer took her books to the clerk at the next register, giving Gina an envious look. It wasn't lost on Gina.

"For tonight," Ben prompted. He didn't appear annoyed that she seemed to have momentarily forgotten. "You said that you couldn't go out after work last night, but that you probably could tonight." He looked at her hopefully. Or was that just her imagination?

She'd talked to Betty, who had checked with her mother last night. Since tonight was a Friday night and Betty hadn't hit the dating circuit yet—her mother referred to Betty as a late bloomer—Gina was assured of a sitter for Jesse.

Now all that remained was taking that final leap from self-proclaimed female hermit to socializing woman. Easier contemplated than done.

For most of her life, she'd loved company, loved going out. She'd always been a people person, until she'd had her trust betrayed at a college fraternity party. McNair had resurrected the leeriness that had come to define and delineate her life for months after her rape, making her hold all men suspect. Looking for ulterior motives.

She hated being that way, and yet...

"Oh, right." Gina beckoned forward the next customer who was about to bypass her. "I can take you here," she told the woman, then looked at Ben. "Um, I'm not so sure that I can, after all. There's the store, we don't lock up until ten tonight—" As she scanned the book, the numbers popped up on the register.

"Don't they let you go out for dinner?" Ben deadpanned.

"I'll lock up for you tonight, Gina," a deep voice on her other side rumbled.

She glanced toward the other register, not surprised to see the slightly superior look gracing the face of the tall, thin, prematurely balding young man. The man with the improbable name of Joe Valentine had regarded her as an interloper when Jon had given her responsibility of the store over him. Joe had been working at the bookstore a total of two and a half years and considered himself not just a clerk, but Jon's assistant. Gina had changed all that and he made no secret of the fact that he didn't care for it.

"After all, it's not like I haven't done it before," Joe said smugly.

There went her last excuse, she thought, secretly glad of it. She liked being divested of excuses, because part of her really wanted to see Ben again, under any pretext. Pretexts made her feel that it was all right. "Thanks, Joe, as long as you don't mind."

"Hey, where else am I going to go?"

"It looks like it's all settled, then," Ben said to her. "Unless you don't want to." He knew if he left it open like that, she wouldn't feel he was trying to pressure her into anything.

Oh, she wanted to, all right. Maybe a little too much. "It's not that—"

"Something else?"

The cop in him rose to the fore. He peered at her, keeping his voice casual, wondering if her resistance involved Andrew in some way. Was she keeping the boy someplace accessible? Was there someone else involved? Was this not just about revenge, the way McNair thought, but a child kidnapping ring with Andrew the latest victim?

It was a horrible thought, but one that was far from new. Ben knew that Cade's own son had been kidnapped for just that reason. It had taken Cade three years to find the boy again. Darin Townsend was the reason ChildFinders, Inc. existed.

She almost said something about Jesse and being reluctant to leave him, but at the last minute decided not to. She was undoubtedly being overly paranoid, but there was no harm in keeping her private life private. No harm and maybe a great deal of good.

"No, nothing else."

Score one for the home team. "Well then it looks like it's settled. How about Wellington's?" Ben asked.

She was familiar with the restaurant. It was a place she'd treated herself to once a month while she'd been attending college. The food was wonderful and the ambience even better. It was a place she could easily see him in, but not for the type of thing she'd thought he had in mind. Suspicions whispered in her ear again.

"Isn't that a little fancy? I thought you just wanted to grab a bite to eat and talk about research."

His smile disarmed her before he said a word.

"Who says the bite has to be in a fast-food place? Or that we have to chew fast?"

He saw the protest forming on her lips, saw the indecision in her eyes. He was winning her over, but he had to talk quickly to sustain his advantage. Getting her to a friendly, neutral place that might seduce her defenses was all part and parcel of his plan to get her comfortable enough to talk to him. The more she talked, the more likely she'd be to let something slip.

"Think of it as partial payment for your time," he told her.

She couldn't help smiling. "Script points and dinner?"

"Right. And anything else you can think of, too."

Her eyes narrowed. *Was* this just an elaborate come-on after all? She didn't want to believe it, yet... "Such as?"

"I'm very handy with my hands."

Her heart sank. It was a come-on. "I'm afraid I really don't—"

He stopped her before she said something he was going to regret. "That didn't come out right. What I mean is that I can fix things around the house. Cracking plaster, doors that stick, things like that."

The small condo she had sublet from Jon's friend could more than use a face-lift, but not from someone she didn't know. She knew the danger of opening her door and her life to someone.

"I don't need anything fixed," she assured him.

"All right," he replied philosophically, "then it'll just be dinner and research."

"Dinner and research," she echoed.

A line was beginning to form at the register again. Joe was looking toward them with a less than friendly expression on his face. Ben began to talk quickly before Gina saw the clerk and retreated to help him. "What time would you like me to pick you up?"

It would keep things simpler if he didn't know where she lived. "Since this is dinner and research, why don't I just meet you at the restaurant?"

He picked up on her reluctance to share her address. The scale tipped against her again. "You really are an independent woman, aren't you?"

The grin that curved her mouth nearly unraveled him. It was completely guileless and captivating. "Whenever possible.'' Hearing Joe clear his throat, she realized that she'd somehow managed to drift away from the register. She began moving back toward the registers. ''Now then, I'm afraid I've got to get back to work.''

He wasn't finished yet. There was one more thing he needed from her. Her prints. Ben glanced toward the section she had directed him toward yesterday. ''Um, I was wondering if you could recommend any other books for me from the store?''

She thought a moment, shaking her head. ''I think we covered that last time.'' Surprise flittered over her features. ''You didn't finish the one you bought yesterday already, did you?''

He nodded. ''Stayed up all night. I thought if there was something else—''

''All right, let's see.'' Because he seemed so eager, she went to check the books listed by subject on the computer. Going over the inventory, she stopped at a particular title. ''Well, there is one more that might help—''

All he needed was one. Because the books were accessible to the public, the idea of getting her prints from the one he'd already bought hadn't occurred to him until after he'd handled it extensively. He wasn't about to make the same mistake again. ''Take me to it.''

She couldn't help smiling. ''You really are eager about this, aren't you?''

He said what he knew she needed to hear, even though there was a part of him that was starting to feel uncomfortable with the duplicity. ''So eager I can taste it.''

Telling Joe she would be right back, she brought Ben over to the American history section and, after a moment, found the book she was looking for. It was out of place. "This one doesn't go into depth on the battle, but it does give you a pretty good background on the tribal life and the people." Turning from the shelf, she started to hand the book to him.

He made no effort to take it from her. Instead, he indicated the register. "Great. I'll take it."

"Don't you want to look through it first?"

"No, I trust your instincts." He began leading the way to the front counter. She had no choice but to follow. "Ring it up for me and I'll be out of your hair until tonight."

"All right." Joe spared her an annoyed look as she went to the second register and scanned in the book for Ben. "Twenty-three fifty-eight."

She took the two bills Ben handed her and made change, then tore off the receipt and slipped it, along with the book, into a bag.

He took the bag from her. "I'll see you tonight, then."

"All right." She said the words, banking down the excitement that popped up unexpectedly. A customer looked at her impatiently and she waved the woman forward.

"What time?" Ben asked.

"Excuse me?"

"You didn't tell me what time," he pointed out, then suggested one for her. "Seven all right?"

Gina hesitated for a moment. It would take a while for Jesse to settle in if he knew she was going out. "Eight would be better."

"Eight," he agreed. "I'll see you then."

A feeling of triumph mixed with something he couldn't quite identify flowed over him as he left the store.

His next stop was a stationery store he'd seen on the next block. He needed a padded manila envelope.

"Where's the nearest post office?" he asked the clerk who rang up his purchase.

The woman thought for a moment, then conferred with the woman at the next register before giving him a location. The branch was five blocks from his motel.

Back in his car again, Ben wrote out ChildFinders' address across the front of the manila envelope, marking it to Rusty's attention, then slipped the book, the receipt and the paper bag inside. The brief note he included asked Rusty to get all three items to the lab to be dusted for fingerprints. Since she'd been a government employee, Gloria Prescott's prints had to be on file somewhere. Between Rusty and Savannah, he figured it wouldn't be all that difficult to find the prints and get a match.

If there was one.

He tried not to dwell on his resistance to the idea. He wasn't getting paid to take sides, but to do a job. So far, the agency had solved every case of a missing child. He didn't intend to be the first one to fail.

Jesse scrutinized Gina with sharp green eyes. "Are we going out, Mommy?"

She'd been anticipating the inevitable barrage of questions all through dinner, especially since she hadn't eaten, just kept him company while he'd had his. "Not we, kiddo, me."

Uncertainty imprinted itself on his small face. "You're leaving me?"

She knew that ever since they'd uprooted from the only place he'd ever called home, he'd felt uneasy and threatened. She turned from the mirror that a number of earthquakes had managed to warp ever so slightly and looked down at him. "No, I'm not leaving you. I'm going out for a few hours. Like I used to, remember?"

He nodded, his small head bobbing up and down. "When we lived in Bedford?"

She stooped down to give him a quick hug meant to reassure him. And maybe herself, just a little. "Yes, baby, when we lived in Bedford."

He disentangled himself from her, giving her his most grown-up look. "I'm not a baby, Mommy. I'm six."

"Right, practically a man." She rose to her feet again. "Sorry, I keep forgetting." Slipping on her heels, she smoothed the sides of the dress, then looked down at her kindest critic. "So, do you like it?"

He cocked his head, doing his best to look as if he was scrutinizing her. "It's okay. Is it for somebody special?"

She wasn't taken in by the noncommittal tone. She knew what was on his mind.

"You're the only somebody special in my life, kiddo. And don't you forget it." Catching him by the shoulders, she tickled him. He dissolved in a fit of giggles. "How about me, am I the only somebody special in your life?"

He worked his bottom lip with baby teeth. "Maybe."

Pretending surprised indignity, she fisted her hands at her hips and gave him a penetrating look. "Oh, 'maybe' is it? Okay, spill it, kiddo, who's the hussy who stole your heart? Out with it. What's her name?"

He laughed, knowing she was only kidding. His mom was a great kidder. "Judy. Judy Camden."

"Judy, huh?" Even as she teased, she searched Jesse's eyes for signs of things she anticipated. He wasn't going to be hers exclusively forever. The shift had to start sometime. She knew she wasn't going to be ready for it no matter when it came, but for Jesse's sake, she was going to do her best to pretend she was. "So, what's this Judy Camden like?"

"Pretty," he said quickly, then added in a slightly lower voice, "and she's got candy."

Gina stifled a laugh. He was still her six-year-old. "Knew it, an ulterior motive."

Jesse's features drew together in concentration. "What's an ulterior motive?"

Picking up a comb, she did last-minute touch-ups to her hair. "A reason that you're doing something that isn't always obvious."

He was quiet for a moment. "Like why we moved away, Mommy?"

She was careful not to let him know how much she worried about the way all this was affecting him. At no time had she ever said anything to lead him to believe he was in any danger. "We moved away because I wanted to live in San Francisco for a while, and be not that far away from Aunt Sugar." Smiling brightly, she trusted herself to look at him. "You like Aunt Sugar, don't you?"

The grin was wide and infectious. "Yeah, she's nice. And she makes good cookies."

"That she does." Finished, she took his hand in hers. It felt so small, she thought, protectiveness welling up inside of her. "Now, it's off to bed with you, kiddo. Betty's coming, so you call her if you need anything and I'll be back before you know it."

He looked up at her as they walked into his bedroom. "Promise?"

She crossed her heart with her free hand. "Promise."

He beamed at her. "I love you, Mommy."

She picked him up in her arms, needing to hug him to her. ''And I love you.''

Jesse drew back his head so he could look at her. ''Forever and ever?''

''Forever and ever,'' she repeated. ''And a day longer than that.''

Satisfied, he nodded. ''Okay, you can go.''

She laughed and scooted him into his bed, thinking herself to be the luckiest woman who ever lived. ''Thank you, master.''

''You're welcome.''

He giggled at the face she made at him.

Chapter 6

Her perfume seductively preceded her as Gina approached his table. Just the lightest, stirring scent of honeysuckle teased his senses. The promise of spring within the heart of winter.

Ben got his mind back on his job and his role. He smiled at her as he rose in his seat. "I was beginning to think you weren't coming."

Slipping out of her coat, Gina slid into the seat the maître d' held out for her. She tried not to pay any attention to the strange, small quiver in the pit of her stomach. Ben's masculinity was just the slightest bit disconcerting.

His eyes were kind, but he wasn't a safe man. He was a man who could easily rattle a woman's foundation, who could make a woman stray from the clear-and-narrow path. A man who could have her forgetting her thoughts in midsentence. Like now.

"I was beginning to think I wasn't, either. Friday

night's not the easiest night to find—'' Gina caught herself, stopping abruptly. She met his quizzical expression with a soft one of her own as she continued. ''What I was looking for.''

That wasn't what she'd been about to say, Ben thought. ''Which was?''

''A new dress.'' She looked up at him brightly. ''Do you like it?''

His eyes slowly took inventory of what he could see. A simple high-necked turquoise dress that graced her curves as if it had been made with just her in mind.

And stirred a man's mind in directions that were best not traveled, he thought.

''Very much.'' He indicated the plate of stuffed mushrooms. ''I ordered appetizers for us, I hope you don't mind.''

The candle's flickering flame accented the pleased light that entered her eyes. ''No, I love stuffed mushrooms.'' She gingerly picked up one and popped it into her mouth. The familiar taste stirred memories. The last time she'd had stuffed mushrooms was at the art gallery show. When her life had changed forever.

He watched the small appetizer disappear between her lips and entertained the oddest sensation of being envious of a mushroom. And then he smiled.

''What?''

Instead of answering, he picked up his napkin. The tiniest scrap of cheese stuffing clung to the right corner of her mouth.

''Hold still.'' Capturing the point of her chin with his hand, Ben lightly wiped the telltale evidence away.

For just the slightest moment in time, he felt a current pass through him, tightening his belly. Ben dropped the napkin back down on his lap.

The look in her eyes told him she'd felt it as well.

God, but her eyes were blue.

Gina's mind turned to mush as the breath stopped in her lungs.

"You, um, had a little cheese on your mouth," he said.

"Thank you," she murmured, searching for something safe to talk about and trying not to think about the way her stomach had suddenly given birth to a squadron of butterflies just because a man she hardly knew had wiped away a dot of cheese at the corner of her mouth.

The waiter appeared to save her, ready to take their order.

"Would you like more time?" Ben asked. "You haven't had a chance to look at the menu yet."

"Allow me to tell you the specials of the day," the waiter offered, then subtly took a deep breath to launch into a recitation.

But Gina held her hand up, stopping the man before he could tell her the first item.

"That's all right, I know more or less what's on the menu and what I want. I used to come here all the time." It had been one of her favorite places to go. She'd taken Aunt Sugar here one of the few times the older woman had visited her in San Francisco.

"Used to? When?" Ben kept the question casual as he looked over his own menu.

"In another life," she murmured half to herself, then looked up at him, sensing he was looking at her. "I went to college around here."

"But it's not home."

"No, it's not home." Glancing at the menu to make sure the item was still being offered, she ordered shrimp with alfredo sauce and surrendered her menu to the young waiter.

"The same," Ben told him. The waiter nodded and withdrew. "He looked disappointed that he couldn't tell you the specials of the day." There was laughter in her eyes and he found himself momentarily mesmerized and lost. "What?"

She was being silly, she thought. Probably just giddy at the thought of getting out for the evening. She shook her head. "Nothing."

"You're trying not to laugh. Let me in on the joke," he coaxed. "What is it?"

"It's just that the waiter looks a little like Clark Kent." She nodded toward the departing food server. "Superman's alter ego," she prompted when Ben didn't say anything.

"I know who Clark Kent is." She'd given him an opening. He took it and ran with it. "I was just thinking about secrets."

"What about them?"

The shrug was purposely vague. "That everyone probably has one or two."

Gina looked away as she took another stuffed mushroom and eased it onto her small plate.

He was making her jittery. Good, that made two of them. Except that he wasn't supposed to be. He was supposed to be thinking about the case and not about the long legs that were beneath the table, next to his.

"How about you, Gina? Do you have any secrets?" He kept his tone light, teasing. Watching her eyes.

Gina raised them to his as the rest of the restaurant and its occupants seemed to recede. Despite the quavering in her stomach and its new winged occupants, she couldn't help wondering if Ben was fishing or flirting.

She was being paranoid again, she upbraided herself. Why would he be fishing? He had no connection with where she'd come from. No connection to why she'd left.

But looking over her shoulder was what kept her and Jesse free.

"Like you said, everyone has secrets, I think." With effort, she kept her voice as light as his. She looked at him pointedly.

"So, what's yours?" He topped off her glass of wine, though she'd only had a sip or two. "Better yet, what's your secret fantasy?"

A faraway look entered her eyes. That was easy. "Just to be happy."

Ben studied her, intrigued. "That's all? That doesn't sound like such an exotic fantasy."

The last thing she wanted was an exotic fantasy. She'd indulged in fantasy once and been slapped down just as it was about to become a reality.

"It's not. But don't kid yourself, it's harder to achieve than you might think." She'd sacrificed a great deal to that end. The look in his eyes told her he wasn't about to drop the subject. She turned the tables on him. "How about you? Any secrets up your sleeve? Any unfulfilled fantasies?"

He drained the rest of his drink. "Two very different questions," he pointed out.

"Then choose one." Finished with the mushroom, she wiped her fingertips on the edge of her napkin. "And answer it."

He thought a moment, then took his cue from her and embellished in a way he knew would draw her in. A way he actually believed in when cynicism didn't intrude, getting in the way. "I guess being happy sounds pretty good." He paused in just the right place. "And making the world a better place for being in it."

"Very noble." Was he just feeding her a line? She'd rather think that he wasn't, that he was being sincere. "Is that why you've decided to tell the story?"

He was getting lost in her eyes again, he realized. He'd hoped to use his charm on her to get her to open up, but it seemed that the reverse was proving true. And she didn't even seem to be trying. "Excuse me?"

"The massacre. At Wounded Knee. Your screenplay," she finally said when his expression remained ever so slightly bewildered.

"Oh, right." Annoyance at his own lapse rose up within him. He smiled engagingly. Covering. "Sorry, I got lost in your eyes for a second there. I don't think I've ever seen blue that intense before."

And he wasn't now, she thought. At least, not in the way he believed. She was wearing contact lenses. All part of the disguise. The pang of regret was unexpected and Gina blocked it, but not before it had made its presence known.

She struggled to clear her head and not lose her own way amid the lies that were tangled within the truth.

"So, any other fantasies?" she asked brightly. "Besides writing the great American screenplay?"

"No, that would about do it," he replied with a gentle smile. But if he were to indulge in a fantasy, he thought, it would have something to do with a woman who smelled of honeysuckle in the winter and had a waist that begged for a man's hand to slip around it. He reached for one of the breadsticks instead. "I guess I'm just your average, run-of-the-mill, boring guy."

The last thing this man was, was boring, she thought. There was a sexual vitality about him. Just being in the same room with him was enough to make that evident.

She liked the way he looked at her, as if she were the only one in the room instead of just one of many. There was a danger in liking it, but for a few hours, under the protective umbrella of a crowded restaurant, she'd allow herself to enjoy it. Just a little. What was the harm in pretending? As long as she remembered it was just pretend.

The waiter returned with their meals, murmuring something about hoping they enjoyed them before he retreated again.

"You're right," Ben acknowledged, lowering his voice as he leaned in toward her. "Clark Kent all the way." He grinned at her.

It was the kind of grin that went clear down to the bone, Gina caught herself thinking, as it took her hostage. She was going to have to watch herself. She was definitely still too vulnerable to be out with a man she didn't really know.

The evening passed far too quickly and he'd enjoyed it. Enjoyed talking to her, looking at her. The conversation hadn't brought him an inch closer to his investigation. Revolving around impersonal subjects as well as his supposed screenplay's subject matter, somehow it had still managed to give him an intimate image of the woman across the table.

Or maybe it was just a skillfully fashioned image he was meant to buy into. He wasn't certain. Instincts that had seen him through so much had suddenly proved useless. All he knew was that he found himself liking her. More and more.

Guilt ran through his conscience. You weren't sup-posed to like a kidnapper. If she was one.

When the check arrived, he paid it in cash rather than use a card, then rose to his feet to help her on with her coat. As he did, he palmed the scarf she'd worn tucked in at the neck, slipping it into his pocket. Then he leaned in close to distract her and keep her from noticing its absence.

"Sure I can't convince you to go dancing?"

Dancing. That would describe what the warm shiver that was traveling through her was doing. His breath touched her skin as he spoke, creating a longing that was almost overwhelming. A longing that reminded her she was a woman. Regret was abysmal but had to be obeyed.

"I'm afraid I'm sure."

He suddenly regretted that he wouldn't have an ex-cuse to hold her in his arms, even if it was only for three- to five-minute increments. "Maybe some other time."

"Maybe."

The night wind was cold and brusque, as they left the shelter of the restaurant and stepped outside. He wasn't used to weather like this. Living in Southern California had made him soft. "So, can I drive you home?"

"I came in my own car, remember?" She pointed vaguely out into the parking lot.

He turned up his collar, thinking he should have worn something warmer. "How about if I follow you, just to make sure you get home safe?"

The offer amused her. And touched her. It'd been a long time since anyone had concerned himself about her safety.

"Thanks for the thought, but I'll be fine." She touched his face. "Really."

He didn't want to let her go yet. All he'd found out tonight was that he liked the sound of her laughter. But he already knew that. What he still didn't know was how to reconcile two very different Gloria Prescotts he'd been introduced to.

"Here's another thought," he said just as she began to turn away. She raised an eyebrow, silently questioning him. "How about a nightcap? Your place, my place, or somewhere in between. Take your choice."

She raised her eyes to his. They were completely unreadable. All he could read was his own thoughts, his own reactions. And a sudden surge of desire that was as out of place here as ice cubes at a bonfire.

Dammit, he wanted to take her into his arms and kiss her. He bit off an oath in his mind as he shoved his hands into his pockets.

Gina began to say no, he could see the word forming on her lips. "I really don't—"

He needed her confidence, needed to gain access to her house or apartment. "It doesn't have to be anything strong," he assured her. "Water would do." He was losing her. Ben went with the truth. Or part of it. "I just don't want the evening to end."

Gina hesitated, so tempted she ached. But there wasn't just her to think about. She came in a distant second, no matter what this man with the bedroom eyes did to her insides.

Suppressing a sigh, she shook her head. "No, I'd better not. I promised to be home early."

"Promised?" Something twisted inside of him as he repeated the word. "Promised who?"

"Someone," she said evasively.

"Does it have anything to do with those 'complications' you mentioned yesterday?" he guessed.

She smiled then, relieved that he was accepting the excuse. Touched that he could be so sensitive about it. If only...

There was no "only." What there was, she reminded herself, were lies. And safety. "That's very perceptive of you."

"I'm a perceptive kind of guy." Although that seemed to be getting further and further from the truth, he thought. "If I can't see you home—yours or mine— let me at least see you to your car."

That was safe. And nice. "All right."

That same itch he'd felt when she'd first walked in through the door and taken off her coat tonight began to take hold again. Complicating things. He reminded himself that he had his code.

He also had an itch.

As she turned toward him to say good-night, he had another strong, almost overwhelming urge to sweep her into his arms. The candlelit dinner they'd just shared hadn't helped keep his feelings impersonal. Neither did the full moon looking down on them. It made him think of romantic things.

Nothing romantic about looking at a kidnapper, he reminded himself. He was looking for proof, for a missing boy, not romance.

Gina put out her hand. "Good night, Ben. I had a lovely evening."

He slipped his hand over hers, thinking how delicate it felt. "Me, too. Thanks for coming." Reluctantly, he released her. "Tell him he's a very lucky guy, this 'complication' you're going home to."

She thought of Jesse, probably waiting up for her,

dressed in those pajamas with the feet on them. She'd left him in bed, but she knew he wouldn't be asleep. He was stubborn that way.

Gina shook her head. "I'm the lucky one in this case." Getting into her car, she shut the door, then looked up at him again. "I'll see you."

"You've got my number," he called to her. He told himself it was just a phrase as he backed up, watching as she drove off.

Things were just not adding up, Ben thought as he got a beer from the minirefrigerator in his motel room and sat down at the table where he'd set up his laptop and the paraphernalia Megan had talked him into bringing. He'd done some canvassing of McNair's area before he'd left Bedford. The man lived almost in isolation at the apex of a hill in an exclusive neighborhood. His neighbors hardly knew of his existence, much less of Gloria's. Certainly he hadn't found anyone who had seen her leave with the boy the day he disappeared. Rusty had been thorough in the report he'd e-mailed to him.

As pompous as McNair was, he certainly did like anonymity in his private life. Ben frowned, sipping his beer and trying not to think about the woman he'd just left.

Or who had just left him, he amended. Black hair or blond, he could see why McNair had lost his head over her. What he couldn't see was the grasping, ruthless woman McNair had made her out to be.

Maybe her true colors would come out later.

And maybe he should take the weekend to go back down to McNair's area and do some more canvassing.

Or prevail on Chad and whoever else was free to help do it for him.

Chad had to be back from his honeymoon by now, he mused. Who would have ever thought that Chad Andreini would ever fall in love, much less get married? Looked like once in a while, miracles actually did happen.

He was going to need one himself if he hoped to solve this, Ben thought.

This attempt to get close to Gina was leading him into areas he didn't want to go and really beginning to complicate things. He was having some definitely unprofessional thoughts about Ms. Gina Wassel and the sooner he got back on track, the better for everyone.

Especially a small kidnapped boy by the name of Andrew.

Ben glanced at the door he'd just shut, debating going out again. If he confronted her tonight…no, tomorrow morning would be better. He needed a night's sleep and a night's distance from what he'd almost done. Kissing a kidnapping suspect was definitely not in the rule book, not even under miscellaneous.

He leaned back in the chair, balancing himself on two of its legs and stretching. That was when he saw it. The answering machine he'd plugged in to replace the motel's telephone was sitting on the nightstand by the sagging bed. It was flashing.

Setting the barely touched can of beer back down on the table, he got up and crossed to the machine. He pressed the message button. A metallic voice told him that he had one message, then proceeded to let him hear it.

''Ben, it's Carrie. That man whose son you're looking for called three times in the last two days, wanting a progress report. I told him you were out in the field and would get back to him when you could. He's not very happy with that answer. Said you told him you'd keep him abreast of things. He's getting a little belligerent. Maybe you could get back to him?''

A little belligerent. That was his secretary Carrie's shorthand for pompous ass. He had a feeling that Stephen McNair's winning ways did not extend to people he viewed as underlings. Or the ''hired help.''

By rights, he knew he should have already told McNair where he was. But he had a hunch that the man might insist on joining him and possibly ruin everything. Until he found the boy, until he knew what was going on, Ben didn't want McNair showing up.

McNair hadn't exactly struck him as someone who was beside himself with grief over his son's kidnapping, anyway. The calls to the agency seemed almost out of character. Probably just McNair being a control freak, he decided.

Ben frowned, erasing the message. None of the pieces he was juggling seemed to fit in with the others, he thought. Not even when he examined them closely.

Was that because of Gina? Gloria, he corrected himself. It didn't matter what the woman's name was, she was definitely messing up his thought process and it had to stop.

With a sigh, Ben returned to the table, to his beer and to thoughts that were going nowhere.

Chapter 7

Like a small, intent shadow, the little boy followed her from the kitchen to the threshold of the small, crammed garage that was now too cluttered to hold a car, thanks to the condo owner's resistance toward never throwing anything out.

"But why can't you play with me?" He looked accusingly at his mother as she rummaged through first one area, then another. "You promised last night when you went away that you'd play with me today. It's to-day," he announced in case she'd missed that fact.

If dogged determination was the main requirement, this boy who was the light of her life was going to grow up to be a lawyer, there was absolutely no doubt in her mind.

"That was before the kitchen pipe decided to double as a colander."

Where *was* that toolbox? She was sure she'd seen one in here somewhere when she and Jesse had moved in. The condo belonged to a friend of Jon's who was out of the country and glad to be able to sublet it. Since the terms were reasonable, something she had a feeling Jon was responsible for, she felt the least she could do was make repairs when they came up.

Turning around, she looked at her son, still standing in the doorway. "Listen, kiddo, there's nothing I'd rather do than spend time with you, but right now, I need to try to fix the sink. Besides, you had a good time with Betty last night." She picked up a pile that represented laundry waiting to be washed and moved it. No toolbox. "I know you did. She read you all your favorite stories, didn't she?"

Jesse rocked back and forth on his sneakers. "Not all my favorites," he hedged.

She'd had time to talk to Betty while waiting for the baby-sitter's mother to come for her. Betty had given her a detailed account of the evening. "But most of them, right?" Finding a space between the washing machine and the dryer, she looked there. Victory.

"Most of them," he allowed casually, conceding defeat. He was bright enough to know what worked and what didn't when it came to evoking guilt and gaining favors.

"And she played games with you, don't bother denying it." She knew for a fact that Jesse had talked the sitter into letting him get up again after she'd left for the restaurant.

Using both hands, she dragged out the toolbox and carried it to the kitchen. What was in here, anyway? It felt as if it weighed a ton and had enough tools in it to reconstruct the Golden Gate Bridge.

"Not the good kind, Betty said. She likes video games."

Gina spared him a glance. This was an old, familiar tune.

She flipped the toolbox open and began rummaging inside for a torque wrench. "Too bad, we like board games, don't we, Jesse?" When she received no response, she looked up at him. Jesse had sucked in his lower lip pensively and was staring at her, the picture of petulance. "Don't we?" she repeated gently.

"I guess." Huge green eyes looked up at her from beneath wisps of wheat hair that were in the way. "Kyle has a really nice new video set, just like my old one. He's got Race Like the Wind and his mom lets him play it *all* the time."

She smiled sympathetically at him, ruffling the hair she'd so recently cut. She liked his hair longer, but for now, the close-cropped look would have to do. It was the only way she could change his appearance without alarming him. Luckily, Jesse thought he looked "cool."

"I'll get you a new video set when I can, kiddo. Until then, why don't you just enjoy the board games? Lots of kids grew up without video games, you know. They played board games instead."

He sighed dramatically. "Were they poor, too?"

Too. Was that how he felt? Aching for him, she gave Jesse a hug. "We're not poor, kiddo, we're just temporarily not well off."

"I know, Mommy."

He sounded so grown-up just then. Laughing softly, she shook her head. "I'll see what I can do."

Finally finding a torque wrench, she wriggled it out of the box.

Excited, Jesse clapped his hands. "Oh, boy!"

Gina pretended to look at him sternly and failed miserably. "That doesn't mean we're getting one right away," she warned.

"Yes, it does." Because she was on her knees, he could reach her. Jesse threw his arms around her neck and squeezed hard. "You're the best, Mommy."

The words, the embrace, was what it was all about to her. There was nothing more precious to her than this little boy. The single being who made everything worthwhile and bearable. How could she say no to him?

"Yeah, the best pushover." Bracing herself, she got down as far as she could and angled herself beneath the kitchen sink. That the doorbell should pick this time to ring only seemed fitting somehow. Murphy's Law. "Now what?" she muttered irritably. She had half a mind to let it ring.

"The doorbell's ringing," Jesse sang out gleefully. An open, loving child, he loved company. It made no difference if the company was an adult or a kid his own age, he welcomed everyone.

"I hear it, kiddo, but I'm busy right now." Whoever it was would come back if it was important.

"That's okay, Mommy. I'll get it for you," Jesse volunteered.

Crammed into an uncomfortable position underneath the sink, Gina didn't hear what Jesse said at first. But when she called out to him to repeat himself and received no answer, a vague semblance of his words echoed back to her.

He was answering the door.

"Jesse, no!"

But even as she called out, she knew that it was already too late. Time and again she'd instructed Jesse not to talk to strangers or to open the door to anyone, but it was like trying to take wheels off a wagon. Somehow, magically, the wheels always reappeared and the wagon would go merrily on its way. Jesse was the last word in friendliness. Part of her hated to squelch that innocence, especially so early in Jesse's young life, but it was exactly his life that she worried about.

Scrambling up quickly, Gina smacked the top of her head against the cabinet. The impact went right through her, rattling not only her head but jarring the pit of her stomach before traveling clear down to her toes. That one really hurt.

Wobbly, she got to her feet and hurried to the front of the house.

The door was standing open.

"No!" she shouted, launching herself at it. She was about to push back the man she was certain was standing on the other side.

But it wasn't who she thought it was.

It was Ben.

Wavering, she stared at him, confused. Fear began to trickle in. She hadn't told him where she lived. What was he doing here?

Had he followed her last night?

The single question flashed through her mind, dragging up all the dark implications that went along with it.

Gina felt her throat begin to close up.

"What are you doing here?" she demanded.

Ben had had less than half a second for the image of the little boy answering the door to register. Intent on seeing Gina, he hadn't expected to be looking down at a little boy. A little boy who, with longer hair, would look a great deal like the little boy he'd been sent to find.

She had Andrew.

He had to get in touch with McNair.

The thought telegraphed across his mind, then faded. Instead of saying anything to her, he stood there, trying to come up with some sort of explanation for what he was so obviously seeing.

There wasn't one. He didn't have enough input to form one, yet he couldn't quite make himself believe that he was seeing what he thought he was seeing.

Her insides shaking suddenly, still wobbly from the blow to her head, Gina got in front of Jesse. She pushed the small boy behind her protectively, his resistance to the act vaguely registering.

"I said, what are you doing here?"

Putting his hand into his pocket, Ben pulled out the scarf he'd purloined from her last night.

"I came to give you this. The waiter came out with it just as I was getting into my car."

Gina spared the scarf a glance. She hadn't even realized it was missing. "That still doesn't explain how you knew where I lived."

"Simple. I stopped by the bookstore. Some guy named Miles said you weren't coming in, and then he volunteered to give me your address."

Miles. That explained it. She thought of the slightly developmentally challenged young man who Jon kept around to do menial work. Beneath Jon's brusque exterior beat the heart of a kind man. He just didn't like people knowing about it. Miles was always eager to be helpful. She was sure that he'd been more than happy to volunteer where Ben could find the information he wanted.

Ben made eye contact with the boy she was attempting to hide behind her and smiled at him. He was rewarded with a huge grin. The boy looked none the worse for the ordeal. As a matter of fact, he looked as if he was thriving. Any way Ben tried to look at the situation, it just didn't make sense to him.

Gina raised her chin in what could only be taken as a challenge. He blocked the image of nibbling on that chin that suddenly flashed through his mind.

"You went through all that trouble to return my scarf?"

"Seemed like the thing to do." He nodded toward the wrench she held at her side. "Is something wrong?"

Jesse peered out from behind his mother's hip, volunteering to field the question. "Mommy's a pushover and she's fixing our sink because it's a calendar."

The boy called her "Mommy." Had she brainwashed him? Ben knew it wasn't out of the question for kidnappers to force children to answer to different names, to scrub their memories of the lives they'd led before their kidnapping in order to reshape their identities. Those children were taken with the intention of never being returned to their homes.

Was that what she had in mind? Was Andrew filling some hole left in Gloria's life, replacing a child she'd lost? Or was there something else going on here, something he was being kept in the dark about?

Instincts warred with common sense. He needed more input.

"Hush, Jesse." She kept her hand against the boy. Exasperated, she slanted a look toward Ben. "He's telling you things out of context."

Jesse. She called the boy Jesse and he responded to the name. Could it be possible that he'd made a mistake after all? Ben wasn't really certain one way or another. But one thing at least seemed to ring true. Especially since she was holding a torque wrench in her other hand, and now that he looked, he noticed that the edge of her shirt was damp.

"What's wrong with your sink?"

"It's leaking." She fought to keep her voice from taking on a nervous edge. "Now, if you'll excuse me, I was in the middle of trying to fix it."

Rather than leave, Ben moved around her and into the house. "Let me have a look at it. I'm pretty good at fixing things, remember?"

She recalled his offer to trade handyman services for her help. "So am I. Usually." Although, she had to admit that at the moment, she was out of her depth.

The feisty spark in her eyes got to him. He liked women who could hold their own. "I'm sure you are, but do you mind if I take a look? It's this macho gene in me. I try to squelch it, but it seems to rise to the surface whenever I'm around any tools."

"Tools?"

He reached for the wrench she was holding, his hand meeting hers. "Wrenches, hammers, screwdrivers, things like that."

Drawing her hand away, Gina blew out a breath. After an incredibly short internal debate, she relented. Temporarily. "Are you really any good?"

The boy was regarding him with unabashed interest. One of the straps of his overalls was sinking down his shoulder. Ben pushed it back into place, then ruffled the boy's hair. A wide smile met him.

"Worked summers for a general contractor while I was in college. My uncle," he added, hoping that would sway her. He'd been pretty good at it, too, but working with his hands had never been more than a means to an end for him.

Gina wavered. She really didn't have the money to

pay for a regular plumber. That was why she was trying to fix the leak herself in the first place. Beyond applying plumber's putty to strategic places and running an auger down a plugged pipe, she was pretty much in the dark when it came to plumbing problems.

"Okay, I guess you can't do any harm." At least, she hoped not. With Jesse running on ahead, she started to lead the way to the kitchen, then stopped just short of the threshold and looked over her shoulder. "Can you?"

"Never lost a sink yet," he told her cheerfully. He edged around her again, deliberately moving her aside. "Let's see what you've got here."

Crouching down, he surveyed the offending pipe. He was aware that he'd been joined by a pint-size shadow who was mimicking his every move. The kid was definitely none the worse for whatever had happened to him. That was a good sign.

Ben sat back on his heels. "It's leaking, all right."

Gina crossed her arms in front of her. Macho gene, huh? "That much I could figure out for myself."

"The next thing we have to see is if it's leaking from a hole or a fitting that's come loose." As she watched, Ben lay down on his back and snaked his way under the sink. "Got a flashlight?"

"Right here!" Jesse announced. Grabbing it from the drawer where he'd seen it being put away the other day, he shoved it into Ben's outstretched hand.

"Thanks." Ben managed to cock his head slightly, just enough to look at his undersize assistant. "My name's Ben."

"Pleased to meet you, Ben," Jesse said, just the way he'd been taught. "My name's Jesse."

The boy said his name as if he believed it. He needed

time to sort this out, Ben thought. He figured fixing the leaking pipe might just buy him a little.

"Yes, I know." Moving from side to side, Ben snaked his way out again. He sat up, looking at Gina. "Well, the pipes haven't come loose. There's a hole in one of them. You need to have it replaced."

So much for hoping that it was just a matter of having to tighten something or slapping on a liberal application of plumber's putty. She peered at the guilty pipe, though from her angle she couldn't detect anything. "Is it expensive to replace?"

"Shouldn't be, unless you want to use a pipe made out of gold." He got up a scant few inches away from her, brushing himself off. He couldn't help noticing that she'd done a quick survey of his body, even though she was trying not to be obvious about it. Ben tried not to dwell on the fact that it pleased him. He wondered if she knew just how close she'd come to being kissed last night. "If you tell me where the hardware store is, I can have you leakless in about an hour or so."

She couldn't overcome the suspicion that kept scratching away at her. She longed for the days when she could just accept a favor without wondering what the price tag, or ulterior motive, was. Very deliberately, she placed her hands on Jesse's shoulders to keep him from gravitating to Ben's side.

"Why would you fix my sink?"

"Because it's broken," he replied simply. And then he flashed a grin at her. "Besides, you're helping me with research, the least I can do is return the favor."

Ben Underwood was simply too good to be true. Handsome, friendly, helpful and, from the looks of it, handy with his hands, and basically good with kids. That made him every woman's dream come true. But she'd learned the hard way that when things seemed too good to be true, they usually were.

And even if he was as altruistic as he was trying to come across, she didn't want to be in debt to him. "I'd have to pay you."

"You can pay for the pipe," he agreed, tucking in his shirttail, which had come out as he'd gotten under the sink. "The rest we can negotiate." He could swear that he saw fear flash briefly through her eyes. Why? What had he said? It was just a joking, offhand comment. "You could feed me lunch," he added, just in case the pale color of her cheeks was an indication of some sort of fear that he might attempt to take advantage of her.

"Lunch?" she echoed.

"Yeah." He slipped his jacket back on. "That thing between breakfast and dinner. A sandwich will do if you have it."

Jesse tugged on the bottom of his jacket. "I like sandwiches," he told him. "Ham and cheese are my favorite."

This was one adorable kid. He shuddered to think how many people would pay a great deal to have a son like Jesse. Was that it? Was this some sort of black-market stolen-child ring he'd stumbled across?

Glancing at Gina, he just couldn't reconcile his thoughts with his instincts.

"Sounds good to me, Jesse." He fixed his collar and then turned to Gina. "So, where's the hardware store around here?"

She thought a minute, trying to remember the location of the one she'd passed the other day. "There's Harold's Emporium at Sequoia and Main. I don't know the exact address, but the building looks like a big red barn. You can't miss it.''

''I know where it is, I know,'' Jesse told her excitedly.

There were times that nothing Jesse said surprised her. She humored him. ''How do you know?''

''I saw it when we were coming home from the movies last week.''

Last week. But McNair said the boy had been taken only a few days ago. More discrepancies, Ben thought. *Was* he barking up the wrong tree after all? In which case, Andrew's trail had become exceptionally cold. But somehow, he didn't think he was that far off.

Jesse was moving from foot to foot, his excitement building. ''I can show him where it is. Can I go with Ben, please, Mom?''

''No!'' The word had come out too emphatically. But there was no way she was about to let him out of her sight with a man who was essentially a stranger. Gina pressed her lips together, trying to sound calmer. ''I need you here, Jesse. You can help me make lunch for Ben.''

Jesse clearly would have rather accompanied his new friend on the field trip, but he nodded his blond head, forlorn and crestfallen as he looked at Ben. ''I guess I'd better stay with Mom and help.''

The boy's command of the language impressed him. McNair had told him that his son was six. Most six-year-olds, at least those he had come in contact with, were a rowdy bunch who barely had a nodding acquaintance with manners unless they were force-fed down their protesting throats. McNair hadn't mentioned that the boy was bright, or lively. The man's description of his son had been just the bare minimum. Without the photograph to go on, Ben would have said that the description could have fit any number of boys.

He bent down to the boy's level. "I'd like mustard on mine," he told him. "And I'd like you to watch that pipe for me while I'm gone. Let me know if the leak gets worse. And don't let your mom," or whoever she was, Ben added silently, "use the sink while I'm gone."

Jesse nodded as if he'd just been entrusted with a solemn duty. "Okay," he promised.

"I'll be back as quick as I can," he told Gina, rising to his feet again.

"You really don't have to put yourself out this way, you know," she said, walking with him to the door. She noted that rather than go with them, Jesse remained behind, watching the pipe intently. Ben had found a way to temporarily cap Jesse's exuberance.

"There's nothing in my refrigerator. Call it working for my lunch."

She watched him leave, wondering if she was being overly trusting.

Chapter 8

Frowning, Gina picked up the cloth and wiped the bits of clay from her hands. She couldn't give the bust she was working on her full, undivided attention. Not with Ben Underwood lying flat on his back just a few feet away in the kitchen, fiddling with pipes beneath the sink that had seen better days.

Giving up, she threw down the towel and walked into the kitchen to see just how he was doing. He'd returned from the hardware store approximately half an hour after he'd left, armed with enough things, in her opinion, to replace all the pipes not only beneath the kitchen sink, but the ones in the two bathrooms as well.

The man had the air of an overachiever about him, she thought with a smile.

She'd be the one to know about that, she thought ruefully. When she'd graduated from school, she'd been all set to conquer the world. Instead, it had conquered her.

Not yet, she thought fiercely. *Not yet.* She'd deal with those thoughts later, when she felt they actually were safely in her past.

She looked at Jesse, crouching on the floor beside Ben's outstretched legs, ready to jump in and help at the slightest sign from his newly adopted mentor. In an incredibly short amount of time, Jesse had taken to Ben as if he'd been waiting for a man like him to come along all of his young life.

Maybe he had.

This, she had to admit to herself as she slanted a look in Ben's direction, was the kind of man she would have chosen to be Jesse's father. If she could have chosen. She thought of Jesse as the most fortunate accident of her life. He'd been conceived in the worst of all possible circumstances, but despite his beginning, Jesse had turned out far better than even her wildest dreams.

His father had been a smart man, at least as far as book intelligence went. But genes only went so far, even erudite, sophisticated ones, she thought wryly. Environment counted for something. She'd tried desperately to provide everything that a sensitive, impressionable child like Jesse might need, but in her heart, she'd always known that it wasn't enough. What Jesse truly needed was a man by his side he could look up to.

Didn't they all, she added silently.

She was trying very hard not to notice that the would-be screenwriter had a body that had been fashioned in someone's sculpture class on a good day. Firm and rippled. Certainly better than any of the male models that had been recruited to pose in her art classes all those years ago. But then, those were boys, this was a man with a capital *M.*

Although looks had never really been that important

to her, they certainly didn't hurt, either. And this man had his share. Any way you cut it, from the top or the bottom, Ben was very easy on the eye.

As long as that didn't lead to a softening of the brain, Gina reminded herself. She'd been that route once, and though she had Jesse to show for it, once was definitely enough.

Gina glanced at the clock on the stove. Ben had been at this for more than an hour. Her eyes rested on Jesse's crouched form. Of course, he'd had help and she would be the first one to agree that small helping hands had a tendency to lengthen the time it took to do a project rather than shortening it.

"How's it going down there?" Not that she could actually see for herself, but Gina bent her head down to look in, anyway.

The flashlight Ben was using managed to also illuminate his chest and the T-shirt that was draped tightly over it. Even lying down, the man had pectorals to spare.

God, but she would love to capture that in clay. She could almost feel his chest forming beneath her fingers, the clay falling back to allow that firm, muscular body to emerge.

Her fingers itched.

She was romanticizing again, she upbraided herself.

Turning his head slightly away from what he was doing, Ben saw a long, curvy silhouette encased in well-fitting jeans that underscored the shapely legs beneath. Her breasts were straining against her blue sweater as she leaned in toward him.

He had the sudden urge to tangle his fingers in her short, dark hair, to bring her face down to his and find out if her lips really did taste of wild strawberries, or if they only looked that way.

He was going to need a shower after he finished here for more than one reason, he thought. A particularly cold one, even if it was chilly this time of year up here.

"Almost done," he told her, retreating back under the sink.

It would be safer all around, he told himself, if he just looked at the pipes and concentrated on what he was doing. He had to stop letting himself be distracted.

She looked at the clock again. "I guess I'm lucky you don't charge by the hour."

"But I do." His voice floated out from under the sink. "A sandwich an hour." Ben looked out to the left where Jesse squatted by his feet, eagerly awaiting his next request. "How about you? Does a sandwich an hour sound fair to you?"

Jesse shook his head up and down with vigor. "Very fair."

He probably meant that, too, Ben thought, grinning as he tightened the pipe seal slowly, careful not to crack it. The kid looked as if he actually had a handle on what he was being told.

Cute, smart and helpful. What more could a parent want?

The return of their child, that's what, he reminded himself sternly, thinking of McNair. But in the last couple of hours, it had become so natural to think of this towheaded boy as belonging to Gina, not McNair. They had this easy relationship, this give-and-take that he would have thought would have taken time to develop.

Gloria had been Andrew's nanny, he reminded himself. That was time enough to develop a rapport. As for calling her Mommy and responding to being called

Jesse, for all he knew that was a game she'd told the boy they were playing. A pretend game. Kids were good at games. Especially smart kids.

There were a thousand possibilities within the framework of what was going on. A thousand ways to fit the jagged pieces together.

Until he had some more facts he could work with, facts he could make sense out of, he was going to have to keep up this charade, and if that meant fooling around with corroded pipes in order to get the information, so be it. He'd certainly been called on to do worse.

For the time being, however, he'd dragged out this particular fix-it project as far as it could go. With little effort he could have had the sink back together in half the time. Ben couldn't remember ever working so slowly in his life.

But he'd done what he'd set out to do. Created a rapport with Jesse. The boy had talked a blue streak. Unfortunately, none of it was actually helpful in piecing together what had happened. He hadn't even mentioned his father, but that could have been due to his feeling like an outsider in McNair's home. The man had told him he'd had trouble adjusting to his role as father. Andrew, or Jesse, had probably picked up on that. Asking the boy any direct questions about his father was out of the question. Gina was too close and would hear everything. For now, he had to keep a low profile.

Relieved to finally be out from under the sink, Ben scooted out and retired the wrench that Jesse had given him a few minutes ago, putting it on the floor beside him.

"I think we're done, partner."

He watched as Jesse picked up the tool and placed it back into the toolbox. Glancing to the side, he noticed that the boy had also replaced the lid on the plumber's putty the way he'd asked him to. Hell, the kid was neater than he was.

Rising to his feet, Ben dusted off his hands. His shoulder, the one he'd been wounded in, ached a little. He rotated it automatically, then looked at Jesse. "Okay, ready to see if she flies?"

Jesse's brows came together in a puzzled blond line. "It's supposed to fly, too?"

"That's just an expression, kiddo," Gina told him, coming up behind Jesse. Looking at Ben, she draped her arms on either side of the boy. The gesture wasn't lost on Ben. She was silently establishing boundaries. Silently saying that the boy was under her protection.

"Oh. An expression." Jesse nodded his head sagely, as if committing another thing to the vast catalog of his memory.

Damn cute, Ben affirmed. He gestured toward the faucet. "You want to do the honors? You turn it on and I'll watch to see if it leaks."

"Okay." But even standing on his tiptoes, Jesse still couldn't reach the faucet to turn it. Frustration creased the concentration on his face.

Gina moved to pick him up so that he was closer to the faucet, but Ben stopped her. "Tell you what, let's switch jobs. You watch, I'll turn."

The reversal brought out a broad smile. "Sure." Holding the side of the sink just the way Ben had a moment ago, Jesse squatted down. His eyes were trained on the new pipes.

Ben had the water running full blast. "See anything?" he asked the boy.

"Just pipes," Jesse replied solemnly, his gaze never wandering.

Ben bent down to inspect his handiwork for himself. He shone the flashlight from one end of the new pipes to the other. No telltale leaks, squeezing themselves out of almost invisible spaces, appeared.

"How about that, you're right. Just pipes. Looks like we fixed ourselves a sink, pal." He rose to his feet again, Jesse popping up like golden toast beside him. "Put 'er there." Ben stuck out his hand.

Surprised and pleased, Jesse slipped his hand into Ben's, shaking it as if he were Ben's equal. Only his dancing eyes gave away the combination of pride and joy he was feeling at being treated this way.

"Now it's time for you to do your part." Ben turned to look at Gina. "Got those sandwiches ready for a couple of hungry men?"

"Yeah, hungry men," Jesse echoed, standing close to Ben.

Jesse was having the time of his life, Gina thought. She'd taken him to Disneyland last summer and she could swear he was having more fun now than he had then. Had she known, she thought wryly, she could have just bought Jesse a toy sink to fix and saved herself a lot of time and money.

She knew it wasn't just playing with tools that had brought that wide smile to Jesse's lips, it was feeling that he'd been helpful and treated like an adult by an adult.

He was a good kid. And maybe, just maybe, Gina thought, Ben Underwood was a good man. A really good man.

There had to be at least one around, didn't there? It wasn't just a fairy tale she'd been buying into all of her life, was it? Somewhere, men who were kind and good really did exist. She still believed that, needed to believe that. And maybe one had gotten loose and found his way to her doorstep.

Her mouth curved with just a touch of self-mocking. She was going to have to stop buying into those bedtime stories she read to Jesse.

"Already taken care of. The sandwiches are waiting for you right there."

Gina pointed to the tiny breakfast nook where she and Jesse took all of their meals. The table in the dining room had been taken over by a computer on one side and the bust she was currently working on when she found the time on the other.

From where he was standing, Ben thought he caught a glimpse of something that looked like a mountain of clay. He edged over just a little, still looking, trying to get a better view.

Gina saw where he was looking. Self-consciousness slipped over her. "Your sandwich is over here, on this table." She thought of moving and blocking his view, but he was faster than she was.

"Just a sec."

He realized that she could take it as a clear invasion of privacy, but curiosity had him walking into the other room to get a better look at the unfinished work.

It was a bust of the little boy. As he studied it, Ben saw that even though Gina hadn't finished it, she had somehow managed to capture the essence of the boy, the lively spark in his eyes. He didn't think that was possible with clay.

Impressed, he looked at her as she came in after him. "You do this?"

She sculpted to let out feelings, to work through emotions. In part, she considered it to be like therapy. But, until it was finished, it was a private thing she didn't want viewed by strangers. Elbowing Ben out of the way, she picked up the towel she'd used earlier and draped it over the bust.

Ben looked at her. It wasn't so much a desire for privacy, he thought, scrutinizing her expression, as intense embarrassment that had prompted her covering the bust.

"It's not very good," she murmured. Not yet. But it would be, she promised herself. When it was finished.

"Not good?" How could she say that? Even unfinished, it looked remarkable, and he wasn't one impressed by works of art. "It's fantastic." Something from his childhood nudged itself forward. "All I ever managed to do with clay was make those thin, long snakes. You know, the kind you get by taking a hunk of clay and rolling it between the palms of your hands over and over again." One eye on her face to see if he had her silent permission, he removed the cloth again and then dropped it to the side. Subtle nuances, like the dimple in the corner of the boy's mouth, rose to meet him. She had real talent. "This sure beats that."

"Lunch" was her only response as she turned on her heel to lead him back to the kitchen. But he thought he detected the hint of a pleased smile flirting with her lips.

He thought of flirting with her lips himself, then banked down the intruding urge.

Again, he wondered what a woman like Gina was doing, mixed up in something like this. She was not only beautiful, but talented. Why jeopardize all that? Though his first allegiance was to his client, Ben felt he had to get to the bottom of this before he made any calls. Otherwise, it might go badly for her, and he didn't want that happening unless it was absolutely unavoidable.

Once they were brought in, the police department was not going to go out of its way and take mitigating circumstances under consideration. That was for the courts to deal with.

And even then it might not go well for her. He'd seen too many trials won by the sharpest lawyer, the one who played tricks and pulled rabbits out of a hat. Truth got lost somewhere along the way. But while the case was still his, he intended to take on the parts of both law enforcement and judicial system until he got some answers that at least partially satisfied him.

Jesse pushed his chair over, bringing it closer to Ben before scrambling up on it. The huge grin on the boy's face when he looked at him was infectious. "You were a great help today, partner," Ben said.

"After lunch, can we fix something else?" Jesse asked.

Ben popped the top of the can of soda Gina had put out and raised his eyes to hers. "I don't know, what needs fixing around here?"

The thing that needed fixing most, Ben couldn't do anything about, Gina thought. She gave Jesse a slight reproving look. He knew better than to pester. "Mr. Underwood has better things to do than to hang around here fixing things, Jesse."

"Actually, I don't," Ben contradicted. He saw that his response seemed to throw Gina off a little, but sticking around here for the rest of the afternoon was better than he could have hoped for.

She didn't want Jesse making too big a deal out of this. If Ben stayed, if he just hung around as if he belonged, Jesse might get the wrong idea. He might get used to this and she didn't want him to. Not when he was going to be disappointed in the end.

"No scenes to write?" she asked Ben pointedly.

"I thought I'd take the day off, let things just simmer in the back of my head for a while." He paused to take a drink.

Out of the corner of his eye, he saw Jesse do the same. When he bit into his sandwich, chewing slowly, Jesse aped his every movement. Ben couldn't help being amused. He also couldn't help seeing that Gina noticed Jesse's actions as well.

"Jesse, Mr. Underwood doesn't need you to ape everything he's doing."

He smiled, then winked at Jesse who, pleased, fluttered an eye shut in response.

"That's okay, Gina. I don't mind. It's kind of flattering, I think." It was, he realized. He'd never been anyone's hero before. "I think you've got yourself a real winner here."

Unable to resist, Ben ruffled the boy's hair again. It felt incredibly soft to the touch. Ben couldn't help wondering if Gina's hair felt the same. He pulled himself up short. For a minute, he'd forgotten that the boy wasn't actually her son.

"I don't think I've ever met a kid who's better behaved or more willing to help. You've done a great job raising him." He watched her face for any sign of some sort of discomfort at the praise.

There was none. Either she was one hell of an actress, he thought, or…

Or what?

"Jesse's just a naturally good kid," she told him. "When he wants to be," she added affectionately, thinking of times when he'd been less than angelic. But for the most part, he was the joy that kept her life centered. Very deliberately, she shifted the focus away from her and her son to Ben. "So, how long have you been a writer?"

The question caught him off guard. He'd been getting lost in her eyes again, in the soft, supple curve of her neck, in watching the way the ends of her hair brushed along the outline of her face.

Ben cleared his throat, rousing himself. "All my life, really. I just decided to get serious about it a few years ago."

"And you've just been working on this one screen-play all this time?" Was he a procrastinator, she wondered, or had there been some day job to sap his time, the way there had been with her.

Ben looked appropriately embarrassed. "No, there've been others, but nothing that seemed sellable."

"But this will be." It was half a question, half a general assumption.

"I think so. I think the story of Wounded Knee is a story whose time has come. If I get it right," he added with a touch of modesty he knew would go over well. "Which is where you come in."

The thought was not without its merits. It also produced a smile that seemed to form deep within her. If she wasn't careful, he was going to charm her just like he'd managed to charm Jesse.

Going to? Hell, he'd already done it. All she needed was to be stuffed into a box and tied up with a big, plump pink ribbon.

"I'll do my best."

"Me, too," Jesse chimed in, a dab of mustard smeared on his chin. "I'll do my best."

Ben lifted the boy's chin with his hand and wiped away the mustard with the tip of his thumb. "It does a man's heart good to know he's got a good team behind him,'' he said solemnly.

Gina both loved and worried about the way the boy's eyes lit up when he looked up at Ben.

Chapter 9

She had to admit she was impressed.

Ben had helped her clear the dishes away and then dried while she washed. And when Jesse asked him to watch a videotape with him, the one he'd almost worn clean through in the last few weeks about a celebrated mouse and his duck friend, Ben hadn't begged off with some spur-of-the-moment excuse. Instead, he'd sat down with the boy and actually watched the tape. Twice.

When it ended the second time, Gina walked over to the television set and switched it off. Jesse looked up at her in surprise. "Mom."

"Twice is enough for now, Jesse. You've already watched that tape so many times, we both know the dialogue by heart." She looked at Ben on the floor beside her son. It was a scene she could too easily let herself get used to. And so could Jesse. She needed to nip this in the bud before it went too far. "It's not fair to make Ben watch it a third time."

Playing peacemaker, Ben asked Jesse, "Got anything else you'd like to watch?"

"Yes." Jesse began to run to his room for his other prized videotape.

"No," Gina said firmly. Jesse stopped in midstep and looked at her. "I think we've detained Ben here long enough."

Which was his cue to leave. Ben rose to his feet inches away from her, wondering what had caused her to suddenly do a one-eighty. He kept his expression and remark amiable. "You know, if I didn't know any better, I'd say you were trying to get rid of me."

Relieved that he wasn't going to try to talk his way into staying longer, Gina was already leading the way to the front door. It was one thing to spend a little time with him at the bookstore, or even over dinner, but having him in her home was a whole different ball game. She'd allowed his engaging manner and the leaking sink to mitigate her resolve. Watching him with Jesse had almost made her forget it entirely. But it was because of Jesse that she couldn't afford to let her guard down. She'd already established that she could never tell where the next threat was coming from, and though it seemed unlikely, it might be from him. For Jesse's sake, she had to be cautious.

"I'm not trying to get rid of you but, um, I've got some things to do and I'm afraid that I don't have the time to entertain a guest."

Though she'd started to open the door, he lingered just a moment. He needed to be invited back. To make her trust him enough to be willing to open up. There was this feeling in his gut he had to work through and he couldn't do it without concrete evidence to refute it.

"Gina, I've held your corroded pipes and plugged up your leak. I'd think that puts me beyond the realm of a guest. Maybe somewhere in the area of student and teacher, seeing how you're helping me get my story straight. Or maybe," he added more softly, "with a little luck, we could be friends." He looked into her eyes, seeing her soften. Trouble was, he was feeling the same way himself. And that wasn't good. Especially since he was fighting off the very real, very intense urge to kiss her. "Friends don't need to be entertained. I can hang out with Jesse."

For a second, she wavered. It took effort to remind herself that she'd heard that before. Pretending to enjoy her son's company when it was all a ruse just to get to her.

At a loss, that same nervous feeling slipping over her, the one that warned her something was out of kilter, Gina put her hands on her hips and looked Ben squarely in the eye.

Could you tell if a person was lying to you just by looking into his eyes? She'd never been very good when it came to uncovering the truth. Until it was too late.

For Jesse's sake, she had to make herself sound distant. "Why are you so intent on staying here?"

There it was again, he thought. That look. The one that telegraphed fear. What was she afraid of? It couldn't be him. He was deliberately being his most harmless, most charming. And yet, he could swear there was a leeriness in her eyes, as if she thought perhaps he was the devil himself, or one of his minions.

"Not intent," he said, beginning to correct her, then

deciding to play it more simply. He looked at her with concern. "What is it, Gina?"

She stiffened, raising her chin, her body language warning him off. "What's what?"

"You look like an inexperienced soldier who just sighted the enemy and you don't know whether to shoot or retreat." She began to protest, but he added gently, "I'm not the enemy, Gina. Why would you think I was?"

For just a second, when he looked at her like that, she felt her mouth go dry. She couldn't let him get to her. But he was. So quickly she could hardly draw a breath. It wasn't even anything he said, it was just the way he looked at her. The way he smelled. It had been a very long time since she'd been with a man, and up until Ben came along, it hadn't really bothered her.

But it did now. That made her nervous, too. Because she didn't want primitive yearnings coloring her judgment or making her drop her guard.

"I don't think of you as the enemy. You're letting your imagination run away with you," she told him shortly. Gina opened the door, her message clear. "Now, I don't want to be rude, but I'd really appreciate it if you left."

Hands raised, he stepped outside. "I never overstay my welcome. Well, hardly ever," he amended just before she closed the door in his face.

Definitely more going on here than met the eye, he thought, walking back to his car. One minute she was friendly, the next, it was as if her own actions surprised her and she became distant and formal.

Guilt did funny things to people, he thought. But if she felt guilty about taking the boy, why didn't she attempt to contact McNair and return him? For that matter, why hadn't she contacted McNair at all, at least to torment him? That had been the man's implication, and he knew that if McNair had received any word from Gina—no Gloria—Ben corrected himself, McNair would have been on the phone immediately, reporting this latest event to the office, which in turn would notify him.

No one was notifying anyone, which meant she hadn't called. Why not? What was her game? *Did* he have the right woman, or was there some sort of colossal blunder going on?

The only blunder, he told himself, would be if he allowed himself to get sidetracked by this woman. He was already feeling far too kindly toward her.

One way or another, he intended to get to the bottom of this. He hoped that the bug he'd planted in her kitchen phone while she'd been busy in the other room would tell him what he wanted to know. Maybe she wasn't in on this alone, and whoever her silent partner was, he or she would get in contact with her in the next few days. It was something to hope for. He was grateful now that Megan had insisted they all keep surveillance equipment with them, just in case. At the time he'd thought carrying it around was rather melodramatic.

Live and learn, he mused, watching the condo in the middle of the block become smaller and smaller in his rearview mirror.

That had been his real reason for showing up on her doorstep with the scarf he'd taken last night—to plant the bug. When Jesse had become his miniature shadow, he'd been afraid that he wouldn't get the opportunity, and as long as Jesse was with him, Gina was never far away. But he'd finally managed to plant the bug when Jesse had gone to the bathroom and Gina was out of the kitchen. The few minutes he'd been alone in the kitchen had been all the time he needed.

He just hoped it would bear some fruit.

"I want to apologize."

Ben had been uncertain how to proceed given the way things had ended on Saturday. The day and a half he'd spent waiting for any incoming or outgoing calls on Gina's line had amounted to an exercise in futility. The only call out she'd made was to a theater that played children's movies. That had been early Sunday morning. There had been no incoming calls. The woman was a nun. It should have frustrated him, and it did, a little. But it also pleased him. More than a little. That in itself worried him, because he felt it was getting harder and harder to hang on to his objectivity.

But here it was, Monday, and he needed to find a way to get himself back into her good graces and remain there until at least he had positive confirmation from the prints he'd sent in to be analyzed. So he'd walked into the bookstore a little after noon, prepared to do any damage control necessary to get to his goal.

She was glad he'd come into the store. She hadn't thought he would, after the way she'd brushed him off. She'd tried to talk herself out of regretting it later, but hadn't quite managed to get there. Seeing him here now brought with it an elation she hadn't been prepared for.

There was almost no one in the store. Mondays were notoriously slow. The browsers tended to come in the latter half of the week, as did the college students who suddenly needed books for weekend assignments they'd put off to the last minute. Monday saw only diehard book lovers and people who had nowhere else to go for half an hour.

She motioned Ben over to the side, away from Joe, who wasn't even trying not to look as if he was listening.

"Apologize?" she asked, curious. "For what?"

"For making you uncomfortable," he began, feeling his way around slowly. But Gina cut him off before he got his footing on the path he was searching for.

"I'm the one who should apologize." This wasn't easy for her, but just because she'd taken a few wrong turns in her life and had paid the consequences for it was no excuse to be rude to someone whose only fault was being nice. "For being so abrupt on Saturday. I mean, you did go out of your way to fix the sink and you saved me more than a few dollars. I know what plumbers cost these days. It's easier to marry one than to pay one." She was digressing. Gina forced herself back to her apology. "I shouldn't have pushed you out like that."

She was wearing it again, that vague stirring scent that made him think of long, cool spring evenings under the stars. Of stretching out on bright green shoots of grass made velvety by the night and holding a woman in his arms. "I don't recall any pushing."

"Not physically." A rueful flush washed over her cheeks. "But you know what I mean."

Gallantry was the best inside track and he knew it. Women appreciated a man who was willing to forgive quickly. "Consider it forgotten."

"Good."

That over with, Gina was about to get back to work. Except that she couldn't. She'd behaved in a manner she would have taken Jesse to task for if she'd caught him at it. Ben was being incredibly gallant about it. The least she could do was give him some sort of explanation. She knew it shouldn't matter one way or another, and that after he was finished with his research, she would probably never see him again, but she didn't want him thinking of her as some moody, mercurial woman.

Gina forced herself to turn around. He was still looking at her. She pushed the words out before she stopped herself. "It's just that...when you showed up on my doorstep like that...I guess in a way it really freaked me out. I..."

She trailed off, feeling helpless and hating the feeling. Helplessness was something that was new to her. It'd become her jailer in the last few months. She didn't like what the twists and turns of her life had made her become. She wanted to be free to be open again. To not look for hidden meanings in words and hidden agendas in people. To stop looking over her shoulder all the time and just enjoy her life for a change instead of being forced to guard it zealously.

He saw her struggle. Something beyond practicality had him saying, "That's all right, you don't have to explain if you don't want to."

Because he didn't press, she told him. Told him what she hadn't shared with anyone. Because no one would have probably believed her. The deck had been stacked against her right from the start, she'd just been too naive to realize it at the time.

Even so, she tempered her story so that Ben couldn't piece it all together. She had to be careful. Even with the truth.

"I was stalked once. It lasted several months. When you showed up like that on Saturday, it sort of brought everything back. I'm sorry if I took off your head."

The would explain her initial behavior, but not why

she'd suddenly all but asked him to leave. For the time being, he figured it best not to point the fact out.

"I'm very resilient. Head's still attached," he told her, moving it from side to side to illustrate. And then, slowly, his smile faded on the off chance that she was telling him the truth. "I'm really sorry. I didn't mean to drag up any bad memories. I had no idea."

Having him apologize made her feel worse. "Of course you didn't, how could you?" She shrugged, looking around the bookstore. And then her eyes came back to his. Was she making another mistake, letting him know about this? She hadn't even told Jon or Aunt Sugar about this. Neither one of them had pressed for an explanation, either. So why was she sharing this with Ben? Why was there this feeling that this almost-stranger could actually be someone to her, if things were just a little different?

"A lot of people think you bring it on yourself, being stalked," she heard herself saying. "Or that you're just imagining it, turning harmless attention into something sinister."

She wasn't making this up, Ben thought. The look on her face when she spoke was real. Unless she was a better actress than he'd ever come across. He restrained the urge he had to put his arm around her shoulders and comfort her. "Did they ever catch the guy?"

Her expression changed right before his eyes. Growing distant again. "I'd rather not talk about it. I just wanted you to know it wasn't you, it was me."

This time, as she began to leave again, it was his words that stopped her. "My sister had the same problem."

Gina looked at him. Was he just fabricating something to put her at ease? "Really?"

"Really." It had been his youngest sister and he could still remember the fury that had gripped him when she'd finally told him about it. "She was in college at the time. Guy wouldn't leave her alone. Followed her around, memorized her schedule. Would constantly pop up, chase away any guy she would start seeing."

It took effort for Gina not to shiver. Except for the college part, he could have been talking about her. It had gotten to the point that she'd been certain her every movement was being monitored. And then the final threat had come, sending her hurrying with Jesse into the night.

"What did she do?"

"Cindy went to the police and they took care of it for her." He didn't add that he was the police Cindy had gone to and that he had taken the stalker aside to describe, at length, in great detail, exactly what would happen to each of his body parts if he didn't stop bothering Cindy. That had been the last Cindy had ever seen or heard from the guy.

Gina laughed shortly. He noticed that her mouth remained set firm. "I guess she had a more sympathetic police department where she lived."

"Maybe," he allowed offhandedly. "Did you try going to the police at the time? Get a restraining order?"

Gina shook her head. She hadn't bothered. She knew what the results would have been. "It was just my word against his."

"So?" In his experience, the police tended to be more sympathetic toward women in these cases. Unless she was lying simply to take him in for reasons that were unclear to him.

"So he was someone with clout. I wasn't. End of story." She heard the electronic doors opening as the buzzer went off. Customers. It was time to get back to work.

But she hadn't ended it, he thought. "He just stopped stalking one day?"

"Let's just say…." But saying anything would be giving away too much. Giving away information she didn't want him to have. "Yes," she finally said. "He did. Now I've got to get back to work."

"I still have some questions." While monitoring her phone, he'd spent the time reading the other book he'd bought. And making notes so that his conversation on the subject wouldn't sound uninformed. "Could we try dinner again tonight? I could have you back and in bed by ten. Your bed. Alone," he emphasized, knowing she'd turn him down if she thought he was hitting on her. He laughed ruefully and not completely for effect. "I guess I've got a long way to go before I get to be smooth."

"Not such a long way," she contradicted. And he knew it, she thought. Still, maybe he was trying to put her at ease. She appreciated it.

"I'm afraid tonight's not a good night." Betty, she knew for a fact, was busy. The girl had told her all about the sweet sixteen party one of her friends was having, even though it was a weeknight.

"Going out?"

She knew she was within her rights to tell him that was none of his business, but she didn't want to. Instead, now that he knew about Jesse, she told him the truth. "I don't have a sitter."

"That's all right, I'll bring dinner to you. Enough for all three of us," he added to forestall any protest. "How does pizza sound?"

He'd hit upon Jesse's favorite meal. And one of hers, too, if she were being honest.

"You don't take no for an answer, do you?"

"Not unless no's the answer I want to hear." His smile was engaging, seductive. Gina felt herself weakening. "So, is that a yes?"

She gave in and felt herself smiling. From the inside out. "It's a yes. I know Jesse certainly wouldn't mind seeing you."

"Great." *Score one for the home team.* "Pizza it is."

"Not so fast," she interjected. "There's one condition."

He tried not to look wary. "And that is?"

"That you bring some of your screenplay with you." Maybe she was taking too much of an interest in him, but she found herself wanting to know things about him. Small, intimate things. The way he wrote was definitely a major part of that. "I want to read the kind of work you do."

We've got trouble, right here in River City, he thought to himself, feeling like the famous huckster in *The Music Man* once the jig was up. "I haven't polished it yet."

His sudden shyness struck her as sweet. "I'll keep that in mind."

There wasn't a single word on paper to offer her. His mind scrambled for viable excuses to give her in place of the screenplay. "The truth of it is, I don't really feel comfortable about letting someone see the unfinished product...."

The more he resisted, the sweeter he seemed. Gina grinned. "I'll keep that in mind, too. Unless this whole thing is a hoax," she teased.

There was a smile on her lips, but he had the feeling

that she might be more than a little serious. He had to produce something in order to keep this charade alive a little while longer, at least until he received word about the fingerprints one way or another. If he pulled the plug now, without the final proof he was waiting for, without getting to the bottom of what he felt was a problem, she might just take the boy and disappear on him. She'd already done it once; there was nothing to prevent her from doing it again.

Which meant he had to come up with something on paper between now and tonight.

"All right," he agreed reluctantly, hoping magic would strike somehow, "I'll bring a few pages—but don't say I didn't warn you."

She grinned. The buzzer sounded again and there was someone at the register. Joe was nowhere to be seen. "Don't worry, I'm sure it's wonderful. You're probably a lot better than you think."

Great.

Feeling less than triumphant, Ben was already striding toward the door. He had work to do.

Ms. Parsons had once told him he had potential, if only he learned how to apply himself. Ms. Parsons had been his eleventh-grade English teacher, strict in her own way but extremely supportive if she felt there was a reason to be. She'd found that reason in him, or so she'd said, except that he'd never done anything to justify that faith. And he'd never quite figured out what she'd meant by saying he should "apply" himself.

The most he wrote these days were the reports that Cade insisted on at the end of each case. And even that was like pulling teeth.

He just wasn't the literary sort.

But Ms. Parsons had thought he could be.

Ben sat at the computer, scowling at the void that comprised the blank screen. God had taken a void and created an entire world in six days. All he had to do was create a few pages in six hours. How hard could it be?

Very, he discovered after an hour had elapsed.

Disgusted, Ben surrendered and got on the telephone, tapping out the number to ChildFinders. He was big enough to admit he needed help. Fast.

"ChildFinders, Inc."

"Carrie, this is Ben. Give me Savannah."

"She's out of the office, Ben," the secretary told him. "She said something about needing to take a few hours' personal time."

Murphy's Law, he thought. "Damn."

"Will Eliza do?"

"Maybe. Wait a minute, how are you at writing?"

There was a pregnant pause. "Writing what, checks?"

He had a feeling this was leading to another dead end. "No, creative writing."

Ben heard a groan on the other end of the line, followed by a laugh. "I took English pass-fail in college. Does that answer your question?"

He was right, another dead end. Mentally, he crossed his fingers. "Give me Eliza."

"Good choice."

Eliza listened patiently to his problem, then regretfully informed him she wouldn't be of any help to him. "Not on this kind of short notice, at any rate. I'm afraid I don't know anything about the subject of your screenplay."

He was pacing now, trying to think as he talked.

''Got any suggestions? She's expecting to see at least a few pages.''

''Level with her. Tell her the dog ate it.''

It took no effort on his part to visualize the smile on Eliza's face. He could hear it in her voice. ''Very funny. Nice to know psychics have a sense of humor.''

''I'm sorry, but—hold it, didn't you once tell me one of your friends was a screenwriter?''

''Would-be screenwriter,'' he corrected her. ''Yeah, Nick Paraskevas.''

''All the better, that means he probably won't be busy. Maybe he could help you out.''

''Yeah, maybe.''

At least it was worth a shot.

Chapter 10

He couldn't reach Nick.

In the end, he had no choice but to write the handful of pages himself. It was either that or show up at Gina's house tonight without them. That would be difficult to explain, not to mention awkward, especially since she had made a point of mentioning it.

Finished, Ben got up from the crammed desk and dropped onto the sofa, then bit back a curse. The rain was bothering his shoulder. He thought back to all the times he'd teased his grandfather whenever the latter complained about the weather affecting his aches and pains.

"Wish you were around, Granddad, so I could tell you I was sorry. I know how you must have felt now." Grabbing a throw pillow, Ben tucked it under his back and tried to get comfortable for a minute.

His brain felt as if it were in the middle of a fog. What he needed, he thought, was to go out for a good jog. Jogging always cleared his head and got him back on track.

No chance of that happening right now, he thought, glancing out the window. It was coming down in sheets outside.

Ben reached for the telephone. He needed to talk to Savannah before she left the office for the day. Time had slipped away from him as he sat at the computer, agonizing over the pages.

"You just missed her," Megan told him when she answered the phone on the fourth ring. "She went home to take care of one of the girls. Some kind of post-Christmas flu going around. I'm the only one here."

"Where's Carrie?"

"Dental appointment, she left early. Why, what's the matter, don't want to talk to me?" He heard her laugh softly. "Might be your only chance. I'm going out of town tonight."

"New case?"

"Nope. Long overdue honeymoon. Garrett and I finally got our schedules to coincide."

From what he'd heard, it'd only taken over a year. Megan and her man from the DEA had been married before Ben ever came to the agency. "What do you need a honeymoon for? By now the two of you should have it down pat."

"Ever hear the saying practice makes perfect?" Her laugh was low, husky, anticipating things to come. "So, what can I do for you?"

"Do you know if Rusty and Chad had any luck showing Andrew McNair's photograph around?"

They were aware of each other's cases, always on the alert for any crossover. It wasn't as uncommon as it might seem. He heard her shuffling paper.

"Adorable face," she commented. "Chad mentioned earlier that so far, there hasn't even been so much as a nibble. Same goes for this Gloria person's photograph. Savannah posted Andrew's photograph and description on the Internet site as soon as we got the case," she reminded him, "but you know that's just a shot in the dark."

He knew. There was a disheartening wealth of photographs on the nonprofit site. It was one of two. Both sites attempting to locate children who had either been kidnapped, or were simply runaways. ChildFinders had only one success story tied to the site, and that had come about sheerly by accident.

Most cases were solved that way, he thought. Hard work, long hours, skill, at times none of that seemed to matter. Luck played the biggest hand. He could use a healthy dose of it himself right now.

That, and maybe a larger helping of common sense. Whether or not he admitted it, he was playing with fire.

Sitting up, he felt the pillow slip down behind him. He had to get going. "All right, well, tell them I appreciate the help. I was just checking in—"

"I'm glad you did. McNair's been calling, harassing Carrie."

The man didn't give up, did he? "Harassing her? Why?"

"Because she won't give him your number up there. Carrie can hold her own with the best of them, but she said McNair is threatening to sue the agency for some sort of breach of promise if you don't get in contact with him immediately."

Ben grimaced in disgust. "Damn him, there's no breach of promise. I told him that I'd call when I had something."

There was a pregnant pause. "Well, don't you?"

It was curiosity, not judgment he heard in Megan's voice. There was a time, when he was on the police force, and she was with the firm, that they had gone head to head. But those days were behind them. He realized now what she'd had to contend with, working the cases she did.

"What I have right now is a situation. I want answers."

Reading between the lines was a habit of long-standing for someone who'd once been with the FBI the way Megan had. "We're not supposed to rehabilitate anyone, Ben, we're supposed to just bring kids together with their families."

"Yeah, I know. But there's something more going on here, Meg. I can feel it. But if I press too hard, I'm not going to get anything. It's like the Golden Goose story you read as a kid. Striking at the source might kill it, while coaxing it can get you everything."

Megan laughed. "Well, if anyone can coax things along, I guess you can." And then her tone shifted. "Listen, I hate to ask, but will you give McNair a call? Carrie said he sounded serious and I don't want to worry Cade with this."

He picked up on the note of concern. This was more than just one partner looking out for another. "Why, what's up with Cade?"

"His wife's having a tough time with the last stages of her pregnancy, and he's got enough on his mind without having to deal with a pompous jerk like Stephen McNair, no matter how important the man thinks is."

It looked as if McNair had no fans at the agency, despite his being the parent of a kidnapped child. "Consider it done. Oh, and give Cade and McKayla my best when you talk to them.''

''Thanks, Ben. One of us'll give you a call if anything crops up about the case on our end.''

''Appreciate it. And try not to wear Garrett out on your honeymoon.'' He laughed when she told him what she thought of his comment, then hung up.

The smile faded the moment he thought of McNair. Ben had never liked being forced to do anything. He'd planned to call his client in his own good time. He didn't appreciate being kept on a short leash.

Ben glanced at his watch. He wasn't due at Gina's for another hour. He blew out a long breath. Might as well get this over with.

Taking McNair's phone number out of his pocket, he tapped out the numbers on the keyboard. The phone on the other end rang several times. Ben was about to hang up, glad of the temporary reprieve, when he heard the crackle of static and then McNair's voice.

''McNair here.''

So much for the reprieve. ''Mr. McNair, this is Ben Underwood.''

McNair's tone shifted from assertive to angry. ''Well it's about damn time you checked in with me, Underwood. Where the hell have you been?''

Ben had always considered himself relatively easygoing, but that didn't mean he was anyone's lackey. Mentally counting to ten, Ben waited before answering. Telling the client where to go wasn't considered to be in the agency's best interest.

''Working, Mr. McNair.''

McNair gave his opinion of that by using an expletive. ''If you are working, and I'm assuming you mean working for me, why haven't you called?''

Edges of his temper began to unravel. Ben struggled to remain civil as he answered, "I said I'd call you if there was anything to report."

"And I said I wanted you to check in periodically. I'm not paying you to be coy with me, Underwood. Where is she?"

Ben felt his jaw clench in response to the demand. "She? You mean 'he,' don't you?"

"Don't tell me what I mean. I said she and I mean she," McNair snarled. "*She* has my son, remember? Now, where the hell is she?"

If it wouldn't have reflected badly on Cade and Megan, Ben would have gladly told McNair to go to hell in no uncertain terms. But though he'd been made a partner, the agency was Cade's baby and he had to respect that. Even if the man he was talking to was an absolute jerk. "I don't know yet."

"Don't know yet? I thought you people guaranteed results. What the hell have you been doing these last few days?"

Allegiance to Cade notwithstanding, Ben was just inches away from telling McNair what he could do with his case. There was just so much a man could be expected to put up with.

"Sometimes these cases take more time than others," he told him through clenched teeth.

"I'm not interested in excuses, Underwood, I'm interested in results."

Ben had a feeling the CEO addressed stockholders, employees and boards of the directors in the same manner he was using now. As if he was entitled to absolute obedience and demanded nothing less. Well, it might work with everyone else, but the abrasive, condescending manner didn't cut it with Ben.

"Now, have you located that woman or haven't you?"

"I said not yet," Ben repeated. "Listen, Mr. McNair, if you're not satisfied with the quality of service you're getting from ChildFinders, specifically from me, you're welcome to go anywhere else you think might do a better job. Or the police, for that matter."

It still bothered him that the only reason McNair hadn't gone to the police was because he didn't want the notoriety it would bring. What did notoriety matter when his son's life hung in the balance? Maybe the boy had wanted to run away from his self-centered, despotic father and Gina had helped him get away because she'd seen abusive behavior on McNair's part.

He kept thinking of her as Gina, not Gloria. He had to stop that and remember to keep not only his distance but a healthy perspective in this.

There was silence on the other end of the line. It lasted so long that Ben thought McNair had hung up and the line had gone dead.

But McNair was still there. Ben heard his voice just as he started to hang up. The voice he heard was subdued. "I'm sorry, I didn't mean to fly off the handle that way. It's just that I'm worried about the boy. There's no telling what she might do to get even."

"I thought you said you weren't worried about Gloria harming Andrew."

A hint of McNair's annoyance returned. He obviously didn't like having his mistakes pointed out. "I was basing my response on past performance. But a woman who would steal a child right out of his own home is liable to do anything if she's desperate enough."

Personally, Ben didn't buy into that. He'd always believed there was a basic core within everyone. They were either decent, or they weren't. Some people were incapable of the final act of murder no matter what. Others…

He let the thought go, wondering only which category Gloria Prescott fell into. According to McNair, she was a coldhearted witch capable of anything, while everyone else had presented Ben with the opposite picture. Which was the real Gloria? He knew which he believed it to be. What he'd witnessed hadn't jibed with McNair's characterization.

Is that your head you're thinking with, or some other part? an inner voice mocked him.

"Look," McNair was saying, "accept my apologies. Just let me know if you find anything. Anything at all," he emphasized. "I might not be the best father and I am new at it, but the boy is still my blood and my one claim to immortality."

"Right. I'll let you know," he said, then dropped the receiver into the cradle. "One claim to immortality." It was still all about McNair, wasn't it? Ben thought.

The hot water felt better than good as it ran down in steamy rivulets along Gina's body.

Because she was alone in the house, she allowed herself to savor the moment. Jesse was playing three doors down with his new best friend, Kyle. She'd taken him there less than half an hour ago. It had been a spur-of-the moment invitation from Kyle, backed by Grace, Kyle's mother. Gina's first inclination had been to say no because Jesse hadn't finished his homework.

But Jesse had been persistent. He'd promised to do it at Kyle's and Grace had told her that she would see that both boys completed their assignments.

She'd given in, the way she knew she would. It wasn't in her to say no to him. But she hadn't told Jesse that Ben was coming over for dinner. That would have put him in the position of having to choose. She'd chosen for him. It was better this way.

She'd already detected a touch of hero worship in Jesse's eyes when he looked at Ben. The boy was so hungry for male companionship, it broke her heart. With Jesse here, Ben might not leave when she wanted him to.

And she didn't want him staying too long.

Gina turned the hot water up a little higher. She felt the tension leaving her, felt herself relaxing. Her eyes drifted shut. A myriad of rivulets ran along her body, zigzag patterns caressing every part of her. Like exploring fingers of a man's hand.

She missed that. Missed the feel of a man's hand touching her.

It had been so long, so very long since she'd loved and let herself be loved.

Yearnings rose to the surface again, reminding her that she was something more than just a mother, something more than just a person who worked in a bookstore. She was a woman, with needs that she had been valiantly struggling to ignore.

How much longer did she have to continue pretending they weren't there? How much longer before she would feel safe enough to let herself care about someone again?

She couldn't think about that. There was no point. She had her son to think about. His safety to worry about. If she allowed herself to get sidetracked, to feel responses when a man looked at her...

With a sigh, she shut off the hot water.

There was no use in torturing herself like this. Someday, she could be herself again. But not yet. Not today. Not until she was sure that Jesse and she were both safe.

She stepped out of the shower and began to quickly towel her hair dry, deliberately making her mind a complete blank. Otherwise, she might begin to visualize Ben in the role of the man who was missing from her life.

The thought brought her head up with a jolt.

Ben? That was almost as ridiculous as having a fantasy lover. Yes, he was good-looking and personable, but he was just someone passing through San Francisco. Someone passing through her life. He could be gone by next week.

Unless he decided to stay...

Why should he? He'd told her that he lived in Southern California, not here. She wasn't even sure where in Southern California. He'd mentioned Bedford, but he hadn't actually said he lived there.

Wouldn't that have been a coincidence...?

Gina tossed aside the towel. Still naked, she reached for a comb and began pulling it through her short, wet hair. What kind of a possible relationship could she have with any man, given her present circumstances? Her whole existence was a cobweb of lies.

Leaning forward, she examined her hair. Were those blond roots beginning to show? She frowned. Maybe it was the light in here, playing tricks on her eyes. She would have thought that hair dye would last longer than just two weeks. Even so, she made a mental note to color her hair the first opportunity she got.

The jarring noise had her heart slamming against her rib cage automatically. The doorbell.

That couldn't be Ben. It was too early.

She took a deep breath to steady nerves that had gotten dangerously frayed over the last few months and hurried into her clothes. There was no time to dry herself off. If she had to flee, she didn't want to make a run for it in a towel.

Sliding her hand along the banister, she rushed down the stairs and reached the front door in a matter of seconds. She held her breath as she stood on her toes, peering through the peephole.

The air left her in a huff, ushering in a surge of relief in its place. Gina pulled open the door. "You're early."

Ben walked in. "I was taught it was impolite to be late. Where can I put this?"

"This" was the umbrella he'd leaned against his neck and his shoulder as he'd hurried from the car to her front step, carrying the pizza box. Waiting for an answer, Ben turned around to face her as she closed the door.

The overhead light fixture was illuminating the drops of water that still clung to her neck and hair. He saw small, dark stains where her cotton shirt made contact with skin that was far from dry. She'd missed a button while putting on her blouse and she wasn't wearing a bra. Her nipples were pushing against the fabric with every breath she took. And with each breath, the material beneath the buttonholes spread apart just enough to tantalize him with a glimpse of firm, moist skin. Maybe an inch, maybe less. Just enough to arouse him.

Ben slowly realized that if he held on to the pizza box any more tightly, his fingers were going to go through the cardboard.

With effort, he forced himself to pull back mentally. He was here to get information from the woman, to pull the pieces of the puzzle into some sort of order, not indulge in erotic fantasies about her.

The fantasies did not go gently into the dark night.

Turning away, he pretended to look around. ''Where's Jesse?'' There was safety in numbers, and right now, he figured they both needed that safety.

Leading the way to the kitchen, Gina pulled out the edge of her hair from the collar of her shirt, brushing her fingers against her neck at the same time. She should have taken the time to dry off, she upbraided herself. But she'd been afraid, afraid of using up precious time. Of being caught unaware.

Struggling with her thoughts, she banked down vivid memories of a break-in and a face so contorted with anger, it haunted her nightmares. McNair had thought she was with another man and had broken down the door when she hadn't come to answer it quickly enough. Afraid, angry, she'd sent him away. McNair had managed to not only violate her home, but her mind as well.

''He's at Kyle's house.'' She saw the look of surprise on his face.

''Who's Kyle?''

''Kyle Abernathy. Jesse's new best friend. He called around four o'clock, asking if Jesse could come over and play. I didn't have the heart to say no.'' Why was she explaining herself to him? There was no reason why he needed to know her thought process. She felt nerves beginning to shuttle forward again. ''I know he'll be sad he missed you.''

Ben placed the pizza down on the table. He couldn't shake the feeling that she'd sent the boy away on purpose. But why? Was she afraid he'd find a way to be alone with the boy and that Jesse would say things she didn't want him to?

That had to be it. Nothing else made sense. "Why, what time is he getting back?"

"After you leave."

Rather than take offense, humor curved his mouth. "Would it make you feel better if we get an egg timer and clock my visit? I can leave when the timer buzzes."

Gina blew out a breath, then laughed herself. "I'm sorry if that came out wrong, Ben. It's just that—"

"You don't trust me."

"It's not that." At least, not exactly. It was far more complex than that.

Opening up the pizza box, he slanted a look in her direction. "Well, it's certainly not that you don't trust yourself, because from what I can see, you're a pretty together lady who doesn't let life just sweep her along."

A smile curved her lips. "Are you trying to flatter me?"

Experience had taught her to hold flattery from good-looking men suspect. Yet there was a tiny part of her that warmed to the words like a kitten coming in out of the rain and lying down in front of a fireplace.

Could flattery turn her head? He had his doubts about that. She seemed much too down-to-earth to be the type to hang on to a man's word. Besides, the picture McNair had painted in his interview had been that of a cold, calculating woman who knew how to use her body to get what she wanted.

Ben tried to remember that, but it wasn't easy. Other thoughts kept crowding in the way. Thoughts he kept telling himself he could handle.

"I'm trying to do whatever it takes to make you feel comfortable with me," he said.

Suspicion, never far away, rose up as the first line of defense. Was there some ulterior motive at work here after all? Her eyes narrowed as she looked at him. "Why?"

There were napkins on her table at the nook. He took several and brought them over to the counter where the pizza was.

"Because you're an attractive lady, Gina, and I'd like to spend some time with you. And it'll make my picking your brain easier. Things always flow more smoothly if people are comfortable with each other."

He saw the momentary struggle in her eyes, saw the instant her guard went down. For the time being, he knew he'd won.

There should have been a sense of triumph. But there wasn't.

Chapter 11

"More likely than not, you'll be going back to Los Angeles soon."

Gina said the words as much for herself as to put him in his place. Maybe more.

She wasn't immune to this man and therein lay the problem.

No, she argued with herself, the problem was that she'd been alone too long, and emotionally, that made her a prime target. If she let herself feel anything for this man, she was bound to be disappointed. He was just passing through.

"Yes," he agreed, trying to keep it light. "But not *too* soon. I like it here. There's an energy in San Francisco that helps me create." His eyes met hers. The words seemed to come out of nowhere. They certainly weren't anything he'd considered on his own. "And even if I was leaving soon, that doesn't mean we can't enjoy each other's company." The smile he offered her was engaging and he knew it. "People usually find me pretty nonthreatening."

Gina took a deep breath before answering. "I don't find you threatening."

Yeah, she did, he thought. And that was exactly what he had to try to get her over, if he was going to get any information out of her.

A part of him was liking this assignment less and less, even though his intentions were for the right reasons.

"Then why do you look as if you're about to shrink back?" He studied her for a moment, trying to get into her head. Not for the first time, he wished he had Eliza's knack of reading people. And then it came to him. "Just when did this stalker thing happen?"

"A while ago." The answer was evasive, her tone dismissive.

For a moment Ben wondered if she could be making the whole thing up, using it as a convenient cover to throw him off, but she looked so sincere, he couldn't seem to help himself. He believed her. More than that, he wanted to protect her.

He had to remember to keep things in perspective.

"Excuse me." Physically moving her aside, Ben reached into the cabinet behind her where he remembered she kept the dishes. Stretching, he purposely brushed his body against hers.

What he hadn't counted on was his own reaction to the calculated movement. He felt his gut tightening in a response that was far more pronounced than what he'd expected.

Startled by the brief contact, Gina moved even farther out of the way. She felt heat rising up her torso, like fire eating its way through dry leaves. What was the matter with her? This was less than nothing. Strangers brushed against one another while passing on a busy street all the time.

But they were something other than strangers.

She cleared her throat, looking at him. "What are you doing?"

Ben was the soul of innocence as he answered, "Getting plates." He took two dinner dishes down and looked at her. "I thought we could eat and talk at the same time. That way you can be rid of me faster."

He made her feel guilty. She hadn't really meant to make him feel unwelcome, it was just that...

Just that suspicion seemed to govern every moment of her life, she acknowledged, and she hated it. Ben was just being open and friendly and she was acting as if he was the enemy. What was wrong with her?

She watched him as he brought plates and silverware over to the small table. If she was in the market to reenter the world of dating and intimate relationships for even a short length of time, he would be a perfect candidate for her to begin with. There would be no consequences to face, no need for any real explanations, because there would be no future. Just two people enjoying themselves in the present, in the moment.

Right, she laughed at herself. Since when was she such a free spirit? Fleeting relationships had never been her style. She needed more. She needed commitment, a future, the promise of tomorrow.

In her present frame of mind, having been through what she had, Gina knew she could never trust anyone long enough to lay the foundation for that. At least, not yet.

And you had to walk before you could run.

Run.

She suppressed a sigh. She was so tired of running. Of fleeing mentally if not physically. Was it ever going to be any different?

Time, she told herself, *give it time.*

"I don't mean to sound as if I'm trying to get rid of you, it's just that it's hard for me to trust anyone on a personal level."

His eyes held hers for a long moment. "The stalker."

She felt as if he was looking into her soul. "The stalker," she agreed.

He slid a napkin on the right side of each plate. "Why don't you tell me about him? Like I said, I'm a good listener."

Not a good idea, no matter how much part of her wanted to unburden herself. She just couldn't afford to be too trusting.

As politely as she could, Gina shrugged away his offer. "But I'm not a good talker, not when it comes to this."

"All right." Moving the pizza box to a better position, Ben took out a slice and placed it on her plate, then took one for himself before sitting down. "So let's dig in and then get to work—if you don't mind."

"No," she said quietly. "I don't mind." She looked at him for a moment, trying to picture him as a writer, as someone who bet his future on what he put down on paper. She couldn't exactly explain why, but it seemed like far too iffy a proposition for someone like him. "No offense, but do you really think you'll be able to sell this screenplay once you finish?" It occurred to her that he hadn't even told her what his "day job" actually was, or how he managed to put food on the table and keep a roof over his head. He'd told her very little about himself and she found herself wondering and wanting to know.

He grinned at her. "Absolutely," he said. And then he winked. "You have to have faith, Gina."

Faith. There'd been a time when she'd had faith, when she'd believed that the world was a warm, wonderful place. Even after her parents had died when she was thirteen. Aunt Sugar had swooped down, enveloping her in love and taking her back to live with her. It had taken her time, but thanks to Aunt Sugar, she'd gotten there. Her feeling had been that, all right, she was a single mother, but she'd had her career and a future that was finally beginning to look up.

Until she had to leave everything behind.

"Maybe you do, but I don't," she murmured, taking two cans of soda out of the refrigerator. Collecting two glasses, she set them all down in the center of the small table.

He raised his eyes to hers, waiting until she took her seat opposite him. The table was so small, her knees brushed against his. He felt the same response, the same electricity he had minutes ago, and forced himself to concentrate on the situation at hand.

"Why, Gina, I would have never pegged you as a pessimist."

She smiled at that. "Funny, neither would I." But things had a way of changing. Through no fault of her own. Or maybe, it had been. Maybe if she hadn't been so trusting, so blind… "But that was before."

"Before…?" Ben deliberately let his voice trail off, waiting for her to fill an event in.

"Before," she repeated with finality, firmly closing the door on the subject. "And this is now." She glanced out the window. The darkness was underscored by sheets of rain. It gave no indication of letting up any time soon. It made her feel lonely. She struggled to shut out the feeling. "So, you're planning on being a big-time screenwriter."

Ben inclined his head. "Something like that."

How many dreamers were there out there? she wondered. But some of them wrote screenplays that were produced, why shouldn't Ben be among their number? "What are you going to do with all the money you make?"

He shrugged. "I hadn't really thought about that part of it. Getting the story told is the main thing."

For her, perforce, it was all about the money right now. She thought of her great-aunt and the money she'd borrowed just to come here. Though it wasn't easy, she'd started setting a tiny bit aside each week, to pay Aunt Sugar back. The kind of money Ben was talking about would have definitely set her on her feet, debt free. The way she'd once anticipated her career as a sculptor would do.

"And the money doesn't tempt you at all." Money represented security to her, but for most people, she'd come to realize, it was the end-all, be-all. Even Stephen had always wanted more, and he had enough money to buy his own small country if he wanted to.

But not enough to buy her, she thought.

"Oh, don't get me wrong, money's great. But I just don't believe it's its own reward. Money just buys you peace of mind. But if you don't know what that is…" She was smiling at him and he congratulated himself on picking the right path to embellish. He just wished her smile didn't sink straight into him so deeply. Made it hard for a man to think. Hard for a man to remember his lies.

"You're so different," she said.

Finished with his slice, he wiped his fingers on his napkin and cocked his head, looking at her. He tried not to wonder what it would be like to kiss her. He wondered, anyway. "Different from what?"

"From what I would have expected, looking at you."

Ben rested his chin on his fisted hand. "And what would you have expected, looking at me?"

She laughed then, looking down, a little embarrassed. She shouldn't have said anything. "Someone who knows how to enjoy himself," she allowed. "And would spend money like water, given half a chance."

He wondered if she was just making idle conversation, or if that was really the impression she had of him. And why any opinion she had should matter. He was just gathering information to help him unravel what was going on and, ultimately, to reunite McNair with his son. He ignored what the consequences of that would mean to Gina.

"I guess you can't always tell a book by its cover."

"I guess not," she agreed. Something was stirring inside her. A yearning she didn't want. Digging into her pocket, she took out a list. She glanced at it, though she knew every book there, before she handed it to him. "I used the computer at the bookstore and made up a basic list of books you might find useful in your background research. I'm not sure just how deeply you want to go into the material, or how much you know, for that matter. So don't get insulted if some of these strike you as elementary."

He glanced over the list quickly and noted her handwriting. It was very precise. Every "i" dotted, every "t" crossed, not a thing like his.

"I'll hold on to my temper," he promised, his mouth

curving. He nodded at the list. "This looks pretty extensive."

"It is. Some of the books might be hard to find, but, like I said, if you want to be thorough—" He hadn't really told her the basic focus of the story, other than bandying the word *epic* around. It might have been just to catch her attention. "Do you?"

He was flying by the seat of his pants here. "As thorough as possible without putting the audience to sleep."

She had no idea why that tickled her as much as it did. "That would depend on your protagonist—I take it it's a he."

He grinned, spreading his hands. "Write about what you know, right? At least to some extent, although the guy's an orphan, so right there, we have a parting of the ways." He was deliberately baiting her, waiting for her to launch into a story about her "sister"—the woman he'd met at social services.

Instead, he saw her eyes cloud over just a little. "I might be able to help you with that, too."

Was this a lie or the truth? He didn't know what to believe. He had no choice but to continue playing along. "You're an orphan?"

"Not to begin with, but I lost my parents pretty early in life. Too early." Even the simple words brought a hitch to her throat. She could never think about her parents without experiencing a mixed bag of emotions.

He took another slice of pizza, but his eyes held hers. "What happened to them—if you don't mind my asking?"

Gina wasn't sure what had come over her. Maybe it was the weather. Rain always made her sad. It'd been raining the day she lost her parents. Normally, she kept it all bottled up inside, but this evening, for some reason, she needed to talk.

"They died in a car accident." A sigh at the loss, at the grief she would always feel, escaped. "I was raised by my late grandmother's sister." She smiled affectionately to herself. Where would she have been, then and now, without Aunt Sugar? "Her name's Sugarland."

"Sounds like there's a story behind that." His smile was kind and coaxed her to continue.

"A very short one. There was an old song she liked to sing as a little girl. One of the lyrics mentioned a place called Sugarland. The nickname stuck. I don't think I actually know what her real name is."

"Maybe she doesn't, either, anymore." The comment had just slipped out in the ease of the conversation they were having. She looked at him, her brows narrowing, and he realized his mistake. "Just a creative guess."

"Good one. She doesn't." The one time she'd actually asked Aunt Sugar, the woman hadn't been able to tell her, promising to look it up in a family bible "soon." That had been several years ago.

"What was it like, growing up without your parents?"

That was the writer in him asking, she told herself, trying not to take the question personally. Trying not to see it as a sign that he was interested in the answer in any other way than intellectually—even though right now, she wanted him to be.

"For the most part, I managed. Aunt Sugar did everything she could to make it up to me. But there were times I still felt disconnected. I guess I was just trying to find my place in the world after they died."

"And did you?"

She thought for a moment. If there had been somewhere she was finally coming together, it would have been the house back in Bedford. The place she'd had to leave so quickly. But that was in her past. She had to think ahead.

Gina smiled with a half shrug just before she took a bite of her slice. "I'm still working on it."

Picking up his napkin, he leaned forward. "Hold still."

"What?" She did as he instructed, wondering if there was a spider crawling on her. It took effort not to shiver. "Why?"

To her surprise, he took her chin in one hand. "Never met a woman yet who liked to wear tomato sauce on her cheek."

This was the second time. "I guess you bring out the messy part of me."

He smiled. "I guess so." Ben wiped away the small, telltale red streak that had smeared on her cheek with the corner of the napkin. "I kind of like you messy. Makes you human."

"At times, I'm all too human," she replied quietly.

His strokes were deliberately slow, deliberately meant to arouse her. But he realized too late that he was getting tangled up in his own trap.

He was trying to get to her, he reminded himself, not the other way around.

It didn't help.

She raised her eyes to his and he felt the last of his footing go.

One moment he was wiping her cheek, the next, he was bringing his mouth in closer to hers. Hardly daring to breathe, he kissed her. Lightly. Just enough to excite her.

And himself in the bargain.

Ben leaned back, the napkin slipping from his lax fingers. Very slowly, he ran just the tip of his tongue along his lips. "Never had pizza served quite that way before."

"I find that very difficult to believe." Good, she could still talk. For a second, she'd thought that she'd completely lost the ability to form coherent words. Other than wow.

"Would you mind if I kissed you again?"

"Yes," she whispered, using the last thimbleful of air that had been left in her lungs.

The smile that she watched slip over his lips was slow, sexy. She couldn't draw her eyes away from his mouth.

"Yes, you mind, or yes, I can?"

Her mind went blank. "I—"

"Never mind," he said softly, taking the decision out of her hands. "Forget I asked."

Asking wasn't his style. It took control of a situation out of his hands, and right now he wanted to be in control. He wanted to hold her. To kiss her. She was the chief suspect in this kidnapping case, but somehow, the fine line between good and evil, black and white, had gotten blurred for him. He'd gotten himself lost in her eyes, in her smile. He wanted to kiss her before he found out things that might make moments like this impossible.

His mouth came down on hers.

Rising to his feet, his lips still sealed to hers, Ben held on to her shoulders and brought her up with him until they were both standing.

Ben could feel her heart pounding hard and he knew his was doing the same, beating double time.

Damn, but she tasted tangy and sweet, with the promise of things he couldn't even begin to fathom. He could feel his body responding in ways he couldn't allow it to.

But for a moment longer, he savored. Drawing her into his arms, he drew her further into the kiss and followed willingly himself.

Why did it have to feel this good?

And why couldn't she have just been someone he'd met by chance on an evening when he was free to think of nothing else but making love with her?

She couldn't breathe. She didn't care. Threading her arms around his waist, all she could do as she kissed him was hang on to this man who was making the room tilt at a forty-five-degree angle.

Her head was spinning.

Gina knew she should draw away while she still had a prayer of being able to think, but she couldn't make herself do that. More than anything, she wanted this feeling, this wild, heady feeling that she hadn't felt for longer than she could remember. Certainly since before her son had been conceived.

For two cents she'd...

For two cents, she'd what? She'd make love with him? Wasn't that where this was heading? To a few stolen moments of mindless ecstasy?

The thought startled her, making her pull back from him in stunned wonder. What was she thinking? She hardly knew the man.

Shaken, she tried to get her bearings. "What just happened here?"

She looked afraid, he thought, the realization bothering him. He ran the back of his hand slowly against her cheek. Blocking out everything else except the way her skin felt. Soft. Like newly fallen snowflakes.

"I'm not sure." He refrained from kissing her again, not particularly pleased that it was harder than he'd anticipated. "I think we might have discovered a new natural phenomenon."

Her eyes crinkled at the corners in response.

He wanted to share her amusement. "What?"

"You're good. Oh, you are very good," she said.

She was smiling at him, but he couldn't help wondering if that was some sort of a put-down. "I have a funny feeling you're not talking about what just happened here."

That was part of it, but she tried not to focus on it. "I'm talking about your gift of turning a phrase—and a woman's head."

"I wasn't trying to turn your head." It was a lie, but he managed it well. That was part of the job. However he didn't have to like it. "If the earth had moved, I wouldn't have been surprised."

Her smile widened. "Neither would I, this is San Francisco. Every doomsday prophet keeps warning us we're about due for another major quake."

He wasn't ready to let her sit down just yet. Instead, he tucked his arms around her waist and held her with just a space between them. If he had his way, there wouldn't have been any space between them, but he knew he had to go slow here. "That notwithstanding, you had to have felt that jolt between us."

There was no point in lying. He'd sensed her reaction. "Yes, I felt it."

"I'd like to see you. Socially. Without a pizza or an unfinished screenplay between us."

And probably any clothes, too, she'd be willing to

bet. And that, she knew, was much too dangerous a scenario to leave herself opened to. Especially since she wanted it herself so much.

She shook her head. "Sorry, you're going to have to settle for this." She disengaged herself from him. "For the research and the pizza and the screenplay. You're just passing through and I'm not."

"Maybe I could stay." He was as surprised to hear the words coming out of his mouth as she was.

It was just part of his cover, he reminded himself.

But if he were being honest with himself, he knew that there was a part of him that would have been willing to give it a try without the case looming over him.

Even if she wasn't guilty, if, by some stroke of luck, she wasn't who he thought she was, what chance did he have with her once she knew of the deception he'd perpetrated? Once she knew he was here to trap her?

She turned the words around to her benefit. "And maybe you could go. This wasn't a good idea."

He didn't want to leave yet, even if he wasn't playing by the rules. "Gina, what are you afraid of?"

She drew her hands away from his. "More things than you could possibly begin to imagine."

She said it so earnestly, he believed her. But it seemed unlikely that she was telling him the truth. After all, McNair had ultimately discovered that Gloria had lied about her references, and when Ben had checked them out himself, he had discovered that Gloria Prescott had never been anyone's nanny. It had been a calculated maneuver to get close to McNair and his money.

Maybe Gina or Gloria or whatever name she chose to go by was lying to him now, too.

Chapter 12

For a fleeting moment, Ben thought of pressing his advantage. Instinct told him he definitely had one and that he could.

All he had to do was reach for her again.

Somewhere in his mind, the phrase about discretion being the better part of valor surfaced.

With a smile, Ben lightly touched her cheek with the back of his hand again. "All right, I'll go. Thanks for the list." He touched his shirt pocket. "Tell Jesse I'm sorry I missed him."

She was getting a reprieve. From what, she wasn't sure, but the feeling was there nonetheless. Pulling herself together, Gina nodded as she accompanied him to the front door.

"He'll be sorry he missed you, too." Maybe because she still hadn't gotten her complete bearings, she admitted a little more to him than she ordinarily would have. "He's always been a friendly kid, but I've never

seen him take to anyone as quickly as he has to you.''
That goes for Jesse's mother, too, she thought, except
that in her case, she was doing her best to block out her
response to Ben.

He flashed a grin. ''He's a great kid.''

She touched his cheek, tempted, yearning, then let
her hand drop. ''Thank you, I think so.''

A gust of wind assaulted her, ushering in rain the
second she opened the door for him. Reflexes had her
pulling the door shut.

Gina blew out a breath in surprise, then looked at
Ben. ''Wow, they didn't say it was going to turn into
a storm. Maybe you'd better wait it out.'' She didn't
want to send him out when it was coming down like
this. It was close to flash-flood conditions. ''It can't last
this way all night.''

Temptation reared its head. Temptation that had nothing to do with furthering the case. Ben hesitated, then
made a decision that was based on nothing that remotely
had to do with common sense or his work ethic. Just
his sense of decency.

''That's all right, I think maybe it's better if I do go
now.'' He looked out the narrow window next to the
front door. ''Does look pretty bad out there, though.
Want me to go pick up Jesse for you?''

''No.'' The answer was immediate. She knew it had
come out too emphatic, too loud. The next moment, she
tempered her tone. ''That's very nice of you to offer,
but I'd really prefer to get him myself.'' She added a
coda to make it sound more believable. ''I have something I need to drop off with Kyle's mother.''

Maybe it was just his nature, making him suspicious,
but he had a feeling she was making the last part up.
Something had her nervous and it wasn't just him.

"Thanks, anyway," Gina said.

"Well if I can't be of any use, I might as well leave." He turned up his collar, then picked up the umbrella he'd left standing in the corner, a small pool of water gathered at its tip where the rain had dripped down.

Ben paused just before opening the door. "Would you mind if I dropped in at the bookstore sometime? To work out the knots? In the screenplay," he added after a beat.

She couldn't believe that he was actually asking permission. No one had ever treated her with such care before, such consideration. Gina couldn't help the smile that rose to her lips, coaxed there by the feeling that she didn't want to begin to identify. It was better if it remained without a name. Things without names stood a better chance of being ignored.

As if.

"No, I don't mind." She bit back the urge to tell him to come tomorrow. "We'll play it by ear."

He nodded. "Should be exciting." With that, he opened the door. The gust that came in ruffled his hair and sent drops of rain all through it. The umbrella would be useless against the wind. He'd waste his energy fighting the wind for possession of it and get wet, anyway. Leaving it closed, he hunched his shoulders forward and made his way into the darkness.

Her cheeks were stinging, but she didn't retreat immediately. "Drive carefully," she called out after him. Ben raised his hand over his head to indicate he heard her, but didn't risk turning around again. If he did, he just might rescind the noble act he was presently trying to pull off.

And if he rescinded, if he turned around and walked back into her house, he knew he was going to cross that invisible line he'd set down for himself. The one that separated his professional life from his personal one. And while being with Gina might not exactly be classified as sleeping with the enemy, it wouldn't be entirely ethical, either.

Drenched, he laughed shortly to himself as he got in behind the wheel of his car. Entirely? Who was he kidding? It wouldn't be ethical at all—even if it did bring her to the point where she could trust him enough to tell him what was really going on.

He jabbed his key into the ignition.

Any way he looked at it, the woman he'd just left behind just didn't strike him as someone who would break the law even in a minor way, much less kidnap a child. Yet she'd stolen someone else's name and created a fictitious life around it.

And then there was the boy, the boy who called her Mommy with no hesitation whatsoever, as if he'd always done so.

What was Ben supposed to believe?

Was he letting his feelings color his judgment or refine it? At this point, he wasn't sure of anything.

Except that he liked the taste of pizza when it was enhanced by her lips. And that he wanted to make love with her in the worst way.

Emphasis, he told himself, on "worst." Unless there were extreme extenuating circumstances, he'd never believed that the ends justified the means.

He allowed himself one last look at her condo. Maybe the rain and the streetlights were playing tricks on his eyes, but he thought he saw Gina standing in the window, watching.

Probably just shadows melding with wishful thinking. Ben stepped on the accelerator and drove to his motel.

* * *

The wind fought him for the door when he unlocked it. He slammed it shut behind him, exerting more force than he'd anticipated. Peeling off his jacket, he tossed it aside on the floor and began unbuttoning his shirt. Both had gotten soaked in the short distance from Gina's house to his car. Shedding the shirt, he shivered.

The room felt cold. As he made his way to the thermostat, he took out his cell phone and looked at the number still visible on the screen. The phone had rung while he was driving, but the rain and wind had made keeping his car within the lane a challenge, requiring both his hands on the wheel and his full concentration. He'd let the call go unanswered.

The number belonged to Erika, his next-to-youngest sister.

He hit the fifth number on his automatic dialer, then dragged one hand through his drenched hair. Raindrops scattered in all directions. The weatherman on the radio had boasted that it'd rained more in the last twenty-four hours than it had the entire rainy season. He didn't doubt it.

He heard the phone being picked up on the other end. "Hello, Erika?"

"Benji!" A myriad of excitement and joy vibrated in the single salutation. That was Erika. Enthusiasm was her credo. "I wanted you to be the first to know. Well," she amended almost faster than he could process her words, "the second, really. I told Mom first. You know how she gets when she doesn't know things immediately—"

If he didn't stop her now, he knew he'd be trampled in the onslaught of words. "Slow down, E. The second to know what?"

"I'm getting married. Justin just asked me. Isn't that

the greatest news you ever heard? Tell me that's the greatest news you ever heard.''

With Erika's exuberance filling his ear and his head, Ben made his way to the small refrigerator in the corner and looked inside. A lonely bottle of beer, only half full, sat forlornly on the shelf, its only company the eerie light from the bulb above.

Why should there have been anything else? He hadn't gone shopping and the last he'd heard, the food elves didn't make house calls this far north. If he'd been home, there would have been a fifty-fifty chance his mother might have made a pit stop, filling his refrigerator with food he'd reimburse her for the next time he saw her, over her loud protests that he was robbing her of one of her few remaining joys.

He had to get better organized. With a sigh, he reached in and took the bottle, letting the door close again.

''Greatest news I ever heard,'' he said, echoing her words back to her.

''You don't sound happy for me.''

With no effort at all, he could close his eyes and visualize the pouty lower lip making a fleeting appearance before another wave of exuberance kicked in. He had years of experience to fall back on.

''I'm happy. Happy for you, happy for Justin and most of all, happy for Mom. She loves to cry at weddings.'' And divorces, he recalled. She'd taken his hard. It hadn't stopped her from launching into a campaign to try to find him a wife before his divorce decree was cold. ''But I'm also wet and clammy.''

There was a beat of silence on the other end, as if his words were registering belatedly. ''Are you getting sick, Benji?''

He looked down. His shoes were probably ruined, thanks to the small lake that had formed next to his car when he got in.

"No, just don't have enough sense to come in out of the rain." He had to get out of these clothes and into something dry. "Look, can I call you back in a few minutes?"

"Sorry, Justin and I are going out to celebrate. I can call you later. Oh-oh-oh, wait, don't hang up," she cried, anticipating his next move. "Justin wants you to be best man."

It struck him as odd. He'd spoken to the man maybe three times and hadn't been all that impressed any of those times. "Why, doesn't he have any better men in his life than me?"

"Nobody's better than my big brother," Erika declared playfully.

This was a far cry from the little girl who had periodically shouted that she hated him. If Erika sounded any happier, he had a feeling it would probably have been ruled illegal.

"You're only saying that 'cause it's true. Look, E, I'm really thrilled for you, but if I don't get out of these clothes soon—"

"Got it." Again he heard noise, as if she was suddenly yanking the receiver back from meeting the cradle. "If you get sick, I'll have Mom send you up a huge bowl of chicken soup."

He stifled a groan. "Not a word to Mom," he warned. "Not even a hint." They both knew what their mother was like. Maureen Underwood was probably the prototype for earth mother. She counted it an incomplete day if she hadn't mothered at least one person and made their world a better place for them.

"She won't hear it from me," Erika promised. "I love you!" she crowed.

He was happy for her. He just wished she had slightly better taste in men. But who knew, maybe it would work out. God knew Erika would give it her best.

"Love you, too, E."

The connection was gone before he had a chance to hang up.

Ben dropped the receiver into the cradle. Well, at least someone was happy, he thought, walking into the bedroom.

There was a shower waiting with his name on it.

He heard the low, soothing sound of her voice as he walked into the bookstore the next day. Feeling oddly like one of the sailors who'd been lured to their demise on the rocks by the sound of a mythical siren's song, he followed Gina's voice to the small alcove that comprised the children's section.

She'd taken a chair at the small table, her knees tucked temptingly against her chest, a large book in her hands. Surrounding her on both sides were ten small children who looked to be between the ages of three and eight. All seemed to be held spellbound by the misadventures of a cat named Scrappy and his best friend, a nearsighted, loyal dog named Hawkeye.

Ben paused, leaning against a bookcase, listening not so much to the story as to the animated cadence of her voice. He found it soothing, yet oddly arousing at the same time, which he knew was far from her intention. But then, he figured he was reading a great deal more into it than the kids were.

She was enjoying herself, he thought. He could see it in her face. How could someone like this be a kidnapper? Every instinct he'd ever developed told him she wasn't. But he didn't know if he could trust his instincts anymore, not when it came to her.

Turning a page, she happened to look up in his direction. He saw surprise in her eyes. Surprise that turned to pleasure. It pleased him and he wished it wouldn't, but he savored the feeling for just a moment.

The rollicking tale was suddenly interrupted as she started to cough. Holding up her hand, Gina set the book down.

"I'll be right back," she said before she got up and went into the back office for a glass of water.

Ten small faces turned to look at Ben, the only other adult in the immediate vicinity.

"Is she going to come back?" a petite strawberry-blonde in forest-green overalls asked.

"I'm sure she'll be right back," he assured her.

A little boy tugged on his pant leg. "What's going to happen to Hawkeye?"

"Well, I don't know—" he began.

Another child thrust the book into his hands. "Mister, can you read to us until Gina gets back? It's almost time for my mommy to come for me and I want to know what happens next."

"Please?"

Several other voices joined the chorus.

Which was how Ben suddenly found himself sitting on a bright green chair that was far too small for him, reading to a pint-size audience. He figured with any luck Gina would return before he got to the bottom of the page.

It took three pages before she made her appearance. When she did, she kept her distance.

His mouth dry from reading, he was quick to offer her the book. "Here."

But Gina made no move to take it from him. Instead, she smiled encouragingly. "No, you're doing fine. Why don't you finish the page?" She pointed to the bottom. "It's the end of the chapter."

He had no choice but to go along with it. Feeling self-conscious for perhaps the first time in his life, Ben read to the end of the page.

"What happens next?" the strawberry-blonde asked. She clearly seemed like the self-appointed leader of the group.

"You'll have to come back next week for that," Gina told her.

The girl sighed dramatically and rose to her feet. She was all smiles when she looked at Ben. "Will you be here next week to read to us?"

He wanted to say "Not if you're lucky," but knew the response would be lost on someone so young. So he took the coward's way out. "Maybe."

"I'll be here too." The little girl beamed at him and then joined her friend as they both went to where their mothers were waiting for them.

As the children shuffled away, Gina began to gather up the books that they left behind and leaned her head close to his. Perfume, sweet and tempting, began to fill his senses before he could block it.

"I think you're about to be on the receiving end of a gigantic crush," she whispered.

He stared at her. "From whom?"

In response, she shook her head, doing her best not to laugh.

"It's true what they say about men. They are all

dense.'' She moved a little closer to him so that her voice wouldn't carry. ''From Emily.''

Bewildered, he looked around. ''Who's Emily?''

''The strawberry-blonde who all but made a date with you for next week.''

Ben looked toward the front of the store. Several of the children he'd just been reading to were clustered there. He picked Emily out by her strawberry hair that seemed to be in perpetual, independent motion, even when she had been sitting down. She was blatantly staring at him. When she saw that he was looking, she covered her face with her hands and giggled.

Ben looked back at Gina. ''You're kidding.''

Men *were* dense, even the good-looking ones. ''Takes very little for a girl that age to give her heart away to an older man.''

''But I just read a few pages of a short story—not even a complete one,'' he protested.

''And you paid attention to her.'' The main point was that he was kind, sensitive and good-looking, not necessarily in that order. Gina could see that it just didn't compute. ''What's the matter, didn't you ever have a crush on anyone older in your life when you were a kid? Maybe a teacher?''

Ben almost laughed out loud at the thought. ''All my teachers were Dominican nuns. I was lucky to make out eyebrows on them.''

''Well, most kids get crushes on someone older in their lives.'' She thought back to her major one. ''I had a fierce crush on Mr. Novak.'' She saw him look at her with interest. ''Tall, blond, blue-eyed, with the soul of a poet.'' In retrospect, he didn't, however, hold a candle to the man standing next to her. ''He was my tenth-grade English teacher and I would have run off with him in a heartbeat.'' Her smile widened.

He looked at Gina. The sun, finally out in full force, filled the reading area, shimmering all around her. ''I guess I'd better watch my step, then, seeing as how I like older women.''

She cocked her head. ''Older women?''

''Older than seven.'' He paused, his eyes sliding along her skin. ''A lot older than seven.''

A sudden fluttery feeling entered unannounced and took up residence in her stomach. She was beginning to like the feeling, she decided. And gave herself permission, guardedly, to like the man who was the cause of it as well.

''Well, since you came to my rescue just now, the least I can do is offer you dinner.''

''A working dinner?'' he asked. ''A real one this time. We didn't really get all that much done last night.''

She caught her lower lip between her teeth. ''No, I guess we didn't. Did you have a chance to look at any of those books on the list I gave you?''

''Not yet, that's why I'm here. I wanted to see how many of these you had in stock and buy them.''

She didn't want him to think she was pushing the books here. That wasn't why she'd made up the list. ''You could go to the library—''

He shook his head. ''No card.''

She found herself fighting back a smile. ''They can issue you a temporary one—''

''My permanent address is in L.A. I don't think a San Francisco library would be eager to issue me a card, temporary or otherwise.''

''No, but I could—''

God, but he wanted to hold her. To draw her against him and just drink in the feel of her. He was grateful they were standing in a public place. "Are you deliberately trying to get me not to buy books?"

"I'm trying to get you to save your money."

She was, too, he realized. "Thanks, but I like underlining and dog-earing. Can't do that with someone else's property."

Rules, he went by rules. She liked that. "Okay, let's see what we've got."

Trouble was, he thought he already knew and it didn't work itself into the framework of an investigation, at least, not in its present ramifications.

"When would you like me to come over?"

Gina thought a second. "Make it six. I've got to stop at the store on my way home."

He didn't want her to go to any trouble. "I could just as easily take you out to dinner."

She shook her head. "No, this is my treat and I can't afford a restaurant. Besides, I promised Jesse I'd help him with a school project." It was a lie, but one she knew she could be forgiven for. She didn't want to give away too much because it might make things seem other than they were. "Six," she repeated.

"Six," he echoed, and tried to tell himself he wasn't looking forward to it.

Chapter 13

He was early.

She was late.

Or at least not as on schedule as she would have liked to have been, she thought as she went to answer the doorbell. She'd barely finished changing, hurrying into her clothes just as she'd heard the doorbell.

But at least Jesse was ready. He'd gone over the things in his backpack a total of three times to make sure he had everything he needed for the anticipated night ahead—a spectacular sleepover that had very little sleep worked into the actual game plan.

As Gina opened the door to admit Ben, the first thing she saw was the grocery bag he was holding in front of him.

''I told you I was taking care of dinner. What did you bring?''

She hadn't answered the door the first time he rang

the bell and he'd begun to think that maybe he'd gotten his evenings confused.

Seeing her wearing a simple black dress that none-theless flattered every single curve he wanted to get acquainted with temporarily fogged up his brain. It took him a second to reclaim his orientation.

He looked down at the bag, as if to check before answering. "Well, I wasn't sure what you were serving, so to be on the safe side, I brought a bottle of white wine and a bottle of red."

The last time she'd had wine had been at the fund-raiser that had wound up changing her life. "You didn't have to—"

He wasn't finished. "Plus something to keep Jesse from feeling left out."

To illustrate, Ben reached into the bag and produced a bottle of sparkling cider that had only bubbles mixed into the apple concoction.

If Ben had bought her diamonds, he couldn't have warmed her heart any more than he had just now. Gina stopped midprotest and just looked at him, her mouth shutting as an afterthought. And then she just shook her head, more to herself than to him. Where had men like this been when she'd been ready to give her heart away? Before she'd built up her arsenal of suspicions?

"Maybe he'll have a quick 'drink' with us before he goes," she remarked.

"Goes?" Ben followed behind her as she walked back into the kitchen. He'd thought it was going to be the three of them tonight. "I thought you were helping him with a project. Jesse's not going to be here for dinner?"

"Project got postponed," she told him vaguely.

Her son, lured by the sound of Ben's voice and lugging his stuffed backpack down the narrow stairs, made his appearance in the kitchen. Coming up behind him, Gina placed her hands around the boy's neck and held him to her. To his credit, Jesse squirmed only marginally.

"My son is about to embark on his first sleepover tonight."

And Jesse had no idea what allowing him to go was costing her, she added silently. But that was for her to know and wrestle with, not Jesse. No matter what was going on in her life, she was determined that her son was going to grow up a normal, well-adjusted boy.

That meant, among other things, slowly allowing him a measure of his own independence to discover his identity—no matter how much she wanted to keep him tied to her for her own peace of mind.

"This true, partner?" Ben asked solemnly as he made eye contact with the boy.

The blond head bobbed up and down with enthusiasm. "It's Kyle's birthday."

"Wow, are you going to have fun. I can remember my first sleepover." Ben glanced up to look at Gina. "It was at my best friend Nick's house. I don't think I closed my eyes all night."

Gina's sympathies immediately aligned themselves with Nick's mother. Ben looked as if he'd been quite a handful at Jesse's age.

He looked as if he'd be quite a handful now.

Jesse's high voice broke into the moment. "I've gotta be at Kyle's house in ten minutes."

Just before he was actually supposed to arrive, Ben thought. He wondered if Gina was clearing the way for them to be alone tonight, or if he was reading too much into this. Maybe it was nothing more than just a coincidence.

Not for the first time, Ben wished the case wasn't getting in the way of things. But it was the case, not his attraction to Gina, that was supposed to be getting center stage, he reminded himself for the umpteenth time. He couldn't lose sight of that. The safe delivery of a small boy depended on his keeping that foremost in his mind.

"Ten minutes, huh?" Walking past Jesse, Ben placed the grocery bag on the table and took out the cider. "Okay, so what do you say we make a toast and then we'll take you over to Kyle's house?"

Not waiting for an answer, Ben began taking down three glasses from the cupboard.

He was making himself at home, Gina thought. As if he'd always been coming here to visit them.

As if…

Everything was just transitory, she reminded herself. She couldn't get carried away. There would be nothing but disappointment if she followed that route—disappointment and perhaps something far worse. She'd had her guard down once and barely gotten out alive. It wasn't going to happen again. This time, she was keeping her eyes wide open, her instincts on alert.

Jesse accepted his glass, now filled with a golden liquid that fizzed and had bubbles rising in it, and looked at Ben with solemn eyes. "What are we going to toast?"

Thinking a minute, Ben raised his own glass of cider. "How about to the future?" His eyes swept over Gina's face before coming to rest on Jesse's. "May it be everything we want it to be."

That sounded wonderful to her.

If only.

Gina raised her glass up, clinking it against the side of Jesse's and then Ben's. "To the future." For a moment, her eyes locked with Ben's before she lowered them.

"The future," Jesse echoed. He took a sip of his drink and then giggled when the bubbles came up to greet his nose. "It tickles," he explained.

Ben pretended to nod solemnly. "Just like champagne," he confided.

Jesse's eyes grew larger and he looked into the contents of his glass with new reverence. "*Is* this champagne?"

Ben fought hard not to smile. "Sure. The G-rated version."

Delighted, Jesse drained the rest of his glass, then set it down on the counter with a contented sigh. "Wow, wait until I tell Kyle."

Anticipating problems, Gina warned, "Make sure you tell him it was cider." That was all she needed, repercussions from Kyle's mother that she was giving alcoholic beverages to her six-year-old son.

"Okay, Mom," Jesse promised.

Ben set his own glass, still half full, down. "You about ready, Tiger?"

With barely harnessed enthusiasm, Jesse looked over toward his backpack. "Sure."

About to usher Jesse out, Ben heard the bell go off behind them. He turned around, looking at the stove. "Is that the end of round one?"

"No, that's dinner announcing itself." For a second, looking at Ben and toasting the future, she'd almost forgotten all about the chicken in the oven. "Just give me a minute, sweetie, and I'll be ready,'' she promised Jesse.

Jesse looked uncomfortable at the nickname as he slanted a glance in Ben's direction. Antsy, the boy shifted from foot to foot, anxious to get to the new adventure waiting for him at his friend's house.

Ben didn't need to be an expert in child psychology for him to read between the lines. He caught Gina by the arm before she could open the oven.

''Look, I came early and threw you off. The least I can do is take Jesse over to Kyle's. No need for you to rush.''

The protest that rose to her lips was automatic, but she swallowed it. Ben was only trying to be helpful. There was no earthly, tangible reason to feel uneasy at his offer. Look how well he fared with the children at the bookstore today. If she couldn't get herself to trust him, she really was a hopeless paranoid.

But the final call was Jesse's. She looked at the boy. ''How do you feel about that, Jesse?''

''Cool!'' he crowed.

''Well, no margin for confusion here.'' She shook her head, pretending to be mystified. ''I had no idea I was so uncool and cramping your style.''

''Oh, no, Mom, it's just that Ben—''

Laughing, Gina touched her son's nose with the tip of her forefinger, reminiscent of a game she'd once played with him.

''That's all right, kiddo. I understand. You've got wings, you want to try them. You're free to go.'' She waved him off. ''Just remember to thank Kyle's mother for having you—and behave.''

''Yes, ma'am.''

Excited, Jesse was nearly to the doorway before he

remembered. Doubling back, he stood on his toes, pulled Gina down to his level and then gave her a huge hug, adding a little more feeling to it because he knew it had to last her all night.

But when she went to kiss him, he whispered "Not in front of Ben" out of the side of his small mouth.

Ben could remember those days, trying hard to look macho for the immediate world. It had taken ten years to outgrow. He was still apologizing to his mother. "I still kiss my mom."

"Really?" Jesse asked.

Gina could have kissed Ben when, very solemnly, he drew an X over his heart. "Cross my heart and hope to die."

"Wow. Okay." And with that, Jesse gave his mother a good-sized, loud smack on the cheek before retreating to the doorway where he had left his backpack. "I'm ready," he needlessly announced.

"Don't forget your coat," she warned, and was rewarded with an "Aw, gee, Mom."

"Not negotiable," she informed her happy wanderer.

Jesse sighed mightily, taking the coat he had helped pick out off the hook where he'd hung it up earlier.

Ben slipped on his own windbreaker, then picked up Jesse's backpack. It was heavier than he'd anticipated and he groaned for Jesse's benefit. "Gee, what do you have in here?"

"Stuff," Jesse informed him, stifling another fit of giggles.

Ben hooked one strap over his arm, his other hand around the boy's shoulders. "How long are you planning on staying over? A month?"

Gina heard Jesse giggling as the two went out the front door.

For a fleeting second, she allowed herself to pretend that this was a typical scene in her life. The life she'd always wanted. With a child and a husband sharing a moment while she looked on with a warm heart.

If only.

Suddenly remembering their chicken dinner was still in the oven, she quickly donned oven mitts and removed the pan from the rack.

Her daydreams, she thought, banishing them, were only that. Daydreams.

Ben was back before she had a chance to finish setting the table.

The sound of the front door opening and then closing again softly had her freezing in place, listening. Busy, she hadn't stopped to turn the lock on the door when Ben and Jesse had left. Now, her fingers icy, she wondered if that had been a mistake.

She raised her voice. "Ben?"

"Right here."

And he was. Right there. Standing in the doorway between the living room and the small dining room.

She couldn't stop the pleasure from filling her. Surprised by her reaction, she didn't even bother to try to block it. Going with the moment, she simply allowed herself to enjoy it. What was the harm in pretending, just for an evening...?

"So, how did it go?"

He crossed to the cabinet. "Great. The boys were off and running up the stairs before I had a chance to say goodbye." Reaching into the cupboard, he took out two glasses and carried them into the next room. "Does Kyle's mother have X-ray vision?"

He just did things without waiting to be asked. Gina

liked that and couldn't help wondering if he'd grown up with a houseful of women. Men weren't usually that intuitively helpful.

"No." She laughed at the question as she placed the large bowl of mashed potatoes on the tablecloth she'd ironed less than an hour ago. "Why?"

"Well, she was looking at me as if she had." Dogging her steps, he got the silverware. "As if she was trying to see everything down to what color shorts I was wearing."

With the question raised, she squelched the impulse to ask him for an answer herself. Instead, she wrapped her hands around the salad bowl and went back into the dining room. "She was probably just wondering if I had a new man in my life."

"New man," he echoed, a fork poised in his hand. "As opposed to an old man in your life?"

The half shrug was meant to hide her self-consciousness but only underlined it. "As opposed to no man in my life."

That there was no one in her life made all this a lot easier for him, but still left him wondering. "Why is that?"

A dozen standard answers occurred to her. Because he'd brought her son faux champagne, she told him the truth. "Takes a lot to make a connection. A real connection. I don't believe in casual flirtations."

And he did, he reminded himself. Enjoying his freedom, casual flirtations were, up until now, the only kinds of relationships he did indulge in.

Until now.

The phrase, his own phrase, echoed back at him. He tried not to attach too much significance to any of it. He couldn't afford to.

"Very admirable."

She shrugged that off, too. "Nothing admirable about it. It might even be easier if I did." At least, that would fill the loneliness that crept up on her at times like a deep, black void, threatening to swallow her up. "But I just don't believe in wasting someone's time, or mine, I guess." She gave it a practical spin. "I've got precious little of it as it is, and what I do have, I prefer giving to Jesse. Moving was kind of hard on him."

Okay, they were getting closer to the story. He kept a casual expression on his face. "Why did you?"

To save him. "It seemed the right thing to do" was all she said.

She placed the platter she'd arranged in the center of the dining room table, between the salad and the potatoes. She'd made too much, she thought. Nerves had done that, she hadn't been paying attention.

"Hope you like chicken parmesan."

Looking at the meal, he could feel his mouth watering. Looking at her had the same effect. "Right now, I'd like anything that didn't slide right out of the box into the microwave."

She slipped the serving utensils beside each bowl or plate. The garlic bread she made added its aroma to the mix. "Sounds like you don't get to eat many home-cooked meals."

Ben broke off a piece of the bread and put it on his plate. "Only when I visit my mother."

"How often is that?"

"Not as often as she'd like." He liberally spread margarine on one side of his bread. "Sunday dinners once a month, except now she serves them on Tuesdays because my sister Cindy can't make Sundays. Attendance is mandatory,'' he added with a grin Gina found utterly endearing.

"And you go."

"I go. But only after she promises not to have some-one sitting next to me at the table I don't know.'' He saw Gina raise her brow in a silent question. "She used to try to fix me up every time I came over.'' In his heart, he knew his mother wouldn't give up subtly try-ing until he finally had a life partner. Seeing as he wasn't in the market for one, she was going to have a very long wait. "My sister Erika's getting married, so that turns the heat off the rest of us for a while.''

"How many is 'us'?''

"Three." He grinned. "I've got two more sisters be-sides Ericka.''

"All single." It was a conclusion, not a question.

"All single." He paused, then raised his eyes to hers and added, "Now.''

Gina wasn't quite sure if she interpreted his meaning correctly. "Now?''

He told himself he was just trying to make small talk, to fill in spaces until she volunteered something he could work with himself, or he could subtly ask her questions. But he knew that he wasn't making small talk, he was sharing. Something he didn't do all that readily, especially not with someone involved in the investigation of a case.

"I was married at eighteen.'' God, could he have been any dumber? Ben thought. His mother, who'd sensed his secret intentions of eloping with Susan, had begged him not to do anything foolish until he knew what direction his life was going in. He'd deliberately ignored her just because she was his mother and couldn't know what it felt like to be in love so badly that her very body ached.

"Straight out of high school, just before college." A self-deprecating smile curved his mouth. "Made a pit stop at a Vegas chapel and married the girl I'd been going with since the tenth grade."

There was a time Gina might have believed in happily ever after. Now she knew better. "What happened?"

He laughed to himself. At the time, no one could have told him anything. He had to learn lessons for himself. He supposed that made the lessons stick better that way.

"I found out you don't make lifetime commitments based on what you know in tenth grade. Things have a tendency of changing." He thought of Susan. There was no malice. No feelings of any kind, really. "We grew up and then grew apart."

"I'm sorry."

He heard the note of genuine sincerity in her voice and was glad that here, at least, he was telling her the truth. "Don't be. It was a great learning experience."

His optimistic view of what a lot of men would have taken as a failure and/or an annoyance, surprised Gina. "Any children?"

He shook his head. "None. Thank God we didn't make that mistake."

But he was so good with Jesse. Was that all an act? "You think kids are a mistake?"

"No, but broken homes are." At the time a part of him had been sad at the break-up, sad that there hadn't been any children, but he'd learned to look at it differently over time. "I want my kid to have a complete set of parents residing on the premises, on call at all times.'' And then he realized who he was talking to. A woman claiming to be a single mother. His words had to sound rather callous. ''Hey, I'm sorry. I didn't mean—''

''I know you didn't. There's nothing to be sorry for. It's a good philosophy.'' Gina thought of the circumstances surrounding Jesse's conception. ''I wish I would have had a chance to implement it.''

Ben backpedaled, striving for damage control. ''Sometimes it's better for the kid if the parents do get a divorce.''

She knew what he was trying to do and appreciated the effort.

''I'm not divorced. And before you guess widowed, I'm not that, either. I was never married.'' One hand on each, she moved the two bowls closer to him. ''Potatoes or salad?''

He looked at her for a moment. The woman knew how to shift gears without missing a beat.

''Both.'' He moved the first bowl closer to him and served himself. When he continued talking, there was only mild interest in his voice. ''You and Jesse's father come to a parting of the ways?''

''You might say that.'' She shrugged carelessly, her eyes growing flat as she thought back to the first time her life had been turned upside down. ''He was just someone I knew fleetingly. This football jock with a million-watt smile who invited me to a fraternity party.'' She recited the details as clinically as she could. ''Somewhere during the night, he slipped something into my drink. I came to in my dorm, my clothes lying in a heap on the floor.''

''Date rape?'' He said the words quietly, so she could

pretend not to hear if she didn't want to tell him. Damn, but he could almost believe her.

The shrug was small, almost vulnerable, though from her expression he guessed she was trying to distance herself from the event.

She hated attaching the word *rape* to something that had given her Jesse. "Let's say it was the first step of my education in the ways of the world. Jesse came nine months later."

She told her lies convincingly. So convincingly that Ben was tempted to believe her. He had to keep reminding himself that the child she was talking about was really McNair's. For the sake of argument, he pushed the questions a little further.

"Why did you go through with it? You could have just as easily—"

Her head jerked up, her eyes pinning him. He couldn't have looked away if he'd wanted to.

"Just as easily what? Swept him away? Rubbed him out like an annoying stain on my dress? No, I couldn't have." A weary sigh escaped her lips. "Oh, I'm not a saint. I did think about it. But it didn't matter how Jesse came into being. He was my baby and I had to take care of him. Do anything I could to make sure he had a decent chance at life."

It took effort to squelch the compassion he felt rising up within him. "What about Jesse's father?"

She laughed shortly. "Disappeared out of my life without a trace."

If the scenario had been true, he would have had no doubt about that. Jerks like that never took responsibility for their actions. "Did you ever tell him about the consequences of what he did?"

"And have him deny it?" The very thought angered

her. "What for? I knew what happened, he knew what happened. Jesse happened." She looked up at him. "And Jesse is the very best thing that ever happened to me in my life. I love that little boy more than anything in this world. I've never regretted his being born, not from the moment I first saw him."

If he looked into her eyes, stripped away everything else, the case, his suspicions, McNair, everything, and just looked into her eyes, he would have found himself believing her.

He only wished he could.

Chapter 14

She hardly remembered eating. Oh, she went through the motions, and food met the fork with a fairly rhythmic regularity until her plate was empty, but she didn't remember chewing or swallowing. She just remembered looking up into his eyes and getting lost.

They talked about the pages he'd brought the other night. The pages she'd finally gotten to read after he'd left. She'd told him that she was impressed and he seemed genuinely flattered. She liked the modest way he accepted compliments. She liked a great deal about him. The way he smiled, the way he treated her son like a person, the way he wasn't afraid to read to a group of children he didn't know just because they'd asked him to.

If she'd been Sleeping Beauty, he would have been the prince she'd been waiting for.

But she didn't believe in princes anymore, she told herself. Trouble was, she wasn't listening.

Anticipation hummed through her the entire time they were in the dining room like a tuning fork perpetually sentenced to vibrate.

Maybe she was crazy, she thought, setting everything up this way. Setting herself up this way. But if she were being honest with herself, the first time she saw Ben, she'd felt something. She'd been too busy trying to mask it, trying to ignore it, to admit that it was actually there.

But it had been.

And still was, only now that feeling, that attraction, seemed to be more intensified. So much so that it became almost another entity in the room with them.

She supposed she'd always had a weakness for heroes. And Ben had come to her rescue that first day in the bookstore and wanted nothing in return. That made him a hero in her book. There was no billowing cape, no black mask, no bold *S* emblazoned across his chest, but there didn't have to be. He was still a hero.

And for tonight, maybe he would be hers.

They cleared away the dishes together and she heard herself doing most of the talking. Small talk, amounting to nothing.

Nerves, she supposed. There were no guarantees that the evening would go the way she hoped. Maybe she'd even back out herself, surrendering to the comforting banality of familiarity instead of taking a leap of faith and leading with her feelings.

The last dish safely put away, Ben took her hand. She looked at him. "What are you doing?"

Instead of answering, he placed his finger to his lips. "Shhh." And then he led her to the living room.

The room was the last word in cozy. The first in sensuality.

Gina purposely left the lights off. The fire, which she'd started just before changing for dinner, was still burning brightly in the fireplace. She paused to stoke it before sitting down next to him.

Her body felt tense and she willed it to relax. It didn't listen.

"I could stare into a fireplace for hours," Gina murmured, her voice low and husky.

And he could look at her for hours. At the way the light from the fireplace seemed to lightly graze her skin, darkening the hue just a little. Just looking at her like this, sitting beside him on the sofa, made his gut tighten and his body yearn for things that weren't even scribbled into the margins of the list of rules. Rules he was ignoring.

What he was doing, what he wanted to do, was outside the parameters that he had mentally set down for himself. He didn't believe in using underhanded means to gain information. Not from good people, and Gina was good people.

If there were nagging feelings and glaring facts trying to prove otherwise, he ignored them. Sometimes, you had to lead with your gut.

He didn't want to disrupt her life.

Even though her very existence here tonight was disrupting his.

"Why?"

His voice was as quiet as hers, fading into the darkness that existed just beyond the small space they inhabited. She hadn't turned on any of the lights when they'd entered the living room, preferring the glow of the fireplace to anything artificial.

She took a deep breath. If she wasn't careful, she

could let herself become mesmerized. By the fire and by him.

"If you look into it long enough, everything else disappears. Problems, worries. Inventories that don't tally," she added with a smile as she turned to look at him.

Kiss me, Ben. Please kiss me. I need so badly to be kissed tonight. To be held and made to feel that there's something more to me than just that bit that exists right now.

He liked longer hair, yet he found her short hair very sexy. He tended to gravitate toward blondes, yet the petite brunette next to him made him think of a fiery gypsy. A gypsy who held his fortune, at least for this moment, in the palm of her hand.

He toyed with a strand of her hair, sifting it through his fingers. His eyes were on hers as he drew closer. "What kind of problems?"

She didn't move, didn't breathe. "Just problems," she replied, her mouth scant inches away from his. "Day-to-day, mundane, nothing-special problems."

He could taste her words on his lips, feel the delicate tickle of her breath as it feathered along his face. Better men than he had succumbed to far less.

All the promises he'd silently made, to himself and to her, about keeping things aboveboard and honest faded in a puff of smoke.

In the heat of needs and reality.

Before he could think it through and force himself to stop, he slipped his hands around her face, his fingers tangling in her soft hair, and lowered his mouth to Gina's. The wine she'd had with dinner intoxicated him.

Wine, hell, *she* intoxicated him and he lost his way immediately.

Lost his way and found his soul, the soul he hadn't even realized was missing until this very moment.

The kiss deepened. His hands left her face and he drew her onto his lap and still the kiss went on.

The little she'd drunk at dinner had barely registered at the time. Now she felt her head spinning as if she was experiencing some sort of delayed reaction. Or she'd suddenly found herself on some sort of wild amusement park ride that left her breathless, giddy and wanting more.

Her heart pounding, she threaded her arms around his neck. Focusing, Gina reversed their roles. She became the giver not the receiver, determined not to be swept away before she left her mark on him. Because she was going to be swept away, she knew that. There was no doubt in her mind. He had a way about him, a presence, a mastery. She knew without being told that there were women back where he came from who numbered themselves among his lovers. Women who had given him wild, memorable nights. She was in competition with all of them.

She wanted to make him forget. Forget anyone whom he had made love with before. For the space of an hour, an evening, a night, she wanted him to think and feel and breathe only her. Though she never had before, she needed the validation now.

She needed him.

He felt as if he'd been hit in the solar plexus by a two-by-four. Worse than that. And better. The woman was like some mind-altering drug, opening up all his senses, bringing bright colors and heat in her wake. Making him aware of everything. The hum of the air, the crackle of the flames in the fireplace, the scent of her hair.

But as alive as it made all his senses become, it also closed him off to everything beyond the small perimeter that they had staked out.

And even that shrank down around him until there was nothing else but Gina.

And his craving to have her.

He heard her sharp intake of breath as he cupped her breast in his hand, gently, as if he was afraid that she might break if his touch was too rough, his impatience too quickly unbridled.

Excitement thundered through him like the tide pounding against the beach during a fierce storm. Very slowly, his hand began to move, massaging the soft mound as his mouth roamed over her lips, her face, her throat. He lingered over the pulse he found there. It jumped as he lightly stroked it with his tongue and he felt her hands tighten on his shoulders.

His own body was humming in time with hers, for each caress, each touch, he felt a kindred vibration within his own. In a minute, he wasn't going to be able to think clearly anymore or have even the vague desire to navigate through the clouds around his brain. In a minute, all there would be, would be her.

If he was going to do anything, it had to be now.

Trying to catch his breath, he drew his head back from hers. "Gina, if you want me to stop, tell me now." He couldn't force himself to stop touching her, to stop tracing the outline of her lips with his fingertips. She had to be the one to tell him, to call an end to it. "A minute from now it'll be too late."

"It already is," she whispered, bringing her mouth up to his.

Maybe it didn't make any sense and it certainly wasn't the way she'd always conducted herself, but

Gina didn't care. Ben brought things out of her she hadn't realized were there. Awakened things that, like Sleeping Beauty, slumbered quietly, waiting for the right moment. The right man.

Whether Ben was the right man no longer mattered. He was *the* one, the one who could awaken all these feelings within her, and she needed him to make her feel whole again, even if for only a little while.

He wanted to be noble, he wanted to have a clear conscience. Above all, he didn't want her *on* his conscience.

But none of that mattered at this moment in time. What mattered was making love with her. What mattered was having her.

Damn it, he was supposed to have more control over himself than this.

The war raged inside of him. And nobility was definitely losing.

Ben peered into her eyes, looking for some sort of sign. Looking for absolution. "Are you sure?"

"This is no time to filibuster," she breathed. She didn't remember ever feeling like this before. Itchy. On fire. "Do you want me to sign a permission slip? Give it to me and I'll sign it, but for pity's sake, don't stop now or I'm liable to self-destruct."

He saw the honesty in her eyes.

There was no turning back, no noble intentions large enough that could possibly stand up to what he was feeling right at this moment.

He pulled her back into his arms and kissed her as if all they had left in time was this one moment. Over and over his mouth slanted across hers, arousing her, arousing himself.

Reaching behind her, he felt for a zipper and found

none. He could feel her mouth drawing into a smile against his. With desire licking at him more fiercely than the flames were licking the log in the fireplace, he drew his head back and looked at her.

"I give up. Do I say magic words to get you out of this?"

She shook her head, her amusement lighting up her eyes. "The dress comes up, over my head."

It was he who felt as if he was in over his head. It was a first.

Rising to his feet, he brought Gina with him. Gathering the dress at her waist, he slowly raised it up and then gently tugged it until the material cleared her body. And left him looking at the most enticing creamy white bra and panties he'd ever seen. Only extreme control kept him from swallowing his tongue.

Her dress dropped from his limp fingers.

His eyes swept over her. Devouring her.

She smiled at him. A smile that went straight to Ben's belly and twisted it until his every thought began and ended with her and the warmth he felt right at this moment.

He placed his hands on her hips, his fingers dipping beneath the few strands of material on either side. Gina began to unbutton his shirt. Her eyes never left his as she worked one button free after another. The slower she moved, the faster his heart pounded. When she pulled out the shirttails, he realized he'd stopped breathing. As she splayed her hands over his bare chest, teasing the hair there, he began again. Double time. Gina slid the shirt down off his shoulders, pushing the material down along his arms until it fell to the floor.

Unable to maintain even a small distance between them, he pulled her deep into his arms, kissing the column of her throat, relishing the way her pulse beat just as wildly as hers.

She was having trouble concentrating, trouble not surrendering entirely and just letting herself absorb all the delicious sensations beating against her. But she wanted this to be memorable for both of them, not just her. And for that, she couldn't be passive. Couldn't just let him take the lead without trying to switch their positions. With effort, she undid the buckle of his belt and flipped open the button at his waist.

She felt herself getting giddy again, a hot giddiness that made her head swim. She stilled her hands as she tried to recover.

"Don't stop now," he coaxed against her ear.

Gina shivered just before he closed his lips around her lobe and nibbled on it. She felt blood rushing through her veins, the crescendo of a wild, moving symphony. When she felt him guide her hand to the apex of the zipper, she could barely breathe.

She hardly remembered moving the metallic tongue down. But she heard the groan that escaped Ben's lips, felt the enticing swell form beneath her fingers and it empowered her. This wasn't just a one-way street. She was as much in charge of the trafficking of sensations as he was.

The power was heady. His kiss was even more so.

Her mouth sealed to his, Gina pushed both sides of his jeans down his taut hips. The denim dragged his underwear down with it. He kicked them both aside. She felt the heat of his body as it pressed against hers and lost her hold on the last thin strand of realty.

Everything began to whirl around her as an eagerness took possession of her. And of him.

She felt the clasp at her back open, the bra came

sliding off a beat before she felt her underwear slipping down past her knees. It was all happening in a bright red, blazing inferno.

Somehow, her mouth questing over his, she stepped out of what remained of her undergarments.

She felt the imprint of his body against hers. A rocket went off inside of her, setting all of her ablaze as demands slammed against needs that had been blanketed and denied for so long.

She didn't want to deny them any longer.

Ben couldn't get enough of her.

It was as if he were in some sort of race, needing to get his fill of her before the final buzzer sounded. Before the clock struck twelve and everything around them would return to what it was before, taking the magic, the exhilaration with it. Before he woke up to find that this was just a dream.

He wanted time to stand still.

He wanted this to go on forever. To feel this passion, this need, this anticipation endlessly. Ben lowered her to the floor before the fireplace, eager to explore this new terrain that was suddenly before him. Eager to sample, to taste, to touch. To caress and hold. She was the first undiscovered country and he the first explorer. The past did not exist, the future was too far away. All there was, was now.

And Gina.

She throbbed all over, her body a symphony of desires, of demands begging to be addressed and satisfied. She wanted to feel his body over hers, to join with him so they could search for the final peak together. But he persisted in his exploration, skimming his lips here, teasing her with his tongue there. Reducing her to a pulsating mass as she grasped at him, at the rug beneath her, at anything that could serve as a conduit and let her hang on just a little longer.

Several times, she'd had to struggle to hold back, to keep the explosions that begged for release at bay, because she wanted the excitement to continue. The love-making to continue.

And then he was over her, his body poised and wanting, his eyes looking down into hers. There was something there she couldn't read. A sadness that defied definition.

Was it regret?

An apology?

She didn't know, she didn't understand, but she ignored it, afraid that it would intrude and rob her of the last bit of stardust she was reaching for.

Ben framed her face with his hands, looking only at her eyes, her lips.

"You're beautiful," he whispered. *And this is wrong. But, heaven help me, it feels so right.*

He felt her arch her hips against him. He swore silently as the last sliver of decency that he was still husbanding slipped through his fingers.

He was only human and never needier than he was right at this moment.

Parting her legs, he slid into her. Ben groaned as he felt Gina's muscles quickening around him. He began to move and she mimicked him, tempo for tempo, rhythm for rhythm, until he no longer knew where he ended and she began.

Knowing somehow didn't seem all that important.

Moving faster and faster, he rushed with her to the final consummation, the final celebration.

Like the aftermath of a cork launching itself from the

mouth of a bottle of champagne, the resulting shower covered them both at the same time.

Feeling unbelievably contented and drained, Ben sagged against her and felt her arms tighten around him. With effort he tried to balance his weight not to crush her. Euphoria kept him light.

Gina sighed. For one moment in time, she felt as if she finally belonged somewhere.

And that somewhere was here. With him.

Chapter 15

There should be guilt.

The thought slowly penetrated the haze that still swirled around Ben's brain.

He knew there should have been guilt, knew that he should be feeling guilty because of what he'd done and what he'd just allowed to happen.

And there was guilt. But it was to such a small extent he would have missed it entirely if he hadn't been looking for it.

Instead, there was this incredible feeling of all-pervading contentment. Contentment with himself, with life and, most especially, with the woman whose supple body lay tantalizingly just beneath his. A contentment that bore the descriptive label of "afterglow" and bordered on a euphoria the like of which he couldn't remember ever experiencing before. Or, if he had, it was buried so far back in the past, it no longer counted.

With a heartfelt sigh, he let it envelop him. He hadn't the strength left for anything else.

Very slowly, her chest rose and then fell as she released the languid sigh that echoed his own. Gina felt as if a thousand rose petals were caressing her skin. Making her feel soft. Silky.

She struggled to hang on to the feeling a microsecond longer, trying not to think that she'd obtained it under false pretenses.

Where there were roses, there were thorns. For her, the thorns were just a hairbreadth beyond her reach.

But they would draw closer.

She knew that.

She knew that Ben might leave very soon, when he was finished with what he had to do, but that he had made love to a lie. Had joined his body with a woman who didn't exist.

At least, not as he thought he knew her.

Not now, not now, she pleaded with herself silently. It had been so very long since she'd felt like this: hopeful, joyous. At peace.

Gina felt him shifting against her and her eyes fluttered open. Until that moment, she hadn't realized that they were closed. She became aware that her fingers were tangled in his hair. Stroking.

She hadn't realized that, either.

She smiled. Nothing like a good man to turn a woman into a blithering, mindless idiot with a brain the consistency of pudding. But it did feel good. So indescribably good.

He looked at her for a long moment, his eyes holding hers. The guilt grew until it became recognizable. And prickly as it chafed against him. How had he let things get out of hand like this?

He knew damn well how. He'd allowed himself to lead with a part of him that had nothing to do with intellect—and everything to do with feelings. He had feelings for this woman, and that didn't bode well for the case, for him and maybe even for her.

Very carefully, he framed Gina's face with his hands and looked for words he couldn't form.

Still, he had to try. "I didn't mean for this to happen."

The shot was clean and drew blood immediately. Wounded, she shrank back. Hurting.

"I didn't notice anyone holding a gun to your head, Ben." He shifted from her and she drew herself up on one elbow, wishing for all the world she had something to cover herself with besides her shaky dignity. "Are you saying that because you're afraid I'm going to dash into my bedroom and pull out a wedding dress, or because you realize you've temporarily taken leave of your senses and now regret what just happened between us to the soles of your feet?"

Jokes, she thought, she was making jokes to hide the all-pervading hurt that had reared up, large and stinging, out of the well of her happiness. Her eyes stung and she silently threatened herself with bodily harm if so much as a single tear made a hesitant appearance. She was going to carry this off, damn it.

"Regret?" Is that what she thought? Hell, how could she? "As in sorry I held you? Sorry I kissed you? Sorry I spent what just possibly could have been the best half hour of my life? No."

A smile began to form in the center of her being. "Forty-five minutes," Gina corrected him, the smile rising to her lips, "but keep talking. You might just pull this out of the fire after all."

How could she think he regretted making love with her when already he felt himself being aroused again? Regret? Were all the men in her world born stupid?

With honesty nagging at him, he gave her a half truth. "It's just that I sensed this vulnerability about you and I shouldn't have taken advantage of it. And you."

Her mouth curved. In his own way, the man was hopelessly gallant. Maybe white knights did exist. Or at least off-white ones. "As I noticed, no one was holding a gun to my head, either."

"Gina—"

Something tightened in her chest almost instantly. She wished he wouldn't use that name. It just made things that much worse.

"Shh." To forestall anything he was going to say, she pressed her finger to his lips. "No apologies, no explanations. We're two adults, having a very adult time." His brow furrowed and she deliberately smoothed it with the tips of her fingers. Would he think she was crazy if he knew that she wanted to make love with him again? Now, while her body was still warm from his. While the glow still held. "In case you haven't noticed, you're not the Neanderthal type. You didn't—and wouldn't—force me to do anything I didn't want to do."

She sounded far more convinced than he was. The firelight was playing on her skin again, kissing it the way he found himself longing to. "How are you so sure what type I am?"

Her smile broadened. She ran her fingers along his forehead. "For one thing, you don't have the low, protruding brow." Raising her head, she kissed his forehead. "For another, you are a very, very gentle, considerate lover."

The grin began in his eyes as they teased hers before spreading to encompass his face. "Wait until you find the chocolate mint on your pillow."

"I'd rather find your head on my pillow." Her own words surprised her. She was asking him to stay until morning. She'd never done anything like this before. But it felt right. "No strings attached."

"My head doesn't come with strings," he told her wryly before feathering a kiss to her lips, then rising to his knees.

The next thing she knew, she was caught up securely in his arms and he was rising to his feet.

Laughing, she threw her arms around his neck. "What are you doing?"

"It's called playing room service," he replied, stealing another kiss. Carrying her, he began walking toward the stairs. "I'm taking you to your room."

She was completely naked, after having made love to a man she hadn't known two weeks ago. Shouldn't she be feeling the slightest bit awkward or uncomfortable?

The word *no* whispered softly along her mind in reply to her own question.

"Why?"

He took the stairs slowly, looking only at her. Banking down any stray thought that didn't involve this moment and this overwhelming feeling that came rushing back to him. "Because if I'm going to make love with you again, it should be in your bed."

He wanted her as much as she wanted him. The realization was exhilarating. "See, considerate." She wove her arms more tightly around his neck, then laughed as his lips teased the slope of her neck.

* * *

He was stalling and he knew it. Stalling under the guise of telling himself he was just trying to gather more information. To look for a way out for her.

Ben frowned, a general annoyance pervading him as he looked for an outlet.

Until the other night, when they'd made love, he would have never doubted himself. He would have said, with no hesitation whatsoever, that he couldn't be bought off.

But had he been?

Had he been bought off by eyes that seemed to look into his soul, by lips that tasted of all things delectable and tempting, and by a woman who seemed to anticipate his every need while creating needs where he hadn't even been aware any had existed?

Had he been bought off by the promise of what was and what was to be?

He couldn't say and it made him angry. Angry at himself and the quandary that had brought him here to this juncture.

He'd spent all of that night and then most of the next day as well with Gina. She'd taken a personal day because Jesse had no school that day. When she went to pick up Jesse at Kyle's house, he'd come with her. Because it was a holiday, the three of them, much to Jesse's delight, had made a day of it. Ben had taken them to a fast-food restaurant and then to the zoo. Jesse'd had a ball. There was nothing in his manner to suggest that he was a child who'd been recently abducted. Everything about his manner went against every single textbook sign Ben had been taught to look for.

The only time his conscience had actually put in any sort of a tangible appearance was when Jesse had remarked that he was wearing the same clothes he'd had on the day before.

At a loss for an answer, he'd been saved by Jesse himself who'd followed up his own question with another. "Is that your favorite outfit?"

Relieved, he'd nodded and purposely avoided looking at Gina. "Yes, yes it is."

Jesse had nodded knowingly. "I've got one, too, but Mom doesn't let me wear it more than one day at a time. You're lucky."

He exchanged looks with Gina then, and smiled because he knew she'd expect him to. But he hadn't felt lucky. Not where it counted. Because this was all an illusion and he was beginning to dread the moment when he was going to have to put it to rest. The moment the magic would stop and he had to let her know that he wasn't Ben Underwood, hopeful screenplay writer, but Ben Underwood, private investigator. The private investigator who was going to bring her to justice.

One way or another, the moment was coming. And though he intended to help her any way he could, it still didn't put any of this right. In his experience women did not take kindly to being lied to.

He felt stymied everywhere he turned. When he tried to find a reason for why she might have done what she did and brought the conversation around to her past, Gina strayed from it almost immediately.

"There's not much to tell, really. It sounds a little like a boring movie. The kind the critics walk out on and studio executive turn down when they see the script come across their desk."

"Can't be that bad," he'd deliberately teased to put her at ease. "Look how you turned out."

The remark had brought roses to her cheeks and he'd

hated himself for it. Hated, too, the way he responded to seeing the color creep in along her face. He wanted to kiss each cheek. To steal off somewhere and peel away her clothing, inch by inch, layer by layer, until he could let his fingers roam around her body, memorizing every dip, every rise, every nuance of a curve.

Damn, but he wanted her. At the end of a long day, while playing a game of chess with her son on the living room floor, he wanted her. What the hell had come over him?

He was glad that the boy was there as a deterrent. Otherwise he had a feeling his willpower would have been quickly overpowered.

"Maybe I turned out this way despite everything," Gina replied quietly.

When he looked at her oddly, she shrugged away the mood that threatened to overtake her and came over to survey the game board. Ben's king was about to be checkmated. There was no way out of the situation. She smiled at him and wondered if he was just a bad chess player, or if he'd done that on purpose. The latter, she guessed. With affection she ruffled Jesse's hair. He probably wouldn't let her do that much longer, she mused. Little boys were sensitive about looking like a "mama's boy."

"Looks like my little genius beat you again."

Chess had never been Ben's game, though he played it better than this. But his mind hadn't been on the game this evening. It'd been on her.

He put his hand out to Jesse. "Looks like," he agreed. "Good game, my man."

Jesse beamed at the compliment.

"Time to get ready for dinner," Gina informed the

boy. "Help me pick up these chess pieces and then go and wash up for dinner."

"Sure thing, Mom." Nimble fingers began gathering up the pieces and depositing them into the brand-new box.

He wanted to be part of this, Ben thought. The thought had snuck up on him, surprising him. But there was no getting away from it. He wanted this illusion to be his reality.

He found himself hating his job.

Gina's leg brushed against him just as she crouched down to help Jesse with the chess pieces. Her head was bent and Ben found himself staring at the crown of her hair.

He saw the roots that were just hinting at coming in. A faint blush of light color amid the deep, rich darkness of midnight black hair. Everywhere he turned, there was more evidence facing him. Mocking him. He couldn't pretend to fall back on coincidence. There was only so much coincidence to go around and he'd used up his fair share.

Gina raised her head and saw him staring at her. He had the oddest expression on his face, as if there was some sort of internal debate going on. She carefully replaced the last four pieces and slipped the lid back on the box. "What is it?"

Ben shook his head. "Nothing. I was just thinking you work too hard." Getting up, he picked up the box and placed it on the coffee table.

There was something more on his mind than that, she thought as she watched him, but she let it go. Maybe she didn't want to hear.

"Picking up chess pieces is hardly hard work," she quipped, smoothing down his collar. Behind her she heard Jesse running off to the bathroom to wash up. "Stay for dinner?"

More than anything, he wanted to say yes, but he knew he needed a little breathing space to think about things. If he stayed, he'd only make love to her again after the boy was asleep. Not a good idea.

Ben glanced toward the door and told himself he had to be going. For everyone's sake. "I'm going to eat you out of house and home."

"Possibly, but I think I can spring for one more meal."

Not quite out of the room, Jesse turned around to peer up at him from the doorway, adding his silent entreaty to the set.

He was about to turn her down, to make up some excuse and leave. But his feet seemed glued to where they were, as was his resolve. Working together, Gina and Jesse were far too lethal a combination for him to withstand.

So he didn't.

Instead, he stayed, he and his troubled conscience, and he pretended, for the remainder of the evening, that he was who he said he was and there was no case, no evidence and no consequences waiting to face them both.

He left after reading Jesse one bedtime story, feeling progressively worse about himself and what he was doing. And damned troubled about all of it.

When he arrived at the motel, Ben went directly to the telephone and punched out a familiar number. He'd wrestled with his conscience, with bits and pieces of facts that were not coming together, all the way to the motel, and nothing had cleared up, nothing had gotten resolved. Everything remained in a state of confusion.

Maybe once the results of the fingerprint tests were in, he'd feel differently.

The youthful voice that greeted him on the other end only made him feel nostalgic for a time when everything was exactly as it seemed, there had been no need for lies or pretenses and the only crimes he was aware of took place in the movies his mother would allow him to watch once he'd completed his chores to her satisfaction.

But those days were gone and he knew that better than anyone.

"Mom?"

The light note left Maureen Underwood's voice immediately. He could almost see her hand tightening on the receiver. "Benjamin, what's wrong?"

Apart from Eliza, his mother was the closest thing to a psychic he had ever known. He deliberately made his voice sound lighthearted.

"Nothing's wrong, Mom. Can't I call my mother without there being something wrong?"

"You can, but you don't. Not usually."

She had him there, he thought, but he tried to divert her for a second, anyway. It was that same stubborn streak that once had him deliberately breaking curfew, just to be perverse. "I could be calling you about Erika."

"Yes, but you're not."

He laughed softly, shaking his head. If she'd been Caesar's mother, the man would have never ventured out on the Ides of March. "And how do you know that?"

"I'm a mother, I've made a science of listening to

your voices and filling in all the blanks you and your sisters thought you were too clever to tell me. All right, come clean. What's wrong?''

He hadn't called to go over the case, only to hear the sound of her voice. Somehow, there was comfort in listening to her go on and on about things. Even if that ''thing'' turned out to be him.

''Nothing's wrong, ma.'' He smiled to himself as he tucked the telephone between his ear and his shoulder. ''Just working the knots out of a case and I got home-sick for the sound of your nagging.''

''I don't nag, I repeat.''

His grin grew larger. ''And repeat and repeat and repeat.''

She pretended to bristle, though he knew she took no offense. ''How else are you and your sisters going to hear me if you insist on tuning me out?''

''How else?'' he echoed with a laugh. Why was there this homesickness pervading him? He never got home-sick. ''So, everything's okay on your end?''

Because she instinctively knew, without knowing why, that her son needed this, Maureen played along. ''I'm not complaining. Your sister says she's getting married. I'll believe it when it happens.''

He kicked off his shoes and got comfortable on the sofa. ''You don't believe her?''

He could hear the skepticism in his mother's voice. ''Erika's been in love before.''

That much was true. Erika did fall in and out of love far more than the average person. But he had a feeling it was different this time. ''She never asked me to be best man before.''

''Huh. Well, maybe this time she is serious.'' Never one to stand on protocol, Maureen pushed a little.

"Benjamin, why don't you drop over tonight? We can talk better face-to-face."

He would have liked that, he thought. To sit in the kitchen where he'd spent so much time when he was growing up, letting his mother fuss over him now the way he wouldn't have then. "Can't. I'm not exactly in the neighborhood."

"Whose neighborhood are you in?"

"I'm in San Francisco." He heard her sigh on the other end. He knew that sound and knew what she was thinking. "San Francisco, Ma, not downtown Beirut. You told me you'd stop worrying once I got off the force."

"I lied. Although I'd sleep better at night if I knew you weren't going around wielding a gun."

They'd had this discussion before. In every conceivable fashion. "I don't go around wielding a gun, Ma."

"But you own one."

Suddenly too tired to debate, he searched for an analogy she could relate to. "You own a TV set, but it's not always on."

"No one was ever shot with a TV set, Benjamin."

"Ma—"

"All right, I'll stop." She paused, and he thought she was regrouping for a sneak attack, one parting shot before she retreated, but she surprised him. "I don't want you hanging up, thinking your mother was nagging you again."

He laughed. "Never crossed my mind."

"Ha. You can never lie to your mother, Ben. I see right through you." There was silence for a moment as she debated whether or not to ask. "Are you all right? Really," she pressed, wanting the truth. "Without going into details I know you can't go into, although why it should be privileged from your mother is beyond me. It's not like I'm about to go running off with it and spread it on the Internet. But without going into those kinds of details,'' she continued hurriedly, cutting off a protest she knew was coming, ''can you tell me if you'll be all right, because what I'm hearing right now, between the 'ma's' and the other words, there's something weighing on you. Is it going to be all right for you?''

She'd done her job, and lightened his moment. ''With you as my mother, how could it not be?''

''Flattery isn't going to get you anywhere. I'm immune, remember?''

His lips twitched. The hell she was. Maureen Benvenuti Underwood could melt faster than the wax on a birthday candle when she heard the right words from any of her children. But he let her have the lie.

''I remember.''

''All right then, do what you always do. Get the bad guy and keep safe.''

If it were only that easy this time. ''I'll do my best, Ma.''

''Fine.'' Worried, Maureen added, ''I'm here if you need me.''

''I know, Ma. I know.''

''You're a good man, Benjamin. Trust your instincts to see you through.''

The problem was, he thought as he hung up, he wasn't sure of his instincts. Just as he didn't know who the ''bad guy'' was right now. Was it the woman he called Gina, the woman he'd made love with and wanted, even now? Or was it him?

Ben sighed as he dragged his hand through his hair. He remained where he was, staring at the telephone for a long while.

And not liking what he was thinking.

Chapter 16

Shadows obscured most of the office, robbing it of its lavish appearance, hiding most of the expensive decor.

Anger resided in its place.

He'd dimmed the lights before he'd sat down. It suited his mood.

Everyone else had gone home. Or off to celebrate. The merger he'd predicted, the merger he'd made them all sacrifice their private lives for, had finally gone through. IndieCorp and Mercury Electronics had united. Less than fifty minutes ago. And he was the man of the hour.

As he should be.

Accolades from fawning underlings and jubilant board members had surrounded him, buzzing around his ears like the sound of so many insignificant bees. The words had meant nothing to him.

Closing his hand around the small, chunky glass, he

tossed down the amber liquid and waited for the raw taste to find him. To mellow him.

It failed.

Just as the feeling of triumph failed to find him. His biggest career victory and it was marred. Marred because she wasn't at his side, as she should be. Wasn't there to celebrate him with the others, wasn't there to be with him and form that perfect standard by which others would envy him.

"Bitch."

The word echoed around the empty office, ricocheting off the African carvings that hung on the wall.

He poured another drink and downed it. The anger boiled within him, sizzling like beads of water on a burning hot skillet.

Damn her, damn the bitch, he was going to make her pay for this, too, just as he was going to make her pay for the rest of it. For spurning him. For disappearing with that brat in tow, making him miserable because she wasn't here to see how important he was. How without him, there was nothing.

But she'd see that. Once he had her back, she would see that. And he would enjoy hearing the words come from that ripe mouth of hers.

"I'm sorry." "Forgive me." "I was wrong." She'd say all that, and more. And then she'd beg, beg for mercy.

Before he took his final revenge.

With a guttural shriek that was barely human, he grabbed the bottle from his desk and hurled it across the room. It shattered against the bar, raining bourbon and shards of glass onto the imported carpeting.

The silence absorbed the sound, making it disappear

into the darkness.

He would make her pay.

One hand on the door, Ben was about to leave when he heard the telephone ring. It was the regular line, not his cell phone. Ben debated ignoring it and just continue walking out.

He couldn't have said why, but something made him hesitate picking it up. The same something that told him he wasn't going to like what he heard on the other end of the line.

But there was no use in trying to evade it. Whoever was calling would try his cell phone next. Besides, hadn't he been the one who'd said that nothing was ever solved by running away? He'd preached it to enough runaways during his career. You would have thought the axiom would have sunk in by now.

Crossing back to the bed, he yanked up the receiver and fairly growled his name. "Underwood."

"Ben, it's Rusty."

Hearing the younger man's voice, Ben did something he normally never did. He tried to dodge. "Look, I'm in a hurry right now, so if you—"

"You're going to want to hear this," Rusty assured him.

Ben could hear the pleasure in the other man's voice. Fresh out of college, Rusty still approached everything he did with gusto. He and ChildFinders, Inc. were a marriage made in heaven.

"Go ahead." Hoping for the best, Ben braced himself for the worst.

"I just finished running those fingerprints you sent in. The ones on the book were smudged and I couldn't get a clear print."

"Well, you did your best—"

"Wait, there's more. The ones on the book were smudged because a lot of people must have handled it before you got it, but there was a faint thumb and fore-finger on the receipt you sent along. It was the only set of prints on it. Good thinking."

That all depended on which side of the rickety fence you were sitting on, Ben thought, trying to curb an unexpected surge of annoyance.

"And?" He wanted to tell Rusty to cut the flattery and get to it, but jumping down Rusty's throat for doing exactly what he'd asked him to do wasn't going to change the results the other man had gotten. Crossing his fingers mentally, Ben prodded. "Whose are they?"

"The suspect's. Gloria Prescott," Rusty added in case there was any confusion. "You found her, Ben. You found the kidnapper. Is the little boy with her?"

He thought of Jesse, of the bright, eager face with its laughing eyes. How could he be that happy and still be a kidnap victim? How could he call her "Mommy" so soon after the abduction? It didn't add up. "Yeah, the little boy's with her."

"Great, looks like the agency's chalked up another one. Or rather, you did." Rusty paused for a moment as if waiting for him to say something. Ben heard paper being shuffled in the background.

"Looks like."

There was another pause on the line and then Rusty asked in a voice that was somewhat less exuberant, "So why do you sound as if someone just died?"

"Maybe someone did," Ben answered.

There was a knot in the pit of his stomach the size of a boulder. Maybe the woman he thought Gloria, or Gina, was, had just died with the verification of the prints. It certainly felt that way to him.

He wasn't one to grasp at straws, but he was grasping now. "There's no possibility that this is a mistake, is there, Rusty?"

"No. Went over all the tests myself to verify the lab's results. They're Gloria Prescott's prints, all right." Again, he paused, waiting. Listening. "Ben, is there a problem?"

Yeah, there was a problem. A hell of a problem. He'd broken the first cardinal rule of investigative work and let himself fall for a suspect. Suspect, hell, a bona fide kidnapper.

Ben sighed, not knowing if he was angrier at himself for his unprofessionalism, or at Gina for doing the deed. "No, no problem. Thanks, Rusty. I'll be in touch."

He let the receiver slip from his fingers onto the cradle. He wanted to throw it across the room. Cursing, he shoved his hands into his pockets, feeling impotent. Feeling like a fool.

Damn it, he hadn't wanted it to be her. With all the evidence pointing her way, with no other possible explanation as to why there were so many coincidences to deal with, he hadn't wanted it to be her.

Even now, he couldn't reconcile himself to the facts. She didn't seem the type.

Seem. Illusion. It was all just illusion. He'd seen and believed what he wanted to see and believe. What she'd wanted him to see and believe.

Ben reminded himself of the stories he'd read. The ones about perfectly nice people who suddenly went off the deep end and did terrible things no one would have thought them capable of doing. Time bombs, waiting to go off. Was that Gloria's/Gina's story? Had she been a time bomb?

But even time bombs didn't go off by themselves, something set them off.

She'd been thrown over by McNair, he remembered. That could have easily triggered her.

Still, he hesitated. Could his instincts have been so off?

But were they his instincts, or had he been thinking with another part of his anatomy? Had he been reacting to clues, or to the scent of perfume, to the set of a mouth, firm and inviting?

He honestly wasn't sure.

What he did know was that he needed to get his mind back on what he was being paid to do and not on some fairy tale he was spinning for himself. He was supposed to find Gloria and Andrew and he had. Only they answered to Gina and Jesse.

He looked at the telephone.

Ordinarily, he would have called McNair long ago, but there was nothing ordinary about this.

He needed more, Ben decided. The cop in him needed more. He needed some kind of explanation, some kind of clue as to why she'd stolen someone else's child. Try as he might, he just couldn't get himself to buy into McNair's story about revenge. Gina, or Gloria, whatever name she wanted to go by, just wasn't the revenge type. He was willing to bet his life on it.

He might as well, he thought, walking out of the motel room and closing the door behind him. He sure as hell was betting his career.

There were things about being an investigator that the cop in him would have balked at—if he'd been one to follow the rules at all times. But that had been one of the reasons he'd left the force. Rules sometimes got in the way of doing the right thing. The spirit of the law rather than the letter.

Right now, the spirit had him breaking and entering, trying to unearth something that would keep the "letter" from locking Gina up.

Careful not to attract any attention, Ben glanced both ways to make sure there was no one looking his way before he picked the lock of Gina's condo door. The lock was embarassingly simple and he thought that she should have invested in something more substantial before moving in.

The woman was a kidnapper and he was thinking of ways to keep her safe, he mocked himself. That would make him the last of the simple-minded Boy Scouts.

A moment later, he let himself in. Ben slipped the lock picks back into his pocket and quietly closed the door behind him. It was a little after eleven o'clock in the morning. Gina was working at the bookstore. He'd deliberately taken the long way to pass by the store on his way to her condo so he could be certain she was gone. Her car had been parked in the lot.

Even so, he took a second to listen for any noises that might warn him that there was someone else in the house.

There were none. He was alone.

Ben reached into his back pocket and took out a pair of surgical gloves. He intended to be painstakingly thorough and he had no intentions of leaving any of his own prints behind just in case they needed to sweep through here later for any reason. There was already enough confusion involved.

He began the process in her bedroom. Ben had no idea what he was looking for, only a vague feeling that he'd know it when he finally found it. "It" being something that would absolve her of the crime she appeared to have committed. If he was going to champion her the way he wanted to, he needed something to go on. Unless he found that ''something,'' he had no choice but to call McNair and tell him his son had been found.

As he searched, a frustrated emptiness pervaded him. There was no one to go to with this, no one's advice to ask. He couldn't very well tell Cade about the unorthodox turn the case had taken for him. In all the years he'd always relied on his own instincts, he'd never felt less certain of what he was doing than now.

The closets and drawers were next to empty. Except for the furniture, the small condo was almost spartan in appearance. No knickknacks to draw attention to the accumulation of events and experiences that went into making up a life, no real touches to prove that this was the home of a family that had any intentions of putting down roots. No photo albums of any kind. It was almost like a movie set, made to look real but ultimately make-believe.

Well, what did he expect? It *was* make-believe.

And yet...

Half an hour of methodical sifting and he'd found nothing to help him support his theory that Gina wasn't responsible for what had happened, that there was some different, plausible spin on the events that seemed to have transpired than the one he'd been given.

Instead, in her bathroom, Ben found only things to further give credence to the theory that Gina had gone out of her way to bury the person she'd been a short while ago. He found a box of brunette hair dye in the cabinet beneath the sink and contact lens solution in her medicine cabinet. An extra pair of contacts was stored beside it. When he opened the tiny container, he found that the second pair of lenses were the same shade of cobalt blue as her eyes. Tinted contacts to hide her true eye color.

The same eyes that had looked into his soul when they'd made love.

Ben closed the case and placed it back into the medicine cabinet. He felt disgusted and angry and cheated all at the same time.

Replacing the hair dye beneath the sink exactly the way he'd found it, he went to the nightstand at the side of her bed. He fought against images that insisted on returning to him. Images of the two of them, making love. Images of the way she'd looked, nude and radiant, in his arms just before she'd drifted off to sleep.

Instead he forced himself to go through the drawers. The first one was empty except for a pad and pen. The second drawer contained a book she was obviously reading. The pages seemed to all fan out, as if they'd been somewhere humid, like the beach on a foggy day. When he picked the book up to examine it, he saw that there was a folded eight-by-ten white sheet of paper beneath it. Setting the book aside, he unfolded the paper.

In the middle of the page, in a bold block font, was a single underlined sentence: I'll make you pay for what you did to me.

The words echoed back at him. They were the words McNair had told him she'd shouted at him when he'd told her she was being let go. Had she meant to leave it behind for McNair to find and instead she'd just forgotten?

Swallowing a curse that burned on his tongue, Ben folded the paper and slipped it back under the book, then shut the drawer again.

He was nearing the end of the trail.

As if trying to fabricate hope where none would be sustained, Ben made his way into the kitchen next. The cabinets contained nothing more than dishes and glasses that had obviously been left behind by the man who had sublet the condo to her, and there was nothing out of place in the pantry. There was nothing that could even remotely be construed as something appearing to be in her favor.

He found her driver's license in the refrigerator.

It was in a sealed plastic sandwich bag taped to the bottom of the vegetable crisper. The driver's license that belonged not to dark-haired, blue-eyed Gina Wassel, but to blond, green-eyed Gloria Prescott.

Ben stared at the license feeling as if a knife was twisting into his gut. He couldn't keep denying it, couldn't keep hoping to find something that would clear her. There was nothing that would clear her. She was the kidnapper of Stephen McNair's son.

There was nothing to keep him from making the call he didn't want to make.

He thought of putting the license back where he found it and just walking away. But he knew he couldn't do that. So he carefully folded the plastic bag around the license and slipped it into his pocket.

Leaving, he closed the front door quietly behind him. He hated what he knew he had to do next and was angry at the woman who had put him in this kind of gut-shredding position.

Cold water didn't help.

Her eyes still stung.

Gina leaned against the small, utilitarian sink in the bookstore's bathroom, staring into the mirror. Her eyes looked as bloodshot as if she'd pulled two all-nighters back to back, or at the very least, found her way into the bottom of a bottle of liquid comfort.

More than anything, she was dying to pop out the contact lenses. The trouble was she had a sinking feeling that if she did, there was no way she'd be able to get them back in again. Her eyes would be too irritated to permit it. It'd be like taking shoes off swollen feet. Putting them back on would be self-inflicted torture. Not to mention damn near impossible.

It was the San Francisco smog that was doing it, irritating her eyes so. That and the fact that she just wasn't used to wearing lenses. But she hadn't had the luxury to break herself in slowly. She'd needed to quickly change her appearance, and a different eye color had been one of the fastest ways to go. To match the real Gina Wassel's description.

Taking a tissue, she dabbed at her eyes. Nope, she was stuck. There was no easy way to explain how she'd suddenly gone from being blue-eyed to green without raising suspicions. Especially Ben's if he happened to drop in this afternoon the way she hoped he would. She could, of course, tell him that she had just been adventurous and decided to go with a different eye color, but the truth was far too close to the lie for her to risk it.

Better that she put up with the discomfort and he think she was reacting to the city's smog or having an allergic reaction to something.

She shook her head as she peered more closely at herself. If this got any worse, she was going to be able to pass herself off as a big white rabbit, pink eyes and all.

It was a small-enough price to pay when it came to

Jesse's safety. And in the end, it was all about Jesse, not her.

Walking out of the bathroom, her eyes still damp from the water she'd splashed into them in an effort to make them hurt less, she automatically looked around at the store's clientele. Searching. This time of day, just after the lunch crowd had thinned out, the store was usually rather empty.

The familiar form registered a half beat before the smile rose to her lips. Ben. He must have come in while she'd been in the bathroom, trying to make herself presentable.

The joy she felt at seeing him faded several notches when she saw the look on his face. She crossed to him quickly.

"What's the matter? You look as if you lost your best friend."

The muscles on his arm tightened in response to the touch of her hand. Not his best friend, he thought, but he'd lost a woman he hadn't thought his life incomplete without until now.

Before he could answer her, she formed her own theory about what was responsible for the expression on his face. "Wait, is someone else doing the same story as you are?"

Completely preoccupied by the events of the last couple of hours, Ben could only stare at her uncomprehendingly. "What?"

"The screenplay. Did you just find out that someone else is doing the same story?" Because his expression wasn't changing, she pressed on, hoping that was it. Hoping there was nothing more serious wrong. Something in her belly tightened. "Because even if they are, that doesn't mean that there isn't room for two versions of the same thing, even coming out around the same time.'' She was talking faster and faster, trying to out-race whatever else there might have been on his mind. ''A television version of the last day aboard the *Titanic* was shown on television just before the movie version came out and that made box office history, so—''

He couldn't bear to have her go on like this. ''No, it's not about the screenplay.''

She'd never heard him sound angry before. A nervousness began to take hold, a nervousness she'd almost managed to banish since he had come into her life. ''Well then, what?''

Conscience had made him come. A guilt he couldn't shake, that made no earthly sense to him. Somehow, he felt he owed her fair warning. But he couldn't tell her here, in front of the people she worked with. ''Is there somewhere we can go to talk?''

She automatically glanced over toward Joe at the register. He nodded, making no effort to hide his curiosity. ''All right.''

Ben took her arm, ushering her over to where the periodicals were kept. For the moment, there was no one else around.

''No, in the back,'' she prompted, leading the way to the room they all used to stash their things when they arrived in the morning. The room that doubled as Jon's office and where he took naps on occasion.

She closed the door behind her, nearly bumping into the coatrack where she'd quickly hung her purse this morning, running late. The room was crammed with boxes, books that had yet to be inventoried before they were put on the shelves.

Gina tried to read Ben's expression. The solemnity,

the deadness of his eyes, unnerved her even further. Was he going to tell her it was over between them?

She felt her heart shrink a little in anticipation of the death blow. She'd known when she'd gone to bed with him that this couldn't be permanent. And yet, a part of her had hoped…

"Ben, you're scaring me, what is it?"

There was no way to say this but to say it. The words felt like poison on his tongue. "I know who you are."

Her voice was very still. "What do you mean?"

Did she want him to spell it out for her? All right, he would. "I know your name isn't Gina Wassel, that you're really Gloria Prescott."

Chapter 17

She backed up, bumping against the coatrack again. It hardly registered. Gina stared at Ben as if he'd just sprouted horns and a tail.

"Who are you?" she whispered hoarsely, her mind too numb to form connected thoughts her soul didn't want to admit.

"I'm Ben Underwood."

There was a finality in his voice, as if the name was synonymous with a death knell.

Gina continued to stare at him, hardly daring to breathe, afraid of the answer to her question. Even more afraid not to ask.

"Who *are* you?"

There was a dangerous look in her eyes he didn't know how to interpret. "Stephen McNair hired me to—"

Stephen. It was as if Ben had aimed a nail gun straight at her heart and fired. It took everything she had not to begin to shake with anger and fear. "Did you call him?" He didn't answer. Her voice rose. "Did you tell him where I was?"

"Gina—Gloria," he corrected himself, frustrated at the way his tongue tripped over her name, not knowing what to call her. Knowing only that in his mind, she was still Gina to him. The woman he'd opened up to far more than he had ever intended. "You know that you can't—"

A deadly panic began to take hold of her. *"Did you tell him where I was?"*

"Yes."

He'd gotten off the phone with the man almost two hours ago, then spent the time between then and now wrestling with his conscience. He'd come here to see her because some part of him, the part that wanted to believe she was somehow innocent, had felt she deserved to know what was about to happen. To prepare herself.

Icy needles ran up and down along her body. He'd called Stephen. He'd told Stephen where she was. Where Jesse was. Her breath came in short, shallow pants. "What have you done? Omigod, what have you done?"

Paralyzed, she stood with both hands covering her mouth, trying to think, trying to will a thought, a course of action into her brain.

Jesse.

She had to get to Jesse. Before it was too late. She felt tears forming and damned herself for the weakness even though she knew they were tears of fury.

Ben saw the tears and something twisted inside of him. He reached for her. "Look, I'll help you get through this, I'll—"

She backed away from him again. Out of the corner of her eye, she saw the tower of boxes.

"You'll help me get through this?" Gina cried incredulously, edging toward the boxes. "Don't you understand? You've ruined everything."

He reached for her again, but she managed to shrug him away before he could touch her. Level with the boxes, she suddenly pushed hard against the middle one. The tower toppled, coming at him. Caught off guard, Ben tripped and fell backward.

She didn't stop to look back, even though something within her wanted to make sure that Ben wasn't hurt. *No time, no time.*

Instead, she grabbed her purse from the rack. The sudden yank made it fall onto the pile behind her.

Gina bolted from the room.

His attention drawn to the back office by the loud noise, Joe had rounded the front counter and was on his way to the rear of the store when she flew by him, nearly knocking him over. Joe managed to get out of her way just in time.

"Gina, where are you going?" Joe called after her as she ran out of the store.

She didn't even try to answer him. Every thought was focused on getting to her car and then getting to Jesse. Before it was too late.

Groggy, Ben scrambled to his feet calling her name. He pushed his way through the boxes and made it out of the back room just in time to see Gina rushing out through the electronic doors. She was moving so fast, they barely seemed to open in time to let her pass.

When he ran by the other salesclerk, Joe tried to grab him. "Hey, why are you running after her? What the hell's going on here?"

The shouted demand fell on deaf ears as Ben ran through the doors. He saw Gina pulling out of the parking lot, the tires of her car screeching as she made a sharp turn. She came within inches of colliding with another vehicle. The next second he saw her car fishtailing as she fought to regain control.

Ben pulled his own key out of his pocket as he sprinted across the lot for his car. The next moment, he went tearing out after her in hot pursuit. He knew that the best course of action to follow was to call 911, but there was no time to reach for his telephone. He couldn't afford to take his eyes off the road for even the split second it took to dial the number. He needed to see where she was going, and even a moment's diversion could seriously cost him.

She was pushing sixty in a thirty-five-mile zone. Cars pulled out of her way right and left. He held his breath as he followed.

Where the hell were the police when you needed them, he thought in exasperation.

He knew where she was going. To get Jesse. Andrew, he corrected himself. Either name, he had no idea where the boy went to school. Every casual question he'd tried to pose asking her for the information had been artfully stonewalled. Without knowing where she was going, there was no way of taking another route and getting there first to cut her off.

All he could do was keep her in his sight and pray that they both got there without crashing into another car. People got reckless when they were cornered and she was flying through yellow lights like a bullet.

Watching her, he couldn't help marveling how well she maneuvered in and out of traffic. It was as if she'd taken that defensive driving course Cade had made each of them complete recently. A lot of things came into play when you were dealing with recovering kidnapped children and Cade had wanted each of them to have every advantage possible available to them.

"Damn good thinking, Cade," he muttered under his breath, staying on Gina's tail. Without the course to have sharpened his reflexes, he wasn't sure if he would have been able to keep up.

Gina looked in her rearview mirror, perspiration beading down her back despite the cold and the chill in her heart. She'd run out with her coat, but hadn't been able to put it on.

Damn, he was still following her. She wished there was time to lose him, but she couldn't risk it. There was no time to lead him on a wild-goose chase. Every second she delayed getting to her son was a second more that Stephen had to make it there ahead of her.

She didn't know how much Ben had found out about her, if he'd tailed her when she was bringing Jesse to school and if he'd given that location to Stephen, too. She didn't think Ben had followed her, but she couldn't be sure. Even though she'd begun to grow secure—she upbraided herself for ever being so stupid as to believe she was out of danger—she'd taken precautions, kept alert for any signs that someone was following her.

Her mouth twisted in a cynical, mocking smile. Being stalked did that to you. Heightened your senses until paranoia all but ruled your life.

She felt tears welling up again.

It served her right for slacking off. She'd started to relax, to think that maybe, just maybe, she could lead a normal life. Only to be shown that she was an idiot. That she'd never be able to have what other women had.

Not until Stephen was permanently out of her life.

In her desperation to be free, she'd even thought of killing him, but it wasn't in her. Not even if it meant saving herself.

But if it meant saving Jesse…

The irony struck her even as hysteria grappled for possession of her. She automatically thought of her son by his middle name now. Not Andrew but Jesse, the name she'd made him answer to when they had shed their former identities and fled from everything they knew. To have a life.

A life that was now just a hopeless illusion.

Where did they go this time? She didn't know. All she knew was that it had to be somewhere away from here. Away from Stephen and away from the man she'd fallen in love with.

Taking a corner, she wiped away the tears that refused to stop with the back of her hand. She should have never let her guard down. Never deluded herself into believing that she could fall in love, get married. Be normal.

Forget that. Forget him. Nothing else matters but getting to Jesse.

She had barely cut off the engine and stopped the car before she was leaping out of the driver's side, rounding the hood.

The car was parked askew at the curb. Two beats later, Ben pulled up behind her. She heard rather than saw his car. Desperation had her sprinting up the steps to get to the school's double doors.

Ben raced after her and caught up before she could open them. He grabbed her wrist and spun her around to face him.

"Let go of me," she ordered. Struggling, she tried to yank her wrist out of his iron grip.

He fought against the very real urge to pull her into his arms. To hold on to her until she stopped struggling. Until she would tell him the truth. Instead, he continued to hold tightly on to her wrist. "You can't keep running this way."

"Yes I can. Now, let go of me. Do you hear me? Let *go!*"

"Hey, lady, you need any help?" An older man, walking his dog at the curb, had stopped to look up at them. "Want me to call the cops?"

That was the last thing she wanted. Cops. She already knew they wouldn't take her side.

Ben pulled Gina in close to him, as if to hug her. "Just a family argument," Ben told the man mildly. "Thanks for your concern, but I'd keep walking if I were you—unless you want a lawsuit slapped on you."

Taken aback, the man closed his mouth and put down his head. Tugging on his dog's leash, he quickly walked down the block.

Using the diversion, Gina kicked Ben's shin as hard as she could. Still holding on to her, he lost his footing and nearly went down the stairs, dragging her with him. At the last second, Ben managed to grab the handrail. His hold on her never slackened.

"Dammit, Gina, you're not going to get away with this. Now, stop fighting me."

He dragged her in his wake until they were at the foot of the stairs again. Still holding her he ushered her off to the side, out of the way of casual passersby. He didn't want any more Good Samaritans butting in.

Ben pushed her against the wall, his body blocking any retreat. "I'll do everything I can to help you—"

She curbed the urge to spit in his face. "I don't need your help, I just need you to let me go."

Frantically, her eyes searched his face, looking for a sign that the man she'd made love to had not been a complete fabrication, a complete lie. That he still existed somewhere inside this stranger who threatened to destroy her life and the life of her son.

"Please," she begged. "If there's an ounce of decency somewhere inside of you, let me go."

Despite everything, he felt an inner struggle between what he knew was right and what his instincts told him was right. "*Decency* is a hell of a word for a kidnapper to be throwing around."

Her mouth fell open. "Kidnapper? What are you talking about? Who's a kidnapper?"

He could almost believe her surprise. But he'd lied to her and had carried it off without a hitch. And she had lied to him. Which meant she was still lying.

"You. You kidnapped McNair's son. The son you were supposed to be taking care of." With each word he uttered, Ben saw the bewilderment and horror intensifying as they took hold of her features.

For a moment, she couldn't absorb what Ben was saying to her. It sounded like so much gibberish assaulting her ears.

"Kidnapped? His son?" Reflexively, she shook her head as if she were trying to clear it, trying to make sense out of what he was telling her. She couldn't. "I still don't know what you're talking about."

"Stephen McNair hired my firm to get his son back from you."

"That's not possible." She felt as if she was trapped inside of some macabre nightmare. "Stephen doesn't have a son."

He'd expected her to lie, but not so implausibly. "Then who's Jesse? Andrew, dammit," he corrected himself. The boy had been Andrew on a piece of paper. The boy he'd interacted with, laughed with, read to, was Jesse. It was hard to shake that. "Who the hell is Andrew?"

"Andrew is *my* son." Without realizing it, she gripped his arm as if to drive home her words. "He's always been my son."

There were too many clouded issues, too many things he needed to have cleared up even at this point. "Then why are you calling him Jesse? And why did you assume a dead woman's identity? Why did you change the color of your hair so you could look like her?" With his free hand, he sifted his fingers through her hair. Trying not to remember the last time he'd done that. Instead, he nodded at her eyes, noticing how red they looked. Was she going to cry again? Damn it, he hoped not. He couldn't handle tears. "Why did you change the color of your eyes?"

"Simple." She raised her chin defiantly. "To get away from Stephen. Before he hurt Jesse."

McNair's questions, all centered around his finding Gloria, not the boy, played across Ben's mind like the echo of a haunting refrain. From the very beginning, it hadn't felt right. Still, he continued to grill her. "And why would he do that?"

He wasn't going to believe her, she thought. But all she had left was the truth. And a prayer that Ben had an ounce of mercy within him. "Because I refused to marry him."

His eyes narrowed as he looked at her. She seemed so sincere. But so did actors. That's what they gave out awards for. "He said he rejected you."

To hear it all turned around stunned her. "He—I—oh, God."

Gina closed her eyes to gather herself. She knew she had only one opportunity to convince Ben that she was telling the truth. One opportunity to make him release her to get her child and flee.

When she opened her eyes again, they were directed straight at him. He'd never seen anyone look so earnest in his life.

"Listen to me. Stephen McNair and I met at an art showing about a year ago. I had some pieces on display. He flattered me, told me he had connections, that he could help me. He said that the office building that housed his company was doing some remodeling and he could get me a commission to sell my work to the decorator. He painted a tempting picture, saying that everyone entering the building would see my sculptures. I got carried away with the thought of finally being successful, of making a good living for Jesse and myself."

She'd been so foolish then, so eager to believe that things were finally turning around for her. Looking back, she couldn't believe she'd been that naive.

"At first he was very kind, very attentive, very proper. But he got tired of the role he was playing, tired of waiting for me to come around. He made it very clear that if I wanted him to use his influence, I was going to have to 'trade' something for that help." She looked away, ashamed that she had been taken in the way she had. "He wanted me to become his mistress. When I refused, he upped the ante and asked me to marry him. By then, I knew I had to get away from him."

She couldn't tell if Ben believed her or not. Gina had

no choice but to continue and hope that he'd come around.

"Stephen tried everything he could to get me to change my mind. There were flowers, and gifts, lots and lots of expensive gifts—he thought he'd overwhelm me." She smiled ruefully. "Or maybe just buy me outright, I don't know. But I sent everything back. When I sent back the diamond engagement ring, he became enraged. Said that no one had ever turned him down before and I wasn't going to be the first."

She closed her eyes again, trying to press back the tears. She wasn't going to cry in front of Ben, wasn't going to humiliate herself that way. Tears were for manipulation, and she wasn't about to use that, either.

"He told me that if I didn't give in to him, he'd hurt Jesse."

He watched her face intently, looking for some crack in the veneer. There wasn't any. "Did you go to the police?"

She laughed, but there was no humor there. "And say what? That a multimillionaire—a captain of industry as he liked to refer to himself—was trying to get me to go to bed with him, to marry him, and if I didn't, he threatened to harm my son?" Didn't he realize how ludicrous that sounded? "I was a nobody who dreamed of being a successful sculptor. He could buy and sell his own city. Who would you have believed?"

And then she grew very still, her eyes penetrating his. "Who *do* you believe?"

He wanted to believe her, knew what his heart was telling him to believe, but in all honesty, he still didn't know. "Gina—Gloria—"

"See? You don't know who to believe—the man paying your expenses or me, the woman you slept with to lower her defenses.'' She was never going to forgive him for that, for using her heart against her.

Guilt and anger rose, fighting for his self-respect. ''It wasn't like that.''

Her eyes grew cold. ''Wasn't it? Weren't you just doing your job, trying to get me off my guard?'' And to think that she had thought she was falling in love with him. How could she have been so stupid? ''What I can't understand is why you didn't call Stephen immediately. Was I that good at fooling you? Or did you just want a tumble in the hay before you turned me in?''

His anger was red hot. ''What happened between us had nothing to do with the case.''

''Didn't it?'' she challenged. ''Then why didn't you call him when you found me?''

He told her the truth. What had been bothering him since the beginning. ''You didn't seem like the kidnapping type.''

''Because I'm *not*.'' Oh, why didn't he just let her go? Why was he making her suffer this way?

''Then why was there a copy of a threatening letter in your nightstand?'' he wanted to know. ''I found it under your book. McNair told me that you'd shouted that threat at him.''

''I shouted…'' Her voice trailed off as she tried to think what he was referring to. And then it came to her. ''That was his note to me you found. I kept it to remind myself not to let my guard down.'' She looked at him pointedly. ''Too bad I didn't remember.''

''Gina—''

She threw away her pride. Pride had no place in this when it meant Jesse's safety. ''Please, please, just turn away. Let me get my son and get out of here.''

He couldn't do that. "Don't you understand that if what you say is true, you can't keep running?"

"Oh, but I can," she insisted. She looked toward the stairs. She was so close, so close. If there was just a way to get him to let go for just a minute. But he was holding her fast and standing so close that she couldn't get a good swing in anywhere. "And it *is* true. You have to believe me."

"Keep running and what? Go somewhere else where he'll send someone else to find you?"

She tried her best to convince him. "Maybe they won't this time. I'll hide our trail better." Desperation entered her voice again as it built momentum. "We'll disappear."

He could feel her eyes imploring him. It would be so easy just to open his hand and let her go. But then what? And if what she said wasn't true, then he would be an accessory after the fact. "I can't let you do that. The next person who looks for you might not be willing to listen."

"And you are?" She peered at him. Just what was he saying?

"Gina—" He stopped. It wasn't her name, yet he couldn't think of her any other way. "What the hell do I call you?"

She was losing precious time. "I don't care, just let me go."

"I can't, either way, I can't." She began to pull again, but he held her fast. "Listen to me, Gina—" He pulled her around when she started to look away. "*Listen* to me. The one thing I didn't do when I took this case was investigate McNair. It's not our policy to investigate the client. We assume that the person coming to us is telling the truth. Maybe we shouldn't," he added. "Come back with me and I promise I won't let him near you or the boy until after I get this all sorted out."

She didn't know whether to believe him or not. Even if she didn't, even if he meant what he said, she knew Stephen. She wasn't safe anywhere near him. "He'll find a way to get to me. He's done it before."

"If it turns out you're telling the truth, I swear I'll protect you." His eyes held hers. "I can't do any better than that, Gina."

"Yes, you can." She raised her chin, her eyes pleading with him. "You can let me go. You can turn your back now and walk away."

She curbed the anger bubbling up inside of her, the urge to scream names at him for having deceived her so. For having used her. Instead, she tried to play up to that tiny fragment—if indeed it did actually exist—that had been so tender to her. That had made her feel as if the world was finally in the right place for her.

"If that night we spent together meant anything at all to you, you can just walk back to your car, call Stephen and tell him you made a mistake. That you didn't find Gloria Prescott or her son. That it was two other people entirely." Her whole being was pleading with him now. "Please."

He'd never been so tempted to turn his back on what he'd been schooled to do. But there were reasons why he couldn't.

Especially if he believed her.

"No."

Chapter 18

"Where are we going?"

Eager, Jesse strained against his seat belt in the back seat, trying to lean forward. His small hands didn't quite make it to the back of the seat where his mother was sitting.

She twisted around to look at the boy. Ben had insisted on using his car, saying he'd send someone to get hers later. She had no choice but to agree. When they'd left the school, she'd started to get in the back with Jesse, but Ben had stopped her. He'd wanted her sitting in the front where he could keep half an eye on her. He figured if he kept Gina and Jesse separated, she wouldn't do anything foolish like try to leap out of the car with the boy.

Risky or not, there was a look in her eyes that he didn't quite trust.

But if there was an edgy nervousness about her, there was clearly an excited one about Jesse. The idea of being taken out of school before the end of the day purely tickled him.

"Are we going to a park?" Jesse asked hopefully, looking from one adult to the other.

How could McNair have remained indifferent to this kid? Ben just didn't understand it. He'd only known Jesse a few days and had caught himself thinking that when he finally got around to having kids of his own, he'd want them to be just like Jesse. Bright, lively and just all-around neat. That McNair could maintain an emotional distance from the boy didn't speak well of the man.

Did anything? a small voice within him demanded. He couldn't come up with a single thing.

Ben's conscience was chafing him.

"Maybe later, partner," Ben told him. "Right now, we're going to get a few things cleared up." Raising his eyes, he glanced at the small, inquisitive face in the rearview mirror. Though part of him really didn't want to, he knew this had to be asked. "Do you remember your dad, Jesse?"

Confusion creased the small, delicate features. He shook his head. "No."

Gina bit back an oath. What was he trying to do? Hadn't Jesse been through enough? "Of course he doesn't remember his dad. He never knew his dad."

Twisting around again, she looked at Jesse, worried that Ben's question had upset him. Children were sensitive and could easily intuit when something was wrong, when their parents were upset. They were a great deal more tuned in than adults gave them credit for.

She struggled now not to let on that anything was amiss, but it wasn't easy, not with her heart jumping

around the way it was. Just as it hadn't been easy going
to the school's main office and pretending that there was
a family emergency that necessitated her taking Jesse
out of class unannounced. With Ben beside her every
step of the way, not giving her any space, she'd had to
walk a fine line between appearing concerned but in
control. The one thing she wasn't right now.

Her mind raced, trying to figure out a way to escape
this man who had attached himself to her and her son.
It struck her that, unlike Stephen, she wasn't afraid of
Ben.

Maybe she should be, she thought, slanting a covert
glance in his direction. But somehow, despite everything, despite the deceit, she felt he wouldn't hurt her.
Not the way Stephen would.

But what Ben intended to do *would* hurt her. Turn
her over to Stephen.

"Is that true, Jesse?" Ben was asking. "You never
knew your dad?" He raised his eyes to the rearview
mirror again.

Jesse slowly shook his head. "No."

Still, she could have coached the boy, found a way
to make him deny knowing McNair. It wasn't your average, run-of-the-mill father-son relationship. "Not
even for a little while?"

Why was Ben belaboring the point? Was he trying to
talk Jesse into giving him the answer he wanted to hear?
"Now what are you saying to him?" she demanded,
forgetting to keep her voice low. "What 'little while'?"

Ben took a corner. There weren't as many cars on
the road anymore. He wouldn't have been able to explain why there was this sense of urgency eating away
at him. Maybe Gina's edginess was rubbing off.

''McNair said that he hadn't known about Jesse's existence until almost ten months ago.''

Which was about the time they'd met, Gina thought. ''Well, that fits.''

He knew she didn't understand what he meant. ''That he received a letter from the boy's late mother, saying he was the father.''

Gina's mouth dropped open. For a moment, she was too stunned to say anything.

''Late, like Santa Claus was this year?'' Jesse asked. He pulled against his restraint again, wanting to join them in the front. ''Mommy said he had a little trouble finding where we were because we had to move so fast.''

Gina felt tears forming suddenly. She'd had to postpone Christmas for Jesse until they were settled in at the condo and she had an opportunity to buy him gifts with some of the money Aunt Sugar had given her. Jesse had behaved like a little adult, so brave, so understanding. Just remembering made her want to cry all over again. He didn't deserve to have this happening to him because she'd become the object of one man's obsession.

Neither did she.

''Not that kind of late,'' Ben explained. He searched for words that would make a six-year-old understand the euphemism.

Gina cut him off before he could find them. ''*I* am his mother.'' She splayed her hand across her chest. ''Late or on time,'' she added, glancing toward Jesse and giving him what she hoped was an encouraging smile.

She knew he had to be thrown off by all this. By being yanked out of class and made to roll up his world again with no warning. Just like the last time. The only difference was they weren't doing it in the dead of night. But Jesse was a trouper and went with the punches no matter what they were. At times, she took her strength from him.

"I've always been his mother," she said with as much pride as she did with veracity.

Ben pretended to be teasing. "This true, Jesse?"

"Uh-huh. My one-and-only Mom." He ended the affirmation with a giggle.

But Gina didn't feel like laughing. "Why are you badgering him like this?" she demanded in hushed anger.

"Because I need to be sure," he answered simply. He floored the gas pedal, just making it through a yellow light that began turning red.

Gina took a deep breath. All right, he wanted proof, she'd tell him where to find it. Maybe then he'd be satisfied and let them go.

"I can give you a whole list of people who could tell you he's my son—starting with the hospital where he was born. Harris Memorial in Bedford, California," she recited. In her mind's eye, she could still see the tall, modern building with its flag flying from the uppermost tower. It had been like an unattainable goal to her that morning. "He was born on a Friday afternoon at 4:10 p.m. after a five-hour labor. It was raining that day and I didn't think I was going to reach the hospital on time."

He picked up her meaning. "You drove yourself?"

"I drove myself," she answered with no fanfare, as if women in the throes of labor made the fifteen-mile journey every day to deliver their children. "Dr. Sheila Pollack was the attending physician. Jesse's pediatrician is, was," she corrected herself, "Dr. Rafe Saldana." She looked at him with an expression that was distant enough to place them on two separate continents. "Would you like their phone numbers?"

She was beginning to convince him. He had to admit that he'd been halfway there to begin with this afternoon. Granted, as his nanny Gina would have had access to some of this information, like the name of his pediatrician, but not the rest of it.

And if that was the case, then that meant he'd been duped. Royally.

For now, he kept that to himself. "No, for the time being, let's just say I believe you."

He'd made her grow leery of him. Gina studied his profile and found no reason to take heart. "Then you'll let me go?"

Duped or not, that was the one thing he couldn't do. "No, because if I can find you, McNair can hire someone else to do it, too." His way impeded by a sudden bottleneck of traffic, Ben cut in front of someone else, crossed through a parking lot and made it to the other street. It was one-way. The time he'd saved was lost again.

"So what's the plan?" For the first time, Gina actually focused on the streets they were driving by. Recognition set in. He was taking her back to her place. Or was he? "We're going back to the condo?"

Ben nodded. "Just to get your things, like you told Jesse." He spared a glance back at the boy, who smiled at him in return. "I'm taking you both back with me."

"Back?" she repeated warily. Had she fled one fire only to be engulfed by another? "Back where?"

He hated the tone in her voice, hated the fact that he

was instrumental in placing it there. But he had no choice.

"You said you were from Bedford, didn't you? Well, so am I. I'm taking you home to my place, Gina. Once we get there, I'll call the police."

"I already told you, the police won't listen to me. It's a matter of my word against his."

"Our word," he corrected her.

There was silence in the car for a long moment. "Then you do believe me?"

He needed to maintain his professional distance, now more than ever. "Let's say I'm getting there. And I intend to investigate this further so that we have proof on our side when we go to the police." It was the best he could do.

Going down the next block, he pulled up in front of the building.

The second Ben turned off the engine, Jesse unbuckled his belt.

"There's Kyle's mother!" He pointed excitedly to the woman carrying groceries. Opening the door, Jesse was halfway out when he stopped to look at Gina. "Can I say goodbye to Kyle and tell him we're going on a trip? Please, Mom? Please? I didn't get to say goodbye to my friends the last time we went away."

She thought of the misery she'd seen in Jesse's eyes when they had left their home, a home she had worked so hard to provide for him. The first real home she had ever had herself. How difficult it had been for him to leave all his friends behind without saying goodbye. She couldn't put him through that again.

Gina got out of the car, aware that Ben had quickly done the same, rounding the hood so that he could stand behind her.

"All right." She took Jesse's hand in hers. "Let me talk to his mom for a minute."

It had been on the tip of her tongue to say no. Ben would have bet his life on it. He could read people that much. And yet, she'd given in to the boy because it had meant so much to him. She'd placed her fear and everything else on hold for the boy. A lot of questions were suddenly answered.

Calling out to Kyle's mother, Gina hurried over. She didn't have to look over her shoulder to know Ben matched her step for step. Until this was resolved, he was going to be her shadow.

Quickly, she fabricated a story for Grace, using the same one she'd given to the principal of Jesse's school. Jesse stood by, not saying a word to contradict or question her. She didn't have time to worry about the example she was setting for him by lying, didn't have time to feel guilty over lying to a woman she had taken a genuine liking to. Her son's life could very well lie in the balance. As well as her own.

Grace smiled warmly at them, curiosity in her eyes as she looked at Ben.

"Sure, Kyle's in the house, playing a video game. You know the one," she said to Jesse. "Earth Conquerors. Can't get him away from it." Shifting the grocery bag to one side, the way a mother did with a small child she carried on her hip, Grace slipped her arm around Jesse's shoulders and began walking with him toward her own condo. "Just stop by when you're about to leave," she called over her shoulder. "I'll have him ready for you."

"Okay, let's go," Ben urged.

Holding on to her arm, Ben ushered Gina up the steps to the condo. "You don't have to hold on so tightly,

I'm not going to run away." She looked toward the other condo. Jesse and Grace were just taking the stairs. "I'm not going anywhere without Jesse."

"You don't have to run away," he told her, stopping at the front door. "I believe you."

Gina stopped hunting for her key and looked at him. Was this just another ploy to get her to drop her guard again? "Without checking out my story?"

"Without checking out your story."

She found the key and took it out. "What changed your mind?" Gina couldn't help the sarcasm that had entered her voice.

"I guess watching the two of you together." They couldn't have faked that. Not that well. "It's not enough that you genuinely care for the boy, it's obvious he cares for you." He thought back to the conversations he'd had with McNair. Even the last one. He'd never had the feeling that the boy was anything more than an ornamental prop in all this. "And McNair didn't seem as interested in getting his son back as he was in my finding you." Ben took the key from her and inserted it in the lock. "When I brought it up to him, he said it was because you had something that belonged to him."

That didn't surprise her. "Yes, his pride. I stole it from him," she said simply as Ben opened the door. She stepped through first. "As I said, he doesn't like to be turned down."

"I still don't."

Gina froze in the doorway.

Like the key figure in a hostile takeover, Stephen McNair was sitting on the sofa in the center of the small living room.

She struggled to stifle the scream that rose in her throat. She'd hoped, prayed, never to have to see him again. Had Ben known he was going to be here, waiting like this? Had he been just talking at her door to distract her?

Not knowing what to believe, staring at McNair, she backed away from Ben.

"How did you get in here?" she asked, her voice deceptively calm as she ground out the question.

McNair rose to his feet. "That's neither here nor there." He looked at Ben contemptuously. A smirk curled his thin lips. "I take it she's already told you her side of the story." He waved aristocratically long fingers in the air, as if conjuring magic. "Some fantastic fabrication about the boy really being hers."

"Maybe not so fantastic," Ben corrected him. "I tend to believe her."

McNair laughed shortly, being magnanimous for the moment. "Don't feel bad, she has that kind of effect on men. I assure you, it's damn near hypnotic." He drew closer and Gina stepped back, maintaining the same distance. McNair's brow clouded. "Certainly managed to hypnotize me. But she's a con artist, through and through, and she'll do anything to get what she wants."

Ben kept an eye on Gina, not wanting her to do anything stupid. "Funny, she said the same thing about you."

Her heart lurched in her chest. Ben *was* siding with Stephen. "Ben—" she began, but he held up his hand to silence her.

But it was McNair who interrupted. "Surely you're not going to believe her."

Ben had just about had his fill of this pompous ass. Everything Gina had said about McNair played itself through his brain at once. "Why? Because you're rich and she's not?"

Ben could see McNair struggling with patience as he drew himself up. "No, because she's lying and I'm not."

"Well, we'll have to see about that, won't we?" Ben began to reach for Gina.

The next moment, Ben found himself looking down the barrel of a weapon that fit so neatly into McNair's hand, it looked as if it had been made expressly for that purpose. Ben didn't doubt that it probably had.

"Sorry, but I don't have time to play games, Underwood." McNair held out one hand, fingers beckoning, indicating Gina. "Send the lady over to me and we'll call the case closed."

Ben's own gun was tucked into the holster strapped to his ankle. There was no way he could get to it without McNair getting off a clear shot. Ben stalled for time. "What? Before you see your son? Or aren't you concerned about him anymore?"

Anger began taking over, dissolving the last remnants of patience. "No theatrics, Mr. Underwood. They're beneath you. We both know what I want. And you've delivered it. Admirably, I might add." The smirk looked almost evil. "You've earned every penny of the fee."

It killed Ben that ethics had caused him to lead the man to Gina's door. "You know you can't get away with this."

"On the contrary." McNair's voice was deliberately singsong, deliberately mocking. "I can get away with anything I want. Or haven't you heard? Rich people can buy almost anything or anyone." His eyes became malevolent slits as he turned them on Gina. "Now, get over here," he ordered.

Trapped, with nowhere to run, Gina remained exactly where she was. Defiant, she fisted her hands at her sides. She wasn't about to stroke Stephen's ego. "No."

The mocking smile disappeared instantly, burned away in the heat of McNair's rage.

"I said get over here. Get over here or I'll shoot you where you stand, you bitch!" And then a strange look came into his eyes as he shifted them toward Ben. "Did she sleep with you? Is that it?" His voice rose, growing high. Growing hysterical. "That is it, isn't it? You slept with him when you wouldn't sleep with me, you whore."

Fury contorted his face until he looked almost demoniac. Screaming obscenities at her, McNair raised his gun a fraction of an inch.

Ben read murder in his eyes and knew he meant to kill Gina. He hurled himself against her, pushing Gina out of the way as the gun discharged. The shot missed her and sank into his shoulder.

He'd felt this pain before. Red-hot waves exploded in his arm, burning him.

Forcing himself to block out the pain, Ben didn't stop to see if Gina was all right. Dropping to the ground, he rolled into McNair. The gun went off again, firing wild as McNair fell backward.

Scrambling to his feet, Ben grabbed Gina's hand. He was running for the front door before he fully regained his balance. Behind him, McNair was shooting at them again. Ben could have sworn he felt a bullet whizzing by his head, missing him by inches.

He'd always been pretty lucky.

The air still knocked out of her, Gina realized they

were running for the car. Terror sliced through her as she tried to twist and get away.

"I have to get Jesse," she cried. "I can't just leave him here."

She tried to pull free, but he held on to her hand. The ache in his other arm was growing prodigiously. "Jesse'll be safer where he is. McNair doesn't know where we left him. Besides, it's you he wants. And I don't intend for him to get you."

Biting off a curse at the pain, he pulled open the passenger door and pushed her inside, then slid over the hood to his side and got in.

He jammed the key into the ignition and gunned the engine. Gina's eyes widened as she looked at him. There was a thick, red ooze soaking through the sleeve of his jacket.

"You're bleeding. You've been hit."

"Tell me something I don't know." Turning the wheel, he peeled away from the curb. As he did, he automatically looked down at the gas gauge. It was below the quarter-full mark. Way below. "God, I wish I'd remembered to fill up the tank."

She looked at the gas gauge. They had enough to hopefully lose Stephen before they had to stop at a gas station. Maybe.

"So do I." Gina twisted around in her seat and saw that Stephen was already out of the building and running toward a car.

Her stomach contracted in a knot.

"What I can't figure out," Ben said, "was how he got here so fast. I only called him a couple of hours ago."

When Ben had come to her in the bookstore, she'd thought he'd just made the call to Stephen. Had she known otherwise, she would have never let him take her back to the condo.

"He has a corporate jet at his disposal, and his own helicopter on standby," Gina said. He'd taken her on a ride in the latter once, preening like a peacock over his "toys." She'd begun to sense then that he was a man she needed to distance herself from. But she'd never dreamed at the time how dangerous he could become. "A couple of phone calls would be all it'd take to arrange things."

There was a catch in her voice. He knew what she was thinking. She was worried about Jesse. Ben spared a glance in her direction as he wove his way in and out of traffic. His head was beginning to spin.

"Don't worry, Jesse'll be all right. There's no way McNair could know about Kyle." He saw her reaching for the cell phone in her purse. "Don't."

Ignoring him, she began to dial. "But I have to call Grace and give her some sort of an excuse. She has to keep Jesse overnight—and not let him go outside to play with Kyle."

"Kyle's glued to the video game, remember? He's not going anywhere and neither is Jesse." Ben put his hand over the cell phone. The movement cost him dearly. Fresh flames traveled up and down his arm. "Wait until we get to a pay phone. Cell phone calls are incredibly easy to intercept and I've no doubt that Mr. Technology back there can pick up every word you say. We want to keep Jesse safe."

"Yes," she said softly, grateful that he'd just kept her from making a fatal mistake. She slipped the phone back into her purse. "We do."

Ben didn't answer. He was struggling to keep the road in focus as he took another sharp turn. The pain in his arm was getting worse.

The tanker truck seemed to appear out of nowhere.

Chapter 19

His head felt as if it was going to explode.

Ben jammed down on the brakes. Gina's scream melded with the shriek of tires and the crunch of metal meeting metal as the front of his car made contact with the tanker truck's cab.

Clipping just the edge, his car spun around drunkenly in almost a complete circle.

Breathing hard, Ben managed to regain control over the car. Gina had ceased screaming. Maybe a whole two seconds had passed, no more. Two seconds that felt like a lifetime.

His heart pounding, his body weakened and aching, Ben pressed the gas pedal as far as it would go and flew down the street. The tanker truck in his wake was turned askew, its cab and body forming a shaky letter *L*.

More important, in its present state, the vehicle blocked the intersection.

He tore through the next intersection, leaving the

near-accident far behind him. "How do you feel about driving?"

"Ask me when my heart stops racing." Peeling her fingers away from the dashboard, Gina looked at him and realized Ben wasn't just making a wisecrack. His face looked too pale even for the fading light. She immediately looked at the soaked jacket sleeve. He was losing too much blood. They had to do something fast. "Pull over," she ordered.

Turning his head in her direction took effort. The world insisted on tilting at a dangerous angle when he took his eyes off the road. "Why?"

He looked as if he was going to lose consciousness at any minute. "Because I think I should drive."

The wry smile was feeble at best as it inched across his lips. "Are you criticizing my driving?"

He'd forgotten he'd just asked her how she felt about taking the wheel, she realized. Fresh panic came in the wake of fear.

"I wouldn't dream of it," she said softly. "You drive like a pro." They were coming to a strip mall. "Now, pull over."

Ben guided the car to the curb. It was all he could manage. "Yes ma'am," he muttered, raising his hand to his forehead. The salute was never completed. Ben slumped in his seat.

Bolting out of the car as if she'd been ejected, Gina ran to the driver's side. She could feel the draft of cars whizzing by her as she pulled open Ben's door. She pushed him over to the seat she'd just vacated.

Thank God they weren't bucket seats, she thought, getting in behind the wheel. There was no way she could have managed to slide him over to the opposite end if they had been.

Taking the wheel, she glanced at the gas gauge. Stunt driving took a toll. The car needed gas badly. Impatient, she waited for a break in the stream of cars. When it finally came, she pressed down hard on the gas. "Hang on, Ben, I'll get us through this."

His eyes fluttered as the words came to him through a haze as thick as New England clam chowder. He managed a ghost of a smile. "My hero."

"Shut up and save your strength," she retorted, valiantly blocking out the salvo of fear that shot through her again. "I haven't forgiven you for this yet." She would have meant it, too, if she hadn't been so worried about him. She fought against panic taking hold of her. It wouldn't do either of them any good if she fell apart now. "I've got to get the car to a gas station and you to a doctor."

"Better than the other way around," he mumbled, and then her words penetrated. He tried to sit up straight and couldn't. But he could still voice a protest. "No, no doctor."

"I'm not having you bleed to death in the car. Red doesn't go with the upholstery."

"You do it," he rasped, his hand clutching her arm. "You bandage it. Can't risk hospital." It hurt to talk now. Ben pushed the rest of the words out. "McNair'll be checking. Looking for you."

He was right.

There was a near-empty gas station at the corner. Gina brushed away tears with the back of her hand as she pulled up in front of one of the pumps. She'd risked going as far as she could. The gas gauge needle was beyond Empty and was now hugging the extreme end of the gauge. They'd driven the last block on fumes.

Getting out, she looked at Ben. He was unconscious but breathing.

Telling herself that he'd brought all this down on himself didn't change the fact that she was afraid for his life. Afraid that the bullet Stephen had fired had hit something vital and that it was just a matter of time before she lost him.

How could you lose something you never had? she mocked herself. He'd just been pretending all this time. The words, the actions, the lovemaking, all pretense.

She shoved her credit card into the slot, then pulled it out quickly. A message to begin pumping traveled across a tiny screen above the slot. Gina flipped up the retainer and pushed the nozzle far into the gas tank. Using the card was risky. It left a trail for Stephen to follow, but she couldn't afford to waste the time it would take to run into the small convenience store where the cashier was ensconced and pay for the gas in cash. Every second counted.

Nervously, she looked around her as she waited for the tank to fill up. Her heart was pounding so hard, she could feel it slamming against her rib cage. Every lengthening shadow represented a potential danger.

Slowly, the world began to come back into focus. Ben realized that he'd been fading in and out of consciousness for a while now. It took a minute for him to become aware of Gina. She was taking his arm and draping it around her shoulders as she half dragged him out of the car. The heavy breathing belonged to her. One hand was wrapped around his waist.

"C'mon, dammit, Ben, I can't do this alone. One step at a time," he heard her telling him. "You can do this, Ben. Walk for me."

He was trying. God knew he was trying his best to hold up his weight. But it wasn't easy.

Frustration ripped at him, punching its way through the haze surrounding him and breaking it up. "This is bull," he growled more to himself than to her. "I'm supposed to…be…taking care of…you, not the…other way…around."

"We'll take turns," she panted, leaning him as best she could against a wall. She used her shoulder to brace him as she inserted the key the smirking clerk in the dismally dark front motel office had given her. "Yours'll be coming up soon, I promise."

Ben realized that he was being brought inside somewhere. Into a dingy, oppressive-looking room. Stale air surrounded him, refusing to move. The scent of cheap perfume clung to the peeling wallpaper and to the faded drapes that sagged against window frames made crooked by a succession of earthquakes, large and small.

The next thing he knew, he was sagging himself, falling backward onto a bed. The mattress embraced him, taking on his shape. Sliding Gina into him. He realized that she was still holding on to him. He managed to turn his head toward her.

Disengaging herself, Gina got back up to her feet. Ben found himself staring up at a sprackled ceiling that had captured more than its share of dirt and hapless insects. "Where are we?"

Gina brushed herself off automatically. The room gave new meaning to the phrase "two-bit dive."

"In a motel," she told him. "I'm not even sure of the name. Most of the letters in the sign in front of the lot were out."

By the sound of it, she was moving around the room.

He heard running water. Her voice was even farther away. "I hid the car in back," she said, raising her voice above the water. "I think we're safe. Stephen probably expects us to be driving straight through to Bedford."

She was beside him again, and he felt her tugging on his jacket. Pain shooting through him, Ben did what he could to raise himself up on his elbow and help her. It wasn't much, but at least he didn't feel as if he was going to pass out again. That was something.

Gina tore the remainder of his shirtsleeve away from his arm. Ben winced and tried to cover the onslaught of pain he felt with banter. "I had no idea you were so eager. You're going to have to give me a minute or two to collect myself."

She'd found a cracked plastic basin in the bathroom and had filled it up with water as far as she was able. Dabbing gently at his wound with the edge of a towel, Gina could almost feel the pain traveling through his arm. "Shut up, Ben."

A deep chuckle struggled to the surface. "You keep saying that."

"Because you keep not listening. Now, lie back and be still." She washed away some more of the blood and he winced again, though not a single sound escaped his lips. It made her feel awful. "I'm sorry. I've never cleaned a gunshot wound before."

"You're doing fine." Clenching his fists, he exhaled the words.

"No, not fine." Exasperation colored each syllable as she continued bathing the wound, trying to see how extensive the damage was. She was way out of her league here. "Fine would be if I could take you to an emergency room."

He couldn't allow her to do that. "Gunshot wounds have to be reported."

She rinsed out the cloth and began again. The wound looked better than she'd first thought.

"So, the hospital'll report it and we'll get the police." Gina tried to remember the first aid course she'd taken when Jesse was born. They hadn't covered gunshot wounds. "Maybe they'll listen this time."

And maybe, as she'd pointed out before, they wouldn't. He didn't want to waste the time. "I'd rather do it on my home territory where we don't have to prove we're the good guys." There was a question in her eyes. He put his own meaning to it. "I used to be a cop."

She smiled wryly, suddenly tired and drained. "And I used to not look over my shoulder all the time."

He could see the strain on her face, hear it in her voice. She shouldn't have had to be put through something like this. And he hadn't helped, Ben reminded himself. He'd been part of it.

"We'll get through this, Gina. I promise. And then you won't have to look over your shoulder anymore."

She made no comment. Ben was making promises she didn't know if he could keep. If anyone could keep. Stephen had gone completely out of control, throwing caution away and behaving like a madman. It was as if he no longer cared about his precious position in the scheme of things. She no longer felt safe in predicting anything about Stephen's behavior or taking another moment for granted.

"Not your fight," she told Ben quietly.

The fact that she really believed that stung, but he knew he had it coming. "The hell it's not."

She wasn't about to let herself get carried away by

hopes that had no basis. It was Ben's fault that Stephen knew where she was, but in an absolute sense, Ben owed her nothing. They were strangers. She didn't even know if Ben was his real name. Gina hadn't been hers.

She changed the subject. "I'm no expert, but I think the bullet went clear through." Ever so lightly, she dabbed disinfectant on the small, round exit wound. "There's another hole in the back of your arm." She forced a smile to her lips as she dabbed more peroxide on the small gauze pad, then pressed it lightly against his wound. "You got lucky."

"Yeah, I did." She realized that he was looking at her.

"What's this scar next to the wound?"

"I was shot in the same arm before."

"Maybe you're not as lucky as I thought." Gina got up and crossed to the card table to get the white bag with a local pharmacy's logo on it she'd dropped there when they'd come in.

"How long was I out?"

"Long enough for me to get to a drugstore and buy these." She emptied the bag on the bed. Gauze pads, bandages and tape fell out. "Then drive us to this hole in the wall."

"Holes in the wall can be good." He didn't think that McNair would look for them here. He watched her lay out what she was going to use. He liked the fact that she didn't seem to rattle easily. With a madman pursuing them, she hadn't folded like a house of cards, the way a great many other women might have. "Did you call Kyle's mother?"

Ripping a length of tape to use once she'd finished bandaging him, Gina stopped and stared at Ben. She was surprised that he would think to ask. Now that he believed that Jesse was her son, he no longer had any vested interest in the boy. Jesse was no longer the kidnapping victim he'd been sent out to find.

"Yes. The minute I got to the drugstore." She stuck one end of the tape on the edge of the bed. "I told her the truth because I didn't want to take a chance that Stephen would get to Jesse." She expected some sort of protest from Ben, but he made none. "Grace promised to look after Jesse until I could come to get him." Moving the basin with its discolored water aside, she picked up the package of gauze and opened it. "If I get back."

He lifted her chin with his good hand until her eyes met his. "You'll get back. Nothing's going to happen to you, I swear it."

She was so tired, so very tired. She wanted to believe him, wanted to have someone to lean on. But there was no earthly reason to trust him. "You're in no condition to enforce any promises you make."

"I've been in worse condition than this."

He felt her cool fingers against his skin as she quickly wound the bandage around his arm, keeping it just tight enough to curtail any more flow of blood. The contact made his stomach muscles tighten.

Ben smiled to himself. It was a good sign. He had to be coming around.

"Is that a container of orange juice over there?" He nodded toward the rickety card table where she had deposited all her hasty purchases. He tried to remember when she could have done that. The last few minutes had run together, bleeding into the time he'd spent being unconscious.

But he was conscious now.

Gina glanced over her shoulder at the card table even though she knew what he was looking at. "Yes."

With effort, he raised himself up so that he was half sitting against the headboard, the flattened pillows propped up against his back. "You think of everything, don't you?"

She didn't take it as a compliment, only an observation. Gina bit off another length of tape, securing the bandage in place. "I have to. I'm a single parent on the lam. There's no time for any second-guessing or do-overs."

His strength was returning. Maybe all he'd needed was that short time out to gather himself together. He'd always been fortunate that way. Gina had stopped fussing around him.

Utilizing the opportunity, Ben combed one hand through her hair, cupping the side of her face. "You won't be 'on the lam' for long. This'll all end very shortly. I promise."

More promises.

For a moment, because she needed it, she allowed herself to linger, to absorb the feel of his hand against her skin. To let herself drift and pretend.

But that had gotten her in trouble with him in the first place. Pretending that everything could be normal for her. That she could have a normal life despite Stephen's existence.

A normal life with Ben.

Fool me once, shame on you. Fool me twice, shame on me.

Gina drew her head back, away from him. "So you say. But you don't know Stephen." She rose to her feet as briskly as she could, pretending now to be indifferent to his promises and walked back into the bathroom with the basin.

Ben heard her emptying it, then putting it away. It sounded as if she was opening and closing doors. The next minute, she was back in the room. She stopped to pick up the carton of orange juice before crossing to the bed.

"There's no cup of any kind in the bathroom and I didn't think to get one. You're going to have to drink the orange juice from the container."

"Won't be the first time." As he took the container from her with his good hand, he grinned and laughed softly under his breath.

She didn't see anything particularly humorous about a carton of orange juice. Maybe his wound was making him light-headed again. "What?"

He opened the carton's lip. "Will you write a note to my mother? She was always after me not to do things like that when I was growing up. Said it was the sign of someone who'd been raised in a barn." Tipping the carton back, he drank deep. It made him feel better.

So did having her sit here with him like this.

Gina took the carton from him and set it aside on the floor, then sat down beside him again. "So all that wasn't just made up? You actually do have a mother?"

"It's practically mandatory for every living creature to have one at conception—as well as a father."

Gina shook her head. The image still didn't really compute. "I'm sorry, I just didn't picture you with anything as normal as parents."

It was an interesting choice of words. "Who says my parents are normal? My mother's sixty, going on sixteen." At times, he could swear she acted younger than any of his sisters. "And my father—" Without realizing it, his expression changed. "Hell, I'm not sure what he's up to these days. If the past is anything to go by, he's probably on his twentieth cheerleader by now. Maybe literally." He shrugged and instantly regretted it.

"They're not married anymore?" Even as she asked, she wondered if any of this was actually the truth. Or if he was lying again for reasons that weren't evident to her.

He shook his head slowly. "Not for a very long time." It had taken him years to reconcile himself to that fact. He wondered how long it had taken his mother. She'd never let any of them witness one ounce of bitterness. "My father left her for someone half his age. I've got a half brother named Jason somewhere. My mother raised the four of us on her own."

It was hard not to hear the affection that came into his voice when he spoke of her. Somehow, she found comfort in that. A man who loved his mother couldn't be all bad, right?

"She's a hell of a lady." He laced his fingers together with hers. "In a way, you kind of remind me of her."

Warning signals went up. "Don't try flattering me now. I'm still angry at you." Her actions warred with her words. She made no move to draw her hand away.

"Doesn't change the fact that you are. A hell of a lady," he clarified when she raised an eyebrow.

Because she was so close and he couldn't resist, Ben slid his hand up to her face and cupped the back of her head. The next moment, he brought her mouth to his. The kiss sizzled between them, evaporating what little air there was in the room.

"I'm feeling better now," he murmured against her mouth.

"I can tell."

Against all common sense, Gina brought her mouth back to his.

Chapter 20

This was crazy.

She knew that. But she needed this, needed to feel this wild feeling surging through her veins that only Ben seemed to be able to generate within her. Needed to forget the terror that hovered over her, the threat of consequences, needed to forget everything but this isolated moment in time she found herself in.

Needed Ben.

She didn't want to think, only feel, only respond. And she did so respond to Ben.

Her lips raced tiny, quick butterfly kisses over his face and neck, nullifying his ability to make rational decisions. Numbing his resolve.

"Hey, slow down," he told her softly, drawing his head back. A smile played on his lips. Ben stroked her hair, tucking a stray strand behind her ear. Feeling things he'd never felt before, even about the woman he'd married. Gina drew out emotions from him he hadn't thought himself capable of. "In case you hadn't noticed, I'm a little handicapped here at the moment."

"Didn't think that would stop you." Feeling foolish, she started to get up.

He caught her by the hand. "Who said anything about stopping?" Gina sat down on the bed again. "It'll just slow me down some." His eyes grew serious as he searched her face, worried. With everything that had happened, he hadn't taken the time to find out how she was. "Are you all right?"

The question struck her as almost funny. She pressed her lips together to hold back the sudden surge of hysterical laughter.

"The man who's been stalking me for the last six months, who caused me to uproot and leave behind the best life I'd ever known, has just appeared in my house with murder in his eyes and wielding a gun. No, I am not all right. I am very far from all right." She took a deep breath and then let it out again. When she did, she felt marginally calmer. Letting the situation get to her wasn't going to help her deal with it. "But right now, I don't want to think about anything. Not about him, not about what could happen—"

"Shh," Ben soothed, kissing her lips lightly, once, twice, three times, melting her a little more each time. "Nothing's going to happen, remember? It's going to be all right."

She smiled against his mouth. "You promised."

"I promised."

Kissing her slowly, deeply, Ben began to undo the buttons on her blouse. The edges sighed apart. Very gently, he slipped his hand in between the material and, ever so softly, caressed her breast. He heard her shuddering breath escape, felt her melt against him as the urgency of her response built.

He made love to her slowly, gently, as if she were made of spun sugar, too sweet to be devoured all at once, too fragile to feel the intensity of his desire. The passion that increased with each movement, each passing second, was not a wild thing. Instead, it was a stable force whose base continued to widen.

Gina felt it welcoming her, absorbing her.

His goal, beyond making love with her, beyond creating pleasure for her, was to make Gina feel safe because he was there with her. Having robbed her of the safety net that was beneath the tightrope she was making her way across, he could at least do that for her. Could make her feel that she wasn't alone. That she wasn't going to be harmed. Because he would never allow anyone to hurt her or her son. Ever.

He was doing just what she wanted, spinning a web so tightly around her that her mind was restricted to the moment, unable to touch the past, the future. Living only within each stroke of the clock.

They undressed each other, shedding clothes as they shed barriers until they were divested of everything except the overwhelming need they felt for each other.

Gina skimmed her hands along his flat, tight belly, her excitement feeding on the feel of hard muscles beneath her fingertips, glorying in the embodiment of power she felt radiating from him. Each kiss built in momentum, taking her closer and closer to the place she wanted to be. She could feel the frenzy growing within her.

She was making him crazy.

Nipping at his skin with her teeth, anointing it with her tongue. Covering his torso with wild, inflaming imprints of her mouth. He could hardly keep up with her and the sensations she generated within him.

Looking at her, he would have never guessed about the tigress who resided within. Gina gave every indication of being a proper lady, one who made you remember your manners even if they had been abandoned at the threshold of youth years ago. Yet now she clawed at him with the wild desperation that was the hallmark of someone who was fleeing something.

She set fire to his very soul.

Catching her wrists with his good hand, he held them above her head. When she looked at him in dazed, wide-eyed wonder, rising to the surface after bathing in a sea of deep, wet, openmouthed kisses, he merely smiled at her.

He could almost read the question in her mind. If he'd let her, she would have easily straddled him, initiating the last leg of the journey. In her present state, it would be over with too soon.

"Let me make a first move on my own," he whispered against her cheek.

Moving his body over hers, he began to do to her what Gina had just done to him. Over and over, he kissed her, her face, her neck, the hollow of her throat, the swell of each breast until she was reduced to a mass of quivering, undulating delectable flesh. And when he could hold himself in check no longer, Ben moved her legs apart with his knee. Gently, watching her eyes, he slid into her, careful not to make the final maneuver anything but the rightful joining of two kindred souls.

He had no details of the fraternity party violation that had resulted in Jesse's conception, but instinct showed him the path to take with her. Gentleness until she began to lead the way toward something else.

And when she did, they began the ever-increasing, frantic pace that would bring them to where they both wanted to be.

The explosion rocked them both. Even as the euphoria that had engulfed them slid back into the shadows, he could still taste her cry in his mouth. She'd called out his name, and that, more than anything else, was responsible for the wild, thundering excitement he'd felt in his veins. He'd been uppermost in her mind even in the throes of her climax.

Slowly, he moved off her, taking care not to crush her beneath his weight. As he fell away, he sucked in his breath. The pain radiated through the right side of his body, traveling in both directions. He struggled to even out his breathing.

She was instantly concerned. Guilt pushed forward. She shouldn't have let this get out of hand. He was hurt. "Your shoulder?"

"Yeah." A half shrug accompanied the acknowledgment. "I kind of forgot about it for a while."

Gina was exquisitely drained and reveling in the feeling, hugging it to her. "I noticed."

She turned her head toward him and discovered that there was no space between them. His face was touching hers. She moved back, but not before absorbing the sensation and taking comfort in it. If she let herself, she could get so accustomed to this. Accustomed to having someone to turn to. Someone beside her for the good moments and bad.

All illusion, a little voice warned silently. But the warm feeling persisted, hanging on.

Feeling her pulse grow steadier, she forced herself to concentrate on something beyond his nearness. "So, what's the plan now?"

He'd already thought this out. It had come to him the instant he saw the gun in McNair's hand. Ben pressed a kiss to her forehead, having no idea how much that small gesture meant to her.

"After I catch my breath, I'm going to make a call to the agency and have one of my partners set wheels in motion to swear out a warrant for McNair." He saw the dubious look on Gina's face. "He drew a gun on you in front of a witness. A witness he wounded." For emphasis, he nodded toward his bandaged shoulder.

Gina worried her lower lip. "Do you think it'll stick?"

"Oh, it'll stick all right." He had no doubts of that. "There's no turning back for him now. He made a fatal mistake and we've got him."

Gina looked toward the window. A single neon light, orange and obtrusive, radiated through the dust-laden drapes. She'd learned not to count her chickens. "Not yet," she whispered.

"But we will." Ben knew the only way she was going to have any peace was when they actually brought McNair in. He sat up, a fresh wave of pain rising up with him. Ben looked around to see where his clothes had ultimately landed. "They have a pay phone in the front office?"

Sitting up, Gina thought a minute. "Yes. Well, not exactly in the front office, but just outside on the side closest to the rooms. I drove past it when I parked the car. You're still not going to use the cell phone?"

He shook his head as he reached for his pants and underwear. Shrugging into the latter, he turned to look at her. Desire slammed into him with the force of an out-of-control freight train. Even the muted light from the dim lamps made her look like a goddess. He wanted to make love with her all over again. But there wasn't time. They had to get going.

"No sense in taking unnecessary chances. McNair has to be pretty desperate by now and he's going to use anything he can to stop us." Stepping into his pants, he rose to his feet and pulled them up over his hips. "Want to come with me?" He didn't like leaving her, not even for a few minutes.

Gina got off the bed and began getting dressed herself. Slipping on her jeans, she closed the snap at her waist and looked over her shoulder at him. She wanted a few minutes alone to sort out her feelings. An hour ago, she'd hated him. Now her life seemed to be in his hands, as well as a few other things as well.

"No, I'll just stay in the room and wait for you." She saw his brow furrow. Was he really worried about her? Or was it just his guilty conscience that prompted his concern? She wished she knew. "It's only a few feet away. I'll be all right."

Zipping up his jacket over his torn shirt, Ben looked dubiously at the lock on the door. Flimsy, it represented the bare minimum as far as protection went. He supposed that it could offer some resistance. Certainly long enough for him to get back to her in the eventuality that something went wrong.

Ben ran his hand along the back of his neck, wishing he could shake this uneasy feeling that was dogging him. There was no reason to think that McNair would actually track them to the motel. It wasn't as if this was the only one in the area. Gina wouldn't have been careless enough to have used a credit card to pay for the room and neither one of them had used the cell phone.

He knew that, like Gina, he wasn't going to relax until McNair was in custody. Although, the last half hour they had come pretty close, he thought with a smile. "All right, but lock the door after I leave."

He *was* worried about her. She still wasn't sure if it was because he felt guilty about leading McNair to her or because there was something stronger at play.

Gina masked her thoughts with a show of amusement. "Should we decide on a secret code? Two short raps and one long one?"

He laughed shortly, relieved that she was taking things well.

"I think my yelling 'Open up, Gina, it's me' should be enough of a clue." About to go out the door, Ben suddenly stopped and doubled back as she looked at him in surprise.

Her surprise melted into pleasure as he caught her by the waist with one hand and pulled her to him, then kissed her on the mouth. Hard.

It took her a second to orient herself and catch her breath. He'd all but made the room fade away. "What was that for?"

A slow, sexy smile curved his mouth. "If you have to ask, then we're going to have to do the last half hour over when I get back. I obviously didn't do it right." He looked into her eyes. No, he thought, he couldn't leave it at that, at a flippant remark. Not when he felt the way he did. She deserved more. "I'm sorry, Gina."

She didn't have to ask him about what. She understood and nodded. "I know."

He crossed to the door again and opened it. "I'll be right back," he promised, stepping over the threshold. "Don't open the door to anyone."

Following him, she put her hand on the doorknob, ready to close it. This time, her eyes sparkled as she looked at him. "Not even if they huff and they puff and they threaten to blow the room down."

He heard the nerves in her voice and squeezed her hand. "Not even then." He watched her close the door. "I don't hear the lock," he called out to her.

She twisted the metal latch and the tumbler echoed as it caught. "There. Happy?"

"Happy."

Hurrying to the front office, he saw the pay phone on the wall, just as Gina had described. Fishing through his pockets, Ben came up with a handful of change. He laid the coins out on the tiny counter just beneath the phone. Telephone numbers in different handwriting and different-colored ink and pencils surrounded the telephone like a surreal halo.

He glanced at a few as he tapped out the numbers on the keypad that would connect him to the agency. More than a couple promised the caller a good time.

Ben shook his head and wondered how many lonely people were out there. He'd been in their number, he realized, despite his active dating life. Until he'd met Gina.

Gloria, he corrected himself. Her name was Gloria. He wondered if he could get used to calling her that. Then wondered if she'd give him the opportunity to try.

Ben waited as a disembodied voice told him how much money to feed the phone in order to get his call to go through.

Slipping the correct amount into the slot one coin at a time, he listened impatiently to the melodic tones as they registered. Just as he put in the last one, he thought he heard a noise behind him. Gina.

"I thought you said you were going to stay in the room," he began, turning from the phone.

It was the last thing he remembered. Something hard came crashing down on his head.

They were going to have to get something to eat, Gina thought. Maybe they could stop at a fast-food place on their way. Picking up her purse, she rummaged through it, counting her change and the few bills that were there. It was going to have to be a really cheap fast-food place. She was running out of cash.

Gina whirled around at the sound of the glass breaking behind her. Her breath stopped in her throat, clogging the scream.

Stephen was in the room. She turned to run.

Shards of glass crunched beneath his feet as he ran to catch her. Grabbing her by the hair, he yanked her back before she could reach the door.

"Surprised?" he breathed against her.

Tears from the pain radiating from her scalp sprang to her eyes. She clutched the purse against her as if it were protective armor. "How did you…?"

The laugh made her skin crawl.

"I won't bore you with details. Suffice it to say I have ways." Releasing his hold on her hair, he backed away a step. "I've told you that before. You'll never get away from me, Gloria. I've told you that before, too. If I can't have you, no one can."

The look in his eyes left her no doubt about the state of his mind. The gun in his hand was aimed directly at her.

Stall, she had to stall. "Are you going to kill me?"

"Very good," he mocked her. "Yes, but not here." His mouth twisted in a condescending sneer as his eyes swept over the room. "Not in a cheap motel room. If we're to go out in a blaze of glory, I have something a little more dramatic in mind.''

She heard only one word. ''We?'' Was he planning on killing himself as well? *Dammit, Ben, where are you? How long does it take to make a lousy phone call?*

''Of course, 'we.' Surely you don't think I'm going to wait around for some stumbling policeman to make an arrest. And I'm not about to sit in prison, cooling my heels while some overpriced lawyer keeps making appeals that get rejected.'' He ran the barrel of his pistol against her cheek. ''Smile, darling. Your fifteen minutes of fame is about to come up.'' He saw her eyes dart toward the door. McNair's expression turned malevolent. ''He won't be coming to your rescue this time. I've taken care of him.''

Anger scissored into her fear. ''What did you do to Ben? Did you hurt him?'' she demanded, yelling at him.

''I gutted him like a fish.''

Shrieking, Gina swung around, her nails extended. She tried to gouge out his eye, but McNair was faster than she was and pulled back. Her nails raked across his face instead.

''You bitch. Turn me down for that two-bit nobody? I'll show you who's the better man.'' Grabbing her arm, he twisted it behind her back until she almost fell to her knees. Jamming the gun into her back, he pushed her to the door. ''Now, we're getting out of here and into my car.''

She tried to dig in, but he dragged her with him. ''Move, damn you.''

''If you kill me now or later, what does it matter?''

''Oh, it matters, Gloria, it matters very much. Trust me, being gut-shot is a particularly painful way to die. Now, move!''

Twisting her arm even harder, he pushed her out the door.

"Mister, hey mister, you all right?"

The reedy voice came out in a burst of stale cigarette breath and beer, forcing Ben into consciousness. The overwhelming pressure on his brow transformed into a headache the moment he opened his eyes. Someone was shaking his shoulder. His bad shoulder.

Pain assaulted him on all fronts.

A thin man with a three-day-old stubble, wearing clothes that looked as if they had been slept in for a week, was bending over him, curiosity more than concern written across his face. Ben realized that he was lying sprawled out on the cracked asphalt just beneath the pay phone.

He touched the top of his head and came in contact with a hell of a bump. The wince was automatic. "What happened?"

Extending a bony hand, the motel clerk helped him to his feet. "I dunno, I was coming out to get some ice and found you lying here."

McNair.

Gina.

Panic seized him instantly. Ben swung around to look toward the motel room where he'd left Gina. The door was hanging open. He cursed roundly at his own stupidity. He should have never left her alone.

Ben turned on the clerk. "Did you see anyone driving off?"

The man jerked his thumb toward the office. "There's a pay-for-view wrestling match on. I shelled out forty bucks to get it. Coulda been the circus passing through here with a whole bunch of damn marching elephants and I wouldn't have noticed.''

"Great, just great," Ben spat out in disgust. He hurried back to the room.

"Hey, you ain't gonna sue anybody, are you?" the clerk called after him. "''Cause it ain't my fault!''

Ben didn't bother answering. Running into the room, he saw the shattered window and the glass on the floor. "Gina!"

But even as he called her name, he knew she was gone. He swore again as he looked around. It looked as if she'd put up a struggle, he thought. She hadn't gone peacefully, but she had gone. He felt his heart sinking.

Coming up behind him, the clerk peered into the room. "Damn, but you people sure know how to party." He frowned as he saw the glass by the broken window. "Maybe I should be suing you."

There had to be a clue, some sort of indication where they were going, Ben thought in desperation. Gina would have tried to leave him a sign of some kind.

If she knew where she was going, he thought angrily. Damn it, what did he do now…?

His cell phone rang in his pocket.

He realized his hands were trembling as he pulled the cell phone out. Ben flipped it open, praying it was Gina. Or even McNair, threatening, gloating. Anything. All he needed to work with was a transmission signal. There was a tracking device in his car, courtesy of Megan.

"Hello?" No one answered him. "Hello?" he repeated. A faint noise crackled in the phone.

"Anybody there…?" the clerk asked, nosy.

Ben waved him into silence, listening intently. He could make out Gina's voice. She was talking to

McNair. She must have found a way to secretly dial his number on her cell phone and keep the channel open.

A hell of a woman, he thought, racing out to the back of the lot.

The car was there, just as she said it would be.

''Hey, who's going to pay for all that damage in there?'' the clerk yelled after him.

Turning on the ignition, Ben spun the car around one hundred and eighty degrees and headed for the street. ''I'll mail you a check,'' he called out.

But first, I've got to find Gina, he added silently, praying that neither her battery nor his gave out before he got to her.

Chapter 21

"Figured it out yet?"

Stephen's face was devoid of any sanity. His mouth was distorted as it twisted into a smile that made Gina's blood run cold. Adrenaline raced through her with no outlet, no course of action open to her. She prayed that Stephen had lied to her, that he hadn't killed Ben.

If he had—

She couldn't think about that now. She had to think of a way to save herself. She couldn't let Jesse become an orphan.

In a voice that was far steadier than she felt, she said, "I've figured out that you're crazy."

Headlights from cars passing in the opposite direction shone into the car, contributing to the dangerous, edgy atmosphere as they played along his face.

"Yes, maybe I am at that. Crazy to let a whore like you become an obsession. But all that's water under the bridge.'' He spared her a malevolent look. "And very shortly, we will be, too.''

Gina contemplated jumping from the car, but Stephen was going too fast. She needed to get him to slow down, to get him so angry that he swerved off the road.

"The reason I became such an obsession to you is because I *wouldn't* become your whore.''

McNair flung his fist at her, hitting her across the face with the back of it. Caught by surprise, Gina didn't have time to jerk away. The diamond ring he wore ripped into her cheek. A trickle of blood began to ooze from the gash. Gina pressed her lips together to hold back the cry of pain.

"You became his fast enough, didn't you?'' Stephen demanded. "Didn't you?'' The accusation echoed inside the car.

"That's because he's twice the man you'll ever be.'' Stephen grabbed the gun he'd tucked beneath his thigh for easy access and aimed it at her. Bravado pushed words out of her mouth. She wanted to make him blind with rage, it was her only chance. "Go ahead, get it over with. Shoot me,'' she taunted him. "But that'll spoil your little plan, won't it?''

Dammit, Gina, shut up, Ben ordered silently, listening to the byplay on the cell phone that lay open on the passenger seat next to him. If only there was some way to will his thoughts to her. He wasn't sure how much of a head start McNair had and he was afraid he wouldn't be able to reach them in time to stop whatever it was the man had in mind.

Frustration ate away at him. He couldn't call 911 because he didn't dare break the connection between the two phones. It was the only way he had to track down the other vehicle.

McNair's comment about being underwater soon gave Ben a sickening clue where they were heading. The Golden Gate Bridge. A bridge that had figured so prominently into the suicides of so many people who felt they had come to the end of the line.

The road the other car was following led directly to the bridge. McNair intended to either jump off or somehow drive off the bridge with Gina.

Dammit, he should have killed McNair when he'd had a chance. All he would have needed to do was get to his gun instead of grabbing Gina and running. That was two mistakes he'd made.

Three, he corrected himself. He'd taken the case in the first place.

Sweating profusely, Ben pushed down on the accelerator as far as it would go. The speedometer needle jumped even higher.

Twisting down another street, he passed a police car. Less than two beats later, he'd gained an entourage. Red-and-blue dancing lights flashed demandingly in his rearview mirror.

Now they come, he thought in disgust.

He couldn't stop to talk and explain what was happening. That would eat up too much precious time and they might not believe him without first checking his story out.

Here's hoping San Francisco's finest is an understanding bunch.

The speedometer needle passed eighty.

She could see the Golden Gate Bridge coming up in the distance, ablaze in lights. At night, it was a magnificent sight, like a regal, bejeweled woman going out for an evening on the town. Gina could remember look-

ing out of her dorm window at night and just staring at
it. Seeing it there, night after night, had created a peaceful, reassuring feeling.

Now the sight of it sharpened the fear that was carv-
ing away at her.

She looked at Stephen's rigid profile. She had to find
a way to stall for time. This would all resolve itself well
if she could just stall long enough, she thought frantically, praying that for once her optimism wasn't un-
warranted.

"Why don't you pull over?"

The look McNair gave her was demeaning. "So you
can offer yourself to me in hopes that I'll forget about
all this?" Stephen sneered. "Too late, Gloria, you
should have thought about that sooner. Much sooner."
His voice took on ranting tones. "I could have made
you a queen. You and that brat of yours would have
never wanted for anything. But you had to throw it all
away, make a laughingstock out of me."

They'd reached the foot of the bridge. Gina's heart
sank. At this time of the evening, the rush-hour traffic
had all but disappeared. Traffic itself had thinned out.
There was no one blocking their way, no one to slow
his progress.

It was all up to her.

"No one was laughing at you, Stephen. No one even
knew about me." Her mind was blank. She had nothing
to draw on. "You need help, Stephen. You need to see
a doctor."

"See a doctor? How dare you? How *dare* you?" He
grabbed her arm, holding her in place in case she had
any thoughts about jumping out of the car. He wasn't
going to allow her to ruin this, too. "What I need is to
see you dead."

A faint buzz in the distance transformed into something discernible as it drew closer. He stopped talking and listened.

Sirens.

The air turned ripe with his curses. Gunning the engine, McNair swerved around two vehicles and headed for the center of the bridge. The sirens grew in volume, in number. Coming to a screeching halt, the car fishtailed. He ignored it, ignored everything but the urgency to carry out his plan.

One hand holding his weapon, Stephen grabbed Gina's arm again and yanked her over the hand brake, dragging her into the driver's side.

"C'mon, c'mon," he said, pulling on her arm, "there isn't much time."

She tried to grab on to something to keep from being pulled out, but Stephen was too strong for her. He dragged her out of the car. No sooner was she out than he released her arm and grabbed hold of her waist. He half carried, half dragged her with him as he backed up to the side of the bridge, holding the gun to her all the while.

He indicated the railing. There was nothing on the other side but a tiny ledge. Beyond that was the ocean, its surface a choppy black.

"Climb, damn you, climb."

"No!" she screamed, bracing her hands against the railing to keep him from forcing her over it. "If you're going to do it, do it here! I'm not going to go through this charade with you! You're a self-centered, deluded, pathetic excuse for a human being."

"Shut up! Shut that foul mouth of yours!" Beside himself with rage, sputtering like a rabid dog, McNair raised the gun to her temple.

The sound of a gun discharging resounded in the night air, a macabre sound echoing over and over.

Braced for the shattering pain, Gina was numbed when it didn't overtake her. Instead, she felt McNair's hand loosen from around her waist, felt the friction as he began to slide down against her back.

A silent scream ricocheted in her throat as she stumbled away from him.

"God dammit, you've killed me." The accusation gurgled out of Stephen's mouth even as blood trickled from the corners. He sank down the rest of the way, a nonthreatening heap at Gina's feet.

Colors, voices, people were all coming at her at once, blending in eerily with the sound of sirens in the background.

Someone was holding her.

The scent of the cologne peeled away the numbness that had clamped its jaws around her.

Ben.

"Ben!" She sobbed his name before she could even focus.

"It's me, baby, it's me." Covering her face with kisses, he picked her up in his arms, cradling her against him.

Which was a good thing, because her legs had suddenly gotten too weak to support her. "Your arm," she protested feebly.

He'd shifted most of her weight toward his good arm. "Shh, it's my turn to play nurse."

"He told me he killed you," she sobbed.

He kissed the top of her head. "No, he just gave me one king-size headache."

It was only then that she began to make out people,

words. There were squad cars and police patrolmen all around them.

He'd come in to save her just like the cavalry, she thought giddily. No, like a white knight. "How did you…?"

He didn't want her to talk. He wanted her to save her strength. When he'd seen McNair holding the gun to her head, the whole world had frozen. He hardly remembered pulling out his own weapon and firing. He just remembered the prayer that had crossed his mind. The one that had guided his aim.

"Ran every light from there to here. The police just kind of came along for the ride." He looked at her face as one of the patrolmen moved past him to examine McNair. He'd never seen another living person look as pale as Gina. Except for the welt on her cheek. McNair had done that. Ben struggled to hold on to the threads of his temper. "Are you all right?"

She sighed and leaned her face against his shoulder. "I am now."

A stocky policeman made his way to the center of all the activity. It was clear that he was in charge. "Someone want to tell me what the hell's going on here?" he demanded.

"Well, one thing's for damn sure. It ain't going to be him." The policeman examining McNair rose to his feet, dusting off his hands. "He's ready for a body bag and a date with the coroner."

The stocky policeman turned to Ben. "Then I guess it's going to have to be you."

"With pleasure," Ben replied. He looked at Gina and smiled at her. It was over. Her ordeal was finally over. "As soon as you get a paramedic to take a look at the lady."

* * *

"I can't believe it's all finally over," Gina murmured three hours later.

Leaning her head against the car headrest, she sighed. It felt as if she'd lived an entire lifetime in the last few hours. After the paramedics had seen to the cut on her face and assured Ben that she was all right, she and Ben had given their statements at length several times over to a parade of police personnel, beginning with the patrolmen at the scene and ending with two detectives at the precinct where they were taken. Once Ben's identity and former connection to the Bedford police, as well as his present position with ChildFinders, Inc. were verified, things went a great deal more smoothly.

The detectives had told them it appeared to be an open-and-shut case. Gina had clung to the word *shut*.

They were going back to Kyle's house to pick up Jesse. She and Ben were going to have to be available to the police for at least the next few days in case there were any further questions. But after that, she was free.

Free.

Ben looked at her as he came to a light. He wouldn't have exactly phrased it that way. It wasn't over, at least not yet. "This is going to be all over the front page of the newspaper and the lead story on the six o'clock news for weeks to come, you know that, don't you? A man like Stephen McNair doesn't go quietly."

She thought of the way the man had died, the way he had intended to end it if Ben hadn't arrived in the nick of time.

"No, he certainly saw to that," she answered wryly.

He was still thinking of the news media. He knew how relentless they could be in their quest for a story.

There was no reason for her to have to go through that. He didn't want her to.

"I could find somewhere for you to stay for a while, until it blows over."

"That sounds like heaven. But I'm through hiding. Through putting my life on hold. It's about time I got back to living."

After everything that had happened, he'd been afraid that she would turn into a recluse, afraid to venture out. He'd seen it happen.

"Where?"

She didn't even have to stop to think. "Back in Bedford." That was where home was for her. In Bedford where her career looked as if it was finally going to take wing. Where her friends lived. Where Ben lived.

He hadn't realized he'd been holding his breath until she said that. Relief flooded over him. "As Gloria Prescott?"

"That's my name." Although she'd gotten accustomed to hearing him call her Gina.

He was trying to read between the lines and not give off any unintentional signals that would have her backing away. "So it'll be business as usual?"

Gina laughed softly, surprised she had enough energy for that. "As usual as it can be, given the circumstances."

He felt his way around cautiously. "You might need someone to run interference for you, at least in the beginning."

She picked up something in his tone. Something that heartened her. Not everything about the last several hours had been bad.

"That sounds like a good idea." Gina turned in her

seat to look at him. The seat belt dug into her shoulder. "Do you have anyone in mind?"

"I might." There was a diner just up ahead on the corner. He didn't want to keep glancing at her in small snatches. He wanted to look into her face, her eyes, as they talked. "Want to pull over for some coffee? We could discuss this."

"That sounds good to me."

The diner had seen better days, but everything within it had been scrubbed clean and it was neat. There was a faint scent of disinfectant mixing with the aroma of rich coffee and freshly baked apple pie. Gina had said yes to the coffee and passed on the pie. The knot in her stomach had yet to come undone.

She waited until the waitress's shoes were no longer audible, then set down the coffee cup she'd been nursing. Her eyes met Ben's.

"So, what is it you wanted to talk about?"

He felt like a singer about to kick off a baseball game by singing the national anthem only to realize that he'd forgotten the words. Ben searched for a way to begin.

All he had to do was think of the last few hours and how they could have turned out differently and he knew what to say. "I'm sorry, Gina. So sorry that I put you all through this."

They were sitting in a booth. She glanced at their reflection in the window. They made some pair, he with his shoulder wound, she with the bandage on her face. She covered his hand with hers, making a silent covenant. "You saved my life, so we're even."

Ben shook his head. That wasn't the way he saw it. "No, no, we're not. Because you saved mine, so we're back to being uneven."

"And you don't like that." She could tell by the way he phrased it.

Turning his hand up, he took her hand in his. "I don't like being beholden, no."

Something inside her began to shrink away. Was he trying to give her some kind of message, put her on notice? "Is that all it would be, a payment of a debt? Erasing a balance on some nebulous balance sheet of debits and credits?"

Where had she gotten that from? "No. You know better than that."

"Do I? Maybe you should tell me. Tell me exactly what there was between us."

Was. He didn't like the word. It made it sound as if it was all over. The passion, the desire, everything, over. In the past.

Well, wasn't it? McNair was dead, she didn't need him to protect her from the man any longer. Protect her from the man he'd led to her door in the first place, Ben reminded himself ruefully.

"It was wonderful" he said quietly, taking her hand again. "At least it was for me."

She bit her lower lip as she looked at him. "It was for me, too."

Then maybe, just maybe, it didn't have to be relegated to the past. Maybe it could be in the present as well. And the future. "Then there's no reason that it couldn't continue to be, is there?"

Gina looked at him for a long moment. No, she wasn't going to allow herself to read things into his words, wasn't going to take a single thing for granted. She wanted him to spell it all out for her.

"My head's been rattled around tonight, Ben. You're

going to have to be clearer than that for me. What are you saying?"

"I'm saying that I don't want this to end when I bring you and Jesse—Andrew—finally back to Bedford." He realized he was taking things for granted, that he would be the one to help them with the transition, but he pushed on, anyway. "That I don't want it to end because your name's not Gina anymore."

She cocked her head slightly, like a bird listening to the wind whisper a love song through the leaves. "So you want to what, start dating?"

The question made him laugh. It was a deep, rich sound that surrounded her. That made her feel safe. "I think we're past that point."

Without saying she agreed, she put another question to him. "What point haven't we passed?"

Okay, this was where he went for broke, he decided. He'd thought about it and it felt right. The moment he'd thought about it, he knew it was what he wanted to do. "The point where I get down on one knee and ask you to marry me."

Her mouth dropped open. She'd expected him to haltingly suggest living together. She would have settled for that. "What?"

Instead of answering, Ben slid out of the booth, still holding her hand, and got down on one knee. "I love you and I want you to marry me. I want to give you and your son a new last name, so that no matter what first names you decide to go by, I'll always know how to find you."

"You already know how to find me." The tears were making it hard to see. She blinked them back, wishing she wasn't so emotional. She didn't want him to think she cried over everything. "I'll be the woman right beside you. Always."

He rose to his feet, bringing her up with him. "So what do I call you?"

She hadn't realized, until this very moment, just how much she loved this man that deception had brought into her life. She supposed, in a way, she had Stephen to thank for that. "How does 'darling' sound?"

"Darling," Ben repeated, grinning. "Has a nice ring to it."

The grin disappeared as he kissed her.

* * * * *

Look for A HERO IN HER EYES,
Marie Ferrarella's next book,
available in August 2002 from
Silhouette Sensation.

Sweet Caroline's Keeper

BEVERLY BARTON

THE PROTECTORS

by
Beverly Barton

Ready to lay their lives on the line,
but unprepared for the power of love!

Defending His Own
Guarding Jeannie
Blackwood's Woman
Roarke's Wife
A Man Like Morgan Kane
Gabriel Hawk's Lady
Keeping Annie Safe
Murdock's Last Stand
Egan Cassidy's Kid
Navajo's Woman
Whitelaw's Wedding
Sweet Caroline's Keeper
(in *DANGEROUS TO LOVE*)

COMING SOON:

Jack's Christmas Mission - *December 2002*

For the readers who have made
THE PROTECTORS
series a big success!
And special thanks to my editors,
Lynda Curnyn and Leslie Wainger.

Prologue

Caroline asked the Harpers' chauffeur to drop her off at the back of the house. She had her key with her, knew the security code and could easily slip in through the kitchen entrance. If she went in through the front door, Preston would hear her, learn that she was sick and insist on phoning her mother. Lenore wouldn't like being called away from the Mitchells' party. Caroline had learned through experience that it was best to never interfere with her mother's plans, even if that meant trying to handle things that were difficult for a twelve-year-old to handle alone.

Last year, she had overheard her stepfather and mother arguing and had learned something that she had suspected all her life.

"Good God, Lenore, what kind of mother are you?" Preston's voice had trembled with near rage.

"I'm the kind of mother who gave birth to a child she didn't want simply because her husband and her family left her no other choice."

"Even if you didn't want Caroline, you must love her. You

must care about what happens to her. She's a sweet child. Intelligent and—''

"I endure her presence on holidays and breaks from school," Lenore had said. "But next summer, I'm sending her to my sister-in-law Dixie in Mississippi, so don't you dare bring that brat of *yours* here for the summer. Send him off to camp or tell your ex-wife to keep him."

Caroline banished the memory now as she sneaked through the darkened kitchen and up the backstairs of their Baltimore, Maryland, home. Although she spent little time here with her mother and Preston, her mother's third husband, she loved the house and especially her room. Preston had been the one who'd hired an interior designer to prepare the room for her shortly after his marriage to her mother, five years ago. Caroline had no memory of her real father, who had died when she was barely two. And all she remembered about Bruce Verner, Lenore's second husband, was that he'd always smelled of tobacco and had had a boisterous laugh. During that marriage, Caroline had been cared for by a succession of nannies.

As she made her way up the backstairs, Caroline thought she heard voices in the study, but more than likely Preston was just watching something on television. Lately her stepfather had seemed totally uninterested in the glamorous parties her mother so loved. She had noticed, too, that he had been closing himself off in his study a lot, at least for this past week since she'd been home for the Christmas holidays. She suspected that her parents were having marital problems. Her best friend, Brooke Harper, with whom she was supposed to be spending the night, had told her that she'd overheard her mother and father talking about Preston and Lenore Shaw's imminent divorce. Brooke had asked Caroline what *imminent* meant.

"It means something that's going to happen soon," Caroline had explained.

She didn't want her mother to divorce Preston. She loved

her stepfather. He was very good to her. Better than her own mother had ever been. He visited her at school sometimes. And whenever his own son, Fletcher, came to visit for a weekend, he insisted that she come home so that they could share family time together. Her mother had begrudgingly participated in the picnics, horseback riding and theater excursions. What would happen to her, if her mother divorced Preston? She would lose the closest thing she'd ever had to a father.

Caroline couldn't bear the thought of losing Preston.

Another wave of nausea hit her full force. Just as she rushed down the hall and toward her room, the voices downstairs grew louder. Men's voices. Arguing. Preston's voice. Shouting.

Caroline barely made it to her bathroom before the bile spilled from her mouth. Hurriedly, she flipped on the light switch, then leaned over the commode, emptied her stomach and dropped to her knees. Her sleepover with Brooke had come to an abrupt halt the minute she'd started vomiting. With the Harpers attending the same party as Caroline's mother, the task of summoning the Harpers' housekeeper had fallen to Brooke. When Caroline had asked to go home, the housekeeper had quickly awakened the chauffeur to drive *Miss McGuire,* as she referred to Caroline. Caroline supposed she'd caught a virus of some sort. One of those twenty-four-hour bugs. She'd just sleep here on the bathroom floor if necessary and try not to disturb anyone. Maybe if she did her best not to annoy her mother while she was home during the holidays, Lenore might be nicer to Preston and to Fletcher and maybe even to her. And if they could be a family during Christmas, perhaps Lenore would never divorce Preston.

Caroline scooted across the tile floor, lifted a washcloth from the stack on the wicker tier table and reached up to grab the rim of the sink. Hoisting herself up, she stood on shaky legs, her hands gripping the rim of the sink. She turned on the cold water, wet the cloth and washed her soiled mouth.

Her stomach settled somewhat and she breathed a relieved sigh. She had vomited twice at Brooke's house, then once on the way home and again just now. About every thirty minutes her insides churned and she erupted like a volcano.

Maybe she could lie down for a while. Until the next time. Her bed looked inviting. A white French provincial four-poster decked in baby-pink eyelet lace. If she soiled the bed linen and her mother found out…! Caroline didn't even want to consider the possibility. Of course, the housekeeper, Mrs. Claypool, never ratted on her anymore, not after the first time, when Caroline had accidentally spilled cola on the carpet and Lenore had gone ballistic. No, she didn't dare risk sleeping in her bed tonight. She'd have to settle for the ceramic bathroom floor.

But before she settled in for a long night, maybe she should change into her pajamas and then go back downstairs, to the laundry room, and wash the vomit out of her blouse before the stain set in. There would be no way to hide the garment. Maybe if she hurried, she could go down, wash the blouse and return before another bout of nausea hit her.

She stripped out of her clothes. The blouse came first. She draped it across the rim of the bathtub, then removed her shoes, socks and jeans. These items went into the clothes hamper on the floor of the linen closet. She took off her underwear and stuffed them into the small "delicate items" bag that her mother insisted she use. Her mother had taught her that a lady always washes her own intimate apparel.

As she entered the dark bedroom, illuminated only by the light from the bathroom, she caught a glimpse of her naked body in the cheval mirror. She was round and plump, her body just beginning to develop feminine curves. For all intents and purposes, however, she was still a child. If her hair were blond or red, she might resemble a chubby cherub, but she'd never seen a painting of an angel with black hair.

She rummaged in the dresser drawer, found a pair of pink-and-white-striped flannel pajamas, pulled them on and then searched the closet for her fuzzy pink house shoes. She'd have to be very careful not to disturb Preston. He would be sure to notice that she was sick. Her stepfather had a keen sense of observation. He would take one look at her and surmise that she wasn't feeling well, regardless of what excuse she gave him for not spending the night with Brooke.

After returning to the bathroom to retrieve her soiled blouse, she sneaked down the backstairs, trying her best to be as quiet as possible. When she entered the kitchen, she heard a rather odd noise, as if something had fallen over in the den, which was diagonally across the hall. And from the sound of it, whatever had crashed to the floor had been a rather large object. Should she investigate? she wondered.

Suddenly she remembered what Amelia Randall had told the girls at boarding school about her grandfather. He'd had a heart attack, fallen unconscious on the floor, and if it hadn't been for the quick action of her grandmother, the man would have died. Had Preston had a heart attack? He was old— more than forty. It was certainly possible, wasn't it?

Just tiptoe down the hall and peek into the den, she told herself. It's probably nothing. Preston might have accidentally knocked over something. But you should make sure that he's all right before you go back upstairs. Caroline scurried into the washroom, dropped her blouse in the sink, ran enough cold water to cover the garment, then rushed back through the kitchen and out into the hall. The light in the foyer, at the end of the hallway, spread a long, dim glow over the hardwood floor and cast shadows along the corridor walls. The den door stood open. Caroline crept slowly, cautiously down the hall. Preston usually kept the door to his den closed.

When she reached the doorway, she peered into the room; Preston's large oak desk was the one object in her direct line of vision. The banker's lamp on her stepfather's desk emitted the only light in the room. She dared to take one step over the threshold, just to get a better look. But before her eyes could scan the entire room, she noticed that the huge world globe that sat center stage lay on the floor, along with the heavy wooden stand on which it normally rested. And there, beside the globe, lay Preston.

Caroline gasped. Silently. Mercy! Had he had a heart attack, just like Amelia's grandfather? Panic momentarily controlled her. She knew nothing about helping someone who'd had a heart attack. But she had to do something or Preston might die. *Think, Caroline, think. What must you do first?* Call for an ambulance immediately. Without giving her own sickness another thought, she ran into the room, heading for the telephone on Preston's desk. But as she reached for the phone, she noticed blood seeping onto the wooden floor. Blood pooling around her stepfather's head. And then, just as the reality of what had actually happened began to dawn on her, Caroline heard something behind her. Turning abruptly, she saw a man. Tall. Broad-shouldered. Wearing dark clothes. Black slacks. Black pullover sweater. Black gloves. She caught only a glimpse of his face, the light brown beard and mustache, the hawk nose, the shaded eyes as his gaze narrowed and pinned her to the spot. Her gaze collided with his.

Was he a thief? she wondered. Perhaps, but he was also a murderer. For she knew in that one terrifying moment that Preston was dead. Killed by this intruder. The tall stranger still held the weapon in his hand. Caroline stared, hypnotized by the big gun. He would have to kill her, too, wouldn't he? After all, she had seen him, even if not very clearly, hidden as he was in the shadows.

Instinctively, Caroline opened her mouth and screamed. What else could she do? The quivering began inside her body and quickly spread outside, from head to toe. She kept screaming as she trembled. Her eyes squinched with fear. Her heartbeat accelerated wildly, the rhythm drumming in her head. She was going to die. He was going to kill her.

Seconds passed, agonized moments of sheer terror, as she

waited for the sound of the gun firing. Waited for the bullet to hit her. Waited for her life to come to an end.

Minutes flew by. She kept screaming and screaming, unable to control the hysteria that had claimed her. Her vision clouded with unshed tears. Why hadn't he shot her? What was he waiting for? She blinked several times, clearing her vision enough to see that the man had moved out of the shadows. Where was he?

She scanned the room. No sight of him anywhere. She heard the front door open and close. He had left the house. And he hadn't killed her. But why? Why had he let her live?

Caroline glanced down at her stepfather. She shivered. Then as if in a trance, she picked up the telephone receiver, dialed the emergency number, and the moment she heard another human voice, she asked for help. She told the person her name, her address and that someone had just killed her stepfather. Then, while the person asked her several more questions, Caroline stopped speaking. She dropped the phone. The receiver fell to the floor, dragging the base to the very edge of Preston's desk. She turned her head and vomited into the nearby wastebasket. Her mother would scold her for making a mess. But Preston would take her side. He always tried to protect her from her mother's wrath. He was so kind and good and gentle.

Caroline wiped her mouth with the back of her hand, then walked over and sat down on the floor beside Preston's body. She lifted his limp hand in hers and held it tightly.

"I'll stay right here with you," she told him. "I won't leave you alone."

Aidan Colbert parked the nondescript black sedan in the underground parking garage at Peacekeepers International in Washington, D.C. With expert ease, he removed the 9 mm from his shoulder holster, then lifted the case from the floorboard, placed the weapon alongside the silencer and closed the lid. Following instructions, he left the case on the seat, then got out of the car, locked the doors and walked toward the elevator. He punched the up button. The elevator doors swung open. He removed his ID card from his pants pocket, inserted it into the appropriate slot, and then hit the one-inch-square, unmarked blue panel.

As the elevator rose higher and higher, taking Aidan toward Ellison Penn's office atop the Peacekeepers building, he tried not to think about the child. But he knew he probably would never be able to erase that moment from his mind—when their gazes had locked and she realized he had killed her stepfather. For just a split second he had seen Brendan's little face, Brendan's blue eyes, Brendan's frightened features. Aidan had seen on the girl's face tonight the exact look that had crossed his little brother's face only moments before his father had struck the fatal blow that had ended Brendan's life nine years ago.

The child had thought he was going to kill her.

The elevator stopped. The doors opened to reveal the entrance to the office suite occupied by the current head of Peacekeepers International. Fellow agent Gavin Robbins, another new recruit, waited for him in the outer office.

"Mr. Penn is waiting for you," Gavin said, his dark eyes staring accusingly at Aidan. "Word has already reached him that there was a problem—a witness you didn't eliminate."

Aidan glared at Gavin but didn't respond verbally. There was something about Gavin that rubbed Aidan the wrong way. They had disliked each other on sight the moment they'd met six months ago when they began their training together. Aidan followed Gavin into the ultramodern office, dominated by black leather sofas and chairs, contemporary paintings on the stark white walls and pieces of expensive avant-garde metal sculpture placed strategically on glass-and-chrome desks, tables and bookshelves.

Ellison Penn stood a tad over six feet tall, a good two inches shorter than Aidan, but he possessed a commanding presence. A professional athlete's build. Large. Muscular.

Without an ounce of fat on his body. His all-seeing eyes were a shade lighter than his steel-gray hair, which gleamed like polished silver against his light olive skin.

"We know that Shaw's stepdaughter was at the house," Ellison stated in a matter-of-fact way. "She wasn't supposed to be there. I'm not sure what happened. Our man followed Preston when he took her to the Harper house several hours earlier."

"She saw me," Aidan said. "I don't think she got a good look, but—"

"You should have eliminated her." Standing as if at attention, Gavin puffed out his chest as he issued his opinion. "By allowing her to live, you compromised the mission."

Aidan glowered at Gavin. "I thought it was our job to protect the innocent, not kill them."

"Aidan is right," Ellison said, a world-weary look on his face. "As a Peacekeeper, he could not have murdered that child without going against the very principles on which our organization was founded."

"But if the child can recognize him—" Gavin said.

"The child is traumatized," Ellison told them. "The initial report I received states that she's in shock and has been unable to help the local police in any way." Ellison surveyed Aidan from head to toe. "Shave the beard and mustache."

"Yes, sir," Aidan replied.

"And to be on the safe side, I'll send you to our London office. You can work from there for the next year or so, until Preston Shaw's death becomes just one more unsolved murder."

Aidan nodded agreement.

"I'll keep abreast of the developments in the case and keep tabs on what happens to the child." Ellison shook his head. "Damn shame she was there. She didn't see you kill him, did she?"

"No, I was just on my way out of the room when she walked in."

"We should have sent backup with you," Ellison said. "Someone to watch the house while you were inside. But we thought our information was reliable and we were sure Shaw would be all alone. One man in and out quickly was less of a risk." Ellison breathed deeply, his washboard-lean belly tightening when he inhaled. "We'll never make that mistake again."

"Sir?" Aidan squared his shoulders and stared point-blank into his superior's cool gray eyes.

"Yes, what is it, Colbert?"

"About the child...I'd like to be kept apprised of everything concerning her."

"That's not a good idea," Ellison said. "Regardless of how you feel, there can be no personal contact between you and Caroline McGuire."

"I was thinking of impersonal contact, sir. I believe I have a right to care what happens to the little girl."

"You're in the wrong business if you allow yourself to get sentimental over Preston Shaw's stepdaughter," Gavin Robbins said. "A professional assassin cannot afford the luxury of caring about his victim's family."

"Robbins, I'd like to speak to Colbert alone," Ellison said.

Aidan didn't glance at Gavin, but could sense the man's displeasure as he strode from the office. "If there is anything I can do to help the child...any way I can... All I ask is that I be informed, that I receive frequent updates on her condition."

Ellison rounded his desk, walked over to Aidan and clamped his large hand down on Aidan's shoulder. "I understand what you're feeling. A man's first assignment is never easy. And unfortunately, with your first assignment things didn't go exactly as planned. In time, you won't be as disturbed by mishaps that occur."

"I'm sure you're right. But that doesn't change the facts in this case. Will you or won't you agree to forward all information on the child to me in London?"

Ellison tightened his grip on Aidan's shoulder. "It's against my better judgment…but, yes, I'll see that you learn everything there is to know about Caroline McGuire. However, I must warn you that you can never contact her personally or reveal in any way who you are or—"

"Do you think I'd ever want her to know me, to find out that I'm the man who killed her stepfather?"

"You were only doing your job. Preston Shaw had to be eliminated. He had become a very dangerous man."

"But that little girl doesn't know the facts. She isn't aware of what kind of man Preston Shaw really was. She'll spend the rest of her life believing he was good. And the man who killed him—" Aidan broke off, shook his head and cast his gaze to the floor. He couldn't bear verbalizing his thoughts, couldn't face the truth of how Caroline must feel about her stepfather's executioner. With Preston Shaw's blood fresh on his hands and the memory of the frightened expression on the child's face vivid in his mind, he was having difficulty convincing himself he was one of the good guys.

Chapter 1

Davids Wolfe tucked the file folder under his arm and picked up the mug of steaming black coffee from the kitchen counter, then opened the door and walked out onto the wraparound porch surrounding his log cabin. The drive from Atlanta had been well worth the hours behind the wheel. Even after all these years, nothing felt as right as coming home to the east Tennessee mountains where he'd been born, where generations of his mother's family had lived and died. The Scottish-Irish settlers had claimed these hills as their own, bringing with them their folklore, superstitions and Celtic music. The proud Cherokees to whom this land had belonged long before the first Pilgrim set foot on Plymouth Rock, except for a few who had hidden away, had been transported via the Trail of Tears to Oklahoma in the early part of the nineteenth century. His half-breed mother's ancestors had been among those few who had escaped and found refuge deep within the Smoky Mountains of Tennessee and North Carolina.

David eased into the large wooden rocking chair, which

was constructed of small logs and matched the porch swing and the other chair to his right. Leaning to the side, he placed his mug on the porch floor, then took the thick file folder from under his arm, opened it and spread it across his lap. The face of a child stared up at him. A picture of Caroline McGuire at age twelve, a school photograph taken several months before her stepfather's death. A plump little girl with short, cropped black hair, her bangs hanging in her eyes. A pair of unforgettable blue-violet eyes. Eyes that had haunted him for fifteen years. Hurriedly, he flipped through the folder. Picture after picture came into view, interspersed among data compiled on an unloved and unwanted child whose own mother had tossed her aside, as if she'd been nothing more than an outdated dress.

David knew as much about Caroline McGuire as anyone on earth did. From the size shoe she wore to her favorite brand and shade of lipstick. For the past five years, she had used an expensive label with a seductive name—Passion Pink. And although she enjoyed going barefoot as much as possible, when she purchased shoes, she bought a size 7B. She collected clocks and had an assortment in her St. Michaels, Maryland, home, as well as her Talbot Street photography studio. She had purchased everything from a cheap resin lighthouse clock to an antique mahogany grandfather clock she had acquired at an estate sale.

She didn't smoke. Had never done drugs. And seldom drank. When she did consume liquor, her drink of choice was a strawberry daiquiri, a concoction as sweet as she was. Although she had numerous friends and had dated a variety of men since her first date at seventeen, she had never been married. Lived alone. And at twenty-seven, was possibly still a virgin.

David flipped through the hefty dossier, removed the information and picture Ellison had faxed him at his apartment in Atlanta first thing this morning, just as David had been heading out the door for his long weekend at the cabin. He dropped the thick folder onto the seat of the other rocking chair, then reached down and picked up his coffee. After taking several swigs of the strong brew, he looked at the picture of Caroline at her mother's funeral a week ago. The snapshot, taken at a distance by one of Ellison's flunkies, showed a somber young woman in a dark suit. Surrounding her were her first cousin, Lyle Jennings, her assistant Roz Turner, her stepbrother Fletcher Shaw, and her old friend Brooke Harper, who was Fletcher's girlfriend.

When David swiped his fingers across the picture, down Caroline's cheek, an odd sensation tingled in his fingertips, as if he had actually touched her skin.

He had sent flowers to the funeral, of course, and signed the card simply *David*. He would liked to have been there, to have offered her sympathy and comfort, but of course that hadn't been possible. Any personal contact between them was forbidden.

David couldn't help wondering how Caroline felt about losing her mother, a woman who had shipped her off to her aunt Dixie's in Mississippi less than a month after Preston Shaw's death, and for all intents and purposes had deserted her. From what he knew of Caroline, her kind heart probably wept for the woman who had given birth to her. But how did one ever come to terms with the feelings of anger, hurt and resentment one felt for a parent? God knew he had never been able to accomplish that seemingly impossible feat. But Caroline was a better person than he, so maybe for her it was possible.

He reread the hand-scribbled note from Ellison.

Caroline has inherited the house on Sheffield Street from her mother. I cannot imagine that she'll ever want to go back there. Perhaps she will simply turn the place over to a Realtor. I understand that during the years Lenore leased the house, it fell into disrepair. Gavin assures me that Caroline is holding up well. I did tell you that he

is dating her, didn't I? They met at a charity auction in
Baltimore a few months ago. He's quite taken with her.
But then, who wouldn't be? Your Caroline has grown
up to be quite a beauty.

Fifteen years ago Ellison Penn had cautioned Aidan Colbert not to become emotionally involved with Caroline's
plight, and yet Ellison had taken a keen interest in the well-
being of Preston Shaw's stepdaughter. David had always suspected that Ellison shared some of the guilt that had plagued
Aidan for nearly thirteen years—until Aidan's ''death'' in an
explosion while on a Peacekeepers assignment in the Middle
East more than two years ago.

Aidan Colbert had kept his distance, observing Caroline's
life through pictures and reports, helping her financially over
the years, yet known to her only as her phantom benefactor,
David, a name he had chosen because it had a special meaning to him alone. David Wolfe had been Aidan's maternal
great-grandfather, a man who had been much revered by his
family.

When Aidan Colbert had died, David Wolfe had risen like
a phoenix from the ashes of the bomb explosion that had
officially ended Aidan's existence. Then, with Ellison Penn's
assistance, he had begun a new life, with a surgically recon-
structed face and a fake identity.

I did tell you that he is dating her, didn't I? It was as if
David could hear Ellison's voice speaking the taunting
words. Ironic that Gavin Robbins, who had once asked Aidan
Colbert why he hadn't eliminated Preston Shaw's stepdaughter, was now dating her. David didn't like the idea of Robbins
being involved with Caroline. She deserved better. Robbins,
still a gung-ho agent, had been promoted only this past year
to second in command, directly under Ellison, whom David
prayed never retired. He couldn't imagine someone like
Gavin taking over the reins of Peacekeepers International,
which was a front for an organization of highly trained men

and women who worked as contract agents for the U.S. government and its allies. These handpicked agents lived seemingly normal lives. Their families and friends knew them to be employees of Peacekeepers, experts who worked to secure peace throughout the world, as nongovernment negotiators who fostered humanitarian deeds worldwide. But in truth the job that these men and women performed was to protect the cause of freedom and eliminate any problem that might arise that couldn't be handled through ordinary channels. And a small squad of agents were trained as assassins, prepared to kill on command, when no other alternative existed. Aidan Colbert had been a member of that select few. And so had Gavin Robbins.

David tossed aside the faxed note and picture, letting them sail down and settle on top of the file folder. He rocked back and forth, slowing occasionally to sip his coffee. He would call Ellison tonight. Thank him for the update. And suggest that his old mentor find a way to persuade Robbins to end his relationship with Caroline. He had hoped nothing would come of their dating, had thought she would see through that phony gentleman facade Robbins projected and dump the bastard. He couldn't allow Caroline to waste her life on a man unworthy of her. Out there somewhere was a man he could trust with Caroline's heart and her life. Caroline deserved only the best. And that sure as hell wasn't Gavin Robbins.

Caroline held the key in her hand but could not bring herself to unlock the front door. She had purposely never returned to the house on Sheffield Street and had avoided this area of town whenever she'd come to Baltimore. She wouldn't be here now if Fletcher and Lyle hadn't agreed to accompany her. Of course, she could have simply turned the house over to a Realtor without seeing the place herself. But she felt that this was the final step in putting the past behind her—now and forever. Sometimes she would go days without thinking about that night, but then a memory would flash through her mind and it would all come back to her. Thankfully, with each passing year, the memories faded, became less vivid, and she had long since recovered from the emotional breakdown she had suffered after Preston's death.

You can do this, she told herself. Preston is dead. Your mother is dead. And for all you know the intruder who murdered Preston might be dead, too. None of them are inside this house waiting for your return. Only memories await you, and even the most horrific memory cannot harm you.

"Are you sure you want to do this?" Lyle Jennings asked. "I can handle this for you. Or—" he glanced at the other man "—Fletcher can deal with it."

"No." Caroline reached out and squeezed Lyle's hand. Dear, kind Lyle, who was like a brother to her. Lyle's mother had raised the two of them together in her modest Iuka, Mississippi, home. A loving disciplinarian and fine Christian woman, Dixie Jennings had taken in her brother's child and treated her as if she were her own. "I need to do this myself. But I want to thank you and Fletcher—" she smiled up at her stepbrother "—for coming with me. I don't think I could do this without y'all."

"To be honest, this is something I need to do, too," Fletcher said. "I haven't been back inside the old house since the day of the funeral. I remember going into the study that day. The house was filled with people, of course, and Lenore was center stage as the grieving widow." When he stole a quick, apologetic glance at Caroline, she smiled reassuringly, letting him know she, too, had understood her mother's penchant for theatrics. "I slipped away into the study. I wanted to see where it had happened."

"Oh, Fletch, I never knew you'd done that." Caroline patted her stepbrother's arm. "How awful for you."

"Yeah, it was. The servants had tried to clean the floor, but the blood had stained the old wood and I could see the spot where Father had bled after he'd been shot in the head."

Caroline had not talked about that night to anyone in a long time. Not since she had completed years of therapy with the psychiatrist in Memphis. Her aunt Dixie had driven her across the state of Mississippi every other week to visit the doctor, an expensive therapist who specialized in traumatized children. To this day she didn't know how much those sessions had cost. Far more than her aunt could afford. If it had not been for David, she wouldn't have gotten the help she had so desperately needed. David, her mysterious benefactor. David, a man who had known her stepfather, had contacted her aunt through his lawyer to offer financial assistance for Caroline McGuire.

"No use putting this off any longer." Caroline inserted the key in the lock, turned it until she heard a distinct click, then twisted the doorknob and opened the front door. She breathed deeply, inhaling to fill her lungs fully before exhaling slowly.

Taking a small, tentative step, she crossed the threshold into the foyer. A sour, musty smell assailed her senses. The stench of an old house, closed up and unused for many years. The only light came from the sunshine pouring in through the open front door.

"I understand no one has lived here for the past four years," Fletcher said, as he moved inside and came to a halt near Caroline. "So, there's no electricity. I suppose we'll have to open up the blinds if we want to take a good look at the place."

Caroline didn't budge. Lyle entered, put his arm around her shoulders and hugged her to his side. "Would you like for Fletch and me to open the blinds to let in some light and raise a few windows to air out the place a bit?"

"Just open the blinds," Caroline said. "Enough so that we can see our way around in here."

"Will you be all right here by yourself while we do that?" Fletcher asked.

Caroline nodded. Yes, she'd be fine—if she didn't go any farther into the house. If she didn't go into the study.

Fletcher and Lyle disappeared, one taking the rooms to the left of the wide foyer, the other the rooms to the right. Caroline forced herself to move. Although the floor badly needed refinishing, wallpaper was peeling off the walls and the white painted woodwork was stained and yellowed, the empty foyer still retained a hint of its former beauty. She could remember the first time she had walked into the house. She'd been seven years old. Shy. Awkward. And uncertain whether or not her new stepfather would like her.

Preston Shaw, tall, slender and elegant in a Cary Grant sort of way, had come out of his study when Caroline arrived with her nanny. She had looked up at the big man, into his handsome, smiling face and sparkling blue eyes and breathed a sigh of relief.

"Well, hello, Miss Caroline," he'd said. "Aren't you a pretty little thing. You'll probably grow up to be every bit as lovely as your mother."

Before that day, no one had ever told her she was pretty. With those few words, Preston had won her heart—and her loyalty—forever. And during the next five years, she had grown to love her stepfather more dearly than anyone on earth. He had been her champion, her defender and her friend. When her mother had been cruel, he had been doubly kind. When her mother had rejected her, he had lavished her with attention. And when he had died, she had lost the only father she had ever known.

Tears pooled in Caroline's eyes. No, you mustn't cry, she told herself. You have already shed enough tears to last a lifetime. Preston wouldn't want you to cry.

"You have such a lovely smile, my dear little Caroline," Preston had told her. "You should use it more often."

A fragile smile quavered on her lips. She blinked away the unshed tears and wandered out of the foyer and up the hallway. *Face the worst first. Get it over with. Now!* The door to the study stood wide open. Lyle had already opened the blinds and afternoon light poured through the slats, laying stripes of alternating sunshine and shadows across the dirty wooden floor. Since the room was bare of furniture, it appeared even larger than she remembered. A vast empty space.

But suddenly Caroline visualized the way the room had once looked—the way it had looked fifteen years ago. Warm. Inviting. Richly decorated with the best money could buy. In her mind's eye she could see her stepfather. Laughing. Talking. Joking. A personable man, well-liked by everyone.

The images inside her head darkened, fading from joy to sorrow. Preston's body sprawled on the floor. The world globe and its stand toppled. A pool of blood. Fresh. Bright red. And the hooded eyes of a large bearded man standing in the shadows, his hand gripping the weapon that had murdered Preston. Their gazes had locked for a split second. Paralyzing fear. Numbing realization that she was going to die. Shock when he had left the house without harming her. But why had he not killed her, too?

Caroline could hear her own long-ago screams. Incessant. Terrified. Hysterical. Sounds from years gone by.

Someone touched her. She gasped and jerked away.

"Sorry," Fletcher said. "I didn't mean to startle you."

Caroline swallowed. "A part of me would like to burn this place to the ground."

"It's yours. You can do whatever you want with it."

"I could give it to you. After all, this house belonged to your father."

"Yes, but he left it to your mother and she in turn left it to you," Fletcher reminded Caroline. "My dear, I'm afraid this house is your headache, not mine."

A quirky smile lifted the corners of Fletcher's lips. In many ways he reminded her of his father. Tall. Debonair. Good-looking. And quite charming. She laced her arm through his and sighed. "I think Preston would want to see people living here again. A family. Parents. Children. He did so want us to be a family, didn't he?''

"Yes, he did."

"I think I should renovate this place and put it up for sale." Caroline glanced around and this time she saw the room as it was, not as it had once been. Holding the memories at bay, she led Fletcher out into the hall, where Lyle stood, dusting off his hands.

Lyle sneezed. "Sorry. You know I'm allergic to dust."

"Yes, I know that's your story," Caroline said jokingly. "At least you convinced Aunt Dixie of that fact. I always had to dust and vacuum your room for you."

"Yes, you did," Lyle replied. "But in return, I always washed the supper dishes, didn't I?"

"Only because Aunt Dixie made you do it." Caroline glanced at the staircase, which rose from the entrance hall to the second floor. "I want to go up and have a look at my old room before we leave."

"Have you decided what you want to do with this place?" Lyle asked.

"Mmm-hmm. I think I'm going to hire a contractor first thing next week and have the place fixed up enough to sell. The church's charity programs could use a sizable donation, couldn't they?"

Lyle's mouth formed a surprised oval. "Are you really thinking of donating the proceeds from the sale of this house to the church?"

"Mother wouldn't approve, of course, but I think Preston would. Don't you agree, Fletcher?"

"No doubt he would," Fletcher said. "Father was a generous man."

"Then it's settled." Caroline knew in her heart that she had made the right decision. In coming here today—to face a past that still occasionally haunted her. And for choosing to donate the money from the sale of her old home to the church where Lyle had been a minister for the past several years.

So, Caroline was going to renovate and sell the old house, then donate the proceeds, in Preston's name, to the Congregational Church. A fitting tribute to a man she had loved like a father. Preston would have wholeheartedly approved. He'd been a great one for pomp and circumstance. How he had enjoyed his role as an agent for Peacekeepers International, thought to be only a philanthropic organization established for doing good deeds around the world. But Preston had also enjoyed playing secret agent, taking risks. He had loved the cloak-and-dagger games, the adrenaline rush of outsmarting everyone around him.

Despite his job with the Peacekeepers, Preston Shaw had been an asset to his true friends and associates of the Loyalists Coalition, never forgetting to whom he owed his real allegiance. When given an order, he obeyed. Unfortunately, his adherence to the dictates of a cause controlled by a select few had cost Preston his life. Once the Peacekeepers had discovered the man was a traitor, what else could they do but eliminate him?

Unfortunate that the child had been at home the night Aidan Colbert had assassinated the Peacekeepers' rogue agent. Lucky for Colbert that she had been unable to identify him. And even more fortunate that Preston had not lived to follow through on the threats he had made against the organization to which he'd sworn his first allegiance. For several years after Preston's death, *they* had held their breaths, wondering if he might have found a way to reach out from the grave to wreak vengeance. But with each passing year, they had relaxed more and more as they began to believe that Preston had left behind no evidence to link him to their organization or to expose the identities of its other members.

They had kept a close watch on Caroline, just as the Peacekeepers had. But for entirely different reasons. She was no longer of any interest to them and, since Aidan Colbert's death two years ago, apparently of little interest to the Peace-keepers. But since there was and had been for many years a connection between Caroline and him, he still maintained a personal interest in her and even felt affection, to a certain degree.

Perhaps Colbert should have eliminated her that long-ago night. Even some of the other Peacekeeper agents had agreed. But in the end, there had been no need. Preston had told neither her nor her mother anything about his double life. And despite his threats, he had not bequeathed either of them the secret documents he had sworn he possessed.

Caroline was safe. Safer now than she'd ever been in the fifteen years since her stepfather's death.

Chapter 2

When a Talbot County contractor who attended Lyle's church told Caroline that he would contribute his services for free, other church members, including a plumber and an electrician, volunteered their services to renovate the house in Baltimore. Most of the job would have to be done on Saturdays, but the workforce had turned out en masse last week, so things were moving along quicker than anticipated. This was their second Saturday, and the main focus today was stripping wallpaper and tearing out damaged Sheetrock.

While six men worked on the main project, ripping out the mildewed walls in the two basement rooms—one used as a wine cellar years ago and the other a former minigym—Caroline and three other women stripped old wallpaper off the upstairs bedrooms. As she and her friend Roz, who had been her assistant at the studio for the past three years, concentrated their efforts on Caroline's old bedroom, Mrs. Mabry and Allison Sims worked diligently in the master suite.

As she scraped away at the stubborn wallpaper, Caroline

tried to remember only the happy times she'd spent in this house, but try as she might, bad memories kept creeping into her thoughts. Her instincts had warned her to stay away, to put as much distance between herself and the past as she possibly could. But how could she let others work to restore the house while she stayed away? She couldn't, of course.

"Damn!" Roz cried suddenly, and stuck her index finger into her mouth.

"What's wrong?" From where she sat perched atop the ladder, a wet sponge in one hand and a metal scrapper in the other, Caroline glanced down at her friend, who had been attacking the stubborn paper along the baseboard.

Roz sucked on her finger, then removed it from her mouth and held it up for Caroline's inspection. "The stupid scrapper slipped and I nicked my finger on the edge."

Caroline laid aside her equipment and climbed down the ladder. "Here, let me take a look. I've got a first aid kit in my car, if you need a bandage."

"It's just a scratch, but you know how little cuts can hurt like the devil."

Caroline grabbed Roz's finger and inspected it thoroughly. "It's not even bleeding."

"Okay, so I'm a crybaby." As Roz shrugged, she rolled her eyes toward the ceiling.

Caroline adored Rozalin Turner. Few people understood their friendship, not even Lyle, who knew Caroline so well. But she realized that poor Lyle didn't know quite what to think of the flashy, loudmouthed Roz. She wasn't the type of woman he was used to being around—nothing like Aunt Dixie or Caroline or the good ladies of the Congregational Church. Roz wasn't a Southern lady, not by the widest stretch of the imagination. Roz was…well, Roz was Roz. A liberated free spirit.

Roz had come for an interview three years ago, answering an ad in the newspaper Caroline had placed for an "all-around personal assistant to a professional photographer."

Just one look at Roz and Caroline had thought how easily her appearance might offend some of the studio's wealthier clients. Then as now, her curly bleached-blond hair had been piled atop her head, giving her a sexy, tousled look. She wore shorts, a tank top, an ankle bracelet, three toe rings, six pairs of tiny gold hoops in her ears and a belly button ring. But within five minutes of talking to Roz that day, Caroline had realized that to counter the negative effect of her wild-child appearance, Roz possessed a flamboyant, exuberant personality that could charm the birds from the trees.

They had become fast friends and Roz was, without a doubt, the best assistant in the world. She had a way with adults and children alike. And although she tried to hide her softer side, the woman had a heart of pure gold. Almost everyone recognized that fact and appreciated Roz for the wonderful person she was—everyone except Lyle, who was put off by everything Roz said and did. In the beginning, Caroline had tried to bridge the vast gap between her cousin and her assistant, but had finally given up any hope that the two would ever be friends.

Roz's stomach growled. "Isn't it getting to be lunchtime?"

Caroline pulled her wristwatch from the pocket of her faded jeans to check the time. "It's only eleven. Lunch is at noon. Mrs. Mabry brought two big picnic baskets overflowing with food. Just hang on another hour and we'll have a feast."

Caroline surveyed her tall friend's slender curves. How was it possible for someone to eat like a stevedore and keep a model-thin figure? Every extra bite that went into Caroline's mouth wound up on her hips and thighs.

"Caroline!" Allison Sims cried as she rushed into the room. "Steve just called out to me from downstairs and said to come get you. They've found something in the basement they think you should see."

For a brief moment Caroline's heart stopped beating as an

odd thought flashed through her mind. *Had they found a dead body?* Don't be silly, she told herself. You're letting being in this house spook you. Your imagination is working overtime.

"What did they find? A treasure chest filled with diamonds and rubies?" Roz asked, her large, brown, Bette Davis eyes widening with speculation.

"He didn't say," Allison replied. "But he said for us to hurry."

Roz and Caroline joined Allison and the three met Mrs. Mabry on the landing, where she waited for them.

Steve stood at the bottom of the backstairs and motioned for them to come down, which they did. "Caroline, you're not going to believe this, but when we tore out that back wall in the wine cellar we found a...well, we think it's a secret passageway of some sort."

"You're kidding." Caroline's heart fluttered.

"And that's not all," Steve said.

"What do you mean, that's not all?" Roz asked.

"The guys are waiting for you." Steve grabbed Caroline's wrist. "You'll have to see this for yourself."

The image of Preston Shaw's body sprawled out on the study floor appeared in Caroline's mind, but she brushed it aside, telling herself not to be ridiculous. If there was a dead body downstairs, a skeleton hidden away for years, Steve wouldn't be acting so excited, now would he?

Since their plans included working on the house from early morning to late into the night every Saturday, Caroline had arranged to have the electricity turned on, as well as the water. The stairs leading down into the belly of the old house were well lit, plainly revealing several steps with rotting edges and a wall covered in an accumulation of spiderwebs. Steve brought her to a halt at the bottom of the stairs. The other five men, including Lyle, stood circling something as they gazed down toward the floor.

"She's here," Steve informed them.

Five heads popped up and five pair of eyes focused on Caroline, who stood frozen beside Steve.

Roz gave her a shove. "Go on. I'm dying to find out what they've discovered."

As Caroline moved toward the circle, the men separated and one by one moved away from the object resting on the concrete floor. She stared at the metal box, approximately twenty inches square, and immediately recognized it as some sort of small safe.

"Diamonds and rubies," Roz said.

"Or perhaps some stocks and bonds," Steve suggested.

"Could be cash money," Marty Johnson said.

"Might be nothing but an empty safe," Lyle told them.

"It's closed, and unless you can figure out the combination—" Steve looked directly at Caroline "—we may never find out what's inside."

"Why would you think I'd know the combination?" Caroline asked.

"Because of the initials on the safe," Steve said.

"What are you talking about?" Caroline walked closer to the safe and knelt in front of it.

"What were your stepfather's initials?" Lyle asked.

"P. W. S.," Caroline replied. "Preston Wakefield Shaw." The six men said "Hmm-mmm" in unison.

Caroline dropped to her knees and examined the safe. There, attached to the front, were tarnished silver letters— the initials P. W. S. "This must have belonged to Preston."

"Our guess is that he put this safe in the hidden passageway," Marty said. "Did he ever mention the passageway or the safe to you or your mother?"

Caroline shook her head. "Not to me, but perhaps to Mother. I wouldn't know about that." But as she denied knowledge of the passageway and the safe, a long-forgotten memory tried to resurface. The night he'd been killed, Preston and her mother had gotten into another of their many arguments and her mother had stormed out of the house, on her way to yet another party. Preston had noticed Caroline standing in her bedroom doorway and had come over to her.

"I'm sorry," he'd said. "Don't let the tension between Lenore and me upset you. I love your mother and you very much. Don't forget that."

He had kissed her on the forehead then, as he often did. Preston had given her the only paternal affection she'd ever known.

"I wanted to tell your mother something important, but she didn't have time to listen."

"I have time to listen," Caroline had said. So naive. Such a child.

He had placed his hand on her shoulder and said, "If anything happens—" He had cleared his throat and begun again. "I've put away something downstairs, something important. A sort of life insurance policy to protect your mother and you and Fletcher. But it's not something for you to worry about. I'll tell Lenore about it in the morning."

When Caroline felt someone shaking her shoulder, she glanced up and saw Roz staring at her. "What's the matter with you?" Roz asked. "You're acting like you're in a trance."

"No, I was just remembering a conversation I had with Preston."

"Something about the safe?" Lyle asked.

"I'm not sure. Maybe."

"Do you have any idea what the combination might be?" Steve asked.

"I haven't the foggiest," Caroline replied. "Isn't there another way to get into this thing?"

David dumped his suitcase on the floor beside the simple brass bed, unloosened his tie and removed his sport coat. He reached into the closet and withdrew a wooden hanger, draped the coat around it and returned the hanger to the closet. After whipping off his tie and tossing it in a nearby chair, he flopped down atop the neatly made bed. He had flown in from Miami this evening, after two weeks of playing private nursemaid to a Latin American businessman and his family who were vacationing at Disney World. Jack Parker had been scheduled for the assignment, but at the last minute a client who had used Jack on his previous trip to Egypt had specifically requested him to act as his bodyguard for a return visit. Ellen Denby, CEO of the Dundee Private Security and Investigation Agency, had given David a twelve-hour notice and promised him a bonus, if he'd take the job without giving her a hassle. It seemed a couple of the other agents had worked for this particular businessman in the past and refused to be stuck with his flirting wife and whiny kids, even for a day, let alone two weeks.

David stared up at the white ceiling in his bedroom. He'd done nothing except move in some brand-new furniture when he'd leased this Atlanta apartment six months ago. After taking the job as a Dundee bodyguard fifteen months ago, he'd rented a furnished one-bedroom place, which had suited him just fine. But once he realized he would probably be staying with the Dundee agency for many years to come, he started looking for something larger. With three bedrooms the apartment was spacious, giving him enough room to spread out and move around, which he liked. He hated cramped quarters. A result of having grown up out in the country.

The few people who had seen the inside of this place all said the same thing. That it looked as if he'd just moved in. No pictures on the walls. No personal objects scattered around here and there. A minimal amount of furniture. And not one memento that even hinted he'd had a life before he moved to Atlanta. And in a way, that assumption was correct. David Wolfe had no past beyond sixteen months ago, when he'd been released from a private hospital after enduring nearly a year of surgeries and rehabilitation.

As far as anyone knew—including the other Peacekeepers International agents—Aidan Colbert had died in an explosion in the Middle East. In fact, he *had* almost died. Ellison Penn had had Aidan flown directly to a private hospital where he had been admitted under the name John Doe. Orders were then issued to do everything possible to save the man's life. At this hospital no one asked questions, not even the highly skilled doctors who had performed a miracle and not only saved his life, but had put him back together. Almost as good as new. Except that now he had someone else's face. Not quite as good-looking as he'd once been, but at least his face wouldn't scare small children.

When he'd regained consciousness, after he'd been in the hospital for nearly three weeks, Ellison had paid him a visit and given him a precious gift. His freedom. A new identity. A new life. Few were ever allowed to leave Peacekeepers International. Few actually wanted to leave while they were still in their thirties. But Aidan Colbert had discovered that, after more than twelve years as an agent who was called upon to kill on demand, he had begun to lose his humanity. The killing, which he had once abhorred, had become simply a part of his job. Too easy. Too simple. Not enough regrets or maybe too many.

So, when he'd left the hospital, he had walked away as David Wolfe, with all the credentials to verify his identity to his new employer—the Dundee agency. Ellison had told him that he'd called in a favor from an old friend, Sam Dundee, the agency's retired owner, to get him a good job. As a bodyguard he laid his life on the line every day he was on an assignment, and the job required that he be prepared to kill, if necessary, to protect a client. But he wasn't tied to this job for life. He could leave the Dundee agency anytime he wanted to go. In fact, he already had enough money to last a lifetime—money that Aidan Colbert had earned as a Peacekeepers agent. Money that Ellison Penn had put through a ''laundering'' process before having it deposited in David Wolfe's account. The problem was, David didn't know *where* he'd go. What he'd do.

David unbuttoned his shirt and scratched his chest, then sat up and removed the wrinkled garment. As he rubbed his neck, he glanced down at his suitcase, then scooted to the edge of the bed, lifted the case and set it against the footboard. He unzipped the black carry-on and lifted the small rectangular velvet box out from under the stretchy security straps that held his clothes in place.

He'd gone straight from the airport to Leander & Smythe Jewelers. He had commissioned the gift two months ago and had inspected it thoroughly when he'd picked it up this evening. He flipped open the box. Beautiful. A pearl-and-diamond bracelet.

Next Thursday was Caroline's twenty-seventh birthday— June 21st. Over the years he had limited his gifts to birthdays and Christmases. The only exceptions had been her high school and college graduations. He would sign the card simply *David*, as he had done for the past fifteen years. And through his lawyer, she would send him a thank-you note. Sweet and sincere, scolding him for being too generous.

He couldn't help wondering if she would celebrate this year's birthday with Gavin Robbins. He sincerely hoped not. Why couldn't that cousin of hers—Reverend Lyle Jennings—introduce her to another nice young minister? Maybe a man of the cloth would prove himself worthy of Caroline.

David closed the lid and laid the jewelry case on the bedside table to his right. Last year he had sent her a pearl necklace and the year before teardrop pearl earrings. After she'd turned twenty-one, he had begun sending her birthstone jewelry.

Just once he would like to see her on her birthday—in the flesh, all dressed up for a night out and wearing the jewelry he'd bought for her. But he would never again see Caroline face-to-face. He, of all people, had no right to be a part of her life.

David removed his shirt, tossed it atop his silk tie on the chair and lay down on the bed. The minute he closed his eyes, an image of Caroline appeared. The picture taken at her mother's funeral. Surrounded by caring friends. Never alone. Never lonely. Thank God she had been able to put the night of Preston Shaw's death behind her and build a good life for herself. He had wanted that for her and had done everything within his power to see that from that horrible night forward everything was made right in her world. As right as he could make it. After all the heartache she had been through, she deserved nothing less.

"Caroline," he whispered softly. "My sweet Caroline."

They sat on the floor in the middle of the kitchen, Caroline and her friends, as she tried for the tenth time to open the safe by using a combination of numbers she thought might have had some meaning for Preston. She had tried his birthday, her mother's birthday and their anniversary. Then she'd tried various other number combinations. Their old phone number, or at least the first six digits. The zip code for that area of Baltimore didn't work, either. Now she was trying Fletcher's birthday.

Marty and Steve had carried the rather heavy metal safe up from the basement and Allison and Roz had wiped the black box with rags. For the past hour no work on the house had been done. Everyone was sure that something valuable would be found inside the safe. Why else would it have been hidden away?

Caroline tried the new numbers. Right. Left. Right. Nothing. The safe remained locked. A collective groan signaled the onlookers' disappointment.

"I give up," Caroline said. "Maybe we should just use a stick of dynamite."

Roz giggled. Mrs. Mabry gasped.

"Have you tried every important date in your stepfather's life?" Lyle asked.

"All that I know, including his birthday, mother's birthday and Fletcher's."

"What about your birthday?" Roz asked.

"Mine?" Why would Preston have chosen her birthday as the combination to this safe? Maybe because no one would have guessed that he would choose those numbers. "All right. What have I got to lose?"

Everyone watched with baited breath as once again Caroline turned the knob on the small personalized safe. She tried her birth date. Nothing happened. Then she tried it backward. Still nothing.

"It's no use," Caroline said, then just as she spoke, an idea hit her. Without saying another word, she spun the dial to eighteen, then to twenty-one and back around to eleven. Fletcher's birth date, February 18th. Her birthday, June 21st. And Preston and Lenore's wedding anniversary, the date that had joined two families. January 11th.

The safe opened, pretty as you please.

Chapter 3

"I can't believe it!" Caroline gasped as she turned the handle and opened the solid steel door.

The others hovered closely, and when they got a good look inside, a chorus of disappointed sighs permeated the kitchen.

"No diamonds and rubies," Roz said.

"It's empty." Steve frowned.

"No, it's not empty." Caroline reached inside and grasped the small manila envelope stuck in the back of the safe.

When she pulled the envelope out and held it up, she saw that her mother's name had been written plainly across the top, in a bold, distinctive hand that Caroline felt certain was Preston's. A tremor shivered along her nerve endings.

"Aren't you going to open it and see what's inside?" Roz asked.

With quivering fingers, Caroline ripped open the envelope, then reached in and pulled out a single sheet of stationery.

"It's only a letter," Allison said.

Yes, it *was* only a letter, but instinct cautioned Caroline as she unfolded the message Preston had written to her mother. What if it were something private, a love letter? They're both dead now, Caroline reminded herself. Reading something personal can't harm either of them.

November 30. The letter was dated only a few weeks before Preston's death.

My dearest Lenore,

If you are reading this, then my worst fears have been confirmed and they have killed me to keep me quiet. When you clear out this safe, you will find this letter and the enclosed key. Safeguard this key and the identical one in your possession. They unlock the means by which to keep our family safe, after I am gone. Look inside your heart for the proof of my love for you and the children. If they try to harm you or either of the children, do not hesitate to use what I have left you. This is my last and most precious gift to you, Fletcher and Caroline.

Your devoted husband,
Preston

"What does the letter say?" Roz asked.

Ignoring her friend's question, Caroline turned the envelope upside down and shook it. A key fell out and into her open palm.

"A key?" Lyle stared at the object Caroline held.

"A key to what?" Roz asked.

Caroline closed her fingers over the mysterious brass key. What *did* it open? It was such an ordinary-looking thing. Not fancy. Denoting nothing specific. "I have no idea what it unlocks."

"Didn't your stepfather say in his letter?" Lyle asked.

Caroline shook her head, then stood and held out the letter to her cousin. "I don't understand why Mother left this envelope in the safe. It's apparent that she knew about the hidden passageway and where Preston kept the safe. She must have cleaned the safe out before she moved from the house.''

"We didn't even see the envelope at first," Roz reminded Caroline. "Wasn't it stuck way in the back? It's possible your mother simply overlooked it."

Lyle scanned the letter hurriedly. "Oh, my, my. If what he says in this letter is true, then whoever killed Preston Shaw wasn't some thief trying to burglarize the house."

"If that letter is true, then my stepfather was assassinated," Caroline said. "And this key—" she opened her hand, lifted the key and held it up between her right thumb and forefinger as she stared at the object "—might unlock the identity of his murderer."

"I think you should call Fletcher right away," Lyle said. "He should know about this letter and the key. Perhaps he'll recognize the key and know what it unlocks."

David woke with a start, sweat drenching his naked chest. He rose from the bed, sat on the edge and placed his bare feet on the floor. He hadn't been plagued by that particular dream in a long time. Not in years. He supposed he had finally reached a point where he'd been able to reconcile his guilt with the knowledge that he had acted under orders and done the right thing. Raking his hand through his hair, he stood and walked across the room and into the bath. He left off the light so that only the dim glow of the moon coming through the window eliminated the complete darkness. He turned on the faucets, cupped his hands to catch the cold water and splashed his face, then lifted a towel from the nearby rack and blotted the cool, reviving moisture.

Preston Shaw had been dead nearly fifteen years. Why did he occasionally still dream about the night the man had died? Preston didn't just die, David reminded himself. *You killed him.* Acting under orders from Ellison Penn. The Peacekeepers' secret agents took care of their own, whether to protect them or to dispose of them. If one went rogue, which rarely happened, then he or she met a swift punishment at the hands of the organization itself. Shaw had been under suspicion for several months, but no one wanted to believe the charming man was capable of subversive activity that might threaten the United States. But despite Shaw's blue-blooded background and the respect he had earned over the years, in the end, he had proved himself dangerous to the very government he had sworn to serve.

Only a handful of people knew the truth—the wealthy, suave, sophisticated, gallant and greatly admired Preston Shaw had assassinated U.S. senator Herbert Harwell, under orders from a secret society of insurgent and highly dangerous powerful men known as the Loyalists Coalition. Preston Shaw had been a double agent.

And two months later, the Peacekeepers' special agent, Aidan Colbert, executed the traitor Shaw had proved himself to be by that one atrocious, deadly act.

David padded through the apartment, out into the large open space that combined a living room and kitchen. He plopped down in the black leather easy chair, hoisted his feet atop the matching, contemporary-style ottoman and picked up the TV remote control. At this time of night, when he suffered with bouts of insomnia, he usually watched reruns of black-and-white comedy shows from the fifties and sixties. He had a weakness for the *Andy Griffith Show* and *Father Knows Best,* both depicting an unobtainable ideal of family life. God knew his own family life had been the furthest thing possible from ideal. The horrors his father had inflicted on them might have come from an Edgar Allan Poe tale of torment and fear.

But that wasn't your past, your childhood, he reminded himself. That life belonged to Aidan Colbert. And Aidan Colbert is dead.

David clicked on the TV but kept the sound muted as he flipped through the various stations. As he zoomed from channel to channel, his gaze traveled back and forth from the television set to various other objects in the room. In his peripheral vision he caught a glimpse of the file folder containing the history of one Caroline Lenore McGuire.

What he needed to do was strike a match to the folder, to destroy it completely. Over the years, he had foolishly allowed Caroline to become an obsession. What had started out as a man wanting to help a child, to watch over her and keep her safe, had turned into more. Exactly what, he wasn't sure. But whatever it was, it wasn't good for him. If he'd been smart, he would have let his observation of Caroline's life end with Aidan Colbert's death.

David turned up the sound on the TV just enough to create a racket, then meandered into the kitchen and prowled around in the refrigerator. After retrieving a bottle of imported beer, he popped the cap and walked back into the living room. The program on TV was an old movie with a scene depicting a light snowfall in a metropolitan area.

His mind drifted swiftly back in time. It had started to snow that night, just as he left the Shaw house. Small flakes at first, but by the time he had returned to the Peacekeepers' headquarters, the ground was covered with a light dusting. The first snow of the season. Had Caroline ever realized it had snowed that night or had most of her memories from that time been banished along with the horror of finding her stepfather's body and coming face-to-face with his killer?

Tomorrow morning, he would telephone Ellison and tell him to end the surveillance of Caroline. In all these years no one had tried to harm her, so what was the point of the agency continuing to protect her? *Not the agency,* an inner voice reminded him. The only reason Ellison had continued keeping watch over her was as a personal favor to Aidan Colbert. But Aidan was dead and it was high time to allow his obsession with Caroline to die, too.

It had been three days since she had found her stepfather's cryptic message to her mother, perhaps the last letter he had ever written. And despite everyone's insistence that she not make too much out of what Preston had written, Caroline found that she simply could not let it go. She had discussed the matter with Lyle and Roz, but the minute they saw how upset the revelation made her, they suggested that perhaps Preston had been paranoid for some reason. After all, the police had thoroughly investigated her stepfather's death, hadn't they? And when she had shown the letter to Fletcher, he'd been shocked and at first as convinced as she that someone had murdered his father because he possessed information that could harm someone else. Perhaps someone very powerful. After all, Preston had belonged to a prestigious Washington organization and wielded a great deal of power as second in command at Peacekeepers International. Wasn't it possible that some foreign government had ordered his assassination? Fletcher had immediately contacted Gavin Robbins, who had, as a favor to Fletcher and her, gone straight to Ellison Penn, the head honcho of the Peacekeepers fifteen years ago and now.

"Ellison has assured me that Preston wasn't involved in anything dangerous for the Peacekeepers at the time of his death," Gavin had said. "And the organization conducted their own private investigation and came to the same conclusion as the police—a botched robbery had resulted in the murder of Preston Shaw."

"But what about this letter?" Caroline had waved the handwritten missive under Gavin's nose.

"Caroline, honey, why do you want to dredge up the past this way?" Gavin had asked. "Ellison and I both remember how odd Preston had been acting the last few weeks of his life. Ellison thought he was on the verge of a nervous breakdown because his marriage was in trouble. If Preston's mental state was shaky, then he very well could have become paranoid."

"I do remember the last couple of times I saw Father he

acted rather peculiar,'' Fletcher had said. ''He seemed distracted.''

''I believe that what you both have told me only adds to the evidence in this letter that Preston feared for his life.'' Caroline had paused, looked at the two men, saw skepticism on their faces and then continued, ''And he was afraid for Mother and Fletcher and me.''

''Even if what you suspect is true—and I don't think it is—after all these years, there would be no way to prove it,'' Gavin had said. ''No way to find Preston's murderer. Besides, why put yourself and Fletcher through hell all over again?''

''That's where you're wrong,'' she'd told him. ''I have a key that can unlock the evidence Preston left as an insurance policy to protect his family.''

''Perhaps Caroline is right.'' Fletcher had put his arm around her shoulders. ''If there's any way we can find Father's murderer, then I'm willing to relive that hell, to go back and rehash what happened that night.'' He had looked point-blank at Caroline. ''What about you, kiddo, do you think you can relive what happened? Maybe you'd better think about it before you open that old can of worms.''

Caroline had thought about it. All last night and all day today. And no matter how many times she went over things, she came to the same conclusion. She believed what Preston had written in the letter. Her stepfather had been the victim of cold-blooded, premeditated murder. The bearded man in the shadows had been an assassin. And she had practically witnessed the crime.

Then why didn't he kill you? She had asked herself this question a million times and had yet to come up with a logical answer. If he had been merely a burglar or if he had been a hired killer, why would he have balked at killing a child if it meant protecting himself?

If she could find the lock that the key opened, she might well find the answer to this question as well as all the others surrounding Preston's death. Unfortunately Fletcher didn't recognize the key and she had no earthly idea where to start looking.

Caroline liked parties well enough, although she preferred quiet evenings at home. She loved sitting on her back porch in the evenings partly because she had a great view. The waterfront footage, which was part of the five acres that had come as a package deal with the house, had been one of the reasons she had purchased the nineteenth-century ramshackle wooden structure and remodeled it four years ago. But this was one party invitation she couldn't decline. When Gavin had called to ask if he could be her escort to the birthday party Fletcher was giving for Brooke aboard his yacht, she was delighted that she wouldn't be attending the event alone. Even though she had decided not to date Gavin again, she'd thought one more date wouldn't matter. But after tonight she'd tell him that she couldn't see him again.

When Gavin and she had boarded the *Lenore,* he had pulled her aside and said, "You'll be the most beautiful woman here tonight."

Gavin was always complimenting her, saying all the things she supposed most women liked to hear, which made her wonder if Gavin's womanizer reputation wasn't well founded. They had been dating on and off for the past few months. More off than on, but that was her doing, not his. When she'd made it perfectly clear after their third date that she had no intention of hopping into bed with him, she had assumed he wouldn't be back. She'd been wrong. After that, his pursuit of her had intensified, as if he liked the challenge. Perhaps he believed he could wear her down with his gentlemanly charm. It was past time for her to be totally honest with him. She liked Gavin well enough, enjoyed his company occasionally and was inordinately flattered by his attention, but she wasn't in love with him and never would be. Call her old-fashioned, but she wanted to wait for love, wanted her first time to be with a very special man.

Caroline strolled along the deck of the *Lenore,* the motor yacht Fletcher had inherited from his father. Preston had purchased the yacht new when he'd married Lenore and took her on a honeymoon cruise in the Caribbean. As a child Caroline had loved the three summer vacation trips aboard the wide-beam cruiser. Fletcher had kept the yacht in perfect condition, and the vessel maintained the original cockpit and gorgeous oak interior throughout. Below were three staterooms with their own baths and the galley up layout offered a deck-level powder room, too.

Fletcher kept the yacht anchored at the marina and often loaned the boat to friends for excursions in the bay. Much like his father before him, Fletcher was known to be generous to those nearest and dearest to him.

A balmy spring breeze swept across the deck, caressing Caroline's hair. As the evening had worn on, she'd grown tired of dancing, first with Gavin, then later with Fletcher and several of his friends, each progressive dance partner just a little drunker than the one before him. She had lost track of Gavin in the throng of well-wishers, about thirty minutes ago, shortly after Brooke had blown out the candles on her enormous birthday cake and ripped into the stack of elaborately decorated gifts. Caroline was more than ready to head back to St. Michaels right now and wished she could locate her date. As she had made her way along the congested deck, she had asked people she knew if they'd seen Gavin, but no one seemed to have any idea where he was. She couldn't help wondering if he'd found some willing female and was making use of one of the staterooms.

Why on earth would you continue dating a man you thought capable of having sex with another woman while on a date with you? she asked herself. *Because you didn't want to come to this party alone, that's why.*

As Caroline tried to find a less-congested area on the yacht

so she could at least breathe without smelling liquor or cigarettes, her mind filled with thoughts of her own upcoming
birthday. She had never had a gala celebration like the one
Fletcher was hosting for Brooke, but since she'd turned thirteen, her birthdays had been special events. Made special by
one person. One man. *David.*

Each year a gift. A signed card. A birthday cake delivered
by a local bakery. And balloons equal in number to her age.
Since that first year when she had felt so alone, after her
mother had sent her to live with Aunt Dixie and Lyle, she
had never again dreaded a birthday. Because of David's generosity.

She longed to meet her benefactor, but after years of having her request to meet with him and thank him personally
denied by his attorney, Caroline had finally accepted the fact
that for some reason known only to him, David did not want
the two of them to ever meet. Over time she had played out
more than one scenario in her mind. Perhaps he was very
ugly and even deformed—a true beast of a man. Or maybe
he was married and thought his wife might be jealous of all
he had done for an old friend's daughter. Whatever the reason, David had become a mystery she dreamed of one day
solving. She could not deny that she had built his image into
one of a knight in shining armor, someone who would willingly slay dragons for her.

She couldn't explain to anyone why she loved a man she'd
never met, why she believed that for the past fifteen years
David had been the one constant in her life, the only adult
who had never betrayed her, never left her, never stopped
loving her. As a child she had clung to his phantom image,
thinking of him as a substitute father, a protector and a benefactor. Because she had lost her own father and two step-
fathers, and then her mother had abandoned her, she had
transferred her desperate need for these lost parental figures
and loved David as if he had truly been in her life.

David's presence in her life, albeit from afar, had been like a light at the end of a lonely tunnel and she had developed an attachment to his kindness when she had felt herself to be nothing more than an unloved and unwanted child. Even Aunt Dixie's love and concern had not been enough to fill the void she had felt. But somehow knowing that David cared, that David would always be there for her, he had in an almost miraculous way made her feel less alone, less abandoned, less unloved.

She wasn't quite sure when her affections for David had begun to change, to alter from a child's adoration to a woman's admiration and respect. For many years now, her dearest wish had been to meet this special man who had cared so greatly for her all her life. And she couldn't deny that in her heart of hearts, she fantasized that David would become a real part of her life.

Suddenly someone near her gasped. "We're moving."

Another said, "I didn't know Fletcher was going to give us a trip out into the bay as a finale for Brooke's party."

Caroline sighed and shook her head. Now she was stuck aboard, probably until the wee hours of the morning. She continued making her way around the deck, finding it less crowded toward the aft side. She walked past a handful of couples wrapped in each other's arms as the *Lenore* left the dock. At last she was alone, with only the sea breeze around her and the starry sky overhead. She had never been a party girl, not even as a teenager, and now less than ever. She much preferred small, simple dinners at home with a few well-chosen friends. At this precise moment, she would much rather be sitting on her back porch, barefoot and in a pair of tattered old shorts, than dressed to the nines and bored out of her mind.

Suddenly, without any warning, someone came up behind Caroline. She sensed the hovering body before she actually felt it as it pressed against her back. Was it Gavin? Had he finally come looking for her? As she started to turn around, she found herself trapped, held in place by the man's big arm, which quickly draped around her. She opened her mouth to protest, but before she could make a sound, a foul-smelling rag covered her nose and mouth. She whimpered as her head began to spin. Overwhelmed by complete helplessness, she quickly drifted off into a semiconscious state. The very last thing her fuzzy brain registered was the feeling of being lifted. Raised up into the air and over the railing. Then released.

Floating. Down. Down. Down. And into the water.

Chapter 4

David had no idea why Sam Dundee had summoned him to his island home, but David's gut instincts warned him of trouble. He had met the owner of Dundee Private Security and Investigation Agency the first day he'd come to work there. The big boss had flown into Atlanta to personally introduce his newest agent to Dundee's CEO, Ellen Denby, who normally did the hiring and firing. David had gotten this job because Ellison Penn knew Dundee personally and had called in a favor. So maybe Ellison's involvement with Dundee was the reason David felt so uneasy as he followed along behind Manton, the seven-foot mahogany-skinned guardian of Dundee's private island retreat. David had realized almost instantly that the giant of a man was mute, but his keen black eyes seemed to look into David's very soul. The last thing David wanted was someone seeing past the David Wolfe facade and finding Aidan Colbert.

When they reached the porch of the huge raised cottage that sat perched atop a small hill, which gave the house a magnificent view of the gulf, Manton opened the door and

held it for David. Once inside, David was greeted by Sam
Dundee himself, who apparently had been waiting for him in
the foyer.

Sam offered his hand. "I hope the boat ride from Biloxi
wasn't too bad. The waters are a bit choppy this morning."

David exchanged a handshake with the big man. Although
they were close in height, Sam had the build of a football
linebacker, with massive shoulders and arms.

"The boat ride was fine," David replied.

"Join me in the den," Sam said. "I have another guest
who came in late last night and he's anxious to speak to
you."

David's stomach tightened. Another guest? He vanquished
several thoughts and settled on one. Ellison Penn. There was
no one else it could be. But why would Ellison risk contacting him personally? They had both broken several cardinal
Peacekeepers' rules in order to bury Aidan Colbert and res-
urrect him as David Wolfe two and a half years ago.

Sam led David to the den, which was Caribbean light and
airy. Cream walls. Massive windows, open to catch the
spring breeze and illuminate with morning sunlight. Overstuffed chairs and sofa. An ornately carved blond oak desk,
placed in front of floor-to-ceiling bookshelves, dominated the
room. Behind the desk, in the large cream leather swivel
chair sat Ellison Penn. Ellison's attire of tan slacks and navy-
blue short-sleeved shirt took David aback; he didn't think
he'd ever seen the white-haired gentleman in casual clothes
before. The man's friendly gray eyes were as deceptive as
his healthy tanned face and gregarious smile. Ellison Penn
looked like any affluent American businessman. One would
assume this seventy-year-old gentleman incapable of harming
a fly. But David knew better. This grandfatherly-looking
man, as the commander of the secret squad of Peacekeepers
agents, had over a period of twenty years ordered the assassination of several dozen people.

Ellison rose to his full six-foot height. "Good to see you,

Mr. Wolfe. I appreciate your meeting me on such short notice.''

David stared at his former boss, a man who had served as his mentor for many years. Ellison held a thin file folder in his hand. ''Mr. Penn.'' David nodded.

''I'll leave y'all alone.'' Standing in the doorway, Sam glanced at Ellison and then at David. ''Lunch will be in an hour. Jeannie and I would be pleased if both of you would join us before Mr. Wolfe returns to Biloxi this afternoon.''

''We'd be honored to join you and your lovely wife,'' Ellison said.

Sam closed the den door, sealing the two men together within the privacy of the room.

Inclining his head toward the door, David said, ''He doesn't know who I am...or rather who I was, does he?''

''No one knows, except the two of us. Safer that way.'' Ellison rounded the side of the desk and came toward David. ''I trust Sam implicitly, but he's safer not knowing your true identity.''

''Why are you here?'' David asked. ''Or better yet, why did you have me summoned here?''

''Let's sit.'' Ellison indicated the sofa.

Ellison took a seat, laid the file folder on his lap and relaxed against the enormous cushions. Sitting on the opposite end of the sofa, David stared inquisitively at the file folder.

''As you know, Caroline McGuire inherited the house on Sheffield Street in Baltimore when her mother died,'' Ellison said.

David nodded but remained silent. What was he supposed to say? *Yes, I well remember that house, that December night and what transpired between Caroline's stepfather and me.*

''Unknown to us, the house had a hidden corridor in the basement.'' Ellison ran his fingertips around the edge of the folder. ''It was probably constructed by the original builder, but there are no blueprints on record for the old house, so there's no way of knowing for sure.'' Ellison kept his gaze fixed on the folder. "When Caroline and members of her cousin Lyle's church were working in the basement, they found the hidden passageway and a small, portable safe that Preston had put there."

Now Ellison had gained his attention. David's heartbeat accelerated. A secret passageway? A hidden safe? "Were they able to open the safe?"

Ellison nodded. "Yes, Caroline finally figured out the combination and was able to open the safe."

"I assume there was something inside—something important. Otherwise you wouldn't be here."

"The safe was empty—" Ellison paused for effect "—except for an envelope. And inside that envelope was a letter Preston had written to his wife, Lenore." Ellison lifted the folder and handed it to David. "We didn't get our hands on the original, so this is only Gavin Robbins's account of the letter that Caroline showed him."

David flipped open the folder, scanned the typed page and cursed under his breath. "Goddammit!"

"Somewhere out there Preston Shaw left some damning evidence against some very important people," Ellison said. "People who have, for the past fifteen years, thought they were safe. Leaders of the Loyalists Coalition who ordered Preston to kill Senator Harwell."

"How did Caroline react to the letter? And Fletcher Shaw? What did he have to say?"

"Gavin tried to convince them to let the matter drop. He told them that after all these years—"

"Let me guess…" David bounded off the sofa, slammed the folder against the palm of his hand and glared point-blank at Ellison. "Caroline is determined to find out what the key unlocks. She wants to find out who killed her stepfather and why."

"Since she discovered the letter and the key, she's been relentless in pursuing the search." Ellison rose to his feet. "She's tried the locks on every door in the house on Sheffield

Street, but to no avail. And she is in the process of contacting everyone who ever knew Preston. She even telephoned me, but I was able to avoid taking her call.''

"Sooner or later, you'll have to talk to her.'' Years ago David had feared something like this would happen. During the weeks and months directly following Preston Shaw's death, the Peacekeepers had kept a vigilant watch over Shaw's wife, son and stepdaughter. Then when nothing had materialized, no evidence to point the finger at Shaw's accomplices in the Senator Herbert Harwell assassination scheme, David had hoped that Caroline was safe. That she would always be safe. "If these people find out she has a key that will unlock the evidence against them, then Caroline is in danger. You'll have to keep her under surveillance…make sure she's—'' The look in Ellison's eyes, a mixture of regret and sadness, warned David of bad news. "What's happened? Is Caroline all right?'' David's heartbeat roared in his ears.

Ellison grasped David's arm, manacling his biceps through the material of his shirt. "While Caroline was attending a party aboard Fletcher Shaw's yacht, someone chloroformed her and dumped her into the bay.''

Every muscle in David's body tensed. Every nerve screamed. He jerked free of Ellison's grip, narrowed his gaze and glared at the bearer of evil tidings. "Is she…?'' He couldn't bring himself to say the word. The file folder slipped from his hand and sailed smoothly down to the floor.

"She's alive,'' Ellison said. "No thanks to our would-be assassin, however. If his plan had worked, Caroline's body might not ever have been found. It would have probably been hours before anyone aboard the yacht discovered her missing.''

"She's alive?'' David released the breath he'd been holding. "Does that mean she's all right?''

"That means she's fine and recuperating at home after a brief stay in the hospital. And she's understandably unnerved.'' Ellison shook his head. "I'm afraid the police got involved, but they aren't overly concerned. Considering the fact that the yacht was filled with drunken partygoers, they assume Caroline had been drinking and might have accidentally fallen overboard.''

"If you had someone watching her, why didn't—"

"It seems that Gavin got sidetracked by a rather luscious blonde,'' Ellison admitted sheepishly. "Not conduct I approve of in any of my agents, but as you know, Gavin has a weakness for the ladies.''

"And this is the man who was only recently promoted to the number two position at Peacekeepers?" David wanted to smash something—anything—but preferably Gavin Robbins's face! "Caroline needs a twenty-four-hours-a-day bodyguard. They've already tried to kill her once to stop her from using the key. They'll try again and again, if necessary, until they put a stop to her investigating.''

"You're right, on both counts," Ellison agreed. "These people—whoever they are—will continue their efforts to stop her permanently. Therefore, she needs constant protection.''

"We can dispatch someone from Dundee's... Ah... Has Sam already chosen someone to...?''

"Fletcher Shaw got in touch with his lawyer and told him to find the premier agency in the country and request their best bodyguard for his stepsister, so naturally the lawyer recommended Dundee's. I made a recommendation to Sam last night. That's why he telephoned you and requested your presence here today.''

"I'm afraid I don't understand.''

"I don't know of a man on earth who has a bigger stake in protecting Caroline McGuire than you do." Ellison clamped his hand down on David's shoulder.

David swallowed hard. "No. Not me.'' Surely Ellison wasn't suggesting that he act as Caroline's bodyguard. The idea was out of the question. There could be no face-to-face contact with Caroline. Not ever. *You were ordered not to go near her. You were allowed to be her caretaker only from a distance.*

"Aidan Colbert is dead," Ellison said. "There is no connection between David Wolfe and him."

"It would be wrong for me to take this assignment."

"I thought you'd jump at the chance. You've acted as her secret guardian, her protector, her keeper for nearly fifteen years." Ellison squeezed David's shoulder. "Tell me that you believe there's another man who is capable of keeping watch over Caroline the way you can. Tell me that everything within you isn't chomping at the bit to go to her side as quickly as possible." Ellison released his hold on David and met his gaze. "This is your chance for redemption."

"Do you think I need redemption?"

Ellison held up his hand in a stop gesture. "Don't try to convince me that you haven't been eaten alive with guilt ever since that night. Do you think I don't know what it did to you having to confront Caroline only moments after you had killed her stepfather?"

Ellison was right and he damn well knew it. Of all the assignments Aidan Colbert had completed as a Peacekeeper none had tormented him the way that first assassination had. There had been no doubt in his mind that he had done the right thing, that Preston Shaw had to be eliminated. In that instance as in many that had followed, he had done his duty, had lived by the Peacekeepers' code, and his actions were those of an honorable man doing a dirty job for his country. Innocent people sometimes got in the way and were hurt or killed. But not by him. Never by him. Only that one time when the innocent victim had been Caroline McGuire. Memories of her still haunted him. It was her little cherubic face he saw in his nightmares, that terrified look in her eyes. The look of a child who knew death awaited her. He had seen that fear in another child's eyes once, long before the night of Preston Shaw's execution. When he had recognized the terror in Caroline's eyes, her face had been overlaid with the features of another. His little brother Brendan.

"Are you all right?" Ellison asked.

"What?" David blinked several times, bringing himself out of a bad place, an evil moment from his childhood that plagued him to this day. "Yes, I'm all right. And yes, I'll take the job as Caroline's bodyguard. You're right about me. You know that I would die before I'd let anyone harm her."

"Yes, I'm sure you would." Ellison reached down and picked up the file folder from the floor. "I'll have Sam contact Fletcher Shaw and let him know that a Dundee agent named David Wolfe will arrive in St. Michaels tonight. Sam has arranged for Matt O'Brien to fly you straight from Biloxi to Maryland. And Jack Parker is on standby to join you, if you need backup later on."

"You were awfully sure I'd accept this job."

"My boy, you must remember that I'm the man who has worked as your accomplice in taking care of Caroline all these years. I, better than anyone, know what she represents to you and exactly to what extent you would go to keep her safe."

"If it means breaking every rule in the book, I'll do it," David said in a calm, controlled manner. "Know this from the start—Caroline's well-being comes first, before anyone or anything else. And that includes the Peacekeepers."

Ellison nodded. "While you're guarding Caroline, you'll also be investigating Preston Shaw's death along with her. The key she has holds the one and only possible means of finding any evidence as to who Preston's cohorts were. Those men still exist and have continued their work, even if somewhat less obviously. With enough proof, we could put those men in jail where they belong and eliminate an ongoing threat to this country."

"You make sure I get what I want and I'll do my best to help the Peacekeepers get what they want." David offered Ellison his hand.

"You have a deal." The two men sealed their pact with a powerful handshake.

Caroline felt trapped inside her own home and it was a feeling she detested. Since her release from the hospital yesterday, she had been surrounded by well-meaning friends. Roz, Brooke, Lyle and Fletcher had all four spent the night, and at least two of them had been with her throughout the day. Brooke's parents, Oliver and Eileen Harper, had stopped by while she'd been in the hospital and had driven down from Baltimore earlier today. Eileen had even sent a beautiful bouquet of get-well flowers. Then Gavin had shown up about an hour ago and joined the fearless foursome. Now the five of them sat around in her living room, each one hovering like a mother bird waiting for her chick to hatch. As much as she enjoyed their company and appreciated their concern, she was accustomed to the peace and quiet of living alone. But for some undetermined amount of time, she would have to forego her privacy and greatly treasured solitude. Once the bodyguard Fletcher had hired for her arrived, she wouldn't be alone again. Someone would be at her side, day and night. Watching her. Protecting her from harm.

"What time is this bodyguard supposed to arrive?" Brooke asked.

"He should be here within the next half hour," Fletcher said. "I spoke to the CEO of Dundee's and was assured that they're sending one of their top agents."

"What's his name?" Gavin asked.

"Wolfe," Fletcher replied. "I don't know if that's a first or last name."

"If he turns out to be a big, gorgeous hunk, I may move in with you," Roz said.

Lyle gave Roz a condemning stare. "Is that all you think about, Ms. Turner, men and sex?"

Roz's cheeks flamed red, but she kept her temper in check

as she skewered Lyle with her gaze. "Unlike you, *Reverend,* some of us actually enjoy the sins of the flesh."

"You make that more than obvious," Lyle countered. "Most people have the decency not to flaunt their sins in front of the world. But you seem to have no qualms—"

Roz got right up in Lyle's face, which immediately stopped his condemnation. "Now, you listen here you Bible-thumping, pulpit-spouting—"

"That's enough!" Caroline put one arm around Roz's shoulders and the other around Lyle's, then adeptly separated the two warring parties. "I wish that just once the two of you could be in the same room together without going for the jugular."

"If you ask me, they've got the hots for each other," Brooke said. "If they'd just hop in the sack and get it over with—"

"You're crazy if you think I'd be interested in a holier-than-thou *virgin,*" Roz said, putting special emphasis on the last word. "I like my men rough, tough and experienced."

"I can assure you, Ms. Turner, that you're safe from me." Lyle turned and stormed out of the room.

"Now, look what you two have done." Caroline glowered at Roz and then at Brooke. "You know how sensitive Lyle is."

"I'm sorry," Brooke said. "Lyle is such an easy target, but I forget how serious-minded he is."

"The man can't take a joke," Roz complained, then forced a smile as she wrapped her arm around Caroline's waist. "I shouldn't have gotten into an argument with him. Not tonight of all nights. Lyle and I were able to act civilly toward each other when you were in the hospital, so there's no reason we can't continue to be civil toward each other. The last thing you need is having your cousin and your best friend at each other's throats."

"And I thought I was Caroline's best friend," Brooke said, with a half-joking pout on her lips.

"All of you are my friends," Caroline said. "My dear friends. And although having y'all here is driving me nuts, it's also distracting me from thinking about what happened the night before last on Fletcher's yacht."

"I can't believe someone actually chloroformed you and threw you overboard," Fletcher said. "If I'd thought that damn key would put your life in danger, I'd have insisted you toss it into the bay. I'd rather never know what the key opens if searching for it puts your life at risk."

"Don't you see? Someone doesn't want us to find out what this key opens." Caroline lifted the key, which she had slipped onto a gold chain and placed around her neck. "I truly believe that when we find what the key opens, we'll find proof of who killed Preston and why."

"Perhaps you should give Fletcher the key," Gavin said. "After all, Preston was his father, and if anyone has the right to unearth any secret truth about his murderer, then Fletcher does."

"I don't need the damn key," Fletcher said. "However, my dear sister, I think you should hand the thing over to this fellow Wolfe. His agency, Dundee's, is going to be working with him to investigate Father's death."

"Do you think that's wise?" Gavin asked. "The bigger the stink you stir, the more danger there is bound to be for Caroline."

"I'm not going to back down," Caroline said. "Being almost drowned had the adverse effect on me from what my would-be killer intended. Not only am I still alive, but I'm more determined than ever to find what the key unlocks and retrieve whatever evidence there is against Preston's killer."

The soft tinkle of the doorbell chimed throughout the house. Caroline froze for an instant. All eyes turned toward the foyer.

"Shall I go to the door?" Fletcher asked. "It's probably your bodyguard, Mr. Wolfe."

"Why don't we go together?" Caroline suggested.

Fletcher nodded and with a magnanimous sweep of his hand indicated for her to precede him. By the time Fletcher and she reached the foyer, Roz, Brooke and Gavin were only a few steps behind; then Lyle came out of the room across the hall and halted several feet away from the others. Caroline grasped the brass handle and opened the door.

She wasn't quite sure what she'd been expecting, but the man standing on her front porch wasn't it. He was tall, broad-shouldered and lean, with a bronze tan, thick dark blond hair and tinted aviator glasses that hid his eyes. He wore a cream-colored sport coat and a teal-blue shirt, casually elegant attire that a man with money might wear to project both a fashionable and yet masculine image. He wasn't handsome, but he was devastatingly attractive, in a self-assured way that professed to the world he was a man to be reckoned with. A shiver of apprehension fluttered in Caroline's stomach. She heard an indrawn breath and assumed it came from Brooke. Then a low, soft whistle told her that Roz had just made a comment.

"I'm Wolfe," the man said, his voice dark and rich and distinctively Southern, as he removed his sunglasses and slid them into his pocket.

"Won't you come in, Mr. Wolfe. We've been expecting you. I'm Caroline McGuire."

When she held out her hand, he simply stared at it for endless seconds, then encompassed it within his own huge hand. The moment they touched, a current passed between them. A shocking sensation of awareness. And when their gazes met, Caroline gasped. She had never seen such cold eyes, moss green and void of any emotion.

"Hello, Caroline," he said.

Startled by her reaction to the stranger, Caroline snatched her hand away but couldn't stop looking directly at him in the same way he continued staring at her. Did he feel it, too? she wondered. That odd sense of recognition, as if she had known this stranger all her life, perhaps even in a dozen other lifetimes?

Chapter 5

He couldn't take his eyes off her. She was more lovely than any picture he'd ever seen of her. This was Caroline—his Caroline. He wasn't sure exactly when he'd begun to think of her that way. It had been a gradual thing, taking place so imperceptibly that he had no way of pinpointing the precise moment that his thoughts of her had become possessive. Perhaps if he'd had a family of his own, his feelings for Caroline wouldn't have taken on such monumental proportions. Aidan Colbert had had a few distant relatives, but no real family to speak of, and David Wolfe had no one. There were no parents, no siblings, no wife and no children. Only Caroline.

When he noticed the flush on her cheeks and the way she suddenly broke eye contact, Wolfe realized he had been staring at her for longer than was socially acceptable. In the future, he would have to be careful and take advantage of unguarded moments, when no one else was around, to drink his fill of her. He wondered if a thousand lifetimes would be enough.

Someone cleared his throat. Wolfe glanced behind Caroline to where four people stood guard over her, each inspecting him thoroughly. The two men glowered at him as if they didn't quite trust him. The two women surveyed him from head to toe as if he were an item up for auction. He recognized all four people from photos that had been included in the packet Sam Dundee had given him this afternoon before he'd left Le Bijou Bleu, Dundee's private island. The dossier contained brief bios and photographs of the people most important in Caroline's life.

Fletcher Shaw came forward and extended his hand to Wolfe. He sized up the handsome young man quickly as he reached out to accept his gesture of greeting. They were about the same height, but Shaw was more slender, his handshake weaker. Caroline's stepbrother possessed an air of superiority, one that declared without words that he was the master and considered David the servant.

"Fletcher Shaw."

"Wolfe." He looked directly into Fletcher's blue eyes and noted just a hint of uncertainty there. Most of his adult life he'd had that effect on other men. A wariness they tried to disguise, but couldn't. A primitive fear that admitted a more dominant male had just arrived on the scene.

"I'm the one who hired you," Fletcher said. "Ms. McGuire is my stepsister and I'm quite concerned about her welfare. I've been assured that you're one of the best at what you do. I want only the best for Caroline."

So do I, Wolfe thought. *That's all I've ever wanted.* "I can assure you, Mr. Shaw, that Ms. McGuire's safety is my top priority. No one is going to get to her, except through me."

"Caroline, you lucky girl, you." Tall, fashion-model elegant, Brooke Harper sauntered across the foyer, all the while sizing up Wolfe, flirting subtly as she held out her hand. "I'm Brooke Harper, Caroline's oldest and dearest friend." She sighed dramatically when Wolfe shook her hand. She held on just a fraction too long, then when Fletcher moved to her side, she laughed and said, "Fletch, darling, if I'm ever in danger, will you hire me a Dundee bodyguard like Mr. Wolfe?"

Before Fletcher could respond, Roz rushed forward. "Hi. I'm Rozalin Turner. Since I'm Caroline's assistant, I'm sure we'll be seeing a great deal of each other."

"Ms. Turner." Wolfe acknowledged her presence by looking directly at her.

Caroline motioned for the other man, who hadn't moved since Wolfe entered the foyer, to come to her. "This is my cousin, Reverend Lyle Jennings."

Surprisingly the short, stocky reverend's handshake had more power than Shaw's, and the wariness Wolfe saw in the man's eyes had more to do with concern over Caroline than with masculine dominance. He liked Lyle on sight, which made him second-guess his own judgment. He seldom liked anyone immediately. But reason told him that his knowledge of Lyle Jennings's place in Caroline's heart preconditioned him to like the man who truly was a brother to her.

"Mr. Wolfe, I'm very glad you're here," Lyle said.

Wolfe nodded, then looked past the others to where a third man stood, arms crossed over his chest and his dark, hooded eyes focused on Wolfe. The last time he'd seen Gavin Robbins was a few days before Aidan Colbert had left the country on his final Peacekeepers assignment. Although the two had worked together for nearly thirteen years, neither had ever moved beyond their initial hostility toward each other. David wondered what Gavin would do if he realized Aidan Colbert had become David Wolfe. Not that there was any reason Gavin would recognize him. All resemblance to Aidan Colbert was practically gone.

Caroline turned around and smiled at Gavin. "Come meet Mr. Wolfe," she said.

Gavin made no move to approach. Instead he remained aloof, deliberately setting himself apart from everyone else. "Fletch tells us that you come highly recommended. I think you should know that I have every intention of checking out your credentials.''

Caroline gave Gavin a disapproving look, apparently appalled by his bold rudeness. "I'm certain that's not necessary.''

"On the contrary," Wolfe said. "If I were your boyfriend, I'd want to make sure the man who was to be at your side day and night was someone trustworthy.''

Brooke and Roz giggled. Fletch coughed and cleared his throat. Lyle glanced at Caroline as if wanting to gauge her reaction.

Caroline walked over and closed the still-open front door. "I was just about to prepare some coffee, Mr. Wolfe. Won't you join us in the living room?''

"Thank you," Wolfe replied. "But if you don't mind ending this evening with your friends a bit early, I'd like to familiarize myself with your house and the grounds tonight and go over a few rules with you that can't wait until morning.''

"Oh, I see." Caroline stared at him strangely, as if she didn't quite comprehend the necessity of such discourteous haste. He feared that Caroline would find his abrupt and oftentimes tactless actions disturbing. One of the many things he knew about her was her penchant for good manners. Something Dixie Jennings had drilled into her as a girl.

"Well, I guess we've been asked to leave," Fletcher said, obviously not pleased by Wolfe's take-charge attitude.

"You've hired me to do a job," Wolfe reminded him. "From this moment on, everything I do will have one objective—to protect Ms. McGuire.''

"Yes, of course." Fletcher hugged Caroline, then glanced at Brooke. "Get your things, darling, and we'll leave Caroline in Mr. Wolfe's capable hands.''

"I'm sorry we have to end our lovely evening so early," Caroline said as she scurried around after her guests while they prepared to depart.

Wolfe stood in the foyer, waiting and watching, while she shared hugs and kisses and goodbye waves with her friends. Gavin was the last to leave, but when he did go, he made a production of planting a rather intense kiss on Caroline's lips. Every ounce of Wolfe's willpower came into play at that precise moment, stopping him from jerking the cocky Robbins away from Caroline and forcefully tossing him out into the yard. The very second that the last car left the driveway, she turned to Wolfe, a look of annoyance on her face.

"Was that necessary?" she asked.

"I apologize if I was rude," he said. "But good manners aren't a priority in my business." He glanced around the foyer, taking note of the rooms to the right and left and the staircase that led up to the second level of the roomy clapboard house. "Familiarizing myself with your surroundings as quickly as possible will enable me to do my job more efficiently. I'll need to inspect the house from top to bottom, cover the grounds, check out your security system and do the same thing at your studio downtown."

"I don't have a security system here at the house," she said.

"Yes, I know. One is being installed first thing tomorrow. I'll check out the one at your studio in the morning and then the newly installed one here tomorrow evening."

"I see."

He turned to her and forced himself to avoid direct eye contact. "You won't leave this house, not even to go outside for a walk, without me. Before you get in your car, I'll inspect it. At work and at home, I'll be at your side. I'll require a bedroom directly across from yours and ask that you sleep with your door open…or we can arrange for a cot to be put in your room."

"I prepared the bedroom across the hall from mine."

Wolfe nodded. "I realize this isn't easy for you, Ms. McGuire. But a few minor changes in your lifestyle can help me keep you safe. I've already arranged not only for a security system to be installed at your home tomorrow, but as a precaution, the locks on your doors will also be changed.''

"That seems rather drastic, doesn't it?''

"Someone tried to kill you and will, more than likely, try again. I will do whatever is necessary to make sure any future attempts fail. From this moment until the day you are no longer in danger, my only purpose will be to protect you.''

Caroline's mouth opened on a silent gasp, as if she were startled by his vehement declaration. Did she think he had overstepped his bounds? he wondered. Had what he'd said or the way he'd said it made her suspicious of his motives?

Wolfe cleared his throat. "As a professional bodyguard, it's my duty to put your welfare above everything else.''

"I understand.'' She glanced toward the closed front door. "Do you have a suitcase in your car?''

"I came from the airport in a taxi,'' he told her. "My bag is on your porch.''

"If you'll get it, I'll show you upstairs to your room, then I'll give you a tour of the house. It will be easier to show you around outside in the morning when it's daylight.''

"That will be fine.''

"Mr. Wolfe…I'm going to be honest with you. I feel awkward having you living here in my house. I realize that you're a professional, but you're…you're—''

"A man?''

"Well, yes.''

"I will do my utmost not to invade your privacy. I won't come into the bathroom with you or enter your bedroom without knocking, unless there's potential danger involved. However, I'm afraid that my being with you might cramp your love life a bit. I'll have to tag along on all your dates.''

"Believe me, you won't be cramping my love life.'' Caroline sighed. "I'm not seeing anyone in particular right now.''

"Is that right? Hmm-mmm…what about Gavin Robbins?''

Caroline laughed. Wolfe loved the sound. He'd never

heard her laugh before, never heard the sound of her voice. Never been close enough to reach out and touch her. And he realized that he was finding the sight and sound and scent of her intoxicating.

"I won't be dating Mr. Robbins again."

"Good."

She lifted her eyebrows and stared at Wolfe.

"Your not dating anyone simplifies my job as your body-guard."

"Oh. Yes, of course." She glanced toward the front door. "Please, get your bag and I'll show you upstairs."

Wolfe followed her instructions, retrieved his black vinyl bag, closed and locked the front door and followed his client up the stairs. He tried not to focus on her body as she moved with such easy grace, taking the steps slowly, her round hips swaying to her body's own particular rhythm. She wore gray cotton slacks and an oversize white blouse that hung to mid-thigh. Her only jewelry, other than a simple wristwatch, was a gold chain that disappeared inside her shirt and a pair of small pearl-and-diamond ear studs. He recognized the earrings immediately and his chest tightened. A gift for her twenty-first birthday from her illusive benefactor, David.

When they reached the landing, Caroline turned abruptly and almost collided with Wolfe. Gasping, she took a couple of hasty steps backward in an effort to keep their bodies from touching. Noting the pink flush that stained her cheeks, he came to the conclusion that Caroline blushed easily. Always? With everyone? Or just with him? he wondered. Did she sense the tension between them as acutely as he did? As much as he wanted to deny the attraction as anything phys-ical, as remotely sexual, he knew better than to lie to himself. She was reacting to him as a woman does to a man, and her shy sweetness reinforced his suspicions that she was sexually inexperienced.

She stared at him, seemingly unable to speak. Her chest rose and fell steadily as her breathing accelerated just a fraction. She was a vision. Lovely beyond belief. Flawless, creamy skin. Shoulder-length black hair that glistened with healthy vibrance. Full pink lips, which she licked nervously. Wolfe's body tightened. He gazed into the depths of her blue-violet eyes and lost himself in their mesmerizing power. He broke eye contact suddenly and darted his gaze from one of her earlobes to the other.

"Nice earrings," he said, using any excuse to end the accelerating tension between them.

She took a deep breath. "Thank you. They were a twenty-first birthday gift and are favorites of mine. I wear them quite a lot."

I gave them to you, he wanted to say but knew he couldn't. He had no rights where she was concerned. None whatsoever. He could never be more to her than a bodyguard, an intruder into her private world.

"My room?" He looked right and then left.

"Oh, yes." She moved hurriedly, leading the way into the bedroom on the right side of the narrow corridor. "There are only two bedrooms finished up here. There are two more that I intend to eventually redo, but since I live here alone, I really don't need the extra... Forgive me. I'm rattling. A sign of nervousness."

"I'm sorry if I make you nervous, Ms. McGuire. Perhaps once you become accustomed to my being here, you'll feel more comfortable." He followed her into the spacious guest bedroom.

"You have your own bathroom and I cleared out closet space—" she indicated the closet by pointing "—and the top two drawers of that dresser—" she inclined her head toward the box-shaped, cherry dresser "—are empty."

"Nice room." He scanned the area hurriedly, taking note of very little except the color scheme of neutral shades and the uncluttered simplicity. He hoisted his bag up and onto the foot of the cherry sleigh bed.

"If you'd like to settle in first, we—"

"I'd prefer to check things out now."

"Yes, of course. Where would you like to start?"

"With your bedroom," he said.

She blushed again, and it was all he could do not to slide the back of his hand over her cheek and caress it the way he had her photograph on more than one occasion.

Roz had noticed the car following her about five minutes ago. At first she'd felt uneasy, since there weren't many cars on this lonely stretch of road at this time of night, but when she recognized the vehicle as a Ferrari, she relaxed. Caroline must have given Gavin Robbins his walking papers tonight. And who could blame her? Why would anyone want Gavin, hunk that he was, when a hottie like Mr. Wolfe was sleeping just across the hall? Of course, Caroline wasn't the type to make the most of propinquity. If the luscious Mr. Wolfe was guarding her body, Roz knew exactly what she would do. She'd invite him into her bed ASAP. Roz chuckled softly as she reached out to turn up the volume on the cassette player. She sang along with Faith Hill's latest hit and pressed her foot down on the accelerator.

She liked her music loud, her cars fast and her men hard. She'd bet her life that Gavin was pretty hard right about now. He might want Caroline, but he'd be willing to settle for what he could get. Roz figured that was the reason the VP of Peacekeepers International was chasing her along the back roads, like a hound after a fox. There had been a time when she wouldn't have cared, that it wouldn't have mattered to her that she was second choice. Hell, there had been a time when she'd screwed around indiscriminately and hadn't given a damn whether mutual respect or affection was involved. Odd how she'd changed gradually over the past few years, but especially during the last eight months since her breakup with Jason Stanley. She supposed she could blame Caroline's goody-two-shoes influence, but she'd be lying to herself if she attributed her changed-woman ways to her employer and dear friend.

"Lay the guilt where it belongs," she mumbled under her breath. "You've done something really stupid, Rozalin Marguerite Turner. You've let some man get under your skin. And not just any man."

She whipped her older-model Corvette into the drive at the side of her little house in a quiet neighborhood of other older homes, some well-kept and others a bit shabby. Her own place fell somewhere in between. It wasn't as if she owned the place and could fix it up herself. She'd signed a one-year lease eight months ago when she'd moved out of Jason's place in Easton.

By the time she got out of her car and made it to her front door, the sleek black Ferrari turned into her drive. She hesitated for a moment, then unlocked her door, reached inside and flipped the switch that turned on lights inside her living room. But she didn't go into the house. Instead she waited for Gavin.

He called out to her the minute he emerged from his car. "Roz, wait up."

She turned around leisurely, letting him know that she wasn't surprised to see him. When he approached her, she smiled. "Not driving back to D.C. tonight?"

"That depends." The dimples in his cheeks appeared when he grinned. "If a friend offered me a place to sleep..."

"I have only one bed."

"I don't mind sharing." Gavin moved closer, stopping when only inches separated their bodies.

And I wouldn't mind sharing more than a bed, Roz thought. Being celibate wasn't her thing and she'd gone without for eight months now. Besides, she could sure do a lot worse than Gavin Robbins. She'd bet the guy was a tiger in the sack.

"Come on in," Roz said, giving him a come-hither gesture with the crook of her index finger.

Gavin followed her inside and didn't waste any time putting the moves on her. She had no sooner locked the door when he wrapped his arms around her and pulled her backside up against his arousal. He was hard, all right. Hard as a rock. And ready to rumble.

"You know that whatever was between Caroline and me is over," he whispered against her ear. "You can sleep with me and still have a clear conscience."

"If I hadn't already known that Caroline didn't want you, I wouldn't have invited you in," Roz told him as she turned around to face him. "There's one thing I don't do and that's betray a friend."

Gavin nuzzled her neck as he delved his hands low and cupped her buttocks, lifting her up and into his erection. "I don't want you to think you're my second choice or anything."

Roz kissed him with a passion she forced, with a hunger she felt not for him, but for another man. But her wicked body didn't know the difference, didn't care who was kissing and fondling her. Their tongues dueled as Gavin removed her blouse. She broke free from the demanding kiss to help him take off her bra. When his mouth touched her nipple, she shivered.

"I don't mind being your second choice," she told him. "As long as you don't mind being mine."

He halted momentarily and glanced up at her. "Pretend I'm the freaking Prince of Wales if it'll help you get in the mood."

Just what she wanted to hear—that he was in this for an easy lay. No emotions involved. No commitment beyond tonight. As she led Gavin to her bedroom, an unwanted and totally unbidden thought passed through her mind. If she were with *him* right now, how would she feel? What would *he* say and do at a moment like this?

Roz finished undressing hurriedly and hopped into bed, then opened her arms and invited Gavin to come to her, to take her so completely that all thoughts of any other man would vanish from her mind. When he shucked off his clothes and came down over her, she lifted her hips. He delved deeply with one powerful thrust. As physical pleasure spiraled through her body, tears gathered in the corners of her eyes.

There would never be a moment like this with him, the one she really wanted. He would never want her. She knew she wasn't good enough for him, that he thought she was a tramp and probably always would.

Holding her shoes in one hand, Brooke tiptoed down the hall, hoping not to disturb her parents. Of course, this wasn't the first time she'd come home in the wee hours of the morning, and being well over twenty-one she hardly owed either her mother or her father an explanation of her whereabouts. The antique grandfather clock in the foyer downstairs chimed the hour. Three o'clock. She supposed she should have stayed the rest of the night with Fletch, but her mother enjoyed seeing her each morning at breakfast. And it had been for her mother's sake that she had sublet her apartment and moved back home. Like most children she supposed she had thought of her mother as invincible, but Eileen Harper's recent bout with breast cancer had proved that theory wrong. Although the doctors assured them that they'd gotten it all and her mother's chemotherapy and radiation treatments officially ended a few weeks ago, Brooke intended to live with her parents until she and Fletch married.

She hummed softly to herself as she reached out to open her bedroom door. Fletch hadn't proposed, at least not officially, but she knew it was only a matter of time until he did. After all, they'd been sweethearts since childhood, and even though each had experimented with other romances, they always came back together. They were two of a kind, whether Fletch realized it or not. Both born into old moneyed families, blue bloods by heritage. Former debutante mothers and wealthy, powerful fathers. And since Fletch intended to run for Congress next year, he would need the right wife at his side, someone who was part of the Washington crowd. What more could he ask for? After all, her father was his staunchest supporter, and with her dad's connections, Fletch would be a shoo-in for the party's nomination.

"Brooke?"

She stopped when she heard her father's voice and turned to face him. With a smile curving her lips she greeted him. "What are you doing up at such an ungodly hour?" she asked. "I hope I didn't waken you."

"You didn't." He slipped his arm around her shoulders. "Sometimes old men don't sleep well."

"Dad, you aren't old. You're the youngest sixty-nine-year-old man I've ever known."

"Did you have a nice time tonight?" Oliver Harper asked.

"Yes." She nodded as she slid her arm around her father's waist. "We all stayed with Caroline until her bodyguard showed up. Roz and Lyle stayed and Gavin Robbins dropped by, too."

"What's this bodyguard Fletcher hired like? Did he seem capable?"

Brooke chuckled. No way could she tell her father just how very capable Mr. Wolfe actually looked. She suspected the man was lethal, even in small doses. Pity that all that machismo was wasted on Saint Caroline. Oh, she loved Caroline dearly, but after a while it became rather tedious having a friend who was so incredibly good. Just once she'd like to see Caroline screw up. Maybe then all the men in her life would finally take her down off that damn pedestal they had her on. Fletch included!

"Mr. Wolfe came from the Dundee agency, headquartered in Atlanta," Brooke said. "I'm sure you can ask around and find out all you need to know about this man."

"I may do that," Oliver said. "After all, we don't want just anyone looking out for Caroline. She's practically family...or will be once you and Fletcher are married. And I owe it to Preston to be concerned about the girl. He was quite fond of her, you know.''

"Odd, isn't it, about that letter Caroline found in the safe hidden in the basement of that old house where they lived when Mr. Shaw was killed.''

"I had hoped Caroline would disregard the message," Oliver said. "It's apparent Preston was delusional when he wrote it. The poor man actually thought that someone intended to murder him because he had important secret information. I can't believe an intelligent girl like Caroline has bought into such a ludicrous fabrication.''

"Then you don't think there's any chance that Mr. Shaw was involved in some sort of espionage?''

"Preston Shaw was no more a spy than I am." Oliver hugged Brooke to his side. "How about a brandy with your old man before you head off to bed.''

"I can't think of anything I'd like better. But only one. I want to get some sleep before I have breakfast with Mama.''

"You can't imagine how much it's meant to Eileen having you back home these past few months. You're a good daughter, my love.''

"And you're the best father in the world.''

Brooke considered herself fortunate, far more so than most of the women her age. Few of her friends and acquaintances had not only both parents living, but parents who were still married to each other. And being an only child, she had been the center of her parents' universe. When she and Fletcher had children, she hoped that they could be the kind of parents her own had been. But why shouldn't they be? They were the same type of people, weren't they? And as her mother had told her countless times—blood will tell.

Chapter 6

An overcast sky veiled the morning sun, diffusing the light and cloaking the springtime warmth. Caroline loved it when the weather cooperated enough for her to have breakfast on the back porch as they were doing today. When she had followed Lyle to Maryland's eastern shore after the local Congregational Church hired him as their minister, she'd felt a sense of coming home. She found a serenity and beauty by the bay unlike any she'd ever known. And an unparalleled freedom. After college graduation, she had worked for another photographer in Richmond and then a couple of years later opened her own small studio. She always tried to stay within driving distance of wherever Lyle settled. He was the only family she had left and both he and she were determined to stay together and not allow too many miles to separate them. It was what Aunt Dixie would have wanted. She could almost hear her aunt's voice. *Blood is thicker than water.*

"It's inadvisable for you to be out here," Wolfe said. "You're too accessible. Someone could come out of the woods or in from the bay and get to you. After this morning, all meals will be eaten inside.''

''I realize that you know better than I what's safe and what isn't,'' Caroline said. ''But I'm not sure I can live like a prisoner in my own house.''

''I'm sorry.'' He stared at her over the rim of his tinted glasses, which had slipped down his nose. The moment he caught her looking directly at him, he shoved up the glasses and averted his gaze. ''Let's hope we find what your key opens soon and put an end to the danger in your life. That way you'll be rid of me and can resume your normal activities.''

''Mr. Wolfe, I have a career…a job, with clients depending on me. And I have responsibilities that can't be put on hold.''

''Just Wolfe,'' he said.

''What?''

''Call me Wolfe, not Mr. Wolfe.''

''Oh. All right…Wolfe.'' What was it about this man that repeatedly frustrated her? Was it the way he looked at her through those damn tinted glasses, as if while he remained hidden from her, he could see straight through into her mind and her heart? Or was it the way she felt in his presence—small and vulnerable and totally feminine? Or was it having a stranger know so much about her personal life? She realized that in order to protect her, his agency had to know a great deal about her, but she got the feeling that Wolfe knew a little too much.

Perhaps the problem was that she wasn't accustomed to his type of man. One who sits at the breakfast table wearing a hip holster. An aura of strength and danger surrounded her bodyguard, a man trained to protect others, with both defensive and offensive tactics. Has he ever killed in the line of duty? she wondered, and a shiver of apprehension shimmied along her nerve endings.

''You can go to work,'' Wolfe told her. ''You can go

anywhere that I feel isn't dangerous, anyplace where I can protect you. And if you're insistent on not changing your lifestyle, I can call in another Dundee agent as backup.''

''I'm sure you're costing Fletch a small fortune. I can hardly expect him to pick up the tab for a second bodyguard.'' Caroline shook her head. ''Let's give it a try, doing things your way, and if I find that to be too confining, I'll pay for the second bodyguard myself.''

Wolfe nodded. ''Before I drive you to your studio, do we have time this morning to discuss the reason you believe someone tried to kill you?''

''I thought you already knew.'' She spread strawberry jam on her toast, then offered the jar and knife to him. He declined the offer. ''From some of the things you said last night, I assumed you knew everything there was to know about me.''

''No one knows everything there is to know about another human being.''

''You're right.'' Caroline sighed, realizing that no one would win an argument against this man, especially not her. He was far too logical in his thinking, whereas she usually acted on pure emotion. ''What do you want to discuss?''

''I want to see the letter you found in your stepfather's safe and I'd like a better look at that key.'' He eyed the chain hanging around her neck. ''Fletcher Shaw has given us permission to go through any personal files that he has in his possession that once belonged to his father. I'd like your permission to have a copy of the key made and sent to our lab in Atlanta.''

Caroline lifted the chain and grasped the key in her hand. ''No.'' She shook her head. ''I don't mean to be uncooperative, but I'm not willing to allow copies of this key to be made. The copies could fall into the wrong hands.''

''And just who do you suspect would wind up with the copies, Ms. McGuire?''

''I don't know.'' Caroline scooted back her rustic wooden

chair and stood. She tossed her napkin on top of the table and walked away, down the steps leading out into the backyard, which faced the shoreline.

He immediately followed her, catching up with her quickly, before she had a chance to go more than a few feet. He grabbed her arm to halt her. She turned on him, a protest on her lips. A tingling sensation radiated up the entire length of her arm from where his big hand held her.

"Do you have any idea how much I hate all of this?" she asked him. "For nearly fifteen years I've believed that an intruder, a burglar, killed my stepfather. Now I know better. Now I have the proof, in his own handwriting, that someone assassinated him because he was in possession of some damaging information. Someone ordered Preston Shaw's execution and someone carried out that command." She fingered the chain around her neck. "This key is the only weapon I have against those people. I won't let it out of my possession."

"Then we have no choice but to use trial and error to try to find out just what your key opens." Wolfe tugged on her arm. "Don't run away from me again, Ms. McGuire. Your life could well depend upon my being at your side."

And my sanity might well depend upon putting some distance between us, she wanted to say, but didn't. "Are all the Dundee agents like you?" she asked as he led her back to the porch.

"All the Dundee agents are highly trained professionals," he said. "Their former professions vary somewhat—military, law enforcement and government agents, mostly. Ages vary, too, as do personal histories."

"What description would fit you?" What did it matter? she thought, the moment she asked the question. This man is a temporary fixture in your life. Here today, gone tomorrow. You shouldn't get personal with him. He isn't here to be your friend.

"If you've finished breakfast, let's clear away the dishes and get you back inside," he said.

"Oh, I see. You get to know all about me and my life, but I'm not supposed to ask you any personal questions. Is that how this works?"

"Something like that." He stacked their dishes, laid the silverware crossways atop the plates, then handed them to Caroline. He removed the butter and jam from the table with one hand, then picked up the blue linen napkins and stuffed them into his pants pocket.

"You really think someone is going to appear out of nowhere and try to kill me on my own back porch?"

"It's been known to happen." He nudged her into action, keeping step with her as she walked into the kitchen.

She set their dirty plates and silverware in the sink, then turned to face him and held out her hands to accept the butter and jam. Their hands touched in the transfer, a momentary brush of flesh against flesh. An electrical current sizzled through her. Frozen to the spot by her reaction, she glared at him and found him looking right at her, as if he had been shocked by the same surge of energy.

"Is it against the rules for me to see your eyes?" she asked, her voice uncharacteristically breathy.

He hesitated, then with a slow, precise movement reached up and removed his glasses. But he didn't allow their eyes to meet. Not immediately. She waited, heart thumping in an erratic rat-a-tat beat, as he lifted his gaze from where he had focused on the floor and stared straight at her. The cold, hard glimmer in his daring green eyes paralyzed her momentarily. There was no warmth, no sympathy, no understanding in his gaze. Not one shred of human emotion, almost as if he were a robot. She could not control the involuntary quivering that shook her body from head to toe.

Without saying a word, Wolfe put his glasses back on, then stepped away from Caroline. This time he was extra careful not to touch her. That was when she knew he wasn't as immune to her as he wanted her to believe.

Gavin Robbins was not one of his favorite people, so listening to him brag about his recent sexual conquest didn't go well with Ellison's morning tea. The man was every bit the cocky bastard he'd been fifteen years ago as a young recruit, but he possessed something the Peacekeepers prided themselves on—loyalty to the organization. Robbins had proved himself to be a top-notch agent time and again, and despite Ellison's personal dislike of him, the man didn't have one black mark against his record. When the second-in-command position came open at the unexpected death of the former VP from a heart attack, the other agents had immediately recommended Robbins. When the vote was counted, Robbins had been elected to the position by a landslide. If there was one thing Robbins did almost as well as he did his job, it was kiss ass.

"So, even if things are over with Caroline, I can still keep close enough to her to be apprised of everything going on in her life. Now that I'm bonking Roz Turner, she'll keep me updated on what's happening."

"And using Ms. Turner as an unknowing informant was your sole reason for instigating an affair with her?" Ellison lifted the china cup to his lips and sipped the imported tea that was blended in a small London shop specifically for him.

Gavin chuckled. "Hey, a man does what a man has to do. Right? Besides, it's not exactly a hardship. Roz is one talented lady, if you know what I mean."

Ellison heaved a deep sigh, signifying his displeasure, but the subtle gesture escaped Gavin's attention. Robbins was like many men of Ellison's acquaintance. Self-absorbed. Overly confident. And a bit of a braggart. He dreaded the day when he would be forced by old age to relinquish the reins of Peacekeepers International to a man more suited to the military than diplomacy. His personal choice would have been Aidan Colbert. But the man known as Aidan Colbert was dead.

"So, have you found out everything we need to know about Caroline's bodyguard?" Gavin asked as he plopped down in the chair directly across from Ellison's desk. "Is he somebody we can trust?"

"My sources tell me that Mr. Wolfe is as trustworthy as they come." Ellison took another sip of the delicious tea, then placed his cup on the saucer atop his desk. "Caroline McGuire is in good hands."

"Yeah, well, I'll bet Aidan Colbert is turning over in his grave at the thought of some young stud sharing a house with Caroline. If you ask me, Colbert had a sick obsession with our Ms. McGuire."

"There was nothing sick about Aidan's concern for Caroline. He was a man of principle, a man with a conscience. He deeply regretted that she'd practically been a witness to her stepfather's execution."

"Colbert let his conscience get in the way sometimes," Gavin said. "In my opinion, he'd be alive now if he hadn't tried to get that group of grade-school kids out of the way before that bomb went off. The guy's own actions screwed him."

"I didn't ask you."

"Yeah, yeah. Okay. I know the guy was a favorite of yours and you were priming him to take over your job one day, but face it, Ellison, Colbert never really had what it took for our line of work."

"Until I tell you otherwise, you will now and in the future refer to me as Mr. Penn." Ellison eased back his chair and stood. "Only my family and friends call me Ellison and you, Gavin, are neither."

"You've made your point, *Mr. Penn.* So, how about a look at whatever information you have on Mr. Wolfe?"

"The information I have on him is right up here." Ellison tapped his right temple. "All you need to know is that if

Caroline finds this so-called evidence Preston Shaw supposedly hid away somewhere, we can count on Mr. Wolfe to see that only the proper authorities will have access to the information.''

"I'd like to know how you can be so sure of Mr. Wolfe."

"Suffice it to say that I am sure." Ellison skewered Gavin with a deadly glare that issued a silent warning for his subordinate to back off immediately. He realized that he risked piquing Robbins's curiosity with his evasiveness, but he wanted to postpone sharing any vital information about Wolfe with a man he didn't completely trust.

Photography by Caroline was located in a renovated building in downtown St. Michaels. The waiting area resembled an old-fashioned parlor, with turn-of-the-century reproduction furniture. Two college-aged gofers acted as receptionists and hostesses, booking appointments, welcoming clients and serving coffee and tea as well as pacifying crying babies and entertaining restless children. The pale cream walls in the parlor boasted a lineup of brilliantly photographed babies, children, brides and families. Wolfe knew that Caroline had become a renowned portrait photographer, but until seeing her work today he hadn't fully comprehended how truly talented she was. In each picture she had captured the very essence of her subject.

"She's very good," Wolfe said without realizing he had spoken aloud.

"The best," Roz agreed. "She has clients who come here from all over the country. Every young girl dreams of having her bridal portrait taken by Caroline, and we have expectant mothers making appointments with us for their unborn child's first-year pictures the minute they discover they're pregnant."

Wolfe glanced over his shoulder, checking on Caroline's whereabouts as she padded barefoot across the wooden floor and introduced herself to her first two clients of the day—a mother with a toddler in tow and an elderly gentleman barely restraining the friendliness of his springer spaniel. Caroline bent on one knee in front of the little boy who, judging by his size, was probably no more than three.

"Hello, Justin, I'm Caroline. My, you're a big boy. Your mother told me that you like bugs…spiders and flies and scorpions. Did you know that I have a whole box filled with bugs in my studio?"

The curly-headed child grinned and said, "You've got bugs?"

"Dozens of them."

"You got a scorpion?"

"At least three of them." Caroline held out her hand to the toddler. "Would you like to go with my friend Roz…you and your mommy…and see my scorpions?"

The child jumped up and down, then tugged on his mother's hand. "Let's go now, Mommy. Go see the bugs."

While Roz led mother and child into the studio area used primarily for shots of babies and children, Caroline made her way to her next customer. She sat down on the sofa beside the old man, then leaned over and let his dog sniff the back of her hand. Immediately the spaniel wagged his tail and lifted his front paws onto Caroline's knees.

"Hello, old boy," Caroline said as she rubbed the dog's ears. "What's his name?" she asked the owner.

"Freddy."

"Well, Freddy, you're a sweetie, aren't you?" She glanced at the pet's master. "Mr. Dalton, do you mind if I give Freddy a doggie treat?"

"I don't mind at all. Freddy's like me, he's getting up there in years and one of the few pleasures left to him is eating." Mr. Dalton laughed good-naturedly and patted his potbelly.

"Sandy—" Caroline motioned for the plump redheaded gofer "—will take you and Freddy outside in the garden, and when I finish with little Justin Payne, I'll join y'all. If you'd like coffee or tea or if Freddy needs a bowl of water, then you just tell Sandy.'' Caroline dipped into the deep pocket of her baggy blue slacks and pulled out a bone-shaped dog treat. She waved it under the dog's nose. He caught a sniff and snapped it up immediately.

As soon as Mr. Dalton and Freddy disappeared down the corridor that led to the garden at the back of the studio, Caroline motioned to Wolfe. ''There's only one door in and out of the children's studio, so if you guard that door, no one can get to me.''

''Is that your subtle way of telling me to stay out of your way while you're working?'' Wolfe asked.

''You catch on fast,'' she replied.

He walked behind her down the hallway, past the curtained alcoves young clients used to change clothes and into the large, colorfully decorated room she used as the children's studio. After scanning the area and noting only one window, which overlooked the enclosed garden courtyard where Sandy entertained Mr. Dalton and Freddy, Wolfe closed the single entry door and leaned back against it.

He watched as she maneuvered the lighting, first setting up what he later learned from Roz was a 350-watt diffuser fill light to the front right of the squirming Justin Payne.

''Roz, place that quartz key light behind him while I get the metal deflector in place.'' Caroline made a funny face at Justin, who had his hands filled with an assortment of plastic bugs.

Caroline and Roz worked tirelessly as a team, each in perfect timing with the other. Roz maneuvered the child with expert ease, returning him to a posed position time and again while Caroline checked lighting and angles as she snapped picture after picture of her energetic subject.

Wolfe couldn't take his eyes off Caroline as she worked. Her face glowed with enthusiastic zeal, and any fool could see how much she loved what she was doing. She and the camera became one, joined into a single entity capable of producing photographic masterpieces. If Aidan Colbert had done nothing else of any consequence in his life, he could take some credit for having helped this incredible young woman achieve her goals.

Bubbly, blond Kirsten, the other studio gofer, brought in lunch for two on a tray and placed the tray on Caroline's cluttered desk. "Crab cakes," she said. "Enjoy." Her smile flirted with Wolfe, but he purposefully ignored the girl.

When he pulled a chair up to the other side of the desk, Wolfe glanced at Caroline, who gave him a condemning glare.

"What?" he asked.

"Did you have to be so rude to Kirsten?"

"I wasn't rude," he said. "If I'd been rude, I would have told her that she was wasting her time with me. I have no interest in eighteen-year-old girls."

"Oh, I see. No point in encouraging her." Caroline opened the lid on the food container. "Tell me, just what age bracket does interest you?"

Wolfe lifted the coffee mug off the tray. "Definitely over twenty-five."

"How old are you?" she asked.

"Thirty-six."

"Hmm-mmm."

"Too old?" he inquired.

"For what?"

"For someone twenty-seven?"

Caroline blushed. "I'm twenty-seven, or at least I will be on Thursday."

"Yes, I know."

"You're not too old." She immediately averted her gaze, concentrating on the food before her.

He'd never been particularly adept at playing games with women, certainly not a lighthearted flirting match like the one he'd just exchanged with Caroline. But with her, he felt different. With her, he *was* different.

While sipping his coffee, he glanced around her office, taking note of the photos on the walls, personally significant portraits confined to her private space. There were three shots of Brooke Harper and the same number of Fletcher Shaw. Two pictures of Roz, each capturing a vulnerability that surprised Wolfe. And dispersed among the other framed photographs were half a dozen shots of Lyle Jennings at various ages, from a chunky teenager in a baseball uniform to a majestic shot of him in his minister's garb. Glass-enclosed shelving lined the wall space on either side of the unused fireplace. Wolfe surveyed the contents. Clocks of various kinds and sizes. A couple of sculptures. And on a shelf by itself, a small 35 mm camera.

Wolfe set the mug on the tray, shoved back his chair and stood. As if drawn to the object by some magnetic force, he walked across the room for a better look at the little black camera. He peered through the glass, then lifted his hand as if to touch the object. Was this what he thought it was? Could it actually be the camera Aidan Colbert had bought Caroline for her thirteenth birthday?

He sensed rather than heard her when she came up behind him. She was so close he could smell the sweet scent of her delicate perfume.

"That was my first camera," she said, a trace of nostalgia in her voice. "It's my most prized possession."

"An inexpensive 35 mm camera is your most prized possession?" Inclining his head slightly, he glanced back at her.

"Yes. You see, it was a gift."

He nodded, afraid to speak, uncertain he wouldn't blurt out some sentimental hogwash that she couldn't possibly understand.

"Someone very special gave it to me for my thirteenth birthday." She opened the glass door, reached inside and removed the small camera. "My love for photography began with this camera. Taking pictures with it opened up a whole new world for me.''

Wolfe swallowed hard. Had his insignificant little gift, purchased in London on a whim, actually done so much for the young Caroline?

''Who gave you the camera?'' he asked.

''Someone very important to me.'' Caroline sighed. ''A man I know only as David. He's been my benefactor since my stepfather died. He knew Preston and has sort of looked out for me for that reason. I have no idea who he is or what he looks like or how old he is. But in my heart, I see him as my knight in shining armor.''

Wolfe watched silently as Caroline placed the camera back in its honored spot. When he glanced at her again, he noticed the tears glistening in her eyes and the slight tremble in her hand. Realization hit him like the blow of a sledgehammer.

''You're infatuated with this man,'' he said.

''Yes, I know. But it's a harmless infatuation. My David has made it abundantly clear that we can never meet.''

My David. She referred to him in the same possessive way he thought of her. *My Caroline.*

''What if you could meet him? What would you say? What would you do?'' Wolfe asked.

Would you run into his arms? Would you tell him that you love him?

''That will never happen,'' she said. ''The only place I'll ever meet my David is in my dreams.''

Chapter 7

"So, you think searching through this old place might turn up a clue?" Roz asked

"It's worth a try," Caroline said. "Wolfe and I agree it's possible the key fits something other than the doors."

Wolfe stayed at Caroline's side, constantly alert to the surrounding stimuli. Every sound. Every sight, especially things he caught in his peripheral vision. He even took note of the odors, having learned long ago to use all his senses when safeguarding his life and the lives of others. There was no way to know for certain when another strike would be made against Caroline or from what direction a second attempt on her life would come. Everyone was suspect. The postman whistling as he delivered mail across the street. The taxi driver picking up a fare half a block away. The woman planting flowers along her sidewalk two houses up.

Lyle Jennings came around the side of the house on Sheffield Street, paused and took a deep breath. His freckled face was slightly flushed from having run around the entire yard, back and front.

"The back door's locked," Lyle said, huffing a bit from exertion. "No windows open or broken and no one in sight out back."

"Thanks," Wolfe said, then held out his hand for the door key. "Roz, you take Caroline to the end of the porch and stay there until I have the door completely open."

"Aren't you being overly cautious?" Caroline asked. "What are you expecting—someone to jump out and grab me?"

"That's a possibility." Wolfe removed his tinted glasses. "But I was thinking more along the lines of an explosive device being triggered when the front door opens."

Caroline gasped. Roz grabbed her hand and tugged. Lyle ran toward the porch, then bounded up the steps.

"Come on. Let's do what he says." Lyle came up behind the two women, placing one hand on Caroline's back and the other on Roz's shoulder.

"Please be careful," Caroline called to Wolfe as Lyle led her and Roz to the far end of the wide front porch.

Wolfe felt fairly confident that the door was clean, but he wasn't willing to take any chances with Caroline's life. He slipped his glasses, which corrected his slight nearsightedness, into the inside pocket of his sport coat, then checked the door thoroughly, inserted the key and unlocked the door. He waited for a couple of minutes, then turned the doorknob. Once the door stood wide open, he motioned to the others. Caroline came to him immediately and they entered the house together.

"What's the matter, Rev, the tension too much for you?" Roz asked Lyle. "You're as white as a sheet."

"I suppose I am, but then I have enough sense to realize the danger in this situation," Lyle said. "Of course, you're not the least bit afraid, are you? A wild woman like you, with a tattoo on her leg and holes pierced in various body parts, lives for excitement. Tell me, Ms. Thrill Seeker, if a bomb had exploded just then, would that have given you your kicks for the day?''

"Oh, bite me, Lyle. You're such an uptight, goodie—''

Caroline stopped in the foyer, turned around, put her hands on her hips and yelled, "For heaven's sake, will you two give it a rest. If y'all can't get along while we're here, then one of you can go sit in the car.''

"Sorry.'' Roz breezed past Lyle, her nose upturned as she entered the foyer. "Are you sure that guy—'' she hitched her thumb backward in Lyle's direction "—is a blood relative of yours?''

"If we can proceed—'' Wolfe looked from Roz to Lyle, who stood in the open doorway "—then I suggest Caroline and I search down here and in the basement and you two try upstairs and then the attic.''

"Remind me again what we're looking for,'' Roz said.

"Anything that requires a key to open,'' Wolfe told her. "Before we leave, we'll try it on all the doors again, just to be sure, but my guess is that Caroline's key doesn't open a door. I think it's a key to a drawer, a trunk, a box… something like that. I had Caroline take several snapshots of the key and we've sent them to Dundee headquarters. If it fits any type of standard lock, our lab should be able to identify some definite possibilities.''

"Let's get with it,'' Roz said. "I have a hot date tonight, so I need to go home in time to get ready.''

"Who's the unfortunate man?'' Lyle asked.

"Lyle, that wasn't very nice.'' Caroline frowned, but Wolfe noticed her lips twitching and knew she was on the verge of smiling.

Roz narrowed her gaze, glanced pensively at Caroline and grimaced. "Well, actually, my date is with Gavin Robbins. Gee, Caroline, I hope you don't mind. I mean, you did say that you weren't going to see him anymore and—''

Caroline laughed. "You're more than welcome to Gavin. But Roz, honey, I think you could do better. Gavin's a good-looking charmer, but if you get serious about him, he'll break your heart.''

"Amen," Wolfe said under his breath. Caroline certainly had figured out Gavin's true nature without any warnings from a friend. He couldn't help wondering if Roz were half as astute.

Caroline glared at Wolfe. Had she heard his quiet comment?

"Get serious about him? Not me." Roz stared pointedly at Lyle. "I'm the quintessential good-time girl, just in it for fun."

"One of these days, you'll have to pay a price for having all that fun," Lyle said.

Roz made a face at Lyle, then stuck out her tongue. He just rolled his eyes toward the ceiling and headed up the stairs. Before he made it to the landing, Roz caught up with him. Wolfe could hear them mouthing off at each other as they tramped along the upstairs hallway.

"What is it with those two?" Wolfe asked.

"They're opposites who don't attract," Caroline said.

"Or maybe opposites who do attract and are fighting the attraction?"

"Hmm-mmm. Maybe." She reached out and laid her hand on Wolfe's arm. "You don't like Gavin Robbins, do you? Why? You don't even know him."

"Sorry about my comment," Wolfe said. "You're right, I don't know him, but I have pretty good instincts when it comes to people, and my gut reaction to Robbins was negative." Wolfe glanced at Caroline's hand resting on his arm. "I'm glad you saw through his gentleman facade."

Caroline's fingers tightened around Wolfe's arm. Their gazes met and locked. He jerked away from her abruptly, unnerved by the powerful sexual urges she ignited within him. *Dammit, man, this isn't just any woman. This is your sweet little Caroline!* Ah, but that was the problem—she *was* his sweet Caroline. But she was no longer a little girl.

''Where do we start?'' she asked, obviously willing to overlook his blatant rudeness.

''The kitchen, then the laundry room and the pantry,'' he said. ''After that we'll walk from room to room and look for anything that locks with a key.''

Wolfe tried not to think about the past, tried not to remember the only other time he'd been inside this house. One cold December night nearly fifteen years ago. Fresh snow falling. Christmas lights blinking all over town. On his way down the hall that night, he had passed the living room, noticed the decorated tree and the presents stacked high underneath. Preston Shaw had been sitting behind his desk in the study when he looked up and saw Aidan Colbert standing in the doorway. He'd jumped out of the chair and come forward, his expression one of outrage at first, and then when he'd realized the intruder in his home was an executioner sent by the Peacekeepers, fear etched his classic features.

David wondered how he could now enter that same room…with Caroline? He wasn't the man he had been then, not by appearance nor identity. And there was no way Caroline could know he was the man who had executed Preston Shaw. But God help him, he knew who he really was and what he'd done that night.

There would be no way to avoid going into Shaw's study. Wolfe knew he had no choice but to walk through the door, Caroline at his side, and confront the demons from his past without letting on to her that anything was wrong. But Caroline would be forced to relive that night again, too. Perhaps he could persuade her to stay just outside the door while he searched the room. But if she insisted on coming into the room with him, then he would be her protector, her strong shoulder to lean on if she needed one. However, not by word or deed could he dare let on that he was familiar with any of the intimate details concerning what had occurred in that room when a twelve-year-old child had come face-to-face with her stepfather's killer.

* * *

"We have one last room on the first floor to check before we head down into the basement," Caroline said. She had deliberately left the study for last, dreading to go in there again. It had been difficult enough when she'd opened up the old house a few weeks ago and forced herself to enter Preston's study for the first time since the night he was murdered. How could she possibly go in there again?

"If you'd rather not go into the study, you can wait out in the hall where I can see you, while I check for a lock of some kind," Wolfe told her.

"You know about what happened that night, don't you? Fletcher must have explained to you how his father died."

"When a Dundee agent takes on a case, the persons involved are thoroughly investigated and a dossier put together on them as quickly as possible," Wolfe explained. "I have copies of the police report concerning Mr. Shaw's death, as well as old newspaper clippings. So, yes, I'm aware of the fact that Preston Shaw died in that room." Wolfe glanced up the hall at the open door.

"Do you have a report on me?" Caroline asked. "If you do, then you know that I had a nervous breakdown that night, after I called the emergency number. I saw the killer...was in the room with him...but later I couldn't identify him. I was helpless because I was upset and confused. And my memories were fuzzy. A murderer is probably out there now, walking the streets a free man, because I couldn't give the police a good description of him."

"You can't blame yourself for something you weren't a part of."

"If what Preston wrote in the letter he hid away in the safe is true, then he wasn't killed by some burglar. He was assassinated because he had information that was dangerous to someone very powerful. Don't you understand—the man who shot Preston was a professional killer. So tell me this, why didn't he kill me, too?"

Tears pooled in her eyes. That same old unanswerable question still haunted her. More so now than ever—now that this new evidence had been discovered. She turned away from Wolfe and hurried down the hall toward the study, feeling as if somehow she could solve the mystery only in the room where it had begun.

''Caroline!''

Wolfe was running after her. She could hear his heavy footsteps, could sense him drawing nearer and nearer. But she couldn't stop, couldn't wait. She raced into the study, halting in the middle of the room, at approximately the same spot where Preston had lain sprawled on the floor. She gazed down at the scuffed, dusty wood and could almost see the bloodstains that had, in reality, been removed years ago. Suddenly she looked up and saw a large, dark figure near the door. Her heartbeat thundered in her ears. Moisture coated the palms of her hands. Tremors racked her body.

He was going to kill her. Shoot her the way he had shot Preston. She couldn't escape. And there was no one else in the house she could call for help.

A child's chilling screams echoed inside Caroline's head. The room began to spin around and around. She desperately wanted to find that poor, pitiful screaming child, but how could she? Her feet seemed glued to the spot and her vision was beginning to blur.

Wolfe had seen that look on Caroline's face before. The sheer terror. The fear that she was going to die. Salty bile rose in his throat. His stomach knotted painfully. He couldn't bear seeing her this way. Remembering. Reliving that moment when the two of them had gazed into each other's eyes on a snowy winter night so long ago. Over the years, his nightmares had been filled with that ungodly moment when a little girl had thought he was going to kill her. He had gone over that moment in his mind again and again, and each time he had thought about how ironic it was that he, of all people, had put that kind of fear into a child. Aidan Colbert, who had killed his own father to stop him from murdering a child.

"Caroline." He spoke her name softly. "Don't be afraid. You're not in any danger. No one is going to hurt you."

He recognized the glazed look in her eyes. How many times had he seen traumatized men and women relive a terrifying moment? In her mind, Caroline was twelve again, Preston lay dead on the floor—and Aidan Colbert hovered in the shadows, the deadly weapon still in his hand.

All color drained from her face. She began swaying, just a fraction, the movement almost indiscernible at first. But he knew the signs. She was on the verge of fainting.

"Caroline…Caroline…"

He rushed forward despite the horror he saw on her face as he approached. She opened her mouth on a silent scream. He suspected that in her mind she was screaming at the top of her lungs. Just as she started to topple over, Wolfe reached out and grabbed her, swooping her into his arms. She lay limp as a dishrag. He carried her out of the study, down the hall and into an area that had once been the living room. There nestled beneath the arched bay windows was a window seat. He walked across the room, sat down with Caroline in his lap and very gently patted her cheek. Her eyelids fluttered. He patted her face again. Her eyelids opened and closed. She moaned.

"Caroline?"

This time when she opened her eyes, she looked straight at Wolfe. "What happened?" she asked.

"You fainted."

She lay there in his arms, a delicious weight. Warm and soft. The delicate scent of her flowery perfume permeating the air he breathed. Her silky black hair draped over his arm.

"Oh, Wolfe, I'm so sorry…I was remembering that night and…" She bit down on her bottom lip. "It was you."

"What?" Fear grabbed him by the throat in a stranglehold. No, it wasn't possible. She couldn't have recognized him as the man who'd shot Preston Shaw because he no longer resembled that man.

"I saw you there in the doorway, didn't I? And I thought…oh, God—" She sat straight up and looked at him so sadly. "I thought you were Preston's killer. For just a few seconds I thought I was twelve again and it was that night. I looked up and saw you and thought—" She gasped, then flung her arms around Wolfe and buried her face against his chest.

He held her securely but without force. Everything within him longed to comfort her, to find a way to put an end to her torment. But could he trust himself to act purely as her bodyguard, as an objective employee whose sole duty was to protect her? *There is no rule that says you can't comfort her, is there?* he asked himself. It seemed to him that he had spent a lifetime longing to comfort Caroline, wanting to erase the past and give her a happy future. He had sought any and all means to aid her, hoping that in some small way he could atone for what had happened to her—for what his actions had done to her. In photographs and written reports from Ellison, he had watched her grow up, change from a shy, chubby little girl into a beautiful, successful woman. How many times had he watched the videos Ellison had sent him of Caroline's high school and college graduations? He had freeze-framed her face on both videos so many times he had lost count. Exactly when his concern for a child had turned into an obsession with a woman, he wasn't quite sure.

She mumbled softly, her lips moving against his shirtfront. "Why didn't he kill me?"

Wolfe slipped his hand between her neck and his chest and cupped her jaw. She allowed him to tilt her chin just enough so that he could see her face. He looked into her eyes, the color of the blue-tinted violets that his mother had grown in pots on her kitchen windowsill. Of its own volition, his thumb tenderly raked across her parted lips.

She sighed and said his name. "Wolfe?"

''You won't ever have to come back here again,'' he said. ''I promise.''

''Can you answer my question?'' She stared at him pleadingly. ''In your line of work, you must have been confronted by hired killers more than once. Why would a professional hit man let me live? Why didn't he kill me?''

Because my job was to eliminate a rogue agent who posed a threat to our government, not to harm an innocent child. The explanation swirled around inside his head. The desire to tell her what he was thinking became an overpowering need. Now is not the time for true confessions, he reminded himself. He had joined Peacekeepers, hoping to help others, to save the innocent whenever possible—because he had failed in his efforts to save his own younger brother and his mother from the wrath of a mean drunk. And every day of his life, since he was a boy of thirteen, Aidan Colbert had lived with the knowledge that even though he had taken his father's life, he had acted too late to save the two people dearest to him. If he could have helped his brother, his mother might still be alive, too.

''I'm not sure why he didn't kill you,'' Wolfe said, his voice deceptively calm. ''If he was a professional, then he'd been sent to do a job. You weren't part of that job. And if you couldn't identify him, he had no reason to kill you, did he?''

''But he couldn't possibly have known that I couldn't identify him, that he had been partially hidden in the shadows and—''

Wolfe cradled her face with his hands. ''Stop torturing yourself. I thought you'd gotten over this, that you had put it in the past.''

''What?'' She stared at him, puzzlement written plainly on her face.

Damn! He should have kept his mouth shut. He'd gotten sentimental and said too much. ''I assumed that since you live a very normal life and aren't under any type of psychiatric care that you had dealt with Preston Shaw's death years ago.''

"I thought I had."

Wolfe scooted Caroline off his lap and helped her to her feet as he stood. "Are you all right now? You don't still feel faint, do you?" Get back in bodyguard persona, he thought. And keep it that way. He couldn't afford to let his personal feelings for Caroline show.

She stared at him, a fragile frown drooping her mouth and a wounded expression in her eyes. "I'm fine, Wolfe, thank you."

The moment she moved away from him, he wanted to grab her and pull her back into his arms. He wanted to tell her that he was David. Her David. The man she thought she could meet only in her dreams. How he wished he could admit to being her caretaker, her guardian angel, without having to confess that he was a fallen angel, a man with blood on his hands—the executioner who had killed her stepfather.

"I suppose we should check the basement next," Caroline said, her back to Wolfe.

"Certainly." He had to keep his distance from her, no matter how tempted he was to be more to her than a temporary employee.

After suggesting that she take the rooms on the left while he took the rooms on the right, Lyle had tried to avoid Roz as much as possible. Just being around the woman unnerved him. The first day Caroline introduced them, they had taken an instant dislike to each other. And that bothered him. Then and now. As a general rule, he liked everyone he met. But there was something about Roz, something in her manner, in her speech, in the way she dressed that simply drove him crazy. And it didn't help that she seemed to thrive on annoying him, on poking fun at his appearance, his demeanor and his profession.

But the most disturbing aspect of their unfriendly relationship began a few months ago. The first time he'd had one of those dreams about Roz. It wasn't the sexual content of the dream that had bothered him so much—after all, he was a man as well as a minister—but the fact that the woman in the dream had been Roz. Wasn't she the last woman on earth he would find appealing? Apparently not. If it had been only one dream, he would have dismissed it, but the first one had been followed by more—many more. Now it had reached the point that whenever he was around Roz, his body responded to her. If she ever found out that he was getting sexually aroused whenever he just looked at her, she would take great pleasure in tormenting him.

"Hey, Rev, are you about finished in there?" Roz called from the hallway. "If you are, then let's head to the attic."

"Be with you in a minute," he replied. The attic would be dark, warm and confining. Not someplace he'd want to be with Roz. He could tell her that he'd check the attic without her, but knowing her, she would veto any suggestion he made.

Taking several deep breaths and willing his traitorous body to cooperate, Lyle met Roz in the hall. When she looked at him and smiled, his stomach turned over.

"Ready?" she asked.

Why her, dear God, why her? Lyle prayed. We are totally incompatible. She's the exact opposite of everything I want in a woman. Is this some sort of test? Are you throwing temptation in my path to see if I can resist? Or is this some sort of joke you're playing on me?

"Hey, are you okay?" Roz asked. "You've got this goofy look on your face. What were you doing, praying?"

"Yeah, something like that."

"Odd time to pray, don't you think? You're the only guy I know who's ever taken one look at me and started praying." Roz sashayed closer and closer, her smile slightly sinister. "Were you praying for my soul, Rev? Or for your own?"

When she reached out and ruffled his hair in a playful manner, he jumped away from her. She burst into laughter.

"What's the matter, are you afraid I'll contaminate you, that my evil ways will rub off on you?"

"Yes, as a matter of fact, I am afraid of exactly that."

Her warm, exuberant smile faded quickly, replaced by a killer glare so sharp it could have cut through steel. The minute Lyle saw the hurt look in her eyes, he wished the words back. But it was too late.

"Let's go in the attic and check things out." Roz headed toward the door that enclosed the hidden staircase leading to the third level of the house. "I need plenty of time to get gorgeous for my late date with Gavin. He's the kind of guy who loves being around a woman like me."

Lyle wanted to explain and to apologize, but he did neither; instead he remained silent—hadn't he already said more than enough?—and followed her up the narrow winding stairs and into the attic.

"It's awfully dark up here," Roz said. "If it weren't for that one little window, we wouldn't be able to see a thing."

"Stand aside and let me see if I can find a light switch."

He fumbled around in the semidarkness and accidentally ran smack dab into a lightbulb hanging at the end of an electrical cord that was attached to the ceiling. Amazingly the bulb still burned and gave off enough dim light to partially illuminate the space. Only a fraction of the area had flooring, the rest was a beehive of wooden boards and high arched beams.

"Looks pretty empty to me," Roz said. "I doubt we'll find anything up here."

As Lyle glanced around, he spotted something in a far corner, a large, bulky object. He walked toward what he soon realized was some sort of old trunk. He ran his hand over the battered lid and dust flew everywhere. The particles danced in the air and tickled his nose. Suddenly he went into a sneezing frenzy.

"Bless you," Roz said as she approached him. "Are you okay?"

"I'm fine. Just allergic to dust."

"What have you found?" She eyed the dusty, battered old trunk. "Does it have a lock?"

Lyle knelt down and inspected the trunk. "Yes, it does."

"Well, hallelujah. This is the first thing, other than the doors, that we've found in the house that actually has a lock."

While he was still bent over and without warning of any kind, Roz let out an ear-splitting scream and all but jumped on top of him.

"What on earth?" he mumbled as he toppled to the floor and landed flat on his back.

Roz, who was hanging on to him for dear life, fell on top of him. He looked up to find her face only inches from his. Her slender form draped his body like a blanket.

"There are mice up here." Roz's voice quivered. "I hate mice!"

"You knocked me down and jumped on top of me because you saw a mouse?" *Get off me this minute. Please. If you don't, I'm not going to be responsible for what my body does in the next sixty seconds.*

"Not just a mouse. Two mice. They went scurrying across the floor—over there." She pointed the direction.

God help me, Lyle prayed. His lips twitched. Roz glared at him. His mouth turned up in a smile he could not control.

"Don't you dare laugh at me," she said.

"Sorry."

Their gazes connected and for one timeless moment they stared at each other. Breaths stilled. Heartbeats stopped. The world beyond their two entwined bodies ceased to exist. He couldn't prevent what was happening. Heaven help him! She had to be able to feel his arousal.

Almost immediately she shoved herself up and off of him. "We wouldn't want anybody to catch you rolling around in the dirt with the likes of me, would we?" Forcing a laugh, she shrugged. "What would they think?"

Lyle rose to a sitting position, then looked up at her. "They'd probably wonder why a pretty, sexy girl like you would have jumped my bones."

Roz stared at him, apparently as surprised by his statement as he was. A soft little giggle erupted from her throat, followed by genuine laughter. "Hey, Rev, you actually have a sense of humor, don't you?"

Her good humor ignited his own and he started laughing, too. She had thought he was joking, when he'd actually been dead serious. Why would a girl like Roz be interested in a quiet, self-contained minister, who wasn't anything special? After all, he was a slightly overweight carrottop who most definitely resembled Howdy Doody much more than Tom Cruise. Thank God Roz had diffused the tension between them by injecting the situation with a healthy dose of humor. Lord only knew what he would have done if she'd taken his comment seriously.

When they heard Roz scream, Wolfe grabbed Caroline's wrist and pulled her along with him as he rushed out into the hall and toward the backstairs. "Stay behind me." He undid his holster and removed his Sig Sauer P228.

Together they crept up the stairs, Wolfe cautious and prepared for whatever he might find. He could sense the tension in Caroline, could smell the fear and understood her concern for her friend. He felt an odd sensation of being connected not only to Caroline's thought processes, but to her emotions as well.

Following his instructions, she stayed at his back, close enough to him so that whenever he paused he could feel the warmth of her breath. Suddenly, as they neared the open door that revealed the bottom of the narrow steps that led to the attic, they heard laughter.

"Hey, up there," Wolfe called. "What's going on?"

"Roz, we heard you scream," Caroline said. "Are you all right?"

"I'm fine," Roz yelled. "Come on up. We think we might have found something."

Wolfe stepped back and motioned for Caroline to go first. She nodded and began to climb the tight passageway. Before her feet reached the top step, her head and shoulders cleared the opening. When she hesitated, Wolfe gave her a gentle shove to set her in motion again. A single lightbulb, hanging from the ceiling by a frayed electrical cord, dispersed a dim light. Sitting atop the only visible object in the attic—an old trunk of some sort—Roz waved them forward. Lyle stood at her side, a wide grin on his face. Then suddenly he sneezed.

"Excuse me. Dust is everywhere."

"One of you want to tell me what's going on?" Wolfe asked.

"Look what we found." Roz stood, moved to the side and waved her hand in a gesture of introduction. "Ta-da. It's an old trunk. And it's locked." Her big brown eyes rounded wide with delight, like those of a child who had discovered a treasure trove of toys.

"I think what Wolfe meant was why did you scream?" Caroline looked point-blank at Roz. "I suppose you know you scared me half to death."

"It wasn't anything," Lyle said. "Our wild, fearless Roz saw a mouse run across the floor and screamed like crazy."

"It wasn't just one mouse," Roz told them. "It was two mice."

"Whatever." Lyle shrugged. "She was so scared she tried to climb me like a tree and we wound up falling on the floor and—"

"I suppose that's when y'all started laughing?" Caroline asked.

Roz nodded. "Who would have thought the rev would actually have a sense of humor about the whole thing. Go figure." Roz grinned at Lyle, who smiled sheepishly, as if he were slightly embarrassed.

"Glad you two are getting along better," Wolfe said.

"Now, how about we give the lock on that trunk a try. If the key doesn't fit it, then we might as well leave because we've searched this place thoroughly."

They gathered around the old trunk. Caroline dropped to her knees in front of it and eased the chain over her head, then she tried to insert the key into the lock. It didn't fit. She removed the key, turned it upside down and tried again. Still no fit.

"It won't even go in." Caroline draped the chain back around her neck. "So much for solving the riddle today."

"I thought you were going to Fletch's house after we left here to go through the things of his father's that he's kept stored all these years," Lyle said, then sneezed again. "You might find something there."

"Fletch is in D.C. today, so we're going over tomorrow at lunch," Caroline said. "Fletch wants to be there with us when we check through Preston's things. Besides, tonight is my volunteer evening at the church. Remember?"

Lyle nodded. "People at the church are going to wonder who Mr. Wolfe is and why he's sticking to you like glue. You probably don't want to tell them that he's your bodyguard."

"We'll just tell them that he's a friend," Caroline said.

"If it were me, I'd tell them that he's my new boyfriend." Roz sighed dreamily as she batted her eyelashes at Wolfe.

Caroline's and Wolfe's gazes collided. Tension wound inside Wolfe's gut. Caroline's cheeks flushed a soft pink.

Don't let your mind wander into forbidden territory, he cautioned himself. You are Caroline McGuire's bodyguard, hired by and paid for by her stepbrother. David Wolfe has no past with her and most certainly no future. You are a temporary necessity in her life and that's all. You are here to protect her, to keep her safe. And once she is no longer in danger, you will disappear from her life—forever.

Chapter 8

Wolfe stood in the doorway and watched her while she slept. Moonlight covered her bed like a creamy, transparent blanket. He knew he had no right to invade her privacy this way, no legitimate reason to hover outside her bedroom. But God help him, he could not resist the temptation to observe her without her being aware of his presence. Whenever he stared at her for a moment too long, she gazed at him questioningly and he could give her no explanation for being so fascinated with her. He could hardly say, "I'm David. Your David. The man who has kept watch over you all these years. I gave you the camera that is your most prized possession and the pearl-and-diamond earrings that are your favorites. You have been the most important person in my life for the past fifteen years. Through all the dark and lonely nights, the unemotional and controlled days, you have been my heart…my soul…my secret treasure."

Since coming into her life two nights ago, he had already discovered that Caroline was all that he had believed her to be. He had observed her with her friends, employees and clients and marveled at the way people were drawn to her. At Lyle's church, where they had gone after leaving the Sheffield Street house earlier in the evening, Caroline had spent an hour tutoring an underprivileged child in reading and then worked in the church's cafeteria for two hours serving meals to the homeless. Lyle had told him that she devoted at least one evening a week, occasionally two or three evenings, to her volunteer activities, but her generosity didn't end there. Caroline paid for clothes for needy children and provided financial assistance to deserving students who desperately needed help with college tuition.

"She knows from firsthand experience what having a caring benefactor can mean in a young person's life," Lyle had said. "No doubt she has told you about David. Everyone who knows Caroline knows the story of her David."

Wolfe closed his eyes to shut out the sight of her lying peacefully, innocently in her bed. The sheet and blanket draped her hips, leaving her upper body unveiled. She rested on her side, the curve of one bare arm fitted beneath the swell of her breasts. He felt ashamed that his body betrayed him, reacting to her beauty in a purely physical way. He was here to protect her, not to ravage her. But every instinct he had was urging him to take possession of this woman. The primitive male within him told him that she was his. His alone. In a way she had not—nor ever could—belong to another man.

He envisioned her awakening, looking at him and smiling. She rose from the bed, her gown diaphanous and flowing, her hair hanging in disarray around her shoulders. With her arms outstretched, she came to him and enveloped him in her sweetness. He swept her up into his arms and carried her back to the bed. She whispered his name. "David. My David." And then with her lips a hairbreadth from his, she gazed adoringly into his eyes and said, "I want you. Please, make love to me."

Wolfe's sex hardened painfully, need riding him hard. He

opened his eyes, took one final look at the woman he longed for, then turned and walked across the hall to his room. To his lonely bed. Back to the reality that Caroline was as out of his reach as the stars in the night sky.

Caroline woke with a start, the feeling of having been touched, of a large, strong hand caressing her body overpoweringly real. After tossing back the covers, she sat up and scooted to the edge of her bed. A shiver of longing shuddered through her, a sexual tingling she had never experienced before that moment. She had dated her share of men, had always immensely enjoyed kissing and had even experimented with some heavy petting a few times, but in the end she had always drawn back, always put a stop to things before they got out of control. Whenever that had happened, she had convinced herself she simply didn't want sex without a lifetime commitment, but in retrospect she admitted to herself the real reason. Caroline felt, in her heart, that she could not give herself to a man without loving him.

She flipped on the bedside lamp, slid her feet into her plush cloth slippers and stood. A tender quiet permeated the house, disturbed only by the soft, comforting sounds of night whispers. The distant lull of water lapping against the shore. The hum of springtime insects. The sigh of a nighttime breeze. The gentle creaking of old timbers. She picked up her cotton robe from the nearby chair, put it on, walked across the room and out into the hall. Was Wolfe asleep? she wondered.

Caroline tiptoed across the hall, halting in the open doorway of his bedroom. Moonlight illuminated the area enough for her to make out his shape where he rested flat on his back atop the covers. With his arms lifted to his head and his entwined fingers resting at the nape of his neck, his position accentuated the breadth of his wide shoulders and the muscles in his big arms. Her heartbeat accelerated instantly when she realized he wore nothing but a pair of dark pajama bottoms. An aura of breathtaking power and masculine strength surrounded him and a subtle sensuality exuded from every pore in his magnificently proportioned body.

As if drawn to him by some magnetic force she was powerless to resist, Caroline stepped over the threshold and into his room. Wolfe shot straight up in bed and reached for his weapon hidden under his pillow. Before Caroline realized what was happening, he was beside her, every muscle in his body tense, a look of predatory energy on his face.

"Caroline?"

She released her indrawn breath on a long, relieved sigh. "I'm sorry. I didn't mean to wake you. I shouldn't have come in here. I'll go—"

When she turned to leave, he moved quickly to snap on the bedside lamp and lay his gun on the nightstand. Then he caught up with her and clamped his hand down on her shoulder with gentle strength. "Are you all right?"

Without glancing back at him, she nodded. His hand on her shoulder was hard and hot. His rough fingertips absently massaged her muscles. A man's touch had never taken her breath away. Not like this. Powerless to stop herself, she pivoted slowly until she faced him. He maintained his hold on her shoulder and increased the pressure just a little as he moved his hand down to cuff her bare upper arm. Unable to bring herself to look him in the eye, she cast her gaze toward his chest and what she saw startled her. She gasped, then lifted her hand and laid it on his brutally scarred upper torso. He grabbed her hand and she thought he was going to snatch it away. But instead he held it there where she'd placed it over his heart.

"What happened to you?" she asked, hypnotized by the viciousness of his scars.

"An accident," he told her, his voice low and husky.

"Oh, Wolfe. How awful for you. You must have suffered terribly. You poor darling."

He lifted her hand away from his chest, turned it palm up and brought it to his lips. When his warm, moist mouth grazed her sensitive flesh, she trembled. There was such gentleness in the way he stroked her, the way he eased his hand up and down her arm, caressing her with a lover's touch. Her gaze lifted to his and a tremor of pure undiluted sexual longing spiraled up from the core of her femininity when he looked at her as if he intended to take her, here and now.

She swayed toward him, unable to resist, swept away by the moment and the heady sensual experience. His gaze narrowed, shrinking his eyes to mere slits. His nostrils flared. His breath became labored. She sensed that he was an aroused beast and she was his appeasement. Excitement dulled her fear as pure animal instinct took control of her mind and body, telling her that he was her mate, the man she had been waiting for all these years.

Abruptly Wolfe shoved her away. Startled by the unexpected action, she caught her breath and glared at him, not understanding his sudden rejection of her.

"You should go back to bed," he said, a hint of regret in his commanding voice.

She nodded, then swallowed hard and said, "Yes. Yes, I should." Embarrassment claimed her with a vengeance and she all but ran from his bedroom, across the hall and into her own room. She started to slam the door shut, but remembered his orders to always leave the door open. With her pulse pounding at breakneck speed, her face hot with shame, Caroline hurried into her bathroom, closed the door and dropped to her knees. Tears streamed down her face.

What had she almost done? Wolfe must think her a hussy to have come into his room and all but attack him. He would have no way of knowing that she had never reacted that way to another man. Only to him.

Ellison stood and rounded his desk when Oliver Harper entered his office. He hadn't seen Oliver in nearly a year and then it had been a brief hello at some political function they'd both been obligated to attend. Although they'd known each other since their days at Harvard, they had never actually been friends. More friendly acquaintances than anything else. Ellison had always liked Oliver, despite the differences in their political leanings and the fact that Oliver had all but stolen Eileen from him when they'd been a couple of young bucks vying for her affections.

"What brings you to Peacekeepers International?" Ellison asked as he extended his hand.

Oliver exchanged a cordial handshake with Ellison, all the while bestowing his most charming smile on his old rival. "Nothing to do with international affairs. I can assure you that I leave all that diplomatic stuff to you do-gooders. You know me, Ellison, I'm of the persuasion to bomb 'em and ask questions later."

Ellison chuckled. Oliver never changed and never apologized for his beliefs. He was the same old right-wing, militant conservative he'd always been. "Then to what do I owe the honor of your visit this morning? I'm afraid if there's trouble on Wall Street, you've come to the wrong organization for help." Ellison indicated a chair to Oliver, then stepped back and leaned his hip against the front edge of his desk.

"No financial complaints." Oliver nodded and sat in the proffered leather chair. "What I've come to you about is something of a personal nature."

Ellison's brows lifted as his eyes rounded with curiosity. "Would you care for some coffee? Or perhaps a cup of tea?"

"No, thank you." Oliver relaxed his tall, lean frame in the chair and crossed his legs. "I suppose you know all about the attempt on Caroline McGuire's life recently."

Ellison nodded. "Hmm-mmm."

"I figured Gavin Robbins was keeping you informed. Brooke told me that Caroline dated Gavin for a while and he was actually her date that terrible night aboard Fletch's yacht. He was rather lax in his duty, wasn't he? If he'd been with her—"

"Get to the point," Ellison said, his voice a bit more testy than he'd intended. "What personal interest do you have in Caroline McGuire, other than the fact she and your daughter are friends?"

"Isn't that enough? If not, then surely you recall that Preston Shaw was a friend of mine. Our families have been socially connected for generations. And Preston adored Caroline. You know the poor child had a nervous breakdown after Preston's murder, so naturally Brooke and I are concerned about her mental health now. Caroline seems convinced that there's some credence to that ridiculous letter Preston left."

"What makes you think the letter is ridiculous?"

Oliver laughed. "I knew Preston. He was a bon vivant, a man who loved the good things in life and got a great deal of pleasure out of his role as a diplomat. He wasn't the type to be involved in espionage."

"Perhaps you didn't know Preston as well as you thought you did. Perhaps none of us really knew him."

"Of course it's possible you're right." Oliver sighed. "At this late date, that's neither here nor there, is it? There isn't anything we can do to help poor old Preston, but Caroline is a different matter. Considering the fact that Preston was one of your own, I'm sure you're as interested as my family is in safeguarding his stepdaughter."

"I understand from Gavin Robbins that Fletcher Shaw hired a professional bodyguard for Caroline. I don't see that there's anything else to be done."

"Now you've hit upon my concern." Oliver leaned forward, his gaze connecting boldly with Ellison's. "I'd like for you to use your connections and have an in-depth security check done on this Mr. Wolfe. I've already made some phone calls and found out that the Dundee agency has an exemplary reputation. It's one of the best, if not *the* best, security and investigation agency in the country. But I wasn't able to get any real information on Mr. Wolfe. His background seems to be a mystery and that fact bothers me. If there's the remotest possibility that there is any truth to what Preston wrote in that letter, then we can't afford to trust anyone.''

"Not even each other," Ellison said in a deadpan manner.

Oliver guffawed loudly. "I trust you, Ellison. You're probably the most trustworthy man I know. That's why I've come to you with my concerns. Find out what you can about this man Fletcher hired to protect Caroline. Let's make sure that she's safe in his hands."

"All right," Ellison replied. "As a favor to you and because Caroline is Preston Shaw's stepdaughter, I'll run a check on Mr. Wolfe." Ellison realized that he would have to pacify Oliver with a fake report on David Wolfe; otherwise his old friend was bound to become suspicious. And that was something he couldn't allow to happen.

Oliver rose to his feet. "You'll let me know the minute you get the information on him?"

"It could take a few days."

Oliver stepped forward and clasped Ellison's hand. "A few days would be perfect. We can discuss your findings at the dinner we're having this weekend to raise funds for Fletcher's political campaign. You are planning to attend, aren't you?"

"Didn't receive an invitation." Ellison pulled his hand from Oliver's grip.

"Consider yourself invited." Oliver grinned. "I'll see that Eileen adds your name to the guest list. She'll be delighted to see you again. It's been what—five years or more since you two saw each other?"

"Give or take a year," Ellison said.

"Caroline will be at the dinner, escorted by her bodyguard. If there's any reason Fletcher needs to dismiss Mr. Wolfe, then we can present a united front and I can immediately call in a man from the agency I use. Eastbrook, Inc., out of Richmond. We've used their bodyguards for years, whenever there was any need."

Ellison followed Oliver into the outer office, past his secretary and all the way down the corridor to the private elevator. The door to Gavin Robbins's office, directly across the hall from the elevators, stood wide open and Gavin's assistant, Mike Latham, glanced up from his desk to make eye contact with Ellison. Gavin had hand-picked his assistant, just as Ellison had, and with his legal background, Latham had proved himself an invaluable asset to the Peacekeepers. The minute the elevator doors closed, Ellison reversed directions and headed straight back to his office. He paused momentarily at his secretary's desk. Barry Vanderpool, whose father had been a Peacekeepers agent until his untimely death, was the most efficient secretary Ellison had ever had. The young man had a knack for anticipating Ellison's every need. He was quite proud of the fact that he had handpicked Barry from a long list of applicants and his instincts had proved him right.

"I don't want to be disturbed for the next half hour."

"Yes, sir," Barry replied.

Ellison closed and locked his office door, then removed his cellular phone, which worked off a scrambled security frequency, thus preventing interception. He dialed the number that he had memorized and waited, tapping his foot on the floor, while the phone rang.

When the familiar voice answered, Ellison said, "We've got a big problem."

"I can't believe we didn't find anything, not even a hint of a clue in all these things." Caroline dropped the handful of old, yellowed letters back into the ornately carved wooden box lying in the middle of Fletcher Shaw's attic.

"I felt certain when we finally unearthed this box that the key would fit it," Fletcher said. "But the thing wasn't even locked."

Brooke leaned over the back of the dilapidated chair in which Fletcher sat, among the array of stored antique furniture and boxed family items. She wrapped her arms around his neck and kissed his right temple. "I'm so sorry, dear. I know how disappointed you and Caroline must be."

"Is there anything else that you can think of?" Wolfe asked. "Something that your father could have left somewhere else?"

"Lenore cleared out his safety deposit box," Fletcher said. "So that's ruled out. And the key doesn't fit any locks in the Sheffield Street house that he shared with Lenore, nor does it fit any locks in this house, where he once lived with Mother."

"What about his office at Peacekeepers International?" Brooke asked.

"I'd already thought of that," Fletcher said. "I phoned Ellison Penn and he assured me that every key issued to Father by the Peacekeepers was accounted for shortly after Father's death. Besides, none of the old keys fit any of the new locks in the Peacekeepers building."

"There has to be something we're overlooking." Caroline paced the unfinished wood floor, trying her best to avoid eye contact with Wolfe. Ever since what had occurred between them in the wee hours of the night, she'd felt a keen sense of embarrassment. When he didn't mention the incident this morning, she felt relieved and thankful that his demeanor toward her had returned to robotic efficiency. Their breakfast conversation had consisted of nothing more than the plans for the day. Then at the studio, while she'd photographed four different clients before noon, Wolfe had stood guard quietly, his gaze only occasionally meeting hers and then moving on quickly.

"Everything that belonged to Father is stored right here," Fletcher said. "And as far as I know, when Lenore left for Europe, she didn't take any of Father's personal items, just his money and her jewels."

"By any chance, did your father have an apartment in D.C.?" Wolfe asked.

"No." Fletcher shook his head.

"What about cars? Did Lenore sell his cars or did you get them?" Wolfe glanced first at Fletcher and then at Caroline.

"I have no idea," Caroline admitted. "Mother left for Europe only a few weeks after Preston's funeral and she'd already shipped me off to Aunt Dixie's by then."

"She sold her Mercedes and Father's BMW," Fletcher said. "But I still have the '39 Alfa Romeo coupe. He willed the thing to me."

A flash of color swept through Caroline's mind. Wind blowing her hair. She and Fletcher giggling. Preston smiling happily. Caroline remembered how she'd loved taking rides out to the Maryland countryside with Fletch and Preston in that fabulous old car. Preston had adored antique cars and had bought and sold several over the years, but he'd always kept the Alfa Romeo—the 8C 2900 Sport Spider. Odd that she would remember that tidbit of information. But then whenever Preston had taken them out in the old car, which he'd had repainted a brilliant red, he had raved on and on about it to them. "Where is the Alfa Romeo now?" she asked.

"I stored it in the garage at my grandparents' cottage in Windhaven." Fletch sighed. "I'm afraid I haven't even seen the old car in years. I didn't inherit Father's love for antique vehicles." Fletch's eyes widened as a suspicion came to mind. "I say, you don't think the key fits the Alfa Romeo, do you?"

"I doubt it," Wolfe said. "But there's a possibility that your father could have stored something in the trunk or the glove compartment that requires a key to unlock."

Caroline focused her gaze on Fletcher. "Would it be all right with you if Wolfe and I drive down to Windhaven and have a look at the car?" She glanced at Wolfe, anticipation glowing in her eyes. "I can call Roz and have her reschedule my afternoon appointments and we could leave right away."

Wolfe looked to Fletcher for approval. "Do we have your

permission to check the car over and remove anything we find?''

Fletch disengaged himself from Brooke's clinging embrace and stood. He shoved his hands into the pockets of his tailored slacks and paced across the attic. ''I'd drive down with you, but I have a meeting with Senator Marshall and Congressman Williams at three today.'' He paused, looked directly at Caroline and then reached out to grasp her by the shoulders. ''I want to find out the truth about Father's murder as much as you do, but not at the cost of your life. I'd rather never know than to risk your getting hurt. But if you're determined to continue with the search, then—''

''I am determined.'' She laid her hands over his where he held her shoulders securely. ''I have no intention of letting someone get away with murder, not if there's the remotest possibility that I can bring Preston's killer to justice.''

''Very well.'' Fletcher kissed Caroline's cheek, then released his hold on her. ''I'll call up Teddy Richards, the caretaker there at the cottage, so he'll be expecting you. I'll explain to him why you're driving down. '' Fletch turned to Wolfe. ''You have my permission to tear the damn car apart if you think you can find anything. And whatever you find, by all means bring it back with you.''

''Then we can leave from here?'' Caroline asked Wolfe.

He nodded.

''I'll call Roz right away.'' When Caroline headed toward the attic stairs, Brooke followed her.

When the women were out of earshot, Fletch said, ''I'm holding you personally responsible if anything happens to her.''

''I can promise you that nothing is going to happen to her as long as there's breath in my body.'' Wolfe glared at Fletcher, his gaze and stance vowing as surely as his words that he was completely and wholeheartedly dedicated to protecting Caroline.

Fletcher narrowed his gaze and stared at Wolfe oddly, as

if he couldn't quite figure out what motivated his stepsister's bodyguard. Wolfe didn't give a damn. Let Fletcher Shaw think what he would. David Wolfe was in Caroline's life now, her constant companion, and until she was safe from all danger, only an act of God could sever him from her side.

Chapter 9

Interstate 97 took them to Annapolis. Then Caroline stayed on Highway 2, heading south, until they reached their turnoff onto a county road that would take them to the coast and the tiny village of Windhaven, which wasn't even a speck on the map. Wolfe sat on the passenger side, riding shotgun, while Caroline drove. He read aloud Fletch's directions that would lead them to his maternal grandparents' waterfront cottage— and hopefully to a discovery inside Preston Shaw's antique car stored there in the garage. Nothing would suit Wolfe better than to learn what the mysterious key opened. Not only would that disclosure put an end to the threat on Caroline's life, but it would enable Wolfe to hand over, to Ellison Penn, the unquestionable proof of Preston Shaw's guilt as well as the evidence against Shaw's cohorts. The Peacekeepers had had enough proof of Shaw's guilt to order his death and Wolfe had simply been following orders when he executed Caroline's stepfather. But having recently seen a new perspective of Preston Shaw through Caroline's and Fletch's eyes made him wonder if there was even the slightest possibility that the Peacekeepers had made a mistake. Wolfe's conscience would rest easier when even the tiniest glimmer of doubt was removed from his mind.

The truth would no doubt break Caroline's heart. She still thought of Preston Shaw as not only an honorable person, but as a good and kind man. Wolfe regretted that it would be necessary to ruin her cherished memories of the man she'd thought of as a father. But now that she had found the mysterious key and had become obsessed with locating the hidden evidence, there was no other way to protect her. As much as he would like to see the other members of the highly secret, traitorous group of which Shaw had been a leader revealed and punished, Wolfe would prefer Caroline never know the complete truth about her stepfather. If they found the evidence Shaw had professed to have in his possession, then Wolfe decided that he would do his best to keep her from being exposed to all the ugly details.

But what if they didn't find what the key unlocked? What if weeks went by, even months, without unearthing the damaging evidence? Would Caroline give up the quest? Dear God, he hoped she would. If not, she would live in constant danger from an unknown enemy.

Wolfe would have felt more at ease right now if fewer people knew their whereabouts. Fletcher and Brooke had taken part in making the plans to go to Windhaven, so it was only reasonable to assume that Brooke might tell her parents, despite his warnings to tell no one. Roz knew, too, and it was possible that she had disregarded instructions and had by now told Gavin and/or Lyle. If Gavin knew, then he might have informed Ellison, or if the boss had been unavailable, then Ellison's trusted secretary. It wasn't that Wolfe suspected anyone in particular, but he had learned the hard way that a cautious man trusted no one. Sometimes even the closest friend might prove to be a person's most deadly enemy.

Wolfe spread his right hand and, using his thumb and middle finger, clasped the side of the frames and repositioned his tinted glasses to rest more securely on the bridge of his nose. Without moving an inch and alerting Caroline, Wolfe scanned their surroundings. She slowed her Lincoln LS when a forty-five mile-per-hour speed limit sign appeared along the side of the road. The area in which they had been traveling was definitely rural and was now becoming more coastal with each passing mile.

They had spoken very little on the long ride from Fletcher's home in Baltimore. No idle chitchat. No heart-to-heart conversation. He read the directions whenever necessary. She commented occasionally on this or that roadway scene. He suspected she felt every bit as awkward as he did after their middle-of-the-night sensual exchange in his bedroom. Try as he might, he couldn't get the sight of her, the scent of her, the feel of her out of his mind. It had taken a great deal of willpower to release her, to reject the offer he'd seen in her lavender-blue eyes. She had wanted him as surely as he had wanted her. How was he going to continue guarding her night and day and resist the sweetest temptation on earth?

"Directions, please." She glanced his way hurriedly, then refocused on the road. "Is our turnoff close?"

Wolfe looked over the directions again, then gazed out the window. "Harcourt Road should be about two miles from here. Fletch says we can smell the sea from that point on."

Caroline grinned, then sighed. "I'm desperately trying not to get my hopes up about finding anything in the Alfa Romeo. But it would be just like Preston to have hidden something important in the car he dearly loved. I keep wondering that if he wanted Mother to find the evidence, why would he leave the car to Fletch?"

"Good question."

They remained silent until Wolfe spotted the turn. "There's Harcourt Road."

She whipped the Lincoln off onto the rough, uneven course, slowing almost to a standstill after hitting a rather large pothole. She grumbled under her breath. The narrow two-lane local roadway was in bad need of repair. If they hadn't been traveling at such a slow speed, they would have probably missed the town of Windhaven, which consisted of a gas station-minimart and little else. A row of empty buildings and a few boats docked in the small harbor comprised what had no doubt been a small, active seacoast village years ago. As they wound their way through the remnants of the old town, Wolfe noted a few signs of new life on the outskirts and wondered what group of wealthy investors had gobbled up the place, probably intending to turn it into a tourist mecca.

"We go half a mile and then turn off onto a gravel road that leads to a dirt road that will take us straight to the cottage," Wolfe said.

She nodded. "Looks like Windhaven will be another tourist destination in a year or two. Pity."

In less than five minutes, they found the cottage, located on a dirt road close to the bay and within walking distance of five other old waterfront houses, built decades ago as summer homes. Standing outside the cottage, his hand raised in greeting, stood a man Wolfe guessed to be at least seventy-five, his bald head gleaming in the late afternoon sunlight.

"That must be Teddy Richards." Caroline pulled the Lincoln to a stop in the overgrown driveway.

"And there's the Alfa Romeo." Wolfe pointed toward the garage, which was the exact shade of yellow as the house. On both the paint was faded and peeling. The rather rickety-looking open garage door hung precariously on rusted hinges.

Caroline removed her seat belt, flung open the door and jumped out and onto the ground. Wolfe hurried so that she got only a few steps ahead of him on her way toward the garage.

"Hey there, you Caroline McGuire?" the elderly man asked.

Caroline held out her hand as she approached him. Wolfe

barely restrained himself from halting her friendly greeting. What were the odds that this old codger was a hit man? Slim to none. But pure instinct guided Wolfe as he slipped his hand beneath the edge of his lightweight sports coat to undo the snap on his hip holster. His hand hovered close to the weapon as Caroline shook hands with the man who identified himself as Teddy.

"Mr. Fletcher said to let y'all do whatever you wanted with the car," Teddy said. "So there she is. Like to take a closer look?"

Wolfe grabbed Caroline's arm as she headed straight for the garage. "Wait a minute."

She glanced over her shoulder, giving him a puzzled stare. "We can hardly check the trunk and the glove compartment or whatever else from this distance."

Wolfe looked at the garage. Nestled inside the small structure's belly was a magnificent antique car, its sides and fenders a single molded unit that tapered to a teardrop rear end. The long curved roofline swooped forward to a split and curved windshield. Like an ageless lady of great style and beauty, Pinin Farina's classic automobile outshone any present-day models. Wolfe owned several vintage vehicles himself, having begun his collection shortly after his resurrection from the dead and his move to Atlanta. He kept his '59 Corvette and his Ferrari 250 swb garaged at his home in Tennessee.

"I'll bring her out so you can get a good look at her," Teddy said. "Not much room to maneuver in the garage and no electricity out there, so no lights."

While Teddy made his way, rather briskly for an old man, toward the garage, Caroline turned to Wolfe. "Are you suspicious of Mr. Richards?" A closemouthed smile spread across her face. "My heavens, he's probably eighty years old."

"A professional weakness," Wolfe admitted. "Not trusting anyone. Suspecting even the most innocent-looking person.''

He placed his hand in the small of her back. She stiffened instantly. He assumed that Caroline had been as curious as he to know how they both would react when they touched again. For him it was a blend of pleasure and agony. His instincts told him that for her it was the same.

''Move over to the side of the house,'' Wolfe suggested. ''I'm not sure I trust Teddy's driving skills.''

Caroline laughed softly as she allowed Wolfe to guide her to what he considered a safer location. They both watched as Teddy opened the driver's side door of the antique car and slipped behind the wheel. Suddenly a pure gut reaction prompted Wolfe to call out to the old man. He had allowed the physical contact with Caroline to momentarily distract him and that distraction had sidetracked his normally astute instincts.

''Wait! Don't start the engine,'' Wolfe cried.

Caroline looked at Wolfe, her eyes widening in surprise, as if questioning his sanity. But within seconds, her look changed to one of shock and then of horror. A loud, ear-splitting blast rocked the ground on which they stood as the Alfa Romeo, the garage and Teddy Richards were blown to kingdom come.

''Son of a bitch!'' As the sound of the explosion reverberated in their ears, Wolfe shoved Caroline to the ground and covered her with his body.

Debris sailed high into the sky—pieces of yellow wood, fragments of red metal, gravel, grass, dirt and the minuscule particles that had once comprised a human body. Bits and pieces of the remains rained down on them, peppering Wolfe's body and showering across the yard and the cottage. Fire singed the earth where the garage had once stood and little outbreaks flamed up all around them. Wolfe prayed that Caroline's Lincoln was far enough way from the blast to have survived intact. It was their only means of escape. His guess was that the explosives had been wired to the ignition, set to activate the moment the car was started. Maybe the person who had placed the bomb in the Alfa Romeo was long gone. But what if he or she had waited around to make sure the blast had done its job? Caroline had been the target, not Teddy Richards.

As soon as the dust settled, Wolfe rose to his knees and closely surveyed the destruction all around them. His tinted glasses, which had fallen off when he'd hit the ground, lay broken only a couple of inches from his right foot. His gaze moved to settle on the Lincoln, which was covered with dust and particles from the blast. Flying debris had smashed in the back window and pockmarked the side of the vehicle. Wolfe rose to his feet, then jerked Caroline to a standing position. She shivered uncontrollably. He ran his hands up and down her arms, then shook her gently.

"We've got to get out of here. Do you understand?"

She nodded and obediently let him lead her hurriedly toward the car. He opened the passenger door and shoved her inside, then closed and locked the door and rounded the hood. The minute he slid behind the wheel, she held out the car keys, which she had earlier slipped into the pocket of her slacks. Her hand shook uncontrollably.

"Poor old Teddy Richards," Caroline said, tears in her voice.

Wolfe reached over, caressed her dirty cheek, then inserted the key in the ignition and started the Lincoln. With only one thought in mind—to protect Caroline—he reversed the car, whipped it out onto the road and slammed his foot down on the gas pedal.

When Wolfe pulled the battered Lincoln into the driveway at Caroline's home at fifteen past eleven that night, four people came rushing off the well-lit front porch where they had been waiting. Roz was the first to reach Caroline, with Brooke a close second. Wolfe allowed the two women to push him aside as they rushed to smother their friend with hugs and dampen her with their tears of relief and joy.

"Oh, God, Caroline, when you phoned Lyle from the Calvert County sheriff's office and told him what happened, he called me immediately." Roz brushed strands of Caroline's disheveled hair out of her eyes. "We've been worried sick."

"Lyle called Fletch, too, and the four of us have been out of our minds with worry," Brooke said. "My poor Fletch has been blaming himself for Teddy Richards's death. And he's been frantic about you."

Wolfe glanced over his shoulder at the two men who stood nearby, as if waiting their turn, then focused his attention on the two women flanking Caroline. Someone had passed along information, whether maliciously or innocently, that had enabled a professional to prepare a booby trap for Caroline. Was one of these four dear friends capable of such treachery? He wanted desperately to rule out Lyle, and if not for his cynical nature, he would have. For the life of him, he couldn't see Reverend Jennings harming a hair on anyone's head, let alone willingly helping someone murder Caroline. The other three, each in his or her own way, were a possibility, even though his instincts told him their affection for Caroline was genuine.

"Caroline." Lyle held out his hands as Roz and Brooke led her up the walkway.

Caroline paused, pulled away from her girlfriends and grabbed Lyle's hands, then put her arms around him and hugged him fiercely. Tears streamed down Lyle's cheeks as he clung to her.

"I'm so thankful you're all right," Lyle said. "I've prayed almost nonstop since you called me, letting the Lord know how grateful I am that he spared your life."

"Did you thank the Lord for sending Mr. Wolfe to me?" Caroline asked, as she pulled back from her cousin and searched for Wolfe.

Fletcher came forward but didn't block the path or prevent

Wolfe from being able to see Caroline. With a fragile, tentative tilt of her lips, she smiled at her stepbrother.

"If only I hadn't sent you down to Windhaven..." Fletcher's voice cracked with emotion.

Caroline caressed Fletcher's cheek, then kissed him with sisterly affection. "Stop blaming yourself for what happened. You had no way of knowing that someone would get there ahead of us and plant a bomb in Preston's Alfa Romeo."

Wolfe followed closely, just behind the foursome as they escorted Caroline to her front porch, then he moved around them to unlock the door. He went in first, turned on the lights, punched in the security code and scanned the foyer before motioning for the others to come inside. Once they were congregated in the foyer, Wolfe disengaged Caroline from her quartet of concerned friends. She gasped when he grabbed her arm. The others stood rigidly still, their gazes riveted to Caroline.

"I have a few questions for y'all," Wolfe said. "And after I get the answers, I want all of you to leave."

"What?"

"Now, see here..."

"I had planned to stay...."

"What sort of questions?"

Wolfe jerked Caroline to his side. She went without protest, although the look on her face warned him that she would confront him later.

"Come with me." Wolfe led the way, hauling Caroline with him. He gently shoved her down into an overstuffed easy chair and took his guard post behind her. The others made their way into the living room. The women sat side by side on the sofa. Lyle took the rocking chair to Caroline's left. Remaining on his feet, Fletcher crossed his arms over his chest and glared at Wolfe.

"Only six people knew that Caroline and I were going to Windhaven to search through Preston Shaw's antique Alfa Romeo," Wolfe said. "Caroline and I. Fletcher, Brooke and

Roz. And Teddy Richards. But I think we can rule out Mr. Richards as a suspect.''

"A suspect?'' Brooke gasped and looked point-blank at Caroline. "What is he talking about?''

Before Caroline could speak, Wolfe cut off her reply and asked, "Did any of you tell someone else where Caroline and I were going and why?''

"I didn't,'' Fletcher replied immediately, a smug look of satisfaction on his face.

"I did,'' Roz confessed. "I told Lyle, but that hardly counts. He phoned the studio and asked to speak to Caroline, so naturally I explained where she'd gone and why.''

"Naturally.'' Wolfe focused on the reverend. "Did you tell anyone what Roz told you?''

Lyle's face paled. He shook his head. "No. Not a soul.''

"Anyone else?'' Wolfe asked.

Roz's forehead wrinkled when she puckered her lips in an oh-dear-me pout. She bobbed her head up and down slowly, regretfully admitting that she had gone against Wolfe's instructions and told someone other than Lyle. "I told Gavin. He called to invite me out and just happened to ask if I'd mentioned to Caroline that he and I were seeing each other. I know I wasn't supposed to tell anybody where you two went and why, but it's not as if Gavin is the guy out to kill Caroline.''

Wolfe growled, deep and low, the sound emitting roughly from his throat. Caroline tilted back her head and glanced up at him. He reached down and clamped his hand on her shoulder. She broke eye contact and looked away from Wolfe and at her friends, but she lifted her hand and laid it over Wolfe's for a brief moment.

Wolfe's gaze moved on to Brooke. "What about you, Ms. Harper?''

"I think I might have mentioned it to Mother and Dad,'' she said.

"Either you did or you didn't." Wolfe's voice held a deadly, accusatory tone.

"See here, Wolfe, I don't like your attitude," Fletcher said.

"I don't really care what you like or don't like," Wolfe replied. "Pleasing you is not part of my job description. Protecting Caroline is the only thing that matters. Someone in this room is responsible for giving information about Caroline's activities to the wrong person. That act, innocent though it might have been, could have cost Caroline her life. I cannot allow something like that to happen again."

"Yes, I mentioned to Mother and Dad that Caroline was going to Windhaven," Brooke said. "And it's possible that one or more of the servants overheard me. I didn't think you meant my family when you warned us not to tell anyone. My parents love Caroline."

"Thank you for your honesty, Ms. Harper," Wolfe said.

"You know, come to think of it, Kirsten and Sandy knew why Caroline had canceled her afternoon appointments." Roz shot up off the sofa. "I didn't think twice about telling them. Gosh, Caroline, I'm sorry."

"It's all right," Caroline assured her.

"I have to disagree," Wolfe said. "It's not all right. However, what's done is done. In future, something like this will not happen again. I don't want any of you pressing Caroline for specifics about the plans she has beyond her normal work schedule. Starting in the morning, she will be curtailing her activities until further notice."

"Is that what you want, Caroline?" Fletcher asked. "If not, say the word and I'll fire this overzealous commando."

"No," Caroline said. "If you fire Wolfe, I'll simply rehire him. He and I will work things out between us."

Roz exchanged a quick what's-up-with-those-two look with Lyle, then said, "Since you came by and picked me up tonight, you'll have to drive me home, Rev."

Caroline slipped her shoulder out from under Wolfe's possessive clasp and stood. Lyle nodded agreement to Roz's request, then got up out of the chair. After he and Roz kissed Caroline good-night, they showed themselves out the front door. Brooke stood, walked over to a scowling Fletcher and slipped her arm through his.

"We should be going, too," Brooke said, then dragged her reluctant and angry boyfriend toward Caroline. "If you need us for anything, don't hesitate to call." She glanced at Wolfe. "But I believe we're leaving you in good hands."

Caroline hugged her childhood friend and her stepbrother, then Wolfe shoved them out the door, locked it and punched in the code to secure the house for the night. The minute he turned to face Caroline, he realized she was fighting mad. Angry with him. For being rude to her friends?

"How dare you accuse one of them of being at fault for what happened at Windhaven!"

"I accused no one."

"No, you didn't out-and-out accuse one of them specifically, but you might as well have." She marched right up to him and pointed her finger in his face. "Those four people are the dearest friends I have on earth. Lyle and Fletch are like brothers to me. Not a one of them would ever do anything to harm me."

"Are you willing to bet your life on that?"

"What?"

He manacled her wrist. She glared at him. "From this moment on, until you are no longer in any danger, the only person you can trust one hundred percent is me."

"You? You're a stranger to me. A hired bodyguard. Why should I trust you more than four people I've known and trusted for years?"

With one quick jerk, he hauled her up against him and lowered his head enough so that their breaths mingled. "I think you already know the answer to that question."

Chapter 10

"Thanks for the ride home." Holding the passenger side door open on the minivan, Roz peered inside at Lyle. "You wouldn't want to come inside for a cup of coffee, would you?"

Lyle didn't respond immediately so she figured he was trying to find a tactful way to decline her offer. It had been stupid of her to suggest that he come into her house, even for something as innocent as coffee. Wasn't he the man who had told her that he was afraid she'd contaminate him, that her wickedness would rub off on him?

"Sure. I'd love a cup of coffee. Have you got decaf?" He opened the driver's side door and hopped out.

Too stunned to speak, Roz stood there for a couple of seconds, her mouth hanging open and her eyes slightly glazed from shock. "Oh...yeah...I've got decaf. Got it in three flavors." She slammed the minivan door. "Hazelnut. Macadamia chocolate and French vanilla."

Lyle rounded the van, then stopped hesitantly. "French vanilla sounds nice."

Reverend Lyle Jennings was actually going to come inside her house, at night—heck, at past midnight—for a cup of coffee. Was she dreaming or had some alien being possessed the rev's body?

Oh, God, her house was a mess. She couldn't remember the last time she'd dusted. There were dirty dishes in the sink. Unfolded clothes in the laundry basket on the kitchen table. And her bed was unmade. Forget about unmade beds, Roz, she told herself. Lyle certainly isn't going to be in your bedroom tonight.

As they walked toward the front door, side by side but not touching, Roz began feeling uncertain about having issued the invitation. "Look, I'm not much of a housekeeper. The place is untidy. Actually, it's an unholy mess. Oh, bad choice of words. Sorry."

"Roz?" Lyle halted at the door.

She turned to face him. "Huh?" she replied nervously. She loved that adorable freckled face of his, those sleepy hazel eyes and that shock of wavy red hair. Put him in a cowboy outfit and he'd look like Howdy Doody all grown up. Yet she could picture a couple of adorable kids who looked just like him. One of these days some really lucky woman would give him those kids. Why the heck did she have to wish she could be the mother of Lyle's babies, the woman he loved and wanted to spend the rest of his life with? Of all the women on earth, she'd be his last choice.

"My place isn't very neat, either," he admitted. "When some of the ladies at the church dropped by, they suggested that I needed a wife. I suspect they took one look at my lack of housekeeping skills and figured—"

"I'll bet they've been bombarding you with likely candidates, haven't they?" Roz could just picture the uptight plain Janes the church ladies had paraded before him. Prim. Proper. Pious. Boring. And completely suited to life as a minister's wife.

As Roz unlocked the door, Lyle sighed. "I've tried every

courteous way I know how to tell the ladies that I'm perfectly capable of finding a wife without any assistance. But they do seem determined for me to choose one of the young women they deem suitable.''

She glanced over her shoulder and saw that he was blushing. ''Come on in.'' After turning on the light in the living room, she spread out her arm in a gesture of welcome. ''Be it ever so humble.'' Immediately she flitted about, picking up magazines strewn on the floor, stuffing scattered clothing beneath sofa and chair cushions and jerking up a couple of beer bottles from an end table. Holding the bottles behind her hips, she backed toward the door to the kitchen. ''Make yourself at home. I'll put on that coffee—French vanilla— and be right back.''

''Thanks.'' Lyle chose the sofa, sat and glanced around the room.

She plastered a fake smile on her face and shoved the door open with her butt, then escaped into the small, cluttered kitchen. Breathing a quick sigh of relief, she tried to remember where she'd stored that unopened bag of French vanilla decaf coffee Caroline had given her, along with the other flavors, in a Valentine's Day gift basket. It's got to be here somewhere, she thought. Ah-ha! In the freezer! Caroline had told her to store the small bags of gourmet coffee in the freezer so they'd stay fresh.

Hurrying, she retrieved the coffee, opened the sack and prepared her four-cup coffeemaker. With that done, she rummaged around in the refrigerator and in the cabinets for something to serve with the coffee. Cake? Pie? Danish? She didn't have any of that stuff. Cookies. She had cookies. Oversize peanut butter cookies she'd picked up at the bakery a few days ago.

While the coffee brewed, she cracked open the door and called out to Lyle, ''Cream and sugar or just black?''

''Sugar, please. One teaspoon.''

''Coming right up.''

Damn, she didn't have a silver coffeepot or any good china. She didn't even own a set of matching thrift-store dishes. The best she could offer Lyle was a pink Bitch's Brew mug. When she had seen the mugs in a speciality shop several years ago, she'd thought they were cute, so she'd bought half a dozen. Most of the guys she dated either didn't even notice the feminist logo or got a good laugh when they read it. Lyle was likely to take offense. What the hell! She couldn't serve hot coffee in her Wal-Mart Looney Tunes glasses, could she? Another purchase that she had, at the time, thought was cute.

Five minutes later, she shoved open the door with her hip and emerged from the kitchen carrying a floral metal tray. The moment she entered the room, Lyle stood. What a gentleman, she thought. She wasn't used to guys with good manners. Lyle's Southern charm had a way of disarming her and making her feel inferior. She knew he didn't come from money or anything like that, but he'd had a mama who was a real lady. Caroline's aunt Dixie had instilled old-fashioned rules of decorum in her son and niece.

Roz placed the cheap metal tray on the cocktail table, wishing with all her heart that it was the finest silver. She sat on the sofa, then Lyle joined her, sitting on the opposite end.

"I thought you might like some cookies." She indicated the plate of cookies by pointing at them, then remembered that pointing wasn't polite. "Peanut butter. I hope you like them."

"Did you bake them?" he asked as he lifted the bright pink coffee mug and reached for a cookie.

Roz chuckled. "Me?" She shook her head. "Honey, I've never baked anything in my life." She gasped. "Sorry, Rev, I didn't mean to call you honey. Just a slip of the tongue."

Lyle blushed again, then picked up a cookie and took a bite. After chewing, sipping the coffee and swallowing, he smiled. "The cookie's quite tasty and the coffee's really good. Thank you."

Roz tried to think of something to do or say to make this less awkward for him. She tried to think of a subject to discuss. Surely they had at least one thing in common. "What do you think of Mr. Wolfe?" she finally asked, then picked up her coffee mug.

Lyle stared at the mug she held, seemingly mesmerized by it. Suddenly Roz realized he hadn't paid any attention to his own matching mug and was reading the logo on hers. His mouth curved into a smile. She giggled.

"Sorry. They're all I've got. I bought them a few years back because I simply couldn't resist them."

"Stop apologizing to me for every little thing." Lyle scooted a little closer to her, his gaze never leaving her face. "I may be a minister, but I'm not a saint, not some perfect human being whose job it is to judge you. I think the mugs are cute. They're—" he paused, as if trying to come up with the right thing to say "—they're so you, Roz."

"Oh?" Was that an insult? A compliment? Neither? "Is that good or bad?"

"Definitely good," he said.

"You mean there's something about me that you think is good?"

His smile widened into a sheepish grin. "I suppose I deserve that." He shook his head and laughed. "There's a lot about you that's good. Buying these mugs is an example of your great sense of humor, and a sense of humor is a good thing."

"Does that mean you don't think the mugs' logo suits my personality? Do you think I'm a bitch, Lyle?" Oh, that's it, Roz, ask a leading question. Brace yourself for the answer, she cautioned herself. The rev doesn't lie, you know.

"No more or no less than any other female of my acquaintance," he replied—and with a straight face.

She stared at him for a moment, then realized he was joking. She punched his arm playfully, laughing as she leaned toward him. Their gazes connected. Warmth suffused her body. Sexual heat. *Don't go there, Roz,* an inner voice warned. Just because he's being nice to you for a change doesn't mean he's interested in you in *that way.*

"I…er…I think Mr. Wolfe takes his job very seriously." Lyle cleared his throat. "And that's good for Caroline. I believe Fletch was wrong to take offense at the things Mr. Wolfe said."

"I agree. I think Wolfe would die to protect Caroline."

"That's his job, isn't it? To be prepared to kill or to die to protect her." Lyle finished off the cookie and washed it down with his coffee.

"Yeah, I suppose it is, but I think there's more to it. Didn't you pick up any vibes between them? If I didn't know better, I'd swear he and Caroline have something going on."

"Caroline just met the man," Lyle said. "She is not the type of woman who would—"

"Honey, any woman is the type who *would* with—"

"With a man like Mr. Wolfe, you mean."

Roz shook her head. "No, I wasn't going to say with a man like Mr. Wolfe. I was going to say, with the right man. A woman would do just about anything for a guy who is her soul mate."

"I hardly think Caroline and Mr. Wolfe are soul mates. They have nothing in common."

Roz gazed into Lyle's eyes. "You might be surprised. Besides, I don't think you have to come from similar backgrounds or be just alike to be soul mates. Do you?"

"I don't know," Lyle admitted. "I've never given the subject much thought." He added in a whisper, "Until recently."

"Yeah, I know what you mean. The idea of having a soul mate is sort of sappy and sentimental, isn't it?"

"And romantic," Lyle said.

"Yeah. Very romantic."

Moment by moment, inch by inch, Lyle and Roz drew closer and closer until they were sitting right beside each other on the sofa. Their arms and legs touching, their gazes locked, their breathing labored.

"You're very pretty," Lyle said.

"Thank you. You're pretty cute yourself."

Lyle blushed, yet again. "I've never thought of myself as cute."

"You are." She reached out and ruffled his thick red hair. "You're awfully cute. And as you know, I just love cute things."

They came together, their lips almost touching. Roz's stomach fluttered. Was he really going to kiss her? Please, let it happen, she prayed. *I promise I'll be good for him. So good. Just let him want me the way I want him.*

The telephone rang. Lyle jumped away from Roz as if an invisible hand had shoved him. Roz groaned. Who the hell would be calling at this time of night? She grumbled to herself, cursing the Fates for interrupting at such an auspicious moment. Another ten seconds and all her dreams might have come true. She stomped across the room, lifted the receiver and growled.

"Whoever this is, it had better be a damn emergency!"

"Roz, sweet thing, did I wake you?"

"Gavin?"

She sensed Lyle's movement and when she glanced his way, she almost cried. The look on his face said it all. Disappointment. Anger. Hurt. He rose to his feet quickly and accidentally hit his knee on the edge of the coffee table. Grimacing, he groaned and rubbed his knee. She looked at him pleadingly. *Don't go! I'll get rid of Gavin. The man means absolutely nothing to me. You're the man I want...the man I love.*

"Gavin, this isn't a good time for me," she said.

"Should I be jealous? Are you in the sack with another guy?"

"Don't be ridiculous."

Lyle was heading for the front door. Damn!

"Call me back when it's daylight outside, okay?"

Lyle opened the front door.

"Better yet, Gavin, don't bother calling me again. Ever!" Roz slammed down the telephone and ran toward the door, catching up with Lyle just as he stepped over the threshold. "Wait!"

Lyle turned and glared at her, his face flushed with anger. "You shouldn't have been rude to your boyfriend on my account. Heck, Roz, it's not as if you and I are friends. We don't even like each other, do we? The only reason we're ever civil to each other is for Caroline's sake."

She bit down on her bottom lip to keep from bursting into tears, then bobbed her head up and down to agree with him. "Drive carefully. Okay?"

He nodded. "Good night, Roz. Thanks for the coffee and the cookies."

"Sure. Anytime."

He hesitated, as if he wanted to say more, but instead he turned and walked away. Roz stood in the doorway for several minutes after the red taillights on Lyle's minivan disappeared down the road. Then she slammed the door, leaned against it and sank to the floor. She keened softly as tears trickled down her cheeks, over her nose and across her lips.

Caroline had all but run from Wolfe, and he had allowed her to escape—from him and his brutally honest statement. Of course she knew why she should trust him and him alone. But she couldn't admit that to him. She barely had the courage to admit the reason to herself. She had locked herself in the bathroom, turned on the shower and stripped naked. While standing under the warm, pelting water, she relived every moment of her life since Wolfe had showed up at her front door. She had wondered how it was possible that on such short acquaintance a perfect stranger had come to mean so much to her.

Now, sitting at her dressing table, combing the tangles from her damp hair, she confronted herself about her true feelings for Wolfe. If she trusted him with her life, as she trusted no one else, wasn't it time to be totally honest with herself? A powerful sexual attraction existed between them. She felt it and so did he. It was unlike anything she'd ever known. But that wasn't the reason why she trusted him. There was more to her feelings than sexual attraction. From the first moment she saw him, she sensed a bond, as if she already knew him. Was reincarnation possible? she speculated. Lyle would say it wasn't. Roz would say it definitely was. Brooke and Fletch would say whatever was currently in vogue with their set of society friends.

No matter what she believed or didn't believe, one fact was clear. Wolfe was a man capable of protecting her, a man who had proved that he was dedicated to keeping her safe. In some odd sort of way, his interest in her seemed personal. Was it the sexual thing? she asked herself. Did he, like some primitive male, think of her as his possession, his woman? As a modern-thinking female, with politically correct views on many subjects, she supposed she should resent that type of macho thinking. After all, maybe Wolfe was the kind of man who thought it was his right to sleep with his female clients. Was his desire to have sex with her at the root of his willingness to go to any lengths to protect her?

Caroline laid the silver comb on the dressing table, eased back the satin-covered bench on which she sat and rose to her feet. It was time for her to have a talk with her bodyguard. She had to find out if she was simply one more woman in a long line of conquests.

What if you are? What will you do then?

She donned the matching satin robe that covered her bare arms and swept to the floor. The lace hem glided along behind her as she marched out of her bedroom. Naturally he had left his door wide open. She paused momentarily outside his bedroom, took a deep, fortifying breath and knocked softly on the door frame. She glanced into the room but didn't see him anywhere.

"Wolfe, I'd like to speak to you, please."

His bathroom door opened. She gasped. He emerged with a large towel draped around his hips, the rest of him completely nude. Taken aback by his lack of clothing, she froze to the spot and swallowed hard.

"I'll come back after you've put on something."

She turned and headed toward her room, but he caught up with her before she'd taken more than a few steps. His big hand clutched her upper arm. She whirled around to face him, her breathing harsh, her cheeks flushed with emotion.

"What are you so afraid of, Caroline?" he asked, his cold, jade-green eyes focused on her face. "You must know…you must feel it here—" he laid his open palm over her heart "—that I would never hurt you, that I will protect you, with my life if necessary."

"Because it's your job?" She held her breath, waiting for his reply. His big hand on her chest felt hot and heavy.

"Yes, partly because it's my job." His palm glided upward, over her collarbone, until he spread apart his fingers and gripped her throat with the utmost tenderness.

"And…" she prompted.

"And because I couldn't bear for anything to happen to you."

He lifted the hand at her throat and circled around to grasp the nape of her neck, while he released his hold on her arm to cup her hip. She gazed into his eyes, hypnotized by the intensity of emotion she saw revealed in their depths. He was going to kiss her, with or without her permission. Had he guessed that this was what she wanted? He covered her lips with his, a gentle possession but forceful enough to brook no denial on her part. When she succumbed to the kiss, he pulled her closer and deepened the contact.

This was unlike any kiss she'd ever known. Powerful enough to propel her from pleasurable experience to raging sexual hunger in one minute flat. Every fiber of her being acknowledged this man as her mate. Primeval forces surged through her body, demanding satisfaction of the most primitive nature. Caroline pressed herself intimately against his erection and a sense of feminine power overwhelmed her. She lifted her arms to drape his shoulders and became an equal participant in the carnality of their kiss.

As quickly as he had instigated the kiss, Wolfe ended it. Caroline felt bereft and breathless, as if her oxygen supply had suddenly been cut off and she was smothering. When he stepped away from her, she reached out for him pleadingly.

"Unless you have no doubts about what you want, then I suggest you turn around and go back to your room," Wolfe said.

He wanted her as desperately as she wanted him, didn't he? So why was he rejecting her? *No, he's not rejecting you,* an inner voice told her. *He is giving you a chance to think twice about what you're doing.*

"If you are sure that you will have no regrets in the morning, then come to me." He held out his hand. "I'll make love to you."

Passion tried to overrule common sense. The temptation to succumb to the most basic human desires fought a battle with her self-preservation instincts. Would she regret it in the morning if she gave herself to Wolfe? She honestly didn't know.

Undoubtedly she hesitated a moment too long to suit him. He dropped his proffered hand. "When it's right...if it's ever right between us, you won't have to think about it. You'll know."

"Wolfe, please..."

"You've had a rough day," he said. "You've been through a traumatic experience. You aren't in any sort of emotional shape to make a decision as important to you as this one. You haven't saved yourself all these years to give yourself to the wrong man now.''

''How did you know—''

''That you're a virgin?''

Her face burned with embarrassment. ''Was it that obvious to you? Am I that inept? Is that why you stopped things when you did—because you prefer your women more experienced?''

''You could never be just another woman to me. If I were to ever take you to my bed, you would become my woman forever. I put a stop to things not because of your innocence, but because I'm the wrong man. I'm not worthy of you, my sweet Caroline.''

He left her standing in the hallway, feeling totally dazed by his statement. Heaven help her, she was more aroused and more confused than she'd ever been in her entire life. And in the morning, she would have to confront him again, this powerful, commanding man. How would she be able to control her attraction to him now that he knew she found him irresistible? But hadn't Wolfe proved himself to be an honorable man? He could have taken advantage of her, but he hadn't. It wasn't Wolfe she had to fear, but her own desire.

Chapter 11

Having dealt with stubborn clients before, Wolfe had learned the art of compromise. But being forced to accommodate Caroline's determination not to drastically change her lifestyle had proved difficult for him. He understood that she didn't want someone else dictating what she could do, where she could go and with whom she could associate. But dammit all, couldn't she understand that he had her best interests at heart? If she would let him have his way, yes, he would lock her away from the world until she was no longer in danger. And yes, he would keep her apart from everyone, even those she loved. Caroline trusted too easily, believed the best of everyone, and thus opened herself up to people who might not deserve either her love or her trust.

And God help him, he was one of those people. But the difference between him and all the others in her life was that he knew what motivated him. He might prove a threat to Caroline's heart, but never to her life. There was absolutely nothing he would not do for her. And on some instinctive level, he believed she knew that.

Since the morning after their kiss in the hallway, Caroline had been more reserved with him, as if she thought putting up a barrier between them would prevent any repeat performances. And that same morning, she had made it perfectly clear to him that although she knew her life was in danger, she could not live in a glass bubble and would not alter the basic pattern of her life. He had presented every feasible explanation of why she would be wise to follow his suggestions, and in the end, they had compromised. She would temporarily give up her volunteer work and all social activities—after the dinner party hosted by the Harpers—but she would continue her normal work schedule. And they would continue their search, wherever it might lead them, to find the lock Preston Shaw's key opened.

Wolfe had been totally opposed to this evening's outing, but Caroline had insisted on attending the dinner for Fletcher Shaw. Her unwavering loyalty to her stepbrother was commendable, but exposing herself this way was foolhardy and he'd told her as much.

"It is important to me to be there for Fletch, to lend my support," Caroline had said. "Humor me about this one night and I promise that I'll spend every night from now on under lock and key."

Reluctantly, he had agreed. "I'll need backup for this evening. There's no way I can guarantee your protection without extra agents to help."

He had hoped to talk her out of going but soon realized she would not change her mind. That's why, at this precise moment, they were pulling up outside Oliver and Eileen Harper's mansion in Alexandria, Virginia. He and Caroline sat in the back seat of the Mercedes he had rented for the night and had personally gone over it with a fine-tooth comb. Caroline's damaged Lincoln would be in the repair shop for another few days. Two Dundee agents, who had flown in from Atlanta that morning and would return on a flight the next day, were in the front seat. Matt O'Brien, acting as their chauffeur, would be on hand outside the Harper mansion and alert him to anything that was even vaguely suspicious. Jack Parker, wearing a black tux, black snakeskin boots and a black Stetson, would play the good-old-boy Texas millionaire friend, someone Caroline had supposedly met when she'd taken a family photo for him. Jack would be Wolfe's backup during the buffet dinner, a second set of eyes and ears inside the house. The main players at tonight's little social event would know that Wolfe's relationship to Caroline was professional; however, they would present themselves to the other guests as a couple.

"Mighty fancy digs," Jack said when Matt stopped the Mercedes in the drive directly in front of the white-columned portico. "Almost as nice as my place back home."

"Don't overdo it," Wolfe said. "Play the part whenever necessary, but don't enjoy yourself too much."

"Ah, shucks. And here I was all ready to lasso me a filly or two and tell 'em about my oil wells."

A white-jacketed servant opened the car's back door. Wolfe emerged first, scanning the area as subtly as possible, then he offered his hand to Caroline and assisted her out of the vehicle. He could barely take his eyes off her. She was so beautiful in her simple black silk dress that clung to her curves and accentuated her hour-glass figure. Shirred around a band collar, the bodice covered her completely in front, but her back was bare almost to her waist. She had swept her hair atop her head in a fluffy, loose topknot. Fine tendrils curled between her ears and face. Her only jewelry was her favorite diamond-and-pearl earrings…and, although it was well hidden beneath her dress, the gold chain on which the key was kept.

"How about moseying along," Jack said, "and let a fellow get out of the car."

Realizing that he had stared at her just a little too long, Wolfe took Caroline's arm, draped it over his and moved forward, enough to allow Jack room to step out of the Mercedes. Once the threesome headed up the steps to the veranda, Matt drove off to park the car and join the other chauffeurs.

Inside the house, Jack and Wolfe remained on either side of Caroline. The place was an example of wealth and good taste, and the party itself, which was already in full swing, seemed to be a great success. No doubt Mrs. Oliver Harper had planned and executed countless of these little private dinners—for a hundred guests—on more than one occasion. As Aidan Colbert, a member of Peacekeepers International, Wolfe had attended his share of social functions and had then, as now, felt a bit out of place in a tuxedo. At heart he had always been and always would be just a country boy.

Wolfe surveyed the crowd, then removed his tinted glasses, replacements for the broken ones he had left in the debris at Windhaven. These people were the rich and powerful. The famous and the infamous. Each invitee handpicked because he or she had either enough money or enough influence to help Fletcher Shaw get elected to Congress. Wolfe slipped his glasses into the inside pocket of his tuxedo jacket.

"Caroline, sweetheart." Fletcher zeroed in on them, all smiles and warm greetings. Brooke Harper, in a strapless royal-blue number, a diamond-and-sapphire choker around her slender neck, looked every inch the debutante heiress. She clung to Fletcher's arm as if she'd been born attached to him.

Try as he might to like Fletch, Wolfe found the man a little too smooth, a little too charming. But then country boys were usually suspicious of their refined city-boy counterparts. And Wolfe knew Brooke's type. He'd dated a few just like her and had found rich girls could be amusing, but incapable of surviving in the real world without Daddy's money.

"Fletch thinks you're very brave to come out tonight, considering how dangerous it could be for you," Brooke said to Caroline, but her gaze was fixed on Wolfe. "But I told Fletch that your Mr. Wolfe wouldn't let anything happen to you."

Brooke glanced at Jack Parker and smiled. "Caroline, it's terribly unfair that a good little girl like you winds up with two dates...and both absolute hunks."

"Howdy, ma'am. I'm Jack Parker, from Texas. And you'd be?"

"She would be—" Fletch cleared his throat. "She *is* Brooke Harper, your hosts' daughter and my future wife."

"Fletch, dear..." Brooke all but cooed. "If this is a proposal, I must say it's a strange one."

Fletcher Shaw turned beet red. Wolfe would bet his last dime that the man hadn't been embarrassed since he was in short pants.

"Stop teasing him, Brooke," Caroline said.

Ignoring Fletcher completely, Brooke slid between Caroline and Jack and slipped her arm through his. "Why don't I show you to the buffet and we can get better acquainted, Mr. Parker? That is, if you're allowed to leave Caroline's side."

Jack grinned, exchanged a casual glance with Wolfe and accepted the lady's offer. "It would be my pleasure, ma'am."

As they strolled into the adjoining room, Brooke glanced over her shoulder and called out, "Caroline, do find Mother and Dad. They're eager to see you and to meet Mr. Wolfe."

"And by all means mix and mingle and enjoy yourselves," Fletcher said. "I must meet and greet. This isn't an official fund-raiser, you know, but Oliver has assured me that we'll get at least five million in pledges tonight, maybe more. That's a good start, don't you think?"

"Wonderful start," Caroline said. "Good luck. We'll find you later to say goodbye."

As soon as Fletcher saw new arrivals, he gave Caroline a hurried peck on the cheek and moved on. Wolfe cupped Caroline's elbow. He intended to remain stuck to her like glue throughout the evening. Jack could scope out the partygoers while Ms. Harper entertained him. The man had a knack for keeping a lady's attention while surveying a crowd and picking out suspicious characters. In the year he'd known Jack Parker, Wolfe had learned the man's easygoing cowboy charm was deceptive. In any battle, Wolfe could think of no one he'd rather have at his side.

"What next, Ms. McGuire?" Wolfe asked. "Since you were damned and determined to attend this affair to show your support of Fletcher and he's already acknowledged your presence, who else do you need to impress with your sisterly loyalty?"

Glowering at Wolfe, Caroline jerked away from him, but didn't protest when he grabbed her arm and draped it through his.

"I realize you're upset with me because I insisted on attending this dinner party," she said.

"I'm not upset," he replied. "Furious, maybe, but not upset."

"Do you honestly think that someone will be bold enough to try to kill me at a party with so much press in attendance?"

"It's been known to happen," he told her. "I just don't want it to happen to you."

"Let's go say hello to Oliver and Eileen, get a bite to eat and then we can leave early. Will that make you happy?"

"Not coming here would have made me happy."

"You're impossible to please, aren't you?"

You could please me, my sweet Caroline, he thought. You could heal my wounded soul and teach me how to be happy for the first time in my life. But my dream is as impossible as your fantasy. Neither is destined to be fulfilled.

"Caroline!" Roz Turner called from halfway across the crowded room.

"Roz?" Caroline searched the direction from which the voice had come and said to Wolfe, "I had no idea Roz had been invited."

The exuberant blonde came barreling toward them, Gavin Robbins in tow. Roz's attire seemed out of place in this

crowd of designer dresses. She wore a silver lamé miniskirt
and matching bustier covered by a sheer gray overblouse. A
pair of half-dollar-size silver hoops dangled from her earlobes.

"Isn't this party fab or what? I've already met an oil
sheikh, an English earl, two senators, three congressmen and
a TV soap opera star."

"I didn't know you were coming here tonight," Caroline
said.

"Neither did I, but then Gavin called me at the last minute
and said his date had canceled on him. So I'm doing him a
big favor, aren't I, Gavin?"

"Yes, a big favor," he agreed. "I had already accepted
for myself and a date. Then the lady had a family emergency.
A man hardly likes to admit that he's been stood up."

"Hey, when this shindig's over, what do you say the four
of us go dancing or out somewhere for a sunrise breakfast
or something," Roz suggested.

"I'm afraid that won't be possible," Wolfe said.

"Sorry, Roz." Caroline patted her friend's arm. "I had to
twist Wolfe's arm to get him to bring me here tonight. We're
not staying long. But I had to put in an appearance, for
Fletch's sake."

"Oh, sure thing. I understand." Roz shook her head sadly.
"I wasn't thinking or I'd have known it was a bad idea. I'll
sure be glad when all this cloak-and-dagger stuff is over and
you can get back to leading a normal life."

"Me, too," Caroline said.

Wolfe cupped her elbow again. The sooner she made the
rounds and he got her out of this place the better. He couldn't
pinpoint exactly what was wrong—maybe nothing except in
his overactive imagination—but his gut instincts told him that
something wasn't right. He couldn't leave Caroline's side to
do any investigating on his own, so he had to count on Jack
and Matt to do what they could to spot any potential trouble

before it got too close to Caroline. Anything that came at her, point-blank, he'd deal with himself.

Caroline had decided it was about time to leave the party. With each passing minute Wolfe was becoming more and more agitated. There was no point in prolonging his agony. Just as she started to tell him they could go, she noticed a short, stocky middle-aged man staggering toward her. When he approached, she tried to recall if he was someone she might know. But by the time he came up to her, his face only inches away, she realized two things—he was horribly drunk and he was a stranger.

"Hi, there, boo-te-ful," the guy said, slurring his words as he spoke. "How's about a little kiss."

With a sharply indrawn breath, Wolfe tensed at her side.

The moment the man's damp lips puckered, Wolfe twisted the man's arm behind his back, then shoved him against the nearest wall.

Jack Parker appeared out of nowhere, taking a guard post at Caroline's side. People stopped their conversations to gasp and stare and mumble. Caroline's palms dampened with perspiration. Her pulse raced maddeningly. Everything had happened so fast, she'd barely had time to realize what was going on before Wolfe sprang into action.

"What the hell's wrong with you?" the man Wolfe had just subdued grumbled, his speech slurred.

Wolfe frisked the drunken man, then shoved him toward Jack. "He's just drunk. How about escorting this gentleman to the door? I think our host and hostess would appreciate it."

"Be glad to accommodate you." Jack grabbed the guy by the shoulder. "You're going to cooperate, aren't you?"

The man nodded and made no protest when Jack led him away. Wolfe clasped Caroline by the forearms and inspected her from head to toe.

"Are you all right?" he asked, concern evident in his voice.

"Yes, I'm fine. Really. Don't you think you overreacted just a bit? He tried to kiss me, not kill me, and you practically broke his arm."

"I've told you before, everyone is suspect. Even an inebriated Lothario."

Caroline didn't know how much longer she could bear living this way. Guarded night and day. Increasingly afraid of every noise in the dark. Wary of strangers. Her normal activities drastically curtailed. And Wolfe watching her closely when he thought she wasn't looking. He was like a predatory animal, waiting to strike, constantly in search of danger. And anyone who dared come too close to her might find his life in jeopardy.

How many times had she gone over in her mind what had happened between them the night Wolfe had kissed her in the hallway? Those incredible moments when passion ruled her completely had changed her relationship with Wolfe, making them each careful of what they said and did with regard to each other. Wolfe seemed less patient, more critical and demanding with his orders, while she couldn't help being less cooperative and more argumentative. They were both using discord to keep their sexual urges in check. If they could remain on edge, just a little angry and slightly hostile, then perhaps they wouldn't make another mistake. And kissing each other had been a monumental mistake. At least it had been for her.

Thank goodness Wolfe had called a halt when he did; otherwise she would have given herself to him, willingly, gladly allowing him to take her virginity. And she would have regretted it later. In the cold, hard light of day, when the heat of the moment had passed. As much as she was attracted to Wolfe—and merciful heavens, she was—he'd been right when he had told her that he was wrong for her.

She abhorred violence in all its forms. Since the night of

Preston's murder, she had kept herself as far removed from anything and anyone even remotely connected to violence as humanly possible. She supposed other than the fact he was like a brother to her, one of the reasons she involved herself in Lyle's life and church work was because he and the life he lived represented gentleness and kindness and brotherly love. And she had dated Gavin because he was associated with Peacekeepers International, the nongovernment organization devoted to world peace through diplomacy. Perhaps she had hoped Gavin would be the kind of man Preston had been. Unfortunately, he hadn't lived up to her expectations.

So why had she ever entertained the notion that she could love a man like Wolfe, a man who made his living protecting people from violence and thereby living violently himself? He carried a weapon and knew how to use it. She suspected that in his line of work he had shot someone, perhaps even killed someone. Wolfe had chosen his profession as she had chosen hers—and he was as good a bodyguard as she was a photographer. Despite his often gentle manner and the tenderness with which he touched her, he was a man capable of physical violence.

"Caroline?" Wolfe said her name softly, against her ear.

She shuddered. In her peripheral vision she caught a glimpse of him, alarmingly attractive in his black tuxedo. Standing at her side, his hand cupping her elbow, Wolfe suddenly seemed as threatening as an unknown assailant lying in wait.

"Caroline, are you all right?"

"Yes, I'm fine." She breathed deeply, willing herself not to respond to him in a physical way. Don't look at him, she told herself. If she allowed herself to care about this man, then he *would* be as dangerous to her as a killer. Loving a man like Wolfe would destroy her. "Let's find Oliver and Eileen. I want to thank them for hosting this party to help Fletch raise money for his campaign next year. After doing that, we can leave."

"You don't want to go through the buffet line?" Wolfe asked.

"No. I'm afraid I don't have much appetite." When she moved, he moved with her, staying in step as she led him through a throng of chatting people.

"You're upset about what happened with that idiot drunk, aren't you? He didn't hurt you. I prevented him from—"

"Yes, I know what you did."

He slid his hand from her elbow to her waist before she realized what he was doing, his action immediately halting her search for their hosts. "I did my job, dammit." He kept his voice low so that only she could hear him, but he might as well have shouted at her, so powerful was his statement.

"Let's not argue," she said. "Not here. Not now."

She could sense the frustration, the barely controlled anger within him. The evidence showed on his face, in the tightening of his muscles and in the agitation in his cold green eyes. She held her breath and waited, then began to breathe again when he released his tenacious hold on her.

Across the room, standing by an older, rather attractive man she thought she recognized but couldn't quite place, was Eileen Harper. Eileen Wendell Harper, the wealthy heiress whose family had been New England bankers for the past two centuries. Eileen was tall, elegantly slender and youthfully vibrant for a woman of sixty who had survived breast cancer this past year. Caroline had always envied Brooke because she and her mother shared such a loving relationship.

As Caroline led Wolfe closer to her objective, she felt an odd reluctance in him, a strange tension that made her wonder what was going on inside that mysterious mind of his. Eileen saw Caroline and smiled. The white-haired man standing next to her paused in their conversation to seek out the person who had captured his hostess's attention. When she approached, Eileen reached out, grasped Caroline's hand and pulled her closer.

After planting a light kiss on Caroline's cheek, Eileen said,

''Dear girl, how simply delightful to see you.'' Eileen then glanced at Wolfe. ''This must be your…er…Mr. Wolfe of whom Brooke has spoken.''

Wolfe nodded but didn't reply verbally. Caroline noticed that Wolfe glanced from Eileen to the man at her side.

''Yes, this is Wolfe,'' Caroline finally said when it became apparent that Wolfe had no intention of saying anything.

Eileen slipped her arm through the arm of the tall, well-built man beside her. ''Caroline, do you remember Ellison Penn? He's the president of Peacekeepers International, and knew your stepfather quite well. El was at Harvard when Oliver was there and we've known him for years.''

The man whom Eileen referred to quite intimately as El greeted Caroline with a placid smile and a firm handshake. ''Hello, Caroline. I don't think you and I have seen each other since Preston's funeral. You've grown up to be a lovely young lady, and from what I understand quite a successful photographer.''

When she shook Ellison Penn's hand, she smiled warmly and wondered why her stepfather's former superior at Peacekeepers would even remember her, let alone know any details about her life. She certainly didn't remember him from the funeral. Of course, she had been sedated that day.

''Hello, Mr. Penn,'' Caroline said. ''It's nice to see you again after all these years.'' She turned to Wolfe. ''May I introduce my friend, Mr. Wolfe.''

The two men stared at each other for only a couple of seconds, but in that brief glance, Caroline noticed an odd expression on Wolfe's face. The two men shook hands and mumbled hellos.

''Here comes Oliver,'' Eileen said. ''He will be so pleased that you've come to our little party. He was afraid you'd hide away there in St. Michaels, after those two perfectly horrible incidents.'' Eileen clasped Caroline's hand again. ''My dear, I do wish you'd give up this quest to find whatever it is that key of Preston's unlocks. It seems to me that all that nasty business should be left in the past. Dead and buried with poor Preston. If I were you, I'd throw that key in the trash.''

Oliver Harper slid his arm around his wife's waist and bestowed a wide, gregarious smile on Caroline and her companion. She had always liked Oliver, even as a child. He had, in many ways, reminded her of Preston. Soft-spoken, gentlemanly and devoted to his family. She recalled several times when Brooke's father had treated them with an afternoon trip to the zoo or to a museum or even to a matinee at the theater. Besides being quite wealthy and extremely powerful, he was a handsome man, with graying brown hair and warm chestnut eyes.

''What's this about Preston's key?'' Oliver asked. ''Any new developments?''

Caroline glanced meaningfully at Ellison Penn, wondering just how much the Harpers had told him about the key she had found in Preston's hidden safe. Was it possible that Preston had discovered damaging information about his former boss or about the Peacekeepers organization and Mr. Penn was the person behind the attempts on her life? He certainly didn't look like a criminal. But maybe Wolfe was right. Maybe she did trust too easily.

''Oh, Caroline, you look simply mortified, my dear,'' Eileen said. ''You mustn't be concerned because El knows about the key. He's totally trustworthy. And because of his former association with Preston, he's quite concerned about your welfare.''

''Ms. McGuire, I want to assure you that Peacekeepers International is as interested as you are in finding out just what sort of information Preston might have kept hidden,'' Ellison said. ''And if there is anything that our organization can do to help you—''

''As a matter of fact, there is,'' Wolfe said. A collective silence followed his unexpected statement. ''I'd like to take a look at Preston Shaw's files. Would that be possible?'' Wolfe didn't give a damn about Preston Shaw's files. He and

Ellison had gone over those files with a fine-tooth comb fifteen years ago. What he wanted—what he badly needed—was some sort of cover so that he could meet with Ellison now and perhaps again in the future without anyone being overly suspicious. The unimportant files were the best excuse he could think of.

"Well...er... Yes, I'm sure that could be arranged." Ellison looked straight at Caroline when he replied. "I can assure you, however, that there isn't anything in those files that might prove useful to you."

"What about tomorrow morning?" Wolfe asked. He needed this meeting with Ellison as soon as possible. His gut instinct was telling him that there was something Ellison hadn't told him about Preston Shaw, something that he needed to know. "I can be at your office by nine."

"The young man seems quite anxious." Oliver Harper's gaze rested directly on Wolfe.

"The sooner we discover what Ms. McGuire's key unlocks and reveal that information, the sooner she will be out of danger," Wolfe said.

"I agree." Ellison Penn nodded. "Although I doubt Preston's files will help you, I will make them available to you tomorrow." He lifted Eileen's hand and kissed it, then nodded to Oliver before turning his attention briefly back to Wolfe. "My personal assistant is here tonight. I'll find him now and arrange for him to bring Preston's files out of storage first thing in the morning and have anything that's been transferred to our computer system put on a disk for you."

"My goodness, Ellison, you're being very trusting, aren't you?" Eileen asked. "After all, what do you know about Mr. Wolfe, other than he's a reliable bodyguard?"

"I know a great deal about Mr. Wolfe," Ellison said, making quick yet consequential eye contact with Wolfe. "After all, I did have a thorough check done on him as a favor to your husband."

"You did?" Eileen tilted her regal head and stared at Oliver.

Oliver cleared his throat, then smiled at his wife. "I thought it best to find out all we could about the man guarding Caroline. And I must say I was quite impressed with his résumé. Let me see if I can summarize in just a few succinct sentences. David Wolfe, thirty-six years old. No living relatives. Never married. No children. Dundee agent for less than two years. Before that a CIA agent who lived and worked in Europe, Asia and the Middle East for most of his career." Oliver looked boldly at Wolfe. "You have an exemplary record, Mr. Wolfe. You're almost too good to be true. But Ellison assured me that he dug quite deep and came up with nothing but the most impressive facts about you."

Caroline withdrew from Wolfe, just enough to put a foot of space between her body and his. She looked at him, but he avoided making eye contact with her. She had found his profession as a bodyguard upsetting, knowing it was fraught with violence. But now she had just learned that his former profession had involved violence on a grand scale and at an international level. There was no telling what he had been required to do as an agent for the CIA.

"Well, it's good to know that our dear Caroline is in such capable hands," Eileen said. "Now, let's put all this aside for the time being and see if we can't have an enjoyable evening."

Caroline stood rigidly, her spine stiff, her chin lifted. Her heartbeat drummed in her ears. She forced a smile and waited until Eileen and Oliver moved on to other guests and Mr. Penn had gone in search of his assistant. She had one question to ask Wolfe about a matter far more personal than anything to do with his former profession.

Caroline confronted him. "Why didn't you tell me that your name is David?"

Chapter 12

Wolfe's gut tightened painfully. Hell, why hadn't he told her his name was David? By not telling her, he'd made concealing it a big deal and given her reason to be suspicious. What if she asked him if he were *her David,* her mysterious benefactor? Don't be ridiculous, he told himself. Why should she think he was that David? She had no reason to connect him with the man who had watched over her and provided for her after Preston Shaw's death. His guilty conscience had made that giant leap, but Caroline's mind wouldn't.

"No one calls me David," he replied. "My clients, my associates and my acquaintances call me Wolfe."

"I understand," she said. "But that still doesn't explain why you purposefully neglected to mention that your given name is David."

"It wasn't purposeful," he told her, then when he saw the skepticism in her eyes, he amended his statement. "At least not at first. Then when you told me about your benefactor and what he meant to you and…things happened between us…" He lowered his voice to a mere whisper. "I didn't want you getting me and this other David mixed up in your mind and reacting to me because of the way you felt about him.''

Caroline didn't say anything, she simply stared at him for several minutes, as if judging the sincerity of his words. Finally she slipped her arm through his and said, ''I've changed my mind. I think I'd like to stay a while longer and maybe eat a bite. Why don't we take a look at the buffet? I'm sure we'll both find something we like. Eileen uses only the best caterers and always has a marvelous variety.''

Was that it? he wondered. Had Caroline finished interrogating him? Had his explanation actually satisfied her? If so, he was thankful. But a niggling little doubt chipped away inside his head and that bothered him. She had definitely let the matter drop too easily. So that meant something else was going on in Caroline's mind. But what?

Two hours later, without any more incidents with drunken Lotharios and no other personal revelations, Wolfe escorted Caroline back to the waiting Mercedes. He'd never been so glad to leave a party in his life. Jack Parker, who had been, as he always was, a big hit with everyone—especially the ladies—said his good-nights and followed them outside, without anyone being aware of the fact that he was the rear guard. Jack was smooth. The best of the best. After the three of them were safely ensconced in the car, Matt exited the circular drive. Within no time they were traveling on the Interstate 495 loop that circled D.C. and the outlying cities, heading toward the Annapolis exit.

After what seemed like an endless silence, Jack, who sat in the front seat with Matt, turned around and smiled. ''That turned out to be fairly harmless, didn't it? Other than Wolfe capturing the kissing bandit, everything went off without a hitch.''

''The kissing bandit?'' Matt asked.

''Some drunk took an instant liking to Miss Caroline and thought he'd steal a kiss,'' Jack explained.

"So that was the guy I saw you escorting outside." Matt chuckled. "I'm surprised Wolfe didn't shoot him. You did know that our Wolfe is an expert marksman, didn't you, Ms. McGuire?"

"Yes," Caroline said quietly. "I believe Fletch mentioned that being an expert with guns was one of Mr. Wolfe's credentials."

"We were lucky," Wolfe said, deliberately changing the subject. "Things could just as easily have gone the other way."

"I'm glad Matt and I were both free to come in and help you tonight," Jack said. "It just so happened that we'd both come off our last assignments when you called Ellen and asked for a couple of agents. Sure am happy I got to meet you, Miss Caroline. As a matter of fact, if you get tired of having a bodyguard as solemn and serious as Wolfe, then I'd be more than happy to—"

"Cut the crap, Parker," Wolfe said brusquely.

Jack rolled his eyes and clicked his tongue, his expression saying, *Uh-oh, what's up with him?*

Matt cleared his throat and glanced in the interior rearview mirror to steal a quick glimpse of the back seat's occupants.

Caroline giggled. "You'll have to excuse him. I've found that your David Wolfe is rather proprietary about me. Is he that way about all his clients?"

"David?" Matt glanced in the rearview mirror again, and when he made eye contact with Wolfe, he returned his focus to the road, pronto.

"Yeah, Matt, didn't you know that Wolfe actually has a given name?" Jack chuckled. "And Miss Caroline, I think Wolfe…can be forgiven for being proprietary where you're concerned. It'd be hard for a man not to be."

"Dammit, Parker, I thought I told you to—"

"So, Jack, what time is our flight out in the morning?" Matt asked.

"Nine-thirty," Jack said.

"I'll need y'all to cancel and take a later flight, possibly even stay over another day," Wolfe said. "I have a nine o'clock appointment in the morning with the president of Peacekeepers International. He's given me permission to go through all of Preston Shaw's old files to see if I can come up with any information that might help us."

"How did you manage that?" Matt asked. "I'd have thought those files were confidential."

"Boy, don't you know by now that the Dundee agency has a way of getting a look at whatever files they need to see?" Jack said. "It seems Sam Dundee's got connections with every government agency in the U.S., as well as organizations like the Peacekeepers."

"Wolfe didn't go through the Dundee agency," Caroline said. "He met Mr. Penn tonight and simply asked to see the files."

Jack and Matt said "hmm-mmm" simultaneously.

"While I'm in D.C. tomorrow morning, I want you two to stay at Caroline's studio with her," Wolfe said. "And you might as well wait until day after tomorrow to leave."

"Sure thing," Jack replied. "When you drop us off at the motel tonight, I'll cancel our morning flight to Atlanta and book us for something day after tomorrow. That is if you're sure you won't need us to hang around longer than that, just in case Miss Caroline wants to attend another fancy shindig."

"Your services won't be needed after tomorrow." Wolfe's voice lowered to a feral growl.

Gavin Robbins left Roz with the pudgy, bug-eyed federal judge who seemed smitten with her, despite the fact that Roz was young enough to be his granddaughter. But Roz didn't seem to mind. The silly woman was dazzled by all the important people she'd met here tonight. She'd probably be so grateful later that she would invite him to spend the night with her. Why else would he bother with a no-class, airheaded bimbo like Roz Turner, except for the sex? What he needed for a lifetime mate was a class act like Brooke Harper, a woman with brains and looks who was the heiress to a fortune. Unfortunately Fletcher Shaw had beat him to the punch there, but since his promotion at Peacekeepers, he'd been receiving more and more invitations to all the right parties. It was only a matter of time until he snagged himself a rich wife. He'd thought Caroline McGuire might be his ticket to respectability and the power he longed for, but they had been all wrong for each other. That ice queen needed to find herself a man like her cousin Lyle, somebody as harmless as a fly. Caroline wouldn't know what to do with a real man if she fell over one in the dark.

While the judge kept Roz entertained, Gavin decided to take the opportunity to say hello to his host and hostess, something he didn't want to do with Roz on his arm. He spotted Oliver Harper in the adjoining room, talking and laughing with General Bishop and Senator Howard.

"Gavin," a male voice behind him called.

He glanced over his shoulder and saw Ellison Penn's flunky, Barry Vanderpool, motioning to him. Ellison thought Barry was something special just because he'd graduated from one of those Ivy League schools and could speak half a dozen foreign languages. Well, Barry could enjoy being the big man's favorite while Penn held the top position at Peacekeepers. But sooner or later the old man would either die or retire, and when that day came, Gavin intended to take over. Then he'd ship Barry off somewhere overseas, never to return to D.C., and promote Mike Latham, his own hand-picked man.

"What's up, Barry, my man?"

"I wanted to speak to you about something that concerns me, however…" Barry glanced nervously around, as if checking for eavesdroppers. "You know how highly I think of Mr. Penn."

"Yeah, sure, he's like a father to you."

"I wouldn't go that far, but yes, I do admire and respect

him greatly, as you know my father did when he worked with Mr. Penn.''

''Does this story have a point, Vanderpool? If it does, how about getting to it.''

''My first allegiance is to Peacekeepers International. That's the only reason I'm mentioning this to you.'' Barry took a deep breath. ''Mr. Penn told me that first thing in the morning I'm to put together all of Preston Shaw's files and search the computer system for anything that might be stored there.''

Gavin knew that he was one of a handful of Peacekeepers agents who knew the truth about Preston Shaw's betrayal and about why he was killed and by whom. Was Ellison afraid that something in Preston's files might have been overlooked when they'd gone through them nearly fifteen years ago? Did he just want to make sure that nothing showed up now—that nothing came back to bite them in the butt?

''This thing with Caroline McGuire has gotten old Ellison curious, is that it?'' Gavin asked. ''Or did he seem unduly concerned about something in particular?''

''You don't understand,'' Barry said. ''Mr. Penn asked for those files because he intends to allow Mr. Wolfe, Caroline McGuire's bodyguard, to go through them to see if he can find anything that will help him in his investigation. I must tell you, Gavin, that I find Mr. Penn's willingness to allow a *civilian* to view classified documents highly irregular.''

Gavin nodded. ''Yeah. Highly irregular.'' What was that wily old fox up to? Gavin wondered. Who had persuaded Ellison to give Wolfe a look at the files? Oliver Harper, maybe? Who else with that much power would be interested in Caroline? Surely Ellison planned to check the files himself before he allowed Wolfe to see them. Or was there something else going on? Just exactly who was this Mr. Wolfe? Was it possible that Ellison knew the man? Whatever was going on, he intended to find out. After all, his own future could very well depend on it.

Gavin grabbed Barry's hand and shook it soundly. "Thanks. You did the right thing coming to me. I'll talk to Ellison and find out what's going on. No need for you to worry."

No need for anybody to worry about anything. Gavin smiled. If Ellison Penn was keeping secrets—or giving away secrets—then he intended to catch the man in the act. Best way to find out what you need to know is try the direct approach first. Go straight to the horse's mouth.

When Gavin found Ellison Penn, he was deep in conversation with their hostess, a strikingly attractive woman, for someone of her age. But then Brooke's mama had probably gone under the plastic surgeon's knife more than once. Half the old biddies here tonight had gotten everything on their faces and bodies lifted, tucked or suctioned.

Ellison saw him approaching and gave him a don't-bother-me glare, but Gavin ignored the warning. As Gavin neared him, Ellison disengaged himself from the charming Mrs. Harper and headed Gavin off before he reached their hostess.

"What do you want, Robbins?" Ellison asked.

"I hear you're making Peacekeepers International files open to the public."

"You heard wrong," Ellison said.

"So Caroline McGuire's bodyguard won't be given access to all of Preston Shaw's old files?"

"Allowing Mr. Wolfe access to those files does not constitute opening them to the public."

"Does Mr. Wolfe have a top-priority clearance?" Gavin demanded.

Ellison hesitated. His square jaw tightened. Gavin would give a million bucks for a two-minute glimpse into the old man's steel-trap mind right now.

"As a matter of fact he does," Ellison said, with a hint of a smile playing at the corners of his mouth. "Just between us, Robbins, I've checked out Mr. Wolfe thoroughly. And

I've seen a rather interesting personal file on him. He's former CIA."

Heat crept up the back of Gavin's neck and suffused his face. Damn! He should have known it would be something like this. Wolfe was former CIA, was he? Gavin found that fact very interesting. Interesting enough to do a little checking of his own. And soon.

Caroline placed her shoes on the rack, then unzipped her dress and removed it. Just as she hung the black silk creation on a pink satin padded hanger, she heard a soft rap on the outer door to her bedroom. Without looking, she knew it was Wolfe. Who else would it be but David Wolfe?

She had known several men named David over the years, and other than the fact that the name itself held a special meaning for her, none of those other Davids had meant any more to her than guys named John or Jim or Tom. But David Wolfe was different. From the moment she saw him standing at her front door, she had felt an odd sense of recognition, as if she already knew him. Of course that wasn't possible. She'd never met the man before in her life. But that feeling wouldn't leave her, no matter how hard she tried to reason it away. On a purely emotional level, her body and her heart had immediately responded to him.

There was no way on earth he could be her David. The very idea was ludicrous. So, why did it matter so much to her that his name was David? Why was she so upset that he had deliberately not told her his given name? Dope, she chided herself. He didn't tell you because of this very reason—because he knew you would put too much emphasis on the name. Even before you knew his name, you were practically trying to seduce him. And failing miserably, she reminded herself. Being a femme fatale was not her forte. She had never seduced a man...had never wanted to seduce a man.

Another knock, louder and a bit more forceful, brought

Caroline's wayward thoughts into focus. She grabbed a lavender silk robe off a hanger and put it on over her black bra and half-slip, then walked out of the huge closet. Wolfe stood on the threshold, leaning against the door frame. He had removed his tuxedo jacket and bow tie, undone the top three buttons on his white shirt and taken off his glasses. How was it possible for one man to look so good? she wondered. Large and lean and devastatingly male. With just enough muscles, just enough body hair, just the right amount of self-assurance without coming across as cocky.

"Is there something you want?" she asked, trying her level best to sound cool, in control and totally unemotional.

He looked her over, from head to toe, his gaze pausing a couple of times. Once on her face and then at her breasts, which swelled over the top of her low-cut, black lace bra. Feeling as if he had stripped her naked, Caroline pulled the lapels of her thin robe together and ran her hand around to the back of her waist, searching for the tie belt. When she realized it wasn't there, she simply held the lapels together with one hand.

He lifted his gaze to her face again. "Unless I find something in your stepfather's Peacekeepers files to give us a clue or we can figure out where else to look, I'd say the odds of our finding the object your key opens aren't very good. The Dundee lab hasn't been able to definitely identify the key from the photos we sent."

"And your point is?" She stayed where she was, keeping the width of her bedroom between them. Having learned the hard way how dangerous it was to get too close to an open flame, she had no intention of being burned by the same fire a second time. And for her, David Wolfe was definitely a blazing inferno.

"I suggest that you give it one more week and if nothing shows up, you—"

"I'm not giving up!"

"As long as you have that damn key in your possession,

your life will remain in danger.'' Wolfe stepped over the threshold. ''All I'm suggesting is that you take yourself out of the equation. Give me the key and let me continue the search on my own, until I've exhausted every possibility.''

''I thought you just implied that after looking through Preston's Peacekeepers files tomorrow we will have exhausted all known possibilities.'' She couldn't—wouldn't— let anyone have the key. And she had no intention of stopping the search. Not until she was convinced that it was a hopeless cause.

''Caroline, please be reasonable.'' He took several steps toward her, then stopped in the middle of her bedroom. ''It's only a matter of time before another attempt is made on your life. Is finding the object that your key unlocks worth risking your life?''

She lifted the chain around her neck enough so that she could grasp the key. ''This key will unlock the identity of the person who killed Preston and the reason he murdered him. I owe it to my stepfather to see that his killer is brought to justice.''

''Damn!'' Wolfe stormed across the room, grabbed her shoulders and shook her soundly. ''It's clear from the way he was killed that Preston Shaw was executed. That probably means the man who killed him was simply following orders. He was simply a tool, just as the gun was, in Shaw's killing. The man who pulled the trigger on that gun is unimportant. There is no point in your tormenting yourself this way when you will never know the identity of that man.''

Caroline's pulse raced, her heart beat wildly. She looked into David Wolfe's eyes—no longer cold, but deadly hot— and shivered with a combination of fear and longing. ''How...do...you know? How can you be so sure? And you're wrong about his identity not being important. Even if he was only a trained assassin—''

Wolfe tightened his hold on her shoulders. ''You have to

let this go. If we don't unearth something in another week, I want you to give me the key.''

When she opened her mouth to protest, he lifted his hand from her right shoulder and placed his index finger over her lips. "What if I promise to find your David, a man who knew your stepfather, and give him the key? Would you trust him to do everything in his power to solve the mystery?''

She stared at him, dazed by his question. "Do you think you could do that, find David—*my David?*''

"If it's the only way to get you out of danger, then yes, I'll find your David for you. He will probably refuse to meet with you, to allow you to know who he is, but my guess is that he will want to do whatever is necessary to help you.''

"All right," she said. "We will give it another week, from tomorrow. And if by that time we still haven't found whatever the key unlocks, then you find my David.''

"And you'll let me give him the key.''

"Find him first and then I'll decide.''

His hands skimmed down, over her arms, across her elbows and to her wrists, which he manacled in his tight grasp. "You shouldn't waste your life waiting for a man who's never going to be able to give you what you want and need. You have to stop fantasizing about this mysterious David of yours.''

"You couldn't possibly understand what it's been like for me." Try as she might, she could not break eye contact with David Wolfe. She felt as if he held her spellbound. "To have someone in your life who has somehow become a part of you and yet you can never see him, never touch him, never talk to him. This man whom you say can never give me what I want and need has spent the past fourteen years doing just that. Don't you understand at all? David has been giving me what I needed, everything I needed, since I was twelve years old.

"The money for the best psychiatrist in the South. Money for nice clothes and piano lessons and swimming lessons and school trips. He paid for my senior trip. He put me through college. He arranged for my first job with the photographer in Richmond and he saw to it that I got a bank loan when I opened my own studio. He doesn't know that I'm aware of everything he's done for me, but I am. When Aunt Dixie died, she left me a letter explaining everything that David had done for me.''

Dixie Jennings had broken the promise she had made to him. No, actually, she hadn't. She had said in their one telephone conversation, ''I vow that as long as I live, I'll never tell Caroline how generous you've been to her.'' Apparently, she had not kept that truth hidden after her death.

''All right, so he was a man who took care of an old acquaintance's child. Good for him. But you're a woman now. A successful woman who doesn't need a keeper. You need a man who can love you and marry you and give you children. Your David can never be that man!''

''How can you be so sure?'' Tears collected in her eyes, swimming over the surface.

''Because I'm a man.'' His fingertip brushed across her upper lip as his thumb cradled her chin. ''Believe me, if your David could come to you and claim you for his own, he would have done it already. He can't come to you. Not now or ever.''

Wolfe released her abruptly. ''But just because he can't be a part of your life doesn't mean he won't help you in any way he can.''

Odd, Caroline thought, the way Wolfe spoke of a man he didn't know. But his words hadn't been a revelation to her. In her heart of hearts she already knew the truth—her David could never be a part of her life.

''Even though I understand that what you say is true, I'm not quite prepared to give up my fantasy,'' she said.

He nodded, a sad look in his eyes as he gazed at her. ''Just don't hang on to that fantasy too long, sweet Caroline, and let life pass you by.'' He turned and walked out of her room.

She waited, her breath caught in her throat, until he disappeared across the hall, then she rushed toward her bed, threw herself across it and let the tears fall. The cards that her David attached to her birthday and Christmas presents always read *My sweet Caroline.* Why of all the endearments in the world had David Wolfe chosen to use that one? Her heart was breaking into a million pieces and no one could help her, no one could heal her. Neither of her Davids. Neither of her guardian angels.

Chapter 13

Wolfe arrived at the Peacekeepers International building in Washington, D.C., at precisely ten minutes till nine and was passed through the security check on the ground level. He had left his Sig Sauer in the car. As the lone occupant of the private elevator to the top floor, which housed the president and vice president's suite of offices, he had a few minutes to prepare himself. It had been nearly three years since he'd been in this building, since Aidan Colbert had reported to Ellison Penn. He reminded himself that he must act as if, before today, he'd never been in this building or the suite of offices with which he was so familiar.

When the elevator doors opened, Barry Vanderpool, the boy wonder at Peacekeepers, was standing there like a sentinel. The twenty-four-year-old had piercing black eyes, shortly cropped auburn hair and a lean, hard body that was obvious despite the cover of a business suit.

"Good morning, Mr. Wolfe."

Barry possessed a military stance and carried himself like

a trained soldier. Wolfe halfway expected the man to salute him.

Wolfe nodded. "Good morning, Mr. Vanderpool."

"Mr. Penn is expecting you. If you will follow me, please."

As the highly efficient Barry escorted Wolfe down the hall, Gavin Robbins emerged from his office, coffee cup in hand. Barry paused and nodded to Gavin.

"I hope Ellison's secretary is giving you the red-carpet treatment," Gavin said as he followed them down the hall. "We here at Peacekeepers like to maintain a good working relationship with all the federal agencies, especially you CIA boys."

"Former CIA," Wolfe said. "I'm retired."

"Retired kind of young, didn't you?" Gavin asked.

Wolfe paused and glared at Gavin, but didn't respond to his question. Instead he continued walking, which prompted Barry to do the same. Wolfe sensed rather than saw Gavin stop and stare at his back. Barry knocked on the closed door to his superior's inner sanctum.

"Come in." Ellison's voice rang out clearly.

Barry opened the door, stepped back and indicated with a wave of his hand that Wolfe was to enter. Wolfe glanced across the room to where Ellison rose from his desk. When they met in the middle of the office, they shook hands, then Ellison closed the door.

"I have all of Preston Shaw's files on the table over there." He indicated with a nod. "I had Barry set things up for you this morning." He pointed to the portable table, stacked with file folders, computer disks and an assortment of boxes. "As you know, Preston was with Peacekeepers for a good many years."

"Is there anything on that table that we didn't go over with a fine-tooth comb nearly fifteen years ago?" Wolfe asked.

"You know there isn't," Ellison replied. "So, want to tell

me what this is all about, why you made such a production of requesting to see Preston's files?''

"Two reasons. First, it gave me a front for meeting with you without anyone asking questions. And second, I want to know exactly what you've been concealing about Preston Shaw. And don't try to tell me that you have no idea what I'm talking about."

"You already know that we suspected Shaw of being involved with a secret organization of men who had a long-range plan to gain control of the government, partially by gradually putting their people in place in Congress and top-ranking government positions. Hell, they even infiltrated Peacekeepers International by recruiting Preston."

"As you say, I already know all of this. What don't I know?''

"The proof we were given that Preston was the man who assassinated Senator Harwell might have been falsified."

Wolfe suddenly felt cold, then went momentarily numb. As if something was draining the blood from his body. He stared at Ellison, his mind screaming accusations, but all he said was "Are you telling me that I was given orders to execute an innocent man?''

"What I'm telling you is that there is a possibility the Loyalists Coalition wanted to get rid of Preston and planned to use us as the means by which to achieve that end, then changed their minds when they realized he had damning evidence against them. But somehow…by mistake, the information was sent to us, anyway. It doesn't mean that Preston didn't kill Senator Harwell."

Wolfe closed his eyes momentarily, the impact of this new information dropping like a lead weight into his stomach. God in heaven, was it possible that Preston Shaw had been innocent? If that were true, how could he ever justify what he'd done? "If there's any possibility that Preston Shaw was an innocent man—''

"You're thinking about Caroline, aren't you?"

"Yes."

"Dammit, man, if the truth comes out, you can't protect that girl." Ellison clamped his hand down on Wolfe's shoulder. "Believe me, Preston Shaw was guilty. Even if he didn't actually pull the trigger, he was part of the assassination plot. Once you find the evidence Preston hid away, there's a good chance we can blow the Loyalists Coalition sky-high and arrest their top men. When that happens, Caroline will learn the truth about her stepfather. There's no way to avoid it."

"She will be devastated," Wolfe said. "But it may never come to that. I'm beginning to have my doubts that if there is any such evidence, we'll ever find it. But regardless, I want Caroline taken out of the line of fire."

"And how do you intend to do that?" Ellison released his hold on Wolfe's shoulder and stared at him quizzically.

"She has agreed that if within a week's time we haven't found the object the key opens, she'll consider turning the key over to someone else and allow him to continue the search."

"Who?"

"The man she knows only as David. I've promised her that I'd find this man for her."

"Have you lost your mind? How the hell do you intend to find yourself? You can hardly present yourself to Caroline and tell her that you're the man who has acted as her benefactor all these years."

"I have no intention of introducing Caroline to *her* David. But if I can persuade her that he has been found and is willing to continue this search, in order to free her from danger, then we'll all get what we want. Caroline will be safe. And I can continue the search for the evidence against the Loyalists Coalition."

"You realize this plan of yours will work only if Caroline is convinced that her David is involved in this scheme. And you must know that if you tell her you've found him, she will insist on meeting him."

"And he will insist that their relationship remains the same, that he not reveal himself to her."

"Let's say your plan works and she gives you the key for you to give to her David and then you unearth what the key opens and find the evidence against the Loyalists Coalition. What will you tell Caroline?"

Wolfe looked squarely at Ellison. "I'll tell her everything, except about Preston Shaw's involvement with the Loyalists Coalition. I intend to let her continue believing her stepfather was a hero, that he died because he had gotten hold of evidence against some evil characters."

"In other words, you're going to lie to her."

"Yeah. I'm going to let her hold on to at least one fantasy while she's forced to let go of another."

"And what fantasy would that be—the one she'll be forced to let go of?" Ellison asked.

"The one about her benefactor David. It will be necessary to eliminate him. Once everything else is settled, she will receive a letter from his lawyer telling her of his death."

"You already had this planned, didn't you, before Caroline found the key? You were going to cut your ties to her."

Wolfe nodded. "I should have gotten her benefactor out of her life years ago, once she outgrew the need for him. But selfishly, I allowed things to continue as they were."

"Satisfy an old man's curiosity..." Ellison smiled, but there was a rather sad, lonely look in his eyes. "Is she all that you thought she was, all you had hoped she would be?"

Quiet fell on the office. A hushed stillness. Wolfe breathed softly. In and out, in and out. "Yes," he replied. "All that and more."

"She need never know who you really are," Ellison said. "You could be with her, if that's what you want."

If that's what he wanted! As emotional pain radiated through him, Wolfe shut his eyes, refusing to acknowledge that there was even a glimmer of hope. "I would know the truth—that I killed Preston Shaw—and eventually the lie standing between Caroline and me would destroy me. No, it's better this way.''

''Very well.'' Preston pointed to the table piled high with Preston Shaw's files. ''You'd better spend the morning looking through that mess, just to continue the farce. And in a week's time, if you can persuade Caroline to go along with your plan, we can use some excuse concerning your rechecking those files to arrange another meeting.''

Wolfe nodded agreement, then pulled out a chair and sat at the desk. During the next couple of hours, he would work his way through these files, then he would call Jack Parker and let him know it would be this evening before he could make it back to Caroline's St. Michaels studio. He had several errands to run, certain arrangements to be made and a few decisions to make. Glancing down at the date displayed on his wristwatch, he was reminded of what day it was today. This would be his one and only chance to spend Caroline's birthday with her. Was he wrong to want to make it a memorable event?

Despite her concern about what information Wolfe might have uncovered when he went through Preston's files today, Caroline finished the last photo shoot of the day feeling pleased with the photographs she'd taken. Lindsey Chapman, a June bride-to-be, had driven in from Wilmington with her groom. Seeing the young couple so much in love and so totally devoted to each other had evoked mixed emotions within Caroline. Joy for the couple and a reaffirmation that true love existed. But also a sense of sadness and perhaps a little jealousy because she doubted she would ever share that kind of happiness with someone.

''Weren't they absolutely disgusting,'' Roz said. ''And God, don't you envy them.''

Caroline laughed, thankful for Roz's sense of humor. Somehow her dear friend always knew the right thing to say to lighten a dark mood.

"Do you think either of us will ever be that lucky?" Caroline flopped down in the padded swivel chair, lifted her feet and propped them on her desk.

"You, maybe," Roz said. "If you'll ever quit mooning over that phantom benefactor of yours and start taking notice of what's right under your nose."

"Meaning?"

"Meaning that six-foot-two hottie who's living in your house." Roz opened the compact minifridge sitting on a corner table, retrieved a couple of bottles of lemon-flavored iced tea and tossed one to Caroline.

"I don't think Wolfe is the type for long-term commitments." Caroline twisted off the bottle cap, shot it into the wastebasket by her desk and lifted the refreshing drink to her lips.

"My theory is that no man is prepared for marriage, not until the right woman comes along and he realizes that he can't live without her." Roz uncapped her drink, tossed the lid at the wastebasket, missed by a couple of inches, then shrugged and took a big swig of tea.

Jack Parker suddenly appeared in the open doorway, a friendly good-old-boy smile on his face and a small package in his hand. "Pardon me, ladies, but this little item just arrived special delivery for Miss Caroline."

Caroline eyed the small parcel that Jack laid on her desk, which she could tell had been opened and hastily rewrapped. From the untidy appearance of the shiny paper and the lop-sided bow, she suspected that neither Jack nor Matt was adept at giftwrapping. When she glanced up at Jack, he grinned.

"Sorry about not getting it put back together all pretty like, but I did the best I could," he said.

"You opened Caroline's package?" Roz asked.

"Had to, ma'am," Jack explained. "Never know what might have been in there. Could have been something dangerous."

"Oh, stupid me." Roz grimaced. "I keep forgetting. So, I take it the package is safe."

"Yes, ma'am."

"Go on. Open it," Roz said. "I'm curious to see who's sending you presents and it's not even Christmas."

"No, it's not Christmas," Caroline said. "But it is my birthday. And I'm pretty sure I know who sent this gift."

"Damn, why didn't you remind me it was your birthday?" Roz whined, and gave Caroline an apologetic look. "What kind of friend am I to forget your birthday."

"It's okay, really." As Caroline reached for the gift, she caught a conspiratorial glance exchanged between Roz and Jack and wondered what it was all about. Knowing Roz, she was simply flirting with the Dundee agent. "When this whole mess about Preston's hidden key is resolved and I can resume my normal life, we'll celebrate. You and Lyle, Brooke and Fletch and I. We'll go out somewhere really nice and make a night of it."

"Excuse me, Miss Caroline," Jack said.

"Yes?"

"Wolfe just called about five minutes ago and said he's only a few miles from here. So I just wanted to say goodbye and good luck, since Matt and I'll be heading to the motel as soon as Wolfe gets here."

"Thank you, Jack." She had been waiting all day for word from Wolfe, but he hadn't bothered speaking to her personally either time he'd called his co-agent. He'd simply informed Jack Parker that business was keeping him in D.C. longer than expected.

"I'll be right outside, if you need me," Jack said. "Matt's locking up out there now that Kirsten and Sandy have left for the day." Jack closed the door behind him.

"Texas Jack there is going to make some woman mighty happy one of these days." Roz sighed dramatically. "Actually, he's probably already made quite a few women mighty happy." She giggled. "I was just thinking about the lucky girl who gets him for keeps.'' Roz plopped down on the edge of the desk and eyed the poorly rewrapped gift. ''So, are you going to open it or not?''

Caroline knew before opening the gift or reading the card, which would be lying inside, that the birthday present was from David. Her David. Not once since her thirteenth birthday had he forgotten. With nervous fingers she removed the bow, untied the ribbon and pulled apart the white wrapping paper to reveal a black velvet jeweler's box. Since her twenty-first birthday, he had sent jewelry as a gift. She eased back the lid to reveal a stunning pearl-and-diamond bracelet. Roz let out a long, low whistle. There sitting atop the present was the familiar white card. She lifted it and read the brief message. *Happy birthday, my sweet Caroline.* And below in the bold, flowing script was his signature. *David.*

''I'll say one thing for this guy, he's no cheapskate.''

Caroline lifted the bracelet from its velvet bed, draped it around her wrist and fastened the catch. ''It matches the other diamond and pearl jewelry he's already given me.''

''You've never worn all of them, have you? I'm sure I would have remembered seeing them if you had.''

''I've considered selling them and giving the money to charity,'' Caroline said. ''You know, except for an occasional event that Fletch or Brooke invite me to attend, I'm not much of a social butterfly. And I have so many lovely pieces of jewelry, most of them gifts from David, that I hardly need them all.''

Roz hopped up, came around the side of the desk and gave Caroline a hug. ''Happy birthday, hon. I'll remind Lyle when I get over to the church that today's your birthday. I'm sure he's just so busy with getting things together for this weekend's church yard sale that he let it slip his mind.''

''I'm sure that's it. And Roz, thanks again for taking my place and meeting my obligations at the church until—''

''Don't think another thing about it,'' Roz assured her. ''You may find this hard to believe, but I'm actually enjoying myself. And the rev and I haven't had one single knock-down-drag-out. At least not yet.''

"I'm glad to hear it. Lyle is a great guy. But I have a feeling you already know that."

Roz grinned. "Hmm-mmm. Maybe."

Caroline waved goodbye. Heading out, Roz almost collided with Wolfe when she opened the office door.

"Sorry," Wolfe said. "Are you leaving for the day?"

"I'm on my way over to the church to do Caroline's good deeds for her." Roz winked at Wolfe.

"That's an interesting idea," he said. "Good deeds by proxy."

He entered the office as soon as Roz left. Caroline immediately noticed that he had changed clothes, that he wasn't wearing the charcoal pin-striped suit he'd left her house in this morning. Instead he was now dressed more casually in navy-blue slacks and a white cotton shirt, the top two buttons undone. But the ever present hip holster remained. Caroline rose to her feet slowly and confronted him.

"Did you find anything in Preston's Peacekeepers files?" she asked.

"Yes and no."

"Can't you be more specific?"

"No information that will help us find the object the key opens," he said. "But some information about why your stepfather was executed."

She tensed. Nausea stirred in her stomach. "He *was* executed, wasn't he?"

"Yes. It seems that he definitely had come into possession of some critical information about a group known as the Loyalists Coalition, comprised of unidentified powerful men who posed a threat to our government. These men were probably responsible for Preston Shaw's murder."

"And these men who had Preston executed don't want me to find the evidence against them and that's why they've been trying to kill me."

"Ellison Penn is as interested as we are in finding that evidence," Wolfe said. "He's pledged to do whatever he can to assist me, including contacting your benefactor's lawyer and asking for his help."

"Mr. Penn knows my David, doesn't he?" She had suspected for years that her David was somehow connected to Peacekeepers International, and that her stepfather's boss had always known the identity of her benefactor. And she was just as certain that had she ever asked him about David, Mr. Penn would have denied knowing him.

"We could end this nightmare for you right now, Caroline. Give me the key and then we'll let it be known that you no longer have the key and have given up the search, but that the Peacekeepers are continuing the investigation."

Caroline stroked the chain at her neck and considered her options. "You said you'd give us another week working on this together. I want that week."

"What difference do you think another week will make?"

"If that's true, then you shouldn't have a problem keeping your promise to me, should you?"

Shaking his head, he huffed loudly. "All right. One week."

There, that was settled. One week wasn't long, but if her prayers were answered, a week would be long enough. Enough time to find what the key unlocked. Enough time to come to terms with her feelings about David Wolfe. "Okay, I'm ready to go home and be locked in for the night." What a way for a woman to spend her twenty-seventh birthday, Caroline thought. No dinner with friends. No birthday cake. No presents. No cards. Nothing special. Just another day.

She lifted her wrist and stroked the pearl-and-diamond bracelet. David hadn't forgotten. He never forgot. But what good was an expensive gift when all she truly wanted was to be with her David, to share just one of her birthdays with him?

"New bracelet?" Wolfe asked.

"Yes. A present from my benefactor."

"A birthday gift."

"Yes, but how did you—"

"Your birth date is listed in the file I have on you."

"Of course."

"If you're ready…" He motioned to the door.

She rose from behind the desk, followed him and turned the light off in the office before closing the door. When he led her toward studio one, which she used for all her adult photography, she tugged on his arm.

"I thought we were going home," she said.

"Later."

"What do you mean, 'later'?"

"I have something I want to show you in the studio," he said. "It's something I think you'll like. So just humor me, okay?"

"Would you mind telling me what's going on?"

He took her hand, led her down the hall and straight to studio one. He placed her in front of him, reached around her to open the door, then gave her a gentle shove over the threshold. The moment she entered the studio, she gasped.

Chapter 14

Caroline could not believe her eyes. The studio had been transformed into a magical, romantic scene, complete with soft lighting, mellow jazz and a table set for two. The tune—"Sorry Seems to Be the Hardest Word"—coming from some unknown source was from a CD of hers. The mournful wail of the saxophone wrapped around her, a musical lover's caress. Hundreds of white balloons filled the room. Some floated across the ceiling like bubbly clouds. Others danced around over the floor, covering every inch of space like an airy, undulating carpet. Huge white candles had been strategically placed on two food-laden tables behind the small center table that had been set with china and crystal for two. Cream-white roses in spiraling vases graced all three tables.

"What is all of this?" Caroline asked.

"Do you like your surprise?"

She whipped around and stared at him. The look on his face sent shivers along her nerves. This was a man intent upon pleasing her. She saw it in his eyes, sensed it as surely as if he had spoken the words aloud...*I want everything to be perfect for you.* But why? Why this man and why this moment? He had to know that he was the wrong David to fulfill her fantasies.

"It's incredible," she replied. "How…when…? Is this the reason you've been gone all afternoon?"

He nodded. "I had some help," he confessed. "From Roz and Kirsten and Sandy, as well as Matt and Jack. The girls helped me set things up in here while Roz kept you in your office. And Matt and Jack haven't actually left. They're outside, keeping an eye on the place. This is why I asked them to stay over until morning."

"Was this your idea or—"

"Totally my idea," he said. "I knew it was your birthday, and since you're confined to quarters, so to speak, I decided you deserved something more than a birthday cake."

"I can't believe this." She glided through the balloons, which separated and floated around in every direction. "I would never have dreamed that you could come up with something this sentimental and romantic." She whirled around and around, letting the balloons dance at her feet as she moved to the sensuous rhythm of the music.

"Then you like it?" he asked.

"Like it?" She stopped twirling and smiled at him. "I love it."

Wolfe closed the door behind him, then stood in place, his arms crossed over his chest, and watched Caroline McGuire savor the fantasy world he had created for her. How many times had he longed to do something special for her? How often had he envisioned a moment like this? If it was wrong of him to want this particular birthday to be memorable, then God forgive him. But this would be the one and only birthday he would ever spend with her. He intended to do everything in his power to make the night unforgettable for both of them. Soon the Fates would condemn him to hell, into a world without Caroline. Damned for past sins. Unforgiven.

She reached up and pulled the scarf holding her ponytail

in place and let the small square of lavender silk sail down to disappear in the ocean of balloons at her bare feet. Her hair fell around her shoulders, strands of shimmery onyx that beckoned him to run his fingers through them, to grasp her head and hold her face to his. He had long ago memorized the features of her beautiful face from having spent hours gazing at photographs of her. But no picture could capture the vibrant loveliness of this woman. She swayed to the music, her green-and-lavender floral skirt whirling around her calves.

Caroline held out her hand. He walked across the room, removed his hip holster and laid it on a side table, then went to her. Without a word being exchanged, he took her into his arms. Their bodies came together, touching tenderly, undemanding and totally at ease, as if they had danced together countless times. In tune. Perfectly matched. A man and a woman. A night filled with promise. Unhurried. As if each moment had no beginning and no end.

Wolfe knew he had no right to expect anything beyond giving Caroline pleasure. And that would be enough. It had to be enough! A part of him longed to tell her that he was her David, the man she had turned into a larger-than-life hero that no mortal man could possibly live up to. But with that sort of revelation would come questions that he could never answer, inquiries into a past he must keep secret from her. He had one more week with her and then he would disappear from her life and her David would also cease to exist. It was the only way—for him and for her. She could never have a normal life as long as she clung to the impossible hope that someday her David would become a part of her world.

Caroline's body heat invaded his skin, seeped beneath the surface to warm his muscles and bones and set afire the desire he had been keeping under control. She tilted her head and gazed up at him. A dreamy smile opened her mouth and curved her soft lips. How could he resist the temptation to sample such sweetness? He brushed his lips over hers. She shivered ever so slightly, an almost indiscernible quiver that shook him as much as if a volcano had exploded inside her. He was so in tune to her body, so in sync with every little nuance, every varying shade of Caroline McGuire. Wolfe cursed himself for the doomed fool that he was. She had not been the only one with a fantasy—an unrealistic dream—as equally impossible and with as little hope of existing in reality as his was.

Like her, he had been alone for most of his life, having lost his entire family by the age of thirteen. Although he had pretended to be strong and fearless, to be self-contained, needing no one, there had been a hunger inside him, a deep, human longing to have something—someone—of his own. For the past fourteen and a half years, he had allowed Caroline to become that someone—the center of his universe. From a safe distance he had watched her grow from a child into a woman and his feelings for her had changed just as gradually. In the beginning he had cared for her as a big brother, a generous friend and a man eaten alive by guilt. And then one day he realized that his thoughts about Caroline were the thoughts a man entertained about a desirable woman. Somewhere along the way she had, in his mind and heart, ceased to be his ward and had become his woman.

Always separated. A safe distance between them. It was easy being infatuated with a phantom lover, one who could never reject you, never disappoint you, never leave you. His sexual appetite had been appeased by numerous women, but not a one of them had taken anything from him because he'd given them nothing beyond the moment, nothing except sex. He had risked nothing. Expected nothing. But Caroline was different. She meant more to him than he dared to admit, even to himself.

"This evening isn't real, is it?" she asked as she lifted her hand to the nape of his neck.

Her question brought him to the present, to this moment in time, with Caroline secure and happy in the safety of his arms. "No, this evening isn't real. It's a birthday present that ends at midnight."

She slowed her movements but stayed in his arms. Looking straight at him, a melancholy wistfulness in her eyes, she whispered, "I care about you. I care too much. But you must know that I don't dare love you. And without loving you, I can't—"

He pressed his hand over her mouth, ending her pronouncement, then when she quieted and simply stared at him, he caressed her face. "My sweet Caroline, you're very wise not to throw away your love on me. Save it for a man worthy of you. But don't wait for your David."

She sighed and her fragile smile vanished. "Did you know that's what he calls me, what he's always called me? My sweet Caroline."

Wolfe hadn't realized how easily those words rolled off his tongue. How many times had he referred to her as sweet Caroline? "Then he and I are in agreement. I think that any man who truly knew you couldn't think of you in any other way. You are so very sweet."

"And just what does that mean?" she asked.

He released her, then cradled her face with his hands. "You possess a loveliness that goes beyond the physical. You have a kind heart and a generous spirit. And although you've experienced tragedies and traumas that would have destroyed a lesser person, you came through it all still possessing a goodness I can't even begin to understand."

"Wolfe...David...why can't you be—"

Her words were like a knife stabbed into his heart. How odd that he should be competing against himself, that he was his only rival for Caroline's affection.

"I'm so sorry," she said. "You've gone to so much trouble to make everything wonderful for me, and instead of being grateful, I tell you that I wish you were another man."

She tried to turn from him, but he grabbed her wrist and

jerked her up against him. Their gazes locked. Their heated breaths mingled.

"It's all right," he told her, his voice thick with passion and deceptively soft. He wanted to tell her that all Davids were the same in the dark, but wisely didn't make a joke of the matter. In his case, it was true. He *was* her David. "You may think you love him, but you want me, don't you, Caroline? Even if you feel that you're being unfaithful, you can't help wanting me. Loving a phantom is so much safer than caring about a flesh-and-blood man, isn't it?" He could tell her that he knew only too well the truth of his words. Hadn't he spent years, just as she had, investing all his deepest emotions into a relationship that was nothing more than smoke and mirrors? An illusion of love.

"You're the one who told me that you and I are all wrong for each other," she said.

"We are." *For many reasons, most of which you can never know.*

"Sometimes we want what is bad for us, don't we?" She shut her eyes, breaking the visual link that bound them. "I've never understood that before, not until I met you. I thought desire was a part of love and that love was a simple thing. I believed that you love and are loved in return and the two of you make a lifelong commitment and then…"

"In the best of all possible worlds, that's true."

"But not in our world. Not for you and me. We're both afraid of love, aren't we?"

He didn't respond verbally. There was no need. He saw the acceptance and the disillusionment in her eyes. God help him, he was destroying her dreams. When she eased out of his arms and walked away from him, he did not try to stop her. Had he made a mistake in trying to give them both a moment out of time, one evening that could belong to them alone, that nothing and no one could ever take from them? Had he prepared this surprise more for himself than for her, knowing that he was the one who would need the memory to cling to, not Caroline? She would have a future, free from him and from her David. Eventually she would fall in love and marry and have children. But what would he have? A lifetime alone.

Caroline had to put some distance between them, had to escape from the seduction of his strong arms and hypnotic gaze. It would be so easy to love this man and so very difficult to get over him once he left her. And he would leave her, return to the life he'd had before he had taken the job as her bodyguard. She knew that he wanted her... sexually...just as she wanted him. She couldn't even begin to explain the strange fascination he held for her. Why, after all these years and all the men who had come in and out of her life, was she drawn to this one man? David. But not *her* David. If she hadn't been attracted to him when she'd known him only as Wolfe, she would have suspected that his name alone had seduced her, that she had allowed herself to confuse the two men in her mind. But she had experienced that inexplicable pull, that irrefutable chemistry the moment she met him.

If Wolfe was right—that she would never meet her David, would never be allowed to see him, touch him, love him— then would it be so wrong to experience passion with another? With this David, whom she could see and touch and...love.

How could she show him the way she felt? How did she tell him that she wanted him, but was afraid that if she gave herself to him physically, she would fall in love with him? *You're already halfway in love with him as it is,* an inner voice whispered. But once they became lovers, there would be no going back, no return to the safety of loving her David. Was she prepared to relinquish her dream for reality? Would a few days in David Wolfe's arms, becoming his woman on a temporary basis be worth what she would have to give up?

Yes. Yes. Yes!

Having made her decision, Caroline searched the shelves

that held some of her photography equipment. She knew of one way—a way very personal to her—that she could seduce David Wolfe. Glancing over the variety of cameras at her disposal, she quickly chose her Rollei, one of her favorites, which was easy to operate, thus giving her flexibility and creative control. Even in candlelight, she could count on this camera to capture more than the eye could behold. Before Wolfe became aware of the fact that he was her subject, she aimed and shot, then aimed again, repeating the process several times.

He faced her. Boldly. Surprised by her actions. For several minutes, he stood before her. Unmoving. He was a magnificent man and the camera loved him. The high cheekbones. The slanted shape of his eyes. The hard, chiseled imperfection of his features. The wide shoulders encased in a loose white shirt. The sleek, fluid lines of a superbly honed physique.

Long after he was gone, she would have these photographs to remind her of this special man.

Suddenly she realized that he was coming toward her, an agitated expression on his face. Without hesitation she continued taking pictures. Hurriedly. Furiously. Moving around the studio, keeping just out of his reach. She knew he intended to stop her. When he finally captured her, he manacled her wrist and jerked the camera out of her hand. She gasped aloud the moment he grabbed her by the waist.

"Why did you do that?" she asked. "I took those shots for me. I promise that no one else will ever see them. Please…" She reached down to where he held the Rollei at his side.

He held the camera just out of her reach. "You were trying to make love to me with the camera, weren't you?" He circled her waist and pulled her close, then lowered his head. "As sensual as we both found the experience, it's a poor substitute for the real thing."

She looked up, thinking he was going to kiss her. Hoping

he would. Afraid he would. But instead his tongue touched her throat. Light. Moist. A faint, tingling caress that moved down her throat and onto the flesh exposed by the V-neck of her billowing lavender blouse. When he released his hold around her waist, she didn't move, didn't pull away. He tugged on her blouse until he loosened it from beneath the waistband of her skirt, then he reached underneath, his big hand flattening across her midriff. She sucked in her breath. She quivered as her nipples tightened. He undid the front snap of her bra, pulled back the cups and freed her breasts, still covered by her blouse.

His mouth opened over one breast and his lips encompassed her nipple through the thin barrier of cloth. When he sucked, she leaned her head back as if it were too heavy for her neck to hold upright. He moved to the other breast, giving it equal attention. Caroline began unraveling, coils of pleasure spiraling, swirling inside her like wind-tossed streamers. While she was in the throes of passion, consumed by pure sexual hunger, Wolfe released her. She lifted her head, her gaze searching for him. He stood several feet away, the Rollei in his hand, the lens pointed at her.

"It's my turn," he said. "To make love to you."

She understood his meaning. She would be his subject. The object of his desire. She looked at him, knowing that all she was feeling in that moment showed plainly in her eyes. He snapped the first shot. She began moving, swaying this way and that, to the soft, jazzy beat of the music. He took picture after picture, his actions frenzied. She had never felt so alive. And for the first time in her life she knew she was sexy and seductive.

She lifted her hair in her hands and then let it cascade through her fingers. She turned her back to him and removed her blouse and bra, then glanced over her shoulder. He captured that seductive pose on film, exploring the fantasy and the pure sexuality of the moment. A clutching pressure built between her thighs, a prelude of longing so intense that it overwhelmed her. She licked her lips, moistening them, and looked at David, knowing he would recognize the invitation.

He came toward her, then stopped to lay the camera on the table where their uneaten food awaited them. She held her breath, anticipating what was to come. He eased up behind her and wrapped his arms around her. She leaned her head back to rest on his chest. He lowered his head and placed his cheek against hers. She curved her arms backward so that her hands rested on his hips.

All rational thought ceased to exist for Caroline. She gave herself over completely to the moment and to the man who held her captive. When his hands lifted to cup and then cover her breasts, she rubbed her hips seductively against his erection. Wanton, alive with a desire unequaled by any previous experience, she surrendered and yet simultaneously conquered.

Wolfe turned her to him and took her mouth in a kiss of unleashed passion, as if a dam of control had burst free inside him. She flung her arms around his neck and participated in the kiss with equal abandon. He unzipped her skirt and pulled it down her hips. It fell to her feet, draping over the nearby balloons like a voluminous tent atop quivering white sand dunes. She clung to him, totally nude except for her lavender satin panties.

He touched her. Everywhere. Her face. Her hair. Her throat. His hands skimmed her arms, her waist, her hips and down her legs. He knelt before her and buried his face against her belly. She threaded her fingers through his thick golden hair and held him to her, glorying in his adoration. He made her feel as if she were the most precious thing on earth to him.

When he hooked his forefingers under the elastic of her panties, she waited, breathlessly, for him to remove the last barrier, the last fragment of cloth that covered her. The panties slid over her hips and down her legs. She lifted one foot and then the other. He grabbed the panties and tossed them aside. His mouth touched her intimately, kissing her, arousing her unbearably. As he spread her legs farther apart, she gripped his shoulders to balance herself and within moments succumbed to the passion of his marauding lips and tongue. He held her in place, his palms on her buttocks, as he brought her to the edge of release.

Caroline wanted the fulfillment desperately. Her body yearned for him to take her that final step into completion. "Please, David, please," she whispered, calling him by his given name in her passion.

And he did please her. The intensity of her climax bolted her knees and shook her from head to toe. While the rippling aftershocks trembled through her, Wolfe swept her up into his arms and carried her across the room, sending balloons flying in every direction as he strode through their midst. He shoved open the door to the nearest dressing room and eased her down on a white damask sofa, then stripped off his shirt and tossed it to the floor.

Caroline reached up, her hands trembling as she unbuckled his belt and unzipped his slacks. He removed his clothes and stood there, hovering over her, gloriously, magnificently naked. Only the candlelight from the studio illuminated the dark dressing room, so her view of him was shadowed, but she could see the scars that marred his big body. A crisscross of scar tissue bisected his brown chest hair in several places and zigzagged atop his thighs.

"Be very sure this is what you want," he said, his voice a hoarse, heavy growl. "We have no future together. This will change nothing between us."

Caroline lifted her right arm and reached up with her left hand to undo the closure on her new diamond-and-pearl bracelet. When she removed the valuable piece of jewelry, she dropped it to the floor atop the small lambswool rug beside the sofa. Not without some regrets, she set aside the past, disengaging herself from a dream that she had outgrown.

She held open her arms to Wolfe, beckoning him to come to her. She would accept him on his terms, take whatever he offered. But he was wrong if he thought this would change nothing between them.

Wolfe knelt, dove his hand into the pocket of his discarded slacks and removed his billfold. She watched, sighing when she saw him remove the wrapped condom. Even in this, in a moment of supreme passion, he was protecting her. She gazed at him. He was big and savage-looking and over-whelmingly male. She knew a moment of panic, of uncertainty that she could accommodate him fully, but when his body covered hers, she surrendered to her own needs.

"I don't want to hurt you," he whispered against her ear, his breathing ragged, perspiration dotting his brow.

"I want you so. Make love to me…" *David. My David.*

She felt his fingers touching her between her legs, dipping inside and spreading the moisture he found. Then he slid his hands beneath her and lifted her to meet him. His first thrust was shallow, entering her with only the tip of his sex. Clinging to his shoulders, she lifted her legs, urging him to delve deeper. He took her by slow degrees, careful to allow her time to accommodate the length and width of him. When he encountered her virginal barrier, he paused, but she would have none of it. She lifted her hips higher, taking him deeper into her body as she wrapped her legs around his hips. The moment he broke through, she gasped, then held on to him, whimpering his name. As if he could hold back no longer, he took her completely, plunging himself fully into her.

Tears trickled from the corners of her eyes. He kissed them away. "I've wanted you so much…for so long…."

Their bodies moved together in perfect unison. Unparalleled passion. Indescribable pleasure. An earth-shattering loving. Caroline could not believe that her body was capable of a second climax so quickly following the first or that the second would surpass the first. She fell apart, crying, moaning, her body trembling only moments before his body tensed and his face contorted into an expression of pain. And then an animalistic moan erupted from deep in his chest when he came. Spasms rocketed through him as her body drained the last ounce of strength from his. He kissed her, devouring her with a passion that a thousand climaxes could never appease.

"Mine," he murmured. "My sweet Caroline."

Chapter 15

Lying beside Caroline, Wolfe watched her while she slept.
He intended to savor every minute with her and store up
enough memories to last a lifetime. He had disregarded doing
the decent, honorable thing and done the unforgivable. But
what man, under the same circumstances, could have denied
himself the thing he wanted most in this world? She would
never know his deep, dark secret. He promised her that—a
solemn, heartfelt vow. Even Caroline, as loving and understanding as she was, would not be able to forgive Aidan
Colbert's sins. And if it turned out that Preston Shaw had
been executed because of falsified evidence…! But now was
not the time for soul-searching, for dredging up guilt and
adding more to his already overburdened conscience. He
would not waste these precious days he'd been given with
Caroline. They were a gift from the gods, one he didn't deserve, but clung to tenaciously and with gratitude.

Just being near her aroused him. Her sweet, feminine
smell. Her soft, vulnerable beauty. The steady rise and fall
of her full, round breasts only half-covered by the sheet. He

leaned over and kissed her forehead. Her eyelids fluttered. He kissed each cheek and brushed his lips over hers. She wriggled against him and sighed.

He couldn't justify what he'd done with her, what he intended doing again, as often as possible. But at this point, he was beyond caring. It wasn't as if he planned to stay in her life, become a permanent fixture. One week. One damn week—that's all he was asking for. After that, he would free her and free himself. He had no choice. To ask for more would mean taking a huge risk—a risk that she would discover the truth about him. Not only that he was her benefactor, but that he was Aidan Colbert, the Peacekeepers agent who had killed her stepfather.

Wolfe lifted the sheet, then slipped his hand between her thighs, palming her mound as his fingers curled over her tender flesh. Gasping, Caroline opened her eyes and looked up at him.

"How sore are you?" he asked, his voice heavy with desire.

Smiling, she lifted her hand to clamp the back of his neck, then dragged his mouth down to hers. "Not terribly sore," she said against his lips. "I think my body can survive making love one more time. But after this, you might have to let me recuperate for the rest of the day." She kissed him, not like a lady, but like a woman. Wet and hot. Tongue thrusting, body arching.

"Don't you know that for more of your sweet loving, I'd promise you anything...give you anything?" His heartbeat picked up speed as he fondled her, dipping a couple of fingers into the moisture that told him how ready she was for what he wanted.

"I understand." She closed her thighs, trapping his hand between them, and rubbed her body sensuously against his. "Nothing should be this good...this wonderful...."

Wolfe leaned over and lifted a condom off the nightstand. This was his last one. He always kept one in his wallet, which he had used when they'd made love at the studio. When he was on an assignment there was no need for a supply of condoms, so he hadn't packed any. By the time he and Caroline had left the studio, he realized there wouldn't be a store open where he could purchase more, so he'd been forced to do something he hadn't done since he was a green kid. He'd borrowed condoms from another guy. He'd figured that a ladies' man like Jack Parker would be prepared at all times, on an assignment or not. And he had to give Jack credit, the man hadn't made one rude comment. He had simply handed over three condoms without saying a word.

After preparing himself, David swooped Caroline up and over him, knocking the sheet to their feet as he positioned her on top of him. She straddled his hips. He bucked upward, seeking entrance. Because of her lack of experience, the three previous times he had been the aggressor, but this time he wanted her to set the pace, to take charge.

"Think you can handle me?" he asked.

"Ooh…ooh." The taunting sound came through her puckered lips as she lifted herself up on her knees, ran her hand between their bodies and circled his erection. "I'm willing to try really hard. Later, you can let me know how I did." A tantalizing, bewitching smile curved her lips.

She brought him to her, then positioned herself and took him into her body. Gradually. Inch by excruciating inch. Why the hell didn't she end this torment and take all of him? Now! Before he died from the tension building inside him? But he had taught her well, the art of slow torture. It took every ounce of his willpower not to thrust up and into her.

As her sheath enveloped him, she slid her legs along the side of his body until they were joined completely from their hips down, then she pressed her breasts against his chest and lay there. Still. Perfectly still. Their heartbeats synchronized. Their breathing set to the same rhythm. His sex instinctively quivered inside her, begging for relief.

"I'm warning you, sweetheart," he said. "Don't make me wait too long."

"Is teasing the beast dangerous?" She lifted herself up, gliding over him, withdrawing until her body clutched only the head of his sex. "Will he devour me?"

David grabbed her by the hips and plunged her down so that she was forced to accept all of him. She cried out when he filled her completely, stretching her to the limit. Her body could not resist the urgent pressure, the throbbing need that prompted her to move. Up and down. Appeasing the beast within him…and discovering her own untamed animal nature. Once unleashed, the primitive woman within her took control. While she rode him, hard and fast, he mouthed her breasts. Sucking, nipping, licking. Her sheath tightened around him and she keened, softly at first, then louder and louder until she was all but screaming when she came. The force of her release triggered his and within seconds of her climax, he shuddered with completion. Needing nothing more. Totally fulfilled.

"Yeah, thanks, Art," Gavin Robbins said. "Let me know if you find out anything else."

He hung up the telephone, then slammed his fist down on his desk and cursed. Art Singleton was a friend who worked at CIA headquarters in Langley, Virginia. He and Art had done favors for each other more than once over the years, and neither hesitated when it came to bending the rules when necessary. Gavin had given Art a name—David Wolfe—and asked his old buddy to run a check on the man. That task hadn't taken long, but had yielded nothing of any significance. Wolfe had been recruited straight out of the army and had been assigned overseas for most of his thirteen-year career. Art assured Gavin that the records didn't show anything out of the ordinary, nothing that red-flagged Wolfe as anything other than what Ellison Penn had said he was—a former agent who had retired and gone into the personal security business.

"The guy's record is as clean as a whistle," Art had said.

"What about his personal life?"

"Hell, man, as far as I can find out, he didn't have one."

"No friends? No women?"

"I'm telling you that the guy might as well have not existed. Nobody seems to remember him. And I checked with people who've been around for years."

"What about men who worked overseas the years Wolfe was there? Surely somebody remembers him."

"Some of those guys are dead and others are still out of the country, but I can keep checking, if that's what you want. But so far, nothing."

"That's what I want. Keep digging," Gavin had said.

There was something all wrong about David Wolfe. Gavin would bet his last dime on it. And he intended to find out just what it was. His instincts warned him that Ellison Penn was trying to pull a fast one. But why? For what purpose? He figured that the whole thing had something to do with Preston Shaw. What, dammit, what? Gavin had racked his brain until he couldn't think straight. But he wouldn't let anything get by him. He was too close to achieving his goals to allow anyone or anything to interfere at this late date.

Wolfe remained by the door of studio two, quiet and out of the way, keeping watch while Caroline worked. He found her totally fascinating. Every inclination of her head. Every twist of an arm or leg. Each smile. Each frown. The way her ponytail bobbed up and down as she bent and swerved, leaned and switched directions, all the while snapping away. Pose after pose. Picture after picture. And during the entire process, Caroline captured the playful mischievousness of a five-year-old little hellion named Abigail Faith Lasley. He had to give Roz a great deal of credit for managing not to beat the precocious child within an inch of her spoiled-rotten life as she worked with Abigail to return her to the poses needed for the photographs. Perhaps no one else noticed the maternal potential in Rozalin Turner. But Wolfe saw it. Roz was a natural, the type of woman who would be able to handle half a dozen screaming kids and make the job look easy.

He glanced toward Lyle Jennings, who had arrived ten minutes ago, early for the lunch date he'd made with Caroline. A sort of day-late birthday celebration. Wolfe had asked Kirsten to order something for their lunch and then run out and pick it up from a local restaurant. It was simply easier to guard Caroline within the confines of her studio than it was to keep her safe in public areas. Wolfe noticed that Lyle seemed as captivated as he was—but by another woman. Roz. Wolfe barely suppressed a chuckle. If any man could recognize *that look* in another man's eyes, Wolfe could...today...considering the fact that Caroline had him mesmerized. So, the good reverend had a thing for the wild and free Roz. And from the occasional sidelong glances that she was giving Lyle, Wolfe suspected the feeling was mutual. The bad girl and the preacher. A classic case of opposites.

The photo shoot ran over fifteen minutes, due mainly not to the subject of the session, but because of her demanding mother. Mrs. Bradford Lasley simply couldn't be satisfied, requesting ''just one more shot'' half a dozen times. Finally Caroline politely called a halt and with her Southern charm assured Mrs. Lasley that the pictures of Abigail would be sheer perfection.

The minute mother and daughter had been escorted out to their waiting limo, Kirsten told Wolfe that lunch was set up in the enclosed courtyard, per his instructions. Caroline led Lyle and Roz outside, while Wolfe followed behind. He remained constantly on alert, always mindful of even a hint of danger. The June sunshine was half-hidden behind gray rain clouds and a whisper of wind breezed through the boxed shrubbery and springtime flower beds. The fancy wrought-iron table was spread with sandwiches, chips and colas.

"We'll have to rush," Roz said. "Forty-five minutes won't give us time to do more than gulp down lunch and then get things set up for the afternoon session with Mrs. Welch and her two daughters."

Wolfe pulled out a chair for Caroline. She graced him with a warm smile, then sat and kept her gaze connected to his while he took the chair beside her. Roz tapped her foot, apparently waiting for Lyle to prove he, too, knew how to be a gentleman. Much to Lyle's credit, he picked up on Roz's cue. When he held out a chair for her, she all but cooed.

The foursome sat quietly, unwrapping their sandwiches, spreading apart napkins and inserting straws through the plastic lids on their drinks. Wolfe would have preferred lunch alone with Caroline. Actually, he would have preferred skipping lunch and having Caroline. Ever since his first sexual encounter when he'd been a teenager, he had been a man with a healthy sexual appetite, but as he'd grown older he had learned to control his baser instincts and curtail his encounters. But he was finding out that his hunger for Caroline wasn't easily sated. After having become her lover, he discovered that he wanted her more than ever.

"So, was the birthday surprise Mr. Wolfe planned for you yesterday evening a success?" Lyle asked.

Caroline almost choked on the bite of Reuben sandwich in her mouth. Roz lifted Caroline's arm and slapped her on the back. Caroline coughed until she dislodged the morsel from her throat, then grabbed her cola and slurped down several huge swallows.

"Are you all right?" Lyle inspected his cousin's flushed face.

"I'm fine," Caroline assured him. "And the surprise Wolfe planned for me was wonderful." She glanced at Wolfe, everything that had transpired between them evident in that heated look.

Wolfe had to break eye contact with her. If she kept looking at him that way, he wouldn't be able to stop himself from reaching out and grabbing her. Damn!

Roz giggled nervously. Caroline took a deep breath.

"Is there something going on that I don't know about?" Lyle glanced from Wolfe to Caroline and then to Roz.

"Let's give Caroline her presents now," Roz said, reaching in her pocket and pulling out a small, gift-wrapped box. "No sense in waiting until after we've eaten."

Wolfe realized that Roz was using the birthday present as a means to draw Lyle's attention away from what he had undoubtedly sensed as sexual tension radiating from Wolfe and Caroline. Perhaps it was best that Caroline's minister cousin not become aware of the fact that she had lost her innocence to a man totally unworthy of her.

Caroline grabbed the gift and unwrapped it hurriedly. Just as she opened the lid, Sandy appeared in the studio doorway, the portable telephone in her hand. She looked directly at Wolfe, then motioned to him.

"Finish opening your gifts," Wolfe said. "I'll take the call."

When he approached Sandy, she held out the phone and said, "It's Fletcher Shaw. He asked to speak to you."

Wolfe took the telephone from her and said, "Wolfe here."

"Yes, Mr. Wolfe, this is Fletcher Shaw. I wanted to run this by you before mentioning it to Caroline." He paused, as if waiting for Wolfe to respond, and when he didn't, Fletcher continued. "I was talking to Mother this morning. She's been away on a cruise, she and her husband, Neall, and they just returned to Baltimore yesterday. Anyway, I was filling her in on everything that has happened to Caroline. Her finding the key and the attempts on her life and my hiring you to protect her."

"Is there a point to this story?" Wolfe asked impatiently.

"Of course there is," Fletcher replied. "As I was saying,

Mother and I were discussing the situation. Naturally, she was upset to learn that poor old Teddy Richards had been killed. She'd known him since she was a young girl. But the crux of the matter is this—Mother remembered something, a place where Father could have hidden the evidence he mentioned in his letter to Lenore.''

"What place?" Wolfe smiled at Caroline when she held up a pair of theater tickets, Roz's gift, then laid them aside and began ripping the paper from Lyle's gift.

"It's a hunting lodge, or at least it used to be a hunting lodge years ago," Fletcher said. "I vaguely remember Father taking me there when I was a boy. I'd forgotten all about the place, until Mother mentioned it. She said it's a rather large old cabin. Several of father's friends, including Oliver Harper, co-owned the place at one time. They mostly used it to get away from D.C., just the guys, to do a little fishing.''

"Where is this cabin?"

"Over in the western end of the state, in Garrett County.''

"Do you have any idea when your father went there last?" David asked.

"I can't be sure, but I do remember him getting away by himself for a long weekend, sometime during the month before he died. I can call Oliver and ask him if he still owns the place. He might recall the last time my father went there.''

"After you speak to Oliver Harper, call me back," Wolfe said. "If your father spent any time there the last few months of his life, then it might be worth checking out. But I don't intend to mention this to Caroline, unless there's a good reason.''

"I agree. That's why I asked to speak to you. Caroline has been through more than enough.''

"Thanks, Fletcher.''

"No need to thank me. I care very much for Caroline. Her happiness and welfare are of great importance to me. The sooner we solve this damned mystery about the key, the better for her. The better for all of us.''

Wolfe grunted. "Get back in touch with me after you've spoken to Oliver Harper.''

Caroline waved at Wolfe, motioning him to her. He tossed the portable phone on a nearby chaise longue and walked across the courtyard.

Caroline held up the theater tickets and pointed to the multicolored scarf she'd wrapped around her neck. "The tickets are for next month's performance at the little theater, if things are safe by then. And look at this beautiful scarf from Lyle.''

Wolfe nodded. "Nice.''

"Who was that on the phone?'' she asked.

"Fletcher.''

"And he wanted to speak to *you?*'' Lyle inquired.

"Yes.'' Wolfe sat down beside Caroline and could not resist touching her hand where it rested on the table. "He was just checking on you. I assured him that you're all right.''

"Better than all right,'' Caroline said, her gaze locking with Wolfe's.

Lyle cleared his throat and glanced away.

"You two could be a little more subtle, you know,'' Roz said. "Lyle might still be a virgin, but he's not blind. Even the uninitiated could pick up on the vibes between you two.''

"I do wish you would quit making pronouncements about my assumed lack of sexual experience.'' Lyle lifted the paper napkin from his lap, tossed it on the table and stood, glowering angrily at Roz during the entire melodramatic process. Then, as if a lightbulb came on in his mind, he gasped and turned his attention to Caroline. "Is she saying what I think she's saying?''

"Oh, get real.'' Roz threw up her hands in a sign of exasperation. "Lyle Jennings, don't you dare act shocked.''

"Please, Lyle, sit back down,'' Caroline said. "All Roz meant was that Wolfe and I…we're attracted to each other.''

Lyle glared at Wolfe. "Is that ethical in your line of work, to become romantically involved with a client."

"Technically, no," Wolfe admitted. "But Caroline is different."

"I agree. She's not the type of woman…well…she isn't…she wouldn't…" Lyle stammered, seemingly unable to find the right words to express his high opinion of his cousin's morals.

"For heaven's sake, Rev, every woman's the type," Roz said. "It's just that for some women it takes the right man. If you had a little more experience, you'd understand—"

"What would a woman like you—who apparently finds every man she meets the right man—know about someone with Caroline's moral standards?" Lyle's cheeks flushed scarlet. He balled his meaty hands into tight fists. "I may be a thirty-year-old virgin, but you're nothing but a slut!"

Roz jumped up from her chair, then slapped Lyle. Caroline gasped. The moment Roz's hand fell away from Lyle's cheek, he turned and all but ran from the courtyard. Caroline rose to her feet, but before she took one step, Wolfe clasped her wrist.

"I think Roz is the one who should go after him," Wolfe said.

Roz snapped her head around and stared at Wolfe, a blank look on her face. "What?"

"Lyle's got to be feeling pretty bad right about now," Wolfe told her. "He's probably really sorry for what he said to you. Maybe you should go after him and give him a chance to apologize."

"Oh" was Roz's only response, but she whirled around and raced after Lyle.

"Do you think that was wise?" Caroline asked. "They might wind up killing each other."

"Yeah," Wolfe said. "Either that or kiss and make up."

Caroline's eyes widened in surprise, then a slow, soft smile spread across her face.

* * *

Roz caught up with Lyle in the hallway that bisected studios one and two. "Lyle, please, wait a minute."

Ignoring her, he kept walking. She reached out and grabbed the back of his shirt. He jerked free, then spun around to face her.

"Go away and leave me alone," Lyle said. "Can't you see that you bring out the absolute worst in me? Every time I'm around you, I want to…to…"

"To what?" she asked. "Strangle me? Tar and feather me? Have me run out of town on a rail?"

"No, dammit!" Lyle glared straight at her. "I keep telling myself that you're bad, a bad woman, with the morals of an alley cat, and that I'm an idiot for thinking you would change, that all you need is a man who truly loves you." He took a tentative step toward her.

She stared at him, her eyes round, her mouth agape, totally stunned by what he'd said. "You're right, you know. For a man who truly loved me the way I loved him, I could be good. Oh, so good. And faithful to my dying day."

"Roz, I'm sorry," Lyle said. "I had no right to say such awful things to you. It was just my way of protecting myself."

"Protecting yourself from what?"

"From you," he admitted, his voice a mere whisper.

Before she had a chance to do more than suck in her breath, Lyle grabbed her by the back of the neck, hauled her up against him and kissed her passionately. Roz's knees buckled. Her head started spinning. Butterflies danced in her stomach. She melted against him and returned the kiss, slipped her tongue inside his mouth and placed her hands on his chest. The kiss went on and on until they finally had to come up for air.

Lyle released her. "Stay away from me, Roz. Please, stay away from me."

He turned and ran down the hall, leaving Roz breathless, aroused and deliriously happy. A silly, wicked little smile curved the corners of her lips. The rev had the hots for her. Hot damn!

Chapter 16

As she sat beside Wolfe in the leased Mercedes, Caroline felt giddy with excitement. And if she were totally honest with herself she would have to admit that there was a certain amount of apprehension and nervousness intermingled with the anticipation bubbling inside her. They were on their way to a cabin co-owned by Oliver Harper, located in Garrett County, outside of McHenry. Since the 1920s and the formation of Deep Creek Lake, the isolated county had been gradually turning into the year-round resort area it was today. When she and David had gotten the key and directions from Oliver, who had driven to Fletch's home in Baltimore to save them from making the trip to Alexandria, he had invited them to stay a few nights at the cabin on the lake. And he'd even suggested that they take advantage of the great fishing.

"It would do Caroline a world of good," Oliver had said. "The fishing is at its best this time of year. You can pick up a couple of fishing licenses at any tackle shop. And even if you don't find what Preston's key unlocks hidden away up at the cabin, you wouldn't have completely wasted your time.''

She and Wolfe had left straight from Fletch's home this morning and taken I-70 out of Baltimore, then hit I-68 to Keyser's Ridge and were now heading south on Route 219. Located in the heart of the Allegheny Mountains, Garrett County was a paradise for adventurous sportsmen. Hiking, biking, rafting, skiing, backpacking and camping vied with boating and fishing to lure outdoorsmen from across the country.

Caroline glanced down at the map and written directions that lay in her lap. They should be at the cabin within the next few minutes. Just two more turns and they should be on the road that would take them directly to the cabin. She had used the past three hours on the hundred-and-ninety-mile drive from Baltimore to try to calm down, to prepare herself for the possibility that this trip might very well turn out to be a burnt-run, a totally wasted trip. After all, what were the odds that Preston had hidden away some sort of trunk or box or case at a cabin that had belonged to friends and was used by a variety of people? But Oliver had recalled that Preston made a weekend trip to the cabin less than a month before his death, making it possible that he had stored something there.

''You're awfully quiet,'' Wolfe said.

''Just thinking,'' she replied.

When he stole a quick glance at her, Caroline's stomach did silly flip-flops. Would she ever get used to the way he made her feel? All hot and bothered. Arousing her sexually with something as innocent as a glance, a touch or a smile. Then she remembered that she wouldn't have the chance to become accustomed to this all-consuming passion. Wolfe wasn't going to be a part of her life for very long. She couldn't bear the thought of their affair ending so quickly, when it had just begun. But he had made it perfectly clear that he was a temporary man, unwilling to make a commitment. Wasn't his way for the best? she asked herself. Although her body yearned for his and she was more than half-way in love with him, she really didn't know David Wolfe. He was little more than a stranger to her. Common sense told her that there were hidden depths to him, things she might never know.

"This turnoff?" he asked.

"Huh?" She checked the map quickly. "Yes, this is the one."

"Try not to be disappointed if we don't find anything," he said. "You know the odds aren't in our favor."

"That's just what I was thinking. And I want to thank you for understanding why I had to make this trip, to try this one more possibility. If we don't find anything then—"

"Then we'll spend the night and head back to St. Michaels tomorrow."

"You believe we're wasting our time, don't you?"

"Hmm-mmm. Probably. But I promised you another week to search, didn't I?"

She reached over and laid her hand on his shoulder. He tensed, then relaxed, never taking his eyes off the road. "I can sense that you're concerned. You are anticipating some sort of trouble, aren't you?"

"Always," he said. "Trouble comes with the territory. And it's my job to stay one step ahead of the game."

"In what way specifically?"

"Several ways," he told her. "This Mercedes is equipped with bulletproof glass for one thing."

Why wasn't she surprised? "Then you didn't lease it from just an ordinary car rental place, did you?"

"No."

"What else?"

"Someone has already been to the cabin and checked it out for me."

"What?"

"A necessary precaution."

"How did they get in without a key?" she asked. "And how did they know where the cabin was located?"

"Let's just say I have friends and the Dundee agency has friends with all sorts of talents."

"You realize that it frightens me when you talk this way," she told him. "It reminds me of what you do for a living, of the government agency you worked for in the past and how violent your life has probably always been."

"Don't think about it," he said. "Who I am or who I was won't affect your life in the future."

Did he really believe what he'd said? she wondered. Did he truly think that once they went their separate ways, she would be able to forget him, stop wanting him, no longer love him? And would she be that easy for him to erase from his life, as if she had been nothing more than just another brief affair. He might think so, but he was kidding himself. There was no doubt in her mind that she would leave an indelible mark on his heart, as he would on hers. Perhaps they were unsuited for each other and fate had simply brought them together by accident, but one irrefutable fact remained—they were soul mates. Mismatched soul mates. A contradiction in terms, but nevertheless true. On some basic, instinctive level, she had recognized him the moment they met and he had recognized her, too.

"Check the map," he said. "I think the next turnoff should be coming up soon."

She glanced at the map. "The second road on the left. Probably a quarter of a mile."

That one-quarter of a mile zipped by hurriedly. Wolfe pulled the Mercedes up alongside a two-story log-and-rock structure with a big front porch. Through a thin crop of pines, they had a perfect view of the lake. When Wolfe killed the engine, he threw his arm out to prevent Caroline from releasing her seat belt.

"What's wrong?" she asked.

"Nothing. Just stay here in the car for a couple of minutes, until I make a phone call.'' He removed his cellular phone from the inside pocket of his sport coat, flipped it open and hit a preprogramed number. ''We're here,'' he said, then listened intently. ''Good. Thanks.''

''All clear?'' She placed her hand over his and pressed it to her stomach. A shiver of longing raced up her spine.

He undid her seat belt, then curled his hand over her hip. ''All clear for the moment, but that doesn't mean you can have free rein around this place. You'll stay with me at all times. No strolling on the porch. No gazing out the windows.''

''Just like at home.''

He grinned. ''Yeah, sweetheart, just like at home.''

''They took the bait. Hook, line and sinker,'' he said. ''Of course, I'm sure Wolfe is being very cautious.''

''He'll be one against three,'' the man said. ''Even a hotshot like David Wolfe can't overcome three-to-one odds.''

''Only a fool would underestimate him. Mark my word, there's more to him than meets the eye. He's not just an ordinary bodyguard.''

''You know he's former CIA, so that makes him very dangerous.''

''There's something else,'' he said. ''We'll just have to dig deeper until we find out what.''

''If this plan comes off without a hitch, it won't matter, will it?''

He shook his head. ''Make sure there are no foul-ups this time.''

''There won't be. Just tell me when you want our men to move in,'' the man said.

''Early in the morning. Say around three-thirty. Even if Wolfe is awake, he should be less alert at that time. He is only human.''

''Your plan is a good one. It'll be a lot easier for our men to make a clean getaway from that isolated cabin than it would if we made the hit at Caroline's home or studio. We can go in, strike and get out quickly, with practically no chance of any witnesses. And this way you were able to maneuver things so that you won't be suspected of any wrongdoing.''

''When Caroline and Mr. Wolfe are killed, I shall be shocked and appalled and even blame myself a little that I couldn't have done something to have prevented their deaths.''

''There isn't anything at the cabin they might find while they're searching the place, is there?'' the man asked.

He chuckled. ''Don't be stupid. Our people went over the cabin with a fine-tooth comb the day after Preston was killed. The only thing Caroline and Wolfe will find up there are fishing tackle, old clothes and some books and magazines.''

''When do you want me to contact you again?''

''Not for a few days,'' he said. ''I'm sure I'll get a call as soon as the county sheriff discovers the identity of the two victims.''

''Nothing,'' Caroline said as she tossed the stack of old magazines back into the closet. ''We've gone through every closet, every dresser and chest, every cabinet and cupboard. There isn't anything in this entire cabin that opens with a key, other than the front and back doors.''

David pushed up his glasses, which had made their way down his nose about an inch, then fastened his hand atop Caroline's shoulder. ''I'm sorry we didn't find anything.''

She sighed, then inclined her head to the side, bringing her cheek down on his hand. ''But it's what you expected, isn't it? You didn't think we'd find anything.''

Yeah, sure, it was what he'd expected. His instincts had warned him from the minute Fletcher Shaw telephoned him and told him about the old hunting lodge over in Garrett County that the whole thing was a setup. Not that he suspected Fletcher, no more so than anyone else. It would have been easy enough for someone to have used Caroline's step-brother to put a devious plan into action. All it would have taken was a phone call to Fletcher's mother, Pamela. But trying to retrace things by that route might prove impossible since the first Mrs. Shaw's circle of friends included most of the suspects on Wolfe's list and a few that hadn't been there before, but were now. Fletcher, of course. All three Harpers—Oliver, Eileen and Brooke. Gavin Robbins, whom Fletch's mother actually dated a few years back, despite the difference in their ages. Barry Vanderpool, whose mother had been the bridesmaid at Pamela's wedding to Preston. And Ellison Penn, who had been her lover for a few months, shortly after her divorce from Preston nearly twenty years ago. The only two people who weren't connected to Pamela Shaw Larson were Lyle and Roz, and he'd pretty much eliminated those two from his suspects list.

Wolfe had never intended for Caroline to find out anything about this place, had in fact planned to send a couple of Dundee agents—hopefully Jack and Matt would have still been free—to check the place out and report back to him. But Brooke Harper had opened her big mouth and mentioned it to Caroline, who had immediately gotten excited. Brooke's slip of the tongue might have been no more than that, but then again, she could have had an ulterior motive for passing along the information.

"You're awfully somber," Caroline said as she lifted her head from his hand, turned and wrapped her arms around his waist. "Something you want to tell me?"

He forced a smile. "Nothing for you to worry about right now."

Maybe he should tell her now instead of later, but if he did, she would only worry until it happened and possibly work herself up into being a nervous wreck. If it came from out of the blue, she would more than likely act out of survival instinct instead of fear, at least at first. If he explained that someone—someone she trusted—had sent them up here to be killed, she wouldn't want to believe him. But she would. And then she'd fret over who and drive herself crazy about when. No, he would wait as long as possible before telling her just what he thought was going to come down here at this cabin. Either tonight or in the morning. He would lay odds that it would be tonight. These people had been playing the waiting game for a while now. They had to be anxious to get Caroline out of the way, and him along with her.

He could have told her everything before they left Baltimore and allowed her to decide whether or not she wanted to put herself in the line of fire. Reason told him that she was in no more danger here at the cabin than she would have been at home, so he had made the decision for her. Sooner or later, her stepfather's former comrades would have to come after her again. He suspected that if and when she turned the key over to him, they would still want her eliminated, thinking that without her to urge him on, he would eventually give up the search. He hated admitting that she wouldn't be safe—not ever again—until these people were identified, arrested and stopped once and for all.

"I think we should make use of the hot tub before we go to bed," Caroline said, lifting her arms to twine around his neck. "A good long soak would relax us and make us sleep like babies."

He didn't dare sleep like a baby. A few catnaps, maybe. Just enough rest to be able to function at top capacity when the time came. David planted his hands on her buttocks and lifted her up and into his arousal. "I know a better way to relax."

A throaty giggle bubbled from her throat. "Why not both? Sex in a hot tub is deliciously sensuous."

He rubbed himself against her. "And just how would you know? You've never had sex in a hot tub."

She kissed him playfully. "I want to find out if what I've heard is true."

"Can't do it. Not here. Not now."

"Why not? We're here. The hot tub is inside the house, all safe and cosy. And you've already got a...er...you're..."

"I've got a hard-on," he said. "Don't you know that I walk around with one just about all the time when you are around? All I have to do is look at you and I want you."

"The feeling is mutual."

He gripped the back of her head, his fingers forking through her hair. She stared at him, her eyes wide. Their gazes locked and held.

"What's wrong?" she asked. "Why can't we make love?"

Although he calculated the hit wouldn't come until the middle of the night, he had to stay alert. There was always the off chance that he had misjudged his unknown opponent and something would go wrong.

Instead of replying to her question, he removed his glasses, tossed them on the nearby bed and then urged her closer, until her body aligned with his. He lowered his head and kissed her. She responded immediately, kissing him back with equal fervor. Her hands lifted, gripped his biceps and held on tightly. His lips moved to her throat. She tossed back her head and flung her arms around his wide shoulders. He grabbed the fabric of her green cotton skirt and, inch by inch, bunched the fabric in his hand as he lifted the shirt higher and higher.

He was going to have her here and now. Not in the hot tub. Not in one of the beds in the many bedrooms. He didn't dare risk the time it would take or the vulnerable position they would both be in for the sweet, unhurried loving they both wanted.

"How badly do you want it?" He mouthed the words against her throat as his hand snaked beneath her skirt and cupped her hip. "Badly enough to take it raw?"

"Yes." Her hands went to his zipper and her fingers quickly undid his pants.

He slid her panties down her hips and when they fell to

her ankles, she stepped out of them. He walked her backward, straight to the wall, then lifted her enough so that when he reached inside his briefs, she was positioned to take him into her body. She wrapped her arms around his neck and her legs around his hips as he began thrusting and retreating, bumping her hips against the wall, the frenzy inside them building fast.

They mated hurriedly, stealing kisses between each undulating movement of their bodies. He kept up a steady rhythm, making sure pressure was applied to the right spot. She tightened around him, her body milking his, bringing them both closer to fulfillment. His release came first, then hers. Shuddering, gasping, they clung to each other and Wolfe covered her mouth with a kiss that claimed her body and soul.

While the aftershocks of pleasure subsided, he held her for just one more minute, then slid her down over his body until her feet touched the floor. Reluctantly he released her and stepped away, never taking his eyes off her as he readjusted his underwear and zipped his pants.

"Go wash up." He nodded toward the bathroom. "Then put your panties on and—"

"What's wrong?" She looked at him questioningly. "Why the rush?"

"Nothing's wrong, but I'd feel a hell of a lot better knowing that if for any reason we have to run out of here during the night, we'd both be fully dressed."

"And do you think we might have to run out of here during the night?"

He hated that worried look in her eyes, the tension on her face. He grabbed her by the shoulders, then kissed her forehead. "I'm a cautious man. Humor me. We're out in the middle of nowhere in an area I'm not familiar with, so on the off chance something were to happen, I don't want to be caught with my pants down."

She didn't question him further, but immediately did as he

had asked. When she returned from the bathroom she found him placing his glasses and his 9 mm on the bedside table.

"We might as well see if we can get some sleep." He lay down on top of the bedspread, lifted his arms and crossed them behind his head.

"You're expecting an attack, aren't you?" She stood over him, her gaze riveted to his face. "You think they're going to come after me tonight."

"We told Oliver and Fletcher we'd stay overnight," David said. "That means they'll strike either tonight or in the morning."

"You brought me up here knowing… Are you telling me that you think Oliver or Fletcher—"

"Don't jump to conclusions. I'm not accusing either of them. They could easily have been used by someone else and be totally unaware of the fact."

She slumped down onto the edge of the bed. "So, what do we do, wait?"

"Yeah, we wait until I get a signal. My cell phone will ring as a warning that someone is approaching the cabin."

"Then you have Dundee agents posted as watchdogs, don't you?"

"Jack and Matt and a third agent they brought with them. A guy named Domingo Shea."

Caroline lay down beside David, at his side, but not close enough to touch. "Why didn't you explain all of this to me before we left Baltimore?"

"I put it off to save you the worry."

"Gee, thanks."

"Try to get some rest, even if you don't think you can sleep."

Minutes ticked by, endless, silent minutes. He turned off the lamp, pitching the room into darkness. Light from the three-quarter moon filtered through the closed wooden blinds, shooting thin ribbons of illumination across the wooden floor. He lay there and listened to her breathing. Slow and steady.

Finally, after what seemed like hours, he turned to her and drew her into his arms. She resisted at first, as he had known she would, but when he whispered her name, she cuddled close and buried her face against his shoulder.

This woman was meant to be his, ordained by the forces that be, long before their paths had crossed. But an evil trick of fate had placed him in the role of her enemy. And then he had anointed himself her keeper, her phantom benefactor, her secretive and elusive David. But suddenly fate had stepped in again and given him a once-in-a-lifetime opportunity—to meet her, to get to know her, to become her protector when she needed him most. And he had been unable to resist claiming her, making her his.

She lifted her hand and caressed his cheek. "You had to do this, didn't you? By bringing me here, by walking into their trap, you have the advantage because you knew in advance it was a trap."

"You got it." He grabbed her hand, brought her open palm to his lips and kissed it. "I'm not going to let anything happen to you. I promise."

Time passed slowly, each minute seeming like an hour. Every sound tensed his nerves. He had been in situations like this before. Waiting. Adrenaline pumping. Mind whirling. Dozens of other jobs, with countless lives at stake. But never someone he personally cared for the way he cared for Caroline. He was prepared to do anything, risk anything to keep her safe.

"You haven't been able to sleep, have you?" she asked.

"I don't sleep a lot," he said.

"Goes with the territory?"

"Yeah, a bodyguard learns to get by on less sleep."

"That's one more thing I've learned about you. It isn't fair that you know everything about me," she said, her voice warm and soft. "You have a file that tells you my entire history." She paused. "I don't know anything about you. Only the most superficial things."

"What do you want to know?" he asked.

"Have you ever been married?"

"No."

"Ever been in love?"

"No."

She laid her hand on his chest, then fingered his scars. "How did this happen?"

"A bomb exploded. I didn't get out of the way fast enough."

"Oh, Wolfe."

"A hazard of my old job."

"With the CIA?"

"Hmm-mmm."

She threaded his chest hair around her fingers. "Where were you born? Where did you grow up? What were your parents like? Do you have any brothers and sisters?"

He sucked in a deep breath, then released it slowly. "I was born in the hills of Tennessee. My mother's family had lived there forever. She was part Cherokee. My father was a drunk. He liked using my mother as a punching bag, and after we were born, he started beating the hell out of me and my little brother on a regular basis. But he seemed to get a special pleasure out of tormenting my brother."

Caroline wrapped her arms around David and held him. "Oh, Wolfe, I'm so sorry. So very sorry. Your childhood must have been a nightmare."

"Yeah," he said. "But then so was yours, wasn't it, sweetheart?"

"You know it was."

Why he was baring his soul this way, he wasn't quite sure. He'd never talked about his childhood to anyone. But this wasn't just anyone. This was Caroline. His sweet Caroline, with the loving heart and generous soul, who had survived her own tormented childhood. Once he'd begun, he couldn't seem to stop pouring out the truth about Aidan Colbert's tragic young life.

He pulled away from Caroline and sat upright in bed. "There's something you should know…something I should have told you before…."

"What is it?" she asked, lifting herself into a sitting position beside him. "You can tell me anything and I'll understand."

Oh, God, if only that were true. If only he could truly bare his soul to this special woman. His woman. "When I was thirteen, I killed my father."

Caroline gasped. Wolfe got out of bed. He stood in the center of the room, rigid as a statue, his breathing stilled for a minute. Even though she moved quietly, he knew when she climbed out of bed and walked toward him. He waited. Not breathing. Not thinking. Not daring to hope. Just waiting and praying.

She came up behind him and wrapped her arms around him. "Do you want to tell me about it?"

Not moving a muscle, not glancing back at her, he stood there and let her hold him, feeling inexplicably secure and unafraid. Could he explain to this gentle woman about a violent act for which he had never been able to forgive himself?

"I was just a scared kid." When he spoke, the words came slowly, painfully and quietly. "I knew what he was capable of doing. What he'd done to all of us countless times. But things had been getting worse. I knew that sooner or later he'd kill one of us, probably Brendan because he was so little and weak.

"I warned him that if he ever hit Brendan or Mama again, I'd kill him." He shuddered as the memory of that day came back to him, as vivid and real as if it had happened yesterday. "I was coming in from school that day. Brendan had been sick with a cold and Mama had kept him home. I heard them before I even reached the porch. Him hollering and Mama begging. And then Brendan screaming."

"You don't have to tell me the rest of it." She hugged him fiercely.

He felt the moisture of her tears as they seeped through his shirt and onto his back. "I ran around the side of the house and came in through the kitchen door. Then I went straight to my bedroom, got my hunting rifle and went out to the living room. Brendan was lying on the floor, staring up at my old man, who was slapping my mama around. I warned him. I told him if he didn't stop, I'd kill him.

"He dared me to do it. Told me I didn't have the guts to kill him. Then he kicked Brendan. And when he raised his foot to kick him again, I shot him. Twice." Wolfe knotted his hands into tight fists. "Once in the heart. And once in the head. I was a crack shot, even then."

Holding on to him, she eased around his hard, tense body until she could gaze up into his face. He couldn't bear to look into her eyes. She released him, then reached up and framed his face with her hands.

"Forgive yourself," she said. "You were forced to make a terrible decision and you did the only thing you could have done. You protected the innocent, the helpless. You saved your mother and your brother."

He looked at her then, but could barely see her through the fine mist coating his eyes. "That's just it. I didn't save them. Brendan died from his injuries that night. And Mama never recovered from the trauma of her baby boy dying and her older son killing his own daddy."

Standing on tiptoe Caroline kissed him. With care and sympathy. With understanding and compassion. And with love. Her love encompassed him, wrapping around his wounded soul like a soothing balm. Taking him by the hand, she led him to an overstuffed armchair in the corner of the room. She urged him down, then sat on his lap, laid her head on his shoulder and put her arms around him once again.

She fell asleep that way, nestled in his lap, with him soaking up her sweet, precious understanding and forgiveness. He drifted off into a light sleep. Visions of his mother and Brendan wafted through his mind, followed by images of Caroline. The only three people who had ever been important to him, the only ones he would have willingly died to protect. But he had not been able to save Mama or Brendan....

Wolfe woke with a start. The telephone had awakened him, but the sound of a loud crash had roused him. What the hell? He realized Caroline was in his lap and he was still sitting in the chair. Their gazes collided.

"What was that?" she asked.

"My cell phone," he said. "A signal to alert me of danger."

He shoved her up and onto her feet, then jumped up and hurried to the bedside table to remove his Sig Sauer from the holster. Suddenly another crash and then a third followed in quick succession. He grabbed Caroline's hand and flung open the door into the living room. Flames shot up to the ceiling and spread in every direction. Firebombs! Firebombs tossed through the windows. Dammit to hell and back.

"We've got to get out of here," he told her. "Looks like their plan is to smoke us out and be waiting for us when we come outside. They intend to shoot us like sitting ducks."

Chapter 17

Smoke quickly filled the house, folding in on them from every direction. Black, hot and heavy. Like a thick, smothering fog. Wolfe figured he didn't have much choice. The back door was not accessible because of the fire blazing in the kitchen area. Their only escape route was through the front door. Not that it mattered much one way or the other. There was bound to be a man posted at the rear as well as the front. He had no way of knowing how many there were, but his guess would be no more than three or four. And with three Dundee agents in place, the odds were better than even—in his favor. Tugging on Caroline's arm, he led her toward the front door. As they made their way through the smoke-clogged foyer, Caroline began coughing.

"When I open the door, we're going to drop and roll off the porch," he said. "They'll be wearing night-vision goggles and be able to see us, so they're going to start shooting the minute we come out. Don't panic. Don't think. Just move." He grabbed her shoulders and gave her a forceful shake. "I'm going to be right there with you every minute and my guys will be responsible for half the gunfire you hear.''

He felt her trembling and wished he could take longer to reassure her, but time was of the essence. This old cabin was quickly burning down around them. If the smoke didn't get them soon, the ceiling would cave in on them.

''Ready?'' He squeezed her shoulders, then released her and retrieved his Sig Sauer from his hip holster.

''Ready,'' she said, her voice shaky.

He flung open the door. Gunfire erupted all around them. They dropped to the porch floor. Bullets flew over their heads, splintering wood and sending chips flying, some peppering their skin as they rolled. A barrage of gunfire followed, tearing up the floor behind them. Son of a bitch! The Dundee agents would be moving in to strike their attackers at any moment. All he had to do was get Caroline out of the way, keep her safe and wait.

He shoved Caroline off the end of the porch and came down over her on the rock-strewn ground behind the Mercedes. The earth exploded nearby, too close for comfort. Grass and dirt and gravel danced into the air. Without giving her a chance to catch her breath, David tumbled Caroline past the car, over the driveway and into the ditch. Not a deep ditch, but hollowed out enough to give them some protection. He lifted himself off her just enough to allow her to breathe, but placed his hand down on her head as a warning for her to stay put. With the pistol in his hand, he scanned the area behind them, black as pitch, except for the moonlight that barely made its way through the trees. Toward the lake, the view was brighter because the trees were sparse. And in front of them the blaze from the burning cabin lit up the night sky.

An unnatural silence fell. He could hear Caroline breathing as well as the thumping of his own heartbeat. The usual nocturnal noises had ceased, as if every living thing around them had fallen prey to their assailants' attack. Wolfe sensed Caroline's fear, could smell her terror. His own fear ate away at his gut like deadly acid. He was afraid—not for himself, but for Caroline.

The sounds were faint, almost inaudible. But he heard them. Since boyhood, when he'd been raised to hunt wild game in the hills, he had relied on his acute sense of hearing. Without seeing them, he knew there were two shooters closing in on them, from opposite directions. He sensed no more than two men, so where were the others?

Suddenly a single shot rang out, coming from behind the cabin. About damn time, Wolfe thought. He'd begun to wonder if the Dundee agents were ever going to make their move. As he had suspected, a third man had been posted at the back door, just in case he and Caroline had made their escape by that route. But the guy out back wouldn't be helping his buddies. Not now. One of Dundee's best had eliminated him. The approaching footsteps stopped. Their attackers now had to realize Wolfe wasn't alone, which meant they were aware that they, not Wolfe and Caroline, had walked into a trap.

He wanted just one of them to live. Just one. Whichever man survived was going to do some talking. Whoever ordered the hit on Caroline wouldn't have done his own dirty work, but for a mission this important, he would have sent the best snipers. Please, God, let one of them still be alive. And give me five minutes alone with him. That's all I need. Five minutes.

Caroline tugged on Wolfe's shirttail, which partially hung out of his pants. "What's happening?" she whispered. "Why is it so quiet? And who—"

He clamped his hand over her mouth. Be quiet, sweet Caroline. For just a little longer. He could hear movement again. Heavier. Deliberate. The men moving around now weren't trying to disguise their footsteps. They had the advantage. The Dundee agents were coming in for the kill. That probably meant there had been only three attackers and one had already been eliminated.

Gunfire erupted again. Close enough for Wolfe to see

shadows and hear grunts. A battle that ended almost before it began. Wolfe waited. He eased his hand from Caroline's mouth and down her throat. She trembled.

"All clear," Jack Parker shouted. "There were only three of them and they've been contained."

Caroline wanted to breathe a sigh of relief, but her chest hurt too much to do more than whimper. And a burning ache ripped through her side when she moved. Wolfe grabbed her hands and lifted her up and out of the ditch. Moaning, she fell against him, her legs too weak to hold her. Dammit, don't pass out now, she told herself. You're alive. Wolfe's alive. The bad guys are...*contained.* As if from out of nowhere three large dark figures appeared and surrounded them. For a split second her heart stopped, but when one of the men removed his night-vision goggles and grinned, she recognized his grimy face. Jack Parker, looking for all intents and purposes like a commando. Oh, God, that's what he was, she realized. That's what they all were, including David Wolfe. Men trained for deadly missions, capable of subduing an enemy with superior efficiency.

"You took your own sweet time," Wolfe said, glowering at Jack. "Where the hell were y'all?"

"We had everything under control," Jack said, a wide grin revealing a set of white teeth, bright against the dark war paint he wore. "Your orders were to wound, not kill at least one of them, so that took a little more effort."

Wolfe wrapped his arm securely around Caroline, giving her even more support as she began to tremble. "Well, did you accomplish that goal?" he asked.

Matt O'Brien and another Dundee agent flanked a wounded attacker as they dragged him forward. Jack reached out and ripped the man's dark mask from his face. Caroline gasped. She felt Wolfe tense.

"They get younger all the time," Jack said.

"He's just a kid," Caroline cried.

"We're going to have to get him to a hospital for a little

repair work," Matt said. "That is if you want him to live long enough to tell us who sent him on this little hit-and-run mission."

"Take him to the hospital," Wolfe said, his voice deadly. "I want him to live. Just make sure that one of you guards his sorry ass every minute until he's well enough for my interrogation."

Lifting his head, the young man glared angrily at Wolfe. He cleared his throat and spit on the ground. Bloody drool trickled from the side of his mouth. "Interrogate me all you want, Mr. Wolfe. I'll never tell you anything I don't want you to know." He fixed his gaze on Caroline. "Don't think he can keep you safe forever. He can't."

"Get him out of here," Wolfe said.

"The fire department and the sheriff's department will be showing up soon," Jack said. "I can handle this kid by myself, so if you'd like I'll leave Matt and Dom here to explain to the local authorities what happened. I called Sawyer McNamara in on this, so he can help us out with the sheriff."

"Who's Sawyer..." Caroline's vision blurred. The world began to spin around and around.

"FBI," Jack replied. "Hey there, Miss Caroline, are you all right?"

Wolfe pivoted her in his arms. She cried out as pain sliced through her side. Wolfe lifted his hand from her rib cage and cursed a blue streak. "She's bleeding," he yelled. "Goddammit, Caroline, why didn't you tell me you were hit!"

"Hit?" What did he mean? Why was he screaming at her?

Wolfe swung her up into his arms and ran toward the Mercedes. Matt opened the car door. Wolfe deposited her on the seat, then knelt and lifted her arm so he could inspect her side. She glanced down and saw that a huge red circle stained her tattered blouse. Wolfe grabbed the soiled material and ripped it apart, exposing the bruised and bloody flesh. He probed gently. She cried out in pain.

"Where's the nearest hospital?" Wolfe demanded.

"Follow me," Jack said.

The last thing Caroline remembered was Wolfe slamming his door as he got behind the wheel.

Caroline had been trying to awaken for the past half hour. He'd been at her side constantly since she'd come out of surgery early this morning. The bullet had gone through her side, doing no major damage, but she had lost a lot of blood and she would carry a couple of nasty scars the rest of her life. He'd been wild with worry when he carried her into the local hospital's emergency room. In retrospect, he realized that he'd scared the ER staff half to death with his rage when he had demanded immediate care for Caroline. He had blamed himself for not realizing sooner that she was wounded. But she hadn't said a word, hadn't let on that she was in pain. His brave little trouper. She hadn't even realized she'd been shot.

While he had walked the floor in the waiting room, Jack Parker at his side, he had mouthed and grumbled, blaming himself, blaming the Dundee agents and cursing God for allowing something like this to happen to someone as dear and good as Caroline. At one point, Jack had all but dragged him outside to the parking lot.

"Take a deep breath of fresh air and chill out," Jack had said. "You're not doing Miss Caroline any good by the way you're acting. She's not going to blame you or us or anybody except those damn snipers who attacked y'all. That's who you should be wanting to rip apart, so stop screaming at everybody and stop beating up on yourself."

"That kid is going to talk. He's going to tell me what I want to know or—"

"It may be a few days before we can get our hands on him, if then," Jack said. "We may have to get in line behind the FBI, the local sheriff and maybe even Peacekeepers International."

"What do the Peacekeepers have to do with this?"

"Seems our kid sniper, Seth Horton, is a new Peacekeepers recruit," Jack said. "What do you make of that?"

"If Ellison Penn pulls any strings to get his hands on that kid, he'd better be doing it so he can hand him over to me. Otherwise, he'll be as good as admitting he was involved with the attack. Ellison's too smart for that."

"You talk like you know the guy personally and that you suspect him of being part of the plot to kill Miss Caroline."

"I know Penn by reputation," Wolfe said, realizing how close he'd come to revealing himself.

Ellison wasn't on his suspects list. He had always trusted him implicitly. After all, the man had been his mentor and had done a great deal for him over the years, including giving him a new life. He couldn't see Ellison as a rebel, as a crazed right-wing insurrectionist, but at this point, he didn't dare rule out even the most unlikely suspect. Perhaps he had eliminated Lyle and Roz from his list too quickly. He honestly didn't think Roz was the type. And Lyle's love for Caroline seemed too genuine for him to take part in anything that would harm her.

"Find out who recommended Seth Horton for his job at Peacekeepers International," David had told Jack.

"You don't suspect a network of Loyalists Coalition members within the Peacekeepers organization, do you?"

"Not a network, but possibly a few moles working their way into key positions, the way Preston Shaw did."

Wolfe decided that until he had proof of any kind against Ellison, he would go with his gut instincts and trust his old friend. But Gavin Robbins was another matter altogether. He didn't trust that bastard any farther than he could throw him. Especially not where Caroline was concerned, he thought now, gazing down at her as she slept.

"Wolfe?" Caroline opened her eyes.

He took her hand in his as he leaned over and smiled. He'd never seen a more beautiful sight than Caroline awake and recovering. "How do you feel, sweetheart?"

"Groggy." She wriggled, then groaned. "And sore."

"You'll be sore for a few days and then the stitches will itch awhile, but the bruises will fade and so will the scars, eventually."

She lifted her hand to his cheek. "You look terrible." She ran her fingers over the day's growth of beard stubble covering his face. "How long have I been asleep?"

"They knocked you out before surgery around five this morning," he said. "It's six in the evening now. After surgery, you woke for a few minutes and then went right back to sleep. I was beginning to worry about you, but the nurses assured me that some patients don't come out of it as quickly as others. Your body needed the rest, so you just didn't wake up again until now."

"I'm hungry." She giggled, then moaned. "Even laughing is painful. Isn't it silly that after what I've been through, I'd wake up hungry."

"What do you want to eat?" he asked. "Name it and it's yours."

She caressed his face. "I'm going to be all right, aren't I?"

The fear and pain of losing her lodged in his throat, an emotion that prevented him from speaking. If anything had happened to her... Finally, he nodded.

"Then don't you think you should stop feeling so guilty," she said. "You saved my life."

"I risked your life," he managed to say, his jaw tense. "I knew that damn cabin was a trap and I deliberately took you there thinking I could protect you and look what happened."

"You did protect me," she told him as she framed his face with both hands. "And y'all caught one of the snipers. He must be a member of the Loyalists Coalition, the people who ordered Preston's execution. That means if he doesn't know who killed Preston, he can give you the name of someone who does know."

David clasped her hands, pulled them away from his face,

turned her palms over and kissed each one. "Whoever gave the snipers their order to kill you is the person I want."

"Do you think you can persuade him to talk?"

"You can count on it."

The look of deadly intent she saw in Wolfe's eyes frightened her. What would he do to the sniper, who wasn't much more than a boy, in order to make him talk? She couldn't bear even thinking about the methods she'd heard that certain people used to obtain information from an unwilling captive. Wolfe couldn't…wouldn't… Caroline shuddered.

"What's wrong?" Wolfe asked, gently grasping her shoulders. "Do you need a nurse?"

She shook her head. "Can't the police question him? You don't have to do it yourself, do you?"

"Yes, I have to question him myself," Wolfe said. "But you shouldn't be worrying about that kid. All you need to do is concentrate on recovering and going home."

"Wolfe…?"

"By the way, there are some people outside waiting to see you," he said, obviously determined to change the subject. "Lyle and Roz have already been in, about two hours ago, but of course you were still sleeping. And Fletcher and Brooke got here about forty-five minutes ago."

"How did they know—"

"I had Jack phone Lyle and he took it from there." Wolfe nodded to the door. "I'll go out and let them come in to see you. But I won't be more than a few feet outside the door."

"All right."

The moment he exited her room, Caroline's friends swarmed around him, bombarding him with questions. He held up his hands in a cease-fire gesture.

"She's awake and wants to see y'all," Wolfe said. "But no questions about what happened up at the lodge. And in ten minutes, I'm running y'all out of there until later."

The foursome piled into the room. When Fletcher reached out to close the door, Wolfe grabbed the handle and held the door open. He and Fletcher exchanged a question-and-answer glance, then Fletcher released his hold, nodded his understanding and left the door open.

Jack Parker laid his hand on Wolfe's shoulder and said, "I've got something for you."

Wolfe followed Jack farther out into the hall, but still close enough so that he could see into Caroline's room. "What is it?"

Jack held out a pair of tinted glasses, identical to the pair Wolfe had left behind at the lodge, which had been just like the ones destroyed at the lakeside cottage in Windhaven. "Thought you might need these, so I ordered you several extra pairs after the bomb explosion."

Wolfe grinned, took the glasses from Jack and put them on. "Thanks."

"While I talk, just keep smiling," Jack said. "Sawyer tells me that you and Miss Caroline will have to give statements to the local sheriff. Just the basic facts. He says there won't be a problem."

"I can handle that."

"And it seems there's already quite a bit of interest in Seth Horton. A request for custody."

"The County Sheriff has a deputy guarding Horton and will take him into custody when he leaves the hospital." Wolfe grimaced. "So what agency thinks it can usurp the Sheriff's authority?"

"Peacekeepers International, Gavin Robbins in particular. And it seems that Robbins was the one who recommended Horton for the job at Peacekeepers." Jack tightened his hold on Wolfe's shoulder. "Sawyer says that Horton belongs to the FBI, that the feds want to get their hands on him and the Peacekeepers don't have the authority to save the guy's sorry ass. But he also said that past history shows that the Peacekeepers take care of their own."

Yes, they do, Wolfe thought. The Peacekeepers took care

of its own, but not only in the way Jack meant. They did protect one another, but they also executed their rogue agents. Which motivated Robbins—the need to protect Horton or the decision to execute the man?

Chapter 18

Wolfe lifted Caroline out of the car and into his arms, then carried her up the walkway to her house. Roz and Lyle stood in the open door. Matt O'Brien, Domingo Shea and Jack Parker followed. Matt and Dom brought in the flower arrangements Caroline had received during her hospital stay, while Jack remained on guard duty.

"I'm perfectly capable of walking," Caroline said.

"Humor me." Wolfe stepped up on the porch. "It gives me pleasure taking care of you."

A peculiar sensation fluttered inside Caroline. Whenever David Wolfe mentioned looking after her, protecting her, caring for her—as he had done so often in the past few days—unbidden thoughts of another David came to mind. Memories of the David who had watched over her for so many years couldn't be erased from her mind and heart, not even by the passion she felt for David Wolfe. And not for the first time, a ridiculous thought occurred to her—how perfect it would be if her two Davids were one, if she could somehow combine them and never lose either of them.

"Lyle and I cleaned the house and cooked dinner together," Roz said, as Wolfe brought Caroline into the living room and deposited her on the sofa. "Lyle's quite a cook. He's going to make some girl a really good husband."

"Hey, don't let Roz sell herself short." Lyle grinned at Roz. "She actually baked the apple pie."

"It was a frozen pie, straight out of the box." Roz grinned. "All I did was put it in the oven."

Matt and Dom lingered in the foyer. "Hey, what do you want us to do with these flowers?" Matt asked.

"Oh, let me have one of the arrangements and I'll put it on the table for a centerpiece." Roz rushed over and took the smaller of the two vases that Matt held.

"Please put the others in my bedroom," Caroline said.

Matt nodded, then he and Dom headed upstairs.

After sighing dramatically, Roz whistled softly under her breath. "Those two guys are dreamboats, aren't they?"

Lyle cleared his throat and glowered at Roz disapprovingly. Jack Parker chuckled.

Laughing, Roz shrugged. "Okay, so the habit is hard to break. I've spent years collecting men. You can't expect a girl to stop looking and appreciating, just because she's given up the habit."

"I didn't know you'd sworn off men," Caroline said. "When did this happen?"

"Recently." Roz stared meaningfully at Lyle. "I'm testing my willpower to see if it'll earn me any brownie points with a guy I'm trying to impress."

"Lucky guy, if you ask me," Jack Parker said. "Miss Roz, a man would have to be a first-class fool not to be downright flattered that you'd want to impress him."

"Well, Texas Jack, I appreciate your saying that. Let's just hope the guy I want feels that way." Roz continued staring at Lyle until his face turned red.

"Oh, by the way, Caroline, a delivery came for you this afternoon," Lyle said. "Roz and I had them put the things in the storage area off the laundry room. I hope that was all right.''

"What sort of delivery?" Wolfe asked, tension wrinkling his brow.

"Several suitcases and a couple of boxes," Roz said. "Your mother's husband sent them from Europe." Roz crammed her hand into the pocket of her cutoff jeans and pulled out an envelope. "This came with the stuff."

Wolfe took the letter, inspected it and handed it to Caroline, then glanced at Jack. "You and Matt and Dom take a look at that special delivery." He glanced at Roz. "Would you show them where y'all put the items?"

"Sure." Roz's mouth fell open. "You don't think there's a bomb or—"

"Probably not, but it's best to make sure," Jack said.

Caroline ripped open the envelope and withdrew a one-page letter. While she read the message, Matt and Dom came back downstairs and Jack motioned for him to follow as Roz led the way out into the kitchen.

"It's from Armand Mahieu, my mother's sixth husband." Caroline's gaze remained glued to the letter. "He says that although it wasn't my mother's request that I be sent her personal things, he thought it only right that he send certain items to me since I was Lenore's daughter."

"If it's going to be too painful for you to go through those things, I can do it for you," Lyle said.

"No, thank you, Lyle." Caroline folded the letter neatly and returned it to the envelope, then reached over and laid it on the end table. "I'll go through them myself. Just not this evening. Maybe tomorrow."

"Well, Roz and I have plans, so we won't be staying much longer," Lyle announced. "As soon as we serve your dinner, we're going to a church softball game. Roz has joined the team, and after only a couple of games she's already our star pitcher."

"You're kidding me?" Caroline laughed, then glanced up

at Wolfe, who stood behind the sofa. She raised her arm and gently grasped his hand.

Wolfe looked down at her and smiled, but she could tell that his mind was elsewhere. Was he concerned about the special delivery that the Dundee agents were at this very moment checking over to make sure it wasn't booby-trapped? Of course he was. He was a professional, trained to protect. His first thought would always be regarding her safety. He was a man whom life had taught from the cradle that you could trust no one, that you could count on no one but yourself and that you were smart to suspect everybody. In his eyes, no one was innocent until proved so. Nothing was harmless unless thoroughly inspected.

Roz reentered the living room first, carrying a tray of tall iced tea glasses. ''Refreshments, anyone?''

By the time Roz had distributed the tea, Jack, Matt and Dom reappeared. Jack grinned. ''The delivery is harmless,'' he said. ''Looks like a bunch of old clothes, books, pictures and a jewelry box. Nothing lethal. The jewelry box came with a key, so we unlocked it and checked it out. Hope that was all right with you, Miss Caroline. Seems your mother had some pretty nice jewels. Expensive stuff.''

''Yes, my mother had very expensive taste. Monsieur Mahieu, her sixth husband, is a multimillionaire. My guess is that he kept the jewelry he'd given her and gave me the things she'd brought with her when they married.'' Caroline gazed up at David and squeezed his hand again. ''See, now you can stop worrying. At least until after dinner. The delivery really is nothing more than some of my mother's belongings.''

''Speaking of dinner,'' Roz said. ''We fixed plenty, so if you three guys—'' she looked at Jack and Matt and Dom ''—are staying, I'll set a couple of extra plates.''

''Nothing for us now, Miss Roz,'' Jack said. ''We've got a couple of errands to run and then Matt and I will be taking turns keeping watch outside tonight, while Dom heads back to the hospital to make sure the sheriff's deputy is keeping Seth Horton off limits to any unauthorized visitors.'' When he glanced at Wolfe, Jack inclined his head to one side in a come-with-me gesture.

Wolfe released Caroline's hand. "I'll walk the guys outside and be back in just a minute.''

She hated the secrecy, the cloak-and-dagger tension surrounding Wolfe and the Dundee agents as well as the ever-present danger that was so much a part of her life now. She had no doubt that Wolfe was, at this very minute, discussing with the Dundee agents not only a plan to get their hands on Seth Horton when he left the hospital and was turned over to the FBI, but also the escalation of protection for her. Wolfe insisted on keeping the extra agents on hand, and when she'd asked just how expensive that would be, he had told her that the extra cost had been taken care of. By whom? she had asked. Fletcher? No, not Fletcher. And when she had looked squarely into David Wolfe's eyes, she had seen the answer. Her benefactor had somehow learned about what was happening to her and had once again come to her aid.

Seth Horton wasn't sure exactly what his fate would be, but he felt certain he would fare better being turned over to the FBI than winding up in David Wolfe's hands. The two G-men who had escorted him from the hospital this afternoon told him very little, except that they were taking him to meet with their superior. He realized his only hope of avoiding prison was if the Loyalists Coalition rescued him and got him safely out of the country. He had always been told that the organization took care of its own. He believed wholeheartedly in the cause to which his father had dedicated his life and he would die before he would betray his brethren. The feds might be harsh in their treatment of him, but their methods would remain civilized. If he had been subjected to questioning by Mr. Wolfe, Seth doubted that he would have survived.

The big black car in which he was a passenger pulled into a building that resembled an abandoned warehouse somewhere in the D.C. area, but Seth wasn't sure exactly where. During the trip, he had been confined to the back seat and his view obscured by the dark windows and the screen that closed him and the agents off from the driver. The car doors swung open on either side and he was dragged to the right and escorted inside the warehouse, straight into an empty, unused office.

"What the hell is this place?" Seth asked. "Why did you bring me here?"

"Because I asked them to bring you here," a familiar voice said.

Seth whipped around to face the man who had authorized the sniper mission to Garrett County to kill Caroline and her bodyguard.

"You?" Seth glanced from one FBI agent to another, and the realization of just who these men were hit him. He chuckled. "They aren't FBI, are they? They're a couple of our guys. How the hell did you manage that?"

"You must know by now, Seth, that we can accomplish practically anything we set out to do," he said. "FBI agents were on their way to take you, but our guys, as you called them, intercepted the federal officers."

"So what's the plan now?" Seth asked. "How soon can you get me out of the country?"

"There won't be any need for that," he said.

"Do you think the organization can successfully hide me out here in the U.S.?"

"Actually, no, I don't."

"Then—"

The two phony FBI agents grabbed Seth, one on either side. Adrenaline pumped through his body at an alarming rate. He looked point-blank at the Peacekeepers agent and saw his own fate reflected in the double agent's eyes. These phony FBI agents were members of the Loyalists Coalition.

Seth had failed in his mission. Failure was not acceptable to the Loyalists Coalition. They weren't going to give him a second chance.

"But it wasn't my fault," Seth said. "I had no way of knowing that the trap we set for Caroline and Mr. Wolfe would actually be a trap for us."

"These things happen," he said. "No one's fault. But you have become a liability to us, Seth. Your identity is known and there is no way we can guarantee that you won't reveal privileged information."

"You know that I would die before I'd betray the organization."

He nodded. "I'm glad you understand."

Yes, Seth understood. He understood only too well.

As she headed into her kitchen, Roz lifted the edge of her T-shirt and wiped the sweat from her face. "We whipped their butts good, didn't we?" She jerked open the refrigerator door and searched inside for the beer she hoped would be ice cold.

"You really need to work on cleaning up your language now that you're playing on the church softball team," Lyle said.

"Oops, sorry." She retrieved two frosty bottles of beer, closed the refrigerator and tossed one of the bottles to Lyle. "Is it a sin for you to have a beer to cool off after the game?"

"One beer isn't a sin," Lyle said. "Getting drunk is the sin."

"Then we won't get drunk." She popped the lid on her bottle and lifted it to her lips. She caught a glimpse of Lyle in her peripheral vision and noticed that he was staring at her breasts. She took a hefty swig of beer, then glanced down at her chest. Perspiration and dirt stained her T-shirt and her puckered nipples pushed against the tight cotton cloth.

"Are you hungry?" she asked.

"What?" Lyle's face flushed with embarrassment, like a

kid who'd been caught looking through his father's stash of *Playboy* magazines.

Roz laughed. "Are you hungry...for food? I can fix us some sandwiches."

"Thanks, but a beer will be fine for now," he said. "Would you mind if I cleaned up a bit? Washed my face and hands. I feel pretty grimy."

"Sure thing. The powder room is down the hall and to the right. While you're doing that, I think I'll catch a quick shower."

"Well, it is late...." Lyle backed toward the door. "I should probably head on home and let you get to bed."

"No, don't leave. The night's still young. Stick around and we'll fix some popcorn and watch TV. Do you like old horror movies?"

"Yeah, I love them. To be honest, I'm addicted to them."

Yes, she knew he was. One of the many things Caroline had told her about Lyle that she had stored away for future reference. "There's a movie marathon of classic horror flicks on right now."

"Okay," Lyle said. "I'll wash up while you're showering...." He cleared his throat. "I can fix the popcorn if you'll just tell me where you keep it."

"Top left cupboard over the sink," she replied, then headed toward him. As she passed him, she deliberately brushed up against him, then slowly moved around him to shove open the door.

She hurried into her bedroom, took several deep swigs from her beer, then stripped off her shirt on the way into the bathroom. She set the beer bottle on the vanity, then tossed her shirt in the open hamper before reaching inside the tub to turn on the shower. When she opened the linen closet to get some towels, she suddenly remembered that she hadn't put out fresh towels in the powder room after she had thrown the soiled ones in the washer this morning. She grabbed a pink towel and matching washcloth, rushed through her bedroom and down the hall. She didn't hesitate when she reached the powder room and found the door closed. She knocked twice, then flung open the door, squinted her eyes shut and held out the towel and cloth.

"You'll need these," she said.

"You can open your eyes, Roz. I'm decent."

She lifted one eyelid and then the other. Lyle was decent, despite the fact that he had removed his T-shirt and stood there with his bare chest exposed. Her gaze settled on that broad chest, taking in every inch. Thick swirls of reddish brown hair formed a T that spanned the area between his tiny male nipples and bisected his freckled belly. Her hand itched to reach out and touch him.

God, if I shouldn't do this, then give me the strength to resist, she prayed silently.

Of its own accord her hand snaked out and she laid her open palm over his chest, between those tight little nipples that peeked out from beneath all that glorious manly chest hair. Lyle sucked in a harsh, startled breath. Roz dropped the towel and cloth that she held in her other hand onto the edge of the sink, then zeroed in on Lyle. She brushed against him. Her breasts, covered by only a thin layer of lace, pressed against his naked chest. She sighed, loving the feel of his body so close to hers.

"Roz, we really shouldn't—"

She placed her index finger over his lips. "You know I'm crazy about you, don't you? I mean crazy in love. I've never felt about anybody else the way I feel about you. You've got to believe me."

He kissed her finger and smiled, then lifted her hand and held it securely in his. "I believe you."

"I won't lie to you. There have been a lot of guys. I've made some bad mistakes."

"I don't care about the other guys or the mistakes you've made," Lyle told her. He reached out and ran the back of his hand across her cheek. "I preach about forgiveness and

God's love that washes us clean from past sins. I believe what I preach. I live my religion.''

"I've never known anybody like you. You're the most wonderful, kind, honorable, decent—''

"Enough. You make me sound like some sort of saint, and believe me, Roz, I'm just a man…a very ordinary man who lives one day at a time doing the very best he can.''

"Oh, honey, you're not ordinary. Not by a long shot. You're the most extraordinary man in the world.'' She draped her arms around his neck. "I'd give anything if you'd kiss me again the way you did that day at Caroline's studio.''

"Considering the fact that we're alone in your powder room and we're both half undressed, I'm not sure—''

She kissed him. After huffing loudly, grimacing and shaking his head as if he'd just admitted to himself that he'd lost an inner battle, he pulled her into his arms and deepened the kiss. Their hands went wild, touching, exploring, fondling. And their lips mated passionately, imitating the basic sexual act. When they came up for air, Lyle pushed Roz away and then clasped her shoulders.

"We've got to stop," Lyle said.

"Oh, Lyle, honey, I want you so much.'' Roz knew she was begging him, but she didn't care.

"And I want you.'' He gazed at her with hungry eyes.

"Then what's the problem? Sex between two people who care about each other can't possibly be a sin. Didn't God invent sex? With Adam and Eve.''

Lyle chuckled, then clasped her face between his hands. "I'm a minister who preaches abstinence for unmarried people. That's the reason I'm still a…a virgin. I do practice what I preach. Sex isn't a sin, but for me to give in to temptation would be wrong. Can you understand?''

"Yeah, I understand.'' Roz frowned. "I'm not going to get laid tonight, am I?''

"No.''

"But you'd like to have sex with me, wouldn't you?'' she

asked, hopeful that she could bring him around to her way of thinking.

"No, I wouldn't like to have sex with you. Not tonight or any other night."

She glared at him, unable to believe what he'd said. He was lying. He had to be lying. "I thought you—"

"I do want you," he said. "I want to make love to you, not just have sex with you. But for me sex and love must be one. And that act must take place within the sanctity of marriage. That's the only way it can be right for me."

Roz reached out, flopped the lid down on the commode and sat. "Well, I guess that leaves me out." She looked up at him and smiled weakly. "Don't suppose you can fool around just a little. I know all kinds of things to do without going all the way."

"If I started fooling around with you, I wouldn't be able to stop," Lyle confessed. "So while we're dating, we'd better keep our relationship under control and stop at kissing. But once we're married, I'm going to keep you in bed for at least two weeks without letting you ever leave the bedroom."

"Just kissing while we're—what did you say?" Roz shot up off the commode lid fast as a rocket blast, almost toppling over Lyle's empty beer bottle. "Did you say when we're *married?*"

"Yeah." Lyle blushed a shade almost as dark as his hair. "I'd kind of planned on proposing in a more romantic place, after I'd bought you a ring and—"

"You—" she pointed to him "—want to marry me?" She pointed to herself.

"More than anything."

"Have you lost your mind? What will people say? Those little old blue-haired ladies at your church will never accept someone like me. They'll excommunicate you!"

"The worst the church will do to me is ask me to resign and I don't think they will do that. Not once they see what a wonderful woman you are and how happy you make me.

Besides, with your enthusiasm and energy, you'll be an asset to my ministry.''

"One of us has lost his mind.''

Lyle pulled Roz into his arms and kissed her forehead. "We've both lost our minds because we're crazy in love.''

Chapter 19

Caroline's whimpering cries instantly jolted David from his uneasy sleep. She tossed and turned beside him in bed, obviously having a bad dream. And why shouldn't she? Within a few weeks time, someone had tried to drown her, blow her sky high and gun her down. What he found amazing was that she was able to sleep at all. But he credited himself with her feeling safe and secure enough to rest, even if that rest was plagued by nightmares. She knew he would protect her with his life, and not only he, but the Dundee agents he had charged with guarding the house. He reached out and took her by the shoulders as he whispered to her.

"Caroline, sweetheart, it's all right. You're safe. You're here with me and I won't let anyone hurt you."

She stopped wriggling, but she tossed her head back and forth on her pillow as she continued whimpering. "Please, don't leave me. Don't ever leave me."

He flipped on the bedside lamp. "Caroline, wake up." He shook her gently.

She gasped, then opened her eyes and stared at him. Terror turned to surprise and surprise to relief. "Wolfe?"

"Mmm-mmm." He swept the flyaway tendrils of her lustrous black hair away from her face. "You were having a nightmare."

She nodded, then snuggled against him as he enveloped her in his embrace, being careful not to press too tightly and irritate her healing gunshot wound. "You were leaving me," she murmured against his bare chest. "I needed you, but you wouldn't stay."

"You know that I'll stay with you as long as you need me, as long as your life is in danger."

"But then you'll leave. Once I'm safe." She tilted back her head and gazed at him. "What if I'm pregnant, will you still leave me?"

He closed his eyes and called himself all kinds of a fool, as he'd done again and again over the past few days. He hadn't meant to take her without protection; he had made sure he was always prepared. But the night at the cabin, when he had made love to her quickly, standing up, both of them still dressed, reason had taken a back seat to passion. He had tried not to think about what he'd done or the possible consequences. Surely God wouldn't punish Caroline for his mistake.

"I'm sorry that I didn't take the proper precautions that night." Wolfe kissed her temple. "But I think it's highly unlikely that you're pregnant, don't you?"

"The timing was all wrong," she admitted. "I'm sure I'm not pregnant. I had my period while I was in the hospital. I just wanted to know that if you had gotten me pregnant, would you stay when this is all over?"

He lifted himself up and braced his head with his elbow as he looked down at her. She lay halfway beneath him, gazing up at him as if he were the beginning and end of her world. The last thing he wanted was to leave her. But he would have no choice. Because of who he was, because of the part he had played in her tragic past, they couldn't have a future together. No matter how much he wished for a miracle, there would be no happily ever after for Caroline and him.

If only he could tell her the truth—that he was her benefactor, the man who had safeguarded her from afar, the David who had loved her and provided for her and longed to be near her. But that would be only half the truth. He could not confess to one without confessing to the other. She would want to know why he had taken on the role of her keeper all those years ago. He could never tell her that he was Aidan Colbert, the Peacekeeper executioner assigned the task of eliminating a rogue agent who had just happened to be her stepfather. He could never look her in the eye and say, "I'm the man you came face-to-face with in Preston Shaw's study. I'm the man you thought was going to kill you."

"Wolfe, what's wrong?" Caroline asked. "You have the most peculiar look on your face. Was my question that difficult for you to answer?"

He covered her with soft, light kisses. Adoring her. Worshiping her. Wanting her more than he had ever wanted anything. "If you were pregnant, I'd take care of you and the baby, but—"

She kissed him to silence him, then pulled back, her face only inches from his, and whispered against his lips, "I love you."

Her confession took him aback. Heat swelled up inside him, pervading every inch of his body as the meaning of her words became a part of him. He knew that she cared deeply for him, that she was infatuated with him due to their sexual compatibility. But he figured that was only because sex was new and exciting for her. He had not expected her to fall in love with him. Wasn't she in love with *her David?* Wasn't her phantom benefactor the man she truly wanted? Wasn't he just a substitute for the man she couldn't have?

But you are that David, he reminded himself. And even if

Caroline doesn't realize that fact on a conscious level, isn't it possible that subconsciously she knows that you and he are one and the same?

"You're in love with the way I make you feel when we have sex," he told her. "You've never been with a man before and you're mistaking great sex for love."

"Maybe you can separate the two in your mind and heart," she said. "But for me the two things go together. Don't you realize that without my being at least halfway in love with you, I wouldn't have had sex with you?"

What would happen if he told her that half truth right this minute? What would she do if he told her he was her benefactor? If he did that, then he could tell her how much she meant to him, how deeply he cared. He could find a way to kept the other half of the truth from her, couldn't he? Would it be so wrong to take what she was offering? They could go away together. Far away, where no one knew her and no one had ever heard of Aidan Colbert.

But his conscience got in the way, as it always did. Hadn't he caused Caroline enough harm already? "I can't offer you anything beyond what we have now," he said. "I'm sorry. I wish…" *You don't know how much I wish that I could give you the moon and stars, that I could lay the world at your feet. This is one time, my sweet Caroline, that I cannot give you what you want.*

"Then I have no choice…I'll take what you can give me." She reached for him, all the love and longing she felt alive in the depths of her blue-violet eyes. Eyes that had haunted him for years and would continue to haunt him until his dying day.

"You're recuperating from surgery," he reminded her. "I don't want to do anything that—"

"You won't hurt me," she said. "You know how to make gentle love. I need you so. Once I give you the key and you feel that I'm no longer in danger, you will leave me and we'll both be alone. Let's not waste what precious time we have left together.''

No man alive could refuse such a request. Not from a woman like Caroline. She had no idea how alone he would be once he left her. Although he had been alone most of his life, the loneliness in his past couldn't begin to compare to what lay ahead for him.

Tears gathered in her eyes and spilled down her cheeks. He kissed them away, tasting their sweet saltiness with his tongue. ''Don't cry. Please, don't cry.''

He undid the buttons on her silk pajama top, slowly, prolonging the pleasure for both of them. She lay still, her chest rising and falling with each expectant breath she took. When he released the last button, he spread apart the shimmery, soft garment and bared her breasts.

He touched her. Featherlight. Hesitant. Her nipples puckered. His mouth could not resist. His lips closed over one nipple while his fingers played with the other. She moaned and squirmed. His hands traveled beneath her breasts to the flesh below. Licking. Nipping. Kissing. Careful to avoid the small bandage that covered the stitches in her side, both front and back, and sealed her recent wounds. He hooked his fingers beneath the elastic of her pajama bottoms and eased them down and off, leaving her totally nude.

''You are the most beautiful thing on earth,'' Wolfe said.

''Please...I want to see all of you, too.''

He could refuse her nothing. He lifted his hips and removed his boxer shorts, leaving himself totally exposed. His erection thrust forward as if searching for Caroline's body. She was everything to him. Without her— No! He wouldn't think beyond the moment. She was his tonight.

He touched her everywhere, his hands examining and petting. Her face. Her breasts. Her belly. The inside of her thighs. He eased her to her uninjured side and became intimately acquainted with every inch of her back, her hips and buttocks. He lavished attention on her body, arousing her and at the same time arousing himself. Almost beyond endurance. But this loving was for her. His lips joined his fingertips, kissing her mouth and then moving to explore her neck, her ears, her throat. She shivered and his tongue came out to play, traveling over her arms and legs, painting trails between her fingers; then under, over and around her breasts until she lifted her hips and arched her back as her heels dug into the rumpled covers at their feet. Placing his hand in the middle of her belly, he soothed her while he spread her legs apart with his other hand and lowered his mouth to kiss her intimately.

Only a few strokes of his tongue and she was crying out for him. Close, so very close to fulfillment. He ached to be inside her, free from all barriers, but he had risked too much that one time at the cabin. In the last moment of sanity before he could no longer control his actions, he reached out for protection and found the box of condoms he'd picked up at the drug store the other day when he'd picked up Caroline's pain medication, the day she came home from the hospital. The box was still inside the nightstand. He hurried, his hands unsteady, his fingers fumbling. Need rode him hard. The moment the sheath was in place, he braced himself over her, his knees on either side of her legs, and looked down into her eyes as she gazed up at him and held open her welcoming arms.

"I'll be...very...careful," he said, his words strained.

He lifted her hips, bringing her up to meet him, and took her with one quick, powerful thrust. And then he waited, unmoving, except for his labored breaths. Being inside her was heaven. Her body was home and comfort and incomparable pleasure.

He moved. Slowly. Back and forth. Teasing her with gentle strokes. Tormenting himself. Wolfe made love to Caroline with the utmost tenderness, savoring each moment their bodies were one, knowing that she would be a part of him forever. His sweet Caroline.

Her moist folds tightened around his shaft, squeezing and releasing until he thought he would die. When he sensed that she was on the verge of coming, he increased the tempo and deepened the lunges until she bucked and cried out, her climax hitting her hard. He pumped into her, not letting up until the moment of completion. In those seconds after he convulsed with shattering intensity, their bodies wrung every ounce of satisfaction from the culmination of their mating. It was a moment that Wolfe wanted to last forever.

Completely drained and totally sated, he eased himself up and off her, then settled at her side. Being extra careful, he pulled her close. They shared a kiss that held them bound together beyond the sexual experience.

"I love you, Wolfe." She snuggled against him. "Please, don't ever forget me and what we've shared."

Forget her? Impossible. She was a part of him. His mind, his heart, his very soul. "I won't forget you. I promise."

Long after she fell asleep in his arms, he held her and looked at her and savored each precious second. He stored up memories to last a lifetime. Finally, hours later, he slept.

The quiet tap at the bedroom door woke him the next morning. He slipped out of bed, adjusted the covers around Caroline's naked shoulders and reached for his pants lying in the nearby chair. He zipped up his slacks as he made his way to the door. When he opened the door, he found Jack Parker standing in the hall. He stepped outside and closed the door behind him.

"Sorry to disturb you." Jack glanced toward Caroline's bedroom. "But we just got a call from Sawyer. Seth Horton is dead."

"Goddammit! I was afraid of this. What the hell happened? I thought a couple of Sawyer's men were taking Horton directly from the hospital."

"A couple of Sawyer's agents were killed and whoever killed them took Seth. Dom was there when the feds showed up. He had no way of knowing these guys weren't who they said they were. They showed the sheriff's deputy the proper ID. Fake ID, we now realize. But Dom's blaming himself for not suspecting something.''

''Tell him not to. You're right—there's no way he could have known. But with Horton dead, we're no closer to discovering the identity of his superior in the Loyalists Coalition than we were from day one.''

''Are you going to tell Miss Caroline?'' Jack nodded to the bedroom.

''Later. Before someone else tells her.'' Wolfe looked directly at Jack. ''Screen the calls for a few hours. She needs her rest.''

''I can do that,'' Jack said, then hesitated before saying, ''The boss called. She wanted to know how much longer you were going to need three of her top agents.''

''What did you tell her?''

''I told Ms. Denby not to expect us back until you were a hundred percent sure Miss Caroline was safe.''

''Thanks.''

''After this mess is over and things are settled, are you going to hang around?'' Jack asked. ''If that woman looked at me the way she looks at you, dynamite couldn't blast me from her side for the rest of my life.''

''It's none of your... Truth is that I want to stay with her, but it's not possible.''

Jack nodded, then headed downstairs. David was grateful that the long, tall Texan hadn't pressed him for an explanation.

He grinned with triumph as he laid down the copy of the file he had *borrowed* from another Peacekeepers agent. Someone else had done a good job of finding out everything the Loyalists Coalition needed to know about David Wolfe. With the joy of discovery, he beat on his desk repeatedly, then shoved back his chair and bounded to his feet. At last, all the pieces had fallen into place. He'd known there was something not right about David Wolfe. Now he knew exactly what. He had Wolfe and Ellison Penn by the short hairs and they didn't even know it. A wide, self-satisfied smile spread across his face.

David Wolfe was Aidan Colbert! He had to be. Everything fit too neatly. With the help of a few reliable sources, he had unearthed the truth. And Ellison Penn had known all along, had probably even been the one to contact Wolfe and bring him in to guard Caroline McGuire. God, what irony—the man protecting Caroline was the same man who had executed her beloved stepfather.

Of course he couldn't prove David Wolfe's true identity, but he didn't have a single doubt. After all, two and a half years ago, Ellison Penn had taken a severely injured man to a clinic in Switzerland and admitted him under a John Doe alias. This had occurred only days after Aidan Colbert had supposedly died in a bomb explosion, giving his life to save a bunch of kids. This John Doe character had remained at the clinic for more than nine months, and when he left the clinic, he had walked out as David Wolfe, with all the credentials to prove he was a former CIA agent. The only thing was that there wasn't one CIA agent around who could remember David Wolfe. Hell, Ellison had even called in a favor from an old friend, Sam Dundee, to arrange a job for Wolfe.

He could understand Ellison taking care of a Peacekeepers agent, even falsifying records to show that Aidan Colbert had died and then resurrecting him as David Wolfe. But calling Wolfe in to protect Caroline had been a major mistake. And Ellison Penn didn't make mistakes. So, what was going on?

He snapped his fingers. Of course! That was it. Ellison wanted to make sure whatever evidence might be unlocked with Caroline's key would wind up in his hands. And the Peacekeepers' President didn't completely trust anyone the way he had trusted Aidan Colbert.

Ellison had taken a chance of exposing himself if anyone

discovered Wolfe's true identity, but then Ellison didn't think anyone would be smart enough to figure it out. He had a great deal to do if he was going to stop Ellison and protect the organization. The first step was to get Caroline McGuire away from David Wolfe. And he knew just how to accomplish that goal. One phone call was all it would take.

Once Caroline knew that Wolfe had killed Preston Shaw, she would turn against him and walk away, straight into the arms of the Loyalists Coalition. Then they would have Caroline—and more important, they would have the key to whatever hidden evidence might exist against them.

Caroline lounged cross-legged in the middle of the kitchen, all her mother's belongings spread out around her. Wolfe sat on the bar stool above, watching her as she fingered her mother's lingerie.

"My mother liked the finer things in life," Caroline said. "She bought only the best."

"The best thing in her life was you, but she never knew your true worth." Wolfe returned the smile Caroline gave him.

"People were never that important to Mother, not unless they could do something for her. Things were what mattered to her. The things money could buy."

Caroline neatly folded the lingerie and placed it in the suitcase to her left, then she picked up the jewelry chest. Wolfe watched her as she examined the twelve-inch-square brown alligator-skin case, trimmed and studded in brass. Caroline turned the small key, which was already in the lock, and opened the jewelry box. Inside were more than a dozen pieces of rather nice jewelry. Caroline inspected each piece. A couple of rings, one pearl and the other diamond. She held up the diamond.

"This was Mother's engagement ring...the one Preston gave her." She slipped the ring on her finger and found it a bit too loose. "Funny. I always thought my hands were larger than Mother's. She was so elegantly slender."

Caroline dropped the rings back into the case. She picked up several bracelets, then returned them, one by one. She lifted a necklace, rubies and diamonds, then dropped it back on its velvet bed. The final piece she retrieved was a large heart-shaped pendant on a gold chain.

"Preston gave this to Mother, too. For their anniversary, the year he died." Caroline held up what appeared to be an antique piece, perhaps from the 1920s, with tiny diamonds surrounding an onyx, diamond and gold filigree heart-shaped locket of some sort.

"That's an unusual pendant," Wolfe said. "May I see it?"

Caroline held it up and he reached down to grasp it in his hand, then sat back and cupped the necklace in his palm.

Wolfe's gut instincts kicked into play, alerting him that this piece of jewelry struck a chord in his memory. But why? What was it about this object that seemed familiar? The note! The note Shaw wrote to his wife Lenore. What had it said? Something about looking into her heart.

"Caroline?"

"Hmm-mmm?" She glanced up at him.

"I'd like to read the letter your stepfather left in the safe, one more time," Wolfe said.

"Why?"

"That locket triggered a memory," he told her. "Something in the note to your mother."

"I can tell you exactly what the note said. I've memorized it."

"Tell me the part about keeping the key safe and looking into your heart."

"All right," Caroline said, then quoted, *"Safeguard this key and the identical one in your possession. They unlock the means by which to keep our family safe, after I am gone. Look into your heart for the proof of my love for you and the children."*

''Look into your heart,'' Wolfe repeated. ''For the proof.''

Caroline stared at the pendant, then gazed at the jewelry box. ''Oh, my God! Wolfe, do you think—''

''Lock the jewelry box, then remove the key and compare it to yours,'' he said. ''Then use your key to see if it will unlock the box.''

She followed his instructions. She locked the case, then removed the key. With shaky fingers she slipped the chain from around her neck, opened the catch and slipped the key off the chain. She held her key in one hand and the key to the box in the other, then brought them together.

''A perfect match,'' Wolfe said.

''Do you think…?''

She slid the key into the keyhole and turned, then smiled up at Wolfe when they heard a faint *click*. The box unlocked. She jumped up and threw her arms around Wolfe's neck.

''We found what the key unlocks,'' she said. ''But there are no papers in there—'' she pointed to the jewelry case ''—so the evidence has to be here somewhere.''

Wolfe held up the locket for her to see. ''Look inside your heart.''

''The heart-shaped locket!'' Caroline gasped. ''But what sort of evidence would fit into something so small?''

''There's one way to find out. Shall we open it?''

''Yes, please. Open it now.''

Wolfe examined the pendant, trying to ascertain the exact location of the catch. Just as he found it and applied pressure to open it, Jack Parker stuck his head into the kitchen.

''Sorry to bother y'all,'' Jack said. ''But I've got a rather insistent twosome out here demanding to see Miss Caroline.''

''What twosome?'' David asked.

''Lyle Jennings and Fletcher Shaw.''

''What do they want?'' David glared at Jack.

''I told you, they want to see Miss Caroline. Immediately.''

''Jack, please show them into the living room,'' Caroline

said. "Wolfe and I will be right out." She turned to Wolfe, her face alight with happiness. "See if there's anything in the locket, then we'll be able to show whatever there is to Fletch and Lyle."

"Caroline!" Fletcher's voice called loudly.

"Oh, dear, something must be wrong," Caroline said. "I'd better go see what he's so upset about."

The moment Caroline's back was turned, Wolfe opened the locket. His pulse rate accelerated when he recognized the small dark coil of microfilm hidden away inside the golden heart. He turned the locket over and dumped the microfilm out into his hand. If this tiny photographic film contained the evidence Preston Shaw claimed it did, then Caroline would soon be safe from her stepfather's cohorts. Once the evidence came to light, with names and dates, Caroline would no longer be in danger.

Before Caroline reached the door, Fletcher and Lyle came barging into the kitchen. Right behind them Jack Parker reached out and grabbed both men by the backs of their necks. That's when Wolfe noticed that Fletcher Shaw had his hand in his pocket and the outline of a pistol showed plainly through the cloth. Wolfe slipped the microfilm into his pocket, along with the keys.

"Please, Jack, let them go," Caroline said.

Jack looked to Wolfe for permission. He nodded. Jack released his two captives.

"Wolfe, you're fired," Fletcher said as he straightened his crooked collar. "Or should I call you Aidan Colbert?"

Wolfe's gaze locked with his accuser's glare. At that precise moment, it really didn't matter now how Fletcher had found out who David Wolfe really was. What mattered was how much he knew and what he was going to tell Caroline.

"Fletcher, what are you talking about?" Caroline looked from her stepbrother to Wolfe. "Why does he think your name is Aidan Colbert?"

"Because that's what it is, isn't it?" Fletcher said, brandishing the 9 mm he'd whipped out of his pocket. "Don't get upset by this gun, Caroline. Its sole purpose is to make sure we don't have any trouble getting your bodyguard and his associates to leave."

Ignoring Fletcher and the weapon he held, she focused all her attention on Wolfe's face. "Is he right? Is Fletch right? Is your name not David Wolfe? Is it really Aidan Colbert?"

"Yes," Wolfe said.

"I'm afraid I don't understand why…" Caroline swayed slightly.

When Wolfe reached out for her, Lyle ran to her side. "Don't touch her."

"Please, someone tell me what's going on," Caroline said.

"Aidan Colbert was a trained assassin," Fletcher told her.

"What?" Caroline's violet-blue eyes rounded in disbelief. "Is that true? Is that what you did for the CIA?"

"He was never a CIA agent," Fletcher said. "He was a member of a secret society and his very first assignment was to kill a man who had been falsely accused of being a rogue agent."

"Caroline, please…" Wolfe went numb from the pain. He couldn't bear this helplessness, this inability to protect Caroline from the most devastating agony she would ever know.

"Aidan Colbert is the man who was sent to kill my father," Fletcher said, the hatred and contempt in his gaze practically searing the flesh from Wolfe's bones.

"No!" Caroline jerked out of Lyle's arms and confronted Fletcher. "Where did you get such ridiculous information?"

"I was told in confidence by someone with your best interests at heart," Fletcher said. "But I've been sworn to secrecy. It's a matter of national security. I brought Lyle with me to help persuade you to believe me, to realize that you've put your trust in the man who killed my father. We can't do anything to him because we have no proof that will stand up in court. But we can demand that he leave this house and stay away from you. From now on Lyle and I will make sure you're safe."

Caroline turned slowly and looked point-blank at Wolfe. "It isn't true, is it? None of it. It's all lies, isn't it?"

What could he possibly say or do that would reassure her? Absolutely nothing. He had betrayed her, lied to her, pretended to be someone he wasn't. But if he admitted the truth to her now, she would hate him and she would send him away. Without him, her life would be in danger. He didn't know who he could trust and who he couldn't. Was it possible that one of these men who had come running to her rescue might very well be the one intent on killing her? Or were Fletcher and Lyle simply pawns being manipulated by a brilliant strategist? Right now, his money was on Gavin Robbins, the sorry son of a bitch. Robbins had to have been the one who had somehow discovered David Wolfe's identity and gone to Fletcher. *And if it isn't Robbins?* his intuition asked. God help him. Don't let it be Ellison.

"Answer me, dammit!" Caroline screamed.

"Will you give me a chance to explain?" Wolfe pleaded. "I need to talk to you, just the two of us."

She shook her head. "Wolfe, please, answer my question."

"I can't," he said.

"Oh, God. Oh, God…" she gasped.

Caroline crumpled into Lyle's waiting arms. When Wolfe reached for her, Jack Parker clamped his hand down on Wolfe's shoulder and nodded toward Fletcher Shaw, warning Wolfe that Fletcher had his 9 mm aimed directly at the two of them. Fletch's hand trembled. Without much provocation, he might shoot, and as nervous as he was, he could easily fire the gun accidentally.

Chapter 20

Caroline refused to see him, refused to speak to him. Fletcher had ordered him out of her house, and without risking a confrontation that might end in bloodshed, he didn't have much choice. Caroline knew only half truths, as well as the ugliest, most painful truth. Right now she had to be confused and hurting, in more pain than she'd experienced since the night of Preston Shaw's death. And what made the situation unbearable for Wolfe was that then and now, he was responsible for her agony.

Jack stood in the doorway to the bedroom and watched Wolfe as he flung his clothes into his suitcase. "You know we can subdue Shaw and Jennings. Just say the word and Matt and I will—"

"And what happens if one of them accidentally gets hurt?" Wolfe asked as he whipped the suitcase zipper closed. "You have no idea what Fletcher might do with that damn gun. He could start shooting with the least provocation." Wolfe lifted his suitcase off the bed. "Besides, if Caroline doesn't want us here, then legally we can't stay. If we don't leave she can call the police and have us thrown out."

"The David Wolfe I know wouldn't be tucking tail and leaving without putting up a fight," Jack said.

Wolfe turned on Jack, his gaze narrowing as frustration and anger boiled inside him. "That's just it—you don't know me. Didn't you hear what Fletcher said? I'm not David Wolfe. I'm Aidan Colbert and you have no idea what Aidan Colbert is capable of doing."

"Colbert or Wolfe, I know one thing," Jack said. "You care about Caroline. My bet is that nothing and no one else matters to you, just her. So why leave her unprotected?"

Wolfe glowered at Jack, then headed toward him. Jack stepped back, allowing Wolfe to walk past him, then he followed Wolfe downstairs and out onto the porch where Matt O'Brien still stood guard.

"You two stay with her," Wolfe said. "Do whatever it takes to keep her safe. I have some business to take care of, then I'll contact y'all."

"What do we do if she orders us to leave, too?" Jack asked.

"Try to talk her into letting you stay. But if not, then you and Matt keep a watch on her, even if it has to be from a distance. And if she leaves this house, follow her. She won't be safe until I... Call Sawyer McNamara and ask him to meet me at the Peacekeepers International building in D.C. in two hours. I've got some rat killing to do and I just might need some federally authorized backup. But if anyone wants to know, he's to tell them he's a Dundee agent."

Wolfe got in the leased Mercedes and backed out of the driveway, not once looking back. He didn't have time for regrets or sentimentality. Not when Caroline's life was in more danger now than ever. The only way he could protect her was to find out what was on the strip of microfilm in his pocket and hope there was enough evidence to put the top men in the Loyalists Coalition behind bars. Later, when she was safe, he would face Caroline and accept his punishment. Unfortunately, he had a major problem at present. He didn't know who he could trust at Peacekeepers. His gut instincts told him that Ellison Penn was trustworthy. But on the off chance that he wasn't, David wanted the FBI present when they looked at the microfilm for the first time.

"You're coming with me," Fletcher told Caroline, all the while nervously scanning the room for any sign of a Dundee agent. He clasped the pistol with both shaky hands, as if preparing to shoot. "I don't want you here in this house alone. I've spoken to Oliver and he insists that I bring you to stay with them until we can sort through this mess. Their house is more secure than mine or Lyle's and Oliver has even offered to bring in bodyguards from the company he uses."

Caroline sat quietly in a chair at the kitchen table. A blessed numbness had thankfully taken control of her body and to some extent her mind. She could hear Fletcher speaking, could feel Lyle's hands holding hers, could sense the myriad emotions swirling around her. But only one thing truly registered at a deeper level—David Wolfe was a man named Aidan Colbert and that man had been the trained assassin who had executed Preston. No matter how many times she processed the information, her heart refused to believe it was true. Wolfe would never lie to her. Deceive her. Betray her. He loved her. He had risked his life to save her. Fletcher had to be wrong. But why hadn't Wolfe defended himself? Why had he acted like a guilty man?

Oh, Wolfe. My dear David… No, he wasn't *her David*. He never had been *her* David. And that had been her biggest mistake, allowing her heart to confuse the two men, to mix them together in her mind until they were one being. But if Fletcher was right, David Wolfe didn't exist. The man she had given herself to, her heart and her body, was Aidan Colbert—her stepfather's murderer.

Caroline trembled from head to toe. Uncontrollably. Then

quite suddenly she laughed, the sound alien to her ears. Shrill, hysterical laughter. And just as quickly as the laughter began, it died away and was replaced by gasping sobs. Oh, God, no! Please, help me. Don't let this happen to me again.

Somewhere outside herself, she sensed Fletcher and Lyle hovering over her, could hear them speaking, arguing, discussing. She felt them lifting her to her feet, gently shaking her, calling out her name. But she was too far away from them, buried too deep inside the panic-stricken laughter and tears of her own heartache, to respond to their concern.

"My God, she's gone berserk," Fletcher said. "Just like she did the night Father was killed."

Ellison Penn met Wolfe and Sawyer McNamara at the elevator and whisked them down the hall and to his office. Gavin Robbins and Barry Vanderpool watched with curiosity, but neither said a word.

Ellison closed the door, then turned and confronted Wolfe and McNamara. "What's going on? Do you know the risk you've taken coming here like this?" He eyed Sawyer. "And who is this with you?"

"McNamara. FBI," Sawyer said.

"McNamara is here to make sure what I'm about to turn over to you is kept safe," Wolfe explained.

Ellison's eyebrows lifted. "So, you don't trust me. Is that what this is all about? You've found the evidence Preston hid away and you're concerned that I might not be trustworthy."

"Someone told Fletcher Shaw that I'm Aidan Colbert and Fletcher told Caroline." Wolfe watched Ellison closely, gauging his reaction.

"I see. And you think I'm the one who revealed your identity."

"No, I don't think you would betray me," Wolfe said. "But at this point, I don't completely trust anyone."

"But you seem to have no problem trusting the FBI," Ellison said.

"I trust this particular federal agent. Sawyer's not interested in me or you or any classified Peacekeepers business. He wants what I want—to find out who's been trying to kill Caroline."

"As soon as we take a look at this microfilm Wolfe has in his possession, we should be able to tell who we can and can't trust," Sawyer McNamara said. "And once we have the evidence on these men, we can start making arrests."

"Microfilm, huh?" Ellison smiled. "Preston Shaw was a smart man. Unfortunately, he outsmarted himself."

Wolfe relaxed just a bit, feeling more reassured by the minute. Ellison didn't act like a man who had anything to hide.

"Let's take a look at the microfilm," Sawyer said. "If it contains what we hope it does, I can take things from here. For a very long time, we've been wanting to get our hands on proof that the Loyalists Coalition exists."

He dialed the private number and waited for the familiar voice to answer. His superior would be greatly interested in the news he had for him.

"Yes?" the voice said.

"Sir, I thought you would like to know that David Wolfe is at Peacekeepers International at this very minute and in conference with Ellison Penn and another gentleman."

"Who is this other gentleman?"

"I assume he's another Dundee agent. We suddenly seem overrun with them."

"Do you have any idea what's going on in Ellison's office?"

"No, but—"

"Call me back when you have more information."

"Yes, sir."

* * *

Wolfe answered his cell phone while Ellison and Sawyer prepared the microfilm for viewing on a projector.

"Wolfe, it's me, Jack Parker."

"Is something wrong?"

"Don't know," he said. "But I thought I'd better inform you that Jennings and Shaw didn't take Miss Caroline to Shaw's house in Baltimore."

Wolfe's heart lurched, apprehension tightening his gut. "Where did they take her?"

"To Alexandria, Virginia, straight to Oliver Harper's home," Jack said. "Matt and I are keeping watch. We're as close as we can get to the house without being spotted."

"Why would Fletcher take her to the Harpers'?"

The blood ran cold in Wolfe's veins. Jack was right. Somebody Caroline trusted was probably a member of the Loyalists Coalition. But who? Fletcher Shaw? Lyle Jennings? Or was it one or all of the Harpers?

"If the Loyalists Coalition have Miss Caroline, then it may take a squad of storm troopers to get her away from them," Jack said.

"I should never have let her send me away." Wolfe cursed himself for allowing this situation to happen. "I thought I could get things done here before the Coalition took action. I should have—"

"If you had stayed, at the very least Fletcher Shaw would have called the police and had you arrested. At worst, he could have lost his head and shot you. Or one of us could have been forced to kill him."

"Anything would be preferable to Caroline being held captive."

"We don't know for sure she's being held captive."

"Don't we?"

The doctor emerged from the bedroom in the Harper mansion where Caroline McGuire now slept peacefully. Oliver waited outside in the hallway. He hated the uncertainty, the sense of not having everything under control. But thanks to Fletcher's quick actions, they now had possession of Caroline. Unfortunately, she didn't seem to have the key. He had sent a couple of his men back to her house to search for it, but they had come up with nothing.

"Please, come with me, Dr. Johnson," Oliver said, and led the man across the hall into a private sitting room. "How is she?"

"I've sedated her. She should sleep for several hours."

"What were you able to learn from her?"

"She was rather incoherent, but with the proper medication, she was agreeable to answering all my questions."

Oliver smiled, a sense of relief relaxing the tension in his muscles. "What did she tell you about the key?"

"She and Mr. Wolfe discovered that the key opened a jewelry box that had belonged to Caroline's mother," the doctor said.

"A jewelry box? Then Preston was bluffing. There is no evidence. We've been fools to have worried."

"Perhaps. But it seems Mr. Wolfe thought that there might be something hidden inside a large heart-shaped locket they found among Caroline's mother's jewelry."

"A locket? Nonsense. What sort of evidence could be hidden in—" Damn! Microfilm! Of course. Preston had filmed classified documents for the Loyalists Coalition; why wouldn't he have used the same method to obtain evidence against his brethren? "A small piece of coiled microfilm might fit into a large locket. I can think of nothing else it could be." Oliver grabbed the doctor by the lapels of his expensive suit. "Did Wolfe get his hands on that microfilm?"

Dr. Johnson jerked out of Oliver's grip, then smoothed the lapels of his jacket. "Caroline is unaware of any microfilm. She did mention that Mr. Wolfe had been about to open the locket just as Fletcher arrived this morning. If there was anything in that locket, I swear to you that she knows nothing about it.''

"Wolfe wouldn't have left Caroline's house without checking that locket,'' Oliver said. "That means if there was anything inside, it's now in his possession.''

"Yes, that would be my guess.''

"We'll have to act quickly.'' Oliver paced the floor. "You keep Caroline sedated. I'll inform everyone that you've advised complete rest for her and she's not to be disturbed. In the meantime, I will contact David Wolfe and present him with a deal he can't refuse.''

"And that would be?''

"Caroline's life in exchange for whatever Wolfe removed from Lenore Shaw's locket.''

"Will this hold up in court?'' Wolfe asked, his hands damp with perspiration and his heartbeat racing wildly.

"Oh, yeah,'' Sawyer replied. "What we have here—'' he pointed to the viewing screen that enlarged the documents captured on the microfilm ''—is a journal that lists names, dates and events.'' Sawyer reached out and advanced the film. "And this is a signed confession by Preston Shaw that he assassinated Senator Harwell, following instructions from his superior, Oliver Harper.''

An overwhelming rush of emotion surged up inside Wolfe. Relief. Justification. Consolation. He had not executed an innocent man! Preston Shaw had not only been party to the plot to kill Senator Harwell, he had, as the evidence had shown and the Peacekeepers had acted upon, been the man who had pulled the trigger. But the relief was short-lived. Caroline was at this very moment in the home of Oliver Harper, the head honcho of the Loyalists Coalition!

"I knew Oliver had some extremist political views, but I never imagined him to be a true radical,'' Ellison said. "I've known the man since we were in college together and… When this comes out, it will kill Eileen and Brooke.''

"Harper's not the only bigwig on this list," Sawyer said. "We'll be rounding up ten other well-known citizens. A congressman, a senator and a federal judge among them."

"Are you sure Caroline didn't see the microfilm?" Ellison asked.

"I'm sure," Wolfe replied. "But she knew that I suspected there was something hidden in the locket. And if Harper had this Dr. Johnson use drugs on her, she would have told them whatever they wanted to know. And even without drugs, in her present mental state—" Emotion lodged in Wolfe's throat. He turned away from the other two men, clenched his hands into fists and shut his eyes as the pain and fear he could not control ran wild inside him.

"If Oliver learns about the locket, he will figure out what Preston hid inside it," Ellison said. "It wouldn't take a genius to come to the conclusion that the only evidence that would fit into something that size would be microfilm."

"And Harper's only bargaining chip is Caroline McGuire's life," Sawyer said. "It's his trump card, so he'll play it. And very soon."

The call came in on Ellison Penn's private line. He recognized the voice immediately. The devil himself—Oliver Harper. He would like nothing better than to get his hands around Oliver's neck and squeeze the life out of him. How could a man with every privilege life had to offer become the maniacal leader of a bunch of lunatics?

"I understand David Wolfe is there with you," Oliver said.

"That's right."

"Did he bring you a little present?"

Ellison held his breath. He knew…the damn bastard knew! Was there any point in playing games? "Yeah. All gift-wrapped and with a bow on top."

"I have a little gift-wrapped present of my own," Oliver

said. "I thought perhaps your Mr. Wolfe might like to trade."

Oliver's laughter sent chills up Ellison's spine. Oliver wanted a trade. Caroline for the microfilm.

"And if you're thinking of calling in the feds, I would advise you not to. As far as making copies of whatever evidence you have—don't," Oliver said. "After we've made the exchange, don't consider double-crossing me. If you do, you should know that I have no intention of going to jail. I'd kill myself first. And I wouldn't die alone. I find the Egyptian custom of burying the pharaoh's wife with him rather interesting, don't you? You see, David Wolfe isn't the only one with something valuable to lose. You do still love my wife, don't you, Ellison?"

"Why, you son of a bitch!"

"Tsk-tsk," Oliver said. "Now that we understand each other, put Mr. Wolfe on the phone. I do so love bringing a big man to his knees and hearing the fear in his voice. Tell me, Ellison, how long has it been since someone put the fear of God into you?"

Chapter 21

Caroline wanted David. Where was her David? She was alone and frightened. She'd been calling for him for what seemed like days, but someone kept telling her that she would have to wait. Whose voice was that? she wondered. She tried to open her eyes, but her eyelids felt heavy. She tried to move, but her limbs seemed to weigh a ton. What was wrong with her? Why couldn't she open her eyes and get up? She had to find David. He was lost and if she didn't find him soon, he would be lost forever. *Her David,* who had seen to all her needs. He had provided for her, protected her and loved her.

She could almost feel his strong arms around her, holding her, keeping the evil world at bay. He would never let anything bad happen to her. When everyone else failed her, disappointed her, hurt her, she could count on David to be her knight in shining armor.

Suddenly Caroline realized that someone was talking, issuing orders in a harsh voice. But who? And why? And what were they doing in her bedroom? Was she dreaming?

"Bring her around," the harsh voice said. "We're making the exchange in two hours. I want her up and walking by then."

Where am I? What's happening? Who are these people? Is this another nightmare or is this real? I need to know. Help me. Please help me. David...David...David!

Wolfe sat beside Ellison Penn in the back seat as the driver breezed the big black limousine toward the Mount Hope sanatorium and health spa in Montgomery County. Every nerve in Wolfe's body screamed, every muscle strained. Adrenaline pumped through him, preparing him for the most important battle of his life. Everyone else involved in this rescue had an agenda of their own, but for Wolfe the only thing that mattered was saving Caroline.

"We've done all we can," Ellison said. "Everything is set in place, and with a little luck, both your lady and mine will be saved from Oliver Harper."

Harper had to be a monster if he were willing to use his own wife as a bargaining tool. Wolfe had never seen Ellison as distraught and worried as he'd been since Harper's threatening phone call. But then Wolfe knew only too well how Ellison felt—they both had a great deal to lose if anything went wrong.

"We need more than luck," Wolfe said. "We need divine intervention. For our plan to work, everything has to come together perfectly. We have to take Caroline out of the sanatorium while the FBI take Brooke and Eileen Harper into protective custody. Since Harper isn't aware the FBI is involved, we'll have the element of surprise on our side. He's counting on our not bringing in outside help."

Ellison looked directly at Wolfe. "I understand how you must feel because I know what's at stake for you."

"Once Caroline is safe, I know you'll want to deal with Harper yourself. But if Robbins turns out to be the traitor within Peacekeepers, then I want to be allowed to deal with him personally.''

''With this exchange coming down, it's reasonable to assume the traitor will tip his hand and we will discover his identity,'' Ellison said. ''There are only a handful of men within the organization close enough to the top to be truly useful to the Loyalists Coalition.''

Yeah, Wolfe thought, only a handful. Robbins. His assistant, Latham. And Barry Vanderpool. They had ruled out Ellison's top agents, most of whom were out of the country on assignments at the moment. That left only the three suspects.

Wolfe's cellular phone rang. He responded. ''Yes?''

''Dom just reported in with some interesting information. Barry Vanderpool left the Peacekeepers building about an hour before you and Mr. Penn,'' Jack Parker said. ''Want to guess where he went?''

''To Mount Hope.''

''You got it.''

''Then he's—''

''Probably,'' Jack said. ''But guess who's on your tail? Robbins left the building shortly after y'all did, along with a couple of Peacekeepers agents, and he's been keeping a discreet distance behind Mr. Penn's limo.''

''Damn! If Robbins was in this with Harper, he wouldn't have to tail us. He'd know where we were going. That must mean he suspects Ellison and me of being up to something illegal and he's hoping to nail us and make himself look good. I sure as hell was hoping he was our traitor, but looks like he isn't.''

''I'll make sure Robbins doesn't interfere,'' Jack said. ''He might not be in with the bad guys, but if he gets in the way, he could foul things up for us. Sawyer's people are already in position and ready to strike the minute you get Caroline to safety.''

* * *

An attendant led Wolfe and Ellison into Dr. Johnson's private office and asked them to take a seat. They chose to stand. Wolfe checked his watch. The minute they walked out of here, the FBI would enter the Harper home to take Brooke and Eileen into protective custody, while a squad of FBI agents, led by Sawyer McNamara would swarm the sanatorium and arrest Oliver Harper. Within minutes of Harper's arrest, the other nine Loyalists Coalition leaders would also be arrested.

Oliver Harper entered the office, a charming smile on his face as he looked first at Wolfe and then at Ellison. "Right on time, I see. I appreciate your being prompt. Did you bring the microfilm?"

"We want to see Caroline," Wolfe said.

"She's being brought here as we speak." Oliver glanced into the outer office. "She's been kept drugged, so she'll still be a bit groggy."

It took every ounce of his self-control to keep from grabbing Harper and strangling the man. No matter who the other players were, Harper was the one truly responsible for the threats against Caroline. Wolfe would derive great pleasure out of seeing the mighty Mr. Harper spend the rest of his life behind bars.

"I'm sure you have a few Dundee men outside as backup, but I hope you haven't planned a double-cross," Oliver said. "You see, I have men posted in various positions throughout the sanatorium and even in the health spa that adjoins the sanatorium, so if you're thinking of creating problems, reconsider. Innocent people might die."

Dr. Johnson personally escorted Caroline into his office. Although her eyes were glazed, she walked under her own power, aided only by the doctor's hand on her elbow.

"Here's our little patient," the doctor said.

The sight of her, so fragile and weak, broke Wolfe's heart. She wore a hospital gown and was barefoot. Her hair was disheveled, her face pale. She stared at Wolfe and opened her mouth on a silent gasp.

"Come here, my dear." Oliver held out his hand to Caroline and she went to him willingly.

Ellison reached out and grabbed Wolfe's wrist, stopping him from doing what he knew instinct would tell Wolfe to do—rip Caroline away from danger and to hell with the consequences.

"The microfilm?" Oliver held out his hand. "Once I have it, then she's yours."

"Oliver, what's going on?" Caroline asked. "What microfilm are you talking about?"

"Nothing for you to worry about, Caroline," he said, his tone gentle and fatherly.

Ellison reached inside his coat pocket, removed the microfilm and held it out to the leader of the Loyalists Coalition. The look of triumph on Oliver's face was almost more than Wolfe could endure. Just as Oliver reached for the microfilm, they heard a commotion in the hallway and a voice calling out a warning.

"Don't turn her over to Wolfe! The whole thing is a trap."

Suddenly Ellison closed his fist around the microfilm. Oliver jerked Caroline to his side as he whipped a gun from his pocket just as Barry Vanderpool rushed into the office.

Breathing hard, his face slightly flushed, Barry said, "This place is swarming with agents. I recognized our Peacekeepers agents, including Gavin Robbins. They saw me and know that I saw them. They've already taken positions and my guess is we could already be surrounded."

Damn Gavin Robbins! Wolfe cringed at the thought of the gung-ho agent screwing this deal. Undoubtedly Robbins had somehow found a way to sidestep the Dundee agents.

"I should have known better than to trust you, Ellison," Oliver said. "You're not a gentleman. You never were. Too bad for Eileen. I have men ready to—"

"Eileen and Brooke are safe from you," Ellison said.

Oliver's eyes widened with surprise, as if it had never entered his mind that Ellison would have taken precautions so quickly. He held the gun to Caroline's head. "She isn't safe. Does she mean anything to you, Wolfe? If she does, you'll call off the Peacekeepers and Dundee agents. I can and will kill her in a split second."

"And I'll kill you if you hurt her," Wolfe said, his gaze locking with Caroline's. She stared at him, shock and puzzlement in her eyes.

Gunfire erupted outside, gaining the attention of everyone in the office. Damn! Vanderpool's spotting the agents had tipped their hand and set things into motion before the exchange had been completed. Now with Caroline still in his control, Oliver Harper was twice as dangerous.

Holding the gun to Caroline's temple, Oliver kept a tight hold on her as he pushed her toward the door. "We're leaving. Dr. Johnson has a helicopter pad on top of the building and I'll be taking Caroline with me as my own little insurance policy. Better tell your men not to fire at the helicopter because if I go down, Caroline goes down with me."

The minute Oliver and Caroline disappeared up the hallway, Ellison got on his cellular phone and contacted Sawyer McNamara. Wolfe grabbed Dr. Johnson and shoved him out the door.

"You're going to show me how to get to the roof." Wolfe pulled his Sig Sauer from his hip holster and pointed it straight at the doctor.

All hell had broken loose from the sound of it. The FBI agents were at war with the posted guards, members of the Loyalists Coalition trained in combat. Wolfe knew that the government agents would try their best to protect the innocent patients in the sanatorium and clients in the health spa. But right now, he didn't have time to worry about anyone except Caroline.

When he saw Jack Parker rounding a corner near the stairwell the doctor had indicated led to the roof, Wolfe flung Dr.

Johnson toward Jack and said, "Take this bastard to Mc-
Namara. I'm through with him."

"Wait and I'll—" Jack said.

"Can't wait."

Wolfe ran up the stairs, his heart racing, his thoughts wild
with worry. When he reached the roof, he found Oliver dragging Caroline with him as he headed toward the parked helicopter. Wolfe aimed his pistol, but before he could fire,
Oliver turned abruptly, placing Caroline in front of him as a
shield. Wolfe realized that Oliver was about to open fire, so
he dropped and rolled across the rooftop. Oliver began shooting. Wolfe came to a halt behind a row of empty barrels,
took aim and waited for a clean shot, one that wouldn't endanger Caroline. Suddenly, Oliver pulled Caroline with him
toward the edge of the roof.

"Throw your gun out where I can see it—right now. And
come out with your hands behind your head," Oliver called.
"If you don't, I'll kill her. I can shoot her in the head or toss
her off the building. And I doubt she'd survive the bullet in
her head or the five-story drop."

"No, Wolfe, don't!" Caroline screamed. "He'll kill you."

Everything happened at once. Wolfe tossed aside his gun,
then stood and came out from behind the barrels. Caroline
took advantage of Oliver concentrating on David's movements and aimed her elbow to his mid-section. He growled
with pain and loosened his tenacious grip on her arm, but
before she could run, he grabbed her wrist. A gunshot blast
echoed in Wolfe's head and for a split second he thought
Oliver had shot Caroline. *No! God, no!*

But Wolfe realized a moment later that someone had shot
Oliver. The gun in Oliver's hand fired once, straight down.
A reflex action that happened almost simultaneously with the
other gunshot. As Oliver staggered backward, blood oozed
from the wound where he had been hit in the head, but he
kept a deadly hold on Caroline. She struggled to free herself,
but to no avail. When Oliver toppled backward over the two-

foot high metal railing and off the roof, he dragged Caroline over the edge. She screamed. The sound echoed inside Wolfe's head as he ran forward, adrenaline flooding his body. He wasn't able to reach her in time!

Wolfe cried out, his voice agonized. The roar of a wounded animal. Then he saw two hands clinging to the narrow decorative railing that circled the rooftop. Small, delicate hands. Caroline's hands. An instant prayer rose from his heart. Thank God she was a fighter. Thank God she hadn't fallen to her death. Thank God she was alive.

Wolfe knelt on his knees, reached down and grabbed her arms. "I've got you, sweetheart. Hang on. You're going to be all right."

She clasped his wrists. He dragged her up and onto her knees, then wrapped his arms around her and held her. She clung to him, her body trembling, as she sucked in deep breaths of air.

"You saved me," she murmured.

"You saved yourself," he told her.

He couldn't resist the urge to touch her, to reassure himself that she was alive and well. With shaky fingers, he caressed her face. She closed her eyes and sighed. He lifted her raw, bleeding hands and inspected them.

"Are you two all right?" Jack asked as he came running up to them.

Wolfe nodded. "Did you shoot Harper?"

"No, Ellison Penn shot him."

Jack inclined his head toward the open door that led to the stairwell. Ellison stood there, his pistol still in his hand.

"Miss Caroline, it's sure good to see that you're all right," Jack said. "We've got an FBI lady right over here. She's going to take care of you. She'll drive you to the hospital and stay with you." Jack motioned for the six-foot female agent, who then came forward and identified herself.

"Ms. McGuire, I'm Agent Lucie Evans."

Wolfe lifted Caroline to her feet, then released his comforting hold on her hands and gently shoved her toward Agent Evans. "Take good care of her."

He turned and walked away.

"Wolfe!" Caroline called out to him.

More than anything he wanted to go back to her. But that wasn't an option. As he passed Ellison, the two exchanged a knowing glance. This was the only way it could end. He had known from the beginning that his sojourn into Caroline's life would be brief and that once she was no longer in danger, he would have to leave her.

Wolfe took the steps two at a time on his way down the stairs, hurrying as fast as he could to escape. He had to leave now and put as much distance between Caroline and him as he possibly could. He'd been kidding himself to think he could ever explain to her, ever rationalize his past actions. The bottom line was that he had killed her stepfather and for that she would never be able to forgive him. Better to make a clean break now and not prolong the agony for either of them.

Caroline stayed at the church until the last minute. She threw handfuls of birdseed from the yellow net holders and waved goodbye to the bride and groom as they left for the D.C. airport in their white limousine. If ever two people deserved their happiness, Roz and Lyle did. Even the ladies of Lyle's church, who had so vehemently opposed the marriage in the beginning, had finally come around once they'd gotten to know Roz and saw beyond her flashy facade.

Today Roz had walked down the aisle on her uncle Henry's arm, wearing a pale yellow satin dress that hugged her slender curves. Her tulle veil, attached to a yellow rose headband, puffed out away from her face like a halo. Wearing a canary-yellow dress almost identical to the bride's, Caroline had been Roz's only attendant. Fletcher had been Lyle's best man.

Poor Fletch. He'd been duped by Oliver the way everyone

else had been. And feeling terribly guilty for being so gullible, he had taken more than his share of the blame for trusting Oliver. And he had lost the woman he loved. The day Oliver Harper died, Peacekeepers International had arranged for Eileen and Brooke to drop out of sight. They had left Alexandria without a trace five months ago.

As the limousine disappeared and the crowd dispersed, Fletch came up behind Caroline and slipped her coat around her shoulders. "It's good to see somebody happy, isn't it?"

Caroline sighed, then smiled at her stepbrother. "You miss Brooke, don't you? Do you still have no idea where she and Eileen are?"

"No idea whatsoever. It's as if they vanished off the face of the earth." Fletch walked Caroline to her car, then paused by the hood and took her hands into his.

"It's been five months," Caroline said. "I would have thought she might have contacted you by now." *Six months, two weeks and four days since Wolfe had walked out of her life.*

"Has David Wolfe contacted you?"

Caroline shook her head. "I didn't expect him to."

"Did you want to see him again?"

"I honestly don't know," she admitted. "I suppose a part of me hoped that... I should hate him, but I don't. I still care about him. What sort of person does that make me?"

"It makes you human, kiddo." Fletch squeezed her hands, then released her. "We don't get to choose who we fall in love with, do we?"

Caroline unlocked her car, opened the door and slid behind the wheel. Fletch leaned inside, kissed her on the cheek and smiled. "If Brooke gets in touch with you..."

"I promise that I'll call you if I hear from her."

When Caroline turned the bend in the road, she saw a black limousine stationed in front of her house. Her heart skipped a beat. Was it possible that Wolfe...? She parked her Lincoln in the driveway, then got out just as Ellison Penn emerged from the limo. He came toward her hesitantly, as if he thought she might ask him to leave. She hadn't seen him since the night he shot Oliver Harper and helped save her life.

Gavin Robbins, who never owned up to the fact that his overzealous behavior at the Mt. Hope sanatorium had wreaked havoc with Wolfe and Ellison Penn's plans, had visited Caroline when she'd spent several days in the hospital after her nearly fatal ordeal at the hands of the Loyalists Coalition. Although he had made himself available to answer any and all questions regarding Preston Shaw's death and the Loyalists Coalition, he had also taken the opportunity to remind her that he was one of the good guys, a Peacekeepers agent dedicated to the cause of freedom. And he didn't hesitate to also remind her that David Wolfe, aka Aidan Colbert, had been her stepfather's executioner.

After learning the truth about Preston Shaw, Caroline had spent the past five months, as had Fletch, trying to reconcile her memories of a kind, good man with reality, with the fact that Preston had been a traitor to his country, an assassin and a member of the Loyalists Coalition.

"Ms. McGuire, may I speak to you?" Ellison asked.

She nodded. "Please, come inside. I'll fix coffee."

He followed her onto the porch and into her home, then waited in the living room. After tossing her coat onto a kitchen chair and kicking off her canary-yellow heels, Caroline prepared the coffeemaker. As she removed two cups and saucers from the cupboard, she allowed herself to consider the reasons why Ellison Penn might be paying her a visit. An update on the trials of several prominent D.C. citizens that was sure to end in convictions? Word of another suicide attempt by Barry Vanderpool, who was awaiting his own trial? Perhaps news about Eileen and Brooke, something she could share with Fletch? Or would he actually share information about David Wolfe?

When she brought the cups out on a small serving tray, Ellison stood, took the tray from her and set it on the table in front of the sofa. She sat beside him, then lifted her coffee from the tray.

"Did Lyle and Roz have a nice wedding?" he asked.

"Lovely. A perfect November afternoon, with bright sunshine and clear skies. A church filled with friends, relatives and well-wishers. And a bride and groom deeply in love. Who could ask for more?"

"Indeed." Ellison inhaled deeply, then exhaled and looked directly at Caroline. "I suppose you wonder why I've come to see you."

"Yes, I am wondering what brought you to my doorstep."

"I'm retiring from Peacekeepers," he said. "Gavin will be taking my place, at least temporarily. I don't see him keeping the top job for long. He's not suited to it." Ellison cleared his throat. "I'm flying out tomorrow for London to join Eileen and Brooke. They've been living in my London town house for the past five months. Both Brooke and her mother have needed time to adjust and to recover from the shock they suffered when they found out what kind of man Oliver truly was. At first Brooke didn't want to see anyone, not even Fletcher. And of course, she had her hands full taking care of Eileen. But they're both recovering now. Slowly but surely."

"May I tell Fletch where he can find Brooke?" Caroline sipped her coffee, then set the cup and saucer down on the tray. "Do you think she's ready to see him, now?"

"In my telephone conversation with Brooke only this morning I asked her that very question." Ellison smiled. "I intend to speak to Fletcher tonight and see if he'd like to fly to London with me tomorrow."

Caroline smiled. "Two happy endings. I like that."

"Would you like to know where you can find David Wolfe?"

Caroline's heart skipped a beat. "Don't you mean Aidan Colbert?"

"He followed orders. He did his duty like any good soldier. Preston Shaw was an enemy, a rogue agent who had to be eliminated." Ellison reached out and laid his hand on Caroline's shoulder. "You weren't supposed to be there that night. We would never have sent in an agent to kill a man in front of his child."

Caroline pulled away from Ellison's grasp. "When I found the key and my life was threatened, why did you call in David Wolfe to guard me, knowing as you did who he really was?"

"There's something you have a right to know, need to know. Something more about David. You see, after that night when Preston was executed, Aidan Colbert had a difficult time dealing with the fact that you had found Preston's body and had seen his killer. He was a man with a soft spot in his heart for children. He cared very much what happened to you. I think in the beginning, you reminded him of his little brother."

"Brendan."

Ellison nodded. "I sent Aidan to London, to keep him out of the way until we were sure you couldn't identify him. And during the years he spent there, I sent him reports on you. Pictures, too. And it was while he was in London that he arranged, through a lawyer, to begin taking care of you financially. He was appalled that your mother had abandoned you. I believe he spoke to your aunt Dixie only once and all other transactions were taken care of by the lawyer I arranged for him. Money was provided to take care of your psychiatrist's bills, to pay for your medical and dental bills, as well as clothes and items for school. And of course, there were the birthday and Christmas presents.

"And later on college tuition and a bank loan so that you could open your own studio. Whatever you needed, he made sure you had. He took care of you, became your keeper, but always from afar. So, who else would care more about protecting you from the Loyalists Coalition, who else had a bigger stake in your life than Aidan Colbert, the man you only knew as David.''

Caroline rose from the sofa, her heartbeat thundering inside her head, drowning out all other sounds. ''Are you trying to tell me that Aidan Colbert was my benefactor? That David Wolfe and *my David* are one and the same?''

''Yes, that's exactly what I'm telling you.''

Caroline paced the floor as she tried to assimilate the information. A part of her wanted to deny the possibility, but in her heart she knew it was true. Hadn't she, on a subconscious level, always known? The moment she saw David Wolfe for the first time, her soul had recognized his. She had responded to him as she'd never responded to another man, been swept off her feet by her own unbridled passion for a man who was little more than a stranger. But he hadn't been a stranger. He had been her David. The man who had been her guardian angel for fifteen years.

But her beloved David was also Preston Shaw's killer!

''David lives in Tennessee, in a log cabin in the Smoky Mountains.'' Ellison reached inside his coat pocket and withdrew an envelope. ''Here's the directions, along with his address and phone number. But I would suggest you surprise him, otherwise he might bolt and run.''

''You seem awfully sure that I'll go to him,'' Caroline said.

''Not sure, just hopeful.'' Ellison rose to his feet. ''If ever a man needed to be forgiven, your David does.''

For hours after Ellison Penn departed, Caroline sat alone in her living room looking at the pictures she had taken of David Wolfe the night he'd made love to her for the first time. She had been so desperately in love with this man. And from studying the look on his face in the photographs, she saw the truth—he had been in love with her, too. The sun set and the moon came up and still she sat, as her heart and mind fought a battle. And in the end her soul triumphed.

Wolfe brought in a load of wood and dumped it into the bin by the fireplace. The weatherman was predicting a light snowfall tonight. He had always loved the snow up here in the mountains, but even now, after fifteen years, a light snowfall brought back memories of a December night in Baltimore. Don't think, he told himself. Put the past out of your mind. And forget about Caroline McGuire. She is no longer a part of your life. Not in any way. If Ellison had done as he requested, then Caroline would receive a letter from David's lawyer this week, informing her of her benefactor's death. Once that deed was done, then the last connection between them would be severed.

He had quit the Dundee agency, sublet his Atlanta apartment and moved to the mountains five months ago, hoping to escape from the memories of Caroline. But unfortunately those memories followed him, tormented him, plagued him. More than once he had been tempted to call Ellison to ask about her. But somehow he'd found the strength to resist.

Wolfe sniffed, savoring the smell of the homemade vegetable soup he'd put on to cook earlier in the day. After his long hike, he'd read for a while and then gone out to bring in more firewood, and during all this activity, he'd forgotten lunch. He pulled a big bowl off the open rack, then lifted the lid from the soup pot and ladled up the vegetable concoction. He carried the bowl, along with a handful of crackers, over to the kitchen table and sat down to eat. When he had finished three-quarters of the soup, he heard a car pull into the gravel driveway. Who the hell? he wondered. Somebody lost, no doubt. He wasn't expecting anyone and his was the only cabin on this road. He heard a car door slam. Damn. Now he'd have to go out into the cold evening to give some lost tourist directions on how to get to Pigeon Forge or Gatlinburg.

The moment he opened the front door, he recognized his guest, but he couldn't believe his eyes. He must have fallen asleep after dinner and was now dozing in front of the fire. Dreaming.

"Caroline?"

She lifted her hand and waved, then walked toward him. She was even lovelier in this dream than he remembered. She wore a red wool coat, a black-and-red plaid scarf and a matching cap.

"May I come in?" she asked.

"Yes, please," he replied.

Please, come into my dreams, sweet Caroline, and stay here with me forever.

When she entered the cabin, he followed her. She removed her coat, gloves, scarf and hat to reveal a pair of black slacks and a red sweater. She handed him the discarded items and when she did, their hands brushed lightly against each other.

If this was a dream, then it was a damn realistic dream, Wolfe thought. He laid the coat and other items on a nearby chair, then turned back to Caroline. Her hair shimmered a lustrous blue-black in the firelight. She stared at him, tears in her blue-violet eyes.

"I'm not dreaming, am I?" he asked. "You're really here, aren't you?"

"Yes, Wolfe, I'm really here."

"How? Why?"

"Ellison Penn told me where you were and gave me directions to find this place." She glanced around inside the cabin. "Nice home. But it's terribly isolated. I lost my way several times before getting here. I thought I'd never find you."

I have been lost without you, he wanted to tell her. Lost and alone and afraid that my life was over. "Why did you come here?"

"I know everything," she said. "Ellison told me."

"Everything?"

"I know that Aidan Colbert was my benefactor, David," she said. "I think my heart and soul recognized you the moment we met."

He couldn't bear for her to be kind to him, to be grateful, when what he wanted—all that he wanted—was for her to love him. "Aidan Colbert killed your "

She rushed to him and placed her fingers over his lips. "I know who Aidan Colbert was and what he did." The touch of her flesh against his, the nearness of her body, the smell of her delicate perfume aroused him. If only he could take her into his arms. If only…

"Despite how kind and good Preston Shaw was to me, he was a man capable of doing some very bad things. And he was a member of an evil organization. I understand that you acted under orders to eliminate an enemy of Peacekeepers and a traitor to your country. It's taken me five months, but I have finally come to accept the truth about my stepfather. And about you. Even before Ellison told me that you were my David, I had already forgiven you."

"You've forgiven me?" Was it possible? Dare he believe what he was hearing?

"I've come here because I want to help you learn how to forgive yourself." She reached out and took both of his hands into hers. "Not just for executing Preston, but for killing your father."

Caroline had not come to him because she loved him and wanted to be with him. She had come to help him find redemption. But didn't she realize that without her love, there could be no atonement, no salvation?

"Thank you for coming to see me to tell me that you've forgiven me," he said. "But I think you should go now. Leave before the snow sets in."

"I'm afraid you don't understand." She lifted his hands and pulled his arms around her waist. "I've come here to stay with you."

"For how long?" Did she think he needed daily therapy, with her as his nursemaid?

"For the rest of my life," she said.

"What?"

She wrapped her arms around his neck. "Of course, I'll expect you to marry me, eventually. Before we have children."

"Caroline?"

"Hmm-mmm?" She stood on tiptoe and kissed him.

"If you're doing this because you're grateful—"

"But I am grateful," she said.

"I don't want your gratitude."

"What do you want?"

"What the hell do you think I want?" He jerked free, turned his back on her and walked away.

She came up behind him, close enough to touch him, but she allowed a hairbreadth to remain between her chest and his back. "I think you want exactly what I do. To put the past behind us and accept what can never be changed. And to love each other with all our hearts, to get married and have babies and grow old together."

He closed his eyes as tears clouded his vision. Was it possible? Was she really offering him his heart's desire? "Are you telling me that my dream and your fantasy can become a reality, despite the past?"

"That's exactly what I'm telling you. Oh, Wolfe—my darling David—don't you know how much I love you?"

He spun around to face her and without shame allowed her to see the tears trickling down his cheeks. "And I love you, my sweet Caroline. I always have. With all my heart and soul."

Epilogue

"They're here." Caroline rose slowly from the overstuffed chair by the fireplace and waddled toward the front door. David hurried up from the basement where he'd spent the past two hours puttering in his carpentry shop while Caroline napped.

They spent their weekends and holidays here in David's mountain cabin and weekdays at their house in Maryville, where Caroline had opened her photography studio. David had taken up a new hobby that quickly turned into a new profession—carpentry. He had only a month ago opened his own handcrafted furniture shop.

David rushed to Caroline's side just as she opened the front door. "You stay in here," he ordered. "It's too cold outside for you and—" he patted her protruding tummy "—little Brendan. I'll go help Lyle and Roz with the babies and their suitcases."

Caroline sighed. She loved the way David had become even more protective of her during her pregnancy, but sometimes she wanted to scream at the way he kept her from doing anything these days, to tell him that she wasn't an invalid. But she never said anything, realizing how happy it made him to take care of her.

Roz, decked out in a fake leopard-skin coat and matching hat, came scurrying up the steps, one of the twins in her arms. Lyle followed closely behind with the other twin. Since they were bundled up so securely, Caroline couldn't tell the babies apart.

David brought the two suitcases inside and their guests placed the infant carriers on the sofa while they shucked off their winter coats. Caroline removed the blankets from the babies and cooed to them. Instantly she recognized Dixie as the placid infant on the right and Betsy as the squalling babe on the left. The two redheaded darlings had been named in honor of their deceased grandmothers.

"So, how are you doing?" Roz asked. "You look great, but my God, you're twice as big as you were Thanksgiving when you two came to Maryland."

"I feel wonderful and the doctor says I'm fine," Caroline replied. "And I'll have you know that even though I'm in my seventh month, I've gained only twenty pounds. Not like someone else I know who had gained fifty-five pounds by her third trimester."

"Yes, but I had an excuse. I was expecting twins."

"Both of whom are now awake and hungry," Lyle said. "Three months old and all these girls do is eat, sleep, cry and then eat some more."

"Don't forget diaper changes," Roz said. "Daddy doesn't like changing the dirty ones, but I make him do them, anyway. While we're here, we'll let Uncle David change a few. It'll be good practice for him."

David wrapped his arm around Caroline's shoulders and she snuggled against him. "I'll change every diaper, wet ones and dirty ones. And if Caroline didn't plan to breast-feed, I'd be more than happy to take care of all the feedings, too."

"Boy, do you have him trained right." Roz laughed. "Hey, Lyle, get those bottles warmed up and we'll let Uncle

David and Aunt Caroline feed the girls while we change into our bathing suits and hit the hot tub out on the deck.''

Thirty minutes later, Caroline and David sat side by side on the sofa, Dixie in David's arms and Betsy in Caroline's. Both girls slept peacefully. In unison David and Caroline rose from the sofa, took the babies into the guest bedroom and placed them in matching bassinets. When they returned to the living room, they heard Lyle's and Roz's laughter coming from the deck outside. David flipped the wall switch and turned off the rustic overhead chandelier, leaving the room bathed only in a sparkling glow from the twinkling white lights on the Christmas tree.

He wrapped his arms around her and nuzzled her neck. ''Merry Christmas Eve, Mrs. Wolfe.''

Caroline sighed. ''Life is good, isn't it? Fletch and Brooke called from London to tell us that they've planning a double wedding with Ellison and Eileen for next spring and want us all to fly over there for the big event. Roz and Lyle are happily married and the parents of two perfect little girls.'' Caroline laid her arms over David's, where they crisscrossed her big belly. ''And you and I have everything. Each other and now a baby on the way. Oh, David, I'm so happy.''

''And that's exactly how I plan to keep you for the rest of your life, my sweet Caroline.''

She turned in his arms and they shared a kiss. Baby Brendan drew back a foot and kicked his father. Caroline and David laughed, then kissed again, the love growing stronger every day, their lives complete.

* * * * *

*Look for Jack Parker's story
when Beverly Barton's exciting series,
THE PROTECTORS, continues.
Available in December!*

Heart of Stone

LINDSAY McKENNA

Lindsay McKenna

MORGAN'S MERCENARIES

Morgan's Men are born for battle — but are they ready for love?

For Hal Klopper, Boeing public relations,
Todd Brown, Boeing Apache test pilot,
and Phillip Mooney, Boeing aviation expert.

Thank you for your help, your dedication
and your passion for the Apache helicopter.

Chapter 1

"Morgan, I've got to warn you. Captain Maya Stevenson is a modern-day woman warrior," Mike Houston said as he sat down with his boss at a round table beneath a red-and-white-striped umbrella. "She kicks butt and takes names later."

Morgan sipped his fragrant Peruvian coffee, his gaze restless as he looked down the narrow, red tiled walk toward the entranceway of the India Feliz Restaurant, where they were shortly to meet the clandestine and legendary Maya Stevenson. Directly in front of them rose the massive, loaf-shaped dome of Machu Picchu. It was December, summertime, and the landscape was dotted with orchids.

Morgan and Mike had arrived a half hour earlier by helicopter from Cuzco. Agua Caliente was a small, bustling tourist town, the closest community to the archeological wonder that was Machu Picchu.

"She's kind of like a real-life Lara Croft," Mike continued, using the action heroine and the popular video game to describe Maya.

"My son, Jason, is in love with Lara Croft, the female archeologist in his Tomb Raider game." Morgan chuckled. "He's fourteen years old and plays that game every chance he gets." Quirking one eyebrow toward Mike, he said, "A living Lara Croft. That's saying a lot."

Mike, dressed in the typical tourist gear of a Machu Picchu T-shirt, jeans and hiking boots because he didn't want to draw attention to himself, grinned and sipped from his china coffee cup. "You know, for years while we were out here chasin' the bad guys—the drug dealers—my soldiers and I would come busting into the area north of Machu Picchu. We'd fly in with helicopters, then drop down and start raiding. Our goal was to stop shipments from getting into Bolivia. Every once in a while we'd get outnumbered and outgunned, trapped by the druggies, who were trying to take us out. I knew there was no help coming to save our butts. We performed our missions alone, with the government's approval, but they didn't have the money to bankroll us like we needed. So if we got into trouble, we were on our own." Mike's eyes sparkled. "And out of nowhere would come these black Boeing Apache assault helicopters. Two of them. And I mean out of nowhere."

"You've told me about these unmarked black helos coming in and saving your neck from time to time," Morgan acknowledged. "Way back when, we didn't know it was a spec ops—special operations—that was behind them. Now we do." He looked up at the late morning sky, a pale blue with thin white clouds silently wafting overhead. Every now and again a snakelike wisp would coil around the top of one of the towering mountains that literally surrounded Agua Caliente. At six thousand feet in altitude, the small Peruvian town looked to Morgan like a mystical Shangri-la, hidden deep in the mountainous jungle, in the middle of nowhere. The roar of the mighty Urubamba river, less than a half mile away, was clearly audible from the restaurant patio.

Watching the ceaseless flow of tourists passing the India

Feliz, Morgan heard snatches of German, French, Italian, as well as British and American accents. It was a Tower of Babel, quite literally, a baby United Nations.

Morgan had boned up on Machu Picchu and found out that what drew people from around the world was the spiritual nature of this old Incan temple complex. It was said to be the center of feminine energy on the planet, just as the Tibetan Himalayas, on the opposite side of the globe, were considered the masculine center. New Agers came here, from the looks of it—many on some kind of spiritual quest, he supposed.

"This is a very peaceful place," he murmured. "And drop-dead gorgeous. Look at the thousands of orchids clinging to that lava cliff face in front of us. That's pretty astounding."

Mike grimaced. "Yeah, it is. On the surface it's peaceful." He pointed at the hazy, mist-shrouded canyon, where a whole series of mountains nestled shoulder-to-shoulder along the raging, unharnessed Urubamba. The mountains looked like soldiers at attention to him. "Go twenty miles north or east or west, and you're going to meet drug runners trying to get their cocaine crop across the Peruvian border into Bolivia, where they know they won't be pursued by us."

"At least the Peruvian government let Maya come in here with U.S. support. The records suggest she and her squadron of women pilots are slowing the trade out of Peru more than a little. Fifty percent reduction isn't a bad figure considering what she's up against."

Mike nodded and lifted his chin. "Yeah, she's done one helluva job on a shoestring budget. Normally, spec ops get money thrown at them. Millions of dollars, as a matter of fact. But not her program. It was her idea to start an all-women squadron hidden deep in the mountain jungles to take out the bad guys. The only reason the idea took off was because her father's an army general and backed it. If he hadn't been, she wouldn't be here today or done the incred-

ible job she and her band of women rebels have done.'' Mike
grinned, respect in his tone.

"My wife, Laura, who is a military archivist and history
buff, is very taken with Maya's legend." Morgan waved his
hand. "Not that I've told her that much, but Laura is gung
ho about what she knows, and glad we'll be supporting
Maya's mission now, in place of the CIA."

Rubbing his jaw, Mike sat back and stretched out his long
legs. Two local dogs came up to the table and lay down
between them. One was a black-and-white terrier type and
the other looked like the descendant of a golden retriever
who'd met an ugly mutt in one of the back alleys of Agua
Caliente one night. The dogs sat contentedly near their feet,
hoping for a few handouts. "Personally, I think the spooks
wanted Maya to fail," he stated.

"Of course they did." Morgan chuckled as he finished his
coffee. "She's a woman. And she has a band of women
doing a 'man's job' better, probably, than any male squadron
would do it. Doesn't look good to the Pentagon to have
women outshining men in spec ops, you know?" He smiled
across the white-linen-draped table at Mike, who was also
grinning like a fox.

"I think she'll be happy to hear that her squadron has been
transferred over to you."

Raising his thick black brows, Morgan said, "I hope so.
You've met her, right?"

"Yes, a number of times."

"Anything I should know so I don't put my foot into it
with her? I'd like to get off to a good start with Maya, since
I'm going to be her new boss."

Mike smiled hugely. "She doesn't suffer fools gladly or
for long. She shoots straight from the hip, doesn't waste
words. She was raised an army brat, flew civilian helicopters
when she was just a teenager, and went directly into the
warrant officer program the army offered. Took her training
in Apache combat helicopters at Fort Rucker, Alabama,

which is where everyone takes their training to fly an assault helo. When she volunteered for this spook spec ops, she suggested a very provocative idea to the head honchos—let her choose a band of trained women Apache pilots, handpick the crews, and come down here to stop the cocaine drug trade from getting into Bolivia. They promoted her from the warrant ranks and made her a captain because she was going to be C.O.—commanding officer—for this mission. She makes Indiana Jones look like pabulum compared to what she and her women pilots do down here.''

''And why does she have such determination to do this? That's what I don't understand,'' Morgan murmured. ''It's the one piece of her background I can't integrate.'' He gazed over at Mike. ''Do you know why she would scuttle a potentially brilliant army career and go into a spec ops mission like this?''

Mike moved uncomfortably. ''I know *some* of it. The rest, you'll have to ask her.'' He propped his chin on his folded hands and placed his elbows on the table. ''I know you have Maya's personnel records. She was adopted as a baby. General Stevenson was an attaché in São Paulo, Brazil, for the U.S. ambassador. At that time, he was a light colonel. He and his wife hadn't been able to conceive a child. They'd tried everything and nothing worked. One day, a Brazilian Indian woman came to the embassy asking for Eugenia Stevenson. She carried a baby girl no more than two weeks old in her arms. When Mrs. Stevenson came to the back gate to see the Indian woman, she found the baby lying on the walk, alone. That's how Maya was adopted—she was dropped on the U.S. Embassy's doorstep. Eugenia fell in love with her, and they went ahead with formal adoption, giving her the name Maya, which means 'mystery.''' Mike smiled a little. ''No one knows Maya's real origins. I'd say she was part Brazilian Indian and part Portuguese aristocracy, judging from her features and skin color.''

"So, Maya has a stake down here in South America because of her bloodlines?"

"Yes, I'd say so. Just like bloodhounds need to hunt, she needs to be down here with her people, would be my guess."

"That makes sense with what I know. From what I understand, Inca is her fraternal twin sister," Morgan said. "They were born in the Amazon. Somehow, Maya was taken to the city, while Inca was left behind in the jungle to be raised."

"Yes, and Inca didn't know she was a twin until just recently, when you worked with her on that drug mission in the Brazilian Amazon jungle."

"Which is how we learned of Maya and her spec ops," Morgan murmured. "If she'd never shown up that night after Inca got wounded, we'd still been in the dark about her and her mission."

"I think we got lucky," Mike said. "Fate, maybe."

"What else can you tell me about her?"

"I think you know that Inca belongs to a secretive spiritual group known as the Jaguar Clan?"

"Yes. Does Maya, too?"

"Yes and no. She's a member of the Black Jaguar Clan, a branch of the main clan."

"What does that all mean? I know you have Quechua Indian blood running through your veins, and you're more educated about this mystical belief system than I am."

Mike avoided Morgan's incisive gaze. He knew more than a little, but he wasn't willing to bet the farm that Morgan was ready for the bald truth. Mike's wife, Ann, had had enough trouble grasping what it meant to be member of the Jaguar Clan, when she'd learned her husband was one. Mike hedged. "As I understand it, genetically speaking, there's a strong spiritual mission bred into the people who belong to the Jaguar Clan. They're here to help people. To make this a better world to live in. The Black Jaguar Clan is the underbelly, so to speak. They do the dirty work with the ugliness of our world, handle the confrontations in the trenches.''

"And you think that's why Maya sacrificed her army career to become a pain in the ass to the drug lords down here in Peru?''

Chuckling, Mike nodded. "Would be my guess.''

"She's more like a laser-fired rocket," Morgan murmured. "Almost a zealot or fanatic.''

"Isn't that what it takes to be successful at something like this?" Mike questioned. "And aren't you a little bit of a fanatic yourself? Didn't your own background, your unsavory experiences in Vietnam, turn you into a do-gooder for those who couldn't fight and win for themselves?''

Lifting his hands, Morgan said, "Guilty as charged. I'm the pot calling the kettle black.''

"Glad you can see that you and Maya have the same jaguar spots." Mike chuckled. "It takes one to know its own kind.''

Morgan raised his chin, suddenly alert. "Is that her?''

Mike cocked his head, his eyes narrowing. There, turning into the entrance of the French restaurant, was a woman who stood six foot tall. Her long black hair, slightly curled from the high humidity, swung loosely about her proud shoulders and full breasts. She wore khaki-colored shorts and hiking boots with thick black socks peeking over the tops. Her dark brown T-shirt had a picture of a cream-colored Condor, its wings spread wide, across it. Over her left shoulder hung a fairly large olive-green backpack. A pair of sunglasses on a bright red cord swung between her breasts.

"Yeah, that's her," he told Morgan in a low tone.

Morgan watched Maya with a keen, assessing eye. He knew warriors, and he knew how to size up someone astutely. Captain Maya Stevenson looked like a tourist, plain and simple. She was dressed in what rich travelers from foreign countries wore around here. Only her golden skin and long, rippling black hair suggested that she might be South American. Morgan liked the way she moved; on those firm, long legs of hers—with a bold, confident stride. Maya's eyes were wide and alert. Their emerald depths showed interest, excitement and wariness all at the same time as she pinned her gaze directly on Morgan.

There was no wasted motion about this army aviation officer. Morgan found himself smiling to himself. The energy, the power, the confidence around Maya Stevenson was something to behold. She was at least a hundred feet away from them, yet Morgan could swear he felt her stalwart presence, as if the sun itself was shining directly upon him. No photo did her justice, he thought. She was beautiful and looked very similar to Inca, her fraternal twin sister. But there were dissimilarities, too. Maya was six foot tall and a big-boned woman. She had a slight cleft in her chin, and Inca did not. Her face was oval, cheekbones high, shouting of her Indian heritage. Yet the aristocratic thin nose, flaring nostrils and full mouth were very similar to Inca's features.

Morgan was fascinated with this story of twins separated at birth, one becoming an environmental warrior in the Amazon jungles for the rights of the Indians, and the other a maverick military helicopter pilot. While Inca was calm, proud and quiet there was an edginess to Maya, he noted. Maya wore her brazenness, her strength, without fear. He admired that. Getting to his feet, Morgan was glad he was over six feet tall. Yet as she approached him, he saw Maya's eyes narrow speculatively on him, as if she was using x-ray vision to see right through him. Did she read minds, as Inca was purported to do? Morgan hoped not. If Maya knew that he thought her statuesque and possessing a bold, primal quality few women willingly showed, she'd probably deck him where he stood. This was a woman who brooked no bull from anyone—ever. No, she was an equal and it was obvious in every step she took that she expected to be treated as such.

Mike rose. He moved forward, his hand extended toward Maya.

She glared at him and halted. Glancing back toward the street, she whispered, "Follow me. And don't look so damned obvious, will you?"

Morgan looked at Mike, who lowered his hand, a contrite expression on his features. They both watched as Maya headed into the restaurant. It was 11:00 a.m. and there were few people in the usually popular place.

"Let's go," Morgan murmured, a cockeyed grin tugging at one corner of his mouth.

Mike good-naturedly grinned back and gestured for Morgan to go first.

Inside the restaurant, Morgan saw the owner, Patrick, standing behind the mahogany bar. Maya was leaning up against the counter, speaking to him in fluid French. As they approached, she swung her head in their direction. Her eyes grew slitted.

"Come on. Patrick has a table he reserves for me and my friends when I come into town." She brushed between them and moved up the mahogany stairs, taking the steps two at a time to the second floor.

The restaurant was light and airy, with many green jungle plants and bright red, pink and yellow bromeliads in brightly painted pots here and there. Each table had a starched and pressed white linen cloth across it, and there were fresh flowers on every one. As Morgan climbed the stairs, classical music, soft and haunting, wafted through the restaurant. He shook his head, finding it odd that a five-star French chef would come to Peru and set up a gourmet restaurant in such a little backwater town. He wondered what the man was running from.

Maya was sitting at a rectangular table at the rear of the second floor of the restaurant, her back against the wall. It was a good position, Morgan thought. From her vantage point she could see everyone coming up and down those stairs. She'd put her pack down beside her chair and was speaking in Quechua to the waiter. As they approached, she looked up at them.

"Patrick makes the best mocha lattes in Peru. You two want some?"

"Sounds good," Morgan said, making himself at home across from Maya. "Mike? How about you?"

"Make it three," Mike said in Spanish to the Peruvian waiter, who was a Quechua Indian. The waiter nodded and quickly moved to the bar nearby to make the drinks.

Maya held Morgan's glacial blue gaze. She knew he was sizing her up. Well, she was sizing him up, too, whether he knew it or not. As she folded her long, spare hands on the white linen tablecloth, she said, "Mike said you're my new boss. Is that right?"

Nodding, Morgan said, "I'd prefer to say that you've joined our international team and we're glad to have you on board." He stretched his hand across the table toward her. "I'm Morgan Trayhern. It's nice to meet you." She took his hand. Not surprised by the strength of her grip, he met her cold, flinty eyes. She reminded him of a no-nonsense leader capable of split-second decisions, with a mind that moved at the speed of light, or damn near close to it. Already Morgan was feeling elated that he'd fought to get her spec ops as part of his organization, Perseus.

"Don't bite him, Maya," Mike intoned humorously as they released their mutual grip. "He's the only junkyard dog in town that's friendly to you and your squadron."

Taking the napkin, Maya delicately opened it and spread it across her lap. "It looks like I owe you some thanks, Mr. Trayhern. Mike, here, tells me that my number was up at spook HQ and with the boys over at the Pentagon. You certainly look the part of a white knight. Where's your horse?"

Grinning, Morgan met her humor-filled eyes. Her laughter was husky and low. "I can't ride a horse worth a damn. My daughter, Katy, now, she can," he answered. "I like to watch her, but that's as close as I get to a four-legged animal."

"Got a picture of her?"

Taken off guard, Morgan nodded, moved his hand to the back pocket of his chinos and took out his well-worn, black leather wallet. Opening it on the table, he noted Maya's sudden, intense interest. Her gaze was pinned on the color photos he kept within his wallet. Taking them out, he turned them around for her to look at.

"This is my oldest son, Jason. He's fourteen."

"He looks a lot like you," Maya murmured. "That same dark, handsome face."

Morgan warmed beneath her praise because he could tell already that Maya wasn't one to make small talk or say things just to be polite. "Thanks. This is Katherine Alyssa, my oldest daughter. She's riding her Welsh pony, Fred. And this last one is of my wife, Laura, holding our latest children, fraternal twins…."

Maya picked up the photo, her brows arching with surprise. "So, you have twins…." She studied it with renewed intensity. "You have beautiful children."

"Thanks. My wife and I agree, though we are a little partial toward our children." He said nothing more, realizing that because Maya was a fraternal twin, she would make a positive connection with his children. He liked the fact that despite her being a hardened military veteran, she had a soft heart, too. The more he got to know Maya, the more he liked her.

Handing him back the photos, she looked up. "Ah, here are our lattes. You have no idea how long I've waited for this…." And she reached out to take a cup and saucer from the waiter, thanking him warmly in his own language. He bowed his head and shyly smiled at her.

Mike thanked him also. When the waiter left, he chuckled quietly and sipped his mocha latte. "See? I told you Trayhern wasn't the typical male bastard that you're used to working with."

Wrinkling her nose, Maya again met the solid blue gaze

of her new boss. She sipped the rich coffee with delicious
slowness and allowed the sweetness to run delectably across
her tongue. Placing the flowered china cup on the saucer, she
folded her hands on the table.

"I hope you know what you're getting yourself into, Mr.
Trayhern."

"Call me Morgan. I don't stand on ceremony with my
people."

"All right," Maya murmured. "Do you know anything
about us or did you buy us sight unseen, Morgan? A pig in
a poke, maybe?"

Her direct and uncompromising gaze would have been un-
settling had Morgan not liked that kind of straight-across-the-
board honesty. When she lifted her lips and smiled, it was
with a carnivore's grin. She was playing with him, like a
jaguar might with its helpless quarry. Houston was right: she
shot from the hip. *Good.* "Yes, I saw the bottom line."

"And the fact that I used to have three Boeing Apaches,
but because spookdom decided to strangle me slowly by cutting my budget yearly, I had to cannibalize one to keep the
other two flying?"

"I saw that."

"And that I've got twelve overworked pilots who need
some help and relief?"

"Yes, I saw that, too."

"And that the men don't like us women showing them
up?" Her eyes glinted and she leaned forward slightly.

Morgan wasn't intimidated by her low, furious tone or her
directness. He met and held her stare. "I saw that, too,
Maya." When he used her first name, rolling it gently off
his tongue, she recoiled. At first, Morgan wondered if she
didn't like his informality with her. And then, intuitively, he
figured it out: Maya was expecting a hard-nosed bastard to
show up and try to push her around, keep her outside the
circle, like other men had before him. The look in her eyes
was one of surprise—and then naked suspicion. Morgan

knew he was going to have to sell himself to Maya. He would have to prove that, although male, he was trustworthy. That he would fully support her and the hardworking women comprising the secret squadron hidden in the mountains of Peru.

Leaning down, Morgan pulled out several papers from his own backpack. He looked around. The place was deserted. He wanted no other eyes on the material that he was going to lay out before her.

"Don't worry," Maya said. "Patrick knows who we are. He and I are good friends. He protects me and my women when we come into town and need a little R and R. This is our home away from home. He'll make sure no one comes up here during lunch. We've got this place all to ourselves."

"Good." Morgan placed the first sheet of paper in front of Maya. "This is an acquisition form showing that two Boeing Apache Longbow helicopters have just been purchased for your squadron by me." He put a second paper in front of her. "This is a Blackhawk helicopter to replace the Vietnam era Cobra that you're flying." He put a third document in front of her. "Within a week, you will be receiving three I.P.s—instructor pilots—to train you and your team on the new Apache D model, and three enlisted men who will train your crews in software, armaments and mechanics. And lastly—" he put a fourth piece of paper in front of Maya "—here's your new budget. As you look it over, you'll see the financial strangulation your squadron has been experiencing is over."

Maya took all the papers, intently perusing them. Did she dare believe her eyes? Was this really true? She'd gone for three years with so little, watching her people bear the brunt of their financial distress. The task before them had seemed almost impossible, and yet they'd managed to strangle the drug trade to Bolivia by fifty percent, despite the odds, despite the fact that the U.S. government had practically choked off the mission through lack of funding. Looking up, Maya regarded Morgan through her thick, black lashes. He was at ease, almost smiling. She knew the sparkle in his eyes was not there because he was laughing at her. It reflected his pride in the job he'd done getting her the aircraft and help she so desperately needed.

Cutting her gaze to Houston, she growled, "Is this for real, Mike?" After all, Mike was one of her kind, a Jaguar Clan member, and she relied on him heavily at times like this. No clan member would ever lie to another.

"It's for real, Maya. Every word of it. Morgan is your sugar daddy." And he gave her a playful, teasing grin.

Maya grimaced. "What a sexist you are, Houston."

He scratched his head ruefully. "I was teasing you, Maya. Morgan Trayhern runs a first-class operation known as Perseus. You and your squadron are officially moved under his wing and command." Mike tapped the budget paper. "Look at the bottom line. That's money. U.S. funds, not Peruvian soles."

Maya looked at it. Her heart thudded with excitement. "I'm afraid to believe this," she whispered as she looked through the pages again. "We're really going to get two new D models? The ones with radar? I've heard so much about them.... I tried to get them, but they kept telling me they didn't have the budget to let us have the upgraded model."

Morgan tempered his excitement over the joy he saw in Maya's face. This woman was used to running her squadron her way. And he respected that. Still, he needed to be able to gently move her in the direction that he saw her duties down here heading, now and in the future. Maya's plan had been a greenhouse experiment—an all-woman military contingent doing some of the most demanding, most dangerous work in the world. Despite the difficulties of going up against drug runners who flew the Russian Kamov Black Shark assault helicopters, which were nearly equal to an Apache, and flying in this nasty, always changing weather at some of the highest altitudes on the planet, she'd been more than successful. She'd never lost a helicopter or a pilot in the three years since she'd started this operation, and that was a phenomenal record of achievement in Morgan's eyes.

He knew that it was Maya's careful selection of the right women pilots and crews that made this mission successful. Furthermore, she was a charismatic leader, someone people either hated or loved on sight. Morgan understood that, because he had that quality himself. Only Maya was a much younger version of him; she was only twenty-five years old. She had a lot going for her. And he admired her deeply for her commitment to Peru and its people.

"There's just one hitch," Morgan told her quietly. He saw her eyes narrow speculatively on him.

"What?" she growled, putting the papers aside.

Seeing her tense, Morgan said, "I know you have an all-woman squadron. Unfortunately, I couldn't find women IPs to come down here to upgrade you on flying the Apache D models. Do you have a problem with men coming in for six weeks and staying at your base to teach your people?"

"I don't have a problem with men, Mr.—Morgan. *They* have a problem with *me*. If you can guarantee they won't be gender prejudiced, I won't kick and scream about it."

"Good," Morgan said, breathing a sigh of relief. He turned and dug into his pack again, producing a set of orders that had been cut by the army. "Here's the list of men who will be coming in shortly. We haven't been able to tell them they are coming down here yet, but that's a mere formality. I give you my personal guarantee that they are the best. The army's cream of the crop of teachers, to move your people into the D models as rapidly as possible. Because you are so shorthanded, you can't afford to send your pilots back to Fort Rucker for training. Instead, we're bringing the training to you, so it won't interfere with your ongoing missions."

Taking the list of names, Maya frowned as she rapidly perused it. She knew just about everyone in the training field. The Apache team was a small unit within the army as whole—a tight, select family, for better or worse.

Morgan started to lift the cup to his lips when he heard Maya curse richly beneath her breath. She jerked her head up, her green eyes blazing like the hounds from hell. Her glare was aimed directly at him. His cup froze midway to his lips.

"There's no way I'm letting this son of a bitch anywhere near me or my pilots," she hissed, jabbing her finger at the paper she flattened between them. "You can take Major Dane York and shove him where the sun never shines, Mr. Trayhern. That sexist bastard is never going to step foot onto my base. Not *ever!*"

Houston scowled and took the paper. "Major Dane York? Who is he?"

Maya breathed angrily and sat back in the chair, her arms folded across her breasts. "You didn't do your research, Mr. Trayhern. I'm really disappointed in you."

Carefully setting the cup down in the saucer, Morgan allowed a few moments to stretch between them. The anger in her eyes was very real. Her nostrils were flared, her full lips flattened and corners pulled in with pain. Taking the set of orders, he stared at the name.

"Major York is the most accomplished I.P. in the Apache D model instruction unit."

"Yeah, and he could walk on water, too, and it wouldn't mean a damn thing to me."

"You have words with this guy back at Fort Rucker?" Mike asked, a worried look on his face.

"Words?" Maya clenched her teeth as she leaned toward Morgan. "That bastard damn near had me and all the other women going through Apache training five years ago washed out! Why? Because we were *women*. That's the only reason." She jabbed at the paper Mike held. "I'm not letting that Neanderthal anywhere near me or my crews. Over my dead body."

"Hold on," Morgan murmured. "Major York's credentials are impeccable. I wanted the best for you and your pilots, Maya.''

"I can't believe this!" Maya suddenly stood up, energy swirling around her. She moved abruptly away from the table and walked over to the row of windows that overlooked the busy street below. Hands on her hips, she said, "He's gender prejudiced. He didn't like me. He didn't like my flying skills. He didn't like anything I did because I was a woman. Well—'' Maya turned around and glared at them "—I had the last laugh on him and his not-so-subtle tactics. He didn't know my father was an army general. When York was unable to acknowledge some of the women's superior flying skills and wouldn't grade them accordingly, I got angry. When he did nothing to stop his other instructors from harassing us with innuendos, I called my father.''

Morgan frowned. "What happened then?"

Moving slowly toward the table, Maya tried to settle her rapidly beating heart. "You know, York is like a black cloud that follows me around." She laughed sharply. "Here I am in backwater Peru, and he manages to find me anyway. What kind of karma do I have?"

Houston glanced at Morgan and noticed the worry in his boss's eyes. "Maya, what happened?"

"My father had a 'talk' with York's commanding officer. I don't know what was said. I do know that from that day forward, York straightened his act out. He doesn't like women. At least, not military women pilots.'' Her nostrils quivered. She stood in front of them, her legs slightly apart for good balance and her arms crossed. "He was never fair with any of us. I challenged him. I called him what he was to his face. I'd like to have decked him.'' She balled her hand into a fist. "Just because we were women, he wanted to fail us.''

"But you didn't fail," Morgan said.

With a disgusted snort, Maya moved to her chair, her hands gripping the back of it as she stared malevolently down at him. "Only because I had my father's influence and help. Otherwise, he'd have canned every one of us." Maya jerked a thumb toward the windows where Machu Picchu's black lava sides rose upward. "And you know the funny thing? Every woman in that company volunteered to come down here with me and take this spec ops. They didn't like the odds, the army's obvious gender preference toward males getting all the good orders and bases, while the women got the dregs. Screw 'em. I said to hell with the whole army career ladder and came up with a plan for this base. My father backed it and I got it."

Maya's voice lowered with feeling. "I'm sure the army was glad to see all of us go away. Out of sight, out of mind. Well, that's okay with us, because we have a higher calling than the army. We couldn't care less about our career slots or getting the right bases and orders to advance. We love to fly. All any of us wanted was a chance to fly and do what we love the most. We're linchpins down here, holding the balance between the good people and the bad guys, and we know it. What we do makes a difference."

Morgan stood and placed his napkin on the table. "I'm sorry to hear how tough it was on you and your women friends, Maya. I'm sure the army realizes what assets you are. Your stats speak for themselves." He held her angry green gaze. "But York is the best. You have my personal promise that when he arrives, he will not be the same man you trained under before."

"I will *not* allow him to step foot on my base."

Morgan held her challenging stare. He heard the low, angry vibration in her tone. "You've got to learn to trust me, Maya," he said huskily. "I want only the best for your squadron. You've earned that right. If Major York steps out of line, you call me and I'll take care of it. I promise."

"I don't want him back in my life!"

Her explosion of anger and pain echoed around the room. "If you don't accept him as your I.P., you forfeit everything on those papers.'' Morgan pointed to the table where they lay.

Still glaring, Maya looked from him to the papers. She desperately needed those new D models. Her pilots deserved to have the safety the new copters would afford them. And she was dying without the necessary funds for spare parts for her old Apaches. Swallowing hard, she looked slowly back up at Trayhern.

''Very well,'' she rasped, ''authorize the bastard to come down here.''

Chapter 2

"**M**ajor York, if you don't want to be kicked out of the U.S. Army and asked to resign your commission, I suggest you take this temporary duty assignment."

Dane stood at attention in front of his superior's desk. "Yes, sir!"

"At ease," Colonel Ronald Davidson said, and gestured toward a chair that sat at one side of his huge maple desk. The winter sunshine of December moved through the venetian blinds and painted shadows throughout his large office. Was it an omen of things to come? Dane had a gut feeling it was.

Dressed in his one-piece, olive-green flight suit, Dane took the orders and sat down. Davidson's gray eyes were fixed on him and he knew why. Trying to choke down his fear, he tucked the garrison cap he'd been wearing into the left shoulder epaulet of his flight suit. He sat at attention. The tone in his C.O.'s voice made his heart beat harder. Dane knew he'd screwed up—again—with a woman Apache pilot in training to upgrade to the D model. Was this his death sentence? He tried to concentrate on the neatly typed set of orders before him. Reading rapidly, he felt a little relief began to bleed through him.

"Sir, this is TDY for six weeks down to Peru, to teach some spook ops pilots D model characteristics?" He tried to keep the surprise out of his voice. Dane thought the colonel had called him to this office to tell him to resign his commission because of his latest mistake. Obviously, he'd been wrong, and more of the tension leaked out of him. The last thing he'd expected was an assignment like this.

"That's right," Davidson informed him in a growl. Getting up, his body thin and ramrod straight, he tapped his fingertips lightly on the desk before him. "You'll see I've assigned two other I.P.s and three enlisted men to accompany you down there to train these pilots. You're to head it up—unless you don't want the assignment, Major."

Dane looked up. He got the gist of his commander's warning. Yesterday, Warrant Officer Kathy Juarez had filed a gender complaint against him. Dane had been warned it was coming. Swallowing against his constricted throat, he scowled down at the orders. He'd opened his big mouth without thinking first, and the words had flown out. Dane was trying very hard to think before he spoke after his lesson four years earlier with another student, Chief Warrant Officer Maya Stevenson, and the group of women going through training with her. He'd cleaned up his act quite a bit, but sometimes, when he was dog tired and stressed out from the heavy demands on his shoulders, he'd slip up. And he had.

Davidson was giving him one last chance to shape up. There was no choice and Dane knew it. He either took this TDY or Davidson was going to make sure that this most recent complaint from a female pilot was going in his jacket. And once it got in there, his career was over. He would be better off resigning and saving them the trouble of putting the complaint into his permanent military record. It would be a black mark that would follow him until the day he died, a stain he did not want on his record. The army was on a crusade to make itself genderless. Male and female no longer existed. Just bodies. Just human beings. Well, Dane was having real problems adjusting to that new perspective.

"Just to give you a little background on this spook ops group," Davidson continued in a milder tone, "it's been shifted to Perseus, a Q-clearance organization within the CIA family. They operate on a need-to-know-basis by only a handful of people within the government. Morgan Trayhern is the boss. He's asked the army for the *best* I.P.s we've got. The detachment known as Black Jaguar Base has twelve pilots who need upgrade training. The work they do down there is crucial to stemming the flow of cocaine from Peru into Bolivia. Because they cannot spare their people to come up here to Fort Rucker for training, you're going to go down there and train them, instead."

"I see, sir." Well, Dane really didn't, but that didn't matter, either. What mattered was that his C.O. was yanking him out of this messy and potentially embarrassing situation and tucking him quietly away. Out of sight, out of mind. And out of trouble, as far as he was concerned. Because of Dane's jaded past, Davidson, who was in his fifties, didn't particularly care for him, though he respected his abilities as a teacher and pilot. It was a good thing, for Dane knew his career would have been over with this latest charge set against him.

Not that he didn't deserve it. Warrant Officer Juarez was Hispanic, and he'd made the off-the-cuff remark that no South American could fly as well as a North American one. Stupid, yes, but he'd shot off his mouth to his new class of Apache pilots first without thinking about the consequences. And Davidson wasn't happy about it or he wouldn't be sending him away for a long time to let the situation cool down. Dane's ill-timed comment reflected directly back on the colonel, too. Davidson was protecting his own hind end in this. He was up for general's stars in another month. If this incident took off and the newspapers ran with it, Davidson's stars were down the toilet.

"Sounds interesting, sir." And it did. Dane had never been to South America, although he was born in Del Rio, Texas, a little border town, and grew up bilingual, even though they moved from base to base frequently.

"You're getting the assignment because you speak Spanish, Major," Davidson said heavily. "Everyone chosen is bilingual. This spook ops has Peruvian, and other South American pilots, as well as some on loan from overseas. Mr. Trayhern needed someone who could handle the different languages and get the job done. That is why you're getting this TDY." Davidson glared down at him. He picked up another paper. "And perhaps, while you're gone, Major, I can sweet-talk Warrant Officer Juarez into dropping her legitimate charge against you. I'm *sure* you won't make the same mistake twice, will you? After all, you're going to South America to find out just how good the pilots are down there."

Swallowing hard, Dane said, "Sir, I'll make sure it never happens again."

Scowling, Davidson glared at him. "You're old guard, Major. You're a lot younger than me, but you sound like the army back in World War II. Well, those days are gone and you'd better get with the new program of gender neutrality or your butt is history. You'd best make good on this mission, Major. I'm expecting a glowing report back from the C.O. of that ops about you and your men's white glove behavior. Do you read me loud and clear?"

"Yes, sir, I hear you." Dane stood up at attention beneath the man's drilling, cold look.

"Sit down."

Dane sat. He felt the C.O.'s anger avalanche him.

"I'll be damned lucky if this warrant officer doesn't go to the press with your remarks. Our women pilots are just as good—probably better—than our male pilots. They've distinguished themselves time and again, and you keep working against them. I don't know what your agenda is, Major, but on this TDY, you'd better stuff it and work with the people down there four square.''

''Yes, sir, I will.''

''You and your contingent are leaving tomorrow at 0800. You're taking a navy helicopter carrier down to Lima, Peru. The capital city sits right on prime beachfront property. You're also taking two D model Apaches and a Blackhawk with you. You've got three I.P.s, one for each aircraft. One of the three enlisted instructors will fly with each of you. The aircraft, once assembled inside the carrier when it arrives at Lima, will be flown off it and you'll rendezvous with elements of Black Jaguar at an agreed-upon time.''

''I see, sir.'' Dane felt a little excitement. He'd never been on spook ops before. His world revolved around teaching pilots about the deadly beauty of the Boeing Apache. He lived to fly. And he was a good teacher, to boot—at least with male pilots.

''We've got an agreement with the Peruvian government, Major. Once those D models are assembled and brought up to the deck of the carrier, you will fly them on specific coordinates that will be preprogrammed into the flight computers. You will not, under any circumstances, be carrying hot ordnance on board. The Peruvian government wants those three aircraft to leave under cover of darkness, just before dawn. They don't want any nosy newspaper reporters to get wind of us coming into their country or the president will have a *lot* of explaining to do.

''You will meet two Black Jaguar Apaches at a specific location deep in the mountains, far from the capital. They will then escort you to their base. As I understand it, it is dangerous where you will be flying. There is a drug lord, Faro Valentino, who has two Russian Kamov Ka-50's assault helicopters that ply the same area. If they see you, they're going to try and blow you out of the sky. It will be up to the

C.O. of the base and their Apaches to protect you and fly shotgun. They will be carrying hot ordnance on board, in case the Kamovs jump you. There's no guarantee they will. But the C.O. has informed us that you should expect attack. You need to review the terrain of the area and be ready to cut and run if that happens. You need to know where the hell you're going and what you're going to do to make sure these new D models aren't downed before they get to their new base.''

Frowning, Dane said, ''No hot ordnance for us in a dangerous situation? Isn't that stupid, sir?''

Davidson grimaced. ''Major, choose your words more carefully, will you? Didn't you just hear me? The Peruvian government will *not* allow you to bring these assault helos over their territory with missiles, bullets or rockets. What if you crash into homes and kill people? They're afraid that if the combat helicopters are seen, word will leak back to their press, and all hell will break loose. Having U.S. military aircraft flying in Peru is a political hot potato, anyway. We're stepping on eggs. There is no way to get where you're going, except by helicopter. The jungle where the drug lords produce their cocaine is wild, dangerous, country.''

''But they've got Apaches carrying ordnance.'' Dane tried to keep the irritation out of his voice. ''Why is it all right in one place in Peru, but not another? Why should I open up my crews to possible confrontation with a Kamov and get shot all to pieces?''

''We have a lot of political toes we just can't step on,'' Davidson said slowly, obviously at the limits of his patience with Dane. ''Once you get the D models to the base, you'll be able to train the pilots there. When everyone is up to speed, the D models will join the A models already there, and you can fly with hot ordnance.''

''So, we risk three helos and six people trying to get them to this jungle base?'' Dane frowned.

''You will have two Apache A's escorting you in, Major.

Just follow the C.O.'s instructions, and things should go well. But as mission commander on this TDY, you need to realize that if the Kamovs attack, you have to have a plan on outrunning and outmaneuvering them because they can outgun you. The only thing standing between you and them will be those two A models rigged for combat.''

Unhappily, Dane nodded. ''I see, sir.''

''Good.'' Davidson reached for a folder and handed it to him in a brisk manner. ''Here's more info. Take a look at it.''

Opening the file, Dane nearly choked. The color photo of the C.O. of the Black Jaguar Base stared back at him.

''Problems, Major?''

Heat shot up his neck and into his face. Dane tried to squelch a curse as he sat there, pinned in place by his C.O.'s gaze.

''Sir...'' he rasped, half standing, pointing at the photo in the file ''....this is impossible...this can't be.... I mean—''

''Captain Maya Stevenson is the C.O. of Black Jaguar Base, Major. And she's *your* commanding officer on this mission.''

No! Dane sat down, before his knees buckled beneath him, disbelief thrumming through him. Those cool, half-closed emerald eyes, eyes that reminded him of a jungle cat, stared back at him. Maya Stevenson was the biggest thorn he'd ever had in his side. She'd nearly scuttled his career so many years ago. After she'd graduated into the Apache A model, she'd quite literally disappeared. Not that Dane was unhappy about that. He wasn't. She was the in-your-face kind of woman who made him see red with great regularity. He didn't like her independence. Or her chutzpah. She'd call him out every time he said something wrong—or politically incorrect. There wasn't a day that went by when she was his student that they hadn't flared up and had words, angry words, with one another. Worse, she'd reported him and he'd damn near lost his status as an I.P., had been threatened with losing his army career.

Davidson moved quietly around the desk, trailing his fingers along the highly polished edge of it. All the while, his gaze remained on Dane.

"A word of warning, Major York," he whispered.

Dane looked up. "Sir?"

"Mr. Trayhern of Perseus, and myself, are all too aware of the dog-and-cat fight you got into with Captain Stevenson four years ago. If either of us hear a word from her that you or your crew are not being perfectly behaved down there, then things are really going to hit the fan. Big time. You will be training twelve women pilots, Major. And it's well known you don't get along well with women in the military. The crew you're taking down is going to behave just as you do. So I suggest you clean up your act, accept that women make just as good pilots as men, and get on with your teaching and training down there."

Dane stared down at the photo again, disbelief bolting through him. He felt as if he'd been struck by lightning. Maya was in a black, body-fitting flight suit. There were no insignias on the uniform, nothing to indicate her country of origin or that she was a pilot, much less in the U.S. Army. Her hair, as black as the uniform, was in a chignon at the nape of her slender neck. The look of pride in her raised chin, that confidence he'd always disliked about her, now radiated from the photo. He felt hot and sweaty—an adrenaline reaction. Davidson stood within a few feet of him, and Dane could feel his C.O.'s icy gaze drilling into his back as he looked at the photo.

"I feel like I'm being fed to the lions...sir."

Davidson chuckled. "Maybe you are, Major, but this is going to be your final test to see if you can achieve gender neutral status. You pass this test, and I'm sure your career will continue. If you don't, well...this is your last chance. Do you understand that?"

Bitterness flowed through Dane. He glared up at the colonel, whose gaze was unwavering. "I get the picture, sir. Frankly, this is a no-win situation."

"It doesn't have to be, Major, if you let your prejudice against women in the military dissipate. This can be a real turn-around mission for you. But it's up to you. If you want to keep your caveman mentality about women, that's your choice. Or you can see this as a golden opportunity to drop some old, archaic attitudes and embrace and support women in the military. They pay with their lives just like a man does. They deserve equal treatment and respect. It's that simple."

Sure it is. Dane clenched his teeth, his jaw tightening. *Great. Just great.* Not only would he have a woman C.O. lording over him, it was his nemesis, Maya Stevenson. And her father was still in the army and still a general. Dane felt hemmed in and no way out. Wiping his thinned mouth with the back of his hand, he closed the file abruptly.

"My secretary has everything you need for the trip south, Major. You're to meet your crew at 0800 tomorrow morning at base ops. You'll take a C-130 Hercules flight from here to San Diego. There, you'll board the *USS Gendarme,* one of our navy helicopter carriers. They've already got the two Boeing Apaches and the Blackhawks disassembled and on board. Questions?"

Dane stood. He came to attention. "No, sir."

"Very well, dismissed. Oh, and good luck, Major. I hear that Captain Stevenson has been giving a good account of herself and her women pilots down there. This just might be the eye-opening experience you need to convince you that women can do a job just as well as any man." Davidson's mouth lifted slightly. "And maybe better. But you go down there with an open mind and see for yourself."

"Looks like a right purty city," Chief Warrant Officer Joe Calhoun said in his soft Texas drawl as he stood, his hands resting on his hips. "Never been this far south before."

Dane stood next to the other instructor pilot on the deck of the navy helicopter carrier anchored off the coast near Lima. Because the carrier was so large, it could not go near the shallow coastline. A thick gray blanket of fog had lifted hours earlier, and the sparkling lights of Lima, the largest city and capital of Peru, blinked to welcome them.

"Looks are deceiving at night," he muttered. His stomach was in knots. The last week had been hell on him. Dane hadn't been looking forward to this moment. Below, the mechanics were giving a final check on the Boeing Apaches before they were lifted by elevator to the deck where they stood. Glancing at the watch on his hairy wrist, he saw that in an hour they would be taking off.

Although it was December, it was summer in the southern hemisphere. A slight, humid breeze wafted by them. Around them, navy sailors worked quietly and efficiently, preparing the deck for the forthcoming helicopters. Joe, a Chief Warrant Officer 3, and Craig Barton, a CWO4, were under his command, and would be flying the other two helos. Craig, who had experience flying Blackhawks as well as Apaches, would take the Blackhawk into the base.

"Wonder if the women are as beautiful as they say they are," Craig said, coming up to them and grinning.

Dane scowled. "This isn't a party trip, Mr. Barton."

"Hey," Craig murmured, "I'm only kidding. You've been uptight ever since we came on board, sir."

Warrant officers made up the ranks of most of the army's helicopter pilots. Dane had been a West Point graduate and gone into helicopters aviation as a full-fledged officer, so the other men were beneath him in rank. They stood halfway between enlisted personnel and officers such as himself. They were sharp people with fine skills and had shown their capability to fly these deadly machines. The warrants had a long and proud history.

Dane managed a one-cornered smile. "I'm worried about the Kamovs jumping us."

Joe snickered. "What's there to worry about? We got two Apaches to protect us if things get dicey. From what you said, those lady pilots have had plenty of practice shootin' at the bad guys, so I'm sure they can handle a little action, if need be."

Yeah, like a bunch of women were going to protect them. Dane kept the acid comment to himself. He didn't dare breathe a word of his prejudice to these two warrant officers. He'd worked with them for over a year and neither felt the prejudice against women that he did. Joe was half Commanche, born in Texas and twenty-six and Craig twenty-eight, both single, competitive, type A personalities. So was Dane, but he was twenty-nine and feeling like he was eighty right now. If only Maya Stevenson was not in this equation. Dane was still reeling from the shock of it all. Was she as mouthy and in-your-face as she'd been years ago? God, he hoped not. How was he going to keep his inflammatory words in his mouth?

"Well," Joe said in his Texas drawl, "I, for one, am gonna enjoy this little TDY. I mean, dudes, this is a man's dream come true—an all-ladies base." And he rubbed his large, square hands together, his teeth starkly white in the darkness on the deck of the ship.

Craig grinned. "Roger that." He was tall and lean, almost six feet five inches tall. And when he scrunched his frame into the cockpit of an Apache, Dane often wondered how the man could fly it at all. The cockpit of an Apache was small, the seat adjustable from about five feet three to six feet five inches. Being from Minnesota, from good Swedish stock, Craig was big-boned, even though he was lean. His nickname was Scarecrow. Dane liked his patient nature and softness with students. He was an excellent instructor.

Joe, who was a fellow Texan, was an exceptional instructor because he became so impassioned about the Apache helicopter and passing on that excitement to the trainees. Joe lived, ate and breathed the Apache. Maybe because he was half-Commanche he spoke Apache in his sleep—and made the bachelor officer quarters shake and shudder with his ungodly snoring. Grinning in the darkness, Dane admitted to himself that he had good people around him, and maybe, just maybe, that would make the difference on this nasty little TDY.

The other three crewmen, all sergeants, were experts in the new software, the ordnance and the handling of the 'doughnut' or radar dome that was on the D model Apaches. Those three men, Barry Hartford, Alphonse 'Fonzie' Gianni and Luke Ingmar, would teach the women crew chiefs and mechanics at the base the fine points of the new model. They were all married, so Dane had less to worry about in that respect. However, judging from Joe's gray eyes and the sparkling look of a hunter in Craig's brown ones, Dane would have his hands full with these two lone wolves running around loose in the sheep's pen.

"Well, let's turn and burn," Craig said, as he lifted his hand and started for the hatch that led down to the deck where the helicopters were being prepared.

"Roger that," Joe seconded, following quickly on his heels.

Dane stood alone. He *felt* alone. Watching the last of the fog disperse, he saw the twinkling of stars above him. It struck him that he was seeing the Southern Cross for the first time in his life. It was as famous here as the Big Dipper was in the Northern Hemisphere. Snorting softly, he hung his head and looked down at the highly polished flight boots he wore with his one-piece flight uniform. Alone. Yes, he'd been alone for a long, long time. Ever since his mother had abruptly left him and his father, he'd felt this gnawing ache in his gut and heart. His brows drew downward as memories assailed him. His mother was a red-haired, green-eyed, vital woman who had exuded a confidence he rarely saw in females. She'd had enough of being a "housewife" and had made an ultimatum to his military pilot father to either let her work outside the home or face a divorce.

Only twelve at the time, Dane recalled the fear he'd felt when he'd heard them arguing hotly one night in the living room after he'd gone to bed. His father's shouting had awakened him. Dane had lain on his belly at the top of the stairs, head pressed to the wood, hands wrapped around the banister, as she began screaming back at Dane's father just as loudly. She was tall, athletic, brainy, and had no fear of speaking her mind—ever.

"Damn…" Dane forced himself to look up…up at the Southern Cross, which glimmered like diamond droplets against an ebony sky being edged with the first hint of dawn. His mother had left. She'd tried to explain it to Dane, but at twelve, the message he got was that he wasn't lovable enough for her to stay and be his mother. And from that day onward, he'd felt alone. Well, at twenty-nine, he still felt that way, and nothing would probably ever change it. Or the way he felt about his mother. When he was eighteen, about to graduate from high school and enter West Point, she'd left him forever. His mother had been coming to his graduation, driving from San Antonio, Texas, where she'd settled, and a drunk driver had careened into her car and killed her. Dane would never forget that day. Ever.

He heard the whirring of the elevators that would soon bring the Apaches and the Blackhawk to the deck where he stood. Moving his shoulders as if to rid them of an accumulated weight, Dane turned. As he did so, he saw a bright trail streak across the sky toward the east, where they would be flying shortly. It was a meteorite.

Dane didn't believe in omens. He believed only in what his eyes saw, his hands felt and his ears heard. Scowling deeply, he turned on his heel. *Screw it all.* Did the meteorite foretell of his demise? Would it be because of his mouth? His feelings about women? Or were they going to be jumped by Kamovs? Or left at the mercy of a bunch of renegade

Amazon women warriors who thought they knew how to fight?

"Be my luck that it's the latter," Dane grumbled as he jerked open the hatch door and went below to his fate.

"It's time, Maya...." Dallas Klein poked her head through the opened door of her commanding officer's office. Dallas, who was the executive officer for the base operations, raised her dark brown brows as she looked across the wooden floor at Maya's pitiful excuse for a work area—a dark green metal, military issue desk that was battered from years of use. Maya was pouring over several maps spread across it, her face intense, her hand on her chin as she studied them.

"What? Oh...." Maya looked up. She nodded to Dallas. Glancing down at the watch on her left wrist, she blew a breath of air in consternation. "Yeah, it's time all right."

Dallas moved inside the office and shut the door. She was dressed in the uniform of the day—a black, body-fitting Nomex fire retardent flight suit. Her black flight boots gleamed in the fluorescent light from a fixture above the desk. Running her fingers briskly through her short sable hair, she met Maya's gaze. "Did you sleep at all?"

"What do you think?" Maya grimaced, then straightened and opened her arms, stretching languidly like a large cat. "I've got the nightmare from hell visiting us for six weeks. I couldn't catch a wink." Maya quickly wrapped her loose ebony hair into a chignon at the nape of her neck placing a thick rubber band around her tresses to keep them in place.

"Hmm."

"You aren't upset about York coming?" Maya took her knee board, which she used to write things down if she needed it, and strapped it to her right thigh with Velcro. She reached into a glass sitting on her desk and took out several pens, placing them in the left upper sleeve of her uniform.

"Upset? Yeah. Lose sleep over the guy? Not a chance." She grinned·wolfishly.

"You Israelis are one tough lot," Maya grumped. "Has Penny got the coffee on in the mess hall? I desperately need a cup before we take off."

"Yeah, everyone's up and around," Dallas murmured as she opened the door for her C.O. "*Edgy* is the word I'd use...."

Maya grinned tiredly. "Edgy? As in on edge dancing on the edge of a sword? No kidding. Come on, I need my intravenous of java before we blow this joint and meet our male comrades in arms."

Chuckling, Dallas, who at five foot eleven inches was almost as tall as her C.O., followed Maya down the dimly lit hall of the two-story building. Their headquarters sat deep in a cave, well hidden from any prying eyes that might try and find the complex. Maya grabbed her helmet on the way, stuffed her black Nomex gloves into it and then picked up her chicken plate, which was the name for the bullet proof vest they each wore when they flew a mission. Though they were normally called flak jackets, the army slang name was more commonly used.

Maya moved rapidly down the stairs rapidly and out the door. If not for the lights hung far above them on the cave's ceiling, finding their way out of the place would be impossible. Familiar sounds—the clink of tools, the low murmurs of women's voices from the maintenance area—soothed Maya's fractious nervousness. She felt wired—and suspected it was because she would have to meet her worst enemy today.

"You're jumpy," Dallas observed, coming up and matching her long stride. "You sensing something?"

With an explosive laugh, Maya said, "Oh, yeah. Trouble with a capital *T* in the form of Major Dane York. How's that for a mouthful, Klein?"

Chuckling, Dallas opened the door to the Quonset hut structure that housed the mess hall and kitchen facility.

"Mmm, it's more than that. You usually get this way when you smell Kamovs around."

As Maya made her way into the small mess hall which was lined with a series of long picnic tables made of metal and wood, she saw that about half of her crews were up and eating an early breakfast. She called to them, lifting her hand in greeting, and then picked up a metal tray to go through the chow line. The flight crews had been up and working for several hours. There was ordnance to load on the Apaches, fuel to be put on board and a massive amount of software to be checked out to ensure it was working properly before any pilot sat in the cockpit. Today, Maya wanted a full array of Hellfire missiles on the underbelly of each Apache, rockets as well as a good stash of 30-millimeter bullets on board.

Penny, a red-haired army sergeant with lively blue eyes who was the head chef for their base stood behind the line, spoon in hand.

"'Morning, ma'am," she greeted Maya as she heaped dark orange, fluffy scrambled eggs onto her tray.

"'Morning, Penny. You got any of your famous cinnamon rolls?" Maya lifted her nose and sniffed. "I can smell 'em. Any left?"

Penny blushed a bright pink. "Yes, ma'am. I managed to save a couple for you and Ms. Klein." Penny turned to retrieve the rolls, revealing how the white apron she wore over her green fatigues hung to her knees due to her short stature. Sometimes, when she moved too quickly, the apron would become tangled around her short legs and nearly trip her.

"So you didn't let the condors eat them all," Maya said, pleased. She watched as Penny opened the oven and drew out two big cinnamon rolls slathered with white frosting.

"Oh, we've got a buncha buzzards here, no doubt, ma'am," Penny laughed. She placed a roll on each officer's tray. "But I know they're your favorite, so I told my crew to keep their hands off them, threatening that they'd lose their fingers if anyone stole 'em."

Maya grinned. "Thanks, Penny. We appreciate your being a watchdog." Maya poured some coffee from the tall steel canister into a white ceramic mug and then went over to an empty table. She wanted time to talk to Dallas alone before the flight. Every time she thought of Dane York, her gut tightened. And yet there *was* something else troubling her. Maya couldn't shake the feeling…the premonition that Kamovs were around and hunting them. Sometimes they did. Sometimes Faro Valentino, a very rich Colombian drug lord, who had money to burn and could buy the latest in Russian weaponry and aircraft, would deliberately try and hunt them down to kill them. Most of the time he was making cocaine runs over their jungle and mountains. But sometimes…he turned the tables on them. Sometimes the hunted became the hunter. Was today the day?

Dallas sat down opposite her. "You've got that look in your eyes," she said as she eagerly dove into the scrambled eggs. They had Penny to thank for the fresh eggs. A farm girl from Iowa she had long ago bought a bunch of hens in Aqua Caliente, and built them a chicken coop. Penny had her "girls" laying eggs for the entire squadron. Everyone appreciated farm-fresh eggs. They had a much better taste than any store-bought variety, which were sterile in comparison, Dallas thought. Maya always urged her women to be creative, to make this base more a home than a military warehouse. Little touches like Penny's made staying here survivable. Since Lieutenant Ana Luca Contina had married Jake Travers, and Jake had come to stay with her at the base, he had created a huge vegetable garden that yielded wonderful lettuce salads and other hard-to-get items. Jake also took care of supply and Maya was grateful for the ex-Army Ranger's presence on their base. While Ana flew missions, Jake took care of things on the ground. Everyone, including Maya, was happy with the arrangement.

"What look is that?" Even though Maya was far from hungry, she knew today's flight required her to be alert, and that meant feeding her body. Brain cells needed food to work, and in her business of flying the deadly Apache assault aircraft, she needed every iota of intelligence to stay on top of things.

Dallas sipped her coffee after putting a dry creamer into it. "That 'we're gonna get jumped by Kamovs' look."

"Oh."

Dallas set the cup down. "You always have a sixth sense for this stuff. Are you too exhausted to be in touch with it this morning?"

Having known Dallas for the three years that they'd been at the base, Maya trusted the Israeli pilot with her life. On loan to them from her country, Dallas was a tough, no-nonsense warrior who had many times saved Maya's butt when they'd come up against the Black Sharks that would hide and jump them. And Dallas knew her better than anyone at the base. As executive officer—X.O.—she had almost as much responsibility for this base operating as Maya did. And Dallas was someone she could blow off steam to without it getting around. Giving her a narrowed look, she muttered, "Okay, I have a feeling."

Lips curving ruefully, Dallas said lightly, "Couldn't be that Black Jaguar Clan stuff you're connected with?"

Maya didn't often talk about her spiritual heritage or training. Dallas knew more than most, but Maya's affiliation with the Clan wasn't for public consumption. Over the years, Maya's intrepid and loyal pilots and crews had learned there was something "different" about her, but not *what* was different. Of course, Maya didn't have anywhere near the metaphysical talents her sister, Inca, did. No, the only thing she was good at, when in the right space, was teleportation. And in her line of business, Maya was rarely in the right space to use that talent because it required her to be in perfect harmony within herself in order to initiate it. Nope, on any given day, she was painfully human like everyone else. The other talent she had was intuition. She'd get these "feelings" and when she did, she was rarely wrong.

Maya realized Dallas was patiently looking at her with those golden eyes.

"Okay…I got a bad feeling. I think Faro is going to turn the tables on us again. He's going to be the hunter and us the hunted today. Satisfied?"

Pursing her full lips, Dallas said, "Yep, I am. I'm gonna tell my copilot to play heads up then, more than usual. Damn, I wish we could get a radar signature off them."

Maya nodded in agreement. The Russian helicopter was able to somehow dodge their massive radar array and capabilities. Because it could, the Kamov had the ability to sneak up on them and blow them out of the sky—literally. That meant Maya and her pilots had to stay even more alert than usual. They were fighting one of the most deadly helicopter opponents in the world. Their own sensor equipment was useless against the Kamov unless it showed itself, which wasn't often. The mercenary Russian pilots Faro Valentino hired were hardened veterans of many campaigns and knew the ropes of stealth and combat—just like Maya's crew did.

Each Apache had two HUDS, or heads-up displays—small, television-like screens—in each of its two cockpits. Maya's pilots could use IR—or infrared—a television camera or radar. The HUDs had saved the lives of Maya's crew innumerable times, as well as helped them find the heat of bodies beneath the jungle canopy so they could stop drug runners in their tracks as they carried heavy loads of cocaine toward the Bolivian border. In the sky, the Apache's ability to find its target was legendary. Except the Kamovs had their own arsenal of commensurate hardware, and on any given day, a Kamov could jump one of their Apaches without warning. That was when Maya used her sixth sense to the optimum. She'd not lost a helo crew yet, and she wasn't about to start now.

Maya pulled the warm cinnamon roll apart with her long, spare fingers. "This is one of those days I'd just as soon tell the Cosmos I pass on this mission, you know? That's okay, you don't have to answer on the grounds it may incriminate you, Klein.'' She grinned and popped a piece of the soft, sweet bread into her mouth.

''Well,'' Dallas said with a sly look, ''I'm glad I'm not in your boots today, Captain. Whatta choice—Kamovs or Major Dane York.''

''Humph, with our luck, we'll get hit with both.''

Chuckling, Dallas finished her coffee. ''Yeah, that's what I call Black Jaguar luck at its finest.''

That was true, and Maya nodded as she chewed on the roll. ''If we didn't have bad luck, we wouldn't have any at all.''

Dallas's eyes gleamed with laughter. ''And if I'm reading you right, you'd rather face Faro's Kamovs today than York.''

''Bingo.''

''Damned if you do and damned if you don't.'' Dallas rose, picked up her empty tray and said, ''Meet you out on the apron. Time to turn and burn.''

Maya sat there, feeling glum. The soft sounds of women talking and laughing made her feel a little better. The mess hall was always a happy meeting place for her and her hard-working crews. They pulled twelve hours on and twelve off when Faro and his Kamovs decided to take to the sky and make run after run of cocaine to the Bolivian border.

Rubbing her neck ruefully, Maya grimaced. Today was going to be one helluva day, and she wasn't looking forward to any of it.

Chapter 3

Just the act of climbing up the metal rungs that doubled as a ladder, and then onto the black metal fuselage before ducking into the front cockpit of the Boeing Apache, soothed some of Maya's initial anxiousness. Dawn had yet to break in the east. The cockpit canopy opened on the left side, folding upward and back so that both pilots could climb into their respective positions at once. The crew chief was Sergeant Elena Macedo from Peru. Maya could hear her copilot and gunner, Chief Warrant Officer 2 Jessica Merril, settling into her position directly behind her. Jessica hailed from California. Her nickname was Wild Woman. Though she was twenty-six, she had the look of an impish pixie, her blond hair dyed with streaks of red. The splashes of color were Jess's way of donning warpaint and going off to battle, in a sense. Everyone's got a big bang out of Wild Woman's wild "do." She more than symbolized the highly individualized rebel attitude of the base. Maya liked it and approved of it.

The Apache was a big, ugly looking dog with a bulbous nose that housed the infrared, television and radar equipment.

The cockpits rose upward on a metal frame, the front cockpit Plexiglas hardened to take a 30 mm cannon hit as well as bird strikes. The seat felt welcoming to Maya, the space narrow, with the cyclic positioned between her legs, the collective by her left, gloved hand. Between her and her copilot was a blast shield; in case they took a hit and one pilot was killed or wounded, the other would be protected so they could fly the chopper home.

Settling the helmet on her head, Maya lifted her hand and twirled it in a clockwise motion, signaling the ground crew to start up the Apache. The first thing that came on in the assault gunship was the air conditioning, designed to cool the miles of circuitry that were bundled along the sides of the prehistoric-looking craft beneath the black metal fuselage. The blast of air from the ducts in the front panel, along with the high-pitched whine of the air conditioning cranking up, surrounded Maya. She watched all the instruments in front of her start to blink and flicker on. The two HUD's came to life, glowing a pleasant green color that was easy on the eyes and didn't contribute to night blindness. She pressed some buttons, making sure the related systems were operational. Positioning the mouthpiece within an inch of her lips, she tested communications with her copilot.

"Wild Woman, how are you reading me?"

"Loud and clear, Captain."

"Roger."

Looking up, Maya saw the constant wisps of clouds that embraced the ten-thousand foot inactive volcano where their base was located. The two Apaches faced outward, having been pushed into position from beneath the cave's overhang by the crews earlier. The lip of lava extended out a good four hundred feet in front of them and made an excellent landing and takeoff spot for the birds. Squinting above the cockpit console, Maya noted the lava wall that rose directly in front of them a thousand feet high, like a big rock curtain. The only way in and out of this cave complex was through the "eye of the needle," as they called it.

The eye of the needle was a natural geologic wonder—a hole in the lava wall sixty feet high and eighty feet wide, just large enough for an Apache or Cobra to move very carefully through it. The rotor diameter on an Apache was forty-eight feet, so they had very little clearance at any time.

Clouds also helped hide the base from prying eyes. Far below them flowed the mighty Urubamba River, a continual source of moisture rising upward in the tropical heat. As this humid air rolled up the mountainside, it met and mixed with cooler, descending air—exactly where the cave and their base was located, creating a fog that was nearly constant all year-round.

This morning was no exception. They would be required to lift off and fly out on instruments and radar in order to thread the Eye squarely and not take off a chunk of their titanium-edged rotor blades, risking a crash. The operation wasn't for fools or anyone not paying attention to her flying. After logging three hundred miles on a mission, the pilots were often tired coming back, and this obstacle became even more dangerous in their exhausted state.

Glancing down, Maya positioned her chicken plate, the bulletproof vest across her chest and abdomen, so that it rode as comfortably as possible. The radio in her helmet crackled to life.

"Black Jaguar one, this is Two. You read me?" It was Dallas Klein's whiskey-smooth voice.

"Roger, Black Jaguar Two. Read you loud and clear."

"Looks like we got split pea soup out there as usual, Saber."

Maya smiled as she hooked up her harness. Saber was her nickname, given to her upon graduation from army basic aviation school, when she'd gotten her wings. Everyone got a nickname. She'd earned hers because her company said she was like a fine-bladed army ceremonial sword, slicing through any situation with finality. The name Saber had stuck. Maya liked living up to it. "Roger that, Dallas. Nothing new. The boys comin' up from Lima oughta be real impressed if this stuff hangs around the Eye like it usually does," she chuckled darkly. She made sure the knee board on her right thigh was adjusted, in case she needed to jot anything down.

Continuing her checks, Maya felt her left thigh pocket to make sure that her sister's medicine necklace was in there. Inca had given her the protective necklace soon after they'd met, and Maya always kept it on her during a mission. She couldn't wear jewlery, so she tucked it into a side pocket. It felt warm and secure in there and she gave it a pat of affection. In a way, it reminded Maya that now she had a sister to come home to, and to be careful out there in the skies over Peru.

Chuckling, Dallas said, "Oh, I'm sure they're gonna be *real* impressed, anyway."

"We'll see just how tough the good ole boys from Fort Rucker are when they encounter the Eye. I'd give my right arm to see the looks on their faces when they approach it."

"They've been given prior info on it, right?" Wild Woman interjected from the rear cockpit.

Maya nodded. She was ready. They were ready. Excitement thrummed through her. "Roger that, Jess. But looking at it on paper and seeing it in person, and knowing your forty-eight-foot blade has no room for error, despite the winds that are always whipping up from the river, is gonna make it real interesting for those boys."

Laughter filled Maya's earphones. She grinned mirthlessly. Yes, she'd like to see York's face when he came up against the Eye wrapped in thick clouds that were subject to the whim of the winds in this mountainous region. He'd learn to respect Eye real fast. Maya could hardly wait until they returned and she saw the two new Apaches thread it. There

wasn't a pilot around that didn't approach it slowly and with
a lot of trepidation.

The crew chief moved toward the ladder. "You're ready
to go, Captain," she said, and snapped a salute to the two
pilots.

Maya snapped off an answering salute. "Thank you, Sergeant Macedo."

Macedo then brought down both canopies and locked them
into position, making the cabin of each cockpit secure.

Maya rested her gloved hands in plain sight of the crew
below. Until everyone was clear, Maya would not start the
massive engines of the helo or endanger her ground crew. As
the three of them stepped away, their faces shadowed by the
low lighting provided by a nearby generator, Maya lifted her
hand and twirled her index finger in a circular motion, which
meant she was going to start engines.

"Let's get down to work," she told Wild Woman, her
voice turning businesslike. Maya flipped the first switch,
which would engage the engine on the starboard, or right
side of the fuselage. Instantly, a high whine and shudder
worked through the aircraft. Eyes narrowing, Maya watched
the engine indicator leap like active thermometers, bobbing
up and down. When the engine was activated to a certain
level, she thumbed the second engine switch. The gunship
was awakening. In some sense Maya always thought of it as
an ugly and ungainly looking thing. The image of a Tyran-
nosaurus rex came to mind: king of the dinosaurs and a mean
bastard who ruled its turf—just like the Apache did. She
could feel the sleek shudder that ran through it as the gunship
gained power.

To Maya, her helicopter was a living being consisting of
metal, wire circuitry, software and engine parts. She found
her own power in that machinery. Whatever nervousness
she'd felt about the coming encounter with Major Dane York
was soothed away. When she was in the cockpit, the world

and all its troubles dissolved. Her love of flying, of handling this remarkable machine, took over completely.

As the engine indicators leveled out, Maya engaged the main rotor. The four blades began to turn in a counterclockwise motion, slowly at first, then faster and faster as she notched up the power with the cyclic grasped in her fingers. Her entire left forearm rested comfortably on a panel so that her hand wouldn't cramp up and the cyclic became a natural extension of her hand.

"Jess, switch on the radar. I need to thread the needle here in a moment."

"Right... We're up...go for it...."

Maya saw the full sweep of a bright green set of lines on the right HUD. It looked like a slice of pie as the long, green needle of radar swept ceaselessly back and forth, clearly revealing the hole in the wall directly in front of them, despite the cloud cover beyond.

"Let's go over our checklist," Maya ordered.

"Roger," Jess returned, and they began to move through a sequence they had memorized long ago. Maya reached for her knee board, systematically checking off each station as it was called out. There was no room for sloppiness in her squadron. Things were done by the book. It improved their chances of survival.

They were ready. Maya devoured the excitement still throbbing through her. The Apache shook around her, the noise muted to a great degree by her helmet. She tested the yaw pedals beneath her booted feet. Everything was functioning properly. Proud of her hardworking ground crews, Maya lifted her hand to them in farewell as they moved back to watch the two assault helicopters take off, one at a time, to thread the needle.

"Black Jaguar Two. You ready to rock 'n' roll?" Maya asked.

Dallas chuckled indulgently. "Roger that, Saber. My girl

is checked out and we're ready to boogie on down the road
with you. I want to dance on a Black Shark's head today.''

"Roger. Let's go meet those good ole boys from Fort
Rucker first, shall we? They might have the new D models,
but us girls have got the guns.''

Chuckling, Dallas said, "I don't think Gunslinger is ready
for us.''

Gunslinger was Dane York's nickname, Maya remembered
starkly. He was an aggressive, type A individual who lived
to hunt and kill in the air. Of course, so did anyone who got
assigned to Apaches. They were a breed apart, bloodhounds
in the sky, looking for quarry. Grinning, Maya notched up
to takeoff speed and gently lifted the fully armed Apache off
the lava lip. Smoothly, she nudged the helo forward into the
swirling clouds. Within moments, they were completely embraced by the thick moisture.

"On glide path," Jess called out.

Maya flew by instruments only. Her eyes were narrowed
on the HUD, watching the swiftly moving radar that whipped
back and forth on the screen to create a picture of the approaching Eye. The winds were erratic at this time of the
morning, because when the sun rose, the land heated up and
made air currents unpredictable—and dangerous. Raindrops
splattered across the windshield of her aircraft, falling from
clouds which carried moisture from the humid jungle below.
The Apache eased forward, closer and closer to the opening
in the lava wall.

"On glide path…"

Compressing her lips, Maya tensed a little, as always. The
aircraft was within twenty feet of the Eye. Right now, the
wrong wind current, the wrong move with her hands or feet,
would crash them into the wall. *Easy…easy…* She moved
the aircraft smoothly through the hole and out over the jungle
far below. They were at eight thousand feet now, and Maya
eased away from the cliff to allow Dallas's aircraft to exit in
turn.

"Switching to radar to hunt for the bad guys," Jess called.

"Roger." Maya looked up briefly. She could see nothing but the thick, white mists all around them. It was dark and the Apaches ran with no lights on them. Their instruments were all they had. "Keep a lookout for Kamovs. I got a bad feeling on this one, Jess."

"I thought you might. Scanning beginning now..."

Of course, Maya knew that even with their advanced radar, Kamovs had a certain type of paint on their fuselage that absorbed the Apache's radar signal, so that what little pinged back to the instruments on board was negligible, and therefore unreadable. A Kamov could spot them in fog like this, providing the cloud cover wasn't too thick, and nail them. Plus, their radar could send out a strong signal through thinner clouds and get an equally strong returning signal back from its target. Right now, they were sitting ducks and Maya knew it.

"We're out, Saber," Dallas said.

"Roger," Maya replied. "Let's split up, make less of a target of ourselves. Leave a mile between us and head for the meeting point. Keep your eyes and ears open, ladies."

"Roger that," Dallas said.

Inching up the throttles, Maya felt the Apache growl more deeply as it rose higher and higher. She wanted out of this cloud cover, to get on top of it so her 360-degree radar could detect and protect them from any lurking intruders. The Apache felt good around her. It was sleek and smooth compared to many other helicopters she'd flown. With a full load of ordnance on board, she felt the lethal power of it as well. At a flick of a switch on her collective, the stick between her legs, she could send a fiery hell to earth in a matter of moments.

As they rose to nine thousand feet, they suddenly popped out of the cloud cover. Above, Maya saw the familiar sight of the Southern Cross. She smiled a little at the peaceful looking stars as they glimmered across the ebony arc above them. And yet here they were in a cat-and-mouse game with killers who'd just as soon see them dead as alive. The incongruity of it all struck her.

The helicopter dipped its nose forward as Maya poured in more power, and they swiftly moved along the top of the ever-moving clouds.

"Beautiful out tonight," Wild Woman murmured as she scanned her instruments carefully.

"Yeah, it is," Maya said. "I was just thinking how peaceful it looks up there, above us. And how Faro Valentino probably has his Russian merc pilots in their Kamovs hunting for us right now."

"Ain't life a dichotomy?" Jess chuckled.

Scowling, Maya kept moving her head from side to side and looking above her—"rubbernecking," a term coined by World War II pilots. The Black Sharks were deadly hunters in their own right. When the Soviet Union broke up, Faro Valentino had marched in with his millions, purchased two state-of-the-art Kamovs and hired a cadre of out-of-work Soviet pilots, who liked being paid big bucks to fly cocaine in South America. The pilots were considered mercenaries for hire. And Faro had his pick of the best, waving his drug money under their noses.

Grimly, Maya kept switching her gaze from her instruments to the space around them. Somewhere off to her left was Dallas and the other Apache. Because the gunships were painted black, she could not see them at all. And because of their stealth duties, they ran without outboard lights.

"This time of morning there should be no other aircraft around," Maya said to Jess.

"Roger that. The civilians are still tucked in their beds, sleeping in Cuzco."

Chuckling, Maya returned to her duties. She could fly the Apache blind; she knew each movement and each sensation of this stalwart warrior they flew in. The Apache was a killing machine that responded to the most delicate touch. And had a heart that beat strongly within her. The soothing vibration of the engines moved throughout Maya's body, and to her, it was like a mother holding a child and rocking it; it gave her that sense of completeness and wholeness. The Apache was one of the most marvelous inventions of the air, as far as she was concerned. It had been built by Boeing to protect the pilots, first and foremost, and secondly, to become a sky hunter that had no equal. And it did. The Kamov's ability to sneak up on them was the one Achilles heel of this magnificent machine. And because of the type of flying they did, it was a constant threat. The Russian mercenary pilots were the cream of the crop, and they were hunters just like Maya. They lived to fly, hunt and kill. There was no difference between her and these pilots except that they were on the wrong side of the law, in Maya's eyes. Greed ran those pilots. Morals ran her and her people.

Beneath them, Maya knew, there was thick, continuous jungle. She and her teammates had to constantly fly among precipitous peaks covered in greenery. Most of the mountains were at least ten thousand feet high, some higher. Whatever the altitude, flying was not easy and required intense concentration in order not to crash into one of the unseen obstacles. The radar kept the shapes, elevation and height of the mountains on the HUD in front of Maya so that she could fly around them accordingly.

"Hey, look at that red stripe on the eastern horizon," Jess called out. "Bummer."

Dawn was coming. Maya scanned the bloodred horizon.

"Think it's a sign of things to come?" Jess asked.

Maya took the natural world around her seriously. Maybe it was her background with the Jaguar Clan. Or her innate Indian heritage. It didn't matter. There were signs all around them, all the time. The trick was in reading them correctly. "Damn," she muttered.

"Black Jaguar One, this is Two. Over."

Flicking down the button on the collective, Maya answered, "This is Black Jaguar One. Over."

"See the horizon?"

Mouth quirking, Maya glared at the crimson ribbon. "Yeah, I see it."

"Not a good sign. Over."

"No. Keep your eyes peeled, ladies. I'm betting on more company than was originally invited."

"Roger. Out."

Jess chuckled. "Wouldn't those good ole boys from Fort Rucker die laughing if they heard us looking at a red horizon as a sign of a coming Kamov attack?"

Maya knew that there would be radio silence maintained between them and the new Apaches and Blackhawk coming in to meet them. Only once they met would they all switch to another radio frequency to speak for the first time. Ruthlessly grinning, she said, "Yeah, they're gonna pee in their pants when they start flying with us in those new D models. It will shake up their well-ordered little male world."

Laughing, Jess said, "Speaking of which…here they come. Got three blips on radar and…" she peered closely at her HUD "…yep, it's them. It's showing two Apaches, and a Blackhawk bringing up the rear. What do you know? They can navigate."

Maya laughed. It broke the tension in her cockpit. "Well, we'll give them an A for meeting us at the right time and place. Let's just loiter here until they arrive."

Placing the Apache in a hover at nine thousand feet, Maya watched her HUD with interest. The radar clearly showed the three aircraft speeding toward them. The lead one was flown by Dane York, no doubt. Her mouth compressed. Maya held on to the anger that she still had toward him. Every woman pilot at her base had had the misfortune of being under his training command. That was why, when the idea for this base came about, they had all left with Maya. They wanted no part of the continuing prejudice they knew would be thrown at them. At least down here they were graded on their abilities, not their sex.

The crimson ribbon on the horizon was expanding minute by minute, staining the retreating blackness of the starlit sky and chasing it away like a gaping, bleeding wound. Maya kept looking around. She could feel the Kamovs lurking somewhere near…but where? All she needed was to have three unarmed gunships jumped by fully loaded Kamov Black Sharks, with only two Apaches standing between them. Her mind raced. If the Kamovs were near, just waiting for the right moment to jump them, she wondered how they had found out the meeting location in the first place? Was there a leak in intelligence? How could Faro Valentino have gotten hold of this information? Maya frowned. Her gaze moved ceaselessly now. Her gut was tightening. She smelled Kamovs. *Where? Dammit, where?*

"Black Jaguar One, this is Rocky One. Do you read? Over?"

Maya instantly flinched. It was Dane York's deep, controlling voice rolling in over the headset inside her helmet. Her heart leaped at that moment, beating hard. With fear. Old fear that she had felt at the school so many years ago. Anger quickly snuffed out her reaction. Thumbing the cyclic, she answered, "Rocky One, this is Black Jaguar One. Welcome to our turf." She grinned recklessly because she wanted to let him know from the get-go that he was on *her* turf, *her* base and under *her* command.

There was a brief silence. Then he answered, "Roger, Black Jaguar One. What are your instructions? Over."

Her eyes slitted as she saw the three aircraft coming out of the fleeing darkness. They were all painted the mandatory black, with absolutely no insignias on them. Her lips lifted away from her teeth and she said, "We're worried about Kamovs jumping us. No sign of them yet, but we feel them out there. You know the routine if we're jumped? Over."

"Roger, Black Jaguar One. How do you know there're Kamovs around?"

It was just like York to question her. Maya rolled her eyes. "Major, just accept it as a reality. Over."

"Roger, Black Jaguar One. We know the routine in case we are attacked. Over."

"Roger." At that point Maya, gave them the heading for the base. "Stay above the cloud cover. We'll be flying about a mile on either side of you. Over."

"Roger."

"He hasn't changed one bit," Dallas said over their private frequency. "Maybe you oughta tell him you looked into your crystal ball this morning before you got into the Apache, Maya. Tell him you saw Kamovs in your future." And she giggled.

Maya didn't think it was funny at all. Already York was trying to assert control over her by questioning her authority and ability. "No, I'd rather tell him the truth—that we've got a red sunrise and that means Kamovs are hunting us. Think he'd buy that instead?" Maya heard the other three women laughing hysterically in her headset. The laughter broke the tension among them. They knew from three years of experience that red sunrises were an ominous sign.

The light of day shone dully across the sky. Off to Maya's left, she saw the three new aircraft flying in a loose formation, staying far enough apart that they couldn't be hit as a unit by a missile and destroyed. At least York was smart enough not to fly in a tight formation—she'd give him that. Maya could barely make out Dallas's aircraft, positioned a mile on the other side of the group. They had an hour to go before they reached the base. And an hour would feel like a lifetime when she knew the Kamovs were up and hunting them.

"Break, break!" Dallas called. "We've got a visual on a Kamov at eleven o'clock!"

Instantly, Maya thumbed the radio. "Rocky One, hightail it out of here. We've got company. Over."

"Roger. Over and out."

Maya sucked in a breath and cursed as she saw the long shape of the Black Shark with its coaxial rotors coming down out of the sky toward the fleeing aircraft.

"Damn! Come on, Jess, let's get with it!" She punched fuel into the Apache engines. The aircraft instantly responded, the motors deepening in sound as they flew toward the attacking Kamov, which was trying to get a bead on one of the escaping U.S. aircraft. Right now, Maya thought, York was probably pissing in his pants over this. He was a combat pilot in a combat aircraft with no ammunition. Nada. And he was probably hotter than a two-dollar pistol about it. She didn't blame him.

"Whoa!" Jess yelled. "Another Kamov at nine o'clock, starboard!"

That was two of them. Maya thumbed the radio. "Dallas, I'll take the one at nine. You take the one at eleven. Over."

"Roger, you got it. Out." Dallas's voice was tight with tension.

Maya banked the screaming Apache to the right. She spotted the sleek Russian machine trying to go after the escaping Blackhawk below it. The U.S. aircraft had scattered in three different directions like birds that had been shot at. The Blackhawk had dropped quickly in altitude and was making for the cloud cover. The only problem was that once the Blackhawk entered the clouds, the pilot would have to go on instrumentation in an area he didn't know, while being pursued by a Kamov pilot who knew this territory like the back of his hand.

"Damn," Maya whispered. She sent the Apache into a steep dive. The machine screamed and cranked out, the beating pulsations of the rotors thumping through her tense body. Gripping the controls, Maya grimaced, her lips lifting away from her clenched teeth.

"Put a rocket on 'em, Jess."

"Roger. I got a fix!"

"Fire when ready."

They were arcing at a steep, banking dive toward the Kamov, which was closing in on the slower Blackhawk. Maya knew the shot would be wide. She hoped it would be close enough to scare off the Kamov. Or at least make him turn and pick on them instead of an unarmed helicopter.

"Fire!" Jess cried.

There was a flash of light from the starboard wing where the rocket launched. Maya followed the trail of the speeding weapon as it careened toward the Kamov.

"Fire two more!"

"Roger. One sec...firing now!"

Two more rockets left the pod on the right wing of the Apache.

Maya watched as all three streaked toward the Kamov. Satisfaction rose in her as the first one dived in front of its nose. The pilot had seemed so intent on pursuing the Blackhawk that he wasn't aware of them—until now. The problem with the Kamov was that it was a single seater, and the pilot not only had to fly the damn thing, but work all the instruments, as well. That led to attention overload, and Maya was betting the pilot had been so engaged in downing the Blackhawk that he hadn't had time to check who else might be around.

The Kamov suddenly banked sharply to the left. The other two rockets flew harmlessly past it.

Good. Maya sucked air between her teeth as she pushed the diving Apache to the left now, to follow the fleeing Kamov. In her headset, she could hear Dallas and her copilot talking excitedly back and forth to one another as they engaged the other Kamov. It sounded like they had everything under control.

"We're going after this son of a bitch," Maya muttered to Jess. "Hang on."

The Kamov pilot knew it. In a split second, the gunship suddenly moved skyward in an awesome display of power and agility. It was trying to do an inside loop over Maya's Apache so that it would come down behind her "six" or the rear of her machine and put a rocket into her. The Kamov turned a bloodred color as it arced high into the dawn sky, the twin blades a blur as it rose swiftly and then turned over. Maya knew that few helicopter pilots in the world could accomplish an inside loop. But she was one of them. Gripping the controls, she pushed the power on the Apache to the redline. The engines howled. The machine shuddered like a frothing monster, chasing after its quarry. It shot up well above where the Kamov was making its own maneuver. With a deft twist of her hands and feet, Maya brought the Apache into a tight inside loop. All the while she kept her eyes pinned on the Kamov below her.

Within seconds, the Apache was shrieking into a somersault, the pressure pounding against her body. Breathing hard, Maya felt the sweat coursing down the sides of her face beneath her helmet. The Apache was handling well, the gravity rising as she kept the loop tight.

"I'm going to make that bastard's day," she said through gritted teeth. Snapping the Apache out of the loop, she ended up behind the Kamov.

"Jess?" It wasn't truly a question; it was an order. Her copilot knew what to do: arm a missile and fire at the Kamov.

"I'm on it. Firing one, two…"

Eyes gleaming, Maya watched as rockets on either side of the Apache lit up and sped off toward the Kamov, which was now diving for the cloud cover. They were wild shots, but Maya wanted to let the pilot know that she'd pursue him. It was a ruse, of course, because her first duty was to the three unarmed helicopters.

The Kamov dove into the clouds and raced away. The rockets missed their intended target because of the Kamov's rapid response.

"I think he's gone," Jess said, studying the radar.

Maya blew out a breath of air. Looking above her, she rapidly climbed to gain altitude.

"Black Jaguar Two. What's your status? Over."

Dallas came on moments later, her voice tight. "Black Jaguar One, we just routed the second Kamov. He's heading back north. And you? Over."

"Same here. Let's catch up with our unarmed children. Over."

Dallas's laugh was tense and explosive. "Yeah, roger that, One. Out."

Turning the Apache back toward base, Maya didn't for a moment think that the game with the Kamovs was over, but she kept a sharp lookout as they flew homewards. Adrenaline was making her feel shaky now. It was a common reaction after combat. Wiping her face, Maya saw that the bloodred ribbon along the horizon had turned a deep pink color. Now it looked more beautiful than deadly.

"You think our boys peed their pants yet, Captain?"

Maya chuckled over Jess's comment. "Well, if they haven't, they probably thought about it."

"Helluva welcome to the killing fields," Dallas intoned.

"Yeah, well, it will put them on warning that this is a hot area and they can expect this anytime, day or night."

"Probably killed York to have to run. You know how aggressive he is in the air," Dallas said.

Maya laughed fully. "He probably feels like a coward about now. And gee, he had to leave it to four women to protect his behind. *That* is probably eating at him more than anything."

Jess giggled. "Can you imagine his horror that he's still alive and flying and that we didn't drop the ball?"

"Yeah, what's he gonna do," Dallas said, "when he has to stare us in the face and admit we saved his bacon?"

The laughter felt good to Maya. She knew the letdown after a tense combat situation was necessary. Fortunately, they could talk on a private channel between the two Apaches, so that no one else could pick up their banter. She was sure York would have a hemorrhage if he'd heard them just now. No, it was going to be fun to watch the good ole boys from Fort Rucker get a look-see at the Eye of the Needle. It was going to be even more enjoyable to watch them sweat their way through it for the first time. That made any pilot, no matter how experienced, tense up big time.

"Well, ladies, let's go home and see these guys pucker up."

The laughter was raucous.

Chapter 4

Dane York was nervous as he stood aside, watching the all-women crews hurriedly move the three new helicopters into the maw of the huge cave. His heart was still pounding in his chest from barely squeaking through that damned entrance they called the Eye. His other pilots and crew members stood off to one side on the rough rock surface of the lip of the cave, out of the way, tense looks on their faces. Only one person had welcomed them, a woman with short red hair who introduced herself as Chief Warrant Officer Lynn Crown before hurriedly running off to direct the crews as to the placement of the new gunships.

As the clouds around the high lava wall thinned, Dane gazed at the Eye. He heard the approaching Apaches on the other side of it. Wiping his mouth with the back of his hand, he settled his garrison cap on his head and waited. As the morning sun burned off some of the thicker clouds he could see the entrance better. Shaking his head, Dane realized just how tight that aperture really was. How many times a day did Maya fly her Apaches in and out of that thing? What a helluva "needle" to try and thread. Dane wondered how anyone, man or woman, could muster enough brain power and concentration after an exhausting mission to slip through it without nicking the blades of their Apache on the unforgiving lava walls. His admiration for Maya's pilots rose.

Joe and Craig moved to his side. They all watched as another woman, dressed in an olive-green T-shirt and fatigues, trotted out with red-orange flare sticks in her hands and stood at attention opposite the Eye. One of the Apaches was coming through. The crewmember raised her hands above her head to direct the helicopter into a landing spot once it flew through the opening. Dane's eyes narrowed as he watched. Though he and his men had crawled through, literally, this first Apache came through like the pilot was on a Sunday drive!

"I'll be go-to-hell," Joe gasped in amazement. "That's some purty flying. Will ya look at that? Whoever the pilot is, she just flew through that opening like it wasn't there!"

"No kidding," Craig muttered, scowling.

Dane said nothing, his mouth flattening. The first Apache landed opposite where they stood, on the other side of the massive lava lip. Bruising waves of air buffeted them, kicked up by the rotor blast as the gunship landed. The lip was at least four hundred feet wide and about one-quarter of a mile long, from his estimates. The maw of the gigantic cave was simply mindboggling. Inside the shadowy space, crews were running at full tilt as they positioned the three new helicopters in the maintenance area.

The second Apache flew through smoothly in turn, as if the Eye weren't there, either. It landed so close to the first one that Dane held his breath momentarily. The punctuation of the rotors pounded the entire area; the wall across the cave opening acted like an echo chamber of huge proportions, until his eardrums hurt from the reverberations. Wind kicked up by the rotor blades slammed like a boxer's gloves against his body. Still, as Dane watched the two crews hurry toward the Apaches that had just landed, he was critical of everything.

He didn't think Maya Stevenson could run a squadron. However, from the way the crews worked in almost balletlike precision, that prejudice was blown away, too. As the engines were shut down, the high, ear-piercing whine echoing from the wall began to lessen. The rotors began to slow, and finally came to a stop. Instantly, one crew woman ducked beneath the nose of the first Apache and hooked up the device used to pull it inside. He watched as the left-sided canopies were opened to allow the two pilots from each helicopter to exit.

Morning sunlight shot through the Eye in gold streamers that lit up the murky depths of the cave. Dane ignored the surprised murmurs of his I.P.'s, his gaze fastened ruthlessly upon the two flight crews. Maya Stevenson would be there. His heart squeezed a little in anticipation. What was she like now? Even more sure and confident? More mouthy? He scowled. Why did he have to hold such a grudge against her? If the truth be known, and it wasn't something he liked to think about often, from the first time he'd met Maya he'd been powerfully drawn to her. But once he'd come up against her willful nature, he'd instantly rejected the primal attraction.

The wisps of clouds thinned. He saw fragments of the constantly moving mist weave through the Eye, then dissipate beneath the rays of equatorial sunlight that was growing stronger by the minute. Dane saw the legs of the returning women pilots as they gathered close to one another behind the carriage of the last Apache. They were probably talking over their fight with the Kamovs. That would be typical of any group of pilots, male or female. Impatience thrummed through him. He wanted to see her. As repelled as he was by the assignment, there was something in him that ached to see Maya once again. That surprised Dane more than anything else. How could he miss someone who had been such a thorn in his side? Challenging him? Confronting him daily as she'd done at school?

The crews hurriedly took the two Apaches farther into the cave, where they would be unseen from the air. When they'd slowly rolled by, Dane saw the four women pilots, helmets tucked beneath their arms, standing in a circle, talking animatedly. One of them, to his surprise, was a blond with red streaks through her hair. What kind of base did Maya run that she'd let one of her pilots look like that?

The women were all heights and body builds, but it was easy to pick out Maya, because at six foot tall, she stood above all of them. The body-hugging black flight suits they wore had no insignias on them. They were long-sleeved despite the heat and humidity. He knew the suits were styled that way because in the event of a fire in the cockpit, the Nomex material would protect them against burns. He saw that Maya wore knee-high, polished black boots, while the others had on regulation flight boots that fit snugly up to their ankles. Maya looked every inch an Amazon warrior—formidable in her own right.

The drift of women's laughter made him tense. And then he saw Maya lift her head and look directly at him. Dane felt a heated prickle at the base of his neck—a warning—as her eyes settled flatly on him. He was the tallest in his own group, so he would be just as easy to spot as she was. Unconsciously, Dane wrapped his arms across his chest as he locked onto her gaze. At this distance, he couldn't make out her expression. He could feel the coming confrontation, however. And he saw that a number of crew women were casting furtive looks as if to see when, not if, a fight might break out. The tension was thick. Even he could feel it. Joe and Craig moved restlessly, sensing his unease.

Mouth going dry, Dane watched as the women pilots broke from their huddle and walked toward them. Maya strode with her chin up, her black, hair flowing across her proud shoulders, the black helmet beneath her left arm. The other three pilots walked slightly behind her, in a caliper formation. They looked like proud, confident, fierce warriors even though they were women. As they passed through the bright shafts of sunlight, now shining strongly though the Eye, he watched the golden radiance embrace them.

For a moment, Dane thought there was even more light around them. He blinked. Was he seeing things? He must be rattled from being chased by the Kamovs and then having to get through that hole in the wall to land here in the cave. Mouth compressing, he watched as Maya closed the distance between them. There was nothing wasted in her movements. She was tall, graceful and balanced. The chicken plate she wore on her tall, strong body hid most of her attributes. Locking into Maya's assessing emerald green gaze, he rocked internally from the power of her formidable presence.

She was even more stunning than he could recall. In the four years since she'd left the school where he'd been her I.P., she had grown and matured. Her black hair shone with reddish tones as the sunlight embraced her stalwart form. Her skin was a golden color, her cheekbones high, that set of glorious, large green eyes framed with thick, black, arching brows. But it was the slight play of a smile, one corner of her full lips cocked upward, and that slightly dimpled chin and clean jawline, that made him feel momentarily shaky.

The high humidity made her ebony hair curl slightly around her face, neck and shoulders. Still, she could have been a model strutting her elegant beauty down a Paris runway instead of the proficient Apache helicopter pilot she was. The snug-fitting flight suit displayed every inch of her statuesque form. She was big boned and had a lot of firm muscles beneath that material, but there wasn't an ounce of fat anywhere on her that he could see. She seemed all legs, and slightly short waisted as a result. All Thoroughbred. All woman—a powerful, confident woman such as Dane had never known before now. With the sunlight radiating behind her as she walked toward him, she looked more ethereal than real.

Blinking a couple of times, Dane looked down at the rough black lava cave floor, then snapped his gaze back to her. The corner of her mouth was still cocked. He saw silent laughter in her large green eyes, and he felt his palms becoming sweaty. His heart raced as she closed the gap between them. He felt like they were two consummate warriors, wary and distrustful and circling one another to try and see the chinks in each other's armor, their Achilles heel, so that one of them might get the upper hand, and be victorious.

Maya felt laughter bubbling up her long, slender throat as she approached York's group. The expressions on their faces made her exuberant. All but York had an awed look as they stared open-mouthed at her and her pilots. The men didn't look angry or challenging. No, they looked all right to her. But Dane York was another matter. Her gaze snapped back to him. Her heart thumped hard in her chest. Her hand tightened momentarily around the black helmet she carried.

He looked older. And more mature. In Maya's eyes, he'd always been a very handsome man, in a rugged sort of way. He had a square face, a stubborn chin that brooked no argument, a long, finely sculpted nose, eyebrows that slashed straight across the forehead, shading his large, intelligent blue eyes. Eyes that used to cut her to ribbons with just one withering look. Well, that was the past. Maya locked fully on to York's challenging, icy gaze. He stood with his arms across his chest, his feet spread apart like a boxer ready to take a coming blow. His full lips had thinned into a single line. Those dark brown eyebrows were bunched into a disapproving scowl. There was nothing friendly or compromising about York. His hair was cut military short, a couple of strands out of place along his wrinkled brow. The dark olive green flight suit outlined his taut body. At six feet tall, he had the broadest set of shoulders Maya had ever seen. York was a man who could carry a lot of loads before he broke.

And that stubborn chin shouted of his inability to change quickly. Flexible he wasn't.

Maya came to a halt. So did her women pilots, who created one solid, unbroken line in front of the contingent of men. She snapped off a crisp salute to him.

York returned her salute.

"Welcome to Black Jaguar Base, Major York."

Dane saw the gleam of laughter lurking in Maya's eyes as she stood toe-to-toe with him. He admired her chutzpah. Maya knew how to get into a man's space real fast. She knew she was tall and powerful. Confidence radiated from her like the sun that had embraced her seconds earlier.

"Thank you, Captain Stevenson. I can't say the welcome was what we'd anticipated." Dane decided to keep things professional between them at all costs. He saw the glint in Maya's eyes deepen. Her lips curled upward—just a little. Her husky voice was pleasant and unruffled.

"Get used to it. Around here, we're on alert twenty-four hours a day, seven days a week."

He nodded and dropped into an at-ease position, his hands behind his back. "The report didn't say that." Maya stood easily, her booted feet slightly apart. The other women pilots were looking his crew over with critical eyes. He felt as if they were all bugs under a microscope.

"The report," Maya said crisply, "was meant to be brief and to the point. My X.O., Lieutenant Klein, here—" she motioned toward Dallas, who stood at her right shoulder "—did warn you of possible altercations with druggies once you entered our airspace. And it happened, unfortunately."

Dane held back a retort. "If you'll get someone to show my men to their quarters and where we can set up our schooling facility, I'd appreciate it, Captain."

All business. Okay, that was fine with Maya. It was better than York taking verbal potshots at her pilots. Turning to Dallas, she said, "Take them to their quarters. Feed them.

And then have Sergeant Paredes take them to our Quonset hut, where we've set up shop for them to teach.''

''Yes, ma'am.'' Dallas smiled hugely at the cluster of men in green flight suits. ''Gentlemen? If you'll follow me, I'll give you a quick tour of our base and get you some quarters.''

York didn't move as his men left with Dallas. He remained rigidly where he stood. Maya frowned.

''Aren't you going with them?''

''We need to talk, Captain. Somewhere private. Your office, perhaps?''

Smiling suddenly, Maya got it. Okay, York was going to have it out with her in private. *Fine.* She turned to her other pilots. ''Let's call it a day, ladies. You all have reports to fill out, plus your collateral duty assignments. Wild Woman, see to it that the crews refuel the Apaches and let's get them on standby. Any problems, see me.''

Jess came to attention. ''Yes, ma'am!'' And she turned on her heel and hurried into the cave with the other copilot at her side.

Turning her head, Maya looked at Dane, the ice between them obvious. The sunlight was suddenly shut out as a thick, cloud slid silently over the Eye. ''Well, Major? You ready?'' Her voice was a dangerous rasp, a warning that if he thought she was an easy target in private, he was mistaken. She saw York's eyes widened momentarily and then become slits. Maya felt him harness his anger.

''Ready whenever you are, Captain,'' he said coolly.

Turning, she moved into the cave's murky depths. Within moments, York was at her shoulder, matching her stride, his profile grim and set. Maya could feel the tension within him. As they walked into the maw, the lights overhead illuminated the way, giving the cave a grayish cast with heavy shadows.

''Let me give you a quick idea of our layout, Major,'' she said, gesturing to the right. ''Over there is our HQ. My office and all other collateral offices are located in that two-story building. Just ahead of us is the maintenance area for the helicopters. As soon as they land, we get them inside. Faro Valentino always has his Kamovs snooping around. Luckily, we've got that lava wall between the cave entrance and the jungle out there. Otherwise, I'm sure he'd have come in here a long time ago and tried to use his rockets or missiles on us. The wall prevents that from happening.''

York looked back at the landing area. "It's a perfect, nat-ural defense position," he murmured, awe in his tone. "How thick is that rock?''

"Thick enough to stop radar from getting through it." Maya grinned wickedly as she gestured toward it. "We got lucky with this place. On the other side of this inactive vol-cano is an old mining operation and a shaft that connects us to it. There's no way Faro and his pilots can get access to us. Of course, if we were stupid and left our helicopters out on the landing lip, they might drop a bomb or two, but we don't give them that kind of an opportunity.''

Dane looked around. He felt a little of the tension ease between them. Seeing the sudden pride and excitement in Maya's eyes as she talked about her squadron facilities was refreshing to him. So far, she hadn't lobbed any verbal gre-nades at him. He was waiting, though. There was too much bad blood between them, and he knew she hadn't forgotten a thing he'd said or done to her back in flight school. The depths of her emerald eyes were very readable. Or maybe she was deliberately letting him see her myriad emotions.

"I'm going to look forward to checking out your facility, Captain. Seeing it on paper doesn't do it justice. Seeing it in person…well, frankly, it's overwhelming. Who would ever think you could get a base like this inside a mountain?''

"It took a year for Navy Seabees and a lot of helicopter flights to bring in everything you see here." Maya stopped at the door to the two-story metal building. She took off her gloves and stuffed them into the right thigh pocket of her flight uniform. A number of electric golf carts whizzed around the buildings, coming and going in ceaseless activity. They were the workhorses of the facility.

"And you were here that first year?" Dane found it hard to believe.

She straightened and placed her long, spare fingers over the doorknob, her movements full of grace, like a cat's. "Of course."

He heard the sting in her husky tone. She opened the door and he followed. They climbed quickly up the metal stairs. Looking around, Dane was once more impressed. There was fluorescent lighting in the ivory-painted hallway. The highly polished white tile floor made it even brighter. He saw a number of doors to offices as they walked by—every one of them open. Women dressed in army-green T-shirts and fatigues were busy inside. There were computer monitors, telephones on the desks—just like any other busy squadron HQ. Only this one was situated inside a cave in a mountain. Blown away by the facility, he felt his respect for Maya inch upward.

"In here," she said, and stood aside, gesturing for him to enter the open office.

Dane scowled. "You leave your office door open like this all the time?"

She heard the censure in his tone. "Why not? Who's going to come in here and steal top secret info? One of my people?" She laughed.

"Still," Dane said stubbornly, "it's not a good policy."

Snorting, Maya followed him into the office. She turned and shut the door. The tension between them was there again. Placing her helmet on a nearby table, she shrugged out of her chicken plate and hung it up on a wall hook. Ruffling her hair with her fingers, she moved around her metal desk, which looked like a disaster had hit it, and went to the coffee-maker sitting on a makeshift table behind it.

"Want some coffee?" she asked, without turning around.

Pouring the thick, black brew into a chipped white mug, Maya set it on her desk.

"Yes…I need something to calm my nerves after that attack." Dane stood expectantly behind Maya as she reached for a second white mug and filled it.

Grinning, Maya turned and handed the mug to him. "Cream and sugar are here if you want it." The instant their fingertips touched, Maya wanted to jerk her hand away, but she countered the urge. Smoothly handing the cup to him, she took a seat in her old, creaking chair and leaned back in it, her own mug between her hands.

Dane sipped the coffee. Wrinkling his nose, he muttered, "This is strong."

"So? Around here you have to be or you don't make the grade, Major."

He saw the laughter in her eyes again. There was a thoughtful look on her face. How had Maya grown even more beautiful in four years? Dane sat down on the chair located at one side of her desk. The office was small and cramped. On the wall he saw her flight graduation diplomas. There was a color photo of her father, the general, on her desk, along with another of her silver-haired mother. There was a third photo, of a woman who looked strikingly like Maya and was dressed in a dark green, sleeveless T-shirt, a leather thong with two claws hanging between her breasts. Dane hadn't known Maya had a twin sister.

Family was important to Maya, he realized, even out here in the middle of a godforsaken jungle. He also noticed several spikes of orchids, red with yellow lips, on one edge of her desk—a woman's touch. Color to make the ivory walls and dark metal desk seem less masculine, he supposed. On another wall was a pair of crossed U.S. Army ceremonial swords. He recalled that her nickname was Saber, and he smiled to himself. The swords were a nonverbal reminder of who and what she was.

"That hole you fly through out there is a corker," he muttered as he sipped the coffee.

Chuckling darkly, Maya said, "Yeah, it's an added pucker factor, no doubt." She saw his mouth soften slightly over her joke. One corner lifted. Just barely. Maybe old sourpuss York wasn't going to bust her chops, after all. She remained on guard, however, because he was like a sniping bulldog that would come out of left field and attack her verbally when she least expected it.

"You two flew through it like it was nothing. We inched toward the entrance and then inched our way through. I'm impressed with your ability in such tight quarters."

Maya grinned fully. The cup of coffee felt good in her hands. She wanted to relax a little, but she didn't dare. She felt like raw, exposed nerves with him around. Right now, York's face was losing some of its tension; his broad brow was less wrinkled and the creases around his mouth less deep. But she didn't dare trust that the ease between them would last. "They don't teach that in school, do they?"

She saw him frown.

"We call it threading the Eye of the Needle. If you hear the word, *Eye,* that's what we're referring to. And yes, it's a dangerous maneuver."

"If those clouds are too thick," Dane said, "how can your radar penetrate enough to show you where the entrance is?"

Shrugging, Maya murmured, "We wait until the clouds thin out. My orders to my pilots are not to attempt it if the radar can't scan the opening fully."

"I'm impressed."

"With what? The Eye?"

"No…you. What you've set up here. It's a pretty remarkable facility from what I've seen so far."

Maya didn't let his compliment go too her heart or her head. She saw York struggling to remain distant and polite with her. Well, she was struggling to maintain a professional attitude, too. At least he was trying.

"What's remarkable," Maya told him with seriousness, "is that this is an all-woman operation. It was from the git-go. We have the best flight crews in the world. My pilots can outfly anyone, anywhere and at any time."

Dane opened his mouth and then shut it. The pride in her eyes and in her impassioned, husky voice was unmistakable. "Flying down here would certainly give you skills that most of our other Apache pilots don't have."

"Yeah, there's a real difference between live fire and Ka-movs hunting you, and going out to the practice range to shoot at wooden targets that can't shoot back." She laughed derisively.

Dane sipped his coffee. He bit back another acid comment. She was right. Dead right. The glittering look in her eyes excited him. Maya was a hunter of the first order. Like he was.

"I know I'm stuck here for six weeks teaching, but I'd sure as hell like a shot at that Kamov that was chasing me."

"Stuck here?" Maya's voice dripped sarcasm. "Is that how you feel, Major? That you're 'stuck' here with us?"

Damn! Dane closed his eyes momentarily. He'd done it already. He'd spoken before he'd carefully thought over his reply. Opening his hand, he muttered, "Poor choice of words, Captain. My men and I were looking forward to the assignment."

Snorting, Maya stood up, cup in her hands. She glared down at him. "You haven't changed at all, Major. You're just a little smoother around the edges about it, is all. Aren't you?"

Struggling to control his own anger, Dane met her cool, assessing green eyes. His skin prickled beneath her righteous annoyance. "Look, Captain Stevenson, I'm not here to fight with you. We're here to help you fight an enemy, an obviously powerful one. You've got a war going on down here. I wasn't aware of that. Or at least, not the magnitude of it."

Would she believe him? Judging by the way she lifted her chin to an imperious angle, she didn't. At all.

"Let me make one thing *very* clear to you, York." Maya dropped all pretense of military formality. She saw the shock in his eyes over her deliberate use of his last name only. Ordinarily he, as a major, had rank and privilege over her. But not down here. And not ever, as far as she was concerned. "We have a lot of bad history between us. Most of my flight crews don't know about you, and about your reputation of verbally denigrating women who are in the military. Just the women pilots who trained with you at Fort Rucker." Her voice softened, a grating edge to it as she set the mug down and walked slowly around the desk.

"My pilots risk their lives day in and day out. I have only twelve of them. Three fly combat missions every day or night, on a twenty-four-hour duty. Three are on standby at the ready shack. And the other three get a day off that's really not a day off at all. We're shorthanded around here. I've got fifty-four people and that's it. Everyone works twelve-hour shifts, seven days a week. The demands, the responsibilities, are high enough to choke a horse. And every one of those women out there would give her heart, body and soul to me if I asked for it. We operate under wartime conditions at *all* times. There isn't an hour that goes by that my people aren't busting their tails and risking their lives getting necessary things done around here to keep those birds flying."

Her voice lowered to a snarl. "And if you so dare say something like you're 'stuck' here to them, to their faces, I'll be throwing you on board our Apache and sending your butt out of here so fast it'll make even your seasoned head swim." She jabbed her finger into his upturned face. His eyes were nearly colorless and she knew from past experience they only got that way when he was angry. Maya remembered all too well those huge, black pupils set in a pale blue background glaring back at her when she confronted him at the school when he was out of line. "You even *hint* of prejudice toward my pilots or crews and you're out of here. Is that understood?''

Smarting, Dane rose. Maya stood a few feet away, her cheeks flushed, her eyes narrowed with fury, her voice trembling with emotion.

''Why don't you let our past go? That would help one helluva lot,'' he said.

Jerking her chin up, Maya glared at him. ''You started this, I didn't. I'm more than willing to let our past go. But our mutual history is alive and well now, York, from what I can tell. I won't tolerate a *breath* of prejudice from you.''

He controlled his anger. Dane knew her dressing down was warranted. He had no one to blame for his foot-in-mouth this time but himself. Maya had been pleasant with him up to that point. Formal, but at least not angry or nasty like she was being right now. His anger at himself warred with the words he'd had from his colonel; if Maya called his C.O., Dane's career would be over. Looking around, he took some deep breaths to try and settle his frustration.

''Look,'' he rasped, ''let's start all over. All right?'' He held out his hand toward her in a gesture of peace. ''I promise you that my crew is not like me.''

''Thank God.''

''They're just the opposite. They've been looking forward to this assignment.''

''Unlike you.''

Mouth compressing, Dane glared at her. ''You're not going to give me an inch, are you?''

''Not a chance, York. I won't let you think of hurting my people. I know you. My pilots suffered under you just like I did. We have a long, collective memory. And you're the one on the edge of the sword, not us, this time.'' Her nostrils quivered. Tension swirled between them.

''I promise not to allow my mouth to get in the way of any instruction with your pilots and crews.'' Dane held her blazing green eyes. "Is that enough? I'm sorry. Deeply sorry. Or do you want a pound of my flesh, while you're at it?"

Her fury subsided. She sensed York's honest attempt to lessen the tension between them. "You don't have *anything* I want, York. All I expect from you toward my people is *respect*. And if you haven't realized it already, they've more than earned anything you or your men can give them. Like I said, we're on a wartime footing down here. You boys from Fort Rucker 'play' at war, but we're in it up to our hocks every day." Blowing a breath of air between her lips, Maya moved away from him. Why did York have to be such a bastard? And yet, although she hated to admit it, she was powerfully drawn to the army officer. She had to be loco!

Dane waited until her voice ebbed away in the small, cramped room. "You already have our respect," he told her quietly. "I admit I didn't think women could be warriors...but I'm being proved wrong."

Maya walked around her desk and sat down. "You were wrong four years ago, too."

Wincing, Dane set the cup on the edge of her desk. "I think we understand each other, Captain. I'd like to be dismissed so I can get to my men, check out the training facility and get on with why we're down here."

Four years ago, Maya knew, York would not have been so amenable. He'd ridden her ruthlessly and without letting up. Staring at him, she saw that he struggled to be humble in front of her. That must be a new emotion for him—humbleness. He was arrogant before. Maybe he *had* changed.

"Dismissed, Major."

The weariness in her tone told him she wasn't going to forgive or forget. As he walked to the door, he heard her call out to him. "One last thing, Major."

He turned. "Yes?" Maya was studying him like a jaguar might its quarry. Her full lips were compressed with disappointment.

"You got a problem with anything or anyone around my

squadron, you see me about it *first*. Don't talk behind my back, don't manipulate, gossip or think of doing an end run on me and my command here. Got it?''

There was nothing soft about Maya Stevenson, yet he saw the sadness in her eyes, as if she, too, yearned for a truce as badly as he did. Dane placed his hand on the doorknob. He recalled Maya when she'd first come to his school. She'd been fresh, excited, bright and impassioned. Had he snuffed out all those attributes, and was this the result of his handiwork? A no-nonsense woman who could be as brutal as any man in command could be? Well, he had no one to thank for her stance toward him but himself.

''Yes, I've got it,'' he replied in a deep, dispirited tone.

Maya felt very old and tired. She saw real apology in Dane's eyes and it shook her. The old Dane York would never have admitted fault or apologized, even if he was wrong. ''Leave the door open on your way out, Major York. My people have access to me twenty-four hours a day. When you get a schedule set up, bring it to me and I'll look it over. My pilots must continue to fly every day, so you're going to have to work around their duties.''

''I understand.'' Despondency blanketed Dane as he opened the door, turned and walked down the hall. He wanted to say something more to heal the wound he'd just opened up in her. *Damn.*

A number of women looked up as he passed by. He saw the quizzical expressions on their faces. Had they heard the free-for-all in Maya's office? More than likely. This building was not that substantial; was made mostly of corrugated tin and some steel framing to hold it together. Voices would travel well in this complex, he realized glumly.

Maya sat down dejectedly after York left. She leaned back in her chair, gripping the arms and looking up at the ceiling. Her heart was pounding madly in her chest. She wanted to hate York, but that wasn't the main emotion she was feeling. A part of her felt sorry for him. And she wanted to cry. Deep down inside her, Maya had been hoping for a truce between them. She wanted peace, not war. Her life was nothing but combat, and she yearned for peace with him.

Four years ago, Maya had wanted to slug Dane in his arrogant face. Today, just now, she wanted to see some kind of improvement in York's demeanor. And to give him credit, he was trying. That little slip about being stuck here wasn't much, but it had set her off. Judging from the contriteness in his eyes and voice, he was really sorry about it.

"Maybe—" Maya whispered "—maybe you've changed just enough to make this nightmare six weeks tolerable, York. I sure hope so...."

Chapter 5

Maya couldn't wait any longer. She dropped the pen on her desk amid a clutter of papers that desperately needed her attention. She *had* to go down and take a good, close look at the D model Apaches. Glancing at the clock on the wall, she realized it had only been two hours since she'd locked horns with York. Grabbing her black baseball hat off the peg, she settled it on her head and moved out into the hall. Things were curiously quiet. Why? Maya glanced into each office; no one was around. Where was everyone? This was highly unusual.

On the ground floor, Maya pushed opened the door. To her left, the opening to the cave was filled with brilliant sunlight lancing in from the Eye and above the wall as the sun crept higher in the sky. The new D models and the Blackhawk had been brought into the cave complex, at the opposite end from where maintenance was performed on their Apaches. Moving around the end of the building, she grinned and halted. Dropping her hands on her hips, Maya chuckled to herself.

There, surrounding the new helicopters, was nearly the entire squadron. Everyone spoke in excited, animated tones as they looked at the machines, touched them. Her pilots were mingling with the ground crews, and she saw how the new I.P.'s were passionately engaged in conversation, gesturing toward the new D craft, their faces alight with enthusiasm. Some of the worry slid off Maya's shoulders when she saw that the two I.P.s were like little boys with a new toy—only the new toy was a leaner, meaner version of the A model Apaches Maya and her crew flew daily.

Her brows fell. Where was York? She searched the crowd for him. Over fifty people were gathered in a large circle around one chopper. One of the I.P.s, the Texan, squatted near the side of the fuselage, gesturing to all the snakelike coils of wire beneath the panels he held up, proudly showing the insides to the rapt crowd of onlookers.

Maya's heart thumped hard when she spotted York. Her hands settled on her hips as she lifted her chin and laughed softly. Dane York was on his back, on the cave floor, beneath the 30 mm cannon that was suspended beneath the fuselage just below the first cockpit of the D model. Several of her crew chiefs were down on their hands and knees, peering up as he pointed out various parts of the long-nosed machine gun. She watched with interest, close enough to see his expression, but not enough to hear his voice. His square face was alight with enthusiasm. Why, he was even smiling! That caught Maya off guard. York was smiling. What a difference! In flight school at Fort Rucker, he'd never smiled. Not once. She saw Sergeant Nuria Sedano, a Peruvian mechanic, laughing at something he'd said. Another crew chief, Sergeant Lucinda Huisa, was scrunched down on her hands and knees, her eyes narrowed intently, as York continued to extol the changes on this newest model.

"Miracles do happen," Maya muttered. She remained where she was. It was good to see her squadron so enthusiastic about the new helicopters. The other I.P., CWO4 Craig

Barton, was sitting on the lip of the Blackhawk with his own crowd of interested admirers, pointing out details in the interior of the cabin.

Happiness threaded through Maya's heart. It felt good to see her crews eagerly engaged in welcoming the newest helos to their tiny base. Her team worked hard, relentlessly, and she asked everything of them, heart and soul, to keep the operation at peak performance. She wasn't about to wade into the crowd and order them all back to their offices or maintenance areas. No, let them have this small reprieve. Goddess knew, Maya wasn't able to give them much R and R in Agua Caliente, or even better, fly them to Cuzco for a weekend where they could really rest and have a little fun, dancing and drinking at the local clubs. They were a group of young women, nearly all single and in their early twenties. Maya knew that some had boyfriends in Agua Caliente or Cuzco, or back in the States. They signed up for a one-year gig down here, and she understood how tough it was for them to be separated from loved ones for that long. Yet they did it willingly, with a sense of real adventure, knowing the demands and responsibilities before they signed on.

Maya's heart swelled with pride at her crew. She could tell by the looks on the men's faces, that the questions being asked were professional and knowledgeable. Anyone expecting this group to be slow or stupid would be jolted, because some of the sharpest, most intelligent women in the U.S. Army were here in this cave. Maya had literally handpicked her team, all volunteers, during the years the base had been in operation. She was looking for bright, motivated young women who were competitive within themselves—not with others—and who took pride in doing a job right the first time around.

Unable to resist the laughter, the pleasant talk, Maya moved quietly toward the closest group clustered around the D model Apache. She didn't want to be spotted by the men, so she moved at an angle and stayed at the rear of the group.

She saw Jake, the only man in this squadron, standing with his wife, Ana, and listening to the Texas CWO. Her real interest was centered on York, and she eased around the cluster toward the nose of the Apache, where he was still on his back beneath the cannon, explaining the differences between the old and new models to the three attentive crew chiefs.

Dane felt Maya's presence. Oh, it wasn't anything obvious; he just sensed her nearness. Craning his neck to the left, he saw her standing at the rear of the crowd. Her catlike eyes were fixed on him. For a brief moment, his hand froze in midair, then he said to hell with it and went on explaining the technicalities of the helo to the crew chief who was lying on her side and looking up at what he was pointing at. His skin prickled pleasantly. Answering the crew chief as she pointed at the gun where his hand rested, and asked a question, Dane forced himself to pay attention to her and not be distracted by Maya.

Maybe it was the look on Maya's face that made him breathe a little easier. After all, he was still smarting from her angry words of a couple of hours ago. He cast another quick glance at her. She was gone. How had she moved so fast? Where was she? More than once in the last couple of hours, York had heard Maya's loyal squadron describe her as "different." Well, what did that mean? Everyone seemed to tiptoe around the subject. When he asked, they just laughed and said that he would see for himself, and let it go at that. It was clear they loved her, almost idolized her. They seemed to worship the ground she walked on. Dane found that a complete surprise. Usually, a squadron's C.O. was tolerated, never loved.

Where was Maya? Worried that he and his men were somehow doing something wrong, without her permission, he told the crew chiefs he was done. They all moved from out beneath the carriage of the Apache. Dane was the last to leave. As he rolled onto his right side, he saw Maya's black, shining boots. She was standing beside the helicopter now.

Swallowing hard, he realized she was waiting for him. He rolled easily away from the nose and got to his hands and knees. She was standing there, hands on her hips, looking down at him intently.

Rising to his feet, he dusted off his hands. "I thought we'd come over, since there was a crowd already around this helo," he said.

"My people have been waiting for days to see these girls." Maya saw the distrust in his blue eyes. How she wished they could relax around one another. Trust one another. Inwardly, she laughed at her own idealism. York would never give his trust to her. Not until he could honestly accept unconditionally that women were as good as men. That would be the day.

Dane nodded and allowed his hands to rest on his narrow hips. The crew chiefs drifted to the other side of the Apache where the others were, as if sensing Maya and Dane needed to be left alone.

"They're a little excited." He grinned. "I don't blame them. This helicopter is something else. Beyond your wildest dreams come true." He reached forward and patted the black panel with affection. "I think once your pilots get into the training program and see all the differences, the ease in handling, it's going to blow them away. I know it did me."

Seeing the glimmer of sincerity in his eyes, Maya relaxed a little more. "I can tell your I.P.s are excited. It looks like they can't wait to get into teaching mode with my people. I like to see that kind of enthusiasm. It translates positively."

Grin broadening, Dane said, "Oh, you mean Commanche Joe? He lives, eats, breathes and snores in Apache. He's part Indian and that's what we call him. He's one of our best I.P.s. Craig is the other."

Chuckling, Maya nodded and surveyed the chopper with a knowing eye. "One of my pilots, Akiva Redtail, is Native American. Joe should meet her. They probably have a lot in common. What I'm most interested in is that new radar attachment up there, above the rotor. I've been hearing it gives us a huge advantage over the A model.''

Just getting to talk on the same footing with Maya about the D model helped lessen Dane's anxiety. Stepping closer to the fuselage, he rested his hand on a panel almost affectionately. Pointing up to the radar dome, he said, ''Some people call it a doughnut. Others call it a cheese wheel.''

Smiling, Maya studied the circular radar dome that embraced the rotor shaft assembly. ''Leave it to the army to call it one thing, and the troops in the field to get down to basics. I like doughnut.''

''Then doughnut it will be.'' He saw the warmth coming to her green eyes, and the tension leaving her mouth. Feeling on safer ground with her, Dane added, ''I don't know what you call your Apaches, but the guys...and ladies,'' he added quickly, ''are calling the D model 'Big Rig.''''

''Not Firebird?'' Maya mocked with a curl of her lip.

Dane shook his head and gave her a sour look. ''You know, that movie really hurt the Apache and the army. It was a joke. No, no one is calling it Firebird.''

''That movie was stupid,'' Maya groused. Moving up to the gunship, she slid her fingers along the flat black skirt that was part of the fuselage. ''Big Rig sounds good to me. Strong. I like it.''

''The official name for this D model is Longbow.''

Shrugging, Maya moved her fingers upward, almost sensing the heart of the new Apache. ''Big Rig is good. She's big, bold, and has a magnificent heart beating inside this frame of hers.'' She gazed up at the rotors that hung unmoving above them.

Just the way Maya slid her long fingers across the smooth metal made Dane's throat tightened. It was as if she were stroking a lover's skin. And the softness in her tone caught him off guard. Her gaze was one of awe combined with warmth. Respect. Finding himself wishing she felt the same way about him startled him even more. Maybe it was the way her fingers moved across the surface of the aircraft. Or maybe it was the look in her eyes. Would she ever give him that kind of look? One of respect and warmth? He found himself craving her approval instead of always earning her scorn. More than anything, Dane realized he had to think before he spoke around her. Somewhere in him, he *needed* Maya's approval. And her respect for him as a pilot—and as a man. A tall order, he realized, not too hopeful that she'd give him an inch on any of those things.

Patting the fuselage gently, Maya turned to him. She saw that he was looking down at the lava floor as if in a quandary, darkness clouding his intelligent blue eyes. His mouth was working, one corner quirked inward, as if he were experiencing pain of some kind. Maya allowed her senses to fully embrace him. It was a skill she'd been taught a long time ago, one of the gifts of being in the Jaguar Clan. If she dropped her walls of defense, if she left herself open and vulnerable, she could pick up on another person's emotions. Unlike Inca, her sister, she couldn't read minds worth a damn, but she could sense and feel the other person accurately.

As she allowed her defenses toward Dane to dissolve, she was surprised and taken aback by what she felt swirling invisibly around him. There was confusion. Desire. A gnawing feeling like an ache entered her heart. Taking a step away from him, her hand still on the Apache, she frowned and sifted through the mire of dark emotions he was caught up within at that moment. He had no idea she could feel him out like this, nor was she ever going to admit to having such a skill. No one but Dallas Klein knew of this particular ability, and Dallas had kept it to herself.

Sorting through his emotions, Maya felt Dane struggling to try and please her. That came as a surprise in itself. She hadn't thought he was going to try at all. She figured he planned to just stick it out for six weeks and get the hell out from beneath her command the moment he could. She had been wrong. Just knowing that made her feel less defensive, but her guard remained up.

The next feeling she encountered was desire. For what? She couldn't quite penetrate the extent of that emotion. Was he feeling desire to leave this place? That would be about right, because he saw this assignment as necessary, but wasn't looking forward to it at all. The last set of emotions—the need for support and nurturing—threw her off balance. Looking at him, no one would ever think Dane York needed anyone at any time. The craggy square face, those frosty, almost flinty blue eyes, the hardness of his expression all countered what she was feeling around him presently.

Gently, Maya withdrew her awareness from around him. When she did, he lifted his head and squarely met her gaze. On some level, he'd sensed her presence within his aura of energy. Smiling to herself, she decided York wasn't so blind, deaf and dumb after all. Certainly, he wasn't in touch consciously with what had just happened; but on a more subliminal, intuitive level, he'd felt her presence. Shutting down her sensing mode, she once again lifted those barriers back into place so that he couldn't take a piece of her. York was not to be trusted, unfortunately.

"So," Maya said, trying to sound relaxed and informal, "I'll bet your wife and kids are going to miss you being gone for the next six weeks on this secret assignment. They probably don't have a clue where you're at, right?" When a person in the military took off on a top-secret assignment, most families never knew where in the world they were being sent, or why. Maya figured that all the emotions of York's that she'd just sensed had to do with missing his family.

"Excuse me?" He frowned.

"Er…your family. You must be missing them?" Maya felt alarmed by the look he gave her. It was one of curiosity and amusement.

Dane saw Maya's unsureness. It was the first time he'd

seen her confidence slip. So, even though she appeared to be
like a vengeful warrior goddess, unapproachable and strong,
Maya was human after all. That made him breathe a little
easier. Maybe…just maybe…they could find a sure footing
with one another, where they didn't have to spar all the time.
Lifting his hand, he offered her a slight smile of regret. "I
don't have family—at least, not a wife and kids. I'm still
single."

"Oh…" Maya frowned. So who was he feeling all these
emotions for? Certainly, they couldn't be about her. Maya's
mind raced with more questions. She instantly rejected some
of the answers she came up with, knowing York was incapable of such things. Or was he? Confused, she met his thaw-
ing gaze and that cockeyed half smile. His face had lost a
lot of its hardness, the mask slowly dissolving. Was it because she'd touched his aura, and he realized she wasn't his
enemy, after all, just someone who wanted to be treated with
respect? That was too much to hope for.

"Well—" Maya said, lifting her hand from the fuselage
"—you looked…sad, maybe like you were missing someone. I thought it might be your family. Six weeks is a long
assignment."

Just knowing she was trying to be civil—even thoughtful—toward him made Dane reel. He'd thought Maya incapable of such a response. Not that he deserved any slack from
her. No, he'd more than burned the bridges between them a
long time ago and had realized that everything that had happened back then was his fault—not hers. "I see. Well…"
Dane cleared his throat nervously and thought about what he
was going to say this time, instead of just running off at the
mouth like he usually did. Looking out the entrance of the
cave at the haze sunlight touching the ever-moving clouds,
he let the silence build between them.

Turning his head again, Dane met Maya's measuring gaze.
He saw the wariness back in her emerald eyes, but her mouth

was not a slash. No, her lips were slightly parted. Damn, she had a mouth any man in his right mind would want to kiss.

What the hell was he thinking? Startled over the stray bullet of a thought, Dane found himself scrambling. It was a good thing Maya couldn't read his mind or she'd have decked him right where he stood. Giving her a boyish smile, he said, "Sad. Yeah. I'm sad."

Maya frowned. She saw York trying to be honest with her. "About what? Being here?"

The sarcasm in her low voice wasn't missed by him. To hell with it. He was going to risk it all. He had six weeks here with Maya, under her command, and there was no way in hell he wanted to stay on high guard with her all that time. Looking around, he saw that the crews were well out of earshot.

"I'm sad because..." Dane hunted for the right words. "Because I don't like the tenor between us, Captain. Frankly, I yearn for some peace, but I don't know how to accomplish that. I'm confused. I'm trying to figure out how to be here and not be a pain in the ass all the time to you. I don't want to keep parrying thrusts with you and having you getting hotter than a two-dollar pistol about it."

Her heart pounded with relief. The expression on Dane's face was one of earnestness and desire. So that was what the desire she'd encountered in him moments ago was about. He wanted peace between them. Her surprise that he was not married warred with his other words. Why should she care if York wasn't married? Throwing that question aside, Maya focused on the present problem between them.

"I learned a long time ago, Major, that when there is respect—equal respect—between two people, it makes for a level playing field. And when you have respect, you can begin to build trust. Without respect, there can be no trust."

Dane leaned back against the fuselage, no more than two feet away from where Maya stood. Watching the sunlight strengthen and then wane as the endless clouds drifted in and around the cave entrance, he crossed his arms and thought long and hard about her words. Finally, he glanced at Maya. To his relief, she was not shutting him out. He could tell by the relaxed expression on her beautiful features and the alertness and curiosity burning in her emerald gaze that maybe she wanted to wave a white flag of surrender, too, so that they could get on with what needed to be done around here.

"You're right, of course," he murmured, so that only she could hear him. The echoes of laughter, of people talking, bounced endlessly off the walls of the cave. "I think my men will treat your people with respect. I think you can see that happening already. Sounds more like a party going on in here than a war between the sexes. Don't you think?"

Grinning ruthlessly, Maya said, "Definitely a party atmosphere. It's good to hear people laughing, believe me."

Gauging her from beneath his spiky brown lashes, Dane wanted to say, *What about us? Can you trust me? Can you try?* But he didn't. Her reserve wrapped around her like thick a blanket. Dane knew she wasn't about to drop those massive walls she wore with him. He hadn't proved himself to her— yet. More than anything, he wanted the opportunity to try.

"You know, I'm *really* impressed with your squadron," he said sincerely. "Dallas gave us one hell of a tour. She said you masterminded this whole plan, using the defunct mining operation and shaft on the other side of this mountain as a ruse to hide what's going on in here. I found that incredible."

Maya studied him. She wanted to allow his compliment to wash over her, but she resisted the temptation. York could not be trusted. Not with her or her sensitive emotions, which she hid constantly. Being a base commander meant hiding a lot, carrying a lot, and having no one to cry with, or to tell her own worries and troubles to. She found herself wishing that she could share some of those worries with Dane. More shock rolled through her. What was going on? He was her enemy. The man who had always wanted her to fail, who had tried to destroy her because she was an intelligent and confident woman.

Shaking off her thoughts, she refocused on Dane's words and said, "The Indians of the surrounding villages knew of this place for thousands of years. An old jaguar priestess took me up here to the mining operation. She showed me the lava tube that extended a quarter mile into the mountain. And then we climbed around the mountain to this cave. When I realized that, with some work, we could open up the back of the cave into that lava tube, I knew we could make my vision work." Maya gestured toward the cave's ceiling, wreathed in lights suspended from the lava. "I got a Navy Seabee team down here and they found out that there was only about fifty feet of rock between the cave and the tube." She smiled triumphantly.

"We use the mining area on the other side of the mountain as a cover for our operation. We use civilian helicopters to ferry in all our supplies so they don't raise too much suspicion from the tourist trade in Agua Caliente or around Machu Picchu. In fact, the helicopter service in that little town is our undercover way of getting to and from this base. Our people get R and R every two weeks. They climb into *tourista* clothing and fly out on the civilian helo to Agua Caliente to get a few days of rest and partying."

"It's a brilliant plan," Dane said. "Brilliant."

She arched beneath his roughly spoken compliment. His eyes burned with awe as he regarded her. Maya absorbed the energy, the passion in his statement. She realized reluctantly that she, too, was seeking his approval, whether she wanted to or not. Still, one little compliment was not going to erase their mutual, hellish past.

"This place is inaccessible except by helicopter." Maya eased away from the Apache and began walking toward the lip. Dane followed at her shoulder. "Let's walk out to the Eye. From there, you can see the jungle below."

"Are there villages around this mountain?"

Maya nodded. "Yes, three of them. We're tight with the village leaders. I, uh, well, I share a common heritage with their medicine people, their healers, so I've been able to communicate with them about keeping our presence a secret. Sometimes Faro Valentino will send in a two-man team and start sniffing around the base of this mountain. The villagers know who's local and who isn't. I gave each chief in each village an iridium cell phone so that if they spot strangers, they can alert us."

"And it's always been drug runners?" Dane asked, wiping his brow. The sunlight was hot, the humidity high. He'd rolled up the sleeves on his flight suit to his elbows, but he was still perspiring heavily in the noontime heat.

Approaching the outer wall, with the Eye directly in front of them, Maya said, "Nine times out of ten. Oh, sometimes a young tourist will have followed the Urubamba River from Aqua Caliente, which is twenty miles that way." She pointed. "The chief and his people can always tell a real *tourista* from a wolf in sheep's clothing." She grinned.

"Iridium phones. I'm impressed."

Maya snorted and placed her hand on the black lava, which was welted like water ripples. "I went through hell getting my contact to get me iridium phones, but down here, normal cell phones don't work. The only way we can contact one another is using a GPS—global positioning satellites device—plus an iridium phone."

"You got them in your helos?"

She nodded. "You bet. In all three of them. If we crash, or if we blow an engine or take too big a chunk out of one of our rotors, we have that phone to call to base with."

"That ever happen?" ·

Grinning, Maya said, "Oh, yeah. You noticed our third Apache at the back of the cave? The dismantled one?"

"Yeah, it looks pretty well cannibalized."

"With good reason." She frowned. "My contacts weren't giving me the necessary budget to fly in replacement parts for my birds. I ended up having to sacrifice one of them to keep the other two flying. One time, Dallas blew an engine during a run for the border after some of Faro's civilian helos, which were carrying coke. She had to land in some heavy jungle terrain. About one-quarter of one rotor was whacked off during landing. So we ended up taking the replacement rotors from the third aircraft. Once that happened, we began taking other necessary parts when I didn't get the money to resupply and outfit my Apaches.''

Dane watched the wisps of clouds form and dissipate with incredible rapidity. The sunlight, he was realizing, was a force to reckoned with here. As they stood at the opening of the Eye, he watched a thick wall of clouds form below, just above the dark green jungle, and then move slowly upward to eventually block the view.

''It sounds like you've been doing a helluva lot of juggling over the years to make this base work.''

Again Maya saw respect in his eyes. Twice in one day. She was on a roll. Compressing her lips, she muttered, ''I'd rather fly, if the truth be known. The paperwork's a real pain.''

Chuckling, Dane said, ''Spoken like a true squadron commander. I don't know one who wouldn't trade his, er, her desk, for sitting in an Apache and flying instead.''

Pleased that he didn't just use ''he,'' Maya gave him a partial smile. ''Well, I get plenty of airtime, too. I'm the twelfth pilot around here. I fly every third day, just like everyone else.''

''How long are the missions?'' Dane knew that keeping a place like this on line and functioning, an incredibly heavy responsibility, would take every scrap of a person's energy and focus. For Maya to also be flying combat missions every third day was an incredible demand on her. Admiration for her crept into him.

''We've developed flight plans based upon Faro Valentino's usual patterns of trying to run for the Bolivian border with his coke. The range can mean a three-hundred-mile flight radius at times. And when he's running, it can mean we're flying until we need to return to base. Once here—'' Maya turned and gestured to her right where the fuel depot was located ''—my crews can refuel an Apache in ten minutes flat. If they've used ordnance, it's replaced as soon as the refueling is done. And then they're back in the air again, trying to locate and chase down the bad guys.''

Shaking his head, Dane said, ''I didn't realize that.''

''Just wait,'' Maya said grimly. ''I think you and your I.P.s should hang out with us for about three days and get a feel for the demands on our time, our schedule, which is nothing short of chaos usually, before you try and set up a training program for us.''

It was a wise request, Dane realized. He watched as a massive cloud closed in on the Eye. In moments, they were surrounded with fog so thick that he could no longer see into the cave complex.

''With these kinds of IFR conditions,'' he muttered, ''you're really riding the edge.''

''Tell us about it,'' Maya chuckled. ''The cloud cover around here is constant. My pilots don't take anything for granted, especially visibility. Usually, we're flying on instruments alone, coming and going from this place.''

Just as quickly, the cloud dissipated and Dane could once again see the maw of the cave. ''This place is like magic,'' he murmured, looking around at the massive facility. ''Now you see it, now you don't. It's phenomenal.''

''Yeah,'' Maya said, laughter in her eyes, ''you're right about the magic part.''

Dane walked at her shoulder as they moved back into the cave. Sunlight suddenly streamed through the Eye once again, embracing them with radiance and warmth as they went. ''I've noticed something,'' he told her, catching her distrustful gaze. ''And if this is personal, just tell me to back off.''

Maya went on guard. "What?"

"A number of your crew people have made the same remark about you, and it has me curious."

"Oh?"

He heard the brittleness in her tone. They slowed their pace as they neared the new D model. The rest of the squadron was still on the other side. Dane heard Joe's enthusiastic voice as he continued to explain all the innovations to the engrossed crews.

"Yeah…they all used the same word to describe you."

"What have you been doing? Polling my people about me?"

Dane held up his hands. "Whoa. Easy. We didn't pump anyone for info on you, if that's what you think. No, we've just been talking to them about the D model. They're excited and can't wait to get their hands on it. But every one I talked with mentioned how you'd lobbied the U.S. government to get these new Apaches down here. They clearly think the world of you."

Relaxing slightly, Maya crossed her arms. "They have been excited. And I'm sure my people are bubbling over about these Big Rigs being here." Her curiosity ate at her. She saw the glimmer in York's eyes as he studied her. Maya felt like the tables had been turned, that she was the one under the microscope, not him. So what had her people told him? Uncomfortable, she belligerently returned his stare.

"The people we talked to," Dane said, "all used the same word to describe you—*different.*"

Maya's mouth moved slightly and then compressed. "I see."

"It was a compliment," Dane assured her. "Not an insult. I've heard base commanders called a lot of things in my day, but never 'different.'" He cocked his head, a half smile playing across his mouth. "What does that mean? How are they using it in regard to you?"

Shrugging, Maya muttered, "I don't know." Well, she did

know, but she was darned if York was going to find out. Not that anyone except Dallas and Dr. Elizabeth Cornell, their base physician, knew about her other life as a Black Jaguar Clan priestess. No, there were some things better left unsaid. Besides, most of the people under her command were not the least familiar with metaphysics. Gauging Dane, she saw a bit of elfish play in his eyes, as if he were gently teasing her, without malice.

"You know how any squadron is," she said in a bored tone of voice. "Every commander has a personality. I'm sure that's what it's about."

Dane studied her. Maya was ill at ease. She shifted from one booted foot to the other, her arms across her breasts. His intuition, which wasn't great, told him that she was hiding something about herself. Okay, he wouldn't push it. Judging from the look in her narrowed eyes, she wasn't going to say anything more to him about it.

"Yes," he murmured, "that's probably it."

"Captain Stevenson!"

Maya turned, recognizing Private Sandy Wells's high-pitched voice. Sandy, who was her comms—communications—assistant was barely five feet tall, with curly blond hair cut just below her ears and huge blue eyes. As she ran breathlessly toward Maya, she waved a paper above her head.

"Excuse me," Maya told Dane, and turned to meet Sandy.

Sandy came to a halt, breathing hard. "Ma'am, we just got confirmation that two unidentified civilian helicopters are going to be passing right by here in ten minutes!" she said, handing Maya the transmission from the satellite intelligence unit.

Scowling, Maya rapidly read the information. "Faro's at it again," she said.

"I think so, ma'am. Want me to sound the alarm?"

"Yes, Private, do it now."

Running back into the cave, the private headed back to her

comms Quonset hut. A minute later, a clanging bell sounded, echoing eerily throughout the cave.

Maya looked up to see York moving toward her.

"I've gotta go, Major. I'll see you on the return trip. We've got bogeys—more than likely Faro's men. We're going to intercept."

"Wait!" Dane hurried to her side as she walked quickly toward the Apaches at the other end of the apron. "Let me go with you."

She jerked her head toward him. Her eyes became slits. "You?"

"Sure. Why *not* me? Don't you want me to get an understanding of what's going down here? It will help me in assessing what needs to be taught to your pilots."

It made sense, though Maya didn't want him along. But then revenge entered into the equation. Smiling lethally, she said, "Sure, you can be my copilot-gunner, Major. But I'm the commander. Got it?"

Grinning, he broke into a trot at her side, heading toward the Apaches the crews were hurriedly working around. "You're number one." He surprised himself at how easily the words rolled off his tongue.

"Still think you can work an A model's software?" she taunted as she trotted toward her helo. "Or have you forgotten how to do it the old-fashioned way?"

Dane's grin broadened. "I won't embarrass you out there, Captain. That's a promise."

Her heart was beating hard in her chest as she put her foot onto the metal rung to hoist herself upward into the front cockpit. Four years ago, the tables had been turned. She'd had to fly too many hours with York lording it over her from the back seat. Well, now all that was changed. As Maya swung into her seat, she shouted to her crew chief to fetch her helmet from her office and to bring York one that would fit him.

"Never mind, I brought my own," he told her, and

shouted below to one of the other crew people as to where to retrieve his helmet in his quarters. The woman turned and ran into the cave to find it. Time was at a premium. He felt the tempo. Felt the escalating tension. Maya's voice was calm and terse as she spoke to her crew chief. Below, several women hurried to remove the chalks from the Apache landing gear, release the rotor blades from their tie-downs and then pull the machine out onto the lip area, where it could be prepared for takeoff.

Maya was all business. She concentrated solely on what was ahead of her and tried to ignore the fact that York was in her back seat. Settling her helmet on her head, she strapped it on tightly. Jamming the thin black gloves on her hands, she felt her heart pounding erratically with the adrenaline charge. This was for real. Every time they launched, there was a helluva chance they might not return. Faro's men had Kamovs. The sat intel showed two civilian helicopters speeding toward Bolivia. That didn't mean the Kamovs weren't around only that they were waiting…just waiting to jump them. Would York be up to speed? Kamovs had no signature they could detect with their radar. Could she rely on him to spot them if they were around?

How much of her life was she willing to put into his hands? Was the enemy in her cockpit any less dangerous to her than the enemy they were going to try and intercept?

Chapter 6

Dane tried to push his excitement aside. He was going into combat. Finally. There wasn't an Apache pilot alive who didn't thirst for the blood-pounding danger of combat; they lived, ate and breathed for the chance he was going to get right now. The last time he'd seen combat was during the Persian Gulf War, and that was a while ago. Busy cranking up his HUDs and checking them out, he was only peripherally aware of the hurried activity around them. He heard Maya's cool, low voice in his helmet earphones as she talked with her crew chief on the ground. They had been pushed out on the lip, and now the engines were being put on line, one at a time. The shiver that went through the aircraft made him feel good. It fed his mounting excitement.

There were a lot of dangers ahead, too. The warm sunshine streaming through the cockpit canopy, now lowered and locked into place, was making him sweat. The coolness of the air conditioning moved around Dane and reduced the heat within the cabin. Sweat was trickling down the sides of his ribs beneath his flight suit from anticipation. *Combat.* Adren-

aline was surging through his bloodstream as he tightened
his knee board into place around his right thigh. He grinned
lopsidedly. He was glad Maya had let him come along. Now
he had a chance to prove himself to her in another way.

The rotor engaged, the engine's whine deepened. The
Apache began to shake, a familiar and welcome sensation to
Dane. Off to his left, he saw the second Apache warming up,
as well. Maya had just snapped off a salute to the crew below. They hurriedly backed away.

"Who's in the second Apache?" he asked her as he
punched several codes into the computers that ran the HUDs.
A trickle of sweat dripped down his left temple. He reached
up with his gloved hand and pushed it away.

"The standby crew," Maya said. "Lieutenant Danielle
Gautier. She's on loan from the French Army air wing. Her
call sign is Lobo. Her back seat is CWO2 Ellen Canton,
Goosey. We call her Luce the Goose because she honks like
one when she laughs."

"Roger. Thanks."

"Let's go over our checklist before we hightail it out of
here."

"Roger," he said, quickly pulling out the plastic-enclosed
cards and resting them on his thigh where he'd placed his
knee board. He heard the tension in Maya's tone. His own
voice sounded a little tight.

As soon as they were done, Maya said, "Let's rock 'n'
roll. Lobo, you and Goosey ready? Over."

Gautier's low, lilting French accent came back. "Roger
that, Saber. We're ready. Over."

"Roger. Let's mission launch...." Maya nudged the
power up on the Apache. The first order of business was
flying through the Eye. As she positioned the gunship, the
clouds lifted and she could see the hole clearly. Usually,
around noon, the clouds burned off more rapidly with the
help of direct sunlight, and it was easier to thread. Applying
power and keeping her feet firmly on the yaw pedals, she

moved the gunship quickly through the opening. In her helmet, she heard an intake of breath from York. She grinned a little.

"You'll get used to it, Major."

Shaking his head at the ease with which Maya had just negotiated that tight opening, Dane rasped, "I don't think so. You make it look damned easy and I know it's not."

Chuckling, Maya positioned her gunship to one side and waited for Lobo to appear. "I've lost track of how many times I've flown the Eye. It gets easier the more you do it." The second Apache came through quickly.

Dane pulled down the dark visor that would protect the upper half of his face and eyes from the bright sunlight lancing into the cabin. The Apache felt solid and good around him as he typed in the keywords to bring up the identification of local aircraft.

"I'm scanning with radar to try and find those two bogeys," he told her, as he felt the Apache nose down and surge forward.

"Roger," Maya said. She looked around the cloud-cobbled blue sky. "We're climbing above cloud cover first. That will be at around nine or ten thousand feet. Don't get your nose stuck in those HUD screens, Major. You've got to divide your time and attention between them and the Kamovs. They're out there...and it's up to you to find them first before they find us."

"Roger. I hear you loud and clear." Twisting his head, Dane saw the roiling clouds falling away. Maya was pushing the Apache to its limits of speed, over two hundred miles an hour. They were heading in an easterly direction, toward the Bolivian border. Below, the jungle looked like tight little heads of broccoli all crammed together. There was no place to land if they got into trouble. They'd have to drop into the canopy, and that wasn't a pleasant thought.

"You got anything yet?" she demanded.

"No...searching." Dane twisted another knob and

watched the dark green screen intently. "If we had the D model, it would have already picked them up."

"Nice. But it isn't gonna help us right now." Maya continued to scan the airspace around them. Off to her right was Lobo, a mile away. "Sat intel picked up two helos," she told him. "That means we split up and go after them."

"What's their normal avoidance pattern?"

Maya smiled a little, her intent gaze sweeping across her instrument panel. York was asking the right questions. "It differs. Faro Valentino learned a long time ago not to get into a set pattern of flight or time with us. He found out very quickly we're open for business twenty-four hours a day, seven days a week. As soon as you can locate those helos, I can probably tell you more."

"I hear you." He frowned, studying the HUDs. Just the way Maya was flying the Apache made York feel proud of her. She handled the machine deftly and with such silky smoothness that it was hard to tell he was actually in a combat machine. At least right now. Straight flight was one thing, combat flying another.

"Black Jaguar One," Lobo called.

"What've you got, Lobo?" Maya asked.

"We got two Agusta civilian helicopters painted on our HUDs. Looks to me like Faro's running two smaller aircraft into Bolivia this time."

Damn. Had he messed up? Dane quickly scanned again, barely making out something on one HUD—fuzzy outlines at best. He thought it was radar return from some clouds. How could the other Apache crew already have them identified? Smarting beneath his own expectations of finding the bogeys first, he compressed his mouth.

"How could Lobo ID them so fast?" he demanded of Maya.

Dane heard Lobo's musical voice over the earphones on his helmet. "Luce the Goose is used to looking at fuzzy things that float across her HUD, Major. Don't worry, after a while we can ID a cloud from an aircraft no matter how far away or blurred looking it is. It's a real art, believe me.''

Maya grinned. "Good work, Lobo and Goosey." She heard the frustration and embarrassment in Dane's voice. He was in competition with them. It hurt his pride that he hadn't painted the bogeys first. "Get over it, Major. We have other fish to fry," she told him. "Faro's got quite a mishmash of helicopters in his fleet. Over the past three years, he's bought a lot of different civilian helicopters in an effort to avoid us. The Agusta Lobo is talking about are very similar to the tourist helicopter that is stationed at Agua Caliente. He knows we aren't going to shoot at him until we get a positive visual ID on him. We can't take the chance that we'd be loosing a bunch of rockets into a civilian helicopter and killing all on board. That would become an international incident. We'd get press, political problems from it, and more than likely my base and the operation would be shut down.''

"Visual ID is a must, anyway," Dane agreed fervently.

"Roger that. But in Faro's case, it's a high priority. He'd like to see us make this kind of mistake. It would make his life easier if we were outta here." Maya swung her gunship in a slight bank. Up ahead, she spotted the two escaping helicopters about four miles ahead of them. The Agusta could never keep up with an Apache speedwise.

"Saber," Lobo called. "It's confirmed ID on them. Italian Agusta A119 Koala.''

"Roger. Let me go in for a confirmation of the numbers on their fuselages before you approach. No use in two Apaches taking the fly-by risk," Maya answered.

"Roger.''

Dane saw the helicopters clearly on his HUD now. The screen repeated that they were Agusta helicopters. "Numbers on their fuselage?''

"Yeah," Maya said grimly as she angled the Apache so that there was about half a mile between them and the Agusta. "You've got a set of binoculars there, on your right side, on top of where we keep the optic eyepiece. I want you to get the numbers, type them into the computer and see what comes up. Do it as soon as possible. Those Kamovs might be around...."

Dane found the binoculars. Maya made it easy for him to see through them by holding the helicopter on a steady flight path. The two Agustas were flying in a militarylike formation. "Are Russians flying those things?" he asked as he quickly typed in the first numbers.

"Probably. Why?"

"They're flying in a damn tight formation for civilian pilots."

Maya nodded. "You're right. It's a good observation. They probably are Soviet mercenaries that Faro hired three years ago. I guess the boys can't get out of military-formation flying." She laughed a little.

"Got the numbers," Dane told her. He put the binoculars aside and watched the screen intently after typing them in. Information regarding the helos popped up in a lighter green color. Pressing his gloved finger against the screen, he said, "Okay, what we have is two unidentified helicopters. The numbers on their fuselages don't jibe with any registered in Peru."

"Did you try Bolivia? Italy? Chile? Colombia and Ecuador?"

"No..." Damn. He'd screwed up again.

"Punch it in. See what comes up."

Quickly he typed the info on the keyboard located near his left knee. Sweat trickled down his wrinkled brow. More data popped up on the screen.

"This is strange. These numbers don't jibe with any country you've mentioned."

"Good."

There was sardonic satisfaction in Maya's low voice, and an edge, too.

Dane looked up and then scanned the cloudless sky around

them. Where would the Kamovs be? "What do you do now?"

"Call them on the radio," Maya said, and she switched channels and made the call to the two helicopters in Spanish, English, Italian and Quechua, the second language of Peru.

Dane was surprised at her grasp of so many foreign languages. But then he reminded himself that Maya was Brazilian and would probably know not only Portuguese, but Spanish as well.

He heard no radio response from the helicopters to any of Maya's queries. "They're not answering us."

"No kidding." She moved her Apache in for a closer look. "They aren't carrying big guns on them, but don't put it past the pilot or copilot to open a window and shoot a firearm at us."

Dane blinked as she brought the Apache within a hundred feet of the first Agusta. He could clearly see both pilots. The one in the right seat, the pilot, was glaring back at them. The man was heavyset, with a broad face and a sneer on his lips.

"I don't think he's happy to see us, do you?"

Maya heard the grim amusement in Dane's voice. Her lips twitched. "No, he's not, and I know who that bastard is. Sasha Karlov. Sweet name for the nasty, mean son of a bitch that he is…" Instantly, Maya pulled the Apache up and to the right, away from the Agusta. "All right, Lobo, you take the one on the left, I'm taking Karlov's helicopter. Let's see if these boys will turn back or if they want to stay and play."

"Roger, Saber."

"The border is only five miles away," Dane warned, pushed deeper into his seat by gravity as Maya took the Apache up and in front of the fleeing helicopters.

"Yeah, I know. Hang on. We're going to play sky chicken with these boys…."

Dane's eyes widened. Maya set the Apache squarely in front of where the Agustas were flying. His mouth dropped opened, but he didn't have time to yell out a warning. The

Agustas hurtled toward them. Gripping the airframe, bracing himself, Dane thought they were going to crash.

At the last moment, the Agustas split off, one to the right and one to the left, into a steep, diving bank toward the jungle eight thousand feet below.

"No you don't...." Maya growled.

Dane was jerked to the right and then to the left. Gravity seized him and slammed him back into the seat. His helmet banged into the side cockpit window. Stunned, he took long seconds to realize what Maya had done with the Apache. She'd banked sharply left, nosed down and was redlining the engines in a screaming dive to catch up with the fleeing Agustas.

"Watch for Kamovs!" she barked at him.

Blinking, Dane tore his gaze from the Augusta they were rapidly approaching. The helicopter began to jump around, as if to try and get rid of them. Looking up, Dane scanned the skies around them.

"Warm up the cannon. I want you to put a couple of shells right across Karlov's broken nose."

Slammed one way and then the other within the narrow confines of the cockpit, Dane had trouble getting to the HUD controls that connected with the cannon beneath the belly of the Apache. As soon as the HUD lit up with it as the main weapon of choice, he quickly got it on line. Watching the crosshairs on the HUD, he began to track the fleeing Agusta.

"Okay, got 'em..."

"Watch for Kamovs, Major! Don't keep your nose stuck in that HUD, dammit! This is when they usually jump us."

Stung, he jerked his head up. Right now, they were leveling out and screaming along over the jungle. Everything was a green blur beneath them. Damn, Maya was close to the trees! Dane tensed. He saw the Agusta make a tight turn around one of the loaf-shaped mountains. Instantly, Maya followed him. She cut so close to the mountain, that Dane sucked in a breath.

"Get ready!"

Yanking his attention back to the HUD, he saw the Agusta was no longer in the crosshairs. The shot would go wide.

"Ready?"

"Roger," he rasped, quickly working the HUD and re-configuring the software instructions to the cannon.

"Just fire in front of him," she ordered.

"Ready."

"Do it."

There was a slight vibration beneath Maya's seat. She could feel the cannon, located directly beneath her armor-plated seat and platform, shaking away. There were several tracer rounds, bright red, and she followed them as they arced very close to the nose of the Agusta helicopter. She cackled.

"Great shot! You've rattled him!"

Dane arched beneath her praise as she brought the Apache up, almost brushing the tops of the trees alongside the mountain as she followed the Agusta, which was now turning away from the Bolivian border.

"Why don't you shoot him out of the sky?"

"Because we don't know for *sure* if this is a civilian helicopter or one of Faro's. I'd know Karlov's wreck of a face anywhere. But what if his other pilot is not working for Faro? What if Faro is playing with the numbers on the fuselage to confuse us? If we shoot them down, it could cause an international incident."

Maya leveled out the Apache and eased back on the throttles until the gunship was in a hover. She watched the copter fleeing back toward the jungle area where she knew Faro had one of his many cocaine loading stations. "We do a lot of hunt and chase, Major. We're not just randomly shooting helicopters out of the sky around here."

"And if they fire at you?" Dane kept looking for Kamovs.

"That's a different story. In the past, years ago, they did that. Well, you shoot at me, and I'm firing back with all the hardware this Apache carries. Faro lost four helicopters in a row due to that little piece of aggression on his part, and then he finally figured out if he stopped his boys from shooting at us, we wouldn't fire back at them, either. So now it's usually a Mexican standoff. Sky chicken. Who will flinch first?'' She chuckled.

''And so he repaints the numbers on the fuselage of his civilian helos to confuse you?''

''Yes.'' Maya turned the Apache back toward their base. Up ahead, she saw Lobo's Apache coming toward them. ''He does the numbers game all the time. He's well aware that unless we have an absolutely positive ID, we aren't going to take him or his helos out of the sky.''

''And you have to let them go into Bolivian airspace?''

Maya heard the frustration in his voice. ''No…we just make it tougher for them to get there, like we did just now. Faro has orders for his cocaine,'' she said, watching as Lobo's Apache came closer. She made a gesture with her hand, signaling the other helo to go back to base. Instantly Lobo raised her gloved hand and moved the gunship forward. Maya positioned her helo three rotor blades' distance from Lobo's, and they flew in formation toward home.

''As I was saying, Faro has orders for his cocaine. By turning his ships back, he's not making his deadlines for drug deliveries. That puts a lot of pressure on him to get it out of Peru. So, next time around, he'll either use bigger civilian aircraft or more of them to try and get some of the orders through to Bolivian airspace.''

''How many helos would he put up at a time?'' Dane asked, keeping his gaze switching between the HUD radar and the sky. Even now he knew they were not safe. Kamovs could sneak up and jump them.

''Oh, he's got a fleet, we estimate, of twelve helicopters of varying types and models from many different countries that he can use. Plus, he's got two Kamovs, which really don't make us happy at all. If we could paint the Kamovs on radar, that would be another thing, but we can't. Chasing civilian helos back from the border is bad enough. Having to chase them and watch for Kamovs is totally another. We've had some close calls this last year, since Faro put those Kamovs in the air.'' Maya frowned. ''We haven't lost a ship or crew yet, but I'm worried about it.''

Dane nodded and continued to rubberneck. ''I understand….'' And he did. He shared her worry. He was drenched in sweat, his flight suit sticking to him. During the chase, his adrenaline had been pumping. He was still tense and jumpy from the encounter. Maya, on the other hand, seemed like an old combat vet. Nothing rattled her much. To her, this had been a cat-and-mouse game, and that was all. Plus she was used to the scenarios, and he was not. Still, Dane admired her coolness in the face of danger.

Within twenty minutes, they were back at the base. This time Maya turned the tables on him.

''You have the controls, Major. Take us through the Eye.''

Gulping, he placed his hands around the collective and cyclic. ''You like to live dangerously, don't you?''

Maya chuckled. ''Always. What else is there in life but risk?''

He focused on the opening. The clouds were thinning and he could see it visually. ''Well, this is one helluva risk,'' he muttered as he eased the Apache up to the Eye.

''Think you ought to train those pilots up at Fort Rucker for this little challenge?'' She laughed aloud.

Mouth compressed, he eased the Apache through, his gaze shifting constantly between the rotor length and the sides of the black lava wall crowding in on him. The walls weren't moving of course, but that's how it felt to Dane. Once through the Eye, he saw the crew chief on the right side of the lip indicating with her orange sticks where he was to land the gunship. ''This is more than a little challenge,'' he griped good-naturedly.

Maya smiled and relaxed as York brought them in for a nice, gentle landing. The whine of the engines shut down, and the rotors began to slow. They were home. Looking around, she watched as Lobo followed them through the Eye and came to land a hundred feet away from them. Opening the cockpit frame after the rotors stopped, she felt the fresh, humid air rush in. Taking a deep breath of it, she lifted her hand to her crew and smiled down at them. She was so proud of them, she thought as she looked at them, their expressions full of relief at seeing the flight team return safely.

Climbing out of the front seat, Maya leaped to the ground. She took off her helmet and stuffed her gloves into the right pocket of her flight suit, waiting for York. More than a little curious about how the flight had affected him, she watched as he climbed nimbly down off the fuselage cover to the lava below. His face was sweaty, his eyes almost colorless, the pupils black and large. He looked like the hunter he was, and she smiled to herself.

As he took off the helmet and placed it beneath his left arm, she said, "You didn't do badly for a first time up there."

Dane pushed his fingers through his damp hair and held her assessing gaze. He didn't see any tension or wariness in Maya's features right now. He reminded himself that they'd just been on a combat mission and their adrenaline was still pumping from it. Neither of them was in their usual guarded mode with one another—yet.

"Thanks…I'm still upset I didn't see those birds painted on my HUDs."

Smiling slightly, Maya moved her shoulders to rid them of the accumulated tension. "Don't worry about it. Another week in the back seat with us and you'll know how to read fuzzies on the radar as accurately as Lobo and Goosey did."

Walking with her toward the cave, Dane felt elated. It was the first time Maya had smiled. She had such a beautiful, expressive face. He tried to separate out the combat pilot inside her from her outer beauty. It was impossible. Maya was a complex person and he knew it. More than anything, he found himself wanting to simply stare into those deep, deep, almost fathomless green eyes of hers. She had the kind of eyes a man could lose himself within. It was a disconcerting yearning and he struggled with it.

At HQ, they climbed the stairs together. On the second floor, Maya pointed to an open door near her own.

"In case you don't know it, my head supply clerk, Sergeant Penny Anderson, has assigned this office coming up on your left as yours for the duration of your six weeks with us. If you need anything, ask her. Penny's in the office next to yours."

Dane halted and looked into the small office. It had a dark green metal desk just like Maya's. There were paper, pencils and pens on top of it. And a vase of purple-and-white orchids. A woman's touch.

Maya was standing in the hall, watching him.

"Thanks…" he managed to answer.

"What's wrong?"

"Nothing's wrong." He prickled as her gaze narrowed speculatively on him.

"I can feel it around you."

"What? That women's intuition thing?" Dane closed his eyes. *Damn.* He'd just done it again. When he opened them, he saw the hurt and frustration in her expression. Opening his hand, he muttered, "That came out wrong."

"It always does," Maya grated.

His heart contracted. They were back at square one again. Dane searched for something to say that was not prejudicial sounding. "Look, I'm still edgy from the flight. Not that it's an excuse for what I said, but…"

Maya walked up to him, keeping her voice very low. "In our line of business down here, we need all the help we can get. Now, whether it's from a visual, or HUD, or our gut feeling, we don't like to think of one kind of knowing as being better than any other. And yes, you can bet the farm that we use our intuition just as surely as we'll use our eyes and the instruments in our gunships.''

''I hear you,'' Dane muttered defensively, trying to think of a way to climb out of his mistake.

''You want to know how we knew the Kamovs would attack this morning when you boys came up from Lima?'' she asked in a velvet voice.

Dane grimaced. ''No, but you're going to tell me anyway. How did you know?''

Maya lifted her chin and held his stormy blue gaze. ''The bloodred dawn, that's how.'' She watched her words sink in. Dane gave her a startled look, one of disbelief. Because of it, Maya wasn't going to cut him one inch of slack.

''That's right, a red dawn. We've found that when the sky is that color, we get Kamovs up our tail rotors. Over time, we can call it with a lot of accuracy. I know in your well-ordered little world it sounds like voodoo. You call it what you want. As you and your other I.P.s ride with us this coming week to find out how we work around here, just keep your minds open, okay?''

He felt heat move up the column of his neck and into his face. Blushing. Of all times for that to happen! Swallowing hard, Dane met and held her glare. ''I'm not going to get into a fight with you about intuition, Captain. I'll instruct my other pilots to listen to whatever your pilots have to teach them. Frankly, I don't care how you get your info. We're all in this together, to survive. If a red dawn is a red flag, fine.''

Maya took a step back from him and assessed his scowling features. ''Good,'' she murmured. ''That's the kind of can-do spirit I want to see from you and your men, Major. There are differences between how we operate down here and what you taught us at Fort Rucker.''

He saw a wicked look lingering deep in her eyes. For a moment, Dane thought she was enjoying her power over him. Well, hadn't he lorded his power and control over her at Fort

Rucker? Yes. Smarting beneath her cool gaze, he managed to reply, "We're open to learning new things, Captain."

Flexing her shoulders, Maya stepped aside as a sergeant hurried between them with an apology, on her way to another office. "We're both learning."

Dane watched as she turned on her booted heel and walked purposefully toward her office. Blowing out a breath, he turned and went into his own, shutting the door behind him. The office was small, with no windows. Moving around the desk, he placed his helmet on top of a cabinet and stuffed the gloves into it. There was a polite knock on his door.

"Enter," he growled. Looking up, he saw it was a black-haired woman with dark coppery skin and black, almond-shaped eyes. She looked Indian. Maybe from Peru? Dane wasn't sure. Dressed in baggy green fatigues and a green T-shirt that was stained with sweat under her arms and around her neck, she came to attention.

"Sergeant Paredes, sir. Dr. Elizabeth Cornell requests your presence at her clinic when you get a chance, sir."

"At ease, Sergeant," he murmured. The woman was short and stocky. Dane had no idea who she was. Maybe a mechanic. Wiping his brow, he said, "Tell Dr. Cornell I'll meet her in about thirty minutes. I've got a mission report to fill out first and then I'll be down to see her."

Paredes snapped to attention. "Yes, sir, Major. I'll tell her, sir. Thank you, sir." She saluted.

York snapped off a returning salute. "Dismissed, Sergeant. Thank you."

Paredes nodded, did an about-face and left. The door was left open. He moved around the desk, scowling. He shut the door with finality.

As he turned to go back to the desk, there was another knock. Rolling his eyes, Dane wondered how anyone got anything done around here with these kinds of intrusions constantly occurring. He jerked the door open, a snarl on his lips.

A tall woman stood there, one with blond hair hanging around her shoulders, blue eyes, and a narrow face with a patrician nose. She was in a black flight uniform.

Dane instantly reined in his snarl. This was a pilot. "Yes?"

"Lieutenant Gautier, Major York. Captain Stevenson said you might want this…." She handed him some papers. "Mission report forms."

"Oh…yes. Thanks, Lieutenant…"

She gave him a slight smile as she assessed him. "Just call me Lobo. Around here, we mostly stick to our handles and we aren't very formal."

Standing there, Dane nodded. "Yes…thanks…"

Gautier, who was about five foot eight inches tall, turned gracefully and moved down the hall. He watched her disappear into another office.

Looking at the door, Dane decided to leave it open. Old habits died hard. If he was at Fort Rucker, his office door would be closed. His office was off limits to everyone and everything. A bastion against the rest of the world when he felt the need to withdraw from it and get his act together again. Looking up and down the hall, he saw that every office door was ajar. Even Maya's. Well, he was going to have to adjust or else. "When in Rome, do as the Romans do," he muttered as he turned and went back into his office.

Eyeing the bright purple-and-white spikes of orchids hanging out of a green metal can, Dane stopped and touched one of the flowers. They were real, not some silk flower fake. Looking around at the lifelessness of his office, he began to realize why the orchids were put there. It was a breath of real life. Of nature. One corner of his mouth curved faintly as he dropped the mission report forms on his desk. He knew Maya would sense his consternation over the flowers being put on his desk. At his base at Fort Rucker, he'd never have something like flowers around.

It was a woman's touch, he thought again, as he studied

the full white petals and the rich purple in the center of the orchid. And he was in a woman's world. Shaking his head, he seesawed with the dichotomy. On one hand, Maya knew her business as a combat pilot and squadron commander. Yet the evidence of women's things popped up in the most surprising places. That, and the informality that seemed to pervade her command—a blur between rank and privilege. The way Gautier had treated him—more like an equal, when he was a major and she a lowly lieutenant—had surprised him as well.

He'd heard that women knew how to work as a team a lot better than men did. Maybe that was true. Was it because they didn't keep up walls, the barriers of rank, that this place hummed like a well-ordered beehive? He'd been damned impressed at the short time it took to get those two Apaches off the ground and into the air to chase Faro's helicopters. Shaking his head, Dane sat down on the creaky chair. Maya and this place seemed alien, out of sync with him. He was trying to adjust, but it was hard.

Getting down to the business of penning his flight mission report, Dane decided to stop thinking so much and just let things roll as they might around here. He couldn't afford to be rigid like they were stateside. No, down here, Maya ran her organization differently. Lifting his head, he mused at the word he'd just used: *different*. Maybe that was what her people had meant—that she ran her squadron much more loosely than the military usually did. At least more loosely than they were used to up north.

Sighing, he tried to concentrate on the report in front of him, pulling a pen from the side pocket of the left arm of his flight uniform. What would the next few days bring? Some peace, he hoped...if he could keep his foot out of his mouth long enough.

Chapter 7

The bogey bell clanged gratingly throughout the cave complex. Dane moved from behind his desk and grabbed his helmet from the nearby shelf. He knew Maya had duty today. And he'd been waiting for this opportunity for the last four days, ever since his flight with her. Today she was back on the combat flight roster. Hurrying down the stairs, he ran out toward the lip, where they were pushing out the two Apaches that would intercept. It was late afternoon; the sky was the usual mix of clouds and pale blue. The humidity was high and he was sweating profusely.

The well-trained crews swarmed around the individual gunships, pulling off the rotor tethers as the crew chiefs opened up the cockpits for the pilots, who were running toward them.

Spotting Maya coming from the dispensary, which was located at the rear of the cave complex, Dane slowed until she caught up with him. Since the last flight with her, he'd spent every moment he could in the air, as copilot gunner, on different intercept missions. Maya had given him permission because it would help him set up a realistic training schedule, which would begin next Monday.

"I'm coming with you, if it's all right with you," he said as he jogged at her shoulder.

Maya shrugged and kept up her long stride toward the Apache on the left, nearest the wall. "Fine by me."

Penny handed Maya the sat intel information as she approached the gunship. "They've spotted three helos, Captain. They're forty miles from the border."

"Thanks, Penny." Maya stuffed the printout into her flight suit pocket. Dane had already climbed into the back seat and was busy getting into his harness. Looking to her right, she saw that CWO3 Akiva Redtail, an Apache-Lakota Sioux woman, and her copilot, CWO2 Vickey Mabrey, were already in their gunship and ready to roll. Akiva always wore a bright red scarf around her head, a sign that she was an Apache warrior. In her belt she wore an antique ax and Bowie knife that was given to her when she passed all the demanding tests in her tribe to become a warrior. Maya had allowed her to keep the articles of war on her person not only because she honored Akiva, but because they had been handed down through Akiva's family from her great-great grandmother, who was a warrior and rode with Geronimo.

Climbing into the front seat, Maya automatically went through the motions. In no time, she was lifting off the Apache and threading the Eye of the Needle. This was only the second time she'd flown with Dane since his arrival. She'd heard back from the pilots he'd flown with since, on ten other missions, that he was quickly getting up to speed on the demands of the job. *Good.*

"We're clear, Saber," came Redtail's voice.

"Roger, Chief. Let's rock 'n' roll, ladies…and gentleman."

Dane was busy firing up the HUD radar, searching in the general area that the satellite intel had picked up the helo activity. He heard the irony and amusement in Maya's voice. Since their last head-on confrontation in the hall of HQ, she had left him alone to manage his responsibilities for the training schedule. Sometimes he'd seen her pass in the hall, but she never looked his way or dropped by to talk. No, that steel wall between them was solidly in place.

Mouth compressing, Dane scanned the skies overhead. He had no one to blame but himself. Racking his brain for ways to approach Maya and ask her to trust him was a fool's business. If he'd learned anything in the past four days, it was that she trusted those who proved themselves capable of her trust. Her squadron really did idolize her, he'd discovered. They loved her more like a mother who nurtured them, rather than fearing her as a squadron leader. And there was nothing they wouldn't do for Maya. Yes, the last four days had shown him just how much his own dark prejudice against her, against women in general, was really distorted and inappropriate.

"Got anything on radar yet?" Maya demanded as she pushed the Apache up to ten thousand feet, above the cloud layer.

"No," he murmured. "You got any feelings about this mission?"

Maya chuckled. "Uh-oh, sounds like my pilots have been retraining you on the finer points of using your intuition as radar, too."

He liked the sound of her husky voice. She seemed to have let down her guard. He grinned. "Yeah, you could say that. You sense anything?"

Maya felt him trying to earnestly establish a beachhead of trust with her. She was exhausted by the demands of the squadron, plus having the new I.P.s around and flying combat missions. "I'm too damn tired to sense much of anything right now. How about you?" She looked around, always searching for the lethal Kamovs. In the past four days, since their last attack, the Kamovs seemed to have evaporated from their airspace. That wasn't like them, and Maya was uneasy about it. What was up? What did Faro have up his sleeve?

"I'm not sure it's a feeling," Dane murmured, frowning at the HUDs. He saw a vague outline. That meant it was painting something out there. What, exactly, he wasn't sure. "I've got three bogeys on screen," he stated, giving her the coordinates. Instantly, Maya changed directions, and so did Redtail, who followed two rotor lengths behind her.

"What then?" Maya asked. She felt safe in the cockpit of her Apache, like a child in a mother's arms. She trusted this gunship with her life. Literally.

"I don't know.... I can't explain it...."

"You usually can't define intuition hits that clearly," she said. "You know without knowing."

"Spoken like a true oracle."

Maya laughed outright. It was the first time she'd truly let down around Dane, and it felt good. She heard him chuckling in her headset.

"If I was an oracle, I'd be able to tell you what Faro's up to," she griped unhappily.

"Yeah, Lobo said he's up to no good. He's changing tactics on you—again."

"Yes...and that always makes me nervous."

"I'm scanning for the Kamovs," Dane assured her. All around them rose the lofty mountains, clothed in jungle greenery. Dane was familiar with most of the flight routes now. They'd go due east and intercept somewhere between the lowlands of the jungle and the highlands, which curved steeply up to fourteen thousand feet. Lake Titicaca wasn't that far away, although he had yet to see it. The Bolivian border area was high, arid desert, a no-man's land with harsh conditions.

Just as he lifted his head to scan, he saw something peripherally.

"Wait...."

Twisting his head, he looked again.

"Kamovs!" he barked. "One o'clock high! Break! Break!"

Instantly, Maya peeled off to the left. Redtail sheered to the right. The Apache groaned as she brought the nose up and into a vertical climb, the throttles to the firewall. Jerking her head around, Maya saw the double-rotored Kamovs charging them. Her eyes widened.

"Damn! There's *three* of them!"

Dane sucked in a breath. He saw all three of the black Russian helicopters roaring full speed from behind the mountain where they'd been hiding. They were diving down at them. He and Maya were in trouble. Quickly, he punched up the rockets for launch.

Maya cursed softly and realized that two of the Kamovs were peeling off toward her. Where had Faro gotten a *third* Kamov? Had he bought another one in order to up the ante? The third was after Redtail. Maya was too low. The Kamovs were high. They had the advantage. *Damn!* Sweat stood out on her carved face. Her lips drew back from her teeth as she whipped the Apache around so that they could fire at their oncoming attackers.

"Rockets on line. I've got one painted."

Dane's voice was cool and low. It soothed her. Heart pounding, Maya watched as the second Kamov broke from the first and began to move in for a kill.

"Fire when ready," she snapped.

"Firing."

The white light of the rocket sped from both sides of the Apache. Maya wasted no time watching to see if they hit their target. She had a second Kamov stalking her in earnest. Seeing the winking of gunfire, she knew that he was firing 30 mm cannon shells at them.

Too late!

The front cockpit Plexiglas cracked. It was designed to take a 30 mm hit, but the side panels were not shell resistant. Maya heard the explosion of shattering Plexiglas. She felt a white-hot heat sear her left arm. Several pieces of the canopy slashed against her chest and struck the chicken plate with a thud. The vest had just saved her life.

Jerking the Apache to the right, and moving toward the Kamov, she yelled, "Fire!"

Dane had winced as the shells slammed into the front cockpit and arced above him. Was Maya wounded? He'd heard her groan, but that was all. From the way she was handling the Apache, she didn't seem hurt at all. He quickly thumbed the button. The 30 mm cannon beneath the Apache began thunking out huge rounds at the approaching Kamov. Satisfaction soared through him as Maya held the gunship right on course. The cannon shells were going to find their mark.

In his headset, he heard Redtail yelling excitedly. The crew on the other Apache had their own battle on their hands. Jerking his head around, Dane saw two of the shells impact the right wing of the Kamov. *Good!* Instantly, the helicopter banked to the right, away from them, smoke pouring out of one engine.

Maya rubbernecked around, desperately looking for the other Kamov. It was gone! Breathing hard, she pulled the Apache around to locate Redtail. She was about two miles away. The third Kamov was hightailing it back toward the jungle.

Wind was whipping into the cockpit, through the broken Plexiglas. She saw the shattered, sparkling pieces sprinkled all around her, across her lap and on the floor beneath her feet. And then she saw something else. Blood. Blood was splattered across her instrument panel.

"What the hell..." she muttered. "Take the controls, Dane. I need to check something out. You got the controls?"

Instantly, he placed his hands and feet on them. "I have the controls." He kept searching the sky and twisting around. The Kamovs were gone. They appeared and disappeared like magicians; now you see them, now you don't. Breathing raggedly, he blinked his eyes rapidly. Sweat was stinging them.

He looked up over his console. He could see part of Maya's shattered cockpit. And he could just make out the top of her black helmet. Frowning, he said, "What's wrong? Are you all right?"

Maya felt a vague pain on the inside of her upper left arm. As she lifted her right hand to brush away the Plexiglas, she saw that her uniform had been torn open beneath. Several chunks had been taken out of her chicken plate. Moving her fingers along her chest, she made sure she wasn't injured. She was okay. The wind was making her eyes tear and blur so she couldn't see anything.

"Slow this thing down. I can hardly see up here."

Dane pulled back on the throttles. He saw Redtail coming back to join them. "You want me to hover?"

"No, just head back to base below a hundred miles an hour."

"Roger."

He heard a strange edge in Maya's voice. What was going on? "Are you injured?"

Lifting her left arm, she saw blood pumping out of a deep slash in it. "Damn," she muttered. "I'm bleeding like a stuck hog...."

Frowning, Dane said, "Where? Where are you hit?" His heart began to pound unevenly. They were twenty minutes from base. He resisted the urge to speed up.

"The left arm," Maya muttered. "Cut an artery, I think, by flying Plexiglas. Damn...gotta find something to tie off the area above it...." And she began to search around for something, anything, to wrap around her upper arm. Dizziness assailed her. Maya closed her eyes, then opened them. This couldn't be happening. Of all things...

"There's nothing up there to tie it off with," Dane told her urgently. "Use your right hand and press hard on it, Maya. Use direct pressure, all you have. It'll slow the bleeding down. Can you do that?"

Her fingers became slippery as she tried to squeeze the

opened flesh that was pumping blood. "Yeah...I'm doing that now."

"Are you feeling all right?"

Maya heard the tension in Dane's tone. Leaning her head back, she closed her eyes. "No...I'm not. Call base. Ask the medical team to meet us on the lip. I'm losing blood fast...." And she looked down to realize that it had been pooling below her feet on the deck without her even realizing it. Her heart was pounding in her chest like an overstressed freight train. Her voice sounded weak to her ears, not filled with her usual strong confidence. Was she going to die? *No!* She didn't want to. Trying to press her right hand tighter around her upper arm, she felt coldness creeping into her bones. The wind, although warm and humid, was buffeting her.

"Dane..."

Alarmed, he heard the faraway tone of Maya's voice. It was the first time she'd called him by his first name. He heard an edge of fear in her voice. She was going down. *No! Not her! Not now!*

"I—think...I think I'm going to lose consciousness pretty soon. If I do, I can't hold the pressure on my arm and I'm going to start bleeding out again."

Her voice was growing fainter by the moment. His eyes widened. There was nothing he could do to help her. Frustration ate at him. "Maya, just hold on. Take some deep breaths. Stay awake!"

She heard the raw concern in his voice. Resting her head against the back of her seat, she felt darkness edging her vision. Closing her eyes, she whispered, "Redline this gunship...or I'm not going to make it...."

Those were the last words he heard from her. Instantly, Dane moved the Apache to top speed. He called the base and requested immediate medical standby. As he gave the details of Maya's injury, he knew it was a race against time. She was bleeding out. He knew that if an artery was cut at an angle, in two or three minutes it would close itself off to a bare trickle, and her life would be saved. However, if the artery had been sliced cleanly through, it had no way of closing itself off—and she would bleed out and die. Looking at his watch, he saw they had ten minutes until they landed. Hurry! Hurry! His hands wrapped hard around the controls.

Taking over as flight commander, he radioed Redtail, ordering her back to base as well, as there was no need to put a lone Apache up against the two Kamovs that might still be out hunting them. His mind raced. His heart hurt. Maya was too proud, too beautiful, too brave to die. It couldn't end this way for her. It just couldn't! His mouth compressed into a thin line. As he brought the Apache down to six thousand feet, the sky nearly clear for once, he could see the mountain ahead where their base was located.

"Maya? Maya? Do you hear me? We're almost home. Home. You hear me? We're almost home. You're going to make it. Just hang on. I'll get you help. Just hang on…"

There was no answer.

Son of a bitch! He felt an arcing pain across his chest where his heart thumped wildly. It was frustration mixed with anxiety and something else…something so shadowed and hesitant that he couldn't even name it as he flew the Apache toward the base.

Flying up to the Eye, Dane didn't take a hesitant, slow approach. Instead, he used visual, because the clouds had dissipated, and plunged through the opening, quickly setting the Apache down on the right side of the lip. He could see Dr. Elizabeth Cornell standing near Paredes, her paramedic, and a gurney. Heart pounding unrelentingly, Dane quickly cut the engines.

Without even waiting for the rotors to stop, which was protocol, he unharnessed himself. Shoving the cockpit door open, he climbed out on the side of the helo. The rotation of the rotors was causing a lot of air turbulence. It pounded at him. Gripping the handle to Maya's shattered cockpit canopy, he jerked it open.

Someone else placed a ladder next to where he was crouched and was climbing up it. It was Paredes, her eyes slitted with concern.

Dane gasped as he shoved himself into Maya's tight compartment. Blood was everywhere, on the floor and splattered throughout the cockpit. Maya was unconscious, her head sagging back against the window. Her arms were limp against her form. The left side of her uniform was soaked in blood.

"I'll unharness her," he called to Paredes, who had also climbed up on the fuselage area.

Reaching in, his hands shaking badly, Dane unharnessed Maya. She was a big woman. It was going to take every ounce of his strength to pull her out of that cramped cockpit. Reaching for her helmet, he loosened the chin strap and gently pulled it off her head. Her black hair spilled out across her shoulders and the chest armor. Her face was white. Frightened, Dane handed the helmet to Paredes's outstretched, waiting hands.

Mouth dry, he angled his body so that he faced Maya. Slipping his hands beneath her armpits, he hauled her upward. Grunting, he balanced himself against the airframe and pulled her halfway out of the cockpit. Paredes was there to catch Maya's head as it fell downward.

"I got her!" Paredes said urgently. "We need more hands!" she called to those below.

Another sergeant climbed the ladder. Between the three of them, they were able to pull Maya out of her seat. Dane untangled her feet from around the collective and hoisted the lower half of her body out of the cockpit. Free! She was free. Urgency drummed through him. He looked down. Tears stung his eyes. Every person on the base was standing below. He saw so many hands on either side of the ladder lift upward to receive Maya that it tightened his throat. The fear in their faces, the look in their eyes, touched him deeply as he handed Maya to the awaiting sea of helping hands below.

Wiping his mouth, Dane hunkered down on the fuselage

as Maya was placed quickly on the gurney. He saw Cornell put a tight tourniquet above her left arm, which still had blood pumping out. Issuing orders, Cornell had Paredes push the gurney toward the cave. Once the ladder was clear, Dane jumped down. Looking back, he saw that the rotors were still slowly turning. The blood splattered on the front cockpit was Maya's blood. Cursing softly, he hurried through the dissipating crowd after the gurney.

"Dr. Cornell!" he called, jogging up to her as she walked quickly at the gurney's side.

The red-haired woman gave him a sharp, tight look. "Yes?"

"What are you going to do?"

With a grimace, Cornell managed to get a blood pressure cuff around Maya's limp right arm and pumped it up as they moved into the cave. "I don't know yet…give me a moment…." And she put her stethoscope to her ears and placed it on Maya's arm. Releasing the pressure, she listened as they walked quickly toward the dispensary.

"Eighty over forty," she told Paredes in an unhappy voice.

Dane scowled and watched the paramedic's copper features tighten.

"What's that mean?" he demanded, jogging alongside.

"It's bad. Her blood pressure's too low. If we don't get whole blood into her soon, her heart will cavitate and go into arrest." Cornell looked directly at him for moment. "She'll die."

"Blood? You've got blood on hand here, don't you?" Surely, Dane thought, they would. Especially under the present conditions of daily warfare.

"Of course we do." Elizabeth hurried forward and opened the door to the dispensary. Paredes shoved the gurney inside to a well-lit, white room that was crowded with medical equipment.

Dane slipped in before the door automatically closed. Anxiously, he looked at Maya's slack features. Her once golden skin was washed out now. She looked dead already. Anguish soared through him. He stood helplessly as Paredes quickly followed Cornell's orders to slit away the fabric of her uniform on her injured arm with a pair of scissors. He saw the doctor take scissors to the other arm and slit it from wrist to shoulder. In moments, they had an IV fluids going into her right arm.

Dane moved closer to get a look at the injury. It was a gash about two inches long, and he could see the artery was now dripping only slightly, thanks to the tourniquet.

"It had to be a piece of Plexiglas from the shattered cockpit that cut into her," he told the doctor. He saw Cornell's face. She looked grim as she reached for a series of dressings.

"Doctor," Paredes said, "what's her blood type? I can go get the whole blood to give to her."

Cornell hissed, "Dammit, I just realized we don't have her blood type here, Paredes."

Paredes paled. She halted halfway to the refrigeration unit where the blood was kept. "But…"

Cornell quickly cleaned the wound and threw the bloody dressings down at her feet. She worked like a madwoman.

Dane frowned. He looked at Paredes, whose mouth had fallen open. And then he jerked a glance at the doctor, still working feverishly over Maya.

"What are you talking about, Doctor? You just told me you keep blood on hand here."

Cornell grimaced. "Major, what you don't realize—" she swabbed Maya's left arm with antiseptic "—is that we're on a very limited budget. Maya handles what supplies we get in here. She opted to spend the money for O-type blood, the one that is most common, the one that nearly all our pilots have, instead of keeping any of her type on hand, instead."

Running his fingers through his hair, he approached the gurney, his eyes slits. "You're telling me the type she needs you don't have?" His voice had risen in disbelief. Shock.

"That's right, Major. Dammit! Paredes, take her BP again."

"Yes, ma'am!" Paredes quickly moved between Dane and the gurney.

"Eighty over thirty-nine."

"We're gonna lose her...." Cornell whispered. "Dammit to hell!"

"What blood type do you need?" Dane demanded.

Cornell's eyes were awash with tears. "AB positive, Major. It's not the kind of blood you find just anywhere. It would have cost too much to get it and keep it here, and Maya knew that. She took a risk. She wanted the O on hand for the bulk of her pilots, in case they got injured."

Stunned, Dane stood looking down at Maya. Her lips were colorless, her skin leaching out even more. His throat ached. She took a risk. That's what Maya had done. She'd taken a calculated risk, thinking that she would not be the one to get hit or need blood. The looks on the two women's faces made him feel their anguish.

"I've got good news for you, Doctor," he told her quietly as he rolled up the sleeve of his uniform. "I'm AB positive. You can use my blood."

Cornell's head shot up. Her eyes widened. "You *are?*" Her voice echoed around the room.

"Yes!" Paredes shouted triumphantly, her eyes shining with hope. She quickly ran and got the supplies for a blood transfusion from a cabinet.

Dane grinned. "Maya is gonna be pissed off as hell about it, but right now, I'm her knight in shining armor coming to the rescue. Where do you want me to sit, Doctor? You can take as much as you need."

Paredes quickly swabbed down his left arm and placed the needle into one of his large veins. She was smiling ear-to-ear.

Cornell pulled another gurney next to Maya's. "Lie down on this, Major. Quickly. There's no time left...."

Dane did as he was instructed. Paredes moved like lightning, making the IV tube connection into Maya's right arm. Relief flowed through him. The universe worked in strange and mysterious ways, he thought, as Paredes handed him a rubber ball to squeeze from time to time, to keep the blood flowing out of his body and into Maya's. Finally, he'd found a way to connect with her. He wasn't at all sure she was going to be happy about it. Watching as his dark red blood flowed through the tubing and into Maya's receiving arm, he grinned lopsidedly. Cornell was listening intently to Maya's heart after removing the chicken plate. Her brows were furrowed, her eyes half-closed. Her lips were tight.

Paredes hooked Maya up to a blood pressure gauge that was suspended on the wall behind her head. Both medical people watched it raptly.

"Ninety over fifty!" Paredes whispered. She clenched her fist and yelled, "Yes!"

Dane scowled. "What does that mean, Sergeant?"

Paredes glowed, her teeth white against her coppery skin. "It means that her blood pressure is rising, sir. It means your blood is making the difference."

"It means," Cornell whispered unsteadily, as she placed her arm on Maya's shoulder, "that you're saving her life. Literally. She's lost over two pints of blood, Major. I'm going to take about one and half out of you. Normally, we take only a pint."

"Take what you need!" he repeated fervently.

Cornell shook her head. "Depending upon how Maya's blood pressure responds, I may take more—or less—I don't know yet." She watched the monitors fluctuating above Maya's head.

"I'm not going to die with two pints gone," Dane said.

"No, but you'll definitely feel like a ton of bricks hit you for a good two weeks, until your body can make enough to bring you back to your own healthy levels and needs," Cornell warned.

"I can handle it," he assured her with a grin. His heart soared. Maya's life was going to be saved! Dane couldn't recall when he'd ever felt as good about anything as this. Ever.

Cornell smiled hesitantly, her hand moving in a motherly fashion across Maya's shoulder. "We're treading on dangerous ground here, Major. Maya, judging from her blood pressure, lost closer to three pints of blood. I have to balance it out between you." She began to sew the artery back together, with Paredes handing her the needle and thread. "This is a game of balance, Major. I can't take too much from you, or you'll have problems. And I've got to give Maya enough to recover without having to worry about her going into cardiac arrest. I don't have any AB positive whole blood as backup if you go down on me."

A warmth moved through Dane as he lay there watching them work on Maya's left arm. He was beginning to feel the effects of blood loss from the transfusion. It must have been how Maya felt in the cockpit. Closing his eyes, Dane kept squeezing the ball every few seconds. Maya could have died. She almost had. His heart twinged with anguish. She was too beautiful. Too bold and brave to die. If anyone should live, it should be her, he thought as he placed his free arm across his eyes.

Just remembering the crowd of women surrounding the Apache, their arms stretched high to receive Maya and pass her down the line made his throat tighten again. There was something so special about her that instilled people to surround her and protect her. Hell, even he had. What was it? What was that difference? He tried to figure it out as he lay there, his senses tumbling.

"We need to get ahold of Inca," Paredes said to the doctor. "She can help us."

"Maya's sister? The healer?" Cornell asked.

"Yes, ma'am. When we're done here, can I run over to comms and try to raise her?"

"She's in Brazil."

"I know that, ma'am, but maybe they can fly her over here? You know, she touches someone and they heal up."

Dane frowned, listening to the intensely whispered conversation. He lifted his arm from across his eyes, twisted his head and looked at them.

"What are you talking about?"

Cornell continued to sew the ends of the artery together. "Maya has a fraternal twin sister who is a healer in Brazil. I can tell by the look on your face, Major, that you're a little surprised by our conversation. Inca can lay her hands on a person and heal them. Right now, I could use everything possible, to get Maya stabilized. My bet is she's lost three pints of blood. We're putting only one and a half or maybe two back into her. If Inca can help, we're going to explore that possibility, too."

Stunned, Dane stared at them. "A healer?"

Paredes smiled gamely. "Major, this isn't like other bases you've been at. We practice voodoo, too."

"Paredes!" Cornell said sharply.

"Well, I'm just teasing, Major. It's not voodoo, really. The Captain's sister is well known down here for her healing abilities. She's known as the jaguar goddess by just about everyone."

With a shake of his head, Dane covered his eyes with his arm again. "You're right," he muttered, "this is one hell of a strange place."

"Angel, when I'm done here, get to comms. Make the call."

"Yes, ma'am." Paredes glowed with excitement as she handed the doctor a sponge.

Feeling a little floaty, Dane took in a deep breath. Tiredness was beginning to creep through him.

"Ninety over sixty," Paredes crowed triumphantly. "It's working, Major. Your blood is stabilizing her real well."

Dane nodded. "Good, Sergeant. I'm glad." And he was.

The adrenaline he had felt was beginning to ebb away, leaving him feeling shaky in the aftermath. The urgency was still with him, though. Maya wasn't out of the woods yet, according to Cornell. More than anything, he wanted Maya to live. As he lay there, his heart ached with that same feeling he'd felt before, in the cockpit, after Maya had started losing consciousness.

Frowning, Dane focused on the feeling. When he thought he could put a name to the emotion, he instantly recoiled from it. No…it couldn't be. He couldn't feel that way about Maya. Or could he? His mouth compressed in a slash against the possibility. How could he have these kinds of raw, needy feelings toward a woman who hated the very earth he walked upon? He felt a strong caring feeling flowing toward her, a need to hold her in his arms, kiss her and breathe his life back into her. The thoughts were absolutely shocking to Dane, and yet here they were, alive, vibrant and clamoring to be acted upon.

Great, he wanted her as a woman to his man. He craved to feel Maya's arms around him. He wondered what it would be like to feel the softness and womanly strength of her lips against his mouth. Would the heat in her eyes translate to another kind of vibrant heat that could only come from within her? His need of Maya on that level gnawed at him relentlessly. Maybe because he was weakening from blood loss in the transfusion, he was a little more vulnerable to his buried thoughts and feelings toward her.

Confusion spun around in him. Dane felt light-headed. His raw emotions were bubbling to the surface, and they had his full attention. There was no way he could fall in love with Maya. Or have feelings of love toward her. Could he? *How* could he? Nothing made sense to Dane. Not right now. He blamed his present state on the urgency of his emotions. It was just the possibility of losing Maya at the base, on this mission, which was so important. That was all. It had to be all.

Chapter 8

The first thing Maya felt as she dragged herself out of the darkness was pain. Pain throbbing in her left arm. She heard women's voices, low and whispering. Her shorting-out consciousness then became aware of the warmth of a hand on her right shoulder. What had happened? Blinking, she squinted as she opened her eyes.

"Ah, she's awake."

It was Captain Dove Rivera's soft, melodic voice.

Opening her eyes, Maya saw Dr. Cornell and Angel bending over her.

"Do I look like a bug under a microscope?" she demanded in a rusty voice.

Dove Rivera, who sat on a stool next to her bed, lifted her hand from Maya's shoulder and grinned hugely. Her flashing smile filled the room as she gazed down at Maya.

"Welcome back from the Threshold, Maya."

Barely lifting her head, Maya looked around. "I'm in our hospital. Why?"

Elizabeth placed her hands in the pockets of her white coat.

Her stethoscope hung around her neck. "Because you almost croaked on us, that's why, Maya. Do you remember what happened about two hours ago?"

Closing her eyes, her mouth dry, Maya whispered, "Oh damn...we got nailed by a Kamov...." And then her lashes lifted and worry filled her voice. "Dane? Is he okay? I mean...Major York? Did he get hit, too?"

Chuckling, Paredes hoisted her thumb toward the door at the other end of their four-bed hospital section, which was part of the clinic. "Well, he got hit all right. But he's okay." She traded an amused look with the doctor.

Maya felt incredibly weak. "Then...he's okay...." She had been alarmed that he might have gotten hurt, too.

Elizabeth placed her hand on Maya's left shoulder and squeezed it gently. "You received a deep cut to the under side of your left arm. It sliced your brachial artery wide open. You tried to stop the bleeding and eventually, because of blood loss, you fell unconscious. Major York flew you home."

Dove tittered. "You shoulda seen him come barreling through the Eye, Maya. I mean, that man's tail was on fire. He didn't creep through like he'd been doing before." She slapped her knee and giggled. "It wasn't funny at the time, but it is now. We were all waiting for you on the lip." She gestured toward Elizabeth and Angel. "I mean, that guy came through the Eye like it wasn't there. Even *we* were impressed. He's got guts when he needs them."

Closing her eyes, Maya remembered vague bits of the Kamov attack. "Then why is he hurt?" She heard the collective laugh of the women who surrounded her bed. In each of her arms were IVs feeding her nutrients.

"Because," Elizabeth said quietly and seriously, "he literally saved your life."

Opening her eyes to slits, Maya whispered, "He did a good job of flying us home."

"Oh," Dove said, her thick black, brows arching, "he did

a little more than that.'' Her black eyes gleamed with amusement as she traded smiles with her compatriots once more.

''I don't think you're going to like what I have to tell you,'' Elizabeth said, ''but Major York gave you a blood transfusion of AB positive. We had none on hand, as you well know.'' Elizabeth frowned. ''And you were dumping on us, Maya. I figure you've lost three pints of blood. You shouldn't have even have made it back here. When we got you into the dispensary, your blood pressure was falling through the floor. Major York was hovering over you like a mother hen. When he found out we didn't have AB positive on hand, he told us he was.'' She smiled softly. ''The guy is okay, Maya. He started rolling up his sleeve and asking where he could sit so you could get enough blood into you before you went into cardiac arrest.''

Stunned, Maya stared up at the doctor. ''He—Dane—I mean, Major York—he—you've got to be kidding me!'' His blood in her body. The explosion of shock rippled through Maya. She saw the serious set of Elizabeth's narrow face. At thirty-five, Elizabeth was one of the oldest women on the base. And her heart was one of the largest.

''What was it he said?'' Angel said, laughing. ''That when you woke up and found out you had his redneck blood in your body, that you wouldn't be very happy about it?''

''That's what he said,'' Elizabeth murmured. She smoothed the blue gown Maya wore in a motherly fashion. ''We've got other things in motion, too. I had Angel go to comms and contact your sister, Inca. We just got word that she's being flown out from Manaus on a Perseus jet to Cuzco. As soon as she gets here—'' Elizabeth looked at her watch ''—which should be about five hours from now, Dove is going to take the civilian helo from the mining side into Cuzco to pick her up at the airport. She'll then fly her out here.'' She gently tapped Maya's shoulder. ''You're still not out of the woods, Maya. We've got another flight in at the Good Samaritan Hospital in Lima right now, and we're picking up four pints of AB positive blood. You need more, and I'm afraid Major York is really weakened from giving you two pints of his own blood. As soon as Dallas arrives back here with it, we're pumping both of you to normal levels to get you on safer ground. Until then, you are to just lie here and rest. You're going nowhere." Her voice had turned grim.

Blown away by the news, Maya stared up at the doctor. "I still can't believe this—*he* gave his blood to *me?*"

Sliding off the stool, Dove laughed. Though she was half Spanish, half Q'uero Indian, Dove, who stood a little over five foot five inches tall, was built solidly like her Q'uero ancestors, the original Incas. "Now you got redneck blood in you, too, Maya. Just think—blood of the guy you hated the most, the one who almost did all of us in back at Fort Rucker, is in your veins now. Isn't that something?" She picked up her helmet and placed it under her left arm. "I'm on standby, so I gotta get out of here. I just wanted to be here when you came around. You've got fifty other people who are wanting to see you, too."

"Dove, spread the word that Maya is awake and stable."

"I will," she told the doctor as she headed toward the swinging doors at the end of the small hospital unit. At the doors, she halted. "Oh. Major York has been asking about you. He wants to see you. Do you want to see him? He's just outside in the dispensary, lying down. The man keeps asking about you every five minutes."

Frowning, Maya whispered, "Sure…I'll see him…." And her heart fluttered with a strange, new emotion.

Angel and Elizabeth left her bedside. "We'll give you two some time alone," Elizabeth counseled. She wagged her finger in Maya's face. "But if he upsets you, or you want him to leave, just tell him that. I don't want you stressed. Not right now, okay?"

Compressing her dry lips, Maya nodded weakly. "Doc, I'm in no shape to fight or spar with anyone. I just want to thank him. It's the least I can do."

Pleased, Elizabeth said, "Good for you. Angel will come and check on you every half hour. The buzzer is located near your right hand. Push it and we'll be here in a heartbeat, okay?"

"Yes...thank you...all of you..."

The ward became quiet after they left. It was a small room with two beds on either side. Maya had helped create this small hospital section, but this was the first time in three years she'd been in it. There were windows located on the side that faced the opening to the cave. Everything was painted white, and white cotton curtains hung at the rectangular windows, which allowed feeble light to enter the area.

She was propped up slightly in bed, she realized. Her arm ached dully, and looking down at it, she saw it was wrapped in several bandages. The water sitting on the bedstand nearby looked awfully good. Trying to reach for it, she found, to her consternation, that she was so weak it took every effort to drag her hand across her lap toward it.

Lying back, exhausted, Maya closed her eyes. Dane York had saved her life. His blood was in her body. A lot of it. Emotions roiled within her. How could someone who hated her as much as he did do something like this for her? Confused, Maya didn't have much time to work through her feelings. She heard the door open quietly and then close. Turning her head, she forced her eyes open. Through her thick, black lashes, she saw Dane York, still in his black flight uniform, his left sleeve rolled up above his elbow, come walking into the unit. Her heart skipped a beat.

Dane looked washed out. No longer did he walk with that vital step she'd come to know so well. His face was haggard, and there were shadows lurking beneath his large blue eyes. Warmth moved through her unexpectedly as she met and held his welcoming gaze. There was a slight, hesitant smile on his mouth. His eyes were alive with anxiety and worry in their depths. For who? Her? Maya found it hard to think of Dane York as someone who really cared what happened to her. All of her old assumptions exploded suddenly. As he reached the rail of her bed and looked down at her, Maya realized that for the first time she was seeing him without his armor in place. Right now, his face was so very readable. His mouth, usually so harshly set, no longer turned in at the corners. No, if anything, he had an incredible expression of care that radiated straight through her to her heart.

"I didn't hear any hysterical screaming coming from here when you found out you have some of my blood," he teased, his voice husky with emotion. How badly he wanted to reach out and touch Maya. She looked wan, her once golden flesh leached out. Her black hair lay in thick ebony strands around her face and gowned shoulders. Her lips were slightly parted. The look in her eyes was one of confusion, warmth and something else he couldn't easily decipher.

To hell with it. Facing her, Dane reached over and gently moved his hand across the crown of her head, barely grazing her hair. A look of shock registered in her dull green eyes at his gesture of unspoken concern and care. Dane removed his hand. He realized he shouldn't have tried making contact with her. His heart ached.

Tiny tingles radiated across Maya's scalp where he'd skimmed her hair. His touch was so unexpected that she was speechless for a moment. The anxiety in his face was unmistakable. He cared for *her.* Blinking, she opened her mouth to speak. Only a croak came out.

"Sounds like you need some water?" he teased and, reaching over, he poured some in a glass and held it out to her. Dane wanted to do something—anything—to show how much he was concerned for Maya. Surprise and confusion were alive in her eyes as she stared up at him when he patiently offered her the glass.

"I—I'm weak… Can you…can you help me get it to my mouth? I'm dying of thirst."

She'd asked for his help. His heart soared. A slight, self-conscious grin pulled at one corner of his mouth. "Yeah, hold on. Let me situate myself so I can get you into enough of a sitting position to drink it without wearing it…." He set the glass down and moved toward her head. He was looking forward to contact with her once again. Maybe touch was all he had to communicate to Maya that he wasn't the bastard he'd been four years earlier. Leaning over her, Dane slid his arm beneath her neck and shoulders and eased her upward. Maya didn't protest or struggle. She didn't try and fight him or move away from his supportive embrace. Again his heart soared.

"Here," he murmured, bringing the glass to her cracked, dry lips, "drink all you want." As he pressed the rim of the glass to her mouth, he saw her try to raise her hand, but fail. Alarmed at her weakness, Dane realized that although Maya was alive, she was far from well.

Sucking noisily, Maya drank the entire contents of the glass. Dane's arm felt strong and reassuring around her. When she asked for more, he chuckled.

"Good sign. Anytime someone wants water or food, they're going to live." He poured her another glass and then eased her up into his arms again.

Maya absorbed his care. Right now, she was feeling very weak and out of control. The second glass of water sated her. Leaning her head against his strong, capable shoulder, she whispered, "Thanks…"

Dane didn't want to release her, but he knew he had to. Easing Maya onto the bed, he put the glass aside. Fussing with the pillows under her head, he gazed down at Maya. How beautiful she looked. And how in need of care she was right now.

"There. Better?"

Maya nodded once and closed her eyes. "Yeah…better. Thanks." All sorts of warm ripples were moving throughout her neck and shoulders where he'd held her. A part of her wondered why they had this ongoing battle between them at all.

Dane pulled up the stool and sat down, his arm resting on the rail as he faced Maya. The hum of constant activity outside the room could be heard. He felt like a beggar being given the chance to simply absorb her beauty, her strength and bravery as he sat there in the silence of the room.

"You know," he began awkwardly, in a halting, low tone, "I was so scared out there. I didn't realize when the Kamov started firing at us that your cockpit would shatter. I felt frustrated, Maya. I couldn't reach you or help you." He saw her eyes barely open, her pupils large and black and centered on him. Without thinking, Dane reached out and settled his hand over hers, which lay across her stomach on top of the covers. "I don't know what I expected out of that combat situation. When you turned the gunship to meet the Kamov head-on, I was surprised." He grinned a little, his fingers moving to enclose her cool hand. "You were already wounded. I don't know if you knew it at that time or not, but you turned and faced him." Shaking his head, he whispered, "You're the gutsiest person I know."

The admiration, the respect in his low, husky voice riffled through Maya. It was healing. They were words she had wanted to hear from him for so long. And just the warm, quiet strength of his hand over hers fed her and made her feel less confused. As her eyes widened, Maya realized that Dane was no longer wearing his military mask with her. No, he was just a man. A gentle, quiet man who had moved through her heart and soul like a warm breeze over a cold winter landscape.

Dane removed his hand. He knew he was taking a terrible risk by touching Maya a second time. Yet his intuition gnawed at him to keep contact with her. He saw much of the confusion leave her eyes as he'd placed his hand over hers for that precious moment.

"I—uh, don't remember much…at least, not now," Maya began with an effort. "I couldn't believe there were three Kamovs." Her brows knitted. "Dane…he's got three of those gunships now. That's bad news for us. He must have bought another one.'' Closing her eyes, Maya whispered emotionally, ''That's going to up the ante. My pilots are really going to be targets now. We can't paint the Kamovs, dammit.''

''Hey,'' he soothed as he leaned forward and once more grazed the crown of her head, ''don't even buy into that stuff right now.'' Maya barely opened her eyes, and he saw tears glimmering in the depths of them. His heart contracted. Sliding off the stool, Dane leaned over the rail. Framing her face with his hands, he said quietly, ''Listen to me for once, will you? We've got two D models sitting out there. They're more than a match for the Kamovs. Just as soon as we can get your pilots retrained in them, you're going to have *four* aircraft that can combat anything Faro's got to throw against us out there. Okay?''

All her fears rose to the surface. Maya fought the heat of the tears in her eyes. When Dane gently framed her face, a sob worked its way up her slender throat. Mouth moving, she fought not to cry. How incredibly gentle he was with her. How sensitive to her needs right now. As his hands left her face, her tears drifted down her cheeks. He was smiling down at her, his eyes burning with a tenderness she'd never seen before. Reaching out, Dane carefully removed the trail of tears with his thumbs. His touch was so fleeting, and Maya found herself starved for more of whatever he was feeding her right now. Maybe it was her present medical condition that made her excruciatingly vulnerable to him. She wasn't sure.

''I shouldn't be crying...I can't let my people see me cry....'' And she compressed her lips.

Dane settled back on the chair and gripped her hand within his. ''Listen, you run a squadron, Maya, and I'm sure you've shed a lot of tears in private for your people already. I know you have.'' He gave her a tender look while squeezing her hand. ''Behind closed doors, where no one can see you cry.''

Her fingers closed shyly about his. Dane's heart soared with euphoria. His gut feeling that she needed to be touched, to be held, had been correct, after all. For once he was doing something right by Maya—something good, not combative or argumentative. She was not erecting those walls against him, either. If anything, moment by moment, Maya was becoming wonderfully human with him. It was such an incredible gift that Dane was afraid he'd somehow blow it and ruin the tender, healing warmth that swirled invisibly between them.

Sniffing, Maya closed her eyes. "Your hand feels good, Dane. I'm feeling a little wimpy right now...."

He sat there realizing how much bravery it took for Maya to admit that to him. She'd never given him an inch before, not ever. Patting her hand gently, he rasped unsteadily, "A brush with death always makes us see the world a little more clearly. We begin to value what's really important—and what isn't."

Drowning beneath his warm blue gaze, Maya felt a new strength flowing from him into her. "You're right," she whispered. She understood on a deeper level that he was healing her with his heart. The look in Dane's eyes was one she had never anticipated. It was the look of a man who cared for his woman. She wasn't any stranger to a look like that. How could he even *like* her? None of this made any sense to her. Not at all.

"You saved my life, Dane. I want to thank you—"

"Shhh," he whispered. "I think, right now, Maya, you need to sleep. You've got dark rings under your eyes and they're getting darker by the minute."

Her mouth quirked as she stared up at him. He had that slight, boyish smile now, his head cocked, his eyes a stormy blue as he gazed down at her. How handsome Dane was. How strong. How caring. The nurturing feeling coming from him was undeniable.

"Like you don't?" she managed to retort in a croak.

His grin widened. "We have the time," he told her huskily. Releasing her hand, he eased off the stool. Pulling the covers up a little, to tuck her in, he held Maya's green gaze as it followed his every move. "I didn't lose three pints of blood," he told her lightly. "You did. I'm going to let you sleep. The next time you wake up, that AB blood ought to be here from Lima."

Nodding, Maya whispered, "You're right...."

"If you want me to come back to visit you and make a pest out of myself, let Angel or Dr. Cornell know, okay?"

She saw the hesitancy in Dane's eyes and heard it in his voice as he stood there, one hand on the railing. "You saved my life. I think I owe you something."

Dane shook his head and sobered. "Maya, you owe me *nothing*. You hear me? After what I did to you...to all the women pilots at Fort Rucker...if I can atone just a little by giving you some of my blood, that doesn't justify me thinking you want me around you. It doesn't make up for all the pain I caused you, not by a long shot. I don't expect anything from you." He grimaced. "I'm just trying to help instead of hurting you, this time around...."

She felt his pain within her heart. Tiredness was making her feel very sleepy. How badly Maya wanted to lift her hand and place it over his, but she was too weak to even do that. "Listen," she murmured, exhausted, "we need to talk... later...when we're both feeling better. Okay?"

Nodding, Dane said, "You let me know when, sweetheart. I'll be hanging around like a bad cold." He froze momentarily when he realized the endearment had slipped out of his mouth. Instantly, his gaze settled on Maya. He thought she'd be outraged.

Sweetheart. The word rolled off his tongue like honey. Maya absorbed the warmth behind it. She lapped it up like the starving jaguar that she was. Before she could answer, she heard him walking away. As the door opened and closed, she fell into a deep, healing sleep. Her last thoughts were that when her sister arrived, she would ask Inca to not only heal her, but to heal Dane as well. He deserved it.

Dane jerked awake. He'd been sleeping on one of the gurneys in the dispensary. What time was it? Looking down at his watch, he realized he had slept at least six hours. Hearing voices, he sat up and rubbed his face. When he realized they were coming from the hospital section, he slid off the gurney. Was Maya okay?

Dizziness struck him. Dr. Cornell had warned him that he wasn't going to feel very lively for a while. The blood had arrived from Lima much earlier, and he'd gotten a transfusion of two pints of AB blood and was now medically stable. Maya had been given another pint, so that she was now back at the level she should be.

It was 0300. Rubbing his face, exhaustion eating at him, Dane stumbled drowsily toward the doors. Pushing them open, he saw Dr. Cornell standing with another woman. Halting, Dane stared openmouthed for a moment.

The woman, who was dressed in jungle fatigues, black boots and a sleeveless green T-shirt, turned toward him as he entered. Her willow-green eyes assessed him. He felt as if someone had just scorched him with a flamethrower. Standing there, Dane realized with a jolt that this was Inca, Maya's fraternal twin. Their looks were remarkably similar, and yet he saw the dissimilarity, too. Inca was as tall as Maya, but she was small boned, like a slender bird.

"Come in," Elizabeth invited in a warm voice. "We were just going to come and get you, Major York."

Maya, who was sitting up in bed, leaned forward between the two women. She held out her right hand toward him. "Dane. Come over. Meet my sister, Inca. Inca, this is Dane York, the guy who saved my life."

Feeling as though he were breaking in on a party that he'd not been invited to formally, Dane moved hesitantly. "Inca, it's a pleasure to meet you." He held out his hand in her direction as he approached her. Those willow-green eyes scanned him. Once more, Dane felt heat rock through him. Who was this woman? She was a healer, whatever that meant.

Inca slid her roughened hand into his. "You have saved my sister's life. I am grateful." She gripped his hand solidly.

Surprised at her strength, Dane gazed past Inca to Maya. She looked surprisingly well. There was color back in her face. And her eyes glowed with life again. Even more, he realized she was sitting up on her own in the bed. No longer was she weak as a newborn kitten, as he'd seen her hours earlier.

Releasing Inca's hand, he stood there marveling at Maya's change in condition. "That extra blood really worked," he said to Dr. Cornell, impressed.

Maya grinned wickedly at him. "The blood transfusion helped," she told him in a conspiratorial tone, "but look at what Inca just did for me. She healed me." Holding up her left arm, no longer swathed in bandages, Maya pointed to a slight pink scar where the Plexiglas had cut into her arm.

Inca stepped aside and allowed the army officer to move to Maya's bedside to get a closer look at her arm.

"Look," Maya urged him, and raised her arm so that Dane could observe where the wound had once been. "Isn't that something? Inca is so good at what she does."

Disbelievingly, Dane stared at the slight scar. Reaching out, he gently ran his fingers across her arm where the injury had once been. "Impossible," he breathed. "I saw this less than twelve hours ago. That wound was deep...."

Inca's husky laughter filled the room. "You were right, my sister. He does not want to believe that the power of touch can heal another."

Maya lowered her arm and smiled patiently at Dane. He looked confused. And tired. Her heart went out to him. "If you want, Inca will perform a healing on you, too."

Elizabeth stepped aside and brought the stool up for Dane

to sit on. "If you do, Major, you'd better sit down before you fall down." She smiled over at Inca, who stood near the end of Maya's bed. "Inca's well known for her healing abilities, and people who have experienced it say that it's like lightning striking them. Do you want to sit?"

Dane hesitated.

Maya saw it. "Let him think about it, Elizabeth."

Studying Inca, Dane said, "I don't know that I believe in such a thing."

Inca's lips stretched knowingly. "I have no desire to push myself upon you, Major. I heal only when asked to do so. If you do not want a healing, you do not have to have one."

Again, Dane stared at Maya's newly healed arm. It was impossible that it should look like that. Yet she was clearly more alert, her eyes sparkling once more, and she had that slight, careless smile on her full lips that he had hungered to see.

"Don't be bullheaded about this, Dane," Maya said. "Come, sit down. Just let my sister put her hands on you. I promise you'll feel a lot better than you look right now."

Her cajoling made him sit tentatively on the stool. "I guess it can't hurt anything," he muttered uneasily.

Elizabeth chuckled. "Major, you're in South America now, where magic meets reality every single day of the year. I'm a Harvard-trained physician and I can assure you, when I came down here three years ago I hadn't a clue as to what really goes on around here. This place—" she looked around, giving him a slight smile "—is an incredible place of mystery, magic and real life all rolled into one. You can't take your *norte americano* ideas and force them to work down here." She turned to Inca and regarded her warmly. "Inca is a jaguar priestess. She has been trained to heal. To help. Her works in the villages of Brazil are legendary. They call her the jaguar goddess over there, and with good reason." Elizabeth's forest-green eyes sparkled. "I've seen Inca in action before, so I'm not surprised at what she's done for Maya or her wound. If you really want to understand South America, Major, I would suggest you release your rigid ideas and just go with the flow here.''

"Okay…I'm convinced…." Dane gave Maya a wry look. ''I'll do this because I trust you.''

Trust. Maya's heart fluttered as he spoke that word to her. She nodded and met his serious look with sincerity. ''Trust is earned…and I entrusted myself to you and you didn't let me down. You saved my life. Let Inca work on you. I promise you will feel better afterward.''

Nodding, Dane took a deep breath and settled himself on the stool. Looking up at Inca, who had a very serious expression on her face, he said, ''Okay, Inca, I'm ready. Fire away.''

Inca's mouth barely hitched into a smile. She moved forward and stood behind him, her hands coming to rest on his broad shoulders.

''Very well, Major. You have asked. Close your eyes, take a deep breath and release it. They will do the rest….''

Dane expected nothing. Yet, the moment he released that breath from within him, he felt Inca's hands become like hot brands against his skin. He felt the startling heat flow out of her hands, and within seconds he felt as if he were being consumed in searing flames. Sweat popped out on his forehead. He took in another jerky breath. A deep one. An explosion of colors popped like Fourth of July fireworks behind his eyelids. In seconds, he felt heat. And then, moments later, a cooling breeze moved down through the top of his head and swept all the way down to his feet. The rainbow colors ceased. What he saw next startled him even more: the face of a yellow jaguar with black spots staring back at him. And then the vision was gone as quickly as it had appeared.

''There,'' Inca said, satisfaction in her voice as she lifted her hands away from him. ''It is done. The Mother Goddess has healed you.''

Dane slowly opened his eyes. He felt a new sense of vibrancy, of energy, throbbing through him, like a fountain pulsing with renewed life. He saw Inca move to the other side of the bed and place her hand over Maya's. The sisterly love between them was undeniable. They were both grinning like there was a joke between them, but he didn't know what the punch line was.

Elizabeth came up and placed a steadying hand on his shoulder. "How do you feel, Major?"

Dane sat there for a moment, unsure. Inca laughed huskily. He heard Maya laugh with her. Blinking several times, he looked up at the doctor. "Fine…great…like I just got an incredible kick of energy into me…."

Maya heard the awe in his tone and saw it in his eyes. She squeezed Inca's long, roughened hand. "Thank you…and thank them, too…."

Nodding, Inca said, "I think it is time both of you go to sleep. You each need your rest. Come dawn tomorrow, you will feel good once more."

Maya smiled up at her sister. "Can you stay a little while? I know you have a lot going on in Brazil right now."

"I will stay a day," she said. "But then I must go. My husband misses me. And I miss him."

Maya nodded. How she wished that she could find a man like Roan Storm Walker, who was Inca's partner. She had met him several times, and always she was impressed with his quiet, strong demeanor. Together, he and Inca were working in Brazil to protect the Indians from the miners and those who would cut down the rain forest.

"Good," Maya whispered, releasing her hand. "Because I want to spend at least a little while with you…to catch up on gossip and that sort of thing."

Inca raised one thin, black eyebrow. Her gaze settled on the army officer. "My sister, I think what would be best for your healing was if you were to spend some time with the major, too."

Stunned, Dane got up. "No," he replied, his partial laugh

strained, "I don't think Captain Stevenson wants to spend any more time with me than she has to, Inca." Dane tried to avoid the shocked expression on Maya's face as he lifted his hand in farewell. "I'm going to hit the rack. Thanks, Inca." He held his hand out to her and shook hers warmly. "I'll see all of you later. Good night…"

Chapter 9

"I have wonderful news, my sister," Inca said after Dane left, and the hospital was quiet once more. She reached out and gripped Maya's hands, which rested on her blanketed lap.

Anything was better than having to respond to Inca's statement about her seeing more of Dane York. Still, Maya felt guilt eat at her over the reply Dane had made before he left. Why couldn't she have been a little more sensitive to him? A little more kind, rather than lying here staring at him after Inca's unexpected suggestion? Discarding her morose thoughts, she turned toward Inca and saw joy burning in her sister's eyes. She placed her hand over Inca's long, strong fingers. "What? Tell me. I could use some good news." She laughed a little unsteadily.

"Well," Inca whispered huskily, "when I received word that you were badly injured, I was upset. I talked it over with Roan. I decided to try and teleport and not wait to fly by airplane from Brazil to Peru." She wrinkled her nose and laughed demurely. "Now, I know members of the Black Jaguar Clan have teleporting as their specialty, and others of the Jaguar Clan must work at it for a long time before they learn the skill, *if* they do.''

''You've done it before,'' Maya said, searching her memory. ''You teleported into Peru when Mike Houston's wife, Ann, was in trouble. Right?''

''Yes, that was the one and only time I was able to do it successfully.'' Inca released her hand and pulled the leather thong from around her neck. A jaguar claw was suspended from the end of it. ''When I met Ann, I gave her one of my two jaguar claws. I told her if she ever needed me, to call me, and I would be there.'' She tucked the claw beneath her dark green T-shirt again. Reaching out, she captured Maya's hand once more, her eyes gleaming with excitement.

''It worked! I was so surprised. But I was happy, too, because if I could not have been there, Ann would have died before Michael could have reached her himself.''

''It was very brave of you,'' Maya murmured, knowing the story well. ''And I know Mike Houston is forever grateful to you.''

Inca nodded and licked her lower lip. ''Listen, there is more!'' Eagerly, she leaned forward. ''Roan agreed I should try to teleport. Well, you know how you must be feeling in a very peaceful and harmonious place in order to attempt it?''

Rolling her eyes, Maya said, ''No kidding. Ninety percent of the time when I try to do it, I'm not in a state of harmony. I can't control my emotional state that well to make it happen, so don't feel bad.''

''How true,'' Inca murmured wryly. ''I felt that, to reach you, I could do it, Maya. Roan supported my decision. I went into our meditation room, sat down and closed my eyes. I began to do the breathing exercise that we were taught, when suddenly Grandmother Alaria materialized in the room!'' Her voice was filled with awe. ''Can you imagine my surprise when she appeared? This is the first time she has ever visited me like that.''

Maya's brows rose. "Wow. Yeah, that's extreme all right. Why did she appear to you? What was going down?"

Gripping Maya's hands, Inca grinned broadly. "She told me that I could not teleport to you. That I must take the airplane instead. I was shocked. I asked why. I told her how seriously wounded you were. Grandmother raised her hand and gave me that look she gives us...."

Maya laughed weakly. "Yeah, the 'look.' I know it well."

"She said that you were going to be all right. She had gazed into the future and seen that you would live. And," Inca's voice wobbled slightly as she added, "she said I could not teleport because I was with child! And when one is pregnant, one cannot teleport or it could harm the babies."

Maya gasped. She saw the joy dancing in Inca's willow-green eyes. "Babies? You're pregnant?"

Inca gave her a proud look. "Twins, Maya. Grandmother Alaria said I was carrying twins."

Shocked, Maya sat there, her eyes widening.

Inca moved her hand tenderly to caress her abdomen. "She said our mother's side always had twins, and that we carry this heritage within us." Her eyes shone. "And they are fraternal—one boy and one girl, Grandmother Alaria said."

"Oh, this is *wonderful* news, Inca!" Maya placed her arms around her sister's shoulders and hugged her as hard as she could. They sat there and held one another, laughing and crying together.

Eventually, Maya eased away. She wiped her eyes, sniffed then found a box of tissues and pulled some out, handing them to her sister, who was still sniffling. They blew their noses together and wiped their eyes. Maya's grin was uneven.

"Hey, this makes me an *aunt twice over!* How about that?"

Laughing, Inca blotted her eyes self-consciously. "Yes. You will be an aunt." Reaching out, she gripped Maya's hand. "Do you realize what this means? It means that these babies I carry will have a *family,* Maya. They will know who their mother and father are, who their aunt is...." Inca pressed her hand against her trembling lower lip and stared at her twin. Tears spilled down her cheeks.

"Oh, Inca..." Maya whispered. Leaning over, she pulled Inca into her arms and just held her. She knew all too well the pain of abandonment that Inca's early loss of their parents had caused her. Maya knew that in a way, she had been the lucky one; she had been adopted two weeks after their parents had been murdered, by the colonel and his wife at the American embassy in São Paulo. Inca, on the other hand, had been passed from jaguar priestess to priest, all her life, until she was sixteen years old, when she'd gone to the Village of the Clouds to begin her metaphysical training in the Jaguar Clan.

Pressing a kiss to Inca's hair, Maya squeezed her eyes shut. Hot tears jammed into them. She heard the relief, the pain and the joy in Inca's weeping. All she could do was hold her sister, rock her gently and let her cry. There was such beautiful strength and caring in Inca. And at the same time, such a bleeding wound in her heart from the trauma of being abandoned and not knowing that she had any family at all. Inca had searched all her life for family. And when she'd gotten kicked out of the Village of the Clouds for making a bad decision, she had lost the only close relations she'd known. It had devastated her.

Hurting for her past pain, Maya pressed her cheek against Inca's hair and gently ran her hand slowly up and down her long, strong back. Murmuring words of comfort, she felt grateful that she had her foster family, who loved her, as she loved them. Understanding how much the twins meant to Inca, and to her husband, Roan, Maya knew that this would help Inca heal even more since their marriage. Smiling through her tears, Maya whispered, "You're twice blessed, Inca. I'm so happy for you and Roan. These little babies you carry are gonna be the luckiest kids alive. You'll spoil them rotten. You'll be such a great mother...."

Inca pulled out of her arms and used her hands to wipe the tears from her face. Her eyes were red rimmed, but she was smiling. After blowing her nose, she took several more tissues to blot her eyes. "Grandmother Alaria said I was two months along. I did not realize it. I had missed two moons, but I thought it was because of all the stress we were under."

Maya moved several damp strands of black hair away from Inca's cheek. "How wonderful. I'm so happy for you. Does Roan know yet?"

Inca smiled. "Yes, I told him right away. He picked me up, Maya, and he twirled me around in a circle until we were both so dizzy we fell on the floor. We laughed. We held one another. And we cried. But they were tears of joy, not pain."

Maya leaned back against the pillows. She felt exhausted and knew it was because of the power of Inca's healing. She held her sister's damp, happy gaze. "I can't think of two people more deserving than you and Roan."

"He is going to fly me to his home in North America. I will meet his family. I am excited but scared. I do not know what they will think of me."

"They'll see you as part of their family," Maya murmured soothingly as she reached out and patted Inca's hand. "Don't worry. I'm sure they're going to be as happy as you are about your babies." She grinned a little. "So a girl and a boy? Is that what Grandmother Alaria told you?"

Nodding, Inca put another tissue in the pile collecting on Maya's bedcover. "Yes, she is positive of this." Her lips curved softly. "And I have been in contact with their spirits already, Maya. It is wonderful. They are so excited about coming into the world through me. They are very strong spirits. Spirits with a purpose."

"Hmm, I don't doubt that. Look at you, how strong and mission oriented you are."

Laughing, Inca said, "As if you are not?"

"Guilty as charged."

Looking around the small hospital room, Inca whispered, "When I touched you, to allow the healing energies to come through to you, I felt great loneliness in you, my sister."

Frowning, Maya nodded. She avoided Inca's gaze, resting thoughtfully upon her. Maya knew that during a healing, all aspects of a person—their thoughts, their pain, their joy, their past and present—were available for the healer to perceive. "Yeah, I feel a little alone, I guess."

Inca slid off the bed and straightened her T-shirt. Her gaze never left Maya. "You feel very alone, my sister. Why?"

One corner of Maya's mouth quirked. "It comes with the territory here, Inca. As a squadron commander with fifty-some people under my care, I get a little worried about them, their safety, especially with Faro Valentino's Kamovs out there. That's what got me into this mess—a third Kamov came out of nowhere and nailed me and Dane. We were lucky it didn't blow us out of the sky."

"Sometimes, when a person must carry such heavy loads, having a partner helps," Inca murmured, coming back to the bed and placing her hand on Maya's slumped shoulder.

"A partner?" Maya said. "You can't share a squadron command position, Inca. I have Dallas, and she's a great X.O."

"No," Inca replied, gripping her by the shoulder and giving her a small shake, "I am talking about a partner who can hold you, as you just held me as I cried in your arms. A man who can complete you. Give you a harbor of safety when you are feeling very vulnerable and naked to the world around you."

Maya stared up at Inca. Even though her twin didn't have the schooling or the worldliness that she did, the wisdom in her eyes touched Maya to her soul. She felt a little frightened by how much Inca saw in her, and yet Maya knew she was safe with her sister.

"Even now, I feel your fearful response, my sister."

"Yeah…well, for twenty-five-plus years I've gone on alone in an emotional sense, Inca. Somewhere in myself, before I found out the truth about us, that you were my sister— I felt alone. Alone in a way that most people don't have a clue about." Scowling, Maya whispered, "Just having you around, being able to talk to you, contact you, has helped me a lot, whether you know it or not." She gave her a lopsided smile, tears coming yet again to her eyes.

Inca nodded, her own eyes gentle with understanding. "Our love as sisters is one thing, Maya. I talk of another love. The kind that Roan and I share."

"Oh…that…" Maya rolled her eyes. "Forget it."

"What? That you could love a man? That he would support you, care for you, hold you when you felt so alone and burdened?"

"Inca, you're naive. I know you mean well, but you know the rules of the Black Jaguar Clan. We're here to do the dirty work. We're the dark underbelly of the Jaguar Clan." She looked around and gestured. "This cave, this squadron, is what I do best. This is my mission. It doesn't leave me *any* time for a private life. I'll never be big on marriage, kids and family. In a sense, I'm a big mother hen to fifty-some people. I handle people problems twenty-four hours a day. I have no *time* for something like that, Inca."

"So," she whispered, "who holds you when you feel like crying?"

Wincing, Maya avoided Inca's probing look. "You might be naive, but you aren't dumb," she muttered.

Moving quietly to the window, Inca pushed the white curtain aside and watched the activity within the cave for a long moment before she turned again. When she did, she saw Maya frowning, working hard to keep her emotions at bay.

"When I placed my hands on Dane, he had a similar feeling in him."

Maya snapped her head up and looked across the aisle to where Inca was standing. Her sister had placed her hands on her hips and stood watching her from the shadows. "There are a lot of lonely people around," Maya muttered defensively. "So what?"

"He cares for you, Maya."

Snorting, she dragged in a deep breath and said, "I'm sure it's out of guilt over the way he treated me and the other women pilots who had the misfortune to be studying under him."

Shaking her head, Inca slowly moved from the shadows into the light, halting near the end of Maya's bed. Picking at the coverlet, she murmured, "No, his turmoil is not about guilt. I know the difference between those emotions. He is lonely like you. He is a man with many responsibilities, who carries as many burdens on his shoulders as you do. Perhaps, if you find time in the coming days as you rest and recuperate from this trauma you have endured, you might spend some time with him."

"Oh, and do what? Talk about the weather?" Maya moved uncomfortably. She wanted to get up, get dressed and get back to work. However, Dr. Cornell had ordered bed rest for the next two days. Tomorrow, one way or another, Maya intended to work half a day at her office, whether the doctor approved it or not. She was off the flight-duty roster for a full week. That put an added strain on the pilots who had to keep flying, which bothered Maya greatly.

Inca laughed softly. "Ah, I see you trying to evade me, my sister. No, you do not need to talk of the weather with him. He is a man of deep convictions, of goodness. Perhaps you can explore those things with him?"

"Look, I owe him my life," Maya muttered darkly, "isn't that enough? I think what he did for me more than rights the wrongs from the past, as far as I'm concerned."

"That is good—you are willing to forgive. That is a start." Inca smiled again. "I felt him, Maya. I felt his heart. I grazed his spirit. He has his weaknesses, but do we not all have them?"

Maya gave Inca a strange, unsettled look. "What are you trying to do? Just because you're pregnant and going to be a mommy, do you think you can be a matchmaker, too?"

Inca raised her brows. "The words you use, I do not know them all." She opened her hands guilelessly. "What is 'matchmaker'?"

"Humph."

Laughing, Inca moved to Maya's shoulder. She reached out and smoothed her dark hair into place around her neck and shoulder.

"If I didn't know better, Inca, I'd think you're trying to tell me that Dane York likes me or some such hooey."

"Me?"

"Yeah, you. And don't give me that completely innocent look. We're twins, remember? We can read each other like an open book."

Chuckling, Inca folded her hands together and kept on smiling. "I know how stubborn you are. I am the same. I am asking you to see Dane differently than you have been seeing him."

"Dammit," Maya exclaimed softly, giving Inca an uncomfortable look, "he's prejudiced against women!"

"And you are equally prejudiced against men."

Stunned, Maya stared at Inca, the silence swirling between them. Her sister was grim faced now, her willow-green eyes narrowed. Inca was not teasing. She meant it. Averting her gaze, Maya looked down at the covers, the floor, the doors at the other end of the facility. Working her mouth, she finally turned back and met Inca's eyes.

"You're right."

Reaching over, Inca patted her tightly clasped hands. "If you have the wisdom and humility to acknowledge your own weakness, as he does, then there is hope."

"Dammit, Inca, I didn't need to hear that from you."

"What? The hope or the prejudice?" Inca tilted her head and studied Maya's scowling features. "You are like two jaguars. You both have the same spots, the same color of coat. Sometimes—'' she lifted her hands expressively ''—when one meets someone who is just like them, they fight it—fight the other person, because what they see in them they see in themselves. But they will never admit it, of course.''

''That's called projection,'' Maya growled. ''A psychological term.''

''Oh. Well, am I not correct?''

''Yes, dammit, you are.''

''I would think you would be happy, realizing this weakness you both share.''

''It's complicated, Inca. I know you see the world very simply. I don't. I can't. You don't live out in the real world like I do. It's a helluva lot more complex a situation, believe me. Dane York is like a Gordian knot to me and my world...my life. Recently, it's gotten even murkier, so I'm feeling damned vulnerable toward him right now. I don't know whether he's a good guy or a bad guy. He used to be nothing but bad in my book.''

Sighing, Inca whispered, ''My sister, none of us are either all bad or good. You know that from your training. Why do you not apply what you know to him? I could feel the wounding in you that he created. And when I touched him, felt him, I felt his desire to heal this wound between you.'' She tapped Maya's hands. ''You must forgive and move on now. He is trying very hard to please you. To get you to forgive him. He *is* trying, Maya.''

''Okay, okay.'' Maya made an irritated gesture with her hand. ''I hear you.''

''Part of the Black Jaguar Clan schooling is to learn to forgive. Those born into the clan are learning through their wounding. You have an opportunity here, my loving sister. Why do you think the Great Mother Goddess set up what happened to you? I feel that if you had not resisted Dane's offer to find peace and forgiveness between you in the first place, it would not have come to this—this injury to yourself.'' Inca shrugged. ''Sometimes, when we become too stubborn, too set in our ways, something traumatic must happen in order to allow a door to swing open. When it does, you can choose to walk through it or not with the other person involved.'' She smiled unevenly, tears glimmering in her eyes. ''I do not think it an accident that his blood now moves through your body. He is a part of you, yes? And you cannot war against someone whose blood is part of you, can you?''

''I hear you, Inca.'' Maya whispered unhappily. ''I don't like it, but I hear you. And I know you're right. I also understand why I'm in the Black Jaguar Clan. I'm not so evolved, spiritually, as you are. I'm still learning some of the basics, like not taking revenge, feeling hatred and stuff like that.'' Maya lifted her head and met Inca's softened gaze, now filled with tender compassion for her. ''And I'm not so stupid as to realize, symbolically, what happened between me and him. It's just...a shock, that's all. I feel...right now...like the world's closing in on me. I've got three Kamov's to worry about. I have this training for the D model to get underway. I have Dane's old prejudice to fight in myself every time I lay eyes on him. There's just so much going on right now. I feel so damned raw and vulnerable....''

''My sister,'' Inca whispered gently, ''we all undergo such tests, and you are in a test right now. You have gone through them many times before. All I am saying is do not make Dane your enemy while he is here. If you can forgive him, you forgive yourself. Your prejudice toward men is no less wounding as his is against women. Somehow, you must let all that go. Somehow, you must drop your armor and allow who you are, your vulnerable, good side, to show itself to him.''

''Yeah, right, and he'll gut me right where I stand.''

Inca shook her head. ''You are wrong. You must trust me on this, Maya.''

Giving her a dark look, Maya rasped, ''Dammit, this is

hard, Inca!'' Looking around, she muttered, ''There are days when I want to say to hell with this whole thing. There are days when I don't want to know what I know, metaphysically speaking. I just wish I was like every other blind, deaf and dumb human being down here.'' Maya clenched her fist, her voice turning raw with anger. ''I just want to walk away from the mission at times. Away from being in the Black Jaguar Clan. I get sick of it! I get sick of the responsibility, and knowing I'm damn well going to pay for whatever choices I make, right or wrong, because of my knowing.'' Her voice cracked. ''Right now, it's just too much. Don't spew metaphysical pabulum at me, Inca. I can't handle one more stone on the load I'm carrying on these shoulders, all right?''

Nodding, Inca slid her arm around Maya's tense shoulders and hugged her for a long, long time. When she finally released her, she whispered, ''Sometimes our greatest enemy can become our greatest ally.''

Dane was sitting at his office desk the next morning, working on the fine points of the training schedule that would be initiated shortly. Again and again he resisted calling in at the dispensary to ask Dr. Cornell how Maya was doing. Earlier this morning, Inca had left. He'd been pleasantly surprised when she'd dropped by his office to tell him goodbye. She had shared the news with him that she was pregnant with twins. The look in her eyes made him smile self-consciously. Inca was so open, so available emotionally compared to Maya, that he'd reeled when she'd shared the good news with him. She didn't treat him coldly, or as if he were an unwelcome stranger. Just the opposite. She had gifted him with several sprays of orchids, yellow with red lips, and told him to give some of them to Maya when she got back to her office duties.

Inca's eyes had been sparkling, and Dane could almost feel as if there was some underlying reason for her giving him the orchids, but he didn't know what it was.

Inca had suggested that he visit Maya at the dispensary that morning. He muttered that he might, if he could get the schedule completed, but he made no specific promise. The way Inca regarded him, with those thoughtful, compassionate eyes of hers, made his heart contract with pain and need—for Maya.

Trying to shake off thoughts of the early morning meeting, Dane rested his hand against his brow and studied the complex schedule before him. This was a helluva undertaking, and it wasn't easy trying to fit training time for the pilots in between the missions they flew daily against Faro Valentino's aircraft.

There was a soft knock at his opened door. Dane lifted his head. It was Maya. She was standing there hesitantly, her hand on the doorjamb, looking at him with an unsure expression. Instantly, he was on his feet, his chair nearly tipping over. He caught it, straightening self-consciously beneath her gaze.

"I thought you were supposed to be in the hospital," he blurted, rubbing his hands down the sides of his thighs. Her eyes were soft looking and so was her mouth. She was dressed in her usual black flight uniform, which surprised him. Dane knew that the doctor had grounded Maya for a week, and she couldn't fly. The shadowy smudges beneath her glorious emerald eyes told him that her recovery was by no means a hundred percent.

"I was," she said wryly.

"Does Dr. Cornell know you've escaped the dispensary?"

Maya grinned a little. "No, but she'll find out soon enough when she goes to check on me during her rounds."

"I see...."

"I'm like a horse in harness. You can't put me out to pasture too long or I get bored and antsy."

"Yeah, I know that one, too."

"Are you feeling okay?" Maya asked. Dane looked almost

normal, but not quite. His flesh was still not back to its usual color, and there were hints of shadows beneath his eyes.

"I'm fine…fine. And you?"

"I'm okay…. Feeling a little tired, is all." Motioning toward his desk, Maya asked, "Do you mind if I drop by for a visit…for just a moment?"

"Why, er, no…no, not at all. Let me get you a chair." He quickly moved from behind his desk and brought the only other chair to the center of his small office for her.

Maya's heart opened automatically. She saw a red flush staining Dane's cheeks. He was obviously rattled by her unexpected appearance. She had never come to his office since he'd arrived. Swallowing hard, she made her way to the chair and sat down.

"Thank you…"

Stunned by her friendly behavior, Dane didn't know what to think. His head swam with questions. Had Inca's healing done this to her? Or had the trauma of Maya's injury? Maybe she was just unguarded for the moment, but would return to her normal armored state shortly. He thought the latter, and yet he didn't try to erect his own armor to protect himself from whatever she might say to him.

"Coffee? I have coffee." He pointed to the machine behind his desk. Nervousness thrummed through him. Dane saw the uneasiness in Maya's eyes now. She was nervous, too. He could tell by the way she kept shifting around on the chair. Yet she was hurting and he knew it. Oh, it was nothing obvious, but he could sense it—by intuition, he guessed. Moving toward the coffeemaker, he raised a second cup toward her.

"Yes, I'd like some."

"It's strong," he warned.

"I need a strong cup of coffee," Maya said. "Put a little cream and sugar in it, will you?"

His hand shook as he poured coffee into the white, chipped ceramic cup. Laughing a little to ease the tension over her sudden, unexpected appearance, he said, "Now that you're being funded by Perseus, maybe the supply officer can get you in some decent coffee mugs. These have seen better days."

Maya laughed weakly. "Yeah, you're right." She watched as he carefully spooned sugar and creamer into the coffee. She saw his hand tremble. Maya had never seen Dane like this before. And then she realized that Inca's healing had probably opened him up, just as it had her. In her eyes, Dane was like a little boy trying hard to please her, to get her approval, even over such a small thing as a cup of coffee. Her heart opened more.

As he brought the cup to her and their fingers touched, she felt warmth flow up into her hand and wrist from their contact. She saw his eyes grow a smoky blue. She'd seen that look once before, when he'd visited her shortly after she became conscious. It made her feel safe. And cared for. This time, she didn't try and fight that energy sensation flowing from him. No, this time, she allowed it and, if she were honest with herself, welcomed it.

"Thanks," she whispered, taking the cup. Pressing it to her lips, she took a sip. He was standing there expectantly. "It's fine, Dane. Go sit down."

He grinned a little and nodded. "Okay."

Maya watched him take his seat. "You working on the schedule?"

Nodding again, he said, "Yeah, and I'm afraid you aren't going to like what I've come up with. But I'm damned if I can fine-tune it any more than I have because of the heavy-duty circumstances your squadron operates under." Dane gave her a worried look.

Maya sat with her legs crossed, the cup balanced on her lap between her hands. Did she know how beautiful she looked with her long, black hair curling around her shoulders, showing off that slender neck of hers? He thought not. Maya wore no makeup. She didn't need to. When he saw her fine, thin brows knit, his mouth quirked.

"I know you've been working nonstop on it when you weren't flying missions," Maya said, trying to defuse the worry and anxiety she saw in his blue eyes. "What's the problem?"

With a shrug, Dane dropped the pencil on the schedule and leaned back in his creaking chair. "You aren't going to be happy about this, but based upon how many flights your pilots are making daily, I have no choice."

Hearing the grim tone in his voice, Maya said, "Give me the bad news, then."

His heart shrank. Trying to steel himself against the reaction he knew was coming, Dane eased the chair down and set his elbows on the desk, staring directly across it at her. "We have a six-week training program. I know when we came here I said we'd stay for that amount of time. But given the number of flights, the demands on your people and the fact you're shorthanded, I don't have any choice."

"Choice? In what?"

Grimly, Dane looked down at the schedule. "According to my best estimates, Captain, it's going to take three times as long as anticipated to train all your people."

Maya sat there digesting his quietly spoken comment. She saw the worry in Dane's narrowed eyes. She felt his anxiety over her possible response to his statement. Compressing her lips, she said, "Okay...instead of you being here six weeks, we're looking at an extended training-in period of...eighteen weeks. Is that right?"

Dane marveled at the continued softness in her tone. Maya's eyes held no anger, only interest. Shocked that she hadn't come out of the chair or started to make angry comments, he sat there dumbfounded for a moment. "Er, yes...eighteen weeks."

"I see."

Dane held her gaze. Silence filled the void between them.

She sipped her coffee almost gratefully. Sitting up, Dane said, "And you're okay with that?" He tried to keep the disbelief out of his tone.

Shrugging, Maya said, "I wanted you to assess our flight demands against your training schedule, Dane. You did that. If that's what you've come up with, then I'm fine with it. What's wrong? You look like you just got hit by a freight train."

Blinking once, Dane opened his mouth and then closed it. Maya was giving him a wry look, a smile barely touching her full lips. No anger. No accusations. No…nothing. "Maybe I have been," he admitted in a hushed tone, followed by a nervous laugh. How badly he wanted to just stare at Maya. How badly he ached to have just a normal, human-to-human conversation with her. She looked hauntingly vulnerable right now. Scratching his head, Dane muttered, "I just thought you might be upset that we'd be here a lot longer than you wanted us here, was all. I know we're not all that welcome…well, *I'm* not welcome. The rest of my men aren't like me."

"Honest to a fault," Maya murmured. After sipping the coffee, she set the cup on the front of his desk. "Look, Dane…may I call you by your first name?"

He nodded. "Of course!" He tried to keep the shock out of his voice and face.

"My sister just gave me a good talking to," she admitted, amusement in her tone. "Inca's made me realize that I'm part and parcel of our ongoing problem."

Looking at her quizzically, Dane said, "I don't understand, Captain."

"Call me Maya, if you want." She slowly rose and stood before him. He was looking at her in utter shock—maybe because she was trying to be friendly. Or because she had called him by his first name. Unsure, and equally nervous, Maya opened her hand toward him. "We've both had a lot of water go under the bridge, from where I stand. You were prejudiced against women gunship pilots. Well—'' Maya grimaced ''—I was equally prejudiced against men. The pot calling the kettle black. I know...'' She hesitated. ''I know since you've arrived here you've been trying to bury the hatchet between us, and I haven't let you. Well, that's all changing as of now.'' Maya's voice deepened with barely held emotion. ''You didn't have to give your blood to me. I know that. Inca made me realize a lot of things this morning. I was just as blindly prejudiced against you as you were against us. I'm calling a halt to it, Dane. I want peace between us. Can you live with that?''

Chapter 10

"Maya?"

Dane's voice feathered across her. She felt his large, strong hand move gently across her shoulders.

"Ummph..."

"Come on, you need to get some sleep...."

Barely lifting her head off her crossed arms, which were resting on her desk, Maya forced her eyes open. She felt Dane lean over her, his lips very close to her ear. His moist breath flowed over her temple and brow. Strands of her hair tickled her nose as she looked up at him.

"What...what time is it?" she mumbled, sitting up and rubbing her face wearily.

"Too late," he growled. Easing her out of the chair, Dane pointed her toward the cot in the corner of her office. "Come on..."

Maya had lost count of how many times Dane had found her working late in her office. For the past three weeks, ever since their truce, he was like a big guard dog, always looking out for her, taking care of her in small but meaningful ways.

Right now, Maya appreciated his thoughtfulness as she felt him grip her upper arm, guiding her around the desk and to the cot.

Once she got there, she started to lie down.

"Take your boots off."

"Ohhh…I sleep with them on all the time, Dane."

"Not with me around. Come on. Just sit up and stick out your right foot."

Maya watched as he crouched down in front of her, his hand slipping around the heel of the boot she offered. Sleep warped her sense of time, and when she awakened she was always vulnerable. Somehow Dane knew that, because he always spoke to her in a soft, low tone. Appreciating him even more, Maya whispered, "You don't have to keep doing this, you know. I've been sleeping on this cot for three years straight."

Dane eased the boot off and set it aside. "Give me the other one."

Maya did so. Pushing the hair away from her face, she said, "What are *you* doing up so late?"

"Making sure *you* get some decent sleep under your belt."

Wrinkling her nose, Maya felt the boot slip off. "It's enough that *I'm* sleep deprived. Don't take on any of my bad habits."

Chuckling, Dane straightened. His heart contracted with joy as he watched Maya ease onto the cot and settle on her left side, as she always did. Picking up the blanket from the foot of the cot, he unfolded it and drew it across her form. Her dark hair pooled around her shoulders as she bent her legs up near her body, one hand beneath her cheek. Did Maya know how excruciatingly beautiful she really was? Dane didn't think so. One day, he wanted to tell her that. He spread the blanket over her shoulders, tucking her in.

"Good night, fairy tale princess," he whispered. He lifted his hand and stroked her hair. It was the thing he most looked forward to—touching Maya like this. Instantly, he saw the tension around her mouth ease. Her lips parted. She was already asleep.

Dane leaned over Maya and watched the soft rise and fall of her breasts. He'd made an exhilarating discovery three weeks ago when he'd awakened her after she'd fallen asleep while working on the mission reports and flight data. In her drowsy state, Maya was vulnerable. She seemed to *want* his touch, his nurturing as he helped her from the desk to the cot to catch three or four hours of badly needed sleep. The strain and tension was thick around the base since the third Kamov had showed up in Faro's arsenal. Dane had noticed as he'd take off her boots, pull the cover over her and simply stroke her hair, that all of that tension around Maya would dissolve. Would melt away, just like that.

Smiling tenderly down at her as she slept, Dane realized it was a backhanded compliment that Maya would relax with him so near to her. Her thick, black lashes lay against her golden skin. Her breathing was soft and rhythmic. Dane could see her sinking into a deep, deep slumber. Straightening, he shook his head. He didn't know how Maya managed to keep going on so little sleep. Dallas assured him that this wasn't normal, that Maya usually got six to eight hours. She felt it was due to the worry Maya had for her pilots, with the third Kamov being around. Dane couldn't argue with the X.O.'s logic.

Moving to the door, he closed it partially to stop the flood of light into her quiet office. Outside, the echoing sounds of two crews loading ordnance on the Apaches could be heard faintly. Living in a cave, Dane was discovering, had certain repercussions. Everything echoed. A wrench dropped on the lava floor, a person talking near the outer wall—everything reverberated back through the massive cavern.

Instead of leaving Maya's office, Dane glanced over his shoulder again. Something pulled him to stay. Hell, he needed sleep himself. He had taken on the responsibility of getting Maya away from her desk and to her cot because Dr.

Cornell had mentioned to him shortly after Maya had come back to work that she wasn't getting enough sleep. The doctor was worried and so was he. Scowling, he looked around the shadowy office. On Maya's desk were the yellow-and-red orchids that he'd given her. Orchids stayed in bloom a long time, he discovered—four to six weeks. And Maya had appreciated the spikes of orchids he'd given her. It was a daily reminder to him that she was allowing him to remain in her life, to get closer to her.

A sudden idea came to him. The corners of his mouth lifted and he nodded. Yeah, that was a helluva good plan. He'd see Dr. Cornell about it in the morning, and then spring it on Maya, if the doctor gave her approval.

Dane left her office and walked quietly down the hall toward the exit. He wondered how Maya would react to his creative inspiration.

"Maya, I'm officially ordering you to take forty-eight hours of R and R," Elizabeth Cornell told her sternly.

"What?" Maya sat on her cot, pulling on her boots. It was 0700 and she had overslept. Elizabeth stood before her in her dark green fatigues and white coat, her hands in the pockets, an authoritative look on her face.

"You heard me." Elizabeth tried to look severe, but it didn't quite come off as Maya stared at her, a half smile on her face. "And to make sure you do, I've ordered Major York to fly you to Cuzco. I had comms make you reservations at the Libertador Hotel." She shook her finger at Maya, who paused in the middle of putting on her boots and sat there, thighs apart, her hands resting between them. "The major is going to be your bodyguard of sorts. He'll fly you there in our civilian helo and fly you back. Got it?"

Maya laughed and pulled on the second boot. "Liz, you can't be serious!"

"Oh, she's dead serious," Dane said, coming into the office unannounced.

Looking up when she heard his low, modulated tone, Maya sat back and stared at him. He was dressed in a pair of jeans, hiking boots, a short-sleeved white shirt and a blue-and-yellow Saint Louis Rams baseball cap. The bill was pulled down so that it shadowed his narrowed eyes as they locked with her widening gaze.

"So," Dane told her smoothly, moving around Elizabeth, who was now looking quite pleased with herself and her prescription, "put these on." He tossed Maya some civilian clothes. "You need a shower, but I won't hold that against you. You'll get one at the hotel. It's only a thirty-minute hop from here."

Stunned, Maya picked up the clothes, which consisted of a pair of green nylon slacks and a short-sleeved, pink tank top. Dane handed her her hiking boots.

"Put these on, too," he told her briskly.

"But—"

"No buts," Elizabeth said darkly, a threat in her tone. "You're sleep deprived, Maya. And if you don't have the good sense to get the rest you need, then I, as flight surgeon, will ensure you do."

Dane stood there, a silly grin on his face, his hands draped casually across his hips as he looked at the doctor and then at Maya's nonplussed expression. "I think the doc's right, Maya." He looked at his watch. "Meet me down below in ten minutes. I know it doesn't take you long to change."

Frowning, Maya looked from one to the other. "You two are in cahoots on this. I can tell."

Elizabeth smiled triumphantly and traded a fond look with Dane. "You have two friends who care deeply about you, Maya. Listen to them for once, will you? It's not going to hurt anything if you leave this base for forty-eight hours. You'll be in constant contact, anyway. Dane, here, is just going to make sure you get the shut-eye you need."

"Yes, ma'am," Dane murmured to the doctor. "If I have

to put a padlock on her room at that five-star hotel and bring her room service, it will be done. You can roger that.''

Giving them both a dirty look, Maya muttered, ''Okay, okay…I know when I'm outgunned. Get out of here. Let me change my clothes in peace.''

Someone knocked softly at her hotel room door. Maya made several muffled sounds of protest and slowly lifted her head from the feather pillow. It was dark in her room, but sunlight filtered in around the edges of the draperies. What time was it?

The knock came again. ''Just a moment…'' Maya called sleepily, and forced the covers off her. As she sat up, she felt the dregs of sleep still pulling at her. Stumbling to the door, she fumbled for the knob. Opening it, she squinted in the bright light coming from the hall, holding up her hand to protect her eyes.

Dane smiled. Maya was dressed in a wrinkled, pale pink cotton nightgown that fell to her knees. Her hair was in utter disarray. When she dropped her hand, he saw the puffiness beneath her eyes. ''You've slept for eighteen hours. I thought I might wake you and get some food in you.''

''Uhhh…'' Maya frowned, looked down and then back up at him. Dane was dressed in a bright red polo shirt, tan chinos and his hiking boots. He looked devastatingly handsome. ''What? Eighteen hours? You've got to be kidding!'' She looked at the aviator's watch on her wrist, and was stunned to find out it was 8:00 a.m.

Dane saw several tourists coming down the hall toward them, speaking German. He didn't think Maya would want to be seen in her nightgown by strangers. ''Let me come in for a sec,'' he coaxed. ''Company's comin' down the hall.'' And he eased her back into her room and closed the door quietly behind him.

''Eighteen hours?'' Her voice was thick and scratchy.

Maya looked at the watch again. "I don't believe it…." She stumbled off toward the bathroom.

Dane smiled sympathetically and pulled up the covers on the bed, then sat down. Picking up the phone, he ordered breakfast for both of them. It wasn't long before Maya came back. Her eyes were barely open, and they were still puffy. She was holding her hand against her brow as she walked toward him. He got off the bed and moved aside.

"I can't believe this…eighteen hours. I feel like I've been hit by a Mack truck." Maya sat down on the edge of the bed.

"You needed the sleep," Dane told her. Going to the bathroom, he found her hairbrush on the counter. Coming back, he followed his intuition and settled down next to her.

"Turn around," he told her, and guided Maya so that she sat with her back toward him. "This is something I've been wanting to do for a long time…." And he took the brush and began to pull it through the silky, thick strands of her hair.

Maya made a purring sound as he eased the brush across her scalp. The sensation was delicious. Surprising. And wonderful. Without thinking, she leaned back, and was glad when Dane allowed her to relax against him. He continued to draw the brush gently through her hair. When he was done, Maya allowed herself the luxury of simply being held by him. Pressing her head against his neck, she sighed.

"That was wonderful…thank you…."

Dane's heart was pounding. "You deserve a little care," he told her, his voice husky. He wanted to take Maya into his arms, press her back on the bed and kiss her until they melted into one another. Placing a choke chain on those desires, Dane absorbed the feel of having her tall, graceful form resting against him.

Maya's lips parted. With every moment that passed, she entrusted herself more and more to Dane and his strong, caring arms. How long had she wanted this to happen? Ever since she'd made peace with him over their past. He smelled of lime, probably from his shaving cream. Smiling a little, Maya absorbed his strength and the way he pressed his jaw against her hair.

"I never knew..." Maya whispered, her eyes closing.

"Knew what?" Dane held himself in check, fearful of doing something to scare Maya out of his arms. She was a woman who demanded respect, and he knew that if he overstepped the boundaries, she'd fly away like a startled dove. The sound of her voice was soft and faraway, as if she were still half-asleep.

"That a man could be so caring..."

"Even a man like me, eh?"

Maya laughed softly. "Especially you. I would never have guessed...."

Dane closed his eyes. He felt like a starving wolf having Maya in his arms. If she could read his mind, he was sure she'd run screaming away from him. His heart was pounding. His lower body was in a tortured knot of boiling heat and need. How badly he wanted to kiss her. Just kiss her. What would Maya's lips feel like? How many times had he thought about kissing her?

"I'm full of surprises," he joked softly.

"So am I."

"You? Naw. You're pretty predicable," he teased and smiled. Taking a risk, Dane pressed a small kiss on the top of her head.

Maya felt his mouth come to rest upon her hair. A delicious sensation, an awakening, flowed through her. She felt him laugh. The feeling flowed through her warmly. When he tightened his arms around her briefly, Maya felt incredibly safe. No one had ever given her that sense of safety before. Dane was a natural-born leader, and he had confidence to burn. In the past three weeks, since looking at him differently, Maya realized that Inca had been right: they were more alike than she'd ever realized. He'd worked hard to keep that connection with her. And she'd reciprocated.

It was loco, Maya decided—crazy magic. Somehow, the intense healing Inca had given them had opened up their hearts and their eyes, and now they saw one another differently. Better. More provocatively. Maya stirred in Dane's arms, her eyes still closed. Inhaling the male scent of him, she followed her own primal instincts. Shifting in his arms, she lifted her face to him and looked into Dane's hooded eyes. They were a smoky blue color.

For once, Maya wanted to leave her heritage behind. Just this one time, she wanted to resist past lessons learned, and pretend they'd never happened. For once she wanted to simply enjoy this man, explore him and feel the sense of connection that he was offering her. Maya saw the surprise in his eyes as she turned and lifted her lips to his. Surprise turned to raw desire and his black pupils grew large and intense with longing—for her. She felt his hands upon her arms, pulling her more deeply into his embrace. Her breasts pressed against his chest. With her breath hitching as his head came closer, closer, Maya shut her eyes and eased forward. She'd never wanted anything more than she wanted this moment with Dane.

As he closed his mouth across Maya's, a deep shudder went through Dane. Her lips were soft and tentative. Feeling her hesitancy, he placed massive control over his raging desire.

At first he was surprised. His mind churned despite the fire arcing through his body. Maya was vulnerable, and she was sending out a feeler of trust. Maybe, like him, she was a little afraid of the intimacy that the kiss she offered him signaled. Just knowing that gave Dane the patience to move his mouth tenderly across her lips, to let her know that he, too, was shy for the very same reasons.

Maya moaned softly as his mouth grazed hers with unexpected tenderness. Never in her wildest imaginings would she have thought Dane capable of this kind of sensitivity. Sliding her hand across his chest, she wrapped her fingers around the nape of his neck, wanting more of him. He'd shown that he could take her fear, her hesitancy, in stride. He wasn't about to blunder in.

Just knowing that he was attuned to her needs made Maya hunger for more of him. How could she have not realized that Dane was different from other men? Different in the most wonderful of ways? Lost in the glowing heat spreading throughout her belly, she felt his mouth cajole hers. He teethed her lower lip gently, wordlessly asking her to participate. His breath was ragged and moist across her cheek and nose. Maya felt the sandpapery quality of his face against hers. As he fitted his mouth fully against hers and rocked her lips open, Maya surrendered herself to him.

Easing his fingers through Maya's thick, luxurious hair, and framing her face with his hands, Dane kissed her deeply and thoroughly. She was at once wet, responsive, yielding and bold with him. There was a courageous quality to Maya. Even if she was still afraid, she was trusting him—despite their stained past. Inhaling her soft, sleepy scent, feeling her hair swirling silkily against his jaw, he eased his mouth from hers. Opening his eyes, their lips now barely touching, he looked down into her drowsy emerald gaze. The desire in her eyes, the sunlit gold flecks in them, called to him. Dane felt Maya's hand move across his shoulder to pull him forward so that he could ease back onto the bed, with him on top of her.

Just then, there was a sharp knock at the door.

"Room service."

Maya jumped.

Dane tensed.

She laughed softly as she released him. "Real life intrudes."

He gave her an apologetic grin and reluctantly stood up to

answer the door. "I thought what we were sharing was real life, too."

Maya smiled. "It's a dream."

Tipping the waiter, he took the tray into the room himself and set it on the round table located at the window, which overlooked Cuzco. Dane felt his body aching without relief. He wanted Maya, he didn't want food. Hearing her move around, Dane decided to stash those hopes away for another time and place. As he pulled the lids off the two plates filled with breakfast food, he saw Maya come to the table. She had her pink robe on, the color matching the high blush in her cheeks. Her hair was pleasantly mussed, and her mouth looked well kissed—by him.

"Coffee?" he asked as he sat down opposite her.

Maya nodded and placed the white linen napkin in her lap. Her heart was pounding. She could still taste Dane on her lips. Giving him a wry look as he handed her the china cup filled with coffee, she said, "I didn't mean to kiss you…but I'm not sorry I did, either."

Pouring himself coffee, Dane gave her an amused look. "Don't be looking for an apology from me."

Maya ate in silence. Her mind churned. Her heart somersaulted. There was something so strong, so good in Dane that she sat there feeling like an idiot. Inca had seen it. Why hadn't she herself detected it a long time ago? He was a strong, capable man, a man with feelings. He had an incredible sensitivity, an ability to know her, what she wanted and needed, without her ever saying a word to him. Maya knew how unusual that was in a man. Paying attention to her scrambled eggs and slathering her toast with strawberry jam, Maya knew the answer. She had been projecting all her own stuff onto him so she couldn't see who Dane York really was.

"What do you want to do today?" Dane asked lightly as he spooned eggs into his mouth.

With a slight, embarrassed laugh, Maya said, "Well, after

sleeping eighteen hours straight, I think I ought to get off my duff, don't you?'' She tilted her head and caught his amused expression. ''How about if I show you Cuzco? If you love architecture or history, this is the place to be.''

''I like both,'' Dane said. What he really wanted to do was get up and drag Maya over to the bed to finish the delicious exploration they'd started earlier. Dane knew that it was Maya's call to make. Besides, they needed to get to know one another better. He didn't just idly hop into a woman's bed for the hell of it. No, there had to be a lot more between them than just raw sex and desire.

''Good,'' Maya murmured between bites. ''Let me take a bath and get dressed, after I make a pig of myself here with all this great food, and then we'll play *tourista*.''

Chuckling, Dane agreed. ''I've got the most beautiful guide in the world. My day won't go wrong no matter what we do.''

''So, your dad was an army helicopter pilot, too?'' Maya asked. They sat at El Trucha, one of the five-star restaurants in Cuzco. After a day of touring the beautiful old Catholic cathedrals that graced the central Plaza del Sol, they'd settled on this seafood restaurant as their farewell to the city.

Dane cut into the tender pink flesh of the filleted trout on his white china plate. El Trucha was quiet, the service excellent, the booths very private. ''Yeah, he was a career man. He retired after thirty years.''

Maya tried the tasty yellow potatoes, a delicacy of Peru. ''And your mom? What did she do? Was she a career army wife?'' She smiled at him in the low light, enjoying the intimacy that had remained with them all day long. Sometimes Dane would touch her hand or shoulder, but he never made another attempt to kiss her. The day had been wonderful for Maya. She had never enjoyed anyone's company as much as she did his.

Frowning, Dane stopped eating. "No…she didn't like the idea of staying home and being a mother to me…."

Hearing the pain, Maya stopped eating and looked up, seeing the hurt in his hooded blue gaze. "Did they divorce?"

"Yes." Dane tried to concentrate on the moment, not his painful past. Maya had changed into a sleek black dress with a boat neck and a pale pink bolero jacket. She had bought it this afternoon at one of the many shops around Plaza de Armas, the main plaza in Cuzco. Her hair was caught up in a French twist, a pale pink orchid with a red lip entwined in the strands. It made her look delicious and so very exquisite. Pink shell earrings and a necklace adorned her ears and slender throat. He had bought them for her. And she'd accepted the gift like an excited child. But as she sat waiting for his reply, he knew he owed her the truth.

"My mother was a lot like you," Dane said, placing the flatware aside and picking up his glass of white wine. "She was headstrong, independent. She shot from the hip and didn't like staying home to do housework."

Maya smiled a little. "I don't know of a woman alive who likes doing housework, do you?"

"No, but she could have at least hung around to help raise me. She left us when I was twelve. She told my father that she just wasn't happy being a housewife."

Blotting her lips, Maya heard raw pain in his low voice. She could see that by talking about it, Dane had lost his appetite. "So, you've been alone for a long time, too."

Her words sunk into him. "Alone? I had my dad, but he was away a lot of the time. I had a baby-sitter until I was thirteen, and then I was on my own."

"Did your mother have visitation rights?"

"Yeah…but she moved away, and then my father got transferred, and it was impossible for her to travel two thousand miles to see me. You know how it is when you're a military brat."

Setting her plate aside, Maya thanked the waiter when he

came over and whisked it away. Turning her attention back to Dane, she whispered, "I do know. One camp after another somewhere in the world, moving every two years whether you liked it or not." She smiled bravely. "I learned a lot of German and French when my father was moved around."

"I did, too, but so what?" Dane shrugged and handed his half-eaten plate of food to the waiter. "I swore that when I went into the army, I wasn't going to raise a kid the way I was raised."

"Does that translate into 'I'm not going to marry a head-strong, independent woman who might run off and abandon me again'?"

Dane stared at her across the table. The low lighting emphasized the clean lines of her face. Maya's eyes were warm with compassion. "Probably."

"No wonder," she mused softly, "you saw your mother in me. We're alike, from the sound of it. Only, I don't abandon people."

His mouth twitched. "Yes, you two were a lot alike. She's dead now. Got killed by a drunk driver coming out for my high school graduation."

Maya's heart squeezed with sympathy. "I'm sorry. It sounds like she tried to stay in touch with you?"

"Oh, sure, by letters, phone calls once a week, usually. And sometimes she'd visit when we were stateside, but it didn't help."

"You felt she didn't love you enough to stay and raise you, right?"

"Ouch." Dane scratched his head and gave her a long, intent look. "You're pretty savvy about seeing straight through people, aren't you?"

"One of my better qualities," Maya laughed. "And you know as well as I do how that skill comes in handy when you're a squadron commander trying to make fifty-some people work as a team, going in one direction, all at the same time."

He laughed with her. A lot of the weight from the past seemed to dissolve from his shoulders. Maya's eyes were half-closed, and filled with desire—for him. Dane knew now what that look meant. If only they had time…but they did not.

"What about you, Maya? Why aren't you married? You're beautiful, bright and successful. There's got to be men standing in line waiting for you after this assignment." Dane hoped not, but he wasn't a fool.

Now it was Maya's turn to laugh. The sound was husky and filled with derision. "Most men, when they see me coming, run the other way, screaming." Shaking her head, she sipped the wine. "I scare men, Dane, in case you didn't already know that. They aren't ready to deal on an equal basis with a woman like myself."

"I'm learning to…."

Her lips pulled upward. "I can't decide why you towed the mark with me. And no, you never flinched or backed down from me. I respected you for that—despite our past troubles with one another. You were never scared of me, either."

"I was raised with a mother very much like you in personality. Just because you're strong and confident doesn't mean you aren't feminine. I think, looking back on it, that my father married her because he was so taken with her individuality and charisma."

"It takes a real man to deal with a woman like that," Maya said. "And frankly, I just haven't met that many."

"Mike Houston? Morgan Trayhern?"

"Yes, they qualify. But they're a rare species, you've got to admit."

"So," Dane murmured, "you've got your personal life on hold until…"

Grimacing, Maya finished off the rest of the wine and set the glass aside. "I don't have a personal life. The reason I'm here is to do what I'm doing now."

"But that doesn't mean you can't have a personal life." Dane gave her a quizzical look. Her eyes look troubled, and she wouldn't meet his gaze.

"There's a lot you don't know about me, Dane, and I'm sitting here trying to decide whether or not to level with you about it. I owe you the truth. In my line of work, what I want personally has to come second, not first. I'm dedicated to this mission. It's my life."

He ran a finger aimlessly across the linen tablecloth as he considered her words. "Is this where 'different' comes into play?"

Sitting back, Maya regarded him in the building silence. "Let me tell you a story, Dane. When I was twenty-one, I fell in love with a warrant officer who flew the Apache. I kept a…secret from him until it was too late, and we were completely involved with one another. My secret eventually was revealed. And when it was, he was shocked—and scared. He never came back. I lost him. I was devastated, of course. I had been warned that my uniqueness would cause a lot of pain. My teacher warned me that most people would never accept me—all of me." Maya shrugged painfully and set the napkin on the table. Dane's eyes glittered with intense interest. "Well, I'm not going to make that mistake twice. I learned a lot from that affair. I swore never to enter into any kind of a relationship with a man unless he knew up front the truth about me."

"Okay…so what's the truth that will make me run the other way?"

One corner of her mouth lifted. Dane was trying to tease her into relaxing. The look on his face was placid. Could he accept the truth? Maya didn't think so. "It's not that easy…. The truth, that is…"

"You're a highly complex person," Dane murmured. "It's a large part of what makes you charismatic, I think." And desirable to him, but he didn't say that. He saw the fear and indecision banked in Maya's dark green eyes. She licked her lower lip—and that meant she was genuinely nervous, he knew. "Complex people are fascinating to me," Dane continued. "You never lose interest in someone who's complicated. At least, I don't." Nothing she could tell him would scare Dane off, but he was piqued by the intrigue she presented.

"Don't be so sure," Maya warned, her brows dipping. Opening her hands, she said, "I was orphaned at birth. I was then adopted two weeks later by my foster parents. When I was seven years old, I began to have a dream every night. This very old woman, very regal looking, her face very kind, would visit me. This went on for years. I never told anyone about it because she asked me not to. Her name was Grandmother Alaria, Dane. And she's a real person, not just a figment of my imagination."

"Okay," he murmured. "How did you find out that she was alive?"

"When I was seventeen, I went down to Brazil with my mother, who loved the country. Grandmother Alaria met me in São Paulo. I was blown away when she appeared to me in the flesh. She'd told me that we'd meet there and I didn't really believe it. But when she showed up, everything changed."

"She had the capacity to talk to you in your dreams at night?"

"Yes, she did. Still does. She's a very powerful woman."

Dane placed his elbows on the table and rested his chin on his closed hands as he studied Maya's shadowed face. "Okay, you've hooked me and now I'm interested. Go on."

"I'm going to cut to the chase. I found out that my real parents had been murdered by a drug lord in Brazil. And that they were members of the Jaguar Clan, a worldwide mystical community of people who have metaphysical skills and who work for the greater good of humanity and Mother Earth. There are two branches—the Jaguar Clan and the Black Jaguar Clan. Inca, my sister, belongs to the first. I'm of the Black Jaguar Clan.''

''I see. So how does this help you? What does it do for you?''

Maya could see Dane earnestly trying to understand it all. Opening her hands, she said, ''Grandmother Alaria had trained me via dream work to develop a certain skill that all Black Jaguar Clan members possess.''

''Which is?''

Maya pointed to the small crystal salt shaker with a silver cap on it. ''See that?''

''Yes.''

''Just watch it.'' She folded her hands, closed her eyes and took a long, deep breath.

Dane felt a shift in energy around them. It was nothing obvious, just different. One moment the salt shaker was in front of him. The next, it had disappeared. He blinked. Moving his hand forward, he frowned. Looking up, he saw Maya open her eyes and stare at him, unblinking.

''The salt shaker…'' he began, looking around for it.

''You won't find it, Dane.''

Frowning, he said, ''Why not?''

''Because I teleported it over there.'' And she pointed to the window. The salt shaker sat on the sill.

Dane looked at her, his chin raising slightly. And then he stared at the salt shaker. ''What did you do? Is it a magic trick? Sleight of hand or something?''

Maya shook her head gravely. ''Watch the salt shaker.'' She closed her eyes and took another deep breath.

Staring hard at it, Dane saw it suddenly dissolve in front of him. He gasped. Jerking a look at Maya, he saw that she was just opening her eyes.

''What the hell…''

''Look, Dane.'' She pointed to the table between them.

He looked down at where she was pointing. There was the salt shaker. Scratching his head, he picked it up. It was real.

And it was back on the table. Giving her a wary look, he said, "All right, maybe you had a second salt shaker in your hand, hidden, and put it on the table while I was looking over there at the windowsill."

Maya smiled weakly. "If that was so, why isn't the salt shaker still on the sill?"

Stymied, Dane shrugged. He looked hard at her. "What is going on here? What did you do?"

Leaning forward, Maya kept her voice low as she answered. "It's called teleportation. It is the ability to move an object, any object, from point A to point B."

"But...that's physics...that's changing molecular structures from one form to another—and then back again."

"Yes, it is. And I can do it, Dane. I've got the training to do it, and it comes genetically to me because of my heritage with the Black Jaguar Clan."

Taking a ragged breath, Dane looked at Maya for a long time without speaking. "This is voodoo."

"No, it's metaphysics. There's a big difference. What I did, old Tibetan lamas could do. It's noted in their writings. Same with the teachers of India. This is nothing new. It's just new to you, is all."

"You could have made me disappear?" He said it partly in jest, but he studied her intently.

With a slight laugh, Maya said, "Look, Dane, don't get too serious about this little gift—or should I say curse—of mine. The key is that I've got to be in a very harmonious, balanced state to engage it." Maya rolled her eyes. "And my life in the squadron is anything but harmonious, emotionally speaking. Ninety percent of the time I can't do it."

"I see...and this is what your people know about you?"

"They don't know anything about this, or my life as a Jaguar Clan member. I'm telling you because you deserve to know up front, before anything else happens one way or another between us."

His mouth quirked. "But your people kept using the word

different. If they don't know who you really are, why do they call you that?''

"Because I also have a pretty good sixth sense. When I'm well rested and 'on,' I can feel the Kamovs around—even the direction they're coming from, before we visually spot them. I've gained notoriety for that over the past three years."

Nodding, Dane said, "You've thrown me for a loop, Maya. But from what I've seen, you're terribly human just like the rest of us."

Her grin widened. "I am. Probably more so."

"And that's why Inca has healing ability? Her genetic heritage is from the Jaguar Clan, too?"

"Exactly." Maya was pleased with his insight. Although Dane looked shaken, he didn't look scared. "The most important thing you want to remember is that we're mission driven. Black Jaguar Clan members do the dirty work. We engage the bad guys, face-to-face. The other branch does a lot of healing work for the planet, and for people. We just tear up real estate when necessary." Maya laughed derisively.

"You're the soldiers on the front lines. They're the academic part of it."

"Yes, you got it."

"Okay…I think I can handle all of this…" Dane met her guarded gaze.

"There's one more thing," Maya told him, and she patted the lounge seat beside her. Their booth was in a horseshoe shape, and she gestured for him to come and sit next to her.

"Take off my jacket," she instructed him when he'd done so, and she turned her back toward him.

Maya made sure no one was around. The walls of the booth were high and hid them from prying eyes. She felt Dane's hands on her jacket, and she closed her eyes, knowing that this would scare him off. No one had been able to handle the rest of her secret life. No one.

As the jacket slid off her arms, Dane noticed a dark shape on her left shoulder blade. He took the jacket and put it aside.

"What am I supposed to see?"

"That crescent moon symbol on my left shoulder," she said.

"The tattoo?" He didn't think anything of it. In the low lighting, he saw the curved mark she'd mentioned, but it wasn't any big deal to him.

Maya twisted to look at him over her shoulder. "It's not a tattoo, Dane. Touch it." She held her breath.

He ran his fingertips across her creamy, smooth skin, until they encountered the crescent moon. Instantly, he moved them back and forth several times.

"What is this? Did you paste it on or something? I don't understand."

She heard the frustration in his voice—and the curiosity. "That is the symbol for anyone in the clan. A Black Jaguar has black jaguar fur. I received this when I was initiated into the clan, at age eighteen. It appears there afterward. It doesn't hurt and it's not a brand. It's our way of telling our own kind."

Dane picked at the edges of it with his fingernails, thinking it must be taped on. It was not. Running his hand across her shoulder one more time, he said, "I don't understand how it got there." He was more interested in it than frightened of it. He wanted to figure out *how* it got there, not the fact it was there.

Maya took her jacket and slid it over her shoulders again. "It's a mystery how it got there, Dane. But it's there forever. It won't go away."

Raising his brows, he said, "Interesting...really interesting. Now you've got me going on how it could have happened." He smiled at her.

"All this doesn't scare you?"

"No, why should it? It's an anomaly. Something to be studied and answered."

''Spoken like a true scientist,'' Maya murmured in disbelief. ''You're not scared?''

''No. Perplexed, maybe…fascinated with this skill of yours, the teleportation…but scared, no.''

''Every other man I've shown this to has run like hell, Dane York.''

He caught and held her amused stare. ''Well, I'm not every other man, am I?''

Chapter 11

"Uh-oh," Maya murmured from behind her desk as Dane walked in, "you're a man on a mission. I can tell by the look on your face." She met and held his warm gaze. Instantly, her body responded. So did her heart. He stood, hands on his hips, and gave her a wicked smile.

"You're perceptive, Captain. You ready for the scheduled reconnaisance mission?"

Scribbling on several sets of orders before her, Maya muttered, "Almost..." She forced herself to return to the business at hand. Where had the last two months flown? Since she had boldly initiated kissing Dane at the hotel, her whole world was slowly reordering itself. Not that Dane had pushed her about their burgeoning relationship, or crowded her in any way. No, he wisely had stood back and let her come to him, when she felt ready, when she felt sure of herself with him.

Glancing up, Maya melted beneath his hooded perusal. "Stop looking at me that way, Major. You're blowing my concentration."

His mouth quirked as he leaned against the doorjamb. "Can't help it. You're easy on the eyes." It was another busy day at the base. People hurried to and from their offices. Everyone was always in a hurry around here, but after two months, Dane knew why. They were on a wartime footing.

Maya rose and neatly stacked the papers into her out basket for her assistant to pick up and distribute. Her heart was skittering. Today was the day. They'd planned this little work-play outing for a month. Grabbing her helmet off a peg on the wall, she picked up her chicken plate and moved around the desk.

"Let's saddle up. I'm hungry!"

"So am I, and it isn't for food," he murmured as she moved in front of him and out the door.

Maya laughed throatily. She stopped at her X.O.'s office, poked her head in and told Dallas, "We're going now. You got the controls."

Dallas smiled and looked up from the stacks of paper on her desk. "Okay. Take it easy out there."

"We will. Be back in about three hours."

"Roger. Bye…"

Once out of the building, Maya smiled at Dane. "You got the picnic basket packed in the cargo bay of the Cobra?"

His smile was playful. "Oh, yeah. Got a bottle of really fine sirah wine, and I had Patrick, from the India Feliz, make us a picnic lunch that will put anything I could have put together to shame."

Maya dangled her helmet in her left hand as she walked. All around her, the noontime crews were busy. The Apaches were up and patroling. Off to her right, she saw a number of other pilots working with Craig and Joe over the finer points of the D model. The mechanics were schooling the squadrons on software installation. The sun was bright, the humidity exceedingly high. Wiping her brow, Maya said, "We're in for thunderstorms today. Big time."

Dane saw that the crew had just finished refueling the

Cobra. "Yeah, the meteorologist said that it's real unstable where we're going to do our mapping and surveying work."

As they walked out of the cave, sunlight embraced them momentarily before the white, twisting wisps of clouds closed in once again. "Nothing new for this time of year," Maya assured him. Halting at the Cobra, which like the choppers was painted black, she said, "You be the pilot and I'll do the chart work."

Dane nodded. "Fine by me," He climbed in and took the righthand seat in the cockpit.

"What's this?" Maya asked as she stepped up into the Cobra. She saw that the picnic basket he'd mentioned had been carefully boxed to keep it from rolling around in the wide cargo bay. Blankets, pillows and a checked red-and-white tablecloth were strapped to the rear panel.

Dane twisted in the seat as he strapped in. "Oh, those. Comfort things."

Chuckling, Maya slid the door shut, then bent over and climbed into the cockpit. Unlike the Apache helicopter, the Cobra had a tandem seat, where the pilots sat next to one another. "Looks like you thought of everything," she teased, easing the helmet onto her head.

"I think I have," Dane said, going through his checklist once he got his own helmet on. Outside, the crew chief waited for them to start up the Cobra's engine and engage the rotor.

"Wait till you see this little waterfall and meadow we're going to sneak off to," Maya said, flipping several switches and turning the radio knob to a specific frequency. She placed the map between them and slid it into a holder on her seat for easy access once they lifted off.

"Did you put in your flight plan where we'd be going?" Dane asked.

"Absolutely."

"So, the whole base knows we're going off to have a picnic?" Dane asked wryly, lifting his finger and making a circular motion to the crew chief, who stood to one side of the Cobra's nose.

Maya chuckled. "Probably. I've completed my checklist. You ready to go?"

"Roger." He engaged the engine.

The Cobra shook and came to life. It was an old model saved from the closing days of the Vietnam War. Dane had had the chance to fly the relic a number of times, and looked forward to doing so once more. Today they were going to check some areas to see if new trails were being cut into the jungle. This kind of recon mission took place routinely. Faro Valentino never used the same trails more than two or three times to transport his cocaine over the border. He varied his routes, always constructing new ones. Knowing where they were helped Maya know where to run her missions in order to intercept Faro's supply lines.

More than anything, Dane looked forward to this quality time with Maya. Since their kiss at the hotel, his life had changed remarkably. Any lingering shreds of their past disharmony had dissolved. Yet the last two months had been a special hell for him. At the base, there wasn't time or place for him to talk to Maya on a personal level. He came to realize just how busy she was. Everyone wanted her attention. And as squadron commander, her work was never done. To try and steal a kiss was nearly impossible. They had agreed to keep their relationship, whatever it would become, separate from their duties, at the base. But for Dane it was hell.

As he took the Cobra out the Eye and headed north toward their target area, about seventy miles away, he smiled to himself. Glancing over, he saw Maya placing the plastic-enclosed chart across her thighs. She had a grease pencil in hand and was already beginning to concentrate on the job ahead. Work first, then play, Dane told himself. All around him, he saw rising turrets of cumulonimbus clouds forming massively above the jungle. As they sped toward the new area to be charted, he eyed the thickening thunderheads. The Cobra was not equipped to fly through a thunderstorm, where the winds could toss them around like a flea in a tornado.

Dane was damned if thunderstorms in the area were going to stop him from reaching that nice little picnic area known as Landing Zone Echo. He'd discovered that the LZ was a place many of the pilots and crew flew to for a little R and R. It was a low-threat area, as it was off the beaten trail from Faro's cocaine production and Kamov patrols. The waterfall wasn't big, but the pool below it was great for swimming, and there was a nice grassy spot nearby. The beauty of the place couldn't be rivaled. Dane had discovered it through Wild Woman, who had pointed it out one day when they were flying the Apache D. That had got him thinking and scheming on how to get Maya away from the base, to give them some badly needed time alone.

As he flew, the shiver of the Cobra felt good around him. The shaking and shuddering were part of this intrepid aircraft that had seen so much war duty. Even now, Maya used the Cobra for many things, as a medical air ambulance as well as to carry weapons, food and other needed supplies. It was a real workhorse with a multiple mission purpose. The new Blackhawk was replacing it, but the Cobra was still used.

Glancing left, Dane saw Maya working on the map. They flew at five thousand feet, high enough above the jungle to spot any new trail systems being hacked into it. The forest was so thick and lush that it was almost impenetrable. Over the years, the Quechua villagers had cut a maze of trails through it with their axes and machetes. No one could get through that dense growth without such tools.

The air was becoming increasingly bumpy because of the building thermals. Dane grimaced. From the looks of the dark clouds along the horizon, they were going to be rained out. Damn, he didn't want that to happen. He wanted this time with Maya. He had so many questions for her, so many things he wanted to listen to her talk about and share with him. He hungered for it.

He dreamed of her every night, of loving her fully. What would it be like to love Maya? To undress her? To make her one with him? His body automatically tightened at those heated thoughts. And where was his heart in all of this? Over the past two months, Dane had had to be ruthlessly honest with himself.

Maya wasn't a woman to catch, conquer and then walk away from. He'd never do that to her—or to himself. He'd had a lot of time to accept her other life as a Jaguar Clan member. On the surface, Maya appeared to be just as human as anyone else at the base, except for her charisma, that power that radiated from her like sunlight. Everyone responded to it. Hell, he did, too. And yet Maya seemed supremely unaware of it. What drove her, Dane had discovered, was her mission—the legacy of her clan, which ran in her blood. Now he understood why she'd fought so hard to get this base set up.

In the few conversations they'd had during these rare moments when they were alone, he'd explored her connection with that ongoing mission. Maya didn't care about upward mobility in the army. She would be happy being here for twenty or thirty years, doing exactly the same thing. It was then that Dane realized the seriousness of her commitment to slowing the drug trade and helping the world become a better place. Maya was driven. She had a vision. Could her life include a personal relationship? Dane wasn't sure. And what did he want out of this?

"Looks like rain ahead," Maya murmured. She glanced over at Dane. His profile was strong and clean. Feeling the warmth building in her lower body, she met and held his gaze for a moment. "But somehow, I don't think rain is going to detour you from your target or mission."

"You got that right." Dane frowned. "You okay with a picnic inside the Cobra?"

Smiling, Maya lifted the binoculars and scanned the jungle ahead for new trails. "Sure. Let's go for it."

"Helluva day for a picnic," Dane groused as he slipped out of the harness. The rotors were slowly coming to a halt. Outside, it was pouring rain. The sharp pinging sound against the skin of the chopper reverberated through the cabin. Lightning zigzagged across the jungle above them. Easing out of the seat, he moved into the rear cabin. Maya followed him.

"Spread the blankets on the deck," Maya suggested with amusement. "We're going to enjoy our time together no matter if the rain gods are dancing on our head or not." She smiled at him as she took the picnic basket out of the box.

Within minutes, they were comfortable, chicken sandwiches in hand as they sipped the ruby wine. Maya leaned against the rear bulkhead, her legs spread out before her. Dane sat next to her, his elbow occasionally brushing hers. The thunder caromed around them and the rain intensified. She gazed through the cockpit windows at the blurred landscape outside. They had landed in a small clearing. To their left was the waterfall.

"This storm will pass," she murmured.

He leaned back, tipped his head to the left and smiled at her. She had released her hair so that it flowed around her shoulders. The look in her eyes was one of invitation. Maya was so easy to read. Dane corrected himself; she was easy to read when she allowed him to read her.

"The storm between us did," he murmured, finishing off the sandwich.

Laughing, Maya said, "I'd say it was more than a little storm." Gusts of wind rocked the Cobra slightly. The rain was beginning to slacken off. She wiped her hands on the pink linen napkin that Patrick had provided with his five-star feast. Reaching for a slice of potato covered with cheese and bacon, Maya felt a frisson of fear. In another month, Dane and his crew would be gone. She frowned.

"What's the matter?"

"Oh…nothing…"

Dane sipped his wine and watched her enjoy the potatoes. Peru was famous for having more than two hundred varieties of potatoes, thanks to the Incas. Potatoes had been a staple for the empire and still were in Peru. "You're mulling over something," he murmured. "I can feel it."

She leaned back and settled against his left shoulder, wanting to feel his closeness. "You're getting a little too good at reading me."

"Does that bother you?"

Shrugging, Maya sipped the last of her wine and set the glass back in the picnic basket near their feet. "No…it's just that I'm not used to a man knowing how I feel about something, is all." Her eyes sparkled. "I'll get over it."

Placing his own wineglass in the basket, he lifted his arm and brought her into his embrace. Maya came like a purring cat into the circle of his arms. Smiling, Dane leaned back as she settled against him. As she rested her head on his shoulder and wrapped her left arm around his waist, Dane sighed. "*This* is what I've missed. You."

Closing her eyes, Maya allowed the sound of the splattering rain to soothe her fractious state. "Feels good, doesn't it?"

"Yeah, it's kinda nice to be able to put my arms around you without worrying that someone might see us." He chuckled indulgently. Pressing a kiss to her hair, he added, "I feel like a kid in the back seat of a car. Don't you?"

Giggling, Maya pressed her hand to her lips. "Yes. Exactly."

"Sometimes there's no other place to meet your favorite girl but in your old beat-up car," he mused. Looking around, he said, "In our case, it's a beat-up, antique Cobra helicopter."

"Are we dyed-in-the-wool helicopter pilots or what?"

He laughed deeply, along with Maya. Squeezing her, he

felt the fullness of her breasts beneath her flight suit. She felt good and strong and vibrant in his arms. Inhaling her fragrance, he smiled wistfully. "I don't care where I am, as long as I'm with you."

His words feathered across Maya. She closed her eyes, content to be held and to hear the soothing thud of his heart against her ear. "You kinda grow on a person, you know?"

Opening one eye, he angled his head and looked down into her smiling face. Her emerald eyes were wide and drowsy looking. "Like mold?" he teased.

Hitting him playfully on the shoulder, Maya said, "No, not mold."

Catching her hand, Dane placed a warm kiss on it. "What then? Am I like a lousy head cold that just won't go away? Comes back again and again?"

"You certainly have a low opinion of yourself, Major. Mold. A cold. Why couldn't you see yourself as sunshine for an orchid? Rain for Pachamama, Mother Earth?"

He kept her hand and pressed it against his heart. "Very sensual. I like that."

Quirking her lips, she retorted, "Just like a man to pick a disease, or something else yucky."

"I'd rather be rain for the orchid," Dane decided nonchalantly, a smile playing across his mouth.

"Well," Maya grumped, "we sure got the rain." And she pointed at the cockpit windows.

Dane eased her onto her back against the thick blankets spread across the deck. There was plenty of room for two people to stretch out and be comfortable in the Cobra. He saw surprise and then pleasure flare in Maya's gaze as he lay beside her, his arm beneath her neck.

"You're like an orchid, you know," he whispered as he leaned down. "Mysterious, beautiful, exotic…" And he captured her lips beneath his.

Maya's world melted instantly. How much she'd looked forward to kissing Dane once again. Sliding her hands up his shoulders, she pulled him toward her. Wanting to feel the strength of his body against her own, she savored his hot, exploratory kiss. As he eased away from her mouth, she saw his stormy blue eyes watch her intently. Moving her fingertips upward to caress his hard jawline, she whispered, "I want you. All of you…"

Nodding, Dane eased himself into a sitting position. "I know…" And he began to undress.

Maya heard the boom of thunder. The Cobra shook slightly. More wind pounded against its sides. There might be a storm surrounding them, but the storm inside her was building, making her needy and bold. She saw the lazy smile, the confidence burning in Dane's eyes. This time, there was no uncertainty in his expression. Only the look of a man who was going to claim his woman—her. Excitement thrummed through Maya as she eased out of her black uniform. She never wore a bra with it, so as she slid the fabric off her shoulders, she saw his gaze narrow upon her.

Thick strands of hair fell across her exposed breasts. Dane quickly took his uniform off and pushed it aside. He was naked as he got to his knees and helped Maya slide her feet out of the legs of her flight suit. She wore nothing at all beneath the uniform. Smiling a little, he met and held her bold, heated look. How long he'd waited for this—for her. Everything was right as he lay down at her side and she languidly stretched out before him. Maya was more catlike grace than human to his mind and senses. Her eyes were slightly tilted, sultry looking as she moved toward him to make full contact.

The moment her breasts grazed his darkly haired chest, he groaned. Dane took her deeply into his arms, crushing his hips against hers. Maya was soft, yet strong in womanly ways. Her mouth was hot, searching and hungry against his. Breath shallow, he drank of her offering, and tasted the sweet tartness of the wine on her lips. His heart sang. It opened wide like an orchid blooming. Never had he wanted to please anyone more than her. Her leg wrapped around his and locked him tightly against her. Smiling against her lips, he decided he liked Maya's boldness.

As his hand skimmed her left shoulder, it passed across the crescent moon symbol of her clan. Sliding his fingers down the deep curve of her spine, Dane felt himself spiraling like a hawk on a column of heat and need, eager to fulfill himself within her, to join her and connect with her on the deepest, most intimate levels that a man could with a woman. Maya was just as courageous in loving him as she was in flying her gunship against great odds and danger. She was risking herself once more, not in battle, but on the human frontier of intimacy with him. As he met her searching mouth, he kissed her hard and pressed her against the blankets. With his knee, he gently nudged open her long, firm thighs. His heart was thudding like thunder in his chest. The soft moan that rose in her slender throat as he leaned down and captured the hardened peak of her nipple made him sing with joy. The growling sound, the way her fingers dug frantically into his shoulders as he suckled her, made him soar on wings of happiness. More than anything, he wanted to give Maya pleasure.

Breath hitching momentarily, Maya waited impatiently as Dane moved across her. The feral gleam in his eyes made her raw with need. As his hips moved downward, she lifted hers to meet him. The moment he slid into her slick, heated confines, Maya's eyelids shuttered closed. Something primal, so necessary to her life and heart, rolled rhythmically through her. She gripped his shoulders as he thrust deeply into her. A moan of raw hunger tore from her lips. Arching upward, she invited him into her.

Their bodies were slick and moved with an ageless rhythm. As his mouth captured hers, Maya drowned in the sensations, the taste of him as a man, and dug her fingers more deeply into his tense shoulders. Every movement was escalating her pleasure. She saw his lips draw away from his teeth, and felt an explosion deep within her at that moment.

The heat was lavalike, hurling her into a dark oblivion of incredible pleasure and wavelike rhythm. Lost in his arms, the strength of him as a male, his touch and taste, Maya surrendered herself to him in every way possible. An arcing heat raced through her. It made her freeze momentarily, her pleasure so sharp and deep that she gasped with surprise and joy. Hearing him groan, his head pressed against hers, she moved her hips to increase the pleasure for him as well.

Moments strung together like heartbeats. As the tidal wave of heat receded within her, Maya felt Dane sink heavily against her. Smiling softly, she slid her arms around his back and kissed his cheek. They were both panting raggedly. Dane eased himself off her, onto his elbows, and looked down at her. His eyes were a stormy blue, the pupils huge and black with satisfaction. She shared a tremulous smile with him and slid her fingers up across his face and into his damp hair, her body glowing hotly in the aftermath. Words were useless. When he moved in her, she moaned a little and arched in response.

"You are so beautiful," Dane rasped as he leaned down and grazed her parted lips with his own. "Bold, beautiful and courageous."

His words made her feel good. His face was damp, and Maya wiped the perspiration away with her fingers. "You were wonderful," she managed to murmur.

Dane absorbed her trembling words. Maya's voice was husky with satiation. He saw she was fulfilled. So was he. Moving several damp strands of hair away from her temple, he said, "If I'd only known then what I know now about you…"

Maya shook her head, her dark hair spilling away from her shoulders. "Don't go there, Dane."

It was chilly in the cabin, and Dane eased off of her and then leaned down and pulled one of the blankets up and over them. Bringing Maya into his arms, he welcomed her warmth against him, her hand sliding around his torso to draw them even closer.

Lying with her head in the crook of his arm, Maya closed her eyes, a smile lingering on her well-kissed lips. Gazing down at her, Dane ran his fingers slowly through her hair. "I don't know how I could have been so stupid," he murmured. "I really blew it with you back at Fort Rucker."

Barely opening her eyes, Maya looked up at him. She saw the pain in his gaze and the way his mouth was set. "The time wasn't right, Dane, that's all."

The rain was lessening dramatically now. Dane could see slats of sunlight filtering weakly through the storm clouds, which were now moving away from them. "I guess not," he admitted gravely. Combing his fingers through the thick silk of Maya's hair, he held her drowsy green gaze, which was filled with flecks of gold. "Do you know how happy it makes me to see you smile? To kiss you and know that everything's right in the world again? To touch you and be in heaven on earth?"

She nodded and slid her hand up across his arm and shoulder. "Ever since I first kissed you, my world has been a lot better than it used to be, too." Maya saw male pride gleaming in his eyes and liked the way his mouth curved upward. Dane deserved to know how much happiness he brought to her.

Moving his finger along her hairline near her temple, he followed the sweet curve of her jaw. "I've only got one more month down here." His brows moved downward as he studied the slender line of her neck and how it fit beautifully in her shoulder. "Before our truce, I could hardly wait to leave. Now...every day is going to be like a gift. You're a gift to me, Maya... Do you realize that?" He moved his gaze to her emerald eyes, which widened in response to his honesty. "I've never met a woman like you before. And I find myself being very selfish, wanting you all to myself, though I know that can't be."

"Would it help you to know that I'm feeling very frustrated that I don't have the time alone that I want with you?"

Giving her a tender smile, Dane whispered, "I don't know what to do, sweet woman of mine. I want to stretch thirty days into years."

Nodding, Maya said, "I know what you mean...." Did she have the courage to tell Dane how much she liked him? Maya was afraid to say "love" because that word scared her. If she loved Dane, that would change her life. She had her mission; that came first. All other things must come second...or third....

Grazing her lips with his mouth, Dane rasped, "I'm going to make every minute count with you when we get back. I know we can't show any affection for one another out in public, but I'm going to start closing that office door of yours every now and again...for just a few minutes...."

Maya drowned in the promise of his mouth. His lips were searching, tender and exploratory. Maya moved her arms around his shoulders, realizing she'd never felt happier—and never more afraid. Did Dane love her? What was that look in his eyes? Maya had been unable to decipher it. Or was it her imagination? No. Because she was extraordinarily sensitive, she could feel Dane on all levels.

And if he did love her, did she love him? The answer came as a resounding warmth that flowed through her opened heart when he molded his mouth against hers. His breath was moist, his kiss capturing.

Maya felt his other hand range down along her shoulder and gently cup her breast. She leaned into him, wanting him to touch her even more. They were so well matched to one another. Her mind was shorting out. Her body was singing as he grazed her nipple with his lips. What if she did love Dane? The thought scared Maya. The only other time she had loved, the man had backed off because of her secret life.

Well, her other life didn't bother Dane at all. He accepted her at face value. It mattered not one whit about her Black Jaguar heritage. Dane was brave and accepting in ways Maya knew would never happen again in her life. Why had this happened now? How could she split herself between her mission and her need for him? In turmoil, she shoved all her doubts and needs aside and concentrated on Dane, on him touching her and making her moan with pleasure once again.

The world, the pressures, the responsibilities all melted away from Maya. When Dane eased her on top of him so that she straddled his hips, she smiled down at him and placed her hands upon his massive, darkly haired chest. He met her catlike smile with a primal look of his own. She arched as he moved into her. More than anything, Maya realized in that moment that they were made for one another. He was her equal, and she was his. And the respect they had for one another was as solid as Mother Earth herself. Dane owned her heart. He touched her soul. And he completed her as no one had ever done in her life.

Chapter 12

Maya jerked awake, a scream jammed in her throat. She sat up, her breath choppy and ragged. *No! Oh, no!* Closing her eyes, she leaned forward, rubbing her hands roughly across her face to help her wake up. It was a nightmare. Just a nightmare…or was it? The sounds of the cave complex filtered into her office, where she sat on the cot. She'd fallen asleep around 0300, after Dane had come in and forced her to leave her desk and the mission plans she was working on.

Sitting there trembling, Maya felt a trickle of sweat between her breasts. Running her hands through her thick hair to tame it into place, Maya looked around the quiet office. Glancing down at her watch, she saw it was 0600. Time to get up. She had a mission scheduled with Cam Anderson in the Cobra at 0630. A new trail had been spotted fifty miles to the north, and they had to go in and look at it closely this morning.

The nightmare still hung darkly around her. Making herself some coffee, Maya heard booted feet in the hallway outside. Turning, she saw Dane open the door to her office. He had recently shaved, but she saw telltale gray shadows beneath his blue eyes. As he met and held her gaze, Maya nodded.

"I'm up. I'm not coherent yet…but I'm up."

Dane saw the puffiness beneath her glorious emerald eyes. Her hair was still in mild disarray around her shoulders as she made her very necessary coffee.

"You look shaken," he observed as he came in and shut the door quietly behind him. "What's wrong?" Indeed, she looked pale as hell. He saw fear lurking in Maya's eyes as she turned away, her lips compressing into a line that he'd come to recognize as irritation.

"Oh," Maya muttered defensively, "I had a nightmare, was all…." She felt Dane come to a halt near her, and she absorbed his quiet, strong masculine energy. Somehow, just having Dane nearby always steadied Maya when she got into emotional maelstroms like this one. She flipped the switch on the coffeemaker. "There…coffee in three minutes."

Dane pulled out the chair for her to sit on. "Need a brush?"

She gave him a disgruntled look. "That bad, huh?"

Chuckling, he went to the locker near the cot and opened it. Maya kept her cosmetic kit in there, and he pulled it out for her. The past month, this had become an anticipated routine between them. Dane tried to keep the anguish he felt in his heart at bay as he brought the colorful cloth bag containing her toiletries over to her desk. In two days, he and his crew were scheduled to fly back to Fort Rucker, Alabama. It was the *last* thing he wanted to do.

Reaching for the brush, Maya quickly pulled it through her tangled hair. She saw that cockeyed smile on Dane's mouth as he stood in front of the desk observing her with that warm look in his blue eyes. "Thanks…" she murmured grumpily.

Dane sat on the edge of the desk. "You don't normally have nightmares," he stated as he took pleasure in her running the brush through her dark, glinting hair. "What was it about?"

Shrugging, she said, "Oh…nothing…"

"Don't pull that on me, Maya."

She glared at him and then put the brush down and picked up the comb. "It was my guardian."

"Your guardian?"

"Yes, every clan member has a spirit guardian." She saw the puzzlement in his eyes and explained, "They're like a guardian angel. Does that compute a little better for you and your reality?"

His brows raised. "Yeah, I get it now."

"Only," Maya said in a husky tone, "our spirit guides aren't just ethereal, as most people think of guardian angels. They can literally appear into our third dimension." She pointed to the desk. "And if they materialize, they are *real*— as solid as this is. They aren't a figment of anyone's imagination."

"What's the purpose in their materializing?"

Maya looked at him for a moment. In the last month, she'd told him more and more about her secret life. Dane was always fascinated by it, never put off, and certainly never afraid of it or her. He was an amazing person. And she loved him. How badly Maya wanted to say those words to him, but he was leaving shortly. And they hadn't talked about that, either. Both were putting it off. She knew why: she was afraid to admit she'd fallen in love with him, and was unsure how that would upset the well-ordered worlds they revolved within. Maya knew she would not leave her base or her mission. And she knew how much Dane's army career meant to him. She would never expect him to resign his commission and come back down here to live with her.

"They can materialize for a lot of reasons," she murmured as she combed her hair into place. "Sometimes my guardian comes in on his own, without me asking for him. A priestess always gets a male jaguar, and a priest, a female one. That way, the energy is balanced." She put the comb down and saw to her relief that the coffee was ready. Picking up the pot, she poured two cups. "I don't allow my guardian to materialize around here. It would scare the living hell out of my people. Sometimes, when I go into Agua Caliente on a flight, I'll go down to the Urubamba River and let him materialize there, out of sight of everyone. He loves the water, so I'll walk along the shore while he wades and tries to catch trout." Maya smiled softly and, turning, handed Dane the cup.

"And what are they for?" Dane asked, sipping the coffee. He watched as Maya sat down, placed her hands around the mug and slowly drank, pleasure in her expression.

"Protection, help, support and guidance."

"Like—" he searched his mind "—a big guard dog?"

She grinned slightly. "If I was in serious trouble, yeah, my jag would appear. He'd kill to protect me."

"That's good to know," Dane murmured. "I guess he doesn't consider me a threat or I'd have been so much dog meat a long time ago."

Maya chuckled. "Our guides sense a person's intent. And no, he's not going to bother you."

"Good to know." Dane met her smile. "So, what about this nightmare of yours? What was it about?"

Maya hesitated. She didn't want to worry Dane. "Oh…it was nothing…."

"Want me to repeat the question?" Dane nailed her with a direct look that told Maya he truly wanted to know.

Pursing her lips, she sat back in the squeaky chair, the mug between her hands, and looked up at the wall. "My black jag was fighting darkness. Not the kind of night darkness you know. This darkness…well, it was evil. It's the heavy energy that some people accumulate around themselves, like Faro Valentino has around him. *That* kind of energy."

"Okay…" Dane murmured. "What happened?"

Shrugging, Maya muttered, "My jag got overwhelmed

with fire, explosions, gunfire and thick, black smoke. That's when I woke up. It scared me a little.''

Dane studied her. Maya was clearly more than a little upset by the nightmare. ''Do your dreams come true?''

''Yes.''

''That's great,'' he said in a worried voice. ''Do you know what it was about? Where it happened?''

''No, nothing…just an explosion, fire, and a lot of thick, choking black smoke. I saw my black jag appear and I saw him fighting the smoke. Our guides are very powerful, Dane, but even they have limits on what they can and cannot do, just like us.'' Maya slanted a glance at him. ''Well, I gotta get going. I have to meet Cam down on the lip in about fifteen minutes.''

''Oh, that trail recon mission?'' he asked, easing off the desk.

''Yeah. By the book. It will be an easy flight, thank Goddess. I'm not up for a demanding mission in a D model today.''

Dane grinned and set his empty mug on her desk as she rose. ''Well, you're all now official graduates of the new Apaches. Your pilots were the easiest we've ever trained in on it.''

Maya rummaged around in the locker for a fresh, clean uniform. She'd take a quick shower and then get down to the lip. ''Thanks…I think it's because we're in combat mode already.''

''No argument from me. I'll see you down there,'' Dane said. He wanted to go over and kiss Maya, but he saw she was already into the mission. He saw it in her darkened eyes.

''Fine…see you there….''

''Let's go down for a closer look,'' Maya ordered Cam, who was flying the Cobra. Below them stretched the green jungle for as far as the eye could see. Clouds were swirling just above the trees with sunlight poking through in splotchy patterns.

Out of the cockpit window, Maya sighted the new trail. It looked like it was being hacked out at a good rate of speed, judging by how far they'd penetrated the area. The Cobra banked, and Maya held on to the map across her lap, the grease pencil poised in her right hand. Slats of sunlight shot through the broken cloud layer, temporarily blinding her. She pulled down the dark visor that fitted over the upper half of her face.

Cam craned her neck. "You want treetop level, Maya?"

Grinning, Maya said, "Not quite. Let's keep the skids clean on this trip, shall we?" She saw Cam grin broadly. A wisp of red hair stuck out from beneath her helmet near her shoulder. Her forest-green eyes were alive with mirth. Cam had once put a skid into a tree on another such trip, and she'd garnered the nickname Tree Trimmer as a result of the near accident.

Maya looked down at the trail. She could see newly hacked trees and brush pushed aside. There was no one around that she could spot, but that didn't mean there weren't people down there. They would be hiding from them. Faro would often threaten the Quechua men of a nearby village to work on a new trail or else he would start shooting the women and children.

"Look out!"

Cam's cry filled her ears. Maya jerked her head up. She saw a Kamov come barreling through the clouds, its 30 mm cannon blasting away—right at them. *Damn!*

Maya felt the Cobra lurch. Cam had no room to bank or escape. If she tried, she'd slam the helicopter into the trees. Maya opened her mouth to cry out a warning. She saw the tracers from the cannon moving upward. They were going to be hit!

The first explosion came above and behind them—right into the rotor assembly cuff. Maya automatically winced. Her hands went for her collective and cyclic. Cam tried to steady the wounded helicopter. Impossible!

Smoke poured into the cockpit. Coughing violently, Maya felt the entire gunship groan and began to sink. They were going to crash! Hanging on, unable to see because of the thick, greasy smoke in the cabin, Maya shoved the window open. Air! They had to have air or they'd die! Only briefly did she recall her nightmare. This was it.

The screech of treetops digging into the sinking Cobra's skin began. Everything tipped upside down for Maya. She heard the engine scream and begin to race wildly out of control. The blades began snapping like sheet metal being ripped apart. Automatically, she raised her arms over her face. Above them, she heard the heavy, punctuating rotor blades of the Kamov, gloating over its kill.

The last thing Maya saw was a huge tree limb slamming into the side of the cockpit, lunging at them like a spear as the Cobra tumbled in slow motion toward the jungle floor.

"Well, well…" Faro Valentino leaned over and tapped the shoulder of the woman in the black uniform. "Wake up! Wake up, bitch!"

Maya heard a man's voice, very far away, echoing in her hurting head. She heard laughter. Male laughter. Struggling to come out to consciousness, she dragged her eyes open. The man who met her gaze made her recoil. Faro Valentino, his face narrow, his dark brown eyes alight with triumph, stared back at her from close range. The smile on his thin lips increased.

"Ahh, she's awake, *hombres,*" he crowed. His lips lifted away from his even white teeth. "And if I'm not mistaken, you are the very infamous Capitano Maya Stevenson. No?"

Maya listened to him berate her in Spanish. She was lying on the ground, on her back. Her head ached. Nearby she saw what was left of the Cobra, partly on the ground and partly suspended from some trees, still burning. The billowing black smoke was rising skyward in a dark, ugly column. Where was Cam? Maya struggled to a sitting position. Faro backed away from her and stood looking her over. He was dressed in a short-sleeved, white silk shirt and tan pants, and had a smug smile on his face. Three men, armed with weapons, moved in, the barrels aimed down at her.

"Where's my—"

"Gone," Faro snarled. "Before we could get here, she took off. I have my men looking for her right now." He shrugged elegantly. "We'll find her." His eyes gleamed. "But we have you, Captain. You know, you're very infamous around here. You've really hurt my cocaine trade. I'm not a happy man, *señorita.*"

Glaring up at him, Maya tried to divide her awareness between Faro and her own condition. Was she hurt? Her head ached abominably. Looking down, she saw that there was a rip in her flight suit on her left leg, but that was all. Feeling bruised and shaken, Maya realized she hadn't been seriously hurt. What about Cam? What had happened to her? Maya narrowed her gaze on Faro, who was smiling like the jackal he was. The delight on his face made her nauseous.

"My pilot got away?" she demanded, her voice hoarse.

"*Sí, señorita.* Unfortunately, we got here about five minutes after the crash. My Russian pilot, Sasha Karlov, called me on the radio of my sport-utility vehicle," He pointed to a black SUV nearby. "We got here as soon as we could. We found you here, lying on the ground. Your pilot was nowhere to be seen, but we spotted her tracks." His smile increased. "We'll find her. She won't be able to get through that wall of jungle by herself."

Maybe, maybe not, Maya thought. She eyed the heavily armed drug soldiers. They came from a number of countries, judging by the various shades of their skin. All wore military tiger fatigues of gray and black. Their eyes were merciless, as if they'd just as soon shoot her than look at her. Some of the guards wore bandoleers of ammunition across their chests. All had machetes at their sides, as well as pistols. Any thought of her trying to escape dissolved—at least for now.

They were watching her closely. The pistol she carried under her left arm had been removed from its holster. She was alone. And she was at Faro's mercy.

"Get up, Captain Stevenson. You're coming with me." He bowed slightly and gestured gallantly toward the black vehicle.

Maya slowly got to her feet. Dizziness assailed her. She was still wearing her helmet. Taking it off, she felt a trickle of moisture near her left temple. Frowning, she took off her Nomex gloves and touched the area with her fingertips. When she looked at them, she saw they were smeared with blood. No wonder she was dizzy and her head hurt. It was then she noticed that her dark visor had been shattered. Realizing she was lucky her eye hadn't been put out, Maya was glad to sustain a cut over her temple, instead.

"Come," Faro cajoled in a soft voice. "My physician, Dr. Alejandro Lazaro, will clean you up." His voice deepened with satisfaction. "I want you well, Captain. There's a hunt we must take part in. You must be well enough to participate."

Maya moved slowly. The tallest soldier jerked her helmet out of her hand. She glared at him but kept moving forward. At the vehicle, they placed handcuffs on her wrists before they shoved her into the rear seat. Faro sat up front. A big man with a thick brown beard drove. On either side of her were armed soldiers. There was no escape. Her heart was beating wildly in her chest as the vehicle lurched around in a semicircle and headed back down a dirt road. Yellow dust rose in its wake.

Her mind spun. Pain kept jabbing intermittently at her temple. She had to think. *Think!* Faro would kill her, Maya knew. It was just a question of when and how. Well, this was her death spiral dance come to a close. They had now met and confronted one another. That was the warning in the night-mare she'd had earlier, Maya realized.

Closing her eyes, she took in a deep, ragged breath. Dane. She loved him! Oh, why hadn't she told him that? She couldn't even imagine how he must feel about her, but she knew he'd move heaven and earth to find her once he knew they'd been shot down. The only way her squadron would be able to find her was if they saw the smoke rising on the horizon. One of the Apache crews could spot it, and she knew they would. Once they realized it was the downed Cobra, Dane would institute some kind of search for her and Cam, Maya knew.

Faro lit a cigarette and turned around, his arm resting on the butter-yellow leather seat. He regarded her for a long time through the curling smoke. "You know, I'm looking forward to this little contest, Captain. They say you're the best heli-copter pilot around. Well, we're going to find out what you're really made of." And he grinned.

"What are you talking about?" Maya growled. She hated Faro. She couldn't help it. He had shot Inca and almost killed her. If it hadn't been for her intervention, Inca would be dead. It was then that Maya had sworn ongoing vengeance against Faro. She knew he hated her as well. She could see it in his dark, crafty eyes. His light brown hair was long, almost shoulder length, coifed and carefully set in place, she was sure, with a lot of hair spray. His nails were manicured and his hands long and expressive. To all appearances, Faro was a very rich, handsome man, about five foot ten inches in height. He wore a heavy gold chain with a crucifix around his throat, the cross exposed where his shirt lay open to re-veal part of his upper chest.

Chuckling, Faro took a long, pleasurable drag on his cig-arette and blew the smoke toward the roof of the vehicle. "You'll see, Captain. I think it will be a very fitting and just end to you. I've been planning this day for a long, long time. And now you're mine."

Maya clenched her teeth. It would do no good to snarl back at Faro. She would wait for her chance and make a break for it.

Her head ached. Pain skittered into her left temple, and she closed her eyes momentarily. Any thought of teleporting out of this situation was useless. With the pain in her head so severe, Maya knew she couldn't gather and hold the necessary energy to even attempt it.

She'd probably sustained a mild concussion from the crash, because she felt nauseous. Furthermore, her hatred of Faro, for what he'd tried to do to Inca, was roiling in her like a savage jaguar just begging to be loosed upon him. She knew her jaguar guardian was around, but she could barely feel his invisible presence. This was not the time or place to ask him to materialize. No, at the right time, she'd ask for his help. Her thoughts raced back to Dane. What would he do when he found out they'd been shot down?

Hot tears jammed into Maya's closed eyes. She loved Dane. Why hadn't she admitted it to him? Why? Maya knew she was scared of commitment—that was why. Now, bitterly, she realized her folly. More than likely, she was going to die, and Dane would never know…never know that she loved him, ached for him and wanted him as part of her every breathing moment.

Dane was in the back seat of an Apache D model when he received the news that Black Jaguar One had been shot down by a Kamov. Instantly, the pilot, Jessica Merrill—Wild Woman—brought the gunship over in a hard, right bank, redlined the engines and headed toward the crash site. Dane fought emotions that warred with his focus on the HUDs in front of him. Kamovs were around; he and Wild Woman had already chased one back from the border, along with a civilian helicopter that was carrying cocaine. Throat tightening, Dane blinked his eyes a couple of times. Maya and Cam. They were down. Were they alive? He had no way of knowing until the other Apache gunship, Jaguar Three, could hang around the site and try to look for them with its infrared equipment.

"I'm sorry, Major," Jess said, her voice choked. "I know you and Maya…well…we all know how you feel about each other. I'm sorry…really sorry about what's happened…." She gave a sob.

Dane wanted to cry himself. He wanted to scream. Rubbing his compressed mouth with the back of his gloved hand, he rasped, "They're alive. I know they're alive…." He didn't know *how* he knew it; he simply did. Living with Maya for the last three months, he'd learned to trust his intuition without questioning it.

Just then, the radio crackled.

"Black Jaguar Two, this is Three, over."

Dane instantly recognized Akiva Redtail's strained voice. "This is Three. What can you report, Chief?" he asked, his voice hard and emotionless.

"Gunslinger, we have *no* sign of bodies. No sign of anyone on IR. We can see from our vantage point, two hundred feet above the wreckage, that there are tire tracks leading away from it. Do you want us to follow them? Over."

Relief shattered through Dane, though he was far from elated. What if both Maya and Cam had burned up in the flames, unable to cut free and bail out of the Cobra? The IR would not show that—it would only show heat from a living person or animal. He'd just have to wait and see.

"Roger that, Chief. We'll be there in—" he looked at his watch and quickly calculated the distance "—twenty minutes, over."

"Roger, Gunslinger. We're on their trail. Out."

"Beware of Kamovs," Dane warned darkly. "Over and out."

Maya's nightmare came back to him. He sat there and digested the terror he'd seen in her eyes earlier this morning. Why hadn't they both taken the warning more seriously?

Shaking his head, he muttered, "Dammit." Rapidly scanning his HUDs, he knew the Kamovs had smelled blood today. They'd just blown the Cobra out of the sky. He could feel their triumph, sensed they were scanning for him and Jessica, too. They were hungry and wanted another kill. Dane could feel the bloodthirsty energy of the Kamovs, out there hunting for them in earnest. No, he couldn't let his emotions unravel over Maya, over her possible death. If he did, he would put him and Jessica at risk, and he was damned if the Kamovs were going to take a second gunship today.

"Major," Jess said, clearing her throat and trying to deal with her emotions, "we have an S.O.P. for a downed gunship. Do you want to put it into motion?"

S.O.P. was standard operating procedure, a plan. Dane said, "Yes. Call Dallas back at the base and ask her to institute it. Thank you." He wasn't thinking clearly. *Damn!* All he could think about, all he could see in front of him, was Maya's strong, proud face, her eyes gleaming with laughter, her lips curved in that wry, teasing way that always enticed him. Why hadn't he kissed her goodbye this morning at the office? He'd wanted to. He always wanted to kiss her during stolen moments, and that's all they ever had at the base. Stolen moments. Trying to balance their growing love for one another against the needs and demands of the base and its personnel was hell. And the base and its operation always came first—as it had this morning.

Jamming one fingertip beneath his helmet, he wiped away the sweat, feeling afraid. Scanning the equipment, he lifted his head and eyed the sky around them. It was a hot, humid day, the clouds rising in puffs and turrets, threatening eventual thunderstorms later. Where was Maya? Was she all right? Was Cam with her? Were they wounded? Dying? His mouth grew dry. Frustration thrummed through him. The Apache shook around him as they sped toward the dark column of smoke he could see now across the green carpet of jungle.

Sitting there, his mind racing, Dane regretted a lot. He regretted that he'd never been honest enough with Maya to tell her that he loved her. He'd been afraid. Why? Why hadn't he told her? Closing his eyes for a second, Dane cursed softly to himself. He knew that to admit love would mean he had to make life-altering decisions. Well, what was more important right now to him? His army career or Maya? Opening his eyes, he glared out at the green canopy below. The last three months had been more beautiful, more happy, than any other time in his life that he could ever recall. And he knew it was because of Maya, his loving her and opening up to her, them sharing their lives with one another.

"What a damned fool you've been, York."

"Sir?"

"Uh...nothing, Jess. Just muttering to myself."

He scowled and scanned. The column of smoke looked like a dark scar slashed across the pale blue sky. His heart contracted as they angled in toward it. Eyes narrowing, Dane swept the screen, which could detect heat, and quickly scanned the burning pyre of the Cobra, which hung nose down among several trees it had chopped up as it crashed. Most of the gunship had already burned up. The mangled metal of the cabin and tail had survived, but that was all. The heat of the fire showed up on the HUD, a bright apple-green color. Moving the IR scanner, Dane felt his heart thundering in his chest. If there was a body around, the IR would find it.

"Anything?" Jess asked stiffly.

He heard the tension and worry in her tone as she moved the Apache over the crash site. "No...nothing..." Dane switched to the television camera. Instantly, the HUDs showed the wreckage as clearly as if they were literally standing there in front of it. His mouth quirked. "A bad crash."

"Yes, sir," Jess whispered.

"Take us up about three hundred feet. I want to sweep a broader area with IR."

"Yes, sir."

Instantly, the Apache rose. Dane increased the range of the IR. Nothing. No heat… A moment later he saw heat signatures show up on the HUD, but it was either monkeys or birds, nothing large enough to be a human being…

"Wait!" Dane almost shouted. Anxiously, he studied the HUD. There! Yes! He saw a human being moving slowly through the jungle about five miles away from the crash site. Who? It was a solitary figure….

"I got a fix," he told Jess excitedly, and gave her the coordinates. Instantly, Jess brought the Apache up and headed in that direction.

Within a minute they were on top of the heat signature. Dane saw the human form on the screen—a light green against the dark background of the HUD screen. The jungle was too thick to try and use the television camera to see who it was. Whoever it was, he or she had stopped and was waving an arm wildly up at them.

"It's gotta be one of ours," Jess said excitedly.

"I hope…." Dane rasped. He looked up. "See that break in the canopy to your left? Move the gunship over it. See if this person will follow us to that opening."

His heart rose as he saw the figure turn and work its way slowly toward where the gunship now hovered just above the canopy. The rotors were kicking up a lot of flying debris, leaves knocked off the tops of the trees by the powerful blades. Dane saw a small opening between two trees. He steadied his binoculars over the edge of the cockpit and trained them downward. His mouth grew even drier. Who was it? Cam? Maya? A villager? Hands tightening around the binoculars, he waited, breath suspended.

"It's Cam!" he called out. She was down below, still in her uniform and helmet, her arm raised and waving at them. Dane saw the blood smeared across her tense face. Her uniform was ripped in several places. But she was alive. The look on her face was one of relief, tears and anguish.

"Call in the Blackhawk for rescue," he ordered Jess.
"You bet!"

Back at the base, Dane waited impatiently as the Black-hawk landed, with Cam aboard. They'd performed a sling rescue by lowering a harness on a cable down to her. She'd put on the harness and they'd lifted her up and out of the jungle. Dane had hung around for the rescue, guarding Cam and the Blackhawk, for fear of another Kamov attack. None came. From the Blackhawk, Cam had got on the radio and told the bad news about Maya's capture. At this point, Dane could do nothing more. Now that they were back at the base, the team was able to question Cam further and form a rescue plan for Maya. Dane couldn't wait to talk to Cam, to find out what had happened. As the Blackhawk landed on the lip, he jogged toward it. The door slid open after the rotors slowed. He saw Cam, her red hair in disarray around her shoulders, as she climbed out. She saw him and headed directly toward him, the wind whipping around them.

Ducking beneath the blades, Cam reached toward Dane's offered hand. "Major, I'm sorry...so sorry...." she said brokenly. Releasing his hand, she stood, her eyes filled with tears. "We got nailed by a Kamov. He brought us down with cannon fire. It threw us into the canopy. I never lost consciousness. As we tumbled down toward the ground, Maya got hit in the head by a tree branch shattering the cockpit. It knocked her out."

Cam wiped her eyes with a trembling hand. Blood had dried across her face and jawline. "Once we stopped tumbling, the cockpit filled with smoke. I screamed at Maya, but she didn't answer me. I got unharnessed and fell on top of her, because of the way the Cobra was sitting on its nose and side. I managed to get her out of the burning gunship, sir. She fell about ten feet to the ground. I jumped out and pulled her away from the helo, in case it exploded."

Dane stood there watching her face contort. Cam shakily

ran her hand through her tangled hair. "I heard trucks coming. I tried to get Maya to come to, but she was unconscious. I didn't see any other wounds on her, sir. The side of her helmet was dented where that limb slammed into the side of her head. The helmet saved her from worse injury, but she was out cold. I saw two vehicles hightailing it down the road toward us. I knew they were druggies."

Gulping, Cam, said in a broken voice, "I had a decision to make, Major. I couldn't carry Maya into that jungle with me. It was impossible. I decided to try and escape, to get back here to get us help." Cam closed her eyes and pressed her hands to her face. "I feel like I abandoned Maya, but I know I did the only thing I could do. I'm sorry…just so sorry…."

Dane reached out and placed his hand on her shoulder. "You made the right decision, Cam. If you'll tried to carry Maya into that jungle, the druggies would have captured both of you. It's all right…let's get you to the dispensary. Come on…we'll figure out what to do next after you get taken care of. Come on…."

Chapter 13

"Are you ready to meet your fate, Captain Stevenson?"

Maya sat on a stool as Dr. Alejandro Lazaro finished stitching up the cut she'd sustained during the crash. Her left temple ached, and pain kept jabbing into her left eye. The doctor, a thin, balding man, with a well-trimmed gray beard, stepped away. Faro stood in the doorway of his villa, where he'd brought her. The ride from the crash site, on a series of back roads, had taken over an hour. The villa, unseen from the air because it had been built below the thick canopy of trees, was small and functional.

"Let's get on with it, Faro." She had been stripped of her chicken plate and helmet. Sitting on the wooden stool, Maya felt Faro's intense inspection. His mouth curved indulgently. Anyone who did not know of him would think him a rich Peruvian from Lima. He leaned languidly against the doorjamb, his arms crossed against his chest. It was noon, and Maya could smell the odor of spicy food wafting into the small medical facility.

"So, Doctor, is she ready for her last flight?"

Lazaro peeled off his latex gloves and dropped them into a small basket near the table. "*Sí,* she is, *patron.*"

Eyes narrowing, Maya watched the two armed guards standing near Faro. She'd been waiting for an opportunity to escape, but none had come yet. And with her concussion, she often experienced sudden stabs of dizziness that almost made her fall to the right. If she was going to try and escape, she couldn't have that happening or she'd get nowhere.

"Come, Captain. One last sumptuous meal." He gestured for her to get up and follow him.

Maya eased suspiciously off the stool. The guards lowered the barrels of their guns—at her—as she crossed the red-tiled expanse. Faro chuckled and moved into the spacious, sunlit dining room, where he sat down at the end of a long, rectangular table. There was a five-tiered chandelier hanging above it. Floor-to-ceiling windows on one wall showed off brilliant bougainvillea in bright red, fuschia and orange colors against the dark green foilage around the villa. Beyond that was the thick, dark jungle. No wonder they'd never found this villa!

Two maids, dressed in black dresses with starched white caps and aprons, waited anxiously to serve them. It would just be her and Faro dining, apparently.

"Sit there," he ordered Maya congenially, and pointed to the other end of the table. "You must eat well. It is your last meal."

Maya pulled out the heavily carved, straight-backed mahogany chair and sat down on its burgundy cushion. Faro was smiling like a jaguar who knew he had his quarry. At either end of the bright yellow dining room, guards took their stations on the thick cream carpet. Again, she'd have no opportunity to escape.

The first maid hurried to her and placed a bowl of fragrant vegetable soup before her. It was a creamy yellow color, with slivers of almonds and shreds of orange cheese floating in it.

Genially, Faro dug into his soup and delicately picked up a piece of bread and slowly tore it apart. He dipped it judiciously into his soup with two fingers. "You know," he began in a jovial tone, "you have no idea how long I have envisioned you sitting here, eating with me. Eating your last meal." He waved a piece of bread around to emphasize his words. "You have been my nemesis, Captain Stevenson. Until you moved into your base to stop me, it was very easy to get my cocaine out of Peru and around the world." He sipped the soup noisily and then chewed on the bread, his eyes never leaving her.

Maya ate, though her stomach was tight with tension. She knew that to have any hope of escape, she'd have to have nourishment. Eating was the last thing she wanted to do right now, but it was necessary.

Her mind spun with options. Questions. Fear. Opportunity. What was Dane doing? Did they know by now that she and Cam had been shot down? They must know. Dallas would initiate the S.O.P. for rescue. Would they ever find her? No, Maya didn't think so.

Her head was aching. The pain would increase and then lull. When it worsened, she'd be struck with the dizziness that made her want to fall to the right. *Think!* She had to think. No one at the base, other than Dane, knew about her guardian. It hurt to think of even contacting him mentally, because it took a lot of mind focus and concentration to do so. With the pain and dizziness, Maya found it impossible at the moment.

"Even if you get rid of me, you're not getting rid of our commitment to stop you, Valentino."

Chuckling, Faro shrugged. "Ah, but if you cut off the head of the snake, the body will gradually die, no?"

"No." Maya glared at him and continued to eat. Once the soup was gone, the maid quickly whisked the bowl away. A green salad with croutons was set before her. Maya's stomach rebelled. A sudden wave of nausea made her push it aside. It was instantly taken away. Reaching for the glass of water, she drank deeply from it.

Faro studied her and then ordered his soup to be taken away as well. The small maid, a Q'uero Indian, moved in and took it instantly. Her eyes were full of fear. She set the salad before Faro. He politely thanked her and poured the raspberry vinaigrette over it.

"You know, your twin sister has been a real thorn in my brother's side in Brazil," he told her in a soft, dangerous tone. "And you helped put my brother in prison. That is unforgivable." He stabbed his fork into the fresh salad as if stabbing a living thing. "I thought I'd killed her that night at the compound." He lifted his head and stared down at Maya. "But for whatever reason…she lived."

"Your brother deserves prison, Faro. So do you. We're not as easy to kill as you might think," Maya snarled. Her anger and hatred rose, cleansing away the pain and dizziness momentarily. "And I swore I'd get you for trying to kill her."

"Ah, blood vengeance. Good. Good. Well, that's something I can certainly understand." Faro broke off another piece of bread. Slathering it with butter, he murmured, "We had no idea the two of you were related. Inca hasn't been seen by many people, and never allows her photograph to be taken. And, of course, you…well, I had never seen you except in your gunship, so we didn't put two and two together…until recently. When we did, I told my brother you must both die."

Maya said nothing. A plate filled with vegetables and a huge piece of steaming beef was placed in front of her. This was typical Peruvian fare. They ate only twice a day, and when they did, consumed a generous amount of food. Yellow potatoes, orange carrots and other vegetables surrounded the beef. Maya forced herself to begin to eat.

"You know, there are other drug lords, one from Colombia and one from Ecuador, who are joining forces with me." He gave her a pleased look as he finished his salad. "With our combined money, we are purchasing more Russian mil-

itary aircraft. Pretty soon, you are going to be outgunned
down here. Even with the addition of those new D model
Apaches we've been seeing of late.''

"So the back door to Bolivia is *that* important?''

"*Sí,* it is. That is why you must die, Captain.'' He patted
his lips gently with the white linen napkin and nodded his
thanks as the maid placed the main course in front of him.
"I have good news for you. My men were unable to find the
other pilot who flew with you. Perhaps she is out in the
jungle right now, dying. As soon as we're done, I'm taking
you to our heliport,'' he informed her. He sliced into the beef
with short, precise strokes, like a surgeon performing an operation. "I'm going to be sporting about this, Captain. I'll
give you a helicopter to fly.''

The news that Cam had at least escaped Faro's men made
Maya's heart soar. And at the mention of the copter, she
snapped her head up. Her eyes narrowed on him. "To fly?''
she asked.

"Of course. I will give you a sporting chance to escape.''

She chewed on the potato, not tasting it, and watched him
warily. "You're going to let me fly away?''

He chuckled indulgently. "Well, not exactly. I will have
my three Kamovs up in the air to make sure you fly *El Cañón
de Muerte,* the Canyon of Death, where I will 'hunt' you
down.''

Stunned, Maya sat back. The Canyon of Death. Yes, she
knew it well. It was located in Bolivia, the top rim at fourteen
thousand feet. The canyon was nearly a mile deep, and resembled the Grand Canyon in some respects, with narrow
confines, yellow and ochre walls, and in places, white speck-
led granite. The canyon was forty miles long. And it twisted
and writhed like a snake that had been attacked. The walls
of the canyon were narrow, and with one wrong move, a
helicopter pilot could crash into the rock and die. Furthermore, the winds up through the dry canyon could be wicked

and untrustworthy. Especially around noon, when the radiant heat made thermals rise from the earth.

"You see," Faro told her genially, "I am going to give you a sporting chance to survive this little man…er…woman hunt, Captain. I will be in my favorite helicopter, a Russian Hind. I will have a Kamov stationed at either end of the canyon, and one above it. You will start at the north end and try to fly to the south end of it. If you get there, before I find and shoot you down, then you win. On the other hand, if I catch you first, well…too bad…."

"What kind of helo are you being so generous with?" she demanded darkly.

He gave her a pleased smile and cut up his potato into precise, small bits. "You're very perceptive, Captain Stevenson. I expected that of you, you know? I'm giving you a Vietnam era Huey—a Slick, I think, is how you refer to it?"

A Slick? Maya's mind raced. That was a medical helicopter, a workhorse helo from the Vietnam days. It carried no ordnance and no weapons. Her mouth tightened. "I see," she whispered, "you're in an armed Hind and I'm in a Slick with no way to protect myself."

He grinned hugely and popped a slice of carrot into his mouth. "Ah, you see. Yes, well, you *are* the hunted one, after all, Captain. And judging from your legendary flight skills, I felt that just giving you an unarmed helicopter against my Hind would be fair enough. No?"

"You bastard."

His smile fell. He glared at her. "Such table manners, Captain. Didn't they teach you better in *Norteamérica?*"

"Go to hell."

He grinned ferociously and ate more of the food. "No, Captain, *you* are the one who is going to hell. As soon as we're done with your final meal, I'll take you to the canyon by helicopter. Our aircraft are waiting for us there, as I speak. You will have a three-minute head start and then I will take off after you. If you try to escape or leave the canyon, the

Kamov will shoot you down. The canyon is half a mile deep; 2500 feet. You can fly up to seventeen thousand feet, but that is your limit. You can choose to fly through the canyons or above it with this altitude restriction. Frankly, the slick wasn't made for 14,000 feet, much less anything higher, so my suggestion is you fly within the canyon. But that is up to you. If you go above the altitude I've restricted you to, then my Kamov will be happy to send a rocket into your Slick.''

Maya didn't believe for one minute that Faro would give her a three-minute head start. Still, the idea that he was giving her a helicopter at all provided a glimmer of hope. The Slick was unarmed. It was slow and bulky compared to the Cobra, which was a true gunship. Plus, the high altitude would be very hard on the bird. Faro was right: even at 14,000 feet the helo would labor mightily. It lessened her chance of survival. And the Russian Hind was a huge monster, with a lot of power and enough armament to match the Apache arsenal. Her mind spun. She knew the canyon well. Wondering if Faro knew that, Maya said, "What made you choose that canyon?"

"It's risky. It's dangerous to fly in. I fly it all the time." He placed his flatware on the table and held up his long, expressive hands. "It is where I hone my skills, Captain. I know it like the back of my hands, literally."

She nodded and pushed the plate aside. Maya understood very clearly that if she made it to the south end of the Canyon of Death, the Kamov at the end would shoot her down. There was no way Faro was going to let her escape. And she was sure that the orbiting Kamov above the canyon would have his radar targeted on her Slick at all times.

"What happens if I win, Valentino?"

He erupted into mirthful laughter. "Oh, you won't, Captain!"

"But if I do?" Maya whispered. "Are you going to let me fly free?"

Patting his lips, his eyes sparkling with vast amusement, Faro said, "I am a Spanish gentleman, Captain. Of course, I'll let you go. If I'm down, then more than likely I'll be dead." His lips curved away from his perfect white teeth. "But how you could possibly take me down is a mystery to me. I am the one with rockets on board my helicopter—not you. All you can do is act like a rabbit—running, hiding, ducking and dodging. Your only way to 'win' is to run, not confront. No, I'm not worried about losing our little hunt."

Of course he wasn't. Maya wiped her lips with the linen napkin. "Then let's get saddled up, Valentino, because if you think this is going to be easy, you've got another think coming."

Dane straightened up. Four pilots huddled around the map in the small room and talked in low tones. Rubbing his neck, he listened to them discuss possible search patterns to locate Maya's whereabouts. Cam was there, despite her injuries. She had a broken right arm, now in a cast and sling. These pilots knew the area well, and he had to defer to them.

His heart ached. Where was Maya? Did Faro Valentino have her? His gut said yes. A cold chill worked up his back and he turned away. Opening the door, Dane moved out into the well-lit hall of HQ. It was quiet. The whole base was in shock over Maya's disappearance. He saw it in every woman's face. He felt the thickness of shock rolling through the fortress even though no one said anything. In some women's eyes, he saw tears. Others had sat down and cried outright. Still others had a grim look of determination on their faces. It was clear they were angry. So was he.

Rubbing his eyes tiredly, Dane looked at his watch. It was 1300. The crash had occurred at 0700. It felt like the day was going to stretch out forever, with no resolution. Standing in the empty hall, he looked toward the exit, a good hundred feet away.

Was he seeing things? He blinked. No, it was

there…again…. What was it? He frowned and narrowed his vision toward the end of the hall and the exit door.

A grayish cloud seemed to be hanging there. It would disappear, then reappear moments later. Scratching his head, Dane watched it, perplexed. Was stress over Maya's disappearance making him see things? Again the cloud dissipated into nothingness, then came back. He could almost see a shape….

His mouth fell open. He took a step back and gasped as the cloud darkened. This time he saw four black legs appear out of the churning grayness. Stunned, he watched as the apparition became more solid. Tensing, he saw a black jaguar materialize out of the grayish cloud. It stood there, huge yellow eyes with tiny black pupils staring directly at him.

Gulping, Dane wondered once more if he was seeing things. His mind churned and raced. What the hell was he seeing?

And then the truth suddenly slammed into him: it was Maya's guardian! The black jaguar! Dane sucked in a breath of air. He watched the cat as it stood there, its tail twitching languidly from side to side. It was watching him intently. A sudden sense washed over Dane, as if it a powerful ocean wave had deluged him. The jaguar wanted him to follow it!

That was crazy! Was he going insane because of his worry for Maya? Was he making this up? Dane turned to see if anyone else was in the hall. It was empty and quiet. He started to turn toward the door and call to the other pilots to come and look at the cat—to see if they saw it, too.

The moment he started to turn, he felt an even more powerful message slam into him: he should get into his helicopter and follow the jaguar.

It was so crazy. Dane stared at the cat again. The black jaguar stared back. And then the cat turned and lifted the front of its body, placing its paws against the door. The door opened. Dane gasped. He saw the jaguar leap out and down the stairs. Shaken, Dane trotted down the hall and pushed the door open. Peering down the concrete steps, he saw the black jaguar on the stairs leading to the first floor. It was looking up at him expectedly.

All the conversations Maya had had with him flooded back to Dane. He now recalled that if she was in danger, she could send the jaguar for help. Yes! That was it! She was sending her guide to him to get help!

"Stay there!" he shouted to the jaguar. "I'll be back in a moment! Don't move!" And he spun around on his heel and ran down the hall.

Dane knew he probably looked insane as he ran into the room and told them to saddle up, to get every available Apache into the air and follow him. He didn't tell them *how* he knew where Maya would be, only that he knew.

The women pilots all stared at him, but Dallas leaped to her feet.

"Maya's contacted you, hasn't she?" she exclaimed, and looked around at the other pilots. "I was hoping she'd contact someone. Okay, ladies, let's saddle up." She looked up at Dane. "Major? I'm assuming you'll lead the squadron?"

Dane nodded. "Yes." As he turned and trotted down the hall, he wondered if the black jaguar would still be there. He'd feel like a fool if it wasn't. Shoving open the door, he saw the cat standing expectantly, waiting for him. Relief sheeted through him. The cat leaped down the stairwell, and Dane quickly followed.

He wondered if the people in the complex would run in fear as the jaguar pushed open the last door that lead out of HQ and into the cave itself. As he raced down the stairs, the rest of pilots not far behind, Dane was breathing raggedly. His heart pounded with fear and with hope. Maya had sent her jaguar to him. It had worked. Right now, he didn't care to know how it worked, only that it had. As he hurried out the door, he saw the jaguar running toward the closest D model Apache. To his surprise, no one seemed to see the animal. How could they *not* see him? The big cat was plain as day to him.

As he strapped in, with Jessica as his copilot and gunner, Dane wondered how the jaguar would lead them to Maya. The cat couldn't fly, yet stood expectantly on the cave lip, the white wisps of clouds sometimes swirling around and yet never making him disappear from Dane's view. Within minutes, the Apaches were ready for flight, their combined punctuation of rotors echoing throughout the complex. All four Apaches were going up. Was it a wild-goose chase? Was this all part of his fevered imagination? Because of his desperate desire to find Maya? Dane wasn't sure. As he eased the Apache off the lip, he saw the jaguar suddenly make a leap through the Eye.

It was airborne! Dane decided he was crazy and delusional. But none of them had any idea of where to look for Maya. The crash site had been scoured, with no luck. The set of tire imprints disappeared into the jungle. All he could do was trust.

As he flew the Apache through the Eye, he saw between the noonday clouds wreathing the mountaintops, the dark outline of the jaguar up ahead of them.

"You know where we're going?" Jess asked.

"Kind of…" Dane answered evasively, keeping his eyes on the jaguar, which ran easily in front of them, almost half a mile ahead.

"I got something on radar," Jess murmured, "but the signature is unidentified. Right out in front of us. About half a mile. Do you see it, Major?"

Dane was shaken. The jaguar—or its energy, was showing up on their radar! He wiped his mouth. With a tremor in his voice, he rasped, "Yeah, I see it. Can *you* see anything just ahead of us?"

"Uh…no sir, I don't see a *thing*." Jess added a moment later, puzzlement in her voice, "But something *is* being painted on our radar…"

"Okay, no problem. Punch into the computer that it's friendly."

"Yes, sir…"

"Just keep watching for Kamovs."

"Yes, sir."

So, the jaguar could be picked up on radar. Dane looked down at his own HUDs and sure enough, there was a fuzzy apple-green ball of light on his display. It didn't look like a jaguar, though, just a fuzzy oval ball. He felt a little better knowing that Wild Woman saw something. He felt a little less crazy. If the other pilots knew that he was following Maya's spirit guide, they'd think him certifiable. Yet, when Dane checked where they were going, he realized it was straight for the Bolivian border. What if he was wrong? What if he *was* crazy? Dane was torn. He was a nononsense aviator—nuts and bolts. He didn't believe in stuff like this. Or hadn't until Maya came along. She made the invisible and impossible a part of her living, breathing existence. She accepted the possibility of the unknown. He'd never believed in magic. Not until just recently.

Narrowing his eyes, Dane watched the jaguar bound through the sky at full speed, its stride long and rhythmic as it ran. His heart ached. Maya? What of her? How was she? *Where* was she? Was the jaguar leading them to her? The pain of losing her was too much to contemplate. Dane kept himself busy flying the powerful Apache toward some unknown destination in front of them. And yet, as he flew, he somehow was in touch with Maya on a much deeper level. As he kept the gunship steady with his hands and feet, he felt her. He felt her in his heart, in his head, as a part of his spirit. She was dynamic. Unquenchable. A warrior. A lover. His best friend. And the woman he wanted to spend the rest of his life with. Dane found himself praying for her life, praying for a second chance with Maya. If only…if only she could survive. If only…

Maya sat in the Huey helicopter as it warmed up. The blades were kicking up massive amounts of yellow dust around it. Faro had given her her helmet back, but not her chicken plate. She was without any kind of protection. As she sat in the right seat of the old, olive drab Slick, she watched the gauges. Her heart fell when she saw that she had barely enough fuel on board to make it to the other end of the canyon. There was no way Faro was planning on her surviving this hunt.

Looking up, she saw the Russian Hind, a much larger gunship loaded with rockets on its stubby wings, warming up. Faro was at the controls, and a Russian pilot with him in the copilot's seat. She wondered if Faro was really going to be flying it, or his hired gun, who sure as hell had a lot more experience with the Hind. Faro couldn't be trusted, Maya decided. She cinched up the straps on her shoulders and made sure the lap belt was as tight as she could get it. There was no way in hell, she decided, as she looked out the dusty cockpit windows at the canyon before her, that she was going down without a fight. What Faro didn't know was that she knew this canyon as intimately as she knew herself. And that was her one advantage. She routinely flew all her pilots up here to learn how to fly in tight quarters, deal with uneven winds and gusts.

Above her, she saw a double-bladed Kamov Black Shark moving into position at eighteen thousand feet. It would follow her progress all the way down the canyon. The other two Kamovs were already in place. Her scalp prickled. She stopped for a moment and lifted her head. Feeling her jaguar touch her aching mind, Maya smiled a little. *Good.* Her guide had made contact with Dane. Because of her head injury and the intermittent pain and dizziness, sending her guardian for help had been the only thing left open to her to do. Would Dane follow her jaguar? Would he believe enough in what he saw to act? Maya wasn't sure. But it was her only hope. And it was a long shot. If Dane didn't believe what his eyes saw, if he didn't listen to the urgency of the jaguar's message, she was as good as dead.

A guard outside the Slick made a motion for her to take off. In her headset, she heard Faro's voice.

"Captain, take off. I'm giving you a three-minute head start."

Yeah, right. Maya pressed the mouthpiece against her lips. "Today is a good day to die, Valentino."

His laughter filled her headset. "Yes, a good day for you to die, Captain. You're the quarry. I'm the hunter. Take off!"

Maya tried turning the radio dial to another frequency, but nothing happened. Faro had rigged the radio so he could talk to her, but that was all. There was no way she could send a message to Dane or the other pilots. Faro had foreseen that possibility. Heart pumping hard, Maya eased her hands around the cyclic and collective. The Slick shuddered as she upped the speed to take off. It had been a long time since she'd flown the antique aircraft. In her late teens, she had flown one with her father. She had been taught how to fly in a Slick, so it was fitting she would find herself back in one at a time like this. As Maya lifted off, the jagged, ochre walls of the canyon in front of her, she prayed that the machine was truly airworthy. Glancing down at her watch, she mentally memorized the hands. She had a three-minute head start. Gaining more altitude and leveling off at a thousand feet, Maya tilted the nose forward and headed into the mouth of the Canyon of Death.

The sky was a bright, uncontested blue. The sun was high. Her heart was banging savagely in her chest. Wrestling with the surge of adrenaline through her, Maya used it to her advantage and became supersensitive to her surroundings. She watched the jagged spires of the canyon walls carefully. The Huey shook as it encountered gusting winds when she rounded the first, snaking curve of the canyon. She glanced down at her watch.

One minute.

She had to get moving. Feeling blind without the advanced avionics that were always available to her in an Apache, Maya realized she would not be able to see the Hind stalking her. Only if she risked turning in midair to look behind her, or jinxing around so the tail rotor didn't obstruct her vision, would she be able to see it.

The Hind, in contrast, was full of avionics and would easily locate her.

The Huey shook as she moved it sleekly around the second curve. The granite was yellowed by dust that clung to the canyon walls. Maya was tense, her breath coming in shallow gulps. At fifteen thousand feet the copter labored mightily, for this wasn't an altitude it was used to flying at. Air was thin and the rotor blades were gasping for all the cushioning they could find.

One minute, thirty seconds.

Maya didn't trust Faro. At the next turn, she brought the Slick up and turned just enough to see if he was behind her yet. She saw nothing. But then, the curves were so many and frequent that it would be hard to see another aircraft approaching. Below, Maya saw the sand and rock along the floor of the canyon. Only a few hardy green bushes stubbornly clung to life in the canyon. Compressing her lips, she moved the Slick on and pushed the throttles to the firewall. Her mind raced. What would Faro do? Would he follow her through the canyon or just pop up above it, locate her and fire rockets at her? That's what she'd do if she were in his place. But Faro had this love of hunting. He might snake through the narrow canyon as part of the test, because of this mano-a-mano thing that South American men clung to like a shell of armor around them. In her case, that was good. It gave her a slim chance.

Smiling to herself, Maya bet that he'd take the canyon route. The Hind wasn't the most graceful or quick of the Russian gunships. No, it was a huge behemoth that was actually better suited for wide-open spaces and not the tightness of Muerte. On that point, Maya knew the Slick was a helluva lot better equipped to zig and zag between the curves. Above, she saw the Kamov moving along at eighteen thousand feet, its avionics trained on her.

Two minutes.

Again, Maya halted. Here and there in the canyon were nooks and crannies just wide enough to hide behind to wait and watch. The walls of the canyon sometimes jutted out in a slice of thin rock, and she chose one of them to hover near as she turned to check what was coming.

Her heart dropped.

There was the Hind! It was moving bulkily around the last curve, about half a mile behind her. Faro had cheated! Maya cursed softly and turned the Slick toward the south. Now he would stalk her. She redlined her aircraft. The helicopter groaned and shuddered. She could see the shadow of it against the yellow sand and rock below. The ship shook around her. Up ahead was a long S curve. Maya took a hard right and the Slick literally leaned on its right side as she skimmed as close to the wall as she could. The Hind might fire at her, but the rocket could confuse the thin partition of rock with her signature and hit the wall instead, if the pilot didn't set the rocket correctly.

Gravity pushed her into the seat as she worked the Slick out of the hard right turn. The walls shot past her in a blur. She was breathing raggedly, her eyes narrowed as she snapped a hard left yaw. Instantly, the Slick banked hard. The rotor tips almost struck the overhang of granite. Too much! Instantly, Maya corrected, just a little. The Slick steadied and flew along the wall, the rotor blades inches away from the granite outcropping.

She heard a thundering roar erupt behind her. *Damn!* The Slick lurched forward from the shock wave caused by the explosion of a rocket nearby. Correcting the fleeing helicopter, Maya hit the right yaw peddle once more as the wall raced up at her. Faro had missed her! Jerking a look to her right, Maya saw huge clouds of yellow dust rising into the air where she'd flown seconds before. The Hind burst through the wall of dust, hot on the trail of her laboring aircraft.

Faro was closing in on her. She had to think! She had to do something! The Huey was groaning from the hard, demanding flying. Maya wrenched the collective to the right, and then hard left. The walls raced up at her. The winds were inconstant. They pummeled the Huey one moment and eased off the next. Having to juggle the aircraft in that kind of a wind made it even more dangerous to fly this unforgiving canyon.

Another explosion! This time directly in front of her, to the right. Maya cried out as she saw a huge deluge of dirt, debris and rocks hurtling directly down at her. Wrenching the Slick up, she hit the left yaw peddle and climbed up and out of the canyon. The helicopter strained. Panels popped and groaned in protest. The engine screamed like a wounded banshee. She knew by flying above the canyon rim she was as good as dead. It would be easy for the Hind to paint her on radar and fire a rocket at her. *No way!*

As soon as she'd avoided the cloud of debris caused by the explosion, Maya shoved the nose of the Huey straight back down into the canyon. She heard a hiss. Jerking a look off to her left, she saw a rocket speed by, narrowly missing her. Sobbing for breath, she jammed the Slick back down into the gorge. The S turns were tight. She worked the Slick hard and forced it to bend tightly to the right, then to the left. She was flying so low that the rotors of her aircraft were kicking up huge clouds of sand in her wake. It was one way to stop the Hind—to throw sand in its face, literally, and cloud her escape. Radar could paint her less easily through thick dust, Maya knew. She needed every edge she could get.

A buzzer went off. Her eyes snapped to the instruments. The engine was overheating! She saw the needle slowly starting to move up toward the red portion of the gauge. *Damn!* Fifty percent of her fuel was gone. She'd managed to get halfway through Muerte. Suddenly, Maya had an idea. It was a long shot, but it was probably the only chance she had. Mouth compressed, she kept the Slick at full throttle. She could feel the Hind stalking her in earnest. The game was almost over.

Chapter 14

Maya knew of one place in Muerte that might save her from a fiery death. *Maybe.* She sped toward that point, which was a wall partition that stuck out, literally, like a sore thumb, jutting into the canyon. This was the narrowest part of the entire gorge, and as she slid through it, she turned the Slick hard right. Bringing the helicopter around, she hid behind the wall in a hover and waited. Breathing hard, sweat running down into her eyes, she sat tensely, her hands gripping the controls. The Huey was hovering and shaking all around her. Her grip was so tight that her knuckles were white.

Wait…just wait….

The seconds ticked by.

Maya closed her eyes and tried to be patient. Her only chance was the moment when the Hind slowed down to carefully maneuver between the wall of the canyon and the partition causing the constriction. She had to time her attack just right. The Slick had runners instead of wheels on its undercarriage. They were long and slender rods, made of heavy, impact-resistant tubular metal. She was going to try and time

it so that as the Hind came crawling past her, she would ram
the Slick forward. With the tip of one of the skids, she would
jam into the tail rotor assembly of the Hind. If she could
manage such a delicate assault, she might destroy the Hind's
tail rotor and the chopper would lose control and crash.

It was a horrible risk and Maya knew it. The Slick shuddered around her. When would the Hind show itself? She
jerked a look above her. Off to her right, at eighteen thousand
feet, the Kamov hovered. Would he warn Faro what she was
doing? Even if they told him she was hiding behind the wall,
Maya knew none of them would guess her lethal intent. And
the timing was critical. If she couldn't do it right, then the
Slick would slam full throttle into the Hind itself and they'd
all die in a fiery explosion.

Her last thoughts before she saw the nose of the Hind
inching from behind the wall, was that she loved Dane. Her
only regret was she had never told him that. Gripping the
controls hard, Maya waited one more second as the first half
of the Hind appeared. She saw Faro's face turned toward her.
He was grinning. He had been told by the pilot in the Kamov
that she was hiding there. No matter. Lips lifting away from
her teeth, she tensed. Maya rammed the Slick forward. The
machine groaned. The engines screamed. The temperature
needle shot into the danger zone.

Just as the Hind flew from behind the partition, Maya
lurched the Slick into a slight right turn. She dipped the nose
and aimed the skid right at the tail rotor assembly of the
Hind. Bracing herself, she sucked in a breath of air. The Slick
shuddered. Her neck snapped back. She heard the grating
scream of metal being torn apart. As she slammed back into
the seat, the harness cut deeply into her shoulders. The Hind
shuddered drunkenly. An explosion occurred in the tail rotor,
and then Maya felt the Slick being pulled into the Hind. *No!*
She jammed the left yaw peddle and wrenched her aircraft
away from the Hind. More metal snapped. The Slick labored.
The rotors of the Hind were dangerously close. Maya cringed

and pulled away as she saw the Hind suddenly moving upward toward her. *No!*

Yanking at the controls, she realized her skid had jammed into the Hind's rotor and was now stuck there. She felt the Slick sinking along with the heavier aircraft. *No! Oh, dammit!* She had to get free! *Free!*

Hissing a curse, Maya powered up. The mangled skid pulled free. They were falling! She was fifty feet from the ground. Out of the corner of her eye, Maya saw the Hind suddenly nose up. Its rotors bit savagely into the wall of the canyon. Rock, dirt and dust exploded in all directions. She worked the pedals wildly to keep her own ship from crashing. The Hind slammed into the wall, out of control. A huge explosion of black-red-and-orange flames and smoke erupted all around her.

Maya let out a yell as she hauled the Slick to the left, away from the explosion. She was too close! She knew the shock wave from the holocaust would knock the Slick out of her control. The ground was coming up fast! She braced herself. Her breath jammed in her throat. Eyes bulging, she called on every flying skill she'd ever learned to turn away from the fire vomiting in her direction. If she could just get the nose turned...

The wave from the explosion, hot and searing, struck the wounded Slick. Maya cried out and tried to hold her aircraft steady. She was going to crash! The ground came up swiftly. Jerking the nose up, Maya felt heat searing into the cabin. For a moment she was completely enveloped by a fireball from hell itself. Her skin burned. Shutting her eyes, she clung to the controls and stopped breathing. To breathe meant to drag the fire and heat into her lungs, and she knew it would kill her.

Within seconds, the fireball from the destroyed Hind moved past her. Opening her eyes, she gasped. The ground was still racing up at her. The rotors of the Slick slammed into the sand and rock at an angle. The blades snapped off.

Lethal chunks became flying shrapnel that could take off a person's head. Maya threw up her hands to protect her face. The Slick's nose dug into the sand. The cockpit canopy snapped. Plexiglas exploded inward across her body. The harnesses bit savagely into her flesh. The ship dug its nose in and the tail rotor flipped upward.

A cry was torn from Maya's throat. She felt the machine turning, cartwheeling. But not for long. Maya knew the floor of the canyon was nearby.

At the sound of screeching metal, Maya knew the tail of the ship had flipped into the unforgiving granite wall. Would the helicopter burst into flame? She hoped not. With so little fuel on board, the chances were unlikely. Just let her stay conscious! Maya heard the ship groan, and felt it begin to buckle around her. The ochre wall loomed before her widening eyes. She felt the metal around her booted feet caving inward. Instantly, Maya lifted her legs. The last thing she needed was to be trapped by the torn metal, one of her feet sheared off in the impact.

Within seconds, it was over. Dust made her cough and gag. The Slick settled in a corner of the canyon, metal shrieking and groaning. Fumbling for the harness release, Maya managed to jerk it open. She fell heavily between the seats, her eyes blurred from the dust blowing around her. Blindly, she made for the light she saw at the rear of the cabin. *Escape!* She had to escape. She knew the Kamov would be coming in to finish her off.

Maya tumbled out of the Slick and onto the sand, landing on her hands and feet. The roar of the Hind burning fifty feet away, the continuing explosions, hurt her ears. A black, greasy column of smoke rose around her. Maya realized it was her escape route. She knew the Kamov couldn't paint her through that thick, roiling smoke. Struggling to her feet, she dug the toes of her boots into the sand and sprinted drunkenly toward the Hind. They couldn't locate her, with all that heat. Let them think she'd died in the crash, and they'd leave. Then and only then would she have a chance of getting away.

Gasping for breath, Maya flattened herself against the scorched, blackened sand twenty feet from the burning Hind. She looked up through the smoke, looking fearfully for the Kamov. A startled cry broke from her lips as she saw the Russian craft that had been targeting her suddenly explode in a red-orange ball of fire. Metal and debris rained down upon her. The canyon echoed with clanging metallic sounds. Puffs of dust exploded everywhere as the sheared-off metal struck the rocks.

Within a minute, she saw an Apache D model coming in low over the canyon, right toward her. The canyon reverberated with the thick, heavy beat of its rotors.

A sob of relief broke from Maya's lips. She got to her feet and ran hard, away from the Hind so that the pilots could spot her. Lifting her arms, she waved wildly to catch their attention. Just ahead, Maya saw an area where the Apache could land, and she ran toward it. Sobbing with relief, she realized that her jaguar spirit had gotten in touch with Dane and that he had followed him here, to the Canyon of Death. Hot tears blurred her vision as she ran unsteadily toward the landing spot. She watched as the Apache crew detected her and came in for a landing. Gasping for breath, Maya leaned against the wall, her hands on her knees. She was safe. *Safe.* She'd managed to survive Faro and their death spiral dance. There could only be one survivor in the spiral—and it was her.

As Maya turned away, protecting her eyes from the flying sand and dust as the Apache landed, she suddenly felt weak. Within moments, her knees buckled. Crumbling on the sand, Maya sat back on her heels, sobbing. She didn't care who saw her crying. Life was precious. She loved Dane.

As the Apache landed, Maya tried to see who the pilot was. It was impossible, the dust was so thick. Protecting her eyes with her hands, she waited. When she looked up again, she saw Dane running toward her. He was dressed in a black flight suit, without his helmet. His face was grim, his eyes alive with anguish.

"Maya!" he called out to her. His voice was lost in the sounds of the Hind burning nearby.

"Dane!" Her own voice broke. Maya knew she couldn't stand. The relief at her life being spared had totaled her in a way she'd never expected. Opening her arms, she called to him as he skidded to a halt in front of her.

"Maya!" Dane fell to his knees and gripped her by her shoulders. Her face was bloody. Her uniform was scorched and several strands of hair that had worked their way from beneath the helmet she wore were burned. Her eyes were glazed, and she was clearly in shock. Maya sagged forward into his open arms. He groaned and pulled her hard against him and held her. Just held her. She was shaking like a scared child. He began to talk to her, soothe her and let her know she was safe.

Anxiously, Dane moved his hand down her back and shoulders, searching for wounds. Lifting his head, his saw the crumpled Slick off to one side. What was going on? What had happened? He pulled away and looked into her wet face.

"Are you hurt?" he yelled above the roar of the fire from the Hind.

"No…no…I'm fine…oh, Dane, I love you!" Maya sobbed, holding his narrowed blue gaze. She saw the strength in his face and the sudden fierce tenderness enter his glacial gaze. His mouth softened. She felt his hands come up as he gently removed the helmet from her head. Her black hair tumbled around her shoulders.

Easing his fingers through her hair, he held Maya captive by framing her damp face. Leaning forward, he said, "And I love the hell out of you, too. Just take it easy. You've been through a lot. I've got the Blackhawk coming. Angel's on board. It should land in a few minutes. We'll get you back to base and you'll be okay."

Maya nodded and leaned forward. She pressed a trembling kiss against his mouth. Never had she wanted contact with Dane more than in this moment. Maya wanted to convince herself that she was alive and that he was here, with her. Dane kissed her hard in return. His mouth was hot and seeking against her lips. As he broke the kiss, he smiled down at her and tenderly caressed her cheek. Maya felt shaky. Out of control. Sagging back on her heels, she gripped his hands in hers.

"Cam? How is Cam? Did you find her? Is she okay?"

"Yeah, she's fine. We rescued her earlier. A broken arm is all."

Closing her eyes, Maya whispered, "Thank Goddess. I was so scared for her…I didn't know what'd happened."

Dane took in a ragged breath. Joy surged through him. Maya was alive! He tried to gather his spinning thoughts and fight the wave of emotion that nearly overwhelmed him. In the distance, beyond the Apache, he saw the Blackhawk coming in for a landing. As its rotors stopped turning and the dust and pummeling wind died away, Dane stood and then brought Maya up into his arms. Her legs were rubbery. He patiently held on to her as she struggled to get her strength back. She was still crying. Hell, his eyes were wet, too. He grinned boyishly as he looked at her, his arm around her shoulders to steady her.

"I followed your jaguar."

She sighed and surrendered to his superior strength. Just having Dane's arm around her made Maya feel safe from the hell of the last hour. "I'm so glad. I was afraid you wouldn't…."

"It didn't leave me much choice." Dane laughed out of relief. The Blackhawk's door opened and he eased her forward. "Can you make it?"

Giving him a wry look, Maya said, "One step at a time." Looking up worriedly, she asked, "What about the Kamovs? There were three of them."

''Gone,'' Dane told her with satisfaction. ''It was a turkey shoot. They were otherwise occupied when we painted them on radar. They didn't know what hit them.''

Relief shuddered through Maya as they walked around the stationary Apache. She lifted her hand to Jessica, who remained on board, handling all the controls. No gunship could be left without a pilot on board during a wartime situation. The look on the woman's face was one of joy. ''They were making sure I stayed in the canyon as the Hind stalked me,'' she told him.

Dane turned and looked at the burning gunship. ''You took it down, didn't you.''

Maya grinned a little and wiped tears from her cheeks. ''Yeah, you might say that. Not that my method is in any flight training manual.''

With a shake of his head, Dane realized he'd never met a woman as resourceful or courageous as Maya. As he held her and walked her toward the waiting Blackhawk, Angel stood outside the door, tense and expectant. Because Maya was able to walk under her own power, Angel would remain on the aircraft. Under the circumstances, no one knew if Faro had other gunships around.

''When we get back to the base, you can tell us all about it,'' he assured Maya.

She gave him a hooded look, some of her old strength returning now that the shock was wearing off. ''You know what I want, Major?''

He grinned. ''Name it and it's yours.''

''You and a hotel room in Cuzco. I've got some things to say to you and I'm not going to wait any longer. I've learned my lesson.''

Tears came to Maya's eyes as she left the Blackhawk where it was parked on the lip. On her left, Dane had his grip on her arm to steady her. To her right Parades, otherwise known as the Angel of Death, was grinning broadly. Maya's legs still felt wobbly beneath her, but she was determined to walk back into the base complex under her own power, despite the dizziness that assailed her.

The men and women of the base surrounded her. They cheered and cried out her name. Some jumped up and down. Others hugged one another. Many cried. Maya grinned unevenly and raised her right hand to all of them. She understood her role as leader and squadron commander, but until just now she hadn't realized on an emotional level just how much she as a person meant to those who worked under her command. Many reached out to touch her hand, to welcome her back. When she glanced over at Dane, he was smiling widely.

And when the ranks of the crowd parted and Cam came forward, her eyes awash with tears, her arm in a sling, Maya threw her arms around the other pilot and held her and sobbed.

Dane stood back and watched. A tremendous cheer went up, resonating throughout the cave as Maya embraced her pilot and friend. The expressions of joy, of relief, were everywhere. Selfconsciously, Dane wiped his own eyes. At the edge of the crowd he spotted Joe and Craig. To his surprise, there wasn't a dry eye in the house. Dane knew that a returning male pilot would never do what Maya was doing— or what her people were doing—crying, hugging and cheering for all they were worth. He was humbled by the strength and softness that women possessed.

As Maya released Cam, she whispered, "It's all right, Cam. You did the right thing. You couldn't have carried me into that jungle. You and I both know that." She smiled through her tears and touched Cam's sagging shoulder. "Don't be hard on yourself. If only one of us could escape, that was better than both of us being caught."

Nodding sadly, Cam whispered brokenly, "I feel so guilty, Maya…for leaving you there with them. So guilty…"

Giving her a gentle hug, Maya said, "We'll talk more later, okay?"

Sniffing, Cam whispered, "Sure…you get to the dispensary. You're looking pretty bad."

Laughing, Maya lifted her head and met the damp, proud gazes of her squadron, who were surrounding her in what felt like an almost a maternal gesture of respect. She saw Dane come up, his awareness that she was once again in her role as commander of the base, not just the woman he loved, evident in his eyes. Giving him a tender look, she stepped away from Cam into the crowd of women around her.

"I understand," she said in a clear, strong voice that quieted everyone, "that you moved heaven and earth to find us. Thank you." Maya met each person's gaze. They were smiling and clapping their hands. "We scored a big victory today. Faro Valentino is dead. We've bagged four of his gunships." Maya gave a whoop and plunged her fist skyward. "Thanks to all of you! Now, let's get back to work. In the coming week, we're gonna do some heavy celebrating!"

The crowd cheered raucously, the sounds echoing and reechoing throughout the cave. Maya felt dizziness assail her and she automatically put out her hand in search of Dane's steadying one. She wasn't disappointed as he grasped it, then gripped her upper arm. She grinned up at him as the crowd continued to cheer and yell victoriously.

"Come on," he urged, "I think Liz wants to check you over."

Weariness stalked Maya. She knew she was still living on the last of her adrenaline charge. The crowd parted, allowing them to go to the rear of the complex, toward the dispensary. Angel opened the door to it and Maya walked in with Dane at her side. Elizabeth Cornell was waiting for her.

The silence was welcoming as Maya sat on the edge of the gurney. While Angel took her blood pressure and Elizabeth fussed over her, Dane stood back, his arms across his chest, just holding her gaze, that cockeyed grin on his handsome features. In the Blackhawk, she had lain on the gurney while Angel attended her. Dane had remained at her feet, and she'd told him everything that had happened. Wild Woman had flown the Apache home by herself.

Maya was still glad that Dane was nearby. Right now, she felt emotionally shredded by the last twelve hours.

Later, Elizabeth ordered her to her quarters—not head-quarters—to rest. Maya agreed. The doctor had placed a dressing on her left temple over the laceration and told her she had a mild concussion. There were some first and second degree burns on her neck and hands from the explosion of the Hind, but that was all.

Dane accompanied her to her quarters, a tiny room with a bunk, a locker and a makeshift cabinet, in the Quonset hut reserved for the officers near the dispensary. Plywood walls gave the pilots and other officers a little privacy in what was basically a dormitory. Right now, the place was deserted, and Maya was glad. She went straight to the shower at the end of the hall and washed the dirt, sweat, blood and fear off her. Dressing in a pair of jeans and a bright red tank top, she padded barefoot back to her room.

Dane was sitting on the edge of the bed, waiting for her. "You look like a drowned rat," he teased, getting up and gesturing for her to come and sit down.

Touching her damp hair, Maya said, "I didn't get it too dry."

Dane picked up one of the folded towels on the dresser. "I'll do it for you. Come and sit down," he coaxed. There were dark shadows beneath her eyes. Maya was in shock and he knew it. When she sat down and turned her back to him, he eased the soft green towel across her damp, dark strands. Gently, he began to squeeze the towel against them. Just the small act of doing this helped her relax. He felt her shiver.

"Cold?"

"N-no…just coming down, Dane…."

He sat down and continued to gently dry her hair. "How are you feeling?"

"Right now, I'm scared," she admitted hoarsely. "I keep reliving that flight down the canyon and wondering what possessed me to think I could survive it at all." Maya shook her head. Clasping her hands in her lap, she absorbed his touch. How badly she needed Dane's closeness right now. Just hearing his deep voice soothed the raggedness she was feeling.

"That's what makes the difference," he told her quietly as he finished his work. "Warriors focus above and beyond the fray. If they didn't have the confidence to think they could survive, they wouldn't try." He got up, retrieved the comb and brush from her dresser and sat back down. Picking up a lock of her hair, he eased the comb through it. "And you believed in yourself, your skills. You knew the canyon, and that was enough."

His words fell like soothing rain on her inner turmoil. Maya's scalp tingled pleasantly as Dane continued to comb her hair until it lay in dark waves around her head. "Right now, I feel like a scared little girl."

Hearing the tremble in her voice, Dane put the comb and brush aside, turned her around and framed her beautiful face with his hands. Looking deep into her emotion-filled gaze, he saw tears in the depths of her eyes. Maya's lower lip trembled. "I love you," he rasped, his fingers tightening momentarily on her firm, warm flesh. "You're so very, very brave. One in a million, Maya. I don't know how you did it—how you escaped Faro like that. I'm just blown away. I'm sure I couldn't have done it. He'd have knocked me out of the sky in a hurry."

Dane gave her a slight smile. She tried to smile in return and slid her hands along his forearms. Her touch was warm and inviting. Dane knew it wasn't time to love her fully, man to woman. It was a time to hold her. Maya needed to be held.

"Come here, sweetheart," he whispered, and pulled her into his arms.

With a soft moan, Maya sank into his embrace. She nuzzled her brow against the strong column of his neck and slid her hands around his torso. Having Dane's arms around her, holding her against him, was exactly what she needed. A ragged sigh broke from her lips and she closed her eyes. In every way, she surrendered to Dane because right now he was strong and she was weak. Wasn't that what love was about? When one partner was weak, the stronger one could stand and hold the other until he or she was able to stand on her own once again? *Yes.* She inhaled the male scent of him. The solid thud of his heart against hers provided stability when she felt so wildly out of control emotionally.

"I came so close to death out there," Maya admitted in a whisper. Dane stroked her shoulder and back. "And the one thing I regretted, Dane, was that I hadn't told you how I felt about you. I mean…really felt about you." The words came out with her tears. "I sat in that Slick thinking I hadn't told you I loved you. And I knew I was going to die. And that was the one regret I had—that you wouldn't ever know. I felt so terrible about that. I was mad at myself, at my own cowardice in not telling you."

Dane rocked her gently in his arms as she sobbed. Pressing his cheek against her damp hair, he rasped, "Well, I wasn't any better about it than you. I'm equally guilty, Maya. I was on patrol when the call came in that you were down. My first thought was that I hadn't told you I loved you. And I was so sorry…so sorry. I prayed for a chance to get to tell you that."

Sniffing, Maya raised her hand and wiped the tears from her eyes. She eased out of his arms just enough to look up at him. Dane's eyes were burning with tenderness for her.

"I didn't tell you because I didn't know how it could work," she confessed rawly. "I'm not going to leave here, Dane. This is my life. My work." She scowled and swallowed hard. "And I know how much the army means to you. You get your rank and retirement in twenty years. I had no

right to ask you to give up those things, either.'' She opened
her hands, her voice cracking. ''So, I didn't tell you how I
really felt. I didn't see how it could work, so I kept it to
myself.''

Dane nodded grimly and pulled Maya back into his arms.
She sank against him. ''I know,'' he admitted. ''But this last
couple of hours has made me rethink a lot of things, Maya.
I realized what was really important to me.'' He looked down
at her, at her face glistening with spent tears and the shadowy
darkness in her half-closed eyes. Just the fact that she could
be weak, could come to him and ask for his strength, his
care, made him feel powerful and good. Maya was a strong,
confident woman, but she also knew how to surrender to her
emotions, and to trust him. More than anything, Dane was
glad that she had given him her trust.

''I don't know how it can work,'' Maya said brokenly as
she slid her hand up across his chest. ''I—just don't....''

''Listen, you're really tired. Come on, I want you to curl
up here on your bed and sleep. That's what you really need
now—to sleep off the shock.''

''I wish you could lie with me.''

Dane laughed gently. ''Makes two of us, but I don't think
it would go down very well here at the base. Tongues would
wag.''

Maya felt him squeeze her, and she clung to him for a
moment before he eased her out of his arms. Dane was right:
she needed to sleep off the shock. As he got up and moved
her feet to the bed, she lay down, watching him as he took
the blanket, opened it and spread it across her. Then she
reached out and touched his hand.

''You're such a mother hen.''

Leaning down, he pressed a kiss to her damp cheek. ''Yes,
I am, with you,'' he whispered. Stroking her drying hair,
Dane whispered fiercely, ''Now, get some sleep. That's an
order. Dallas is handling all your duties for now.''

Maya felt the exhaustion pulling her eyes closed. ''And

you? What are you going to be doing?'' She knew that in less than two days, Dane was scheduled to leave. Her heart broke at that thought.

Chuckling, Dane straightened and looked around the tiny room, which was shrouded in gray light. ''Oh, I've got a bunch of details to attend to. I'll drop by later and see how you're doing, okay?''

''You'd better.''

His smile increased. ''Yes, ma'am.''

Chapter 15

Maya felt strong, warm fingers moving slowly across her shoulder and down her blanketed back. Moaning, she barely opened her eyes, clinging to sleep. Someone was sitting on the edge of her bunk. In the low light of the small lamp on the nearby dresser, she saw Dane leaning over, a worried look on his shadowed face.

"Uhhh...what time is it?"

Dane brushed several strands of dark hair away from Maya's drowsy looking face. The white dressing where she'd sustained the cut during the crash was exposed, reminding him once more how close he'd come to losing her earlier today. "Hi, sleepyhead," he murmured. Looking at his watch, he said, "It's 2100 hours. Liz thought I should come in and wake you up. You've slept deep and hard since returning to base. She's worried about your concussion and wanted to make sure you hadn't gone into a coma."

Groaning, Maya turned over onto her back, her hand moving to her brow. "I feel like I'm coming out of a coma," she muttered thickly. In the dimness, Dane's face was sharply etched, accentuating his quiet strength. His eyes burned with that familiar tender flame that wrenched her heart every time he looked at her that way. He caressed her cheek, longing in his expression.

"You look so beautiful when you wake up," Dane mused quietly. Normal noises of the base operation were muted at the moment, with many of the pilots and crews in their rooms for the evening hours. The sounds of doors opening and closing, the murmur of women's voices, filtered through to Maya's room. Nothing was completely private in such a setting.

Maya drowned in Dane's hooded look and pressed her cheek against the open palm of his hand. Sleep was gradually releasing its hold on her. "Do you know how good it is to say I love you?"

Nodding, Dane watched the play of light and dark across her high cheekbones and smooth forehead. "I'm grateful we can say it to one another, face-to-face." Maya was so brave. So incredibly courageous. Dane now understood why her troops were so loyal to her. She was truly a woman's role model of mythic proportions.

Maya eased up into a sitting position with a protesting groan. She'd slept in her clothes, and her hair tumbled in an unruly mass across her shoulders. Rubbing her face, and trying to wipe the sleep from her eyes, she felt Dane get up and leave her side. Her heart cried out. All she wanted right now was his presence, his strength, his love. Dropping her hands, she watched as he moved to the dresser. He picked up a tray of food from the mess hall and brought it over to her.

"Liz said you should try and eat something," he told her as he placed it across her lap. "The head cook made your favorite meal—lamb."

The fragrant, herbed odors drifted toward her nostrils. Maya looked down at the aluminum tray, which was stacked with food. The sumptuous meal included small, tasty lamb chops, thick brown gravy, potatoes and carrots. Dane handed her the flatware.

"Where'd she get lamb? That's not on the food requisition form."

Chuckling, Dane sat down near the end of her bunk and simply watched her. Absorbing Maya's presence was like absorbing sunlight into his starving heart. "Dallas asked Akiva to take the civilian helo down to Agua Caliente. They got some from Patrick, the chef at India Feliz Restaurant and brought it back for you. A kind of we're-glad-you're-alive dinner."

Touched by her people's thoughtfulness, Maya heard her stomach grumble. She hadn't eaten since…since she'd had that meal with Faro Valentino. Giving Dane a wry look, she said, "They shouldn't have…."

Dane watched her cut into the lamb chop with enthusiasm. "They love you. Why wouldn't they go out of their way to do something to show that to you? To celebrate your return?" Maya had the most beautiful, well-shaped hands he'd ever seen. There was nothing not to love about her. His body tightened with need of her. Dane wanted to seal the bond of love between them, but this was not the time or place to do it.

Maya chewed thoughtfully on the fragrant lamb. "I don't know about love, Dane. I know they respect me."

His mouth curved in a smile. "You know, under ordinary circumstances, I'd say you were right, but you've built something here that defies the usual laws of gravity in the army's universe. Did you see the looks on those women's faces after you landed and walked out of that Blackhawk under your own power? And the cheers? The smiles of relief that you were alive?" Shaking his head, Dane whispered, "No, Maya, they love you. Liz was telling me that while we were off searching for you this place was like a tomb. She said every woman here was depressed and anxious. They were really worried about you and Cam."

He could see more life coming back to Maya's dark green eyes as she ate with pleasure, her glazed look disappearing. She'd managed to sleep off the shock. Relief flowed through Dane.

"We're a tight group here," she agreed. Cutting into the potatoes and carrots, Maya felt her hunger being sated. "And it's happened over time, because of the threat of death that hangs over us daily."

"Combat troops are the tightest group in the world," Dane agreed. He saw color flooding back to Maya's cheeks. Her eyes were beginning to lose that exhausted look. She ate voraciously—like the jaguar she was. Smiling to himself, he said, "And no one but me saw your black jaguar. Do you know that? It led me to you. I thought I was seeing things at first until it pushed open the exit door at HQ. That's when I knew it wasn't my imagination."

Maya lifted her head and grinned a little. "I wish I could have been here to see the look on your face." She chuckled softly. Handing him the tray, she said, "I'm done. Thanks."

Dane picked up the tray and sat it back on the dresser. Handing her a cup of coffee he'd also brought from the mess hall, he sat back down and watched her sip it with relish. "So, how do you explain that I could see it and no one else could?"

Maya set the cup in her lap, her hands wrapped around it. Silence stretched gently between them. "When you love someone, Dane, it's easy to send a spirit guide to ask for his help," she finally answered.

"I see…I think."

Clearing her throat, Maya said, "What are we going to do, Dane? I love you. I don't know when it happened—or how—but it did." She licked her bottom lip and frowned as she watched his shadowed face grow serious. "I don't know how love grew out of our mutual dislike of one another. I can't explain it." Maya laughed a little, obviously embarrassed. "Another one of life's mysteries, I suppose." Then she

looked directly at him. "What are we going to do? I never
told you how I really felt because you were leaving, flying
back north. I know how much your career means to you.
And I know how much this place—" she looked around the
room, her voice softening "—means to me. I can't leave
here. I don't want to leave here. This is my life. My mission." Mouth quirking with pain, Maya added in a low tone,
"And I know you feel equally strong about your career. I
would never ask you to leave it. So I don't know what we're
going to do, now that our hands have been forced by this
event."

Dane picked at a small thread on the light blue coverlet.
He heard the unsureness in Maya's voice. And the yearning—for him. It sent a delicious sensation from his heart to
his lower body. Even now he wanted her in every possible
way. Could any man tame Maya? No, not ever. She was wild
and primal. She was a woman of the next century, one who
was confident in herself and her femininity in ways very few
other women were right now. Maya was truly a prototype for
women of the future, who would one day follow in her footsteps. There always had to be a catalyst, one unique individual who cracked the collective reality so that everyone else
could see new possibilities, with new eyes. New vision. The
combination was dazzling to him, testing and challenging.

And yet Dane knew without a doubt that they were equals.
She was someone he could be forever involved with, never
bored with, always challenged by, to grow and become a
better man than he had been in the past.

"Well…" he murmured. "I didn't tell you I loved you,
for the same reasons." He slanted her a glance, his mouth
pulled into a wry smile. "And no, I knew you would never
leave this base, Maya. Your heart and soul are here."

Reaching out, Maya slid her fingers over his, which rested
on his thigh. "You understand that now."

Nodding, Dane looked around the dimly lit room. "Yeah,
I get it—now. I don't pretend to understand the magic of

you, of this place, or your Jaguar Clan relations. I only know that these things are a part of you and that they have become very real to me as a result. I can't explain it, Maya. I probably never will, but that's not going to stop me from loving you, or wanting you...." Dane squeezed her fingers gently.

Sipping the last of the coffee, Maya leaned down and placed the mug on the wooden floor next to the bunk. She saw the angst in Dane's eyes, and the sadness and hope in them, too. Pushing the covers aside, she slid down and wrapped her arms around him, resting her head against his broad shoulder. "So, what are we going to do? How are we going to handle the love that we tried so hard to hide from one another?"

Dane absorbed the warmth and soft firmness of her body as she leaned against his side. Clasping her hands as she slid them around his waist, he smiled a little. "I'm leaving with my team tomorrow morning," he told her in a low tone. "And I've got a few ideas, Maya, but I've got to present them to my commanding officer at Fort Rucker." He squeezed her long, sculpted fingers, enjoying the way her cheek was pressed against his shoulder. Her breath was moist against the column of his neck.

"Ideas?"

"Yeah...but I don't want to say what they are just yet...."

Puzzled, Maya lifted her head and looked at him. When Dane turned and met her gaze, she melted beneath his burning blue appraisal. "Dane, I'll settle for anything we can have. If that means me flying north to see you when I can pull free of the base and the demands here, I will. Or vice versa. I'm not willing to let go of what we have."

Her lips were bare inches from his. Dane eased away so that he could turn her around to face him. "I'm a lot more selfish than you," he told her quietly as he framed her face with his hands. "I'm not willing to settle for seeing each other every three or four months for a few hours, or maybe a day in some hotel somewhere." He searched her eyes, which were now glimmering with tears. "In the last three months I fell in love with you, sweet woman, and I'm damned if I'm going to lose you." Leaning down, Dane captured her trembling lips with his. Maya was on the verge of crying and so was he. His heart was splintering at the thought of having to leave her tomorrow morning. Dane had come to rely on Maya's presence, her strength, her womanly wisdom and her magical, catalytic effect on his everyday life.

Maya choked back a sob. Dane was leaving. He wasn't sure when he'd return. As his strong mouth grazed her lips, she moaned. Lifting her arms, she slid them around his capable shoulders and pressed herself wantonly against him. She wasn't disappointed. His arms brought her close, squeezing the breath from her as he captured her lips and rocked them open. As his breath moved into her body, she drank him in hungrily and tried to absorb every sensation. Just the way his mouth molded to hers, gently and tenderly moved against her, made tears form and fall from her thick, black lashes. Maya felt their hot trails down her cheeks. As the tears dripped into the corners of her mouth and became part of the heated kiss, she tasted their saltiness. And so did he.

Gently, Dane broke their long, searching kiss. Both of them were breathing raggedly. He saw the burning desire in Maya's half-closed eyes as she looked at him in the throbbing silence. His heart was pounding in his chest. Ranging his hands across her shoulders and arms, he managed a one-cornered smile. "I'll be back," he promised her huskily. "I'll be back...."

Maya hadn't known how much love could hurt. As she stood out on the lip near the refueling tanks and equipment, her arms across her breasts, she sighed raggedly. The noontime sun was beginning to burn away the clouds around the base. Crews were getting ready to send off the two D models for routine flight coverage of the area. Since Faro had died, the shipments of cocaine had ceased. There were no more

Kamovs to watch for. There were no more games of hide-and-seek.

Moving restlessly around the area, Maya rubbed her chest above her heart. Dane had been gone for two weeks. Two of the longest, worst weeks of her life.

Dressed in her usual black uniform and boots, her hair loose about her shoulders, Maya scowled as she walked, hands behind her back, toward the cave entrance. It was then that she picked up the sound of an approaching helicopter coming toward the Eye. Frowning, she turned. Who could that be? All her helos were on the lip. She noticed that the crews preparing the D models for flight also stopped their duties to look.

Maya's mind spun with options. Possibilities. The sound was definitely that of a D model Apache. What was going down? Nearly everyone in the cave complex was now watching the Eye with open curiosity. Within moments, in a swirl of clouds, the Apache D model came flying confidently through the opening. The rotor wash blasted Maya, because she was closest to it. Shielding her face, she watched as the helicopter came in for a landing. Who was flying it? She had no knowledge of plans for another gunship to fly into her base today. Frowning, she walked quickly toward it. In the cockpit, the two pilots began to unhitch their respective harnesses. The engines were shut down and the rotors began to move slower and slower.

Maya stayed out of reach of the blades, stationing herself on the side where the pilots would emerge. A shaft of sunlight slanted toward her, and she shaded her eyes to see who they were. Again she wondered why there was radio silence. Whoever they were, they should have contacted her to get permission to land here. As the blades stopped, the front cockpit door opened and the pilot turned in her direction, she gasped. It was Dane! He had the biggest grin on his face as he lifted his hand and waved down at her.

Her heart sped up. Maya gaped. Dane was here! The second cockpit opened and Joe Calhoun stepped out. He, too, was grinning for all he was worth. As soon as the blades stopped turning, Maya ordered her crew to put the chocks beneath the wheels and to tether the blades. The flight crew moved with ballet precision to make the Apache safe for the pilots to disembark.

Once the blades stopped turning, Maya moved forward. She saw Dane ease out of the cockpit, climb along the fuselage and step down from the ladder. As he turned, he took off his helmet and set it on the frame of the helicopter. Running his fingers thorough his hair, he turned and opened his arms to her. Maya didn't care who saw them. Everyone on the base knew of their love for one another, even though she'd tried to keep it a secret.

"Maya!" Dane moved forward, his arms wide. He saw the joy and the questions in her eyes as she ran to him. Not giving a damn who saw them, he laughed and took the full weight of her body as she threw herself into his embrace.

"Hi, stranger," he greeted her with a laugh. Holding Maya, he twirled her around and finally allowed her feet to touch the ground. Her dark hair swirled around her as he pulled her against him and captured her smiling lips beneath his own. The world rocked to a halt. Dane heard Joe's big, Texas laugh, heard people cheering and calling their names, but nothing else mattered in that moment but Maya. Her mouth was warm and eagerly welcoming. He held her against him, felt her breath coming into his starving lungs and heart. She tasted of coffee, of the natural sweetness of herself as a woman. Her moan reverberated through him and he smiled against her mouth.

"I love the hell out of you," Dane rasped against her wet, soft lips. He looked deep into her glistening eyes.

Maya breathed raggedly as she met and held his ice-blue, burning gaze. She felt Dane's hands range tenderly across her waist and up to her shoulders. Smiling breathlessly, she whispered unsteadily, "Welcome home, darling. I've missed you so much…so much…."

Her words cascaded over him and fed his starving heart. Easing her away, Dane looked up to see the assembled women crowding around them. The expressions on their faces made him smile. He called to many of them by name and lifted his hand in greeting.

Maya heard her people shouting a welcome. She turned beneath Dane's protective arm and looked around. The joy and delight mirrored on the faces of her crew was something to behold. They seemed to glow collectively—happy for her and Dane, she realized humbly. Managing a smile of her own, Maya thanked them and then ordered them back to the business at hand. They clapped, yelled and shouted, and then dispersed to their individual duties.

Maya gave Dane a dirty look. "You could have at least let us know you were coming."

Chuckling indulgently, Dane released her. He took off his Nomex gloves and stuffed them in the pocket of his uniform. Joe ambled over. "Nice to see you again, Captain," he greeted, her, shaking Maya's hand.

"Hi, Joe. Welcome back to Black Jaguar Base."

Joe looked around. "Is Akiva here?"

Dane traded a knowing look with Maya. Maya grinned a little.

"She's got the flu, Joe. She's over in the officers' quarters, on orders to rest. But I'll bet she'll be happy to see you. Why don't you go over for a visit? I'm sure she'll feel a lot better real fast when she hears you're here."

Joe blushed good-naturedly and tucked his helmet under his left arm. "Thank you, Captain. I think I'll pay her a call right now." He hurried into the cave.

Maya stood there and gave Dane a wicked, teasing look. "Why are you back here with *another* Apache, Major?"

Dane grinned back. He took her hand. "Come on, let's go

to your office. I've got some things in motion that you need to approve.''

Maya sat behind her desk, her eyes wide as Dane finished explaining his plan. Before her were orders that had been cut and were awaiting her signature. She shook her head. ''I don't believe this,'' she whispered, touching them tentatively.

Dane sat on the edge of her desk, relaxed and at ease. The door to her office was closed for once. He wanted this conversation conducted in private. Maya's eyes gleamed with excitement. He felt it. And he wanted to capture that excitement within him, as well. Two weeks without her vital energy, her sense of humor, her unique perspective on the world, had carved a groove of loneliness so deep within him that he knew he could never be without Maya in his life again.

''Well? What do you think? Will it work? Will your women pilots go for it?''

Rubbing her brow, Maya said, ''This is all so much, Dane. So much! I mean, before, we were the black sheep of the army. They were more than happy to see us shoved away to South America. We were out of sight, out of mind.''

''Well,'' he murmured, pleased, ''that's all changed.''

Giving him a stunned look, Maya said, ''This is…wonderful…more than I dared ever hope for my people. They're such good pilots and crews….''

''Thank Morgan Trayhern,'' Dane told her seriously, pointing at the orders. ''When I left here, I flew into Fort Rucker and got him on the phone. I shared my ideas with him.''

''And he went to bat for us.'' Shaking her head in amazement, Maya whispered, ''This is just incredible, Dane. I'm in shock….''

He reached out and grazed her cheek. ''Good shock, I hope?''

Giving him a tender look, Maya said, ''The best kind. Now

you can stay down here with me. That's what I like most about it."

Dane grinned wolfishly. "Believe me, sweetheart, I was racking my brain as to how to have my cake and eat it, too."

Reaching for the orders, Maya lifted them and read them again. "The army is agreeing to take some of my women pilots for I.P.—instructor pilot—duty along the Mexican border, to teach other Apache pilots night maneuvers against enemy aircraft. They'll start interdiction of flights originating out of Mexico, headed for the U.S.A. And the army will be sending replacement pilots down here for combat training, both male and female. There's even an opening for two of my pilots at Fort Rucker, to instruct on the finer points of combat flying."

"Yes. What I see happening down here, Maya, is far-reaching. Your base provides an excellent opportunity for advanced combat training for our best Apache pilots. We don't get to train for combat except when there's a war going on, and then it's too late. All we do now is shoot down cardboard or wooden targets that can't shoot back. My being down here showed me that this environment, although dangerous, is also a way to finely hone our best pilots in real combat conditions." He laughed derisively. "Just having them fly through the Eye will make them better pilots."

Laughing with him, Maya set the orders on her desk. "This means my officers can have a career now. They're not at a dead end by being down here."

"No, just the opposite. Because of their three years of combat flying, they are in a prime position to turn around and teach others, to redefine our combat training even more. All their knowledge and experience is going to be tapped, Maya. Thanks to you holding on to your vision of this place and the mission you undertook." Dane regarded her proudly. Pulling a small box out of the pocket of his olive-green flight uniform, he said, "And here's the army's way of supporting you...."

Taking the box, Maya opened it. She gasped. Inside was a set of gold major's leaves. Jerking a look up at Dane, she said, "Is this real? Am I going to be a major?"

He smiled down at her as she delicately touched the round gold oak leaves that denoted she was now a major in the army. "Yes. More than deserved," Dane murmured. "And it should have been done a long time ago. Your mother and father are going to fly down to Fort Rucker, where there's going to be a ceremony for you seven days from now. Your dad is going to pin them on your shoulders. And I'm going to be there to see it happen." His mouth curved in a proud smile.

Tears flooded into Maya's eyes. "This is all too much, Dane…too much…." She put the box with the metal insignias aside. "The best of this is you get to stay down here and continue to train formally as an I.P."

"Yes," Dane said, easing off the edge of the desk and coming around to her. He pulled Maya up and into his arms. Their hips met and her arms slid around his waist as he studied her in the warm silence. "And judging from the sat intel that Morgan has picked up, it looks like the Colombian drug lord Manuel Navarro, and his Ecuadorian counterpart, Hector Osoro, are going to come in here shortly and pick up where Faro Valentino left off. Morgan's collected proof that Navarro has just sent an order to Russia to buy more of those Kamovs we just took out a couple of weeks ago. He's going to rebuild the fleet and challenge you again."

Her heart squeezing in fear, Maya said, "I knew it wouldn't last long…the peace here, I mean." She looked up into Dane's strong, quiet face. Her heart blossomed with such a fierce love for him.

"The peace won't last long," he agreed. "But Joe is here, and he's going to be my righthand man, to help set up our advanced combat school here at the base." He leaned down and found her lips. Kissing her softly, he whispered, "And right now, as I speak, Major Stevenson, that Bell helicopter is being readied for us to fly to Cuzco.'' He lifted his head, his eyes glimmering. "Interested in taking me up on a nice, four-day R and R in the city? I've got the best room at the Libertador Hotel reserved for us. The champagne is being chilled as I speak. The whirlpool is being heated. The bathrobes are being laid out for us. Fresh flowers…''

Laughing softly, Maya embraced him hard. "Yes, I am. We deserve this little break, Major York. Don't you think?''

His laughter joined hers. Maya drowned in the joy she found in his eyes—joy that they were going to be together. Somehow, Dane had made it happen. As she kissed him hard and swiftly on his smiling mouth, Maya wanted nothing more than that precious time alone with him. They had more than earned it.

"Strawberries, chocolate and champagne,'' Maya sighed as she languished in the hot, bubbling water of the whirlpool in their suite at the hotel. "This is heaven…." Sipping the golden liquid, she felt Dane's arm around her. Both naked, they allowed the heat of the water to draw out the tiredness of the last few months and reinvigorate them. He lifted a strawberry that had been dipped in chocolate to her mouth.

The look in his eyes was feral, one of a hunter, as Maya took the tidbit in her mouth and then sipped her champagne. Outside the window was the city of Cuzco. The afternoon sun slanted against the barren brown mountains that surrounded the second largest city in Peru. The drapes, gold brocade, swathed the huge window so that it looked like a guilt-framed picture of the city she loved so much.

Moving away, Dane drank the rest of his champagne and set the glass on the dark blue carpet that surrounded the octagonal whirlpool. Their room was sumptuous, with gilded furniture from the period of the Sun King. The bed was huge, with a flowing canopy of gold brocade, plus midnight blue and gauzy white veils of fabric flowing from each of the four white-and-gold carved posts.

He saw Maya smiling at him as he turned and stood up. Her eyes were half-closed with desire in their depths—for him. It made him feel good and strong as he offered his hand to her. As her fingers slid into his, he surprised her and lifted her into his arms. The water splashed around them as she gasped and threw her arms around his slick, wet shoulders.

"Dane!"

Laughing deeply, he carried her up out of the bubbling tub of hot water to the bed. Maya didn't have enough playfulness in her life, he'd discovered long ago. Well, that was going to change with him around. Her laughter was music to his ears. If he wasn't good at much else, he did know how to play. And he was going to teach her. Depositing her wet body on the brocade bedspread, he slid down beside her and pinned her hands just above her head. Her laughter dissolved as he leaned over and caressed her smiling lips. Moaning, she pressed her body urgently against his. Moving his hand down her sleek, firm waist and hip, he brought her fully against him.

"We're getting everything wet," Maya whispered as she placed kiss after kiss along his jaw and the column of his neck.

"So what? We're paying enough for it." Dane eased his knee between her thighs. Her body was strong and warm and sleek against his. They were like two warriors of equal power and skill. Relishing her womanly strength, her boldness and inventiveness as she ran her tongue along his collarbone, Dane closed his eyes.

Giggling, Maya arched as his hand moved around her hip and she felt him press himself against the juncture of her thighs. "You're so cavalier, Major...." she whispered, easing her head back as she felt him press insistently against her dampness. Oh, how long she'd looked forward to this intimacy, this playfulness with Dane. He made her laugh. He made her feel so free, like a child again in many ways. Sliding her fingers along the sculpted muscles of his arms and shoulders, she sighed raggedly. Opening her thighs to him, she felt him thrust deeply into her.

The pleasure shimmered hotly within her belly. An arc of heat throbbed upward. Surrendering to him, Maya lay on her back with him moving commandingly above her. With a smile on her lips and her eyes closed, she arched, sliding her hands down his narrow hips. The moment his lips brushed the tip of her hardened nipple, her mind exploded. She could no longer think, only feel, and then feel some more.

The world and all its troubles vanished, dissolving in the heat of their mutual desire. As he caught and captured her lips with a growl, Maya drank hungrily from his own. The droplets of water helped them move slickly against each other as he thrust deeply and rhythmically into her. Each throbbing pulse created a lavalike heat that pooled through her. She tasted the strawberries on his lips, inhaled the male odor that was his alone, and thrilled to the way his hard, muscled body moved in such joyful rhythm with hers. Where he was hard, she was soft. And where she was pressed wantonly against him, there was such a smooth give and take that Maya felt they had been made for one another, like lost puzzle pieces finally fitted together to complete a beautiful picture.

As her body exploded with the gift of his love, she arched and moaned. His arms came around her shoulders and he gripped her to him, thrusting deeply to prolong the wonderful, sunlit sensations that rippled like waves from the core of her body outward. Seconds later, Maya felt him tense. His growl was male. Dominating. He gripped her even tighter and she clung to him, her face pressed against the column of his neck, lost in the sweet, hot haze of their mutual love for one another.

Moments spun into golden sunlight and silvered moonlight for Maya afterward. She felt Dane move off her and draw her fully against him, dragging the fluffy coverlet across them. Lying in the crook of his arm, Maya barely opened her eyes, a smile lingering on her lips. He was gazing down at her, his blue eyes thoughtful as he eased his fingers through her damp hair.

"I love you, Maya."

The words fell tenderly across her. The deep, husky quality of Dane's voice touched her wildly thudding heart. She reached up and caressed his recently shaved jaw. "I'll love you until I draw my last breath, darling."

"I know you will," he answered. And he did. Maya's commitment was total, encompassing her heart and soul. There was nothing tentative about her loyalty to those around her, Dane knew. "There might be times when we fight like hell, but we'll argue constructively, above the belt." He rubbed a silken strand of her hair between his thumb and index finger. "We're strong people. We know our own minds. But we also hold one another's hearts."

Smiling tenderly at him, Maya rested her hand against his cheek. "I trust you with my life, darling. I have for a long time. And you've never let me down." And he hadn't. Even in her worst moments when she'd known she was going to die, Dane had been flying toward her to try and save her. "You're so heroic in my eyes."

He traced her arched brow with his fingertip. Her eyes were emerald, with sunlight dappling their depths as they clung to his. "Not compared to you," he rasped. "You've got such a brave, brave heart in this loving body of yours…. I just hope I can always see what I see in your eyes now, Maya."

"You will. It takes a real man to admit he was wrong, and then right the wrong, like you did between us."

Grimacing, Dane sighed and said, "Yes, and I'm sorry I did that to you…to the other women…."

"That's past now," she whispered. "We've all forgiven you." She grinned. "After you took off the prejudicial armor, look at the man who was behind it. I fell in love with him!"

He chuckled. "A far better Dane York than the old one,

that's for sure.'' Easing his arm from beneath her, he turned over and opened the small drawer in the bedstand.

Maya looked up. "What are you doing?'' She missed his warmth, his maleness, against her. When he turned back to her, he presented her with a small, gold covered case. "What's this?'' Maya murmured, setting it down between them on the damp coverlet.

"Why don't you open it and find out.'' Dane's heart raced with anticipation. Maya rose up on her elbow and fiddled with the latch, her brow knitted in concentration. She looked beautiful lying naked, stretched out like a sated jaguar, next to him. His breath hitched as she opened the lid. Her eyes widened beautifully.

"Dane!''

He looked down at the solitaire emerald ring set in gold. "Do you like it?''

Gasping, Maya eased it from the box. The light glistened through the small solitaire emerald as she held it in her fingers. Her gaze snapped up to his. "Oh! It's beautiful!'' She looked up at him. "An engagement ring? For me?''

Laughing fully, he said matter-of-factly, "Well, yes...I didn't have any other woman in mind.''

Maya sat up, the coverlet pooling around her hips and long legs. "This is so beautiful! Where...when...?'' She gave him a helpless look. Dane was grinning like a fox.

"Blame Dallas. I asked her who the best jeweler in Cuzco was. I told her what I wanted for you, and she gave me the name of the store. Dallas knew your ring size, so I was all set.''

"And she knew about this all along?''

"Yep. She knows how to keep a secret, too.'' Dane met Maya's wide, stunned eyes. "Well? Do you like it? I tried to match the color of the stone with the color of your eyes. Did I succeed?''

Staring down at the ring, Maya felt a lump forming in her throat. "Yes, yes, it's the color of my eyes.'' She was touched beyond words, knowing that emeralds were expensive. And this one was as clear as could be. An emerald of this quality would cost far more than any diamond would.

"It's yours," Dane told her in a low, unsteady tone. "My promise to you, Maya. It's an engagement ring, but it can mean anything you want it to, between us. I'm not trying to rush you toward marriage. The ring is my commitment to you. To us. I want every day we have left to be spent together."

Tears jammed Maya's eyes as she handed him the ring. "Here," she said brokenly, "put it on me?" And she held out her hand.

Sitting up, Dane slid his fingers around hers. In that moment, as he eased the ring onto her left hand, love for Maya welled up through him as never before. Holding her hand in his, he lifted his other palm and slid it along her clean jawline. His own tears blurred her beautiful face for a moment as he spoke. "I'll love you forever, Maya. Forever."

Epilogue

"Take my hand," Maya urged Dane, excitement in her voice. They stood together in the cloud-shrouded Temple of Balance on top of Machu Picchu, the ruins of one of the most famous architectural wonders ever built by the Incas. Even though the entire complex atop this ten-thousand-foot, jungle-shrouded mountain had been abandoned in the 1500s, those who knew better still used the ley lines—complex flow lines of invisible energy that had been purposely directed through the temples—to this day.

As they stood on the grassy expanse of what had been an old courtyard in the temple, Maya drew in a deep breath, happiness threading through her. Machu Picchu appeared as an ancient temple site to the thousands of tourists who came here, but there was much more to it than met the eye. She had been trained to know where the ley lines of energy intersected one another. Where they crossed, a doorway into another dimension existed. It could be accessed by someone who knew how to do it, opened for transport purposes.

Dane stepped toward Maya. He slid his hand into hers.

They were dressed in civilian attire because of the nature of their visit to Agua Caliente. Inca was giving birth to her twins at the Village of the Clouds. Dane had been with Maya, in their bed at their small house on the mining side of the mountain, near the base, when she'd suddenly sat up out of a dead sleep. He'd awakened instantly, and what he saw stunned him. At the foot of their bed stood a woman who looked like a holographic image. When Dane heard her speak, cold chills had worked up his spine. Maya knew her, however. She was Grandmother Alaria, the head elder from the Village of the Clouds. And she had come to tell Maya that her sister was in labor, and to come as soon as she—and Dane—could.

Dane had sat there staring, his mouth open. Oh, he'd heard from Maya of visitations like this, but he'd never experienced one before. They'd hurriedly gotten out of bed and dressed. Maya had transferred base operations to her executive officer, and they'd taken the civilian helicopter to Agua Caliente, at the base of Machu Picchu.

Dane wondered how they were going to reach the village of the Clouds, the mysterious headquarters of the Jaguar Clan. They had taken a bus up from the small Peruvian town to the temple structure atop the green-clothed mountain. This was not his first time up to the ruins. Once before, Maya had taken him up here and given him a full day's tour of the magnificent remains. She had told him then that there was another way to access the Village of the Clouds, but that it was known only to Jaguar Clan members. She'd patiently explained about ley lines, and how the Incas had knowingly gathered, directed and brought them together atop this complex. As much as Dane wanted to grasp her knowledge of metaphysics and the mountain, it was still just a head trip for him—until this morning.

Now, as he looked around the green, grassy area, the Temple of Balance behind them, he saw before them a huge hole—an old underground entrance. Archeologists at the turn of the twentieth century had discovered that a tunnel system had been dug around the entire complex. They hadn't known what it was for. But Maya did. The entrance had been blocked by a huge boulder to discourage the many tourists from even thinking about trying to go down into the tunnel to explore it out of curiosity.

Dane smiled at Maya. Her hair was mussed by the inconstant wind that moved up the steep slope of the mountain and then blew across the ruins on top. It was 0800, and few tourists were up and about at this time of morning.

"See that tunnel?" she asked him in a low tone as she pointed at it.

"Yeah. It's blocked. Is that where we're going?" He still had it in his mind that somehow the tunnel would take them to this mysterious village where Maya had trained.

"Yes. It doesn't matter if it's blocked or not, Dane. The energy door is still present even if you can't see it or feel it."

He raised his brows. "I feel something…like a pull or tug toward the tunnel?"

She smiled a little. "Bingo." She hitched her thumb across her shoulder. "The Temple of Balance is the opening for us to teleport to the village. You see that beautiful *apu*—mountain—in the distance behind us?"

He half turned. There was a tall, snow-covered mountain at least thirty miles away from them. "Yes."

"That's Apu Mandor. You see that huge black stone slab on the western perimeter of the temple? It's called the Pachamama stone, and the Incas carved out the top of it to conform exactly with Apu Mandor's major features."

There was a huge slab of black granite that was about the length of a car and roughly ten feet high. The stone had been hewn to resemble Mandor's mountainous outline almost exactly, Dane realized upon closer inspection. Then it had been raised and set upright. In front of the stone was a square courtyard of dry, packed earth. On either side were stone structures with thatched roofs, standing two terraces below.

Maya had told him that she would sometimes come to this temple to receive a healing, and that the energy was four-directional. Beyond the tunnel entrance, she'd explained, far out across the Valley, was Apu San Juan, another huge snow-covered summit somewhere beyond their view. Between the two massive *apus* and the Pachamama stone was a powerful, transformative energy link. The two small temples in the courtyard represented right and left, or female and male, energy. The Pachamama stone was the neutral source that brought the right and left together and made it into one androgynous flow of energy. It was then linked to the two mighty mountain spirits. Combined, it created an energy door for teleportation purposes. Only Jaguar Clan members, and the Q'uero people who were trained from birth in the old Incan religion, knew about and used it.

Dane didn't pretend to understand the energy dynamics as Maya had painstakingly explained them to him. But even he could feel the pull of energy upon his body. It wasn't his imagination. He was always trying to figure out Maya's magical world, which defied his third-dimensional, reality-based logic, but he hadn't succeeded yet. Over time, he came to simply accept that he didn't know a whole lot about the unseen world that she was so comfortable living in. That never stopped him from loving her. It simply added a unique and fascinating element. Dane was never bored with Maya around.

"You ready?" she asked as she turned and fully faced the tunnel opening.

"Yeah. You sure this is gonna work? I don't understand how we can physically move from this place to somewhere else. What's at work here? Quantum physics?"

He saw Maya roll her eyes in exasperation at him. They'd had many spirited discussions about teleportation.

"I don't know *how* it works, Dane. I only know that it *does*. I accept it on blind-faith knowing and trust."

His mouth hitching upward in a teasing grin, he said, "I don't have to believe it will work in order for it to work?"

Chuckling, Maya shook her head. "No, because your disbelief and questioning is offset by my belief and intent." Her eyes sparkled wickedly. "And what I *know* will more than make up for your questioning. My intent is like a laser compared to the mild skepticism you have about this little trip. Intent, strong intent, will get the job done. So just sit back, relax and enjoy the ride."

Smiling, he said, "What do I do?" Dane saw the excitement in Maya's features and knew it had to do with the birthing of her sister's babies. She could hardly wait to see Inca and the new infants. Neither Maya nor Dane was sure that they'd arrive in time for the births, but they were going to try.

"Bend your knees slightly. Then close your eyes and take a couple of good, deep breaths into your lungs. I'll do the rest."

Dane trusted Maya with his life. In the seven months since he'd returned to the base, their love had done nothing but grow, transform and become more beautiful. As he closed his eyes and took in the deep breaths of air, he felt a warm, shivering sensation enter his booted feet. The warmth moved quickly up through him. Suddenly he heard a pop and felt an undeniable sense of movement, but it was barely discernible.

"Open your eyes," Maya said.

When Dane opened his eyes, he was standing in the middle of the hard-packed dirt plaza of a village. It looked like any other Q'uero village he'd seen before, except for one thing. Looking around, Dane saw people of all colors, of all races and nationalities. Many were dressed in clothes befitting their culture. Blinking, he gave Maya a puzzled look.

"Is this it? The Village of the Clouds?"

She grinned. It had been an easy teleportation and it left her energized, as it should, in the wake of the event. "Yes, this is the Village of the Clouds. Welcome to my other home. It's yours now, too. Come on, follow me.'' Her voice rose in excitement. ''Inca and Roan will be at the birthing hut.''

Dane kept ahold of her hand. He felt mildly dizzy, but the sensation quickly evaporated as he walked. ''How did you get us here? What, exactly, did you do?''

She chuckled, her stride long as she passed several huts. ''I spent over a decade learning how to do this, Dane. I just hooked us up with the energy that's there on Machu Picchu, at that portal we stood in front of. Once I engaged it, we were allowed entrance, and here we are.''

Dogs and children were playing here and there. A number of people were gathered around one of the cooking pots in the center of the village. The plaza was square in design, and around the circle were many different-sized huts.

Mystified, Dane eyed the mighty Andes, their snow-covered peaks blue in color, rising off to one side of the busy, productive village. A roll of huge white clouds seemed to revolve slowly, all along the boundary where the plowed fields of the village met the steep slopes of the mountains. Turning his attention back to Maya, who was almost running now, he quickened his own stride. It had been more than seven months since Maya had seen Inca, and he knew she was anxious to be with her sister again, especially on such a wonderful occasion.

As they came to a long, rectangular thatched hut, Maya slowed. An old woman, very tall and proud, wearing a long, pink, flowing robe, her silver hair caught up on top of her head with white-and-purple orchids tucked in the strands, walked out to meet them. Maya released Dane's hand and threw her arms around the woman. Dane stood back and nodded deferentially. It was the same woman he'd seen yesterday night at the foot of their bed.

''Grandmother Alaria!'' Maya whispered as she hugged her gently. ''It's so good to see you again.''

Alaria laughed softly and kissed Maya on her flushed

cheeks. ''Welcome, my child.'' She turned her attention to Dane, who stood there uncertain. ''And you are the man who holds Maya's heart.'' She extended her long, frail-looking hand to him. ''Welcome, Dane York. We're glad to have you among us.''

Dane slid his hand into Alaria's. He was surprised at the strength of her returning grip, for she seemed almost ethereal, not quite of this world. He could perceive a distinct glow around her, which he'd also seen last night. There was laughter and warmth in her eyes as she met and held his gaze.

''It's good to see you again, my son. Welcome to our humble village.''

''Thank you, Grandmother.''

Her eyes danced with amusement. ''You have many questions,'' she said.

Dane nodded. He looked over at Maya and grinned sickly. ''Yes, ma'am, I guess I do.''

''Perhaps, later, I may answer some of them for you?''

''I'd like that. Yes.'' As he said the words, he felt a shocking jolt come down through his head and pass through him. Shaken, he felt momentarily dizzy from the experience. Blinking, he saw Alaria smile knowingly up at him. What had happened? Dane wasn't sure. Was it Grandmother Alaria? The kindness in her eyes made him realize that whatever had happened was not harmful to him.

''You are a good man, Dane. One of honor.'' She released his hand and returned her attention to Maya, who was shedding her backpack and placing it against the outer wall of the hut. ''Come, both of you. Inca has just birthed and welcomed the twins into the world. Roan is with her and all went well.''

''Thank Goddess,'' Maya whispered fervently as she followed Alaria into the light, airy hut. ''I was so worried....'' Reaching out, Maya grabbed Dane's hand and gave him a triumphant grin. ''Come on!''

He caught her infectious enthusiasm and followed her into the hut. There were windows everywhere. The day was warm, around seventy-five degrees, he would guess, and the sun was shining through the tropical canopy that surrounded the village on three sides. The scent of orchids was wonderful as he followed them down a hall to a room on the left. Entering it, Dane saw Inca with a baby in each of her arms, her face glowing with joy. The man who sat with her, Roan Storm Walker, looked more relieved at the moment than anything else. He was touching his daughter's small, perfectly formed hand with obvious awe. The infants were swaddled in pale pink blankets woven of soft alpaca wool.

"Ohh," Maya whispered softly as she knelt near Inca's pallet. "How beautiful they are, Inca!" Maya placed one hand on her sister's shoulder in welcome and gave her a gentle hug. Then she reached out and delicately touched each baby's dark hair.

Alaria smiled and stood off to one side. "Roan, I'd like you to meet Dane York. Dane, this is Roan. Inca's husband."

Roan eased to his feet and came around the end of the pallet. Gripping Dane's hand, he said, "I'm glad you and Maya could make it. Take a seat. You'll have to wait your turn to hold little Kayla Alaria and Michael Adair Storm Walker."

Grinning, Dane took a seat on one of the three-legged stools in the room and fondly watched as Maya knelt at Inca's side and cooed lovingly over the first infant. Kayla had thick black hair, like her parents, Dane observed. She was golden-skinned like Inca, and looked like she might have green eyes like her, too. Roan knelt at his wife's side, his arm around her shoulder, a look of pride and love burning in his eyes. He was staring down at the little babies as if they were a miracle. Well, weren't they? Dane watched as Maya's facade as a squadron commander melted away. Right now, she was a woman who loved babies. The aunt to the new children brought into the world with obvious love from those who now surrounded her.

Inca lifted her head and smiled at Dane. "I am glad you came."

"Thanks, Inca. I'm glad to be a part of this, too." And he was. Inca's eyes were warm with emotion. Her hair was damp, the dark strands falling nearly to her waist. Wearing a loose white shift, one shoulder pulled down, she held her daughter gently against her as she suckled noisily and strongly at her breast.

Alaria laughed. "Kayla and Michael have their family here, now."

Roan took his son into his arms while Kayla fed. Michael Storm Walker had black hair and his father's deep blue eyes.

Tears welled up in Maya's eyes as she sat back on her heels and met Inca's willow-green gaze. Reaching out, she slid her hand against her twin's cheek. "Family. You hear that? We're family. Isn't this wonderful, Inca? Finally, we've come full circle. We lost our parents. We lost our way, we thought. But we didn't. Not really. All along, there was a larger, hidden plan for us. But we didn't know it at the time. All we could do was trust and carry on." Tears glimmered in her eyes, and she saw Inca's own lips tremble. "And look at the outcome...."

Sniffing, Inca whispered, "I know...I cannot believe it, Maya. Everything in our lives is so good right now. We passed through our own dark tunnel. We passed the tests that were thrown at us." Inca gazed down lovingly at her daughter. A bead of breast milk formed at the corner of her tiny bud-shaped mouth. Roan leaned over and gently removed it with his finger. She smiled into her husband's face and they held one another's gaze for a long time. Then Inca reached out and tenderly touched her son's flushed cheek as he slept in her husband's massive arms.

Maya sniffed and dug into the pocket of her pants. She withdrew a bright red pouch and carefully opened it while Inca watched. "I think," Maya murmured as she pulled out a necklace with Peruvian blue opals and cougar claws on it, "that this necklace Roan gave to you, and you gave to me, should return to the twins here? You could have it refashioned into two medicine pieces. One for each?"

Smiling softly, Inca took the necklace into her hands. "That is a wonderful gift," she exclaimed. Carefully she draped the necklace, which was much too large for the babies to wear yet, across her pink alpaca blanket. The blue-green gems seemed to glow.

Inca looked up at Roan. "Does this feel right to you? To pass this necklace from your family to your son and daughter?"

Roan gave Maya a grateful look. "Yes," he murmured, "it's a wonderful gift back to us all. Thank you, Maya."

"Hey, your medicine necklace helped save my tail," she told them, grinning. "I figured I'd used up one of its nine lives in the process, and your children should enjoy the protection of it now." Patting Inca's hand, she said, "I feel good that it's going home, with you. It belongs in your part of the family tree."

Gripping her hand, Inca whispered, "Thank you...."

Maya leaned forward and kissed her damp cheek. Then, sniffing, she turned. She held out her hand toward Dane. "Come here, trade places with me. You've got to see Kayla. She's so beautiful!" And she pushed herself to her feet.

Dane gave her an unsure look. "Hey, I'm not exactly a parent type," he said as he slowly knelt down beside Inca.

"You do not have to be to look at a baby or touch her tiny hand."

Giving Inca a nervous smile, Dane turned his attention to the first newborn. Soon he was mesmerized by the baby's little hand, waving energetically from side to side as she noisily fed. "Her fingers are so perfectly formed," he said in a low tone. "It's just amazing, isn't it?" He reached out, and the moment his finger made contact with Kayla's hand, her tiny fingers wrapped strongly around his. "Oh," Dane exclaimed, "she's strong!" And then Roan transferred his son carefully to Dane's awaiting arms. He handled the precious cargo carefully. The babies looked similar, and yet each had slightly different features. Dane rocked the baby gently and grinned uneasily. They laughed. Roan patted him on the shoulder to reassure him that he was doing just fine.

Maya stood back, all smiles. Grandmother Alaria had tucked her hands into the long sleeves of her robe and was standing there, her face serene and pleased. Looking around at Inca, with her dark hair loose and shining; Roan in his short-sleeved, plaid shirt and jeans; and Dane, who seemed hypnotized by little Michael, Maya realized there were no dry eyes in the birthing room. A baby broke down barriers in everyone, she thought, warmth flowing through her heart as it throbbed with joy.

There was a movement at the door, and Maya turned. She saw Mike Houston, dressed in a white, long-sleeved shirt with the cuffs rolled up, tan chinos and hiking boots. He was smiling as he placed his hands on the doorjamb and looked in at all of them. Maya heard Inca cry out his name, saw her lift her hand toward him. Mike nodded to Maya and then to Alaria.

"Hi, gang," he called. "Hey, I hear a little girl and boy were just born."

Dane got up and moved to Maya's side as Mike came over. He shook Dane's hand and then Roan's. Then he lowered himself to his knees, at Inca's side. "Come here, Little Sister," he said, calling her the endearment he'd given her ever since they'd been bound by blood in a ceremony long ago. "Let me hold you...." And he placed his arm around her and gave her a long, gentle embrace. Inca sobbed and slid her arm across Mike's massive shoulders as he hugged her.

"Mike!" she wept. "I am so glad you could come! I wanted you here, to be with us...."

"Hey, what's this?" Mike laughed as he pressed a kiss to Inca's hair. "Tears? You should be jumping up and down for joy. Look at what you did. She's pretty, Inca. Just beautiful. You did good, girl.''

Self-consciously wiping the tears from her eyes, Inca smiled bravely up at Mike. "Even now you joke and tease me."

Chuckling, Mike ran his hand lovingly across Inca's head. He gave Roan a wink. "Hey, I'm just built that way, Little Sister. Everything looks like it went well. You feeling all right?" He gave her a searching look.

Inca responded with a trembling smile. "Yes...even after eight hours of labor." She gazed up at her husband and reached out and squeezed his hand. "I could not have done it without Roan."

Mike nodded. "I'm sure. Well, hey, this little squirt is awful pretty. She looks just like you, Inca." And he touched Kayla's pudgy, rosy cheek. Then, he rose and went over to Dane. Opening his arms, he took Inca and Roan's son into his arms, pride in his eyes as he studied the sleeping baby boy. His voice turned scratchy as he regarded them. "Thanks for calling him Michael. That's a helluva compliment," he said and he grinned unevenly, tears coming to his eyes.

Inca sniffed and smiled at Roan, and then shifted her tearful gaze back to her blood brother. "I swore a long time ago if I were ever allowed to have a son, he would be named in your honor."

Mike leaned down and placed a kiss on the baby's thick, black hair. "Well," he said, his voice strained with emotion. "This son of yours will always have my heart, Little Sister. Thank you...both of you, for this honor." He gazed tenderly down at his namesake and rocked him gently.

Standing back, Maya slipped beneath Dane's arm. He always knew when she needed to be held. Giving her a warm look he saw Maya wipe tears from her own eyes. Dane knew how much Mike meant to Inca. He was her blood brother and they were so very close, like family.

"Think you'd ever want one or two of these little crit-

ters?'' Dane asked, pressing a kiss to Maya's temple. He saw
her smile and raise her gaze to his. There was such happiness
in her emerald eyes.

"Maybe…some day. Not now, though…."

Nodding, Dane understood. Just seeing Roan and Inca together, Roan's arm around Inca's shoulders as she nursed
their baby girl, made him love Maya even more fiercely.
Someday, when she realized that her mission could be fulfilled by others who would come and do a tour of duty at
her base, Maya might connect into her mothering side. Right
now, she used her nurturing skills to mother her squadron,
instead. Smiling to himself, Dane could see them having one
or two children. He'd like the opportunity to try and be a
good father, to work with Maya to help their children grow
up healthy and happy. Coming from a broken home, he knew
what to do to help a child feel safe and secure. And he knew
that because Maya had been a foster child adopted by very
loving people, she had an awful lot of love to shower on any
child she might have.

Dane knew enough of Inca's background, the pain, the
abandonment and loss, to know that little Kayla and Michael
would heal many of the deep wounds left within her soul.
And the way Roan cared for his wife moved Dane deeply.
Roan was a big man, rough-hewn, but his touch was tender
and obviously filled with complete love toward Inca. Looking
at himself in reflection, Dane could see some similarities between him and Roan. As much as Inca was the introvert, the
shy one, the one who hid from much of life and civilization
except for the small world she'd carved out in the Amazon
jungle, Maya had taken an opposite path. She was out there—
extroverted, confident, assertive and combative when she
needed to be. Not that Inca wasn't a warrior, because she
was, in her own way. Still, the softness of Inca's features
told Dane that Kayla and Michael, along with Roan's love
and support, would help her bind the last of her open wounds

from the past. They had a very bright, hopeful future together.

Mike kissed Kayla on the noggin, gave Inca a kiss on the cheek and then handed Roan back his sleeping son. He excused himself. "I need to talk to Maya and Dane for a moment. I'll be back in a little while."

Inca nodded. "Do not be long, my brother?"

Mike nodded. Reaching down, he tousled her hair a little. "Not long," he promised her. He got to his feet and moved over to Maya and Dane. He turned his back toward Inca and Roan, his voice lowered. "I hate to be a wet blanket on such a happy occasion, but if you two have a moment, I need to talk to you about some stuff that's stirring."

Rolling her eyes, Maya muttered, "Even here, we can't get away from the heavy energy."

Mike hitched one shoulder and gave her a wicked look. "The world doesn't stop turning just because we're here. You know better than that."

Frowning, Maya nodded. "Okay, let's go over to the main kettle on the plaza to grab something to eat. I'm starving to death." She didn't want to discuss things in front of Inca that might upset her right now. Inca deserved the happiness of the moment. She didn't need to hear about another combat mission that Mike had more than likely cooked up, judging from the look in his eyes. Inca's life had been one of constant war. Right now, Maya wanted her to enjoy the peace and harmony that she so richly deserved with the birth of her twins and with Roan at her side. Nothing should upset this precious moment for her.

"Inca, Roan, we're gonna grab a bite to eat. We'll be back in a little while," Maya said lightly.

Inca lifted her head, her eyes showing instant worry. "You will come back? Can you stay a little while longer?"

Maya nodded. "Dane and I are planning on spending at least two days here with you." She saw instant relief in Inca's moist eyes. More than anything, after giving birth to her babies, Inca wanted her family nearby, Maya knew. When she turned and looked at Grandmother Alaria, Maya could tell the older woman was aware that something was up.

Quietly leaving the birthing hut, Maya walked on one side of Mike Houston, Dane on the other. There were several logs in the center of the plaza that had been cut in half and positioned in a square around the black tripod and kettle. A fortifying cereal known as *kiwicha* bubbled in the pot over the coals of the dying fire. Maya picked up some wooden bowls from a nearby table. Going to the kettle, she spooned healthy portions into each. They all sat down with their food at the table.

Pouring some honey onto her cereal, Maya took one of the many clean wooden spoons held in a large, rough-hewn cup. "Okay, Mike, you've got that look in your eyes. What's comin' down?"

Dane sat next to Maya. Houston sat across from them, his expression becoming serious. Pouring some honey into his own bowl, he stirred it slowly.

"You ever heard of a Mexican drug lord by the name of Javier Rios?"

Maya nodded and chewed on the grainy-textured cereal. "He's one of the main kingpins in Mexico for drug runnin' from there into the U.S. and Canada. A mean son of a bitch who'd rather fire first and ask questions later."

"Yep, same one," Mike said. He poured some water from a pitcher into his wooden cup. Offering some to them, he filled two more cups. "Morgan has been contacted by the U.S. Border Patrol. They're asking for his and the army's help in putting Apaches along the Mexico-U.S. border. The pilots of drug-carrying planes are flying into the States undetected, and the border patrol doesn't have the facilities to stop the air shipments. Rios knows this. He's got enough money to hire U.S. pilots who are looking to pick up an easy ten grand to fly a couple hundred kilos to dealers in major cities.''

Dane quirked his lips. ''So they want Apaches along the border to pick them up on radar as they fly from Mexico into U.S. airspace. And then what? What do you want them to do? Fire on them?''

''I wish. They deserve it,'' Mike growled, taking a deep draft from his glass. Setting it down, he wiped his mouth with the back of his hand. ''The Apaches are to do interdiction duty from San Diego, California, through Del Rio, Texas. The army is going to provide a certain number of Apaches to fly between point A and B every night with their radar turned toward Mexico. Any flight they pick up that's not got a flight plan is suspect. They are authorized to initiate a second Apache, which will meet the intruder flight carrying the drugs and force it down at the nearest available airport.''

''So, no shooting them out of the sky?'' Maya said. She scraped her bowl and finished off the last of the tasty cereal.

''No. The Apaches are to identify, interdict and ground 'em, that's all.''

''So, where does Maya come into all this?'' Dane queried.

Mike put his empty bowl aside. ''I need three of your savviest pilots, Maya. Women who are used to cowboying around, know drug dealers, can smell 'em coming a mile away and aren't afraid of a little confrontation. There's actually three missions being planned. Two are border patrol related and the third is an undercover one. I also need one to help coordinate the border patrol with the U.S. Army contingent. She will be responsible for setting up a plan of action and coordinating this whole ball of wax—successfully. The others will go to San Diego and work with the agents at the other end.'' He smiled at her. ''You got a pilot like that?''

''I'm thinking of one in particular,'' Maya said. ''Chief Warrant Officer Akiva Redtail. She's trim—an Apache and Lakota woman warrior. She's got that sixth sense you're wanting. She's been with us for three years and she knows the ropes.''

''Is she aggressive?''

Dane chuckled. ''Tell me one Apache pilot who isn't? It's bred into them, Mike. I've flown with Akiva and she puts new meaning into the word 'Apache.' She can teach us a lot about aggressive interdiction.''

A grin softened the hard line of Mike's mouth. His gaze remained on Maya. ''Well?''

''You need three of my pilots,'' Maya began, thinking out loud. ''First of all, I know Rios. I've tangled with him before.'' She frowned and tapped the wooden table with her fingers. ''Will Mexico give us permission to fly in their airspace?''

''Yes.''

''How far from the border?''

''They haven't given us a distance yet. That's still on the negotiating table right now.''

Leaning forward, Maya gave him a cutting look. ''You know as well as I do that bribery of high Mexican government and police officials by drug lords is rampant. What you really need is permission to work without many people knowing what the plan will be, if you want success.''

''Okay,'' Mike said, ''tell me what you're thinking.''

Giving Dane a knowing look, Maya said, ''Interview my pilots—Akiva Redtail and Lieutenant Dallas Klein should be on the list. Dallas is my X.O.—executive officer—and you're going to need someone of her capabilities, her familiarity with mission planning, to coordinate this whole thing tactically. Akiva will be good to go on Mexican airspace interior work, hunting down some of Rios's aircraft on their home turf. Or maybe that undercover mission.''

Nodding, Houston murmured, ''Okay, you got my attention. I'll take this info back to Morgan and he can contact the responsible parties about it.''

''Sounds good to me,'' Maya said.

"They won't mind these TAD assignments?"

She grinned. "Not if I know my women. They like to be where the action is, and right now it's pretty quiet, for once, down in our sector. Until those other two drug lords take over Valentino's turf, it should be pretty peaceful—almost boring—at the base."

Dane placed his arm around her shoulders and smiled over at her. "I like the peace and quiet."

Mike eased off his chair. "I've got to get going. I'll be in touch with you by satcom, Maya. Thanks for your help. Morgan will be sending down someone to interview your volunteer pilots very shortly. So, stand by."

"I'll look for info on these three up-and-coming missions, Mike. Thanks for thinking of us." She watched as Mike moved back to the birthing hut to say goodbye to Inca. Sighing, she rested her cheek against Dane's shoulder. "Just when I think it's finally going to quiet down, something else pops up."

Kissing her wrinkled brow, he whispered, "I know. The only thing we can count on is change."

"Isn't *that* the truth." Maya slid her arm around his waist and kissed the hard line of his jaw.

"Your base is going to become a real international hub for Apache pilots," Dane told her proudly. "We have two from the Netherlands scheduled to come in a month from now. And other countries that have bought Apaches from Boeing are standing in line fighting to get orders to Black Jaguar Base. Everyone wants real-time combat experience and this is the place to get it."

"Once an outcast, now the darling of the military elite," Maya chuckled. "Talk about the twists and turns of life."

Dane squeezed her gently. "Well, life is really all about those little babies in Inca's and Roan's arms. We're doing this for them, for their generation. If we can keep the heat on, if we can make these drug lords pay in their own backyard, maybe we'll make enough of a difference. Maybe their children will see real peace in their lifetime."

Maya saw the worry and the determination in Dane's eyes. She sat up and turned to him. Sliding her hands around his jaw, she whispered, "One heart, one mind. We're a good team, darling." The emerald ring glinted on her left hand. "Why don't we sew up the loose ends on our relationship and make them permanent?" She saw his eyes flare with surprise. Maya had never talked of marriage since he'd given her the engagement ring.

Taken aback, Dane stared at her momentarily. Slipping his hand over one of hers, he brought it to his lips and kissed the back of it gently. "You're serious?"

Her eyes filled with laughter. With tenderness. "Very. You ready to make the leap? To go from single to married, Major York?"

The corners of his mouth quirked. Drowning in the green depths of her sunlit eyes, Dane rasped, "Yeah, if you are, Major Stevenson." And he grinned broadly at her.

Maya looked up toward the birthing hut. "I'd like Grandmother Alaria to marry us, Dane. I know our families would like a wedding, too. We can marry here, and then have a second ceremony at your father's home in Texas, can't we? And my mom and dad can join us there as well." She searched his pensive features.

His blue eyes were warm with love—for her. "Why not? Will that make us twice as married?" he chuckled.

She joined his laughter. "Humor…no matter what the circumstance."

"That's one of the many things you love about me."

Maya's lips curved. "You're so sure of yourself, Dane York."

"Another reason you love me."

"Yes."

"And my unflagging confidence."

"That, too."

He preened a little and squared his shoulders a tad more as he held her warm emerald gaze.

"They broke the mold when they made you, York."

Dane gave her a very proud look, one eyebrow moving upward. "Thank you."

Maya broke into a grin. "You're so full of yourself, York."

"Yeah, I know it." Laughter rumbled from his chest.

Sitting there in Dane's arms, Maya surrendered to his strength and tenderness. Closing her eyes, she rested her brow against his jaw as he held and rocked her. Dane was one of a kind and so was she. Jaguars mated for life. And she wanted him as her mate. Forever.

*   *   *   *   *

SILHOUETTE® SENSATION™

proudly presents

a sensually addictive trilogy,
only from
Kylie Brant

Charmed and Dangerous

With their quick wits and killer smiles,
these men are irresistible.

HARD TO HANDLE
August 2002

HARD TO RESIST
September 2002

HARD TO TAME
October 2002

0802/SH/LC38

SILHOUETTE®

SENSATION™

brings more…much more
from

Suzanne Brockmann

TALL, DARK AND DANGEROUS

These men are who you call to get you
out of a tight spot—or into one!

TAYLOR'S TEMPTATION
August 2002

WILD, WILD WES
March 2003

0802/SH/LC39

SILHOUETTE® INTRIGUE™

presents

two stories from popular author
Sheryl Lynn
set in

McClintock Country

*High up in the Rocky Mountains is a place where
the wind blows fast and fierce, where trust is
precious and where everyone has a secret.*

TO PROTECT THEIR CHILD

July 2002

COLORADO'S FINEST

(a LAWMAN LOVERS story)
August 2002

0702/SH/LC34

SILHOUETTE®
SUPERROMANCE™

is proud to present

The Guardians

An action-packed
new trilogy by

Kay David

This time the good guys wear
black. Join this highly skilled
police SWAT team as they
serve and protect
Florida's Emerald Coast.

THE NEGOTIATOR
(July 2002)

THE COMMANDER
(August 2002)

THE LISTENER
(September 2002)

SILHOUETTE® SUPERROMANCE™

Welcomes you to

RIVERBEND

Riverbend... the kind of place where everyone knows your name — and your business. Riverbend... home of a group of small-town sons and daughters who've been friends since school.

They're all grown up now. Living their lives and learning that you can get through anything as long as you have your friends.

Five wonderful stories:

0802/SH/LC37